Faithful Shep

THE STORY OF A HERO DOG & THE NINE TEXAS RANGERS WHO SAVED HIM

by Don DeNevi

TEXAS REVIEW PRESS
HUNTSVILLE, TEXAS

FIRST EDITION

Requests for permission to acknowledge material from this work should be sent to:
    Permissions
    Texas Review Press
    English Department
    Sam Houston State University
    Huntsville, TX 77341-2146

Library of Congress Cataloging-in-Publication Data

Names: DeNevi, Don, 1937- author.
Title: Faithful Shep : the story of a hero dog and the Texas Rangers who
  saved him : a novel based on a true incident from the Texas frontier / by
  Don DeNevi.
Description: First edition. | Huntsville, Texas : Texas Review Press, [2017]
Identifiers: LCCN 2016047392 (print) | LCCN 2016049515 (ebook) | ISBN
  9781680031195 (pbk.) | ISBN 9781680031201 (ebook)
Subjects: LCSH: Texas Rangers--Fiction. | Dogs--Fiction. | Human-animal
  relationships--Fiction. | Frontier and pioneer life--Texas, West--Fiction.
  | Texas, West--Fiction. | GSAFD: Western stories. | LCGFT: Historical
  fiction.
Classification: LCC PS3604.E536 F35 2017 (print) | LCC PS3604.E536 (ebook) |
  DDC 813/.6--dc23
LC record available at https://lccn.loc.gov/2016047392

For Carrie . . .

. . . in the backyard, basking in the warmth of the sun alongside Shep, Boots, and Blackie, who was bewildered and frightened when left behind as the bus pulled away.

"He had been there alone for fifteen days. His side of bacon was eaten, and the sack of corn getting very low. The Rangers were as much delighted as if it had been a human being they had rescued. He had worn the top of the wall of the old stage stand perfectly smooth, standing off the sneaking coyotes . . . Shep had held the fort. . . . "

—George Wythe Baylor, Captain (Ret.), Company C,

Frontier Battalion

El Paso Herald, February 3, 1900

Contents

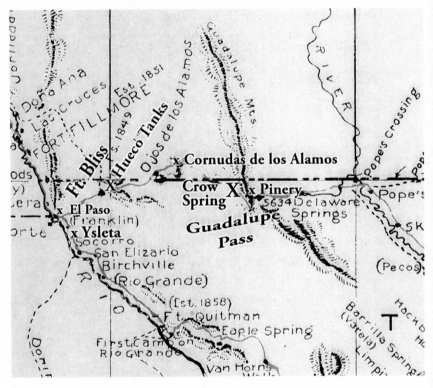

Detail from a map by Roscoe Conkling in *The Butterfield Overland Mail, 1857–1869*, copyright © 1947 by the Arthur H. Clark Company. Reprinted by permission of the publisher.

Faithful Shep

Prologue

The dog scented the cougar before he could see it. One of the loud men with stinking breath looped a rope around the dog's neck and pulled him out of the dark shed with the other dogs, toward the high, walled pen, and the dog could smell the big cat behind the wall. The dog didn't want to go toward danger, but the man had a rope around his neck and wanted him to come.

Long ago, in a time the dog barely remembered, he had been taught by a man who was kind to him. The man taught the dog that he should always obey what humans wanted him to do. That was before the man had gone away, leaving the dog alone. In the many hungry days since, the dog had to get food wherever he could, had to sleep in dark corners out of the wind wherever they could be found. There had been no one to feed the dog, to teach him what to do, or to tell him where to go.

Then, one of the bad-smelling men found the dog and brought him to this place with other dogs. They all stayed in a dark shed until one of the men came to bring one of the dogs outside, to the pen where the mountain lion waited. None of the other dogs had ever come back. Now one of the men had come for the dog, and he was going toward the high-walled pen.

The dog walked beside the bad-smelling man, and the pen got closer and closer. And even though the dog had obeyed the man and had not tried to pull back or run away, when they reached the gate to the pen, the man shoved the dog roughly inside and kicked him, as if the dog had done something wrong. Then the man slammed the gate shut.

The mountain lion was crouched against the wall opposite the gate, staring at the dog, its ears flattened and its teeth bared in a snarl. The dog could smell the cougar's fright, its rage. He could see the muscles bunching in the cat's hindquarters and shoulders as it prepared to spring.

The dog was hungry and weak, because the bad-smelling men had given him nothing to eat. The pads of his right forefoot were raw and bleeding. He looked around, searching in terror for a way out, a place to run. But there was no way out. There was nothing except the dog, the panicked, vicious cougar, and the bloody, lifeless remains of the other dogs that had been dragged in here by the loud, bad-smelling men. The dog's tail curled under his body; he dropped his head and turned his eyes away, to show that he didn't want to fight. He released the contents of his bladder into the dust of the pen, helpless with fear.

The yelling of the men outside the walls got louder. The dog was scared and confused. His senses were assaulted on all sides by the smell of old blood, the stink of his own fear, the acrid odor of the cougar, the noise of the men. A whimper started, deep down in the dog's throat.

The cougar outweighed the dog; it was bigger and stronger. The dog feared the cougar's claws and teeth. He did not want to fight the cougar; he had no chance. But the cougar was scared and angry. It would attack—and soon.

There was another noise behind the dog, more yelling. Then the gate slammed open and another man was inside the pen. He was standing beside the dog, and then he was kneeling. He spoke in a quiet, soothing tone—something no human had done with the dog in a very long time. The man's hands were gentle on the dog and his voice was low.

The cougar was still staring at them, still preparing to charge, but now, because the man was there, it hesitated. The man kept talking, and then the dog knew he would go with the man. The man stood up and started moving back toward the gate, and the dog went with him. He and the man backed carefully toward the gate; they watched the cougar, and the cougar watched them, but it did not attack.

They reached the gate, and another man was there. Like the man who had come into the pen, he did not smell of the foulness that stank on the breath of most of the other men who gathered around the tall enclosure to yell and fight and take dogs into the pen. The two men closed the gate. They kept the dog between them, and the three of them walked past the other, bad-smelling men, most of whom had suddenly become quiet. Many of them were looking at the ground or somewhere else, the way the dog had looked away from the cougar. The man who had come into the pen was angry; the dog could sense it. But he was not angry at the dog. No, he was angry at the loud men, the ones who were standing around the outside of the pen.

The dog and the two men walked away from the pen with the high walls, and the more they walked, the less afraid the dog felt. The two men talked to him in low, quiet voices; their hands were kind.

They went to another place, and there the two men gave the dog food and clean water to drink. They cleaned the wounds in his pads and wrapped his foot so that it could heal and stop hurting. Soon, he could again walk without limping.

The dog was glad to be with someone again—someone who did not smell foul and who was not loud or always fighting. The two men would talk to him and tell him things. They fed him every day and made sure he had water. He was with them now, and he was not scared anymore. The dog would go wherever they went. He would do whatever the two men told him to do.

Chapter One

By the time Joseph P. Andrews and William Wiswall rode into San Antonio on that afternoon in the early fall of 1879, they had already covered some 1,000 miles of rough, dry, and dusty country. They traversed southern Colorado, from their starting point in the mining country of Ouray County, and made their way across the Indian Territory before crossing the Red River into Texas. And even though they had come this far already, they were still many weary miles and, likely, several negotiations away from the goal of their quest.

Still, this fledgling city at the spring-fed headwaters of the San Antonio River was a welcome sight. The heat was unusually stifling for this time of the year; their horses plodded forward with heads down, and Shep, the black German Shepherd who was their constant companion, trotted along in his usual position, twenty feet ahead. It was not long after noon on Sunday, and both men were hungry and in need of beer. Doubtless, their mounts wanted hay, and Shep would probably be content with a bowl of milk and a beef bone.

Slumped in their saddles, Andrews and Wiswall scrutinized their surroundings with curiosity. San Antonio was the principal trading post for hundreds of miles in this part of the vast border region of Texas, and the streets brimmed with hustling men and wagons, the wheels creaking under their loads. Vaqueros from surrounding ranchos rode past or lolled at street corners, laughing and conversing in Spanish with señoritas who hurried by, carrying baskets of corn or buckets of water.

The bustle enveloped the two as they rode into town. In this northern section of the city, home-grown foodstuffs glutted stalls along the streets, the prices low compared to the markets in Denver. To the two mining engineers, the whole of the American Southwest seemed bent on showing its wares in these busy dirt roads and avenues. Street corner hawkers cried for buyers for their vegetables, fruits, berries, grapes, nuts, and eggs.

But it was the people who most captured the attention of the partners. Most of the denizens of this street appeared young, tight-lipped, and dusty. None wore a gun.

Sombreroed braceros trundled barrows past sauntering soldiers from newly built Fort Sam Houston. Cowboys mingled with tradesmen, merchants, and teamsters. Carretas and water wagons trundled past, drawn by horses or burros. Drawled English and staccato Spanish jostled each other in the hot afternoon air.

"Saloons and cantinas up and down the street," Wiswall observed, "but not a ragged, unshaved person or stumbling drunkard in sight. Too busy, I guess. Or too much to do."

"Could be," Andrews said, nodding. "From what I heard tell back in Oklahoma, more than a hundred people are coming from the east to Texas every day. It doesn't look like they're turning anyone away in San Antone."

As they made their way through San Antonio, dogs occasionally approached Shep: some with raised hackles and stiff-legged walks and others with wagging tails and extended noses. The black shepherd received all comers with due caution or good humor, as the occasion warranted. From the angle of his ears and the constant lift of his nostrils, the two men could tell he was as absorbed in the sights, sounds, and smells of this unfamiliar place as they were themselves.

Nearing the center of town, the swarms of people, horses, and stray dogs thinned out. Along these thoroughfares, all of the two- and three-story buildings were constructed of brick or wood frame. A few adobe structures remained in between. Whereas the outskirts had housed a saloon or cantina in every third or fourth building, not one was now seen. All the wide avenues were lined with shiny new rails where saddled horses and teams hitched to clean wagons and buggies. Since it was after noon on a Sunday, vested, cravated businessmen and a few well-dressed women enjoyed an after-lunch stroll before returning home from church services.

"Remember what the sheriff in Austin told us?" asked Wiswall.

"You mean that business about how they stack bricks of gold and silver on the sidewalks outside the banks?" laughed Andrews. "I also remember that he wasn't sure if that was here or in El Paso. He might have had one or two of his facts crossed."

"Maybe we ought to plan a robbery."

"Hew to the line, friend and partner. Any gold and silver we get will come from selling a string of packing burros back up in Ouray County—once we can find and buy them, that is."

Wiswall chuckled.

Past the first-class hotels and restaurants they rode, Shep pacing steadily in front. Andrews and Wiswall passed establishments holding themselves out as manufacturers of jewelry and importers of diamonds, lumber distributors ("Oak, Hickory, Pine, and Redwood for Shingles, Sash, and Doors—Terms Available to Reputable Parties"), and wholesale and retail druggists' offices. They passed physicians' and surgeons' residences; attorney-at-law offices; liveries and saddlers; a commercial college; national banks; a livestock yard; a merchant offering pianos, organs, and coffins; dry goods stores; and sales offices for liquors by the case and Mexican cigars. There were soap and tallow outlets; dentists; marble works; offices for the sale of mineral rights; and vendors of crockery, china, glassware, house furnishing, books and stationery, sewing machines . . . There seemed no end to the commercial enterprises under pursuit by the good people of San Antonio.

"Where should we stay tonight?" said Wiswall.

"I'm game for that hotel on the plaza. It looks brand-new, and the sign out front said it opened only last week. We can get supper right across the street."

"That's fine. Do you reckon they'll allow Shep to sleep in our room?"

"He'll not likely sleep anywhere else."

And so it was that the two men from Colorado decided to room at the American House Hotel. By morning they hoped to decide whether Corpus Christi, Brownsville, Laredo, Eagle Pass, or some other place beneath the Lone Star held the best prospects for their planned purchase of pack burros to satisfy the need of the burgeoning mining enterprises back in Ouray County. With a good supper tucked behind their belts and some scraps fed to Shep, Andrews and Wiswall would perhaps canvass the opinions of the dozen or so men sitting on the hotel's veranda, enjoying their evening pipes.

The American House Hotel was a three-story brick structure situated at one corner of the city center. Standing on the street in front of the gleaming new establishment, Andrews and Wiswall gazed upon the edifice with respect. On their journey through Colorado and the Oklahoma and Indian Territories into Texas, they had often slept in crude log huts or even canvas accommodations. But the American House was built of imported bricks, not adobe. It was a structure of substance and looked to the two weary travelers like a very Taj Mahal.

After securing permission for Shep to enter the hotel and sleep in their room, Andrews and Wiswall registered at the desk, paid $2.00 for a room with bath, and escorted Shep to a blanket on the floor of their quarters. They bathed and then changed their clothes for supper. Then, they made a quick check of the small barn attached to the rear of the hotel, satisfying themselves that their horses were unsaddled, brushed down, watered, and getting fed.

Since there was still at least an hour's worth of daylight, they strolled around the long blocks surrounding and enclosing the city center before entering Link's Restaurant.

Andrews was the taller and more slender of the two. Wiswall, though shorter and a bit more stout, was solidly built. Both of them were accustomed to physical labors in the out-of-doors; neither had any difficulties obtaining and keeping the respect of the persons they customarily dealt with, be they miners with hardened hands and creased faces, or mine owners dressed in linen and seated amid leather upholstery and mahogany paneling.

The two strolled easily along, greeting and stopping to chat with shopkeepers, clerks, and patrons they met along the way. They encountered husbands and wives, arm in arm, with children tagging along behind; farmers and ranchers in business suits; and military men in recently pressed uniforms. Yet, everywhere they looked, they noted incongruities:

music from a hurdy-gurdy sounding from a gambling den deep within one of the old buildings facing the center of the square; loud laughter and noisy talk from every other open window; an Indian man and his squaw squatted against the wall outside an expensive jewelry store. After their rambling walk, Andrews and Wiswall stood finally before the restaurant.

"Are you fellows new to town?" a passerby said to the two. When they told him they were, he informed them, "Well, you won't find a better chop house anywhere around than Link's. It might be the best eatery in all of Texas."

They paused in the doorway to survey the interior. The entire facility was stylish; clearly, the place catered to San Antonio's powerful and well-to-do. An elaborate rosewood bar ran the length of the wall on their left, all the way to a small alcove over a raised stage with footlights. Large mirrors of Spanish plate reflected light into the room. Some twenty-five tables, each seating four patrons, sat at comfortable distances from one another. Crystal goblets and glasses of all shapes and sizes glittered on tables and in waiting pyramids at one end of the bar. The floor was of varnished hardwood. Oil lamps with reflectors shed a buttery glow throughout the room. To the two hard-riding partners from Ouray County, Colorado, the effect was palatial.

The travelers were disappointed, though, to see that all the tables were occupied. A compact group of about six lingered near the center of the bar, and some dozen or so more waited in a vestibule.

Andrews and Wiswall walked to the back of the line in the vestibule, resigned to waiting for their turn. There, at the end of the line, a middle-aged man of erect bearing nodded at them.

"Shouldn't be too long," he offered.

Neatly dressed, he was thin-haired, with leathery, well-tanned skin that started below the stark white hat-brim line just above his eyebrows.

"I'm Joseph Andrews, and this is my partner, William Wiswall. We are just down from Ouray County, Colorado." Andrews took the other man's hand in a firm, dry grip. "We're rooming for the night over at the American House."

"Well, us and our dog," Wiswall added, chuckling.

"Good to know you," the man said, loosing his grip on Andrews's hand to take Wiswall's in turn. "I'm Charley Nevill, and I'd offer you a place to bunk, but I'm afraid I'm camping on the river."

The group in front of the three men took a few steps forward, and they followed along behind. It seemed to Andrews and Wiswall that their new acquaintance was correct in his assessment of their imminent seating at a table.

"You a cattleman?" asked Wiswall. "You have the look of a man who has spent a fair share of his time out in the weather."

"Well, that I have, but I'm not much in the cattle line, no."

"Perhaps you can help us," Wiswall said. "We're looking to buy a hundred or more packing burros to trail back to Colorado." The line moved forward another several paces.

"No, boys, I'm afraid I can't advise you. I'm new to this part of Texas myself."

"I see. Well, what sort of work is it that you do?" Andrews said.

"I'm a Texas Ranger."

Just then, the maitre'd of the restaurant approached. "Gentlemen, I have a side-window table that can seat three, if you squeeze a bit. Do you want it?"

Andrews and Wiswall shrugged and nodded, then looked at Nevill. "Yes, I believe my friends and I will take the table," the Ranger said, smiling. The maitre'd led them to a small, half-round table abutting a window overlooking the city center.

After perusing the offerings, all three decided upon the restaurant's Sunday house specialty, as prominently advertised on the front of the menu's four-page fold-out: *Sunday specialty of Link's—dinner soup, clam chowder; meat, roast pork with green apple sauce; entrée, macaroni and cheese, chicken salad; dessert, tapioca-apple pudding; pastry, summer mince pie and currant cake; coffee, milk, or tea. No alcoholic beverages sold in the dining room.*

As they waited for their food to arrive, Andrews and Wiswall learned that their new acquaintance was 2nd Lt. Charles L. Nevill, acting commanding officer of Company E, Texas Rangers. He had been leading the company less than two weeks. Headquartered at Fort Davis, far to the west, his assigned district covered both Pecos and Presidio counties. Nevill further related that his good friend, Pvt. William Harris of Company B, had been killed during an Apache raid at the head of the North Concho River in July, and Lieutenant Nevill was in San Antonio with the sad duty of calling upon his friend's family.

"I am sorry to hear of the loss of your friend," Andrews said. Wiswall nodded.

"Harris was a good friend and a fine Ranger. He volunteered for many of my expeditions. I owe him a great debt; calling personally upon his relatives is the least I can do."

Dinner, as expected, was a delight. In addition, Andrews and Wiswall enjoyed the lieutenant and his conversation. As they ate, Nevill predicted that a welcome, cleansing rain would soon be upon them, and abundantly so, since virtually the entire southwest was due after three years of inordinate, excessive heat.

"You fellows ought to see how a good rain can transform the deserts and prairies. No Texan ever complains about rain. Even the Apaches will tell you it's coming—and in buckets."

"The Indians set great store by the weather, then?" Andrews said.

Nevill nodded as he speared a morsel of pork. "Rain, in their thinking, is witchery; it brings life to dryness, to all that grows and breathes, and to men themselves."

"We don't have a force like the Rangers up in Colorado," Wiswall said, a bit later. "Police, sheriffs, and posses, for sure, but no lawmen just rambling around the country. What kind of men are you and your fellow Rangers?"

Nevill took a long, slow sip of his coffee. He gave his companions a careful look.

"Five years ago, I served under Capt. L. H. McNelly in a special company of Rangers dispatched to settle some trouble in DeWitt County. In those days, we were so poor that we had to beg for ammunition and horseshoes. But we did what we had to do.

"There were some fellows down there who were hell-bent on continuing to fight the Civil War, you see. And they attracted all the wrong sort of rough men to their cause. But when we went down there, we finally put a stop to it."

"What did you have to do?" Andrews asked.

Nevill fixed him with a steady, green-eyed gaze. "Whatever it took."

After a pause, he continued his narration. "After calming the troubles there, Captain McNelly was asked to form Company A of the organization, and I signed up for it, too. We entered hellhole after hellhole, rooting out the worst of the worst, criminals of every persuasion. I never knew, heard of, or served with such a true and faithful commander.

"And so, to answer your original question . . . What sort of fellows are the Texas Rangers? We're the sort who will do what we must, at any time, to keep order in the state and to make it safe for law-abiding citizens. We will take on any fight, and we will see it through to the end, by whatever means are at hand."

"What's that little gold locket dangling around your neck, Mr. Andrews?" asked Nevill, after a while. "It must mean something to you, since you don't see men wearing them much."

Andrews, without looking up from his coffee cup, answered, "You are correct, sir. It's not a simple memento or a mere piece of jewelry. This locket contains a snippet of my mother's and my father's hair. I lost my parents six years ago. My dearest hope is that one day, I'm laid to rest next to them in Austin."

"If you will permit me a personal inquiry, how did they die?" Nevill said.

"Kiowa and Comanche raiders ambushed them at their homestead, just before the start of the Red River Wars."

"I am very sorry," Nevill said. "I believe the army finally put all that to rights a few years back, but it was too late for your folks." Andrews nodded.

Wiswall said quietly, "Lieutenant, I daresay the decent folk of Texas owe a great debt to you Rangers. I hope you receive the appreciation you ought to have."

Nevill smiled. "Well, we don't serve for the appreciation. It is thanks enough to see the country governed by law and hospitable to the honest efforts of good, enterprising people. But now and then, someone offers a few words of gratitude, and that is awfully nice to hear, I'll admit."

Nevill reached behind him, into a pocket of the short

jacket hanging on the back of his chair. He withdrew a much-handled, often-folded page from a newspaper.

"A schoolmarm from Brenham, a day's ride northeast of here, wrote up a pretty little tribute, not too long ago. It found its way into one of the newspapers, and I keep it with me. Sometimes, when my comrades and I are on a long ride, I'll take this out and read it over again, in the light of the campfire, just to remind myself of why we Rangers do what we do. Would you like to hear it?"

After Andrews and Wiswall gave their encouragement, Nevill cleared a place on the table and spread the newsprint in front of him. "She calls it 'The Texas Rangers,'" he said, and started reading.

It was indeed a lovely piece of encomium. It described the Ranger as he might be situated on a long patrol: astride a sturdy mount, wrapped in an oilskin slicker or a woolen blanket against the cold and wet, tirelessly trailing a band of marauding Indians, or a gang of border desperadoes, or a wily criminal bent on victimizing a remote settlement. The article discussed the early days of the organization: the times when the newly formed territory of Texas was rapidly gaining a reputation for crime, desperation, and massacre. Hence, volunteer companies were organized for protection. These were the first soldiers to be called Rangers.

The piece lauded the bravery of the Rangers, describing how they served without uniforms, took part in no parades, and even avoided the congress of throngs. Rather, they spent their days in the saddle, their nights in the open, pursuing evildoers wherever they might be found and bringing them to justice.

When Nevill finished reading, a lengthy silence followed. Finally, Wiswall, looking past his dining companions and through the restaurant's window onto the town center, said quietly, "I am glad you read that, Lieutenant. And I am pleased that some folks in Texas, at least, realize how grateful they should be for the presence of the Texas Rangers." Nevill inclined his head in thanks.

"What are the matters of most concern for you and your fellow Rangers these days, Lieutenant?" said Andrews.

"Of all we contend with currently, we are most worried about the Apache chief Victorio." Seeing the puzzled looks of the men, Nevill continued.

"A few months ago, Victorio and a couple hundred warriors, along with women and children, broke out of their reservation in Arizona Territory and headed into Mexico. Since then, they have been raiding and terrorizing the country from Fort Davis, all the way west to El Paso and into New Mexico. Victorio is as wily as they come, and my friends in the army tell me he is no mean tactician. I talked to a trooper from the Sixth Cavalry who chased him, and he told me that everywhere Victorio went, he left behind murdered, burned bodies, ruined ranches, and slaughtered cattle and sheep."

"Has he been seen in these parts?" Wiswall said.

"Not around here. But the entire west region of Texas, New Mexico, northwestern Mexico, and Arizona are extremely dangerous places. Pity the people he catches, be they Mexican, US citizens, or even Indians not of his own tribe."

After looking at the two Coloradoans for a moment, Nevill said, "Gentlemen, I think that I will give you some advice about your burros, after all. If you can't find what you need in this part of Texas or farther south and east, then just go back home to Ouray County. Don't risk going west of here."

Chapter Two

With Lieutenant Nevill's warning ringing in their ears, the two partners spent two more days in San Antonio, making inquiries at various liveries and among such persons as they could find who seemed knowledgeable about livestock and where it might be procured. Their hesitancy to leave the creaturely comforts of the American House Hotel somewhat encouraged the leisurely pace of their investigation. Though not lacking in skills or nerve—and having provided for themselves a good arsenal of arms against the dangers they anticipated on the trail—they were uncertain of the best direction to take in pursuing their aim of procuring burros.

Ultimately, the duo judged their best path for the present was as Nevill had suggested; they would point south and east, following the old San Patricio cattle trail that led from San Antonio toward the town founded by Irish immigrants to what was then the northern part of Mexico, nearly fifty years previous, and named for their patron saint. From there, they would strike for the nearby coastal city of Corpus Christi and follow the coast down to the Mexican border town of Matamoros, across the Rio Grande from Brownsville. They reasoned that by working their way from that point gradually north along the river, continuing through the several cities, towns, and hamlets along its banks on both sides, they were likely to come across an adequate supply of the sort of pack animals they sought.

After a fortnight in the saddle and most nights sleeping under the stars, the two partners, with their dog leading the way, finally reached the Rio Grande at the place where it emptied, wide, brown, and flat, into the Gulf of Mexico at the utter tip of the United States of America.

They spent their first night in a hostelry run by a proprietor named Miller, counting themselves fortunate, first, that Shep was once again permitted to sleep in their room, and second, that their room was on the recently constructed third floor of the establishment. The next morning, with Shep trailing along at their heels, they set out for the Matamoros side of the river to begin making inquiries after some burros.

"Where do you reckon we ought to start?" Andrews said as they stepped onto the ferry that would take them across the flowing border between the two nations.

"Well, you're the Harvard man," Wiswall said. "I figured you had a plan."

"You figured wrong, partner. I guess we'll find the first place that looks like a livery and commence there."

"How do you know what a livery looks like in Mexico?"

Andrews stared straight ahead as the ferry pushed off from the Texas side. "I imagine we can follow the smell. That ought to translate pretty easily."

Wiswall chuckled. "You see? I knew you had a plan."

Arriving in front of a likely looking establishment, Andrews, in his best Spanish, asked if there were any pack burros to be had in the vicinity.

The man attending the low-roofed, wooden shed, instead of answering, just stared at Shep, who, standing beside Wiswall, returned the fellow's look with every evidence of intent interest in whatever answer he would make.

"Sit down, Shep," Wiswall said quietly, and the dog promptly sat. "I think you're making this man nervous."

Looking from Shep to Wiswall, then up to Andrews, the man said, in heavily accented but perfectly understandable words, "Señor, why don't you try again in English? I can't make out what you just said."

As Wiswall covered a smile, Andrews said, "We are looking to buy as many as a hundred burros, suitable for service as pack animals. We have means to make immediate payment for the right kind of stock."

The Mexican man nodded slowly. "A hundred?"

Andrews nodded.

The Mexican nodded a bit more. He studied the ground for a few seconds, then looked up at Andrews. "No, señor. I don't know anybody who has that many burros to sell. But I would buy this dog from you; he seems well-mannered and smart, and I could use him to guard the place."

"Shep isn't for sale," Wiswall said. He touched his hat brim. "We appreciate your time, all the same."

The Mexican nodded again. Andrews tipped his hat, and the two men walked on down the street.

After spending the rest of that day making inquiries on both sides of the river—and not receiving the information they hoped for—Andrews and Wiswall determined that the next day they would turn their path along the broad, turbid stream, hoping that they would meet with better success as they made their way through the borderlands.

Well-worn horse and wagon trails led them through Harlingen, McAllen, and all the settlements in between until they reached Rio Grande City in Starr County. On the outskirts of the settlements and along the shallow valleys that extended from the riverbanks, tents, brush lean-tos, and jacales of mud or adobe dotted both sides of the border. Herds of cattle and flocks of sheep and goats grazed the lush meadows and browsed the low scrub.

As Andrews and Wiswall followed the course of the Rio Grande toward the interior, the heat of the late Texas summer began gradually to yield, even so far south, to the cooler nights of autumn. As often as not, a thin, drizzling rain fell on them during the night, driving the men to the imperfectly waterproofed shelter of their small tent, which they shared with Shep. The horses, unsaddled, stood hobbled outside, heads down, the wet dripping off of them in rivulets into the mud. On the damp mornings following such nights, misty air spread an indistinct gray shroud as far as their eyes could see across the flats of scrub mesquite, cenizo, and catclaw.

Now and then, when they were lucky, they encountered a rude posada that offered a roof and perhaps, for a few centavos, a meal of mashed frijoles and tortillas cooked on a flat, baked-clay comal heated over mesquite coals.

One evening, as boisterous autumn winds rattled and whistled around the sills of the simple hut they shared with the family of Lorenzo Quintana and his family—in the brush country about halfway between Roma and Bellville—the after-supper talk turned to the travelers' intentions, direction, and destination. When Andrews informed their host that they intended to follow the river until they found someone who could sell them pack animals, the wizened vaquero shook his head slowly.

"No esta bien, señores, to keep going much more up Río Bravo. Not by yourselves. Es muy peligroso—very dangerous."

"Why is that?" Wiswall asked, glancing at Andrews.

"Victorio," the Mexican said, glancing at the door as the word passed his lips, as though he feared that saying the name of the Apache chief would summon him, demon-like, from the darkness surrounding the tiny hacienda. "This man is muy malo—very bad. He has killed many: gringos, mexicanos, indios . . . Even los Rinches—the Rangers—they cannot catch him. They chase him, but he vanishes like smoke on the wind."

"What else do you know of Victorio?" Andrews said, as Quintana took out his belt knife and began, slowly and methodically, to scrape it across a sharpening stone. "Almost since we entered Texas, people have been speaking of this man. Where did he come from? Who are his people?"

The vaquero shrugged, his eyes never leaving the blade. Metal rasped on stone a half-dozen times before he said, "Es Apache, los Mescaleros, maybe, or maybe Chiricahua. He and his people were on un reservacion farther to the west, maybe Arizona. I think it was a bad place for them. They left to become asaltantes y ladrónes—raiders and thieves. Since then, los Rinches in Texas and la milicia in Mexico have chased him, but no one can catch him."

A coal popped on the fire. Shep, dozing with his back to the glow, flinched upward at the noise, but soon put his head back down.

"Well, we've got to buy some burros, so I reckon we'll keep going, all the same," Andrews said after another few seconds of silence. "We'll keep a sharp eye out."

The Mexican continued sharpening his knife, carefully, deliberately. "No esta bien," he said into his thick mustache, without looking up. "Muy peligroso."

Despite their most earnest efforts, by the time they had passed through Laredo they had still not found anyone who could sell them the burros they needed. They traveled on past Eagle Pass and Piedras Negras, and finally reached as far as the yet-unnamed village gathering up around San Felipe Springs—still with no luck. By this time, the year had leaned over into winter, and the weather was increasingly cold, wet, and windy.

Andrews and Wiswall had entered the wild and extravagant country lying in the Big Bend of the Rio Grande. Palisaded promontories alternated with vistas almost unimaginably broad, expanding to the horizon in such sweeps of vastness that the two travelers wondered how even the Almighty might find them amid the immensity.

On a rare morning when the rain had abated somewhat, they rode along the river on a path that took them through a thicket of honey mesquite. The riders were obliged to duck or lean to this side or that as their horses picked their way along the winding trail.

"Where are those wide open spaces you were waxing so eloquent about just the other day?" Andrews said.

Wiswall swore softly and grabbed at his hat as a low-slung branch raked it off his head.

Suddenly Shep halted in front of them, stiffening as the hair between his shoulders bristled to attention. First Andrews's mount, then Wiswall's, stopped in their tracks as well, their ears perked forward and their nostrils sifting the morning air.

Something large lurked in the thicket ahead of them—large enough that it felt no need to keep its presence a secret. The men heard heavy footfalls on the flinty soil and heard the sound of twigs snapping. Andrews reached for his Colt revolver and Wiswall readied the Springfield he carried, drawing it from its saddle scabbard while keeping his eyes locked on the moving underbrush in front of them.

They could see a shape moving through the thicket, treading in no particular hurry toward the very path they were on. More footfalls, and then a long, tawny head came poking through the branches of the honey mesquite, followed by a curving neck and a mounded hump.

A camel stood on the trail in front of them. It slowly turned its head in their direction and gave a low, guttural bawl.

Andrews's horse exploded skyward and came down on all four feet, humped like a tomcat in an alley fight. Then it put its head down and flung its hindquarters into the air. It sunfished like a devil-horse. Andrews pulled leather for all he was worth, but it was no good; he flew one direction, the Colt he had been holding went the other way. He arced through the air and landed on his left shoulder; the wind huffed out of him. His horse, squealing in terror, went banging off through the scrub.

Meanwhile, Wiswall was fighting to stay aboard. His horse began to crow-hop, but he had the presence of mind to haul mightily on one side of the reins, pulling the horse's head around nearly to his knee. The horse began dancing in a tight circle, and Wiswall turned the air blue with curses as he tried to holster his rifle and keep his mount under control at the same time. As all this was going on, Shep barked at the height of his ability.

The camel watched everything that was taking place with an apparent lack of alarm, or even of curiosity.

Wiswall was finally able to get his horse headed back the way they had come, then to slow it enough so that he could dismount and grab the bridle. He held onto the reins, keeping the horse's head turned away from the source of the panic.

"Andrews! Are you all right?"

Andrews groaned as he levered himself to a sitting position. He rubbed his left shoulder. "I think so," he called. "I'm damned lucky my noggin didn't bounce off one of these trees, though. Did you see which way my horse went?"

"No idea. I was somewhat preoccupied."

By this time, the camel had wandered into the scrub on the other side of the trail, apparently headed toward the river for a drink. Shep stared in the direction the beast had gone but made no move to follow it.

Andrews got slowly to his feet. He took careful stock of all his bones and joints, gradually satisfying himself, much to his relief, that nothing appeared to be more than badly bruised. He scouted around until he located his revolver, and he called Shep to his side. "I'll see how far the horse has gone. Damn that camel and all his tribe."

"If the Arabs show up that belong to him, I'll give them your regards," Wiswall said.

"You do that."

Andrews's horse had left a pretty plain trail of scattered gear and trampled underbrush, so it wasn't long until Andrews came upon the animal, standing in a small clearing with its nose to the ground, cropping the thin grass. When he had straightened the saddle and re-tightened the girth strap, he took up the reins and led the horse back toward the trail where Wiswall waited.

"I reckon we just happened upon a refugee from that little experiment the army conducted, back before the Civil War," Wiswall said as Andrews approached. "They tried using camels out here for a while, thought they might stand the heat and the dry better than horses or mules."

"I think I remember reading something about that, a few years back," Andrews said, massaging his shoulder. "But I surely never expected to be unseated because of a camel in the Texas desert."

"You stayed with him for a couple of hops, at least."

"I never said I was a bronc peeler."

"No, you didn't. Well, here's hoping that's the worst surprise we encounter on this little excursion."

"Easy for you to say; I'm the one with the banged-up shoulder."

"Fair enough."

"Is that damned camel out of the way?"

"Appears so, judging by Shep and the horses. Shall we continue?"

"Lead on. I'll ride drag for a while."

Chapter Three

Andrews and Wiswall slanted northwestward along the slow-moving river, averaging twelve to fifteen miles a day. Once Presidio was behind them, they gradually began to encounter more ranches and haciendas, along with signs of organized cattle operations. Fairly often, they saw riders, either solitary or in groups of no more than three, their saddles rigged for heavy roping. These approached slowly, usually with a carbine held loosely in front of them across the pommel, a finger crooked through the trigger guard. Once they could tell the travelers held only innocent intentions, they typically gave one- or two-word answers when questioned. Their wind-creased faces displayed little curiosity.

Staying close to the river and keeping the Chinati and Sierra Vieja ranges on their right, Andrews and Wiswall rode through endless miles of rough, broken country, dotted with sparse outcroppings of creosote and low-slung juniper. Beneath their slickers, they shrugged under the weight of the near-constant rain, hat brims tilted like drooping plates against the downpour.

Four days out of a hamlet called Gallina, they camped beneath an overhang. From the soot on the low ceiling and the darkened places on the rocky floor, they could tell they weren't the first travelers to shelter there. But there were no signs of recent occupants—human, at least—and it was a relief to gain a night's respite from the relentless tapping of the rain's myriad tiny mallets. There was even enough headroom for the hobbled horses.

The two men made a cold camp; all the wood within a hundred miles was soaked to the core. After knifing open a can of beans and passing it back and forth, they leaned back on their saddles and talked quietly in the early dark of the winter and the rain, their voices just rising above the constant patter beyond the edge of the sheltering overhang. Shep curled up and fell asleep by the back wall.

"What do you calculate Annie is doing, right about now?" Wiswall said.

"Not pining for you, if that's what you're hoping. I imagine she's got the good sense to find herself a man who won't go riding off through the most godforsaken parts of Texas in the middle of a rainy winter."

"Andrews, you can be cruel when you want to be, do you know that?"

Andrews gave a guilty grin. "I'm sorry, partner. I know you miss her. I would be lonesome, too, if I had a gal back home."

"Maybe that's what's wrong with you. Maybe a woman's touch would moderate that razor-sharp tongue of yours."

"Or make it worse." Andrews eased himself back against his saddle, trying to find a comfortable resting place for his head. "Well, this is certain, at least: I will feel a whole lot better when two things have happened: when we have had a bath apiece in a tub of warm water, and when we have secured safe passage back at least as far as the upper Pecos country."

"Amen to that. But we won't have any show of either of those until we reach Ysleta and El Paso del Norte. I, for one, am longing to see the lights of that place as a departed soul yearns for the first sight of the Pearly Gates," Wiswall said.

Andrews nodded drowsily. "We've spent enough time in purgatory; that's certain."

Wiswall grinned. "You fancy this purgatory?"

"It certainly isn't heaven. It might be full-fledged hell, though."

"I don't think Old Scratch himself could kindle a fire hereabout," Wiswall said. "They don't make a brimstone that can stand up to this constant cold and wet."

They both jumped as Shep gave a sharp yelp and growl. They stared into the dark beyond the sheltering rim, their fingers on the triggers of their Colts. But neither of them saw anything, and the only sound was the soft, unbroken drumming of the rain.

"He's already asleep again," Andrews said, looking back at Shep.

"Dreaming, then, I reckon."

Andrews nodded. "Back in that pit, from the sound of it."

"Most likely. Poor old fellow."

After a long silence, Andrews said, "Have you ever considered what it might feel like to be trapped, knowing you faced a hopeless fight?"

"I've thought of little else, since we found him," Wiswall said. "And lately, come to think of it, I've wondered what it might be like to be Victorio. Penned on a reservation, hundreds of miles from the country where you've been accustomed to roaming as free as the wind. I reckon the feeling might be something similar."

Andrews grunted and nodded. "And women and children with him."

After another long spell, Wiswall said, "When a man is hungry and thinks he hasn't got any other choice, he'll do most anything, I imagine."

Andrews ran a hand along Shep's back and scratched behind the big dog's ears. "I imagine you're right."

By the time they were a day's ride past the abandoned buildings of Fort Quitman, the country had broadened out, on the American side of the river, at least. The mountains retreated to the north and east, and the land around the river was unremittingly flat and soggy. It sucked at the horses' hooves with every step, and there was no shelter from the cold wind that drove the rain into their faces and forced it into gaps in their slickers. The last leg of the journey into Ysleta was tedious: the level, monotonous river plain giving way now and then to soaked sand hills bounded on the horizon by hollows, ravines, and gorges filling and releasing the rainwater anywhere it could go onto the prairie floor.

On their left, the Rio Grande, less than a hundred yards from the trail into Ysleta, flowed along as it had forever: a thin sheet of muddy water, less than fifty yards wide, and, at this particular point south of their destination, less than six feet in its deepest channel. Or so it had been, according to the ranch hands they encountered hereabout. If this rain held up, the river would doubtless get deeper and wider. They saw no need to ride into the channel to test the theory.

When they reached irrigated farmlands spreading on both sides of the river around the Mexican village of San Agustín, they knew they were nearing their destination. Soon, in the last of the gray light of day, they saw in the rapidly descending, misty darkness the blurred lights of Ysleta.

But the gates of the old pueblo where the Ranger station was housed were already barred for the night. The old Tigua man crouched in the watchman's hut either could not speak English or didn't want to be bothered by two bedraggled travelers, coming to him after dark. Tired, wet, and chafing at every place where skin passed over skin, Andrews and Wiswall reined their sagging mounts away from the gate and splashed through the puddles toward the village called El Paso del Norte.

To the partners' relief, they happened upon a small hostelry before going too far, and there was a livery stable next door. Though neither building resembled anything new or luxurious, to the travelers it may as well have been Buckingham Palace.

"You boys are about the sorriest sight I seen in a month," the jovial liveryman said as he came outside, raising his coal-oil lantern for a better look as the two dismounted. "You been riding these hosses, or toting them?"

"Friend, you don't have time to listen to our story," Andrews said, managing a weary smile. "Do you have room for our horses?"

"Reckon they can share a stall?"

"They've shared poorer accommodations."

"Well, all right, then. Pull them saddles off and bring 'em inside. I think I got some oats left." He turned away and unlatched the main door of the stable as Andrews and Wiswall tugged loose the latigos holding the cinches.

Inside, they helped the liveryman rub down the horses. Their damp coats steamed in the warm stable, and they were so worn out that the men nearly had to shove them the few steps into the low-walled stall they would share for the night.

"Four bits for each animal for the night," the liveryman said, then held out his hand as Andrews counted the coins into his palm.

"Would you happen to know if the establishment next door will let us keep our dog with us?" Wiswall said.

"Don't rightly know, but you're welcome to leave him here with me. He can sleep on that pile of empty sacks over in that corner yonder, and I got a soup bone or two I can give him."

"We'd be much obliged," Andrews said. "What would that run us?"

"No charge," the liveryman said. "He don't look like he'd be much trouble."

"I don't imagine he will," Wiswall said. Leaning over and looking Shep in the eye, he said, "Go lie down over there, boy." He pointed at the wrinkled pile of burlap in the corner and walked a few paces toward it before turning back toward the dog. "Come on, Shep. Lie down. Over here."

The dog paced slowly in the direction Wiswall had indicated, with a backward glance or two. He sniffed the sacks, looked back at his masters one more time, then lay down with a heavy sigh.

"Well, if that don't beat all!" the liveryman said, grinning. "How long did it take you to train him to do that?"

"He just seems to understand," Andrews said, looking at Shep. "You'll stay, won't you, boy?" he said, addressing the dog.

Shep gave his tail a weary wag, then another. Otherwise, he made no move.

The liveryman let out a cackle. "I do declare he sure enough savvies English! Well, I'll look after him for you, and glad to do it. He'll be right there in the morning when you come, like enough."

Chapter Four

In the morning, feeling considerably more like human be-ings after hot baths and a good night's sleep, Andrews and Wiswall came downstairs and approached the sleepy-look-ing clerk at the shabby bar of the establishment, which also served as the front desk of the hostelry.

"Where might a man get breakfast nearby?" Andrews asked.

The clerk had a neck like a buzzard's. He yawned noisily as he considered the question. "Closest chop house is back toward the pueblo," he said, pointing. "But if you can wait a bit, I'll fix you some eggs, if we've got any."

Noticing the dark crescents beneath the fellow's fin-gernails, Andrews said, "Back toward the pueblo, you said?"

The man nodded, scratching his head.

"One more question," said Wiswall. "Do you have a secure room here where we can lock up our valuables while we go into town?"

"Gents, I believe I can help you with that," came a booming voice from behind them.

Looking past Andrews and Wiswall, the sallow clerk straightened up his posture noticeably. "I was just about to fix them some breakfast, Mr. Corcoran," he said.

"Never mind that, Simpkins." A large man with florid complexion and a black, handlebar mustache came toward them from the front door. "Would our strong box be secure enough for you?" he said in a soft Irish brogue, gesturing to-ward a small office visible through a doorway behind the bar where the clerk sat.

The partners followed Corcoran into the room and saw a large safe that stood chest-height. Shielding the dial from them, Corcoran spun it back and forth a few times and turned the large steel handle. He grunted as he tugged open the steel door. He turned to look at them. "Would this be enough room for your goods, gentlemen?"

Andrews nodded. "I believe so, yes. And would we be able to retrieve them, say, later this afternoon?"

"Certainly. I'll write you a receipt for your belongings, and I'll be close by, all day; Simpkins will know where to find me. Come whenever you like."

Andrews and Wiswall went back to their room and retrieved the two canvas bags containing their rifles and extra ammunition.

Corcoran gave a careful, appraising gaze at the bags. "I believe I see the muzzle of a Sharps sticking out of the top of that bag, don't I? And from the sound and the heft, I'd say that's not the only weapon you fellows brought with you. May I?"

Wiswall nodded, and Corcoran, a pad and pencil in hand, peered into first one bag, then the other, jotting down a description of the contents. When he finished and stepped back, Wiswall swung the heavy door shut, turned the handle, and spun the dial.

"We've had a long ride through a good deal of uncertain country," Andrews said. "We thought it best to be well armed."

"I would say so," Corcoran said, nodding. "Especially these days."

"I presume you're talking about Victorio," Wiswall said.

"The same." Corcoran tore off the sheet on which he had written. "Will this do?"

Andrews studied the receipt for a moment and then nodded. He handed the paper back to Corcoran, who signed with a flourish at the bottom, then passed it back to Andrews, who affixed his customary, small and tidy signature. He folded the paper and tucked it in the breast pocket of his shirt.

"Things will be a good deal more settled, I expect, once the army re-garrisons Fort Quitman, down the river a ways," the innkeeper said.

"We rode past there on our way here," Wiswall said. "Completely deserted."

Corcoran nodded. "The last Buffalo Soldiers rode out of there near three years ago this month. But with Victorio on the loose, I hear they've taken a notion to send a detachment back in, maybe from over Fort Davis way."

"Victorio seems to be on the minds of a good number of folks," Andrews said.

"Damned well ought to be. We've got to get this country cleaned up," Corcoran said. "There's talk of the railroad coming through here, pretty soon. Likely, we'll have new folks coming to town, building houses, buying livestock . . . won't do to have a filthy, marauding savage running loose through the countryside."

"I reckon not," Wiswall said after a lengthy pause.

"We'll be going now," Andrews said, "but we'll be back this afternoon. I imagine we'll want our room for another night, at least."

"Make yourselves at home, gents," Corcoran boomed, clapping them both on the shoulder. "Always have rooms for paying guests."

When they walked in the front door of the livery, Shep bounded up from his corner to meet them, wagging his tail vigorously.

"Boys, I don't know how you done it, but that dog's smarter than some people I met. Stayed right there on them bags, like you told him, and never a peep out of him all night," the liveryman said.

They asked the liveryman if he knew of anyone with pack burros to sell. Not to their surprise, given their luck thus far, he didn't. They paid fifty cents apiece to hire two fresh horses for the day, and the liveryman selected two likely looking mounts from among those stabled inside.

"We'll ride into El Paso and look around a bit, then be back later today," Wiswall said, pulling his saddle off the rail.

"Suit yourselves, boys," the liveryman said. "Leave your dog here with me, if you've a notion."

"No, he'll come with us," Wiswall said.

For the first morning in many, the sky showed patches of blue between the dirty white clouds. The air was cool but with little wind, and their horses were fresh. Andrews and Wiswall set them at a brisk trot toward El Paso del Norte, and Shep paced them easily, loping in his customary position in the van.

The road was level, if pocked with puddles, and they

came to the town in a little over an hour. The ride made them remember their hunger, and they ducked into an eatery that didn't look entirely unpromising. For a quarter-dollar each, they filled up on fried steak, flapjacks, and coffee, saving scraps for Shep, waiting patiently outside the doorway.

Andrews and Wiswall walked across the street toward a large, new-looking guest house called the Central Hotel.

"Looks like everybody in town could stay here," Wiswall said with a chuckle. "Can't be more than seven or eight hundred souls here, altogether."

"Well, you heard our innkeeper; they've got big plans."

They noted the presence of a schoolhouse near the edge of the small business district, a ramshackle sheriff's office, and a bawdy house. An adobe structure called the Pony Saloon featured a stack of empty beer barrels out front. Ox wains, likely waiting for loads of goods to be transported up the old Camino Real to Santa Fe and points north, sat beneath the winter-bare branches of the gray oaks lining the street. They sauntered past the Casa Grande Dry Goods Store and Mundy Brothers, a meat market and wholesaler. Noticing a sign that read, "Lightbody & James / Clothing, Boots, Shoes, Hats," Andrews and Wiswall decided it was time to improve their apparel from the ragged, saddle-and-weather-worn duds they'd had on all across Texas.

"Seems as though no one is going to sell us any burros," Andrews remarked as they stepped through the entry of the clothing store. "We might as well spend a little of our money on some better clothes."

"Lead on, partner," Wiswall said, "I'm close behind."

When they had secured for themselves sturdy trousers, two shirts each, good woolen coats, and crisp, brimmed hats, they decided that new boots were also in order. "What's the use of new clothes if your boots look like something Shep has been chewing on?" Wiswall said.

"I couldn't agree more," Andrews said.

As the clerk toted up their purchases and they made payment, Andrews inquired the direction to Fort Bliss.

"Four miles as the crow flies, northeast of town," the clerk said, pointing.

They tied their parcels to their saddles and aimed toward the army post.

Chapter Five

The northeast route they were advised to take led over to a muddy track named Main Street and past a dozen structures of various sizes, some of adobe, some wood framed. The lane was lined with hitching-rails, saddled horses tied to them; covered wagons of various kinds parked parallel.

"Seems they've got nearly as many saloons as people in this town," Andrews remarked.

"More cathouses than churches, for sure."

"They pay better, most likely."

They slowed their ride long enough to peek inside one of the grog parlors. A large, open room held a bar, several tables and chairs, and a billiards table. Even at this early hour, rowdy patrons filled the place. Stairs ascended the back wall, leading to whatever enterprise—pleasure salon or gambling den—was housed on the second floor.

Just as they were turning to leave, a large, pot-bellied man staggered through the open doorway. Andrews and Wiswall ducked aside to let him pass, but Shep happened to be looking the other way, watching a cat slinking by on the other side of the street. The man stumbled over Shep, barely maintaining his already-impaired balance.

"Get outta my way, you damn mutt!" he said. He aimed a kick at Shep's ribs, and the dog yelped as he leaped aside.

Before Andrews could register what had happened, Wiswall had strode to the much larger man and grabbed two handfuls of his shirt front. "Keep away from my dog, you drunken bastard." He shoved the man roughly, and the fellow fell on his back in the muddy street. He blinked for a moment, and then struggled to his feet, grunting and swearing in a slurred voice. When he stood up, he was a good half-head taller than Wiswall, who stood in front of him, fists balled up at his sides.

By now a few men had strolled to the doorway of the saloon to watch the ruckus. Andrews moved a little closer to Wiswall, keeping one eye on his partner and the other on the observers.

"You son of a bitch, I'll whip you good," the drunk said, pushing his chest toward Wiswall.

"You'll be a damned sight better off trying to whip me than if you kick my dog again," Wiswall said in an even voice.

The drunk stared at Wiswall for a few seconds, and then he peered groggily at the knot of onlookers. He made an exasperated noise and stomped away, his backside covered with mud from the nape of his neck to the heels of his boots. A few of the men behind Andrews snickered as they turned and went back inside.

Andrews went over to Wiswall and handed him his hat, which had fallen off when Wiswall shoved the man. "Well, I reckon we'd best be on our way to Fort Bliss," he said.

Wiswall grabbed his hat and jammed it onto his head. He stared at the retreating drunk for a couple of seconds, and then turned toward his horse. "Come on, Shep," he said.

Just before noon, Andrews and Wiswall hauled up in front of the headquarters of the commander of Fort Bliss. They looped their reins over the hitching rail in front of the handsome, two-story frame building with a broad porch.

"Stay here, Shep," Andrews said, pointing to a spot on the porch next to the front door. The dog settled himself against the wall and laid his head on his front paws. The travelers went inside.

After explaining their errand to the satisfaction of the sergeant major in the anteroom, they were ushered into the office of Major N. W. Osbourne.

"Have a seat, gentlemen," Osbourne said after the introductions were concluded. Settling himself back behind his desk, he said, "How may I be of assistance?"

"Major, we have made a long and, so far, fruitless journey through nearly the whole of Texas, with the purpose of procuring a stock of burros to take back with us to the mining country in Ouray County, Colorado, where we come from," Andrews said. "But we have lately had to admit to ourselves that we are whipped, and now our only aim is to go home by the most direct route and as soon as possible. We are aware of the dangers of such a journey, however."

"Victorio," the major said.

Andrews nodded. "Certainly. And so, Major, our first interest is to know whether, within any reasonable time, you expect to dispatch a patrol or some other movement toward the north and east, especially in the vicinity of the valleys of the Pecos River? If you do, we would earnestly request to accompany them, as far as their orders take them, in order to safely come that much closer to our destination in southern Colorado."

Osbourne had begun shaking his head, even before Andrews finished his request. "I am sorry, Mr. Andrews, but I will not be able to help you in this matter. Not in the dead of winter—one of the wettest and windiest we have had for some years, I might add. To send men out at such a time, absent the direst need, would not be the wisest use of our forces. And besides all that, we have only infantry here—no cavalry."

Andrews thought this over for a few seconds. "Very well, Major; we understand your position. So, then, to our second question: We find it advisable to equip ourselves with a wagon or similar conveyance that might be pulled by a small team. Is it possible that your quartermaster might have such a piece of equipment, perhaps used, that we could purchase?"

Osbourne scratched his chin for a moment. "Now, there, I might be able to help you. Sergeant Foster, could you come in here, please?"

The sergeant-major stepped into the doorway. "Sir?"

"Take these men to Lieutenant Kinzie, and ask him to give them any aid in his power, according to their request."

"Yes, sir."

"I believe that we have something that might be just right for your needs," the major said. "Sergeant Foster will show you the way. I wish you good luck and Godspeed, gentlemen, though I would be remiss if I didn't advise you to winter with us here in El Paso or Ysleta and make your journey in better weather and on safer roads."

"Thank you, Major," Andrews said, standing and shaking the commander's hand, "but we have taken it in mind to go home, and we mean to make the attempt. We are grateful for your time."

"Yes, indeed," Osbourne said, shaking Wiswall's hand.

"This way, gentlemen," the sergeant-major said, gesturing toward the front door.

With Shep tagging along at their heels, the three men strode across the wide parade ground. As they went, Andrews asked their guide if he had any knowledge of the old Butterfield Stage road that led east, past the Hueco Tanks, toward the Pecos River.

"Well, no one goes that way much these days," he said. "It's not judged safe unless you're with an armed convoy."

"Granted, but what about the terrain?" Andrews said. "What kind of rig would a man need to have to manage the trip to the Pecos, going that way?"

"That there is some pretty rough country," the sergeant-major said. "You'd need some good, sturdy stock, I reckon. The terrain is likely why the Butterfield stopped traveling that way, going on twenty-two years ago, near-about."

"It sounds to me as though we had better trade our ponies for a couple of stout draft horses," Wiswall said.

"And the harness for them," Andrews said, nodding.

They arrived at the quartermaster's post. Sergeant Foster made introductions, gave Shep a scratch behind the ears, and left them. Lieutenant Kinzie listened carefully to their intentions and their planned route.

"Gentlemen, how much are you willing to spend on your conveyance?"

They told him that they could hardly afford anything large enough to require a four-animal team—or the animals to draw it, for that matter.

"Well . . . " The quartermaster tapped a finger on his temple as he thought. "I do have one of the Coolidge ambulances in surplus. I don't believe it has been too hard-used. Would you like to come over to the shed and take a look at it?"

The two-wheeled Coolidge was built to accommodate two men on stretchers, lying side by side. It also had a fair amount of shelf space above the bed, it was roofed and curtained against the elements, and best of all, it could be handily drawn by two horses. The lieutenant warned them that this particular model had acquired the unaffectionate nickname "The Avalanche" because of the sometimes bone-jarring ride it delivered, running as it did on only two wheels and lacking much in the way of springs or other suspension. But as a light conveyance that offered a place for sleeping other than the cold ground, Andrews and Wiswall concluded that the Coolidge fit their bill.

"I'll wager we could find a small, cast-iron heating stove that we could rig up inside," Andrews said, pointing here and there at the ambulance's interior. "And those look like iron-hubbed wheels to me."

"If I'm not mistaken, we have some extra harness we can let you have at no cost," Lieutanant Kinzie said. "That will save you some money. And yes, this ambulance has an iron running gear and wheel hubs. You'll need that if you take the route you intend."

By the time they had completed negotiations, the quartermaster made them a price just over $100; Andrews later told Wiswall he calculated that was less than half the price of a new ambulance.

"We don't have any surplus horses," Kinzie told them as he wrote out a bill of sale. "But if I were you fellows, I would ride over to Ysleta. There's a livery right next to a hotel run by an Irishman, and the owner is about as good a judge of horseflesh as anybody I know in these parts. If anyone hereabout has got good pulling stock, he'll know about it."

Andrews and Wiswall realized the lieutenant was directing them back to the livery where they had started earlier that day. "We know the place and the man," Andrews said. "We'll inquire of him, as you suggest."

"Too bad he doesn't traffic in armed guards," Wiswall said, scuffing the toe of his boot on the rough floor planking. "The major informed us that the army wasn't heading our way any time soon."

"Meaning no offense, but you ought to attend carefully to the major's advice," Lieutenant Kinzie said. "Victorio is about as wily as they come. I'm plenty satisfied to sit out the winter here at the fort, and not ashamed to say it."

"I expect you're right about all of that," Andrews said.

"But we mean to go home, and we are still holding out hope of locating some burros we can sell, along the way."

"Well, if you're dead-set, you ought to inquire at the Ranger station, back in Ysleta," Kinzie said. "Civilian escort is one of their usual missions, though I can't say I'd bet heavily on Baylor sending men with you, any more than Major Osbourne did."

"It now seems that we have at least two errands waiting for us back in Ysleta," Wiswall said. "I reckon we'd best be on our way while there's plenty of daylight left."

"We will come back by tomorrow to retrieve the ambulance, once we've secured a team." Andrews said.

The quartermaster nodded. "I'll have your rig greased and waiting for you."

Chapter Six

The old Indian who had denied them entry the night before was nowhere in evidence when Andrews and Wiswall arrived at the entry to the post housing Company C in the Frontier Battalion, Texas Rangers. The gates of the old pueblo stood wide open, and men and horses passed through in both directions, all seemingly intent upon some errand or other.

The Rangers of Company C resided in what appeared to be a warehouse, or block-house of sorts. According to the signage, painted slapdash on a whitewashed board, part of the low, flat-roofed structure housed Chilvers and Keirle Company, Outfitters. The other part, perhaps one-third of the building, was the Rangers' sleeping quarters, mess, and relaxation area. They saw, scattered around the pueblo premises, stables, other small structures and adobe dwellings, and one large, well appointed adobe house fronted by a wide porch.

Unable to catch anyone's attention long enough to obtain guidance as to Lieutenant Baylor's whereabouts, the travelers made for the block-house, which seemed to be the focus of a good deal of activity. With Shep padding along at their heels, they entered a large, well-lit room.

They noticed a man molding bullets near a fireplace on the far wall. Others milled about or sat in threes and fours at plank tables, some cleaning guns or mending tack, and others playing monte or faro with creased cards. One corner of the room held a pile of saddles and harnesses.

"Excuse me, friend, but can you direct me toward Lieutenant Baylor?" Wiswall said to a man sitting by himself, studying a soiled newspaper. He looked up at Wiswall for a moment, then at Andrews. Finally his eyes fell upon Shep, who wagged his tail slowly. One corner of the man's heavy mustache lifted slightly, and he aimed a forefinger over Wiswall's shoulder, through the doorway by which they had just entered. "This time of day, he's generally setting on the porch of his house, yonder." Wiswall touched his hat brim, and they went in the direction indicated. They walked across the muddy yard of the pueblo toward the house, and true to the man's word, they saw a tall, strong figure of a man seated on the porch of the house, draped in a loose-limbed posture on a low bench that somewhat resembled a church pew.

Lieutenant George Wythe Baylor had a narrow, intelligent face, clear blue eyes, and a demeanor of quick and quiet interest in whatever was going on around him. He now focused that interest on Andrews and Wiswall as they approached. "Evening, gentlemen. That is a fine-looking dog you've got with you, there."

"Thank you, sir. I presume you to be Lieutenant Baylor?" Andrews said.

"Guilty as charged," Baylor said with a smile. "And to whom do I have the honor of speaking?" Andrews introduced himself and Wiswall to Baylor, and the three men shook hands all around.

Andrews told the Ranger commander what they had on their minds. Baylor gazed off into the distance as he listened, and for a good, long while after Andrews had finished his request, he continued in what looked like a thoughtful silence.

"No, fellows, I will not be able to send men with you," he said, finally. "And I will also urge you to reconsider your travel plans."

"Thank you, Lieutenant," Andrews said, "and I assure you that you are not the first to question the wisdom of our intentions, with good reason, in all likelihood. But we are firm in our purpose. We have taken care of ourselves thus far on this long journey, and we believe we can see ourselves home on our own, if we have to."

Baylor nodded slowly. "Well, I can't fault your resolve, at least. But may I at least counsel you, as one who has made a careful study of the Mescalero people and their habits and who also knows a little about traveling through this country?"

The lieutenant told Andrews and Wiswall that, if they were determined to go to the upper Pecos country, they should start back the way they had come, but veer sooner to the east, taking the overland stage route to Fort Davis, in the Big Bend country. From there, he told them, they might work their way along Toyah Creek and come to the Pecos drainage by a much safer route.

"That sounds like a lot of backtracking to me, Lieutenant," Andrews said when Baylor had finished. "The way straight to the east would save us a good deal of time."

"What you may save in time, friend, you risk in danger. Let me tell you some of what I have learned in these last months, while I have been pursuing Victorio and his raiders . . . "

As Baylor talked about Victorio and his renegade band, men were steadily passing to and fro across the pueblo yard. Most of those who passed anywhere near Baylor's front porch made enough of a detour to stoop down and scratch Shep's head or rub along his neck. Before long, even Lieutenant Baylor started to notice the dog's spontaneous popularity with his Rangers.

"Your dog has winning ways, I judge," he said, grinning. "How long have you had him?"

"We picked him up back in the spring, on our way down into Texas from Colorado," Wiswall said. He patted a hand along Shep's ribs. "He's made a pretty good companion, all told."

"He is as well-mannered as any dog in my experience," Baylor said.

"Yes, he behaves himself," Andrews said. "We three seem to understand each other pretty well."

"Where did you find him?"

"Fort Sill, in the Indian Territory," Wiswall said. "Some soldiers there . . . had him. We got him from them."

Andrews recognized the hard, flat line of his partner's voice as he recollected the day they'd first seen Shep. He cleared his throat. "Well, Lieutenant, I expect we've taken up enough of your time. We've got some business over at the livery that we need to conclude, so I guess we'll be taking our leave."

"Certainly, gentlemen, certainly. But may I at least invite you to take a meal with me before you strike out on the trail?"

"I'm not in the habit of refusing good food that is freely offered," Andrews said with a wry smile.

"Very well! Why don't you take the day tomorrow to provision yourselves, and then come back here about this same time of the evening? My wife and daughters would enjoy getting to know your dog, there, and I'd relish the opportunity to tuck some good, home-cooked food into you before you head back out into the wilderness."

"We'd be honored, Lieutenant," Andrews said as Wiswall nodded eagerly.

"That's settled, then. I'll look for you tomorrow evening. And my sergeant, Jim Gillett, will be there, too. You'll like him."

The next morning, the livery stable owner proved as good as Lieutenant Kinzie's assessment. He led them to a corral behind his barn and pointed out two heavy-limbed, stocky geldings, one a solid sorrel and the other a bay with a white off forefoot and a blaze down his face. "I just got them from a fellow over Mesilla way. He'll take a hundred for the pair. I guarantee you they're in good shape—at least, I'm pretty sure they are, as much oats and hay as I've put through 'em."

"That certainly seems a fair price," Wiswall said.

"You won't do no better anywhere around here, I promise you," the liveryman said. "These here hosses can pull anything you got, up any hill you're likely to see."

"What can you give us for the ponies we rode in on?" Andrews said.

The liveryman scratched his head. "Well, them hosses are pretty wore out. But they still look sound, and with a little rest and some oats. . . I expect I could go twenty-five each."

After Andrews had patted down both horses, feeling their legs and walking around them a couple of times each, they shook hands with the liveryman. Andrews gave him the trade difference in cash, and they agreed on a time later that morning when they would pick up their new team and take it to the fort to retrieve the ambulance.

They found the ambulance just as Kinzie had promised, and with the team hitched up, it appeared that they would have the means to make the trip to the upper Pecos in at least some measure of comfort. The partners spent the rest of the afternoon securing enough beans, sowbelly, and coffee to carry them to Pope's Crossing on the Pecos and, with luck, a little beyond. Almost as an afterthought, they struck a deal with the liveryman for a saddle horse, reasoning that it might be well for one of them to serve as a kind of outrider on their two-man expedition.

The clouds were starting to close in again as evening began to draw down. The partners even felt a drop or two of rain as they walked across the yard of the pueblo toward the Baylor house, fronted by the broad veranda where they had met the post commander the day before.

Andrews and Wiswall, with Shep following at their side, walked up the steps to the wide porch, and Baylor stood smiling at the front door. "This fellow can come on in with you," he said, nodding toward Shep. "He is one of our guests of honor, after all."

The living room was warm and neatly carpeted. As they entered, a young man rose from his seat on a small sofa near a thriving fire in the brick fireplace. "Gentlemen, meet Sergeant Gillett," Baylor said. "Sergeant, these are Andrews and Wiswall, from up Colorado way, and this is Shep, their four-footed partner."

The sergeant shook hands with the two and leaned down to pat Shep on the head. About then, a middle-aged woman and two girls in their early teens entered simultaneously. Baylor presented his wife and his two daughters. The girls gave pretty curtsies and immediately dropped to their knees on either side of Shep, who welcomed their joyful patter and petting with some vigorous tail-wagging.

Later, discussing the very pleasant evening, Andrews and Wiswall would agree that the sofas, chairs, table, and well-filled bookcases in the Baylor home would not have been an embarrassment to any in New York or Baltimore. A pistol, loaded and capped, lay on the mantelpiece, and through the glass windows of a second bookcase Wiswall spotted a small collection of Indian knives. Mrs. Baylor went into the kitchen and returned with iced water, glasses, and a bottle of excellent claret, a refreshment most welcomed by the mining engineers.

Sergeant Gillett proved an interesting companion. To Andrews and Wiswall's eye, he had an air of distinction about him, a quiet dignity demanding respect. Although there was nothing about him suggesting toughness or ruggedness, there certainly was nothing weak in his demeanor. What impressed them the most was how Gillett's weathered face, though still youthful, held cool, watchful eyes. As the pre-dinner conversation progressed, they learned about his last five years with the Texas Rangers, and especially about his experiences during the recent Red River Wars with the Kiowa, Comanche, and Lipan Apache.

When the small party was called into the dining room a few minutes later, Andrews and Wiswall were pleased to note the care evident in the place settings and the arrangement of the surroundings. A quiet Mexican woman was placing the last pitcher of water on the table when they came in, and the travelers watched as Baylor held his wife's chair while she took her seat. They noted, too, a certain solicitousness in Gillett as he performed the same duty for Baylor's older daughter.

They ate, chattering in politeness on any subject that came to mind: the unusual amounts of wind and rain for West Texas thus far in the winter; the possibility of an economic boom for El Paso now that three railroad companies were in the planning stages of putting lines through the area; the principal problems facing Texas and the nation; the ineptitude and graft presently rampant in Washington, DC. Wiswall made their standard inquiry after the availability of burros for purchase and received the same reply that had dogged them since arriving in Texas. They weren't surprised, as their dependable liveryman had already assured them that no one around had sufficient animals to satisfy their request.

"Well, fellows, you need to eat your fill," Baylor said, passing the bowl of roasted vegetables back to Wiswall. "I don't imagine you'll have similar victuals on the trail."

"Lieutenant, beans and bacon don't make much show alongside a baked Virginia ham, homemade apple butter, hot biscuits, and everything else I see here," Andrews said, raising smiles from the others. "And, ma'am," he said, looking at Mrs. Baylor, "I can't provide sufficient superlatives for the way everything tastes."

"What the Harvard man is saying," Wiswall said as he busily forked vegetables onto his plate, "is that this is the best meal we've sat down to since . . . well, I don't know when."

Everyone laughed. "Mr. Wiswall, I thank you," Mrs. Baylor said, "though we all know that hunger is the best sauce. I expect it has been a while since you had any sort of home-cooked food."

"Yes, ma'am. But I'll carry the memory of this meal all the way back to Ouray County, I can promise you. I'd like to send my fiancée down here to take some cooking lessons."

"Well, I shouldn't put it to her that way, if I were you," Mrs. Baylor said, "but I would be delighted by her company, I'm sure."

Shep was enjoying himself, too. Now and again, Andrews or Wiswall would feel the dog slide back and forth against their legs, beneath the table, as first one, then another would drop tidbits for him. No one seemed to mind at all.

After supper, with the women clearing the table and retiring to the kitchen to wash the dishes, Baylor produced pipes, tobacco, and a leather flask of El Paso port, a special fortified dark wine of rich aroma and sharp taste from the grapes grown along the banks of the Rio Grande. He motioned the three men to the large, comfortable chairs positioned before the fireplace.

As Andrews, Wiswall, and Gillett sat and stretched their legs, Baylor lit his pipe. He took a deep pull and let the blue smoke out slowly. Looking first at Wiswall, then at Andrews, he said, "I must tell you straight from the shoulder; you won't make it if you head up towards the Pecos by yourselves, especially in this cold and wet winter weather. You'll need at least ten days for the 150-mile journey, with Victorio and his band potentially behind every rock or waiting in ambush up ahead."

Shep was curled in front of the fire, and his hindquarters lay near Baylor's feet. The lieutenant gently rubbed the dog with the toe of his boot. "As recently as a month and a half ago, around the end of November, a party of Mescalero Apaches left the reservation after killing an ox and fifteen head of sheep. They packed the meat and headed south on six horses they had just stolen. Inasmuch as the meat is well in excess of their present needs, I think it likely that this is only a foraging party for a much larger force planning to take the field, perhaps in the very area you plan to travel through.

"In our nearby Sacramento Mountains, two miners, Fred Asbecks and William Mann, were chased out during the first week of December. We got word by a telegram from the Adjutant General on the tenth of December that Victorio and his war party were the culprits. Mann knows Victorio well and saw him in person.

"Just a week ago, in the general area you plan to travel through the San Mateo Mountains, there have been skirmishes with Victorio, and he has held his own, maneuvering easily through country so rough that it broke down our US Cavalry men and horses in just a few days of scouting.

"Not long ago, some of Victorio's people jumped a mail coach about sunrise near Fort Cummings, a six-company post about ninety miles northwest, up Deming way. They killed every mortal on the coach; their blood soaked the mail sacks."

The fire popped as a log settled in a cloud of sparks. Baylor looked into the flames for a few seconds, then said, "I tell you gentlemen all this to make you aware of where you are and who you're dealing with, in hopes that I can persuade you against your plan and so that you can retain your scalps."

For a time there was no sound except the soft popping of the fire and the muted talk of the women in the kitchen. "Lieutenant, we thank you for this information and the sincere concern that motivates it," Andrews said, finally. "But we are well armed and adequately provisioned—not to mention abundantly forewarned. I think—and I believe I can speak for Mr. Wiswall, also—we mean to go ahead."

Chapter Seven

Before sunrise the next morning, Andrews and Wiswall had settled their accounts with Corcoran, retrieved their weaponry from his safe, and were at the livery harnessing their new team and saddling their other horse. They lingered in Ysleta only long enough to procure a used, but serviceable small wood stove and rig it securely on the inside of the ambulance. And then, a little before noon on Sunday, January 18, 1880, with the lanky Andrews astride the saddle horse and the stocky Wiswall driving the two-wheeled ambulance, they set out to the east for the Pecos River along the abandoned stagecoach trail that had once been the Butterfield Overland Mail route. Shep, of course, trotted along in front. The two men remarked to each other that, after nineteen years of neglect, the trail was in surprisingly good shape. The coach and wagon tracks were easily visible.

They hoped to come without incident to the old Hueco Tanks station, some thirty miles east of El Paso. With fresh horses in harness and if the terrain didn't become too demanding too soon, they hoped that they might reach the station before dark of the second day of travel.

"Well, what do you plan to say to old Victorio, when we meet up with him on the road?" Andrews asked as the Coolidge ambulance jounced along beside him on the rutted trail.

"I will give him the time of day," Wiswall said, "and inquire after the health of his family. We'll discuss the weather, and I expect we'll both have the same opinion of it. And then, no doubt, we'll part company as great friends and go our separate ways."

Andrews gave a low chuckle. "I didn't think you knew so much of the Apache lingo as all that."

"My Apache is about as good as your Spanish," Wiswall quipped.

"Then we're both in trouble, I reckon."

Wiswall laughed.

On that first day the weather, for once, did them a service; though the sky was gray and the wind blustery, they at least were able to travel dry and on a track that didn't threaten to mire the ambulance to the axles. By late afternoon, the miniature caravan had made its way past the last of the barren hills east of El Paso and had crawled onto the broad, open desert of the Hueco Bolson that separated the Franklin Mountains to the west from the Diablo Plateau, to the east. As far as they could see in any direction, the low scrub of the northern Chihuahua desert stretched away toward the horizon. In the dingy, winter light, the creosote, ocotillo, and three-awn grass surrounded them like a grayish-silver sea.

As the sky darkened and the temperature dropped, Andrews and Wiswall began surveying the terrain for a secluded spot to camp. They calculated they had covered almost half of the distance to the Hueco Tanks since leaving Ysleta, just before noon. But now a slight drizzle had started up, guaranteeing a cold, uncomfortable night. Neither man was interested in spending it on the open trail.

Soon enough, they spotted an arroyo with a few low, sheltering hackberry trees growing along its edges. They pulled off the trail and worked their way down into the little ravine. The bottom was muddy from the recent rains, but it offered some shelter from the wind and at least partial concealment from any unfriendly eyes that might pass in the night.

As Andrews placed hobbles on the three horses, Wiswall made a small fire in the ambulance's tiny built-in stove to heat a supper of bacon, beans, and three-day-old bread. The horses nosed along the ground, cropping such goosefoot and grama grass as they could find on the lower sides of the arroyo.

After supper, Andrews and Wiswall stretched their legs and emptied their bladders and bowels as Shep ranged here and there around the campsite. Presently Wiswall whistled and the dog came trotting back. The three climbed into the ambulance for a night's sleep.

"Well, the Coolidge lived up to its nickname, all right," Wiswall said as the two men settled onto their cots. "Like to have drove my tailbone up through my gizzard, a couple of times. But for all that, this surely beats sleeping on the ground."

Andrews made a few small grunts as he arranged his long legs on the cot. "And tomorrow I'll take my turn in the driver's seat; you can ride the pony."

Shep curled at their feet, just inside the opening of the cart.

"What do you say, Shep?" Andrews said. "Will this little wagon do for our home on the trail?"

Hearing his name, the dog lifted his head and looked at Andrews, then at Wiswall. He laid his muzzle back on his paws and closed his eyes.

"I believe you can mark that as a 'yea' vote," Wiswall said.

"I expect so."

Silence fell, broken only by the occasional click of a horseshoe against a rock.

The next morning, they woke to the all-too-familiar patter of rain on the canvas cover of the ambulance.

"I knew the balmy weather was too good to last," Wiswall said as he yawned and stretched. "Go on, Shep; get up off my feet. We're going to travel damp today; might as well get used to it."

Shep raised himself up and, looking more than a little reluctant, hopped down onto the ground. Andrews and Wiswall rolled up their blankets and stowed them in the shelves above the cots. Wiswall shrugged into his slicker and crawled outside to remove the hobbles from the horses and bring the team to harness.

Andrews found a live coal in the little stove and carefully fed it some dry twigs he found under a tangled windfall. Before too long, the water in the coffee pot was boiling. He took the pot off the stove and let it cool for a bit, then he dropped in a scoop or two of coffee and poured in a little cold water to settle the grounds. By the time Wiswall had the team hitched and the pony saddled, Andrews was able to hand him a steaming tin cup.

"Time we've gone about five miles, I'll need another one of these," Wiswall said as he took his first sip.

"How far do you calculate we are from Hueco Tanks?" Andrews said, handing Wiswall a piece of toasted bread.

"I'd say half a day, if the weather were better," Wiswall said. "But the way the air feels, this rain is liable to turn into snow any time now."

Andrews nodded. "Let's see if we can make it before dark. Maybe there's some better cover there."

"Maybe."

Chapter Eight

"**S**ergeant Gillett calculated we'd have no problem finding wood and water at every stop, especially with the rain runoffs," Wiswall remarked, riding along beside the ambulance. "With any luck, Victorio and his bunch are up in New Mexico, on the west side of the Guadalupes."

"Well, one thing's for sure," Andrews said as he jounced along on the bench of the Coolidge, "there's nothing much in this country for them to hide behind. It's about as flat as any place I've ever been."

"That's so," Wiswall said. "On the other hand, there's not much of any place for us to hide, either."

It was true that they were still in open country, and the wind drove straight across it, pushing the thickening snow flurries into their faces. Fortunately for the travelers, the old Butterfield road was easily discernable, relatively straight, and unhindered.

By midday—at least, as well as midday could be guessed with the featureless gray skies and swirling snow— Andrews and Wiswall could descry the first elevation of the Hueco Mountains rising slowly in the east. Squatting just in front of that low range of mountains, the rocky outcroppings of the Hueco Tanks offered the possibility of a windbreak, and they might even find a partial roof left on the abandoned stage station.

The Hueco Tanks station had been built as a meal and change stop on the Butterfield trail. At one time it had possessed an excellent corral, cabin, storage shed, and blacksmith shop. But the trail had not been used regularly since 1859, when the Butterfield line moved south, trailing the Rio Grande well past Eagle Springs before bearing east for Fort

Davis, then up to the Horsehead Crossing on the Pecos—the route Baylor had so earnestly urged on the two travelers.

Now, twenty years later, Andrews and Wiswall would have to make do with crumbling stone and adobe walls, all that remained of the Butterfield Stage station after nearly two decades of nature's slow, relentless battering. They reached the stark, upthrust crags about an hour before full dark and maneuvered around the four rocky outcroppings that made up the formation until they reached the site of the old station, in a pass between the four hills and an ancient-looking reservoir—now more than half-full of rainwater and runoff.

In the fading daylight, Andrews and Wiswall could make out a few of the hundreds of mysterious paintings that decorated the rock faces and hidden grottos of the Hueco Tanks, said to be the leavings of ancient people who hunted these plains thousands of years before. Of course, there were also more recent graffiti, scrawled by bored Buffalo Soldiers, Butterfield employees, or others with time on their hands, not only on the stone of the Tanks but also across the adobe of the abandoned station.

"My mother used to say, 'Fools' names and fools' faces always appear in public places,'" Andrews remarked as they unhitched the team and prepared their camp in the lee of one of the decrepit station walls.

"Ah, but these are historical markings, don't you know," said Wiswall. "These travelers through the sands of time have left their mark—evidence of their brief sojourn through this vale of tears."

"You might want to save some of that breath for getting the stove lit."

Shep snuffled busily about the camp, pausing at several bushes to lift a leg. After a while, he came to Wiswall's call and received a chunk of bacon, carved off the slab and tossed toward him. He caught it in the air and chomped it eagerly, making short work of the tasty morsel.

"Looks like the snow is slowing," Andrews said a bit later as the two men sat in the shelter of the ambulance to eat their supper. "Maybe we'll make better time tomorrow."

"There's a good deal of water held in the hollows of the rocks here," Wiswall said. "We ought to refill the kegs as best we can before we set out."

In the gray of the next predawn, Wiswall harnessed the team and saddled the pony while Andrews made repeated trips to and from the nearest hollow, hueco in Spanish, for which the entire region was named. After dumping enough fresh water from their wooden pail into the kegs strapped to the outsides of the ambulance, he whistled for Shep and announced to Wiswall that it was time to set out.

Determined to press all the way through to Cornudas del Alamo by sunset, they were relieved to see that as the morning broadened, the sun began peeking through the low-scudding gray clouds, and the snow that had fallen the day before began to melt. On this stretch, the Butterfield road crossed Diablo Plateau toward the Salt Flat. Their only difficulty, initially, was negotiating the winding passage up the western flanks of the Hueco Mountains in order to come out onto the plateau; in this ascent, their sturdy draft horses served them well. Once they reached the more level terrain of the plateau, they made good progress.

"What do you suppose accounts for the cruelty Victorio inflicts on his victims?" asked Wiswall as they trundled along, watching the sun climb the sky in front of them.

"Why would you ask that?" Andrews said. "Do you plan to negotiate with him, if we come upon him?"

"He just stays in my mind, that's all. I suppose I'm trying to come to terms with him as a fellow human being. And it doesn't stand to reason that a man followed by other men is cruel for no reason, unless maybe he's crazy. And it doesn't seem too likely to me that a crazy man would last long, living rough in country like this. So, there must be a method in it, somewhere."

They rode a while in thoughtful silence. Ahead of them, a jackrabbit started from its hiding place under a creosote bush, and Shep kited off after it, giving chase.

"What about those soldiers, the ones who had Shep in that pit?" Andrews said. "What purpose did that serve?"

"Stupidity and cruelty are the province of shiftless men with too much time on their hands," Wiswall said in a grim voice. "I don't fancy Victorio as a stupid man. Or an idle one."

"I didn't take too many philosophy classes back east," Andrews said after a while. "My education focused mostly on the practical matters of the engineering sphere. But I reckon that in Victorio's experience, his treatment of those he vanquishes purchases him some advantage or other. Buys him the respect of his braves, maybe."

Wiswall nodded. His face was tilted sideways and held a pondering look. "Could be. And then there's anger. He can't love the white man for what we have done to a way of life that was a going concern since long before our like first came out here."

Shep was trotting back toward them, his tongue lolling out. Apparently, the jackrabbit would live to fight another day.

"Would you have us all retrace our steps and go back east?" Andrews said. "Get back on our ships and return to England, maybe?"

"I don't calculate that program would get too far, would it?" Wiswall said.

"Quite doubtful. And don't forget; you and I base our livelihood on the assumption that folks will continue to need what comes out of the ground up Colorado way. I don't think the Utes, Apaches, or Cheyenne are going to offer much of a market for coal or lead, do you? Though one might be able to do a little business in silver, I suppose."

"True enough. But still . . . I can't help thinking that if I were pushed into the sort of corner Victorio and the other chiefs are in, shoved onto a reservation nothing like their home country and faced with feeding a bunch of hungry mouths . . . Well, I don't know what I might do."

"I doubt your philosophy would find many takers among the good townsfolk of El Paso del Norte," Andrews said. "They have a railroad to bring in and a population boom to get ready for."

"I grant that's so," Wiswall said. "None of us can turn back the clock. But I can't escape the notion that someday, there will be a reckoning for the way we've treated people like Victorio and the others. I don't know where or when, but it's coming."

"The Almighty grant that we're both pushing up daisies before that great and terrible day," Andrews said.

"Maybe less talk and more watching, then?"

"Point well taken."

By midmorning of that day, there was not a cloud in the blue sky. By noon, the dark, sharp ridges of the Cornudas Mountains rose before the small, one-carriage cavalcade as it wound through the detached hills on the outskirts of the range. As evening began to fall, they spotted the sagging, partially tumbled-down rock walls of the old stage stop. Upslope from it, some 500 feet up the side of Alamo Mountain, was the spring for which the station was named.

"Do you reckon it's worth the hike up that slope with a bucket to refill our kegs?" Wiswall said, eyeing the rocky incline. They could discern a clump of trees above them, about where they guessed the spring issued—likely cottonwoods, to account for the name the Spanish had given the place.

"Before we go all the way up there, why don't we scout among the huecos down here around us and see what they've got to offer?"

"Sound advice, I'd judge."

"That, and I've gotten plumb out of the habit of climbing hills, since we left Ouray County."

"That, too."

"On the other hand, the horses . . . "

They finally agreed that Wiswall would gather water for the casks from such huecos as he could locate more or less in the flat, and Andrews would ride up the slope to the spring on the pony, leading the team. Shep opted to follow the horses.

"Keep your eyes peeled," Wiswall advised as Andrews rode away.

"You do the same," Andrews called over his shoulder.

After an uneventful night, Andrews and Wiswall made an early start and began crossing the desert plain in an easterly direction toward the Guadalupe Mountains and the deserted Crow Spring relay station that lay some six miles in front of them. A light drizzle had begun at about first light, but they were resolved to reach the station by nightfall, and before that if they could.

The road up the slope to the mesa where Crow Spring was situated undulated slightly as it cut through now, a profusion of cactus and yucca, now a long stretch of ocotillo interspersed with honey mesquite. In the distance, they saw the white rumps of pronghorn antelope scampering across the prairie, and closer to the old stage road they could see the round-rimmed entrances of prairie dog burrows with sentinels perched here and there, ready to sound the warning if an intruder approached. Shep tried chasing the little creatures once or twice but soon learned he could never come near them before they vanished underground with a flip of their short, wispy tails. Andrews and Wiswall judged that their laughter at his failed attempts pained the dog; Wiswall declared that he looked downright embarrassed after his second fruitless effort.

Around noon they saw the ruined walls of the station, about a hundred feet off the trail. No roof remained to the structure, but there was an acequia for leading rain run-off water into a tank in what had once been a corral, and the tank was brimming. Scattered on the ground between the roofless walls lay fragments of bottle glass and crockery, a few rusted, crushed cans, strips of decaying leather, and fragments of weather-grayed rope.

The slow rain had followed them all day, but thankfully there was little wind driving it. Huddled beneath their slickers, the partners unhitched the team, took the saddle off the pony, and led the horses to water in the corral tank. They hobbled the animals near the remaining walls of the building where they had maneuvered the ambulance, leaving them to find such grazing as they might. Shep disappeared to explore the surrounding terrain, offering an occasional yip to signify his whereabouts.

Chapter Nine

Before too long, the little stove in the Coolidge had yielded a pot of coffee, some boiled beans, and a good-sized pile of fried bacon, sliced thick off the slab. The rain had begun to slacken, but a cold north wind coursed through the broken walls of the old station, and neither man needed much encouragement to huddle inside and consume the victuals in relative comfort.

"Notice the dinner music?" Andrews asked as they sipped their coffee.

The wind swirled through the cracks in the adobe walls and around the corners, setting up a rising and falling moan.

"I've heard happier tunes," Wiswall said.

"Well, I reckon it'll do for a lullaby, maybe," Andrews said, "as long as we wake up in the morning with our scalps attached."

"Where's the dog?" Wiswall said, after a minute or two. "You heard him lately?"

"Who knows? I hope he doesn't come back carrying a rattlesnake in his mouth."

"Well, that's one good thing about this weather," Wiswall said. "I imagine it's too cold for rattlers."

"No, they've got the sense to be denned up by now," Andrews said with a little laugh. He leaned over to peek out at the sky. "Let the horses graze a bit longer. Then I'll bring them in and picket them along side of the ambulance."

Just then, they heard the sound of Shep's barking coming down the wind.

"Probably still chasing prairie dogs," Wiswall said.

"Now that he knows we can't watch."

Wiswall chuckled and nodded. "He'll come wandering in soon enough, I imagine."

The wind shook the canvas cover of the ambulance. Andrews reached into one of the cupboards and dug out a wrinkled bag of tobacco.

"Good idea," Wiswall said, fishing his stump of a clay pipe out of a shirt pocket. Andrews found a glowing ember in the stove on the end of a pencil-sized twig and set it to his pipe, drawing until he was pulling steady draughts of blue smoke. He passed the twig to Wiswall, and soon fragrant clouds drifted inside the little wagon before wisping out the front flap on the wind.

"Where do you calculate they are?" Wiswall said after a while.

"The Indians?" Andrews took a thoughtful pull and exhaled slowly. "Don't know. If they were around, you'd think we'd have seen something, as wide open as the country is hereabout."

Wiswall shrugged. "Well, if they are around, they've seen us; that's certain."

Andrews nodded. A little later, he reached over to the place where his Sharps lay along the sideboard. He thumbed open the breech and saw the cartridge, ready in the firing chamber. Carefully he closed the breech and replaced the rifle.

A thump and a jostle caused the two men to jerk upright, their hands going to their sidearms. Shep's head poked through the flap of the cover. He grinned at them from his perch on the driver's bench, his tongue lolling back and forth as he panted.

"So you've come home from the chase, have you?" Andrews said. "Lucky you didn't get yourself shot, boy. Next time, knock before you come in the house."

"Never mind him, Shep," Wiswall said, grinning as he ruffled the fur behind the dog's ears. "He's just a little keyed up." Wiswall cut a hunk of bacon from the slab and scooted it toward the shepherd, who gobbled it eagerly.

The men puffed their pipes and the wind rattled on. Shep scooted inside the cover and curled near the front of the wagon bed. Shep raised his head once, peering out the waving canvas flap in the direction from which he had come. Then he put his head back down. The men smoked; their eyelids drooped.

Shep's head jerked up again, his nostrils quivering. He sprang to his feet, barking. At that instant, Andrews and Wiswall heard whooping and shouting, accompanied by the sound of horse whinnies and hoofs striking the ground.

They grabbed their rifles and bailed out of the ambulance, Shep close on their heels. They ran to the opening in the wall and saw a small crowd of Indians—maybe as many as twelve—grabbing at their horses' manes and trying to swing onto their backs. One or two looked like they were cutting the hobbles loose, trying to avoid getting kicked.

The horses had apparently drifted about a hundred yards from the deserted station, and later, the men would guess that the Apaches calculated that was far enough. They were driving the horses across the scrub desert, and to the consternation of Andrews and Wiswall, the horses were making almost as good progress with their hobbles on as if they had been free.

Andrews leveled down with his Sharps and fired. A cloud of dust kicked up beside one of the marauders, but the only other result was that about three of them wheeled toward Andrews and Wiswall, two firing arrows and one aiming what looked like an ancient Enfield rifle.

Andrews and Wiswall hit the dirt as the shafts went over their heads and the shot from the Enfield went wide. Andrews shucked another cartridge into the Sharps as Wiswall, lying prone, opened fire with his Springfield.

The three Indians who had shot at them scattered, and the rest stayed occupied with driving the horses away. By now, a brave straddled each of the three horses, and one of the draft animals was running free, the tattered remains of the leather hobbles flying like a pennant from its off foreleg.

The two rose to chase after the horse thieves, but had to immediately dive for cover again, as the Indians sent another volley in their direction. Andrews and Wiswall returned fire as best they could, but the cause was lost. Soon the horses and the Apaches were out of range.

Shep had stayed near his masters during the melee, barking up a storm but not giving chase. Keeping a wary eye on the retreating band, the men fell back to the station.

"Well, I'll be damned!" Andrews stared at the cloud of dust that was all that was left to be seen of either animals or

Indians by this time. "I should have sidelined those horses! Of all the harebrained . . . " He shook his head and spat in disgust.

"Why wouldn't they have just cut the sideline, like they did the hobbles?" Wiswall said. "Once they decided they could get the horses started without our hearing, it was all up, I expect."

"Maybe so," Andrews said in a grudging voice. "At least they didn't get the dog."

"Wonder he wasn't shot," Wiswall said, looking at Shep. "Standing right out there in the open."

They both stared in the direction their horses had gone. "Well . . . What's our next move, do you think?" Wiswall said.

"I was just trying to decide," Andrews said. "What are we . . . about a hundred miles from El Paso?"

Wiswall nodded. "And at least seventy-five from Pope's Crossing on the Pecos, if our maps are any good."

"And on foot."

"I don't think we can ride Shep, no."

For the rest of the afternoon, they took turns, one standing watch and the other going through the supplies, trying to decide what might be carried and what had to be left behind. Reasoning that their shortest distance to help lay to the east, they decided to leave the Crow Spring station under cover of darkness and get as far as possible across the broad, flat plain before daylight found them.

They rigged a couple of dummies using their spare clothes and stationed them visibly, arming them with boards that might pass as weapons if seen from sufficient distance. "That ought to slow them down for a while, at least, until they realize that the guards haven't moved in a day or two," Wiswall said, admiring their handiwork.

"I don't expect they'll come back tonight," Andrews said, standing with his hands on his hips as he gazed at the surrounding, barren landscape. "They know the dog will give the alarm if they come near, and they know we're armed. And by morning we'll be as far from here as we can get."

"What about Shep?"

Andrews looked at the dog, at Wiswall, and away, across toward the Guadalupes. "I've got a thought on that," he said, finally. "But none of us is going to like it."

Chapter Ten

As twilight deepened, Andrews and Wiswall gathered up such wood as could be found around the old enclosure. A couple of watch fires would make the place look more occupied and would aid their deception. They lit the tinder beneath the two miniature pyres and watched as the flames began to lick upward.

With a heavy heart, Andrews called Shep to his side, standing beside the ambulance. When the dog came, he kneeled down and pointed to the bag of corn and the slab of bacon lying on the ground underneath the little wagon.

"Shep, you have to stay here." He patted the ground under the wagon. "You have to stay here until we get back."

The dog nosed the bag of corn and sniffed the bacon, then looked back at Andrews.

"You've got to stay with the stuff. We'll come back for you—with help."

Wiswall looked at the scene for another few seconds, then turned away, swallowing repeatedly.

Shep's tongue flicked out as he licked his chops. He raised his head slightly, testing the air. Then he lay down beside the bag of corn. He continued to watch Andrews.

"God damn those Apaches, anyhow," Wiswall muttered, his back still turned.

Andrews angled his face toward his partner. "Now, where is all that kindness and understanding you were preaching, not so long ago?"

"That was theoretical. This is personal."

Andrews gave a sad smile and turned back toward Shep. "You'll stay, won't you, old friend? Stay here with our stuff until we come back for you. All right?" He scratched the dog under his chin. Shep licked Andrews's hand and lay his head upon his paws.

Andrews dipped a bucketful of water from one of the casks lashed to the side of the Coolidge and set it on the ground beside Shep. "I guess he can get to the corral tank, when this runs out," he said.

It seemed to take forever for full dark to come. The two men loaded themselves up with all the ammunition and weapons they could carry, along with a blanket and a canteen apiece. They each spent a few moments talking in low voices to Shep, who watched their faces, but never made a move to get up. The dog's ready acceptance of his lonely and danger-ous duty was heartbreaking to both men. Neither thought the other noticed the emotion displayed as they turned from the dog and walked out of the abandoned stage station. Each thought he was the only one who looked back as they went.

The map indicated a ranch of some sort about fifty miles east, around the south end of the Guadalupe range and across the mesa. The stage road would take them past Pinery Station by morning, and there they might find water. They set out, moving along the stage road in the darkness.

The stage road soon became deep with loose sand. It was awful to walk in, and before long, both men were labor-ing and panting beneath their packloads. By the time they reached the broken ridges fronting the Guadalupe slopes, they were drenched in sweat beneath their coats, despite the steady and cold wind quartering into their faces.

"At least we'll be in among the broken country by sun-up," Wiswall panted. "There'll be cover."

The road took them to the right, circumventing the mountains and angling them past El Capitan, the lonely sen-tinel at the southernmost end of the Guadalupes. The stark, abrupt peak rose in front of them, a darker hulk against the spangled night sky. Rounding El Capitan and keeping to the road, they would come to the ruins of Pinery Station—if they didn't collapse along the way.

As the gray of dawn was coming on, they arrived at a foot trail that angled to the left, disappearing into the rocky saddle that separated El Capitan from Guadalupe Peak. "That looks like it's going the way we want to go," Andrews said as Wiswall leaned over, hands on his knees, catching his breath.

Wiswall peered up the path as far as he could see in the near-dark. "And it's not out in the open. I'll follow your lead, though I'm not fond of the thought of climbing, right at the moment."

"We'll rest a few minutes and drink a little water, then we'll go," Andrews said.

A ground-hugging, morning fog rolled slowly toward them as the eastern sky began to pink behind the mountains. "It's coming up pretty fast," said Wiswall. "If it reaches us, we'll not be able to see twenty feet in front or behind. It'll either hide us from the Mescaleros, or they'll use it to jump us."

"Well, we'd better get moving, in any case. Or else die standing still."

They straightened themselves, spent a minute or two helping each other adjust their packs and the straps on their rifles, and then began the trudge up the winding, narrow trail that led up into the saddle.

"If we're lucky, this will let us cut the corner off the mountains and come that much sooner to the Pinery station," Andrews said as they picked their way along. "That puts us some twenty miles from that ranch we saw on the map, I'd judge."

"I hope you're right. But I have an uneasy feeling that you and I aren't the first to walk this path."

Andrews said nothing to this, but Wiswall saw his hand stray down to the Colt revolver holstered at his belt. Wiswall checked his sidearm, also.

Since leaving Shep at the Crow Springs station, Andrews and Wiswall had walked some thirty miles. They hadn't paused to eat; unease had curbed their appetites. They huddled into their coats as the winter wind, channeled by the narrow defile through which they passed, bore down on them with what they considered an unnaturally strong interest.

Reaching an opening in the trail, they paused to take in a sweeping panorama of the desert floor that lay on the other side of the saddle they were traversing.

"That's where we're heading," Andrews said, pointing. "I believe this path leads right down to Pine Springs and the Pinery, a mile on. All we have to do now is descend, and get back onto the Butterfield. I calculate we'll soon be more than halfway to the ranch."

"Lord a'mighty, I hope we can get some help there," Wiswall said, wiping his face. "Even one other man who is a fair shot, and three fresh horses. We could have Shep safe in no time."

"One thing at a time," Andrews said. "Let's get to Pinery, rest up under some cover, and refill our canteens. Then we'll see about the rest of it."

They started down the slope that led to the place where, they hoped, the path opened on the plain to the east of the Guadalupes. Near there they would find what was left of the Pinery station, with water at nearby Pine Spring.

The path wandered back and forth in the manner of any trail that is first made by people on foot, avoiding large boulders and skirting steep slopes as they seek the easiest way. The only sound was that of their boots, striking the rough trail and scuffing along the rocks as they braced themselves backwards for the descent toward the flatlands. Neither of them wanted to think too much about crossing that broad expanse on foot under the glaring light of day, but it was the only way, and they knew it.

The footpath made an abrupt turn that led down into a small draw. Reaching the upslope opening of the draw, the two partners froze, staring dead ahead.

Staring back at them from the opposite end of the draw were what looked like a whole village's-worth of Mescaleros. Three or four of the men were mounted. All were armed.

For an instant, no one moved. And then, Andrews and Wiswall wheeled and ran for all they were worth, back up the trail the way they had come. As they ducked out of the draw back into the defile, they heard arrows clicking against the rocks, near where their heads had been an instant before.

"Is this wide enough for horses?" panted Andrews. "If it is, we can't outrun them."

"There's a sugar loaf butte up to the left!" Wiswall shouted. "If we can get up there we can hold them off, maybe."

Andrews and Wiswall scrambled up the cone-shaped formation, their breath burning in and out of their chests. As they climbed, they could hear the yells and calls of the Apaches, rushing up the trail toward them.

They reached the peak and flung down their packs. "Pull some of these rocks up close," Andrews said. "They'll do for breastworks. You take that side, and I'll cover this one."

The partners crouched behind their impromptu bunkers, readying their rifles. They tried to steady their breathing and sighted down their barrels, waiting for the first target that might present below them. As soon as the leaders came into view, they opened fire.

The Indians quickly scattered off the trail and behind the surrounding boulders. They sent a small swarm of arrows at the two defenders, all of which ricocheted harmlessly off the rocks around them. There was a scattering of gunfire from below that kicked up dust and rock chips near Andrews and Wiswall but otherwise did no damage. Everything grew still—nothing moved.

"Keep a sharp lookout," Wiswall said in a low voice. "They'll be up to something, for sure."

"I think most of them are on your side," Andrews said.

The day was still cool, but perched on the top of the butte, they felt perspiration trickling down their necks and backs. Their eyes relentlessly scoured the slopes below, watching for any sign of their attackers.

There. A stone's throw down the slope from Andrews, a keg-sized rock scooted upward, grinding against the loose shingle on the hillside. He saw a flicker of movement behind it. "They're pushing rocks up toward us, taking cover behind them," he said quietly. "Trying to slip up on us?"

Wiswall nodded. "I see them over here, too. Four or five of them, in a rough semicircle, working their way upslope. Reckon I ought to try and pick them off?"

"No . . . wait. Let's let them get closer. Let them think we don't know where they are. And keep looking for anything else they might try."

For a long time, the only sound was the wind, sighing past the rocks. Now and then, one of the partners would see a stone scoot a little bit, then a little bit more. The day crawled slowly past as the duo bided their time, the Apaches trying to tighten the noose around their necks.

As the afternoon light started to bend toward evening, Andrews said, "Get ready. We may have a break over on this side in a minute."

Without taking his eyes from his surveillance, Wiswall slid an arm through one of the staps of his pack. He said, "Just say the word."

As Andrews peered through his gun sight, a dark shape rose ever so slowly over the edge of the rock Andrews had been watching. He exhaled slowly and squeezed the trigger. The Sharps spoke and the head disappeared.

"Now!" Andrews said in a low, urgent voice. "Down this side; I've knocked over one of them."

Crouching low and clutching their rifles, they scrambled and half-fell down the rocky slope. In twenty strides, they passed an Indian, sprawled on his back in a pool of blood and staring sightlessly at the sky, a clean hole in his forehead. They didn't stop running until they were almost to the plain, where they found a hidden crevice that would admit them both. With solid rock at their backs, they crouched in the crevice, pistols cocked, to wait for full dark.

"I guess they thought we would try to get away back down the trail," Wiswall half-whispered as they made ready for the long walk back to Crow Springs. "Only the one you shot was to the west; everybody else was on the other side."

Andrews's face was grim. "We'll recuperate with Shep. Right now, I feel like hiking all night. Leaving him in the first place was the worst feeling I nearly ever knew."

"How many do you think we killed?"

"Probably just the one."

"Well, the rest of them will have their blood up, for sure."

"No help for it, though. Was him or us."

"That's certain."

Night fell. Andrews and Wiswall eased out of their hiding place and began the long walk, back down the Butterfield Trail toward Crow Spring where, they prayed, Shep was still waiting for them.

Chapter Eleven

Andrews and Wiswall jogged, walked, and stumbled in the dark through the low hills of the western Guadalupe Pass, paralleling the old Butterfield route. They wanted to delay until the last possible moment walking out onto the salt flats. Even in full dark, they felt as if eyes peered out at them from behind every boulder. Once they were out on that plain, with little taller than a man's waist growing on it, they would be completely exposed.

Soon there was nothing else for it; they struck west into the flat. It was overcast, and any other time they would have cursed the lack of a moon. But now, they preferred the concealment, even though it made the going more complicated.

They proceeded almost like blind men, hoping that the bearings they had taken during the fading daylight would carry them across to the abandoned station, or near enough. They took frequent sightings of clumps of bushes or other such landmarks as they could discern in the dark, doing their dead-level best to hew a straight line across to their destination.

They spoke not a word; the only sound of their passing was the scraping of shoe leather and labored breathing. Every so often, by silent agreement, they halted, standing still in the darkness to listen and stretch their eyes vainly into the night for any evidence of pursuit.

They needed to be under cover by daylight. Without question, the Mescaleros could easily track them across the plain. The partners hoped that the Apaches' respect for their superior weaponry would make them pause before attempting the head-on assault of a fortified place—if the two men could get there.

Andrews and Wiswall were weary beyond weariness as the sky began to turn from black to gray behind them. The only good thing about the rising light was that it revealed to them the tumbled hulk of the Crow Spring station, huddled in their direction of travel at the utmost limit of their reduced vision. At least they hadn't strayed too far from the route during their trek through the darkness.

"Buck up, partner; we're almost home," Andrews said, shifting his pack and striding forward with what was left of his determination. Wiswall said nothing, but followed doggedly.

Suddenly, in the silence and solitude of the still-dark desert, they heard the faint but unmistakable sound of a barking dog. Stopping in his tracks to better listen and hear, Wiswall said, "Do you suppose?"

"Yes, without a doubt!"

They quickened their pace, fatigue forgotten for the moment. As they came nearer to the station, they thought they could discern a small, black shape atop one of the broken walls. It was Shep! He was alive!

By the time they were within a stone's throw of the station, the dog was racing toward them. He met the two weary travelers with tail a-wag, bounding and leaping about them and licking their hands and faces.

"Good to see you too, old friend," Andrews said. Despite the dull aches clenching every square inch of his frame, he couldn't keep the grin off his face. Wiswall, too, was rubbing and petting Shep, chuckling quietly.

As they entered the yard of the station, they saw that the two dummy sentinels remained at their posts. The side of bacon beneath the ambulance was gnawed down to less than half the size it had been when they left, but the bag of corn was mostly untouched. As the light broadened, the partners could discover no evidence that any human foot had trod inside the dilapidated adobe walls since their departure, the night before.

Andrews and Wiswall eased their packs onto the ground and lay their rifles in the bed of the ambulance. Andrews sat heavily on the tongue of the wagon, leaning on his elbows and staring at the ground. All at once, exhaustion dropped onto him like a lead-weighted blanket.

"Why don't you crawl inside the wagon and get a little shut-eye?" Wiswall said. "Shep and I will keep watch. Then you can take over for me."

"Partner, I will not dissuade you. Right this minute, I'd pick sleep over a fresh-grilled steak."

Andrews pulled himself to his feet and clambered in beneath the canvas cover of the Coolidge. Within minutes, he was sawing logs.

By noon, Andrews stirred awake to the smell of freshly brewed coffee. He roused himself and scooted outside to find Wiswall sipping gingerly from a tin cup and eating one of the cold biscuits he had stowed in his pack before they left on their ill-fated expedition to the Pinery station.

Andrews poured coffee into the waiting, empty cup and took a careful sip. "I guess a little fire won't hurt anything," he said.

"Not exactly like our presence is a secret, any more," Wiswall said. "I didn't want to bother you with the stove."

"Much appreciated." He fished through his pack and found his own biscuit. "Any sign?"

"Nothing but a buzzard or two. I hope they don't know something we don't."

Andrews gave a low chuckle. He looked down at the toe of his boot, now separated from the badly worn sole along a two-inch gap. "That little hike was bad for our footwear."

Wiswall took another swallow of coffee and tossed the rest on the ground. "Yep. I've got a heel that's about to come off."

"I don't like to think about peeling my boots off, for fear of seeing what my feet look like," Andrews said. "I also don't like to think about walking back to Ysleta."

Wiswall climbed up onto the wagon and crawled onto one of the cots. "Well, I guess we could ask Victorio's bunch to loan us a couple of ponies."

"I'll wake you when it starts to get dark," Andrews said.

"Or if Victorio happens by."

"That, too."

That evening, with Shep curled on the ground between them and giving every evidence of contentment, the two men talked, low-voiced in the dark. They recapitulated everything that had happened to them from the theft of their horses to their narrow escape from the Mescalero band.

Now that they had gotten away from the immediate danger and recovered from the worst of their fatigue, they had the luxury of considering their situation and their options. It was not an encouraging inventory.

"Why do you reckon they didn't come back here?" Wiswall said.

Andrews shook his head. "Maybe the horses were mainly what they were after, and they didn't calculate the rest was worth the risk. Or maybe they just had other fish to fry. I don't hold myself as much of an expert on how Apaches think."

"Do you really think we ought to head for Ysleta?"

"It's either that or wait here for a patrol to come along," Andrews said. "And you heard from both the army and the Rangers about how likely that is."

After a long silence, Wiswall said, "Do you reckon we could wait one more day to start out?"

Andrews stared into the dark. "Yes. Let's rest up tonight and tomorrow, as best we can. Then at dark tomorrow, we'll strike out. If we can make it as far as the Cornudas, we can lay up during the day."

They both looked down at Shep. After another long silence, Wiswall said, "I'll take the first watch with Shep. Go ahead and lie down."

The next morning, they scrounged among the supplies in their wagon and found some gunny sacks they could use to bind up their dilapidated boots. With a little luck, this might carry them to Ysleta.

"Of course, if the Apaches get to us, we won't need boots anymore," Andrews commented grimly.

"Make me a promise, partner," Wiswall said. "If it becomes truly hopeless, put a bullet between my eyes before you do the same for yourself. That seems preferable to me to enduring the tortures we've been told they inflict on their captives."

"I've had the same thought. You can depend on me for that last mercy."

"And you, me."

Several feet away, Shep's head snapped to alertness. The men grabbed their rifles.

They saw a blurred line of motion in the far, gray distance, back toward the Guadalupe Mountains. "Herd of pronghorns on the move," Andrews said, after several seconds of quiet study.

They eased the firearms back down to the ground beside the place where they sat and resumed fashioning their makeshift footwear: wrapping the gunny sacks around their boots and binding them in place with cord.

"I allow these fancy stockings will make us harder to track, at least," Wiswall offered. "I don't imagine our trail will much resemble that of a walking man."

"I don't imagine our feet will much resemble such, either, by the time we come to Ysleta."

For the rest of the day, they ate such of their supplies as they could make ready with no fire and packed what they could into their traveling bags. As the dull gray sky began to dim, they sat on their packs, contemplating what lay before them.

"I suppose it would be too much to ask for the rain to hold off until we make it back." Wiswall said.

"I'd rather walk in the rain if it keeps the Mescaleros in their wikiups and our scalps on our heads."

"Fair enough." After a long silence, Wiswall said, "I guess we'll leave him here again?"

"I don't see any other way, do you? If he barks, he'll give us away. The same if he runs out in front of us; why else would a dog be out in the middle of this country?"

"I reckon it's so. But I hate it, all the same."

"You and me both."

Dark came, and once again, the men gave their dog his orders. They each spent some minutes with him, talking in low tones as they scratched him behind the ears and patted along his back. And when they turned to walk away into the night, down the old stage trail, Shep, as he had done before, stood watching them go, but made no offer to follow.

"It sticks hard in my throat, leaving him," Wiswall said as they shuffled away from the Crow Spring station. "Even if this works the way we plan, we'll be gone for several days before we can get back here."

Andrews said nothing.

Chapter Twelve

They trudged along the trail, gradually ascending toward the low, barren hills of the Cornudas range, less than thirty miles away. They saw no reason not to follow the old stage trail; it was the surest way to avoid getting lost and, by walking at night when Victorio's people were presumably denned up, they thought they might actually make the best time possible.

Arriving at the Cornudas before dawn, they considered making camp in the deserted stage station, but reasoned that if the Mescaleros were hunting them, that would be the first place in the vicinity that they would look. So, instead, the partners scrambled up into the rough granite formations of the hills and found themselves a shelter amid the rocks that would hide them from any prying eyes that might be watching in the daylight. As at the Huecos, they found plenty of cached rainwater in the natural cups and basins of the rocks, and they drank as much as they could hold before filling their canteens.

The beds in their hiding place were hard and rocky, but the men were so desperately weary that whoever wasn't on watch slept like the dead. They passed the day alternating between watching and sleeping, and as night came on they readied themselves for the tramp across to the Huecos, some twenty miles across the Diablo Plateau.

A light rain fell on them, off an on, until about midnight. Even when the rain stopped, a cold north wind drove the clouds across the moon. They huddled as deep in their coats and slickers as they could, but the wind found its way in, chilling them to the bone as they made their way along on sore, bleeding feet.

An hour or so before dawn on the second night back toward Ysleta, they spotted a small ledge off a rocky crest among large boulders overlooking the Hueco Bolson, west of the tanks. With difficulty, they climbed up to the ledge and scooted back in under it as far as they could go. They passed another night like the one they had just had, except that they both admitted it was much harder to keep watch, as exhaustion pressed their eyelids closed with a force that was no less irresistible for its subtlety.

The brief nap the two eagerly sought turned into a full, sound, long overdue night's sleep. They hadn't planned to oversleep, but now didn't regret it. From their slight rocky perch in the first light of sunrise, the two observed the desert below them, all shimmering in whites and silvers in a light fog, as far as their eyes could see.

Nearing the end of the next night's dreary tramp across Hueco Bolson, Andrews said, "How do you figure? Are we far enough west that we might risk traveling in daylight? If we did, we could reach Fort Bliss before nightfall tomorrow, I calculate."

Chewing on a mouthful of dried beef, Wiswall said, "I'm so tuckered out that if Victorio showed up right now, I don't think I could even muster the strength to trot in the other direction. If you're willing to try it, I am, too."

"That's settled, then. We'll rest up for a little while when daylight comes, and then we'll keep moving. The more ground we can cover, the sooner we'll get back to Ysleta."

"Hot coffee, hot food, warm beds, and maybe a few hours of sleep. Then, we go back and get our dog. That's all I want."

By dawn, the temperature had dropped below freezing. Andrews and Wiswall huddled out of the wind in a mesquite-bordered ravine and tried to rest. Soon, though, they had to admit that they were too cold.

"I expect we'll do better if we keep moving," Andrews said. "If we did manage to go to sleep in this cold, we might not wake up."

"Lead on; I'll go as far as these battered feet will carry me. The sooner we get where we're going, the better I'll like it."

By mid-afternoon, and in relatively clear—though still cold—weather, Andrews and Wiswall were ambling past the outlying haciendas to the east of El Paso del Norte. Here and there, sheep scattered across the landscape, seemingly impervious to the cold wind that tormented the weary hikers. Flat-roofed, sandstone dwellings began to dot the countryside, each with its beehive-shaped, adobe horno behind, giving out thin wisps of smoke. Acequia-bordered fields, brown and fallow for the winter, came into view.

By late afternoon they came to Fort Bliss, on the northeast side of the city. They hailed the first sentry they saw and begged for aid. The soldier took one look at the weary, battered travelers and immediately beckoned to one of his fellows. "I can't leave my station, but you'd better get these men in out of the cold. They look like they're fixing to fall over, any minute now."

They were taken to the enlisted men's barracks, though they protested every step of the way that they needed to see Major Osbourne. Within half an hour, they were both lying in tubs of heated water, and twenty minutes after that, they lay on cots under thick, woolen blankets, dead to the world.

They woke the next morning to find clean clothes lying beside their cots. These consisted of rather worn and dated uniforms with all the insignia removed, but they were warm, and Andrews and Wiswall donned them gladly. They bandaged their feet as best they could and slid them, with many a grimace, into the Army brogans they found waiting for them, along with the clothes.

The victuals with which they broke their fast might have been considered bland in other circumstances, but the starved travelers wolfed down the eggs, bacon, and toasted bread as if they hadn't seen food in a month.

"Major Osborne is waiting for you in his office," an orderly told them as Andrews and Wiswall returned their empty plates and utensils for washing by the enlisted men's kitchen detail.

They found the major in the same place they had met with him before, when he had agreed to sell them the Coolidge. "Gentlemen, it seems that you have had a rough go of it," he said as soon as they had all shaken hands and sat down. "I regret to remind you that I indicated such might be the case if you went east on the old stage road."

"Yes, and your prophecy came true in almost every detail," Andrews said with a sad smile. "Victorio's people are the richer for it by three horses, and we are the poorer by most of our supplies and our dog."

"I'm not happy to hear it," Osbourne said. He then urged them to give him the most complete narrative possible of all that had transpired since they had left Ysleta, all those days before.

When they were finished, Osbourne made a number of pointed inquiries about their encounters with the Mescaleros: asking them to repeat where they had first made contact, how many were in the band they encountered in the Guadalupe mountains, what sort of weaponry they observed among the Indians, and other queries on tactical matters.

When they had answered all the major's questions, he sank into thought for several seconds. He looked up at them then, and said, "What are your plans now?"

"As soon as we can, we mean to go back and get our dog," Andrews said. "We were hoping for some aid from the army."

Osbourne looked at them and shook his head slowly. "Mr. Andrews and Mr. Wiswall, with all due respect, we have already plowed this ground, once before. This is an infantry command; we have no cavalry here."

"Indeed," Andrews said, "and yet, we find it prudent to make the request, at least."

"Noted. And my answer remains the same; I will not risk the lives of my men for no other reason than to retrieve a dog—one that ought not to be where he is in the first place, if you take my meaning."

"I understand you, Major," Andrews said. "And if you will inform us what we owe the government for our room and board, we will settle our accounts and inquire elsewhere."

The major's face softened a trifle. "There will be no charge for the small comforts we have provided you." He drummed his fingers on the desk for a second or two. "I don't suppose I can persuade you against what you mean to do?"

"I'm afraid not, Major."

Osbourne sighed and shook his head. "Very well, then. As before, I suppose you may as well inquire of Baylor and his Rangers, over at Ysleta."

"I believe we will do just that. Might we borrow the use of a couple of horses? We have had about all the walking our health will stand, these last few days."

"Never mind that. I'll have my sergeant major drive you over there as soon as you are ready to go."

Chapter Thirteen

As the master sergeant drove Andrews and Wiswall through the central streets of El Paso, the sky began to clabber. By the time they reached the gates in Ysleta, they were slumped beneath their slickers as a cold rain arrowed in from the northwest. The partners bailed out of the buckboard in the downpour and splashed up the steps onto the porch of Baylor's dwelling and headquarters.

Straightaway, a man standing on the porch said to them, "Weren't you fellows here a few days ago? Where's that big, fine shepherd dog you had with you?"

"That's why we need to speak to Lieutenant Baylor. Is he in the vicinity?"

"He went over to the livery on some business, but I expect him back any time," the Ranger said. "That's why I'm waiting for him, here."

Another Ranger strolled over. "You're the fellows that set out on the old Butterfield road, aren't you? How far did you get? Is the dog all right?"

By the time the company's commander arrived, just a few minutes later, a crowd of Rangers had gathered around Andrews and Wiswall to listen to the story of their experiences of the last few days. Baylor stood at the edge of the group for a minute or two, then waded through, coming up the steps to where the partners stood.

"Come on inside, gentlemen. Let's have the whole story, from start to finish. And I'll especially want to know why Shep isn't by your side . . . "

Once inside his office with Andrews and Wiswall, Baylor grabbed the chair from behind his desk and motioned Andrews and Wiswall to a leather couch along the wall.

"I'm relieved you two are safe. I gather you had a run-in with some of Victorio's people. How far did you get? All of us figured you were already pale in death by now. So, tell me!"

Andrews narrated their recent history in as much detail as he could summon, beginning with their departure from the vicinity and ending with their exhausting walk back from Crow Spring. Baylor's eyes bored into both of them as Andrews spoke.

When Andrews finished, the lieutenant sat quiet for several seconds. "Well, that's some story. But thank God, you're safe now." Baylor got up and walked to his office door, motioning for his guests to keep their seats. They heard him give an indistinct order to someone outside, whereupon he came back in.

"So you left Shep in command of the station, did you? And like a good and faithful soldier, he stayed at his post." Baylor shook his head slowly, a look of deep admiration on his face. "Gentlemen, that dog is one in a million."

"You cannot possibly imagine how it tore us to leave him," Andrews said. "And yet, what else could we do? If he came with us, he was almost certain to betray our presence to watching eyes or listening ears."

"Just so," Baylor said, nodding. "I would likely have done much the same, if our positions had been exchanged."

The door opened, and Sergeant Gillett came in. "Thank you for coming, sergeant," Baylor said. "I trust you remember Mr. Andrews and Mr. Wiswall?"

Gillett nodded at the men. "I hear you've had quite a time of it, here of late."

"True enough," Andrews said.

"We were just talking about that fine shepherd dog of theirs," Baylor said.

"Yes, Shep. I wondered where he was," Gillett said.

"Well, that's why we've come to see you, Lieutenant. We intend to go back and get him, one way or another. We applied to Major Osbourne, out at Fort Bliss, but it was a waste of time. He won't help us, he says, because he has only infantry, not cavalry. I gave the dog my word, and the word of Wiswall here, that we would go back and get him, and that means as much to me as if I had said it to a man. If you don't go with us, we aim to go alone, just as soon as we can buy or borrow some horses." Andrews looked at Wiswall, then back at Baylor and Gillett. "We're going within the hour, sir, one way or another. We'll go alone, but we'd surely like to have some help."

Baylor stared hard at Andrews.

"We left him a slab of bacon and half a sack of corn, five days ago. When we last saw him two days ago, everything was half eaten. If the coyotes, the rain and cold, or the Apaches don't get him, he's going to starve to death, because he won't leave the wagon after I asked him to stay."

"Mr. Andrews, Mr. Wiswall, surely you remember me telling you how dangerous it was to go to the Pecos along the Butterfield route?"

After a long silence, Andrews said, "Lieutenant, we have some money. If that isn't enough, I'm willing to work off the debt, here in El Paso."

"That goes for me, too," Wiswall said.

Baylor studied them for a moment, then turned to look out the window. The rain pattered against the panes, and all Andrews and Wiswall could think of was their poor dog, probably hunkered beneath the ambulance—if it was still there—staring miserably out at a hostile landscape.

"You are asking us to ride into considerable danger; I assume you appreciate that," Baylor said at last, turning back to look at them. "As you now have learned, Victorio and his braves might be anywhere in the country east of here. Further, your going has alerted them. And you have killed one of his men."

They silently returned Baylor's look. "We are sensible of the situation, yes," Andrews said, finally. "And we will understand completely if you choose to deny our plea."

Baylor nodded slowly. "And yet, you will still go back there."

"We will," Wiswall said immediately. Andrews nodded.

The lieutenant stared at them a long while. Very slowly, a smile crept across his face. "Well, gentlemen, I can't fault your grit, at least. I believe I'm going with you." Baylor turned toward his sergeant. "Assemble all the men in the outer office, now." Gillett went out.

"We'll soon find out if any of the other men here will

accompany us. We'll leave as soon as we're outfitted for the journey."

Within a minute or two, they heard the sound of boots scuffing across the floor in the outer office. "Shall we go and present our case?" Baylor said. He stepped to the door and opened it, motioning Andrews and Wiswall through.

As the men gathered, several sidled over to Andrews and Wiswall and asked, in half-whispers, about Shep's whereabouts. They answered as briefly as they could, until they were interrupted by Baylor's voice, from the front of the room.

"Our friends here had trouble with the Apaches. They stole their horses at the old Crow Spring station at the foot of the Guadalupes, halfway to the Pecos. They walked back here with gunny sacks over their shoes."

There was a low murmur. A few of the Rangers glanced at Andrews and Wiswall with something like respect in their eyes.

"They had to leave Shep behind because he might innocently have given them away. And we all know what happens to people who get caught by Victorio.

"They've already been to the fort and were denied help because all Bliss has over there is foot soldiers. Now, they are standing here, asking if anyone will go back with them into an Apache-infested area to retrieve the ambulance and fetch Shep, if he's still alive."

If the room was quiet before, it was now as silent as a tomb.

"Now, I realize that not one of you has been in the service for more than three months. Miller, you joined us four days ago. Seaburn, you enrolled and took your oath eleven days back. The rest of you have been with me since December first, just past. I make $2.50 a day; Sergeant Gillett, $1.75, and the rest of you $1.00, and that is surely not wealth enough to justify riding into country where you may well meet with several hundred renegade Apaches.

"Be that as it may, I'm going with these men to retrieve that ambulance and their Shep. I will not ask any of you to join us. I love life as much as the next man, and will not give it up easily. But for that particular dog, I am willing to risk it, as I would for any good friend who is hurting. We're leaving in one hour, after we pack up. We should make the Tanks by tonight, Crow Spring the next day, if we ride at a trot. My hope is that the weather and the Apaches behave. If any of you choose to join us, of course, you'll be welcome."

For the space of perhaps five breaths, not a single muscle moved among all those assembled in the small, crowded waiting room. Then one of the men started for the door with everyone watching him. "I'll get the horses saddled and start sacking up the feed."

Then another man moved toward the door. "We'll likely need the mules and the packsaddles."

Another Ranger turned toward Andrews and Wiswall with a broad grin. "You two fellows have walked a hundred miles in this weather with shoe leather worn down to sandpaper. I reckon I can ride with you at least as far as Crow Spring."

"Well, I'll not let it be said that I let a good dog freeze to death if I could help it," another one said as he started for the door.

Andrews and Wiswall stared about them with jaws hanging slack.

Baylor grinned at Gillett. "Well, Sergeant, looks like you're the one to stay behind and watch over the place."

"Begging your pardon, sir, but like hell I will!"

Baylor laughed. "Well, we need to leave somebody here to watch the place."

"How about the two married ones? Burnes and Thomas?"

"Yes, that'll do. The other nine of us will go, and we need to bring scouts. Sergeant, can you go and summon Simon?"

"Yes, sir." Gillett left. Andrews and Wiswall remained alone in the room with Baylor.

"Lieutenant, what, precisely, just happened here? Do I correctly understand that every one of your men has volunteered to go with us to retrieve our dog?"

"I believe that is correct," Baylor said, a little smile playing about his lips.

"And they understand the danger?" Wiswall said.

"They have learned well that Victorio is not to be trifled with, yes."

Andrews and Wiswall both stood dumbstruck. "We came here to make just such a request," Andrews said finally, "yet hardly dared to hope that even one or two Rangers would return with us. I think I can speak for my partner, here, as well as myself . . . and yet I cannot find the words to adequately say what we are feeling."

"Well, that's all right," Baylor said. "Leave the words for later. Right now, we had best prepare for action."

Chapter Fourteen

Andrews and Wiswall trailed Baylor to the barracks, carrying their rifles and ammunition. The Ranger commander asked for two horses to be brought around for them, and another man who was serving as quartermaster for the expedition pointed them toward a couple of worn, but sturdy-looking saddles.

The main door to the barracks swung open, and five figures dimmed the entrance as they stepped across the threshold. The Tiguas came in, wrapped in furs and cradling Winchesters in the crooks of their arms. Broad-brimmed, brown felt hats, each decorated with a feather or two, were jammed low on their heads.

Baylor greeted them gravely. "Sergeant Olguin, thank you for coming on such quick notice. But Simon, you did not need to bring your brothers. This will not be an easy ride, or a safe one."

"That is why they come," the Tigua leader said. "I tell them what the sergeant has said. They say if I go, they go."

Baylor turned to the partners and beckoned them forward. "Mr. Andrews, Mr. Wiswall, please meet Simon Olguin, our chief scout. You heard me call him 'sergeant,' and he has earned that rank many times over."

Andrews was uncertain as to the custom for greeting an Indian, especially one who carried such a palpable air of authority as Simon Olguin. His dark eyes swept over Andrews's face, then did the same for Wiswall's standing at his partner's shoulder. He inclined his head perhaps two inches; Andrews and Wiswall did the same.

"These are his brothers," Baylor continued, "Bernardo, Ponciano, and Francisco. And this is Domingo, son of

Bernardo. There are no finer scouts, trackers, or fighters between San Antonio and Arizona."

"Mr. Olguin, we are very grateful for your help," Andrews said. "You are putting yourself into a good deal of trouble on our account."

"The lieutenant calls. We come," Olguin said.

The Tiguas wore homespun woolen trousers with buckskin leggings laced up to the knee. They stood in heelless moccasins with calico kerchiefs wrapped around their heads, just visible beneath their hats. Each had a single-edged Bowie knife slung at his waist, and long cartridge belts crisscrossed their chests.

"Simon, here, and his older brother, Bernardo, the tall one next to him, are the backbones, the sturdiest members of the Pueblo Tigua tribe in the Ysleta locality," Baylor said. "These men have kept all of us out of some mighty tough scrapes, I can tell you."

Someone called that the horses were ready, and Andrews and Wiswall, along with the Rangers, hoisted their tack and went outside. Gillett fell in beside them.

"Simon is the Tiguas' tribal war captain, and, in my opinion, the smartest of them all," the sergeant said. "He speaks for all of them, brothers included. He told me that he is going all the way with us, but the three brothers and the young one are only going to accompany us up to the Tanks."

Andrews and Wiswall slung their saddles and blankets across the backs of two ponies Gillett pointed out to them. They cinched and buckled, then fitted the bridles on their mounts after easing the bits between their jaws. Someone handed Wiswall a saddle holster for his Springfield. Andrews motioned away the one held toward him. "The Sharps is too long for that holster. I'll manage without it."

Someone led out two mules, and others began lashing on the supplies they would carry for the convoy: extra ammunition, sacks of grain for the animals, tents, kettles, a couple of fowling pieces, spare tack, sacks of dried beef, coffee, and other needful articles.

"Simon and his brothers will ride ahead, behind, and on our flanks all the way to the Tanks," Baylor announced, lifting his voice above the din. "Simon believes the most likely place for trouble is at sunup tomorrow, when we'll be at Hueco."

"Why would that be?" Wiswall said.

"Sometimes, they'll creep and crawl along the high shelves and into the rocky defiles around a camp," Gillett explained. "They'll hide until first light, then swarm over you all at once. But Simon and his people will scout every inch of the canyons for any hint of moccasin or horse tracks."

"I reckon they have a pretty good idea of how the Mescaleros think," Andrews said.

Gillett nodded. "That's why Lieutenant Baylor was glad to see him."

"Why aren't they all going to Crow Spring?" asked Andrews.

"That is Simon Olguin's wish. They would go, but Simon is worried about this patrol, even if he won't say so. If all 300 of Victorio's Apaches take the field against us, how long can we hold out? Those four are the next leaders of the Tiguas; Simon won't let them go all the way on this patrol."

By the time Gillett had finished his explanation, Andrews and Wiswall wore the most somber faces they had owned since losing their horses to the raiders, days before. They mounted up and watched as Simon Olguin and his kin vaulted onto their blanket-clad ponies. The Tigua looked at Baylor.

"All right, men," the lieutenant said. "Let's ride."

Chapter Fifteen

By the time they were lined out on the road leaving Ysleta, the thick clouds that had threatened rain all through the morning were drifting southwest, pushed by a cold wind that hit the men smack in their faces. They would cut across the desert and pick up the Butterfield trail a mile or two east of Fort Bliss, Baylor had explained. Glancing back at the low, adobe houses slowly disappearing behind them, Andrews recalled to Wiswall how they had made light of the rude little town and its sparse amenities.

"Well, right this minute, El Paso del Norte looks like home, sweet home," Wiswall said. "Given the choice between staying right here and going where we're going, I could make a snug little life hereabout."

The partners noticed that the men of the Frontier Battalion exercised considerable individuality in their selection of trail and battle equipment; there was very little about their traveling companions that appeared to be standard issue. Many of the Rangers rode with two Winchester rifles holstered by their saddles. Most carried bedrolls lashed at the back of the cantle. Some had a small pannier of hardtack tied on behind. Most had rawhide or hemp lariats looped over the saddle horn. Each Ranger, of course, wore a waist holster with at least one pistol; some carried a brace. All had small leather pouches or wallets in a breast pocket or tied on a rawhide thong that they used to carry salt, tobacco, or additional ammunition. Everything was rigged for maximum portability and efficiency.

"Do you notice their faces?" Andrews said softly. "All so relaxed and natural, as if we're headed for a school meeting and barbecue."

Wiswall nodded, looking around him. "These are damned fine men, every one of them."

Gillett reined up beside them. The mules ambled along just ahead, and Gillett pointed to the packs they carried and explained where the extra pistols, knives, and munitions were located. "If we get into a tussle with Victorio, you might need to know where the useful articles are stowed."

"How much road will we cover today, Sergeant?" Andrews asked.

"If we ride double file at an easy trot, we'll be at the Tanks by sundown, depending upon how soft the trail is."

"If this wind holds up, the road ought to dry some," Wiswall said.

"Have you gone often to Hueco Tanks, Sergeant Gillett?" Andrews asked.

"A few times. But I don't especially like it. All those names and pictures, put there by people long gone . . . I don't know. The place has a poor effect on my imagination, I reckon.

"But it's different for Simon Olguin and his people. The Tiguas consider the hills and rocks there sacred. To Victorio and the Apaches, the Tanks are nothing more than a watering hole, but I've heard it said that the Tiguas gather there to worship."

"Well, if you've got to die, I calculate it's best to die in church," Wiswall said.

"Sergeant, please forgive my friend's gallows humor," Andrews said, shaking his head.

Gillett chuckled. "I've heard worse, Mr. Andrews, I can promise you."

The sergeant gave them a bit of the history of the Tigua people of Ysleta Pueblo. They had come there some two hundred years before, he told them, accompanying Spaniards retreating from a revolt among the Pueblo people up around Santa Fe. "They named their village here Ysleta del Sur—Island of the South—after the place they had come from up in New Mexico, which was also named Isleta."

"They certainly seem stalwart men," Andrews said.

Gillett nodded. "None better."

A few rays of sunlight penetrated the broken clouds as they neared the junction with the Butterfield trail; the men could feel perspiration dampening the collars of their shirts. Here and there, Rangers began peeling back layers of garments, bundling them and tying them to their saddles as the convoy jogged along at a posting trot.

Coming to the junction, they angled right, heading northeast along the old Butterfield road, riding two abreast. The Tigua scouts peeled away from the rest, taking up positions ahead, behind, and flanking the Rangers. Simon Olguin rode 150 to 200 yards ahead of the party.

By the time they had ridden into the mid-afternoon, the only other humans they had seen were two Mexicans in separate ox carts, both apparently headed for Ysleta, loaded with firewood. Gillett speculated that they had likely come from Sierra Alto, some twenty-four miles from Ysleta. This boded well, he said: If Victorio's warriors had been nearby— say, in the area of the Tanks—these two woodcutters would likely be deceased and their animals butchered.

"Last month," he said, "Victorio's warriors ambushed a small hay encampment not far south of Ysleta. That night, the lieutenant, myself, and nine other Rangers left immediately for the site, stopping at San Elizario to pick up a guide.

"At dawn, we arrived at the spot of the slaughter and picked up the Apaches' trail; it led across the Rio Grande into Mexico. We crossed the river, and twenty-three Mexicans from a little place called Guadalupe joined us in the search. The Sierra Ventana is mighty hard country, and the raiders ambushed us as we were trailing through a canyon.

"Well, we were pretty well pinned down, and after a long fight we decided we had to fall back. We managed to get back to Guadalupe without losing anyone, and the people there welcomed us for the night."

"So Victoria goes back and forth across the Rio Grande pretty much as he wishes?" Andrews said.

Gillett nodded. "We've chased him on both sides, but somehow, he stays a jump ahead of us—and the militias over in Mexico.

"Just last November, two months ago now, none of us knew where Victorio was hiding. He'd been leading both the US and Mexican armies on a merry chase, both north and south of the river. Then he bushwhacked that group of Mexican workers, fifteen or twenty of them. A second party went to the rescue and he killed them, too."

They rode a while without speaking; the only sounds were their mounts' hoofs striking the trail and the squeaking of saddle leather. "Why do you think Victorio does what he does?" Wiswall said, finally.

Gillett stared into the distance for a long time without answering. "I reckon it's in his blood. The Apaches were bred for fighting, and it's what they do best." He turned to Wiswall. "Did you know that they don't call themselves 'Apaches?' They refer to themselves as 'Nideh,' which means 'the people' in their language. 'Apache' is what the neighboring tribes call them. It means, 'people who fight us all the time.'" He gave a low chuckle, shaking his head.

"So, you would say that Victorio's violence is just in his blood? You don't think it has anything to do with what he found on that reservation the government moved him to?" Wiswall said.

Gillett's face hardened. "I don't go in much for politics, Mr. Wiswall. I was hired by the State of Texas to do a job, and I mean to do it."

Wiswall looked like he was about to reply, but Andrews gave him a tight shake of the head. Wiswall looked away, across the arid, gray landscape.

The weather behaved during the remaining hours prior to sunset. In the dimming light of the afternoon, the Ranger convoy arrived at the ramshackle remains of the Hueco Tanks station. Riders began dismounting; two or three men started unloading the mule packs while others gathered kindling and firewood.

"We're here a little earlier than I expected," Lieutenant Baylor said. "Let's make camp and secure the horses around that overhang, right over there." He pointed to a low cut in the cliff, cast in a golden glow by the last rays of the evening sun.

"By the way, I suppose you all have noticed the mounted lookout, on the shoulder of the hill to the northeast?"

The men around Andrews and Wiswall nodded their heads, but both quickly turned and stared in the direction Baylor had indicated. Sure enough, perhaps a quarter-mile distant and well above them, a man sitting a pony was silhouetted against the skyline, apparently staring down at them as they made camp.

From behind Andrews came Simon Olguin's voice. "Not one. Three." The Tigua scout motioned to points in the hills both ahead of and behind them.

"I expect Victorio will know where we are before sunup," Baylor said. "So I don't need to tell you about staying vigilant tonight. Once we're dug in here, he'll lose men in a fight, and he knows it. But we've got eyes on us, and we will have, most likely, until we've finished what we came to do." Baylor glanced up at the watcher visible above them, then back at the men. "We'll be heading out tomorrow morning while it's still dark."

They suppered on boiled, sundried tripe, hardtack, and hot coffee. The Rangers worked out sentry shifts, with some guarding the animals as others warded the perimeter. As he ate dinner, Wiswall leaned over to Andrews. "I don't see Simon Olguin or any of his kinfolk."

Andrews angled his head toward the rocks rising above them. "I expect they're up there . . . somewhere."

Chapter Sixteen

Twilight slowly coalesced into the solid, almost palpable black of an overcast winter night. The seven Rangers not on sentry duty cocooned in their bedrolls around the dwindling campfire.

Sergeant Gillett arranged his sleeping place, carefully scooping out a slight depression for his hips before spreading his woolen blankets on the ground. Andrews, still seated on his bedroll, said, "I don't see how you fellows ride for nine hours, sleep on the ground, and then get up in the morning and do it all again the next day—and the day after that."

Gillett smiled and shrugged. "It's the life we signed up for," he said. "Now, mind, I'm not at all opposed to sleeping on a feather mattress. But as often as not, there's something bracing about a night spent in the open, eating food you cooked yourself over a campfire." He peered out into the night for a moment. "Of course, it adds considerably to the enjoyment when you don't have to wonder if 300 or so Mescaleros are about to try to lift your scalp while you sleep."

In the dark, one of the horses gave a low nicker. Andrews could see the dim glow of a pipe ember, coming from a nearby dark bundle that marked the resting place of a Ranger.

"Tell me, gentlemen, if you will," Gillett said as he crawled into his blankets and arranged them about him, "how you came to have Shep. He's a fine dog, but as I watched him when you were with us before, I sensed he had a story to tell."

A soft snore came from the ground beside Andrews; Wiswall had already succumbed to the weariness of the day's trail. "Well, since my partner appears to be asleep," Andrews said softly, "I reckon I can tell you about it."

"How's that? Why does it matter if he's asleep?"

"You'll see." Andrews fished his clay pipe out of one shirt pocket and pinched some tobacco from a pouch in the other. He leaned over to fish a slowly burning twig from the edge of the campfire and blew on it until the end glowed. Touching the red spark to his pipe, he puffed the tobacco into life. He took a long, deep draw as he leaned back on an elbow, facing Gillett.

"We were coming down from Colorado, aiming to buy burros in Texas and sell them back up in Ouray County, where we come from. We were most of the way through Oklahoma Territory, and we stopped at Fort Sill. You ever been there?"

"Can't say I have," Gillett said.

"Well, I'll tell you, I don't care if I ever see that place again." Andrews took another deep pull on his pipe. "Most of the time—I'd say nearly one hundred percent of the time, actually—the men you run into on the US Army's premises are good enough sorts. About like the general run of the population, mind you, but mostly hardworking, honest men who are trying to do their duty.

"But at Sill . . . I don't know what it was, sergeant, but I don't think I've ever seen as many shiftless, haphazard cusses in the same place at the same time."

Gillett gave a soft chuckle.

"The one thing that seemed to genuinely interest them was fighting—or watching a fight. And if they couldn't locate a scrape naturally, they'd figure out a way to invent one.

"We could scarcely get out of there quick enough to suit us, Wiswall and I. And on the day we were planning to shake the dust off our feet and ride on to the Red River, we came across the pit."

"The what?"

"Some of the enlisted louts—I hate to call them 'men'— had built a kind of pen, with walls maybe ten, twelve feet high. Big, thick timbers, stood on end, nailed together with planks. Like a small corral, only with solid walls."

"Like something you'd pen a bear in, sounds like," Gillett said.

"You are very close. When we saw the thing, we also saw a crowd of those ne'er-do-wells gathered around, laughing, drinking, and swearing, with money changing hands. We soon surmised that some sort of rowdy wager was afoot.

"We walked closer—should have known better—and in a pitiful shed behind the crowd, six or seven mangy, sorry-looking mutts were tied up. We watched and listened long enough to figure out that these rascals had somehow captured a cougar that they kept penned in their pit; they were throwing stray dogs in there, one at a time, betting on how long it took the cougar to rip the poor beasts apart."

Gillett made a disgusted sound. "I've got no use for wanton cruelty—to man or beast. Surely the officers didn't know what was going on?"

"I doubt it. From what we could tell, the enlisted men had been running their little game for some time, but on the sly, as it were. And, as it occurred during off-duty time, likely the officers didn't make it their business."

Gillett shook his head.

"At any rate, when we got among the crowd, one of them was leading a wretched-looking black shepherd: dirty, feeble, and gaunt from obvious neglect. The poor beast was limping on his off foreleg and whimpering, his tail curled up under him in fear. And yet he went forward willingly; the scoundrel leading him didn't even have to drag him toward the fate awaiting him.

"As the handler, attended by one or two others with clubs and pistols, opened the gate of the pit, the others clustered around the eye-level viewing ports on the sides, eager to see their blood-sport played out. The handler pulled the dog inside, yanked the loop from his neck, and skeedaddled back out as the others slammed the gate closed.

"And that's when Wiswall here sprang into action," Andrews said, glancing down at his slumbering partner. "He yelled out, 'Like hell you will!' and charged for the gate they had just closed. One fellow had the misfortune to be in his path, and he was knocked winding for his trouble. You may not have noticed, Sergeant, but Mr. Wiswall is built approximately like an oak stump."

Gillett chuckled softly in the dark.

"He flung open the gate and dashed inside. By this time, I divined what he was up to and hopped to second him, mostly to guard against mischief from the would-be lion-baiters.

"The dog was cowering just inside the gate, urinating

into the dust in terror. The cougar was crouched across the way, bunching up to spring. Wiswall kneeled down beside the dog and, keeping his eyes on the big cat, started talking in low, soothing sounds to the frightened animal."

"Lord a'mighty!" Gillett said softly. "That was mighty cool-headed, I'll allow."

"I'll never forget it," Andrews said. "He stared at that cougar and talked to that dog as if the two of them were in a parlor by the fireplace. And then I heard him say, 'Come on, now fellow. It's time to get you out of this hellhole.' And Wiswall stood up and backed toward the gate—me watching the cougar and the rabble, by turns—and the dog came right along with him, just as if he understood every blessed word Wiswall had said. In fact, I will confess that maybe he did— and still does.

"Well, Sergeant, we walked through that crowd of no-goods, and not a one of the sorry lot laid so much as a finger on the dog or either one of us—especially if they caught a good look at Wiswall's expression. The dog came right along with us, and he has been with us ever since. We've taken care of him, fed him, fussed over him, and talked to him. He has been our constant companion. And I'll say it again; I believe that Shep understood everything Wiswall said to him in that cougar pit, and I believe he understands what we tell him, to this day."

Gillett gave a low whistle. "That's a story I'll not soon forget."

"And so you can see two things from this, Sergeant," Andrews said. "First, when we told Shep to stay with our supplies at Crow Spring until we came back for him, he took that as an order, just as surely as you would receive an order from Lieutenant Baylor. It came near to breaking our hearts to leave him, but leave him we did. And that's why we have to go back for him—with or without Major Osbourne's infantry, with or without you and your fellow Rangers, come hell or high water . . . though I'm mighty glad Lieutenant Baylor agreed to help us out."

There was a long silence. Then Gillett said, "What's the second thing?"

Andrews turned his face toward Gillett's resting place. "My partner can't abide injustice, be it offered to a stray dog—or a stray Apache chief." Andrews let that sit for a while before adding, "He means no disrespect to you or your mission, Sergeant. And we all know how unlikely it is that the Indians will get to keep their way of life, with the changes happening in this country. But Wiswall doesn't like it. And he won't ever like it. I hope you can understand that, even if you don't agree with it."

"Sometimes hard things have to be done," Gillett said, finally.

"I suppose so," Andrews said, tapping the ashes out of his pipe and lying down on his bedroll. "I lost my mother and father to an Indian attack, so I certainly see the other side of it." As he lay on his back, looking up at the crow's-breast sky, Andrews fingered the gold locket on the chain around his neck. "But, still, even I wonder sometimes . . . How many wrongs does it take to make a right?"

Chapter Seventeen

Before sunrise early next morning, everyone was up, their snug bedding folded neatly and packed, the mules re-packed, and the horses unhobbled, saddled, bridled, and ready for the trail. Some of the Rangers had built a small fire and were having steaming coffee with warm biscuits. Talk was sparse and low in the pre-dawn dark, limited to communication regarding the day's journey.

Simon's three brothers and nephew prepared to depart for Ysleta. Andrews and Wiswall surmised that the Tiguas had not slept, instead scouring the Huecos for hidden attackers and then watching through the night. Now they squatted by the fire, eating biscuits and sipping coffee beside the other Rangers. As Andrews and Wiswall watched, Lieutenant Baylor came over and spoke to each one of the men who would leave.

"Thank you, good friends, thank you. I wish you safe journeys home." The four heavily armed Indians stood and each shook Baylor's hand in turn. Simon Olguin clasped each man on the shoulder. Then they went to their ponies and vaulted onto their backs. They reined their mounts out of the firelight; the sounds of their going faded into the dark.

"Home for peaceful sleep," Gillet said quietly, standing beside Andrews and Wiswall. "Too bad the rest of us can't ride back with them."

"Why, Sergeant," one of the other men said, "can't you nap in the saddle?"

"Not today, Seaburn," Gillett said. "Or I might wake up with an arrow in my throat."

"We look and watch or we die," Simon Olguin said as he drank the rest of his coffee. "Like the coyote, like the pronghorn. Like all life on the desert."

A few minutes later, everyone was mounted and ready to decamp. Glancing at Lieutenant Baylor, Simon Olguin rode out first; the rest of the Rangers, with Andrews and Wiswall, reined their horses after him. Day came on without true sunrise, but merely a gradual shading from black into a grudging, dull gray. Clouds lowered threateningly; it looked like a wet day's ride. As they went, the patrol loosened their slickers from saddle packs and slid them on over coats.

"If we ride through the rain, we can make Crow Spring by late evening," Baylor said. "And if those fellows out there, just beyond rifle range, don't get a lot of reinforcements."

Andrews stared hard, as far as he could see, but could pick up no sign of Apache observers. Then Wiswall said, "There. Just right of that far butte."

Andrews looked. Perhaps three-quarters of a mile distant, a mounted figure picked its way along, followed by two more.

"Lieutenant, I've got a Sharps," Andrews said. "They'd be in range for me. Shall I see if I can knock one of them down? I'm told that turned the trick for the defenders of Adobe Walls."

Baylor smiled. "The Sharps . . . The Indians say it's the gun that shoots today and kills tomorrow. But no." He shook his head. "Simon advises against it. Let them be for now; no need to pick a fight this early in the day. It may come to that, but maybe it won't. In the meantime, we'll ride as though we have no reason to fear or care who sees."

Andrews took his hand off the stock of the Sharps and peered back out over the desert, toward the butte. Now there was no rider visible.

"As bold as brass, we're on our way, boys," Baylor said, raising his voice to carry to the entire troupe. "There will be no forgiveness, reconciliation, or redemption for sloppiness of attention, lack of concentration, or outright recklessness. Let it not be you who fails to focus, leading to our entrapment. If not for your own safety, then for the life of the man riding next to you—pay attention."

They rode along, and once more, Andrews studied the men around him. To a man, they carried themselves as if they were riding through a town park rather than through a bleak desert populated by hostiles. Only their darting eyes betrayed that they were not completely at ease. This is just another day's work for them, Andrews thought.

A cold mist began to sift down on them; soon the horses' coats were slick with moisture—and surely not sweat in the chilly air. "Well, at least we don't have to worry about rattlesnakes in this weather," said one of the Rangers, a short, balding, middle-aged fellow named Cloyes. "I'd rather make a bed in the snow than have to worry about a snake crawling into my blankets during the night. They'll do that, you know."

"Ain't a snake this side of the Brazos River that'd sleep with you, Cloyes," one of the other men said. Several laughed at this. Cloyes's face reddened. Andrews heard him mutter under his breath, "All the same. I don't cotton to snakes."

Simon Olguin rode some seventy-five to a hundred yards in front of everyone else. As Andrews watched, he saw the scout's head turn left, watch for a while, then swivel back to the right.

"Three flanking us to the left now, four on the right," Gillett said, riding along behind Wiswall. "And always just out of Winchester range."

"You think they'll attack?" asked Andrews.

"Only if Victorio tells them to," answered the sergeant.

By now they had left the Butterfield trail; Baylor and Gillett had made the decision to cut directly across the desert expanse rather than follow the longer upper trail. They calculated this would put them at the Crow Spring station that much quicker. Also, concealment would be more difficult for ambushers in this open terrain. Of course, that also meant that the Rangers traveled in open view.

"How long have you and the army been dealing with Victorio?" Andrews asked.

"Well, let's see if I can recall the history," Gillett said. "Victorio is chief of a branch of the tribe sometimes called Warm Springs Apaches. In years past, I've heard, he rode with Geronimo, Mangas Coloradas, and maybe one or two others. He and his people were up around Fort Craig, New Mexico, and the order came to move them to a reservation in Arizona Territory.

"Victorio balked, gathered up his braves, women, and children, and lit out for Mexico. This was sometime around the summer of 1877. And for the last two years or a little more, he's been making a nuisance of himself here, in northern Mexico, and eastern New Mexico."

"Looks like the nuisance is growing, Sergeant," a trooper named Fitch said, nodding toward the south. Andrews and Wiswall looked to their right; now there were six braves flanking them, where four had been not long before.

"Our odds are dropping by the minute," Wiswall said.

"So I guess the Mexican authorities would like to see him gone just about as much as you would," Andrews said.

"Oh, I reckon. The milicianos want to see the last of him, too."

The cold mist continued to fall as they rode across the desert, all through the dreary morning. Now and then a jackrabbit would flush from cover in front of them, loping away in zigzags. "If old Shep were with us, we'd have the very devil of a time restraining him," Andrews remarked. Wiswall smiled.

"We ought to raise the Cornudas within the next couple or three hours," Gillett said. "From there, it's still a good thirty-odd miles across to Crow Spring. But we can make it tonight if we ride into the dark."

"I wish it was dark now," Cloyes muttered. "I don't like riding along with them Apaches watching every damned move we make. Pardon the language, Sergeant."

Up ahead, Baylor shouted for Simon Olguin. The scout wheeled his mount and trotted across the desert toward the rest of the column. After a quick conference, the lieutenant turned to the others, gathered in a loose semicircle behind him.

"Sergeant Olguin thinks this is as good as any place for a quick rest for the horses and ourselves. It's just about noon, so let's take a half-hour, at most. Seaburn, you stand watch on the left flank, and I'll take the right. Let's give the horses and mules some feed, and eat a little ourselves. Then we'll resume our ride."

As the Rangers began to dismount, Gillett commented, "Our audience is still growing."

Andrews and Wiswall peered out toward the northern and southern horizons. "I make ten on this side," Wiswall said after a few seconds.

"The same, at least, over here," Andrews said.

"Well, better to eat lunch now than in battle formation, I guess," one of the other men said.

"Is Victorio out there, do you suppose?" Andrews said.

"I doubt it," Gillett said. "If he was, we'd likely already know."

After filling feed bags with oats and strapping them on their mounts, the men pulled hardtack and cured beef from their packs and saddlebags and ate while standing beside their horses, washing down the hasty meal with a few swallows from their canteens. Then, as quickly as they had dismounted, they were all back in the saddle and pointed east by southeast.

By this time, Ojos de los Alamos was well behind them, off to the left. The party was moving well, despite having to slog through the occasional water-filled washout. They pressed on at a brisk walk or easy trot into the mid-afternoon, and the Cornudas rose up to their left. As the sky began to darken, and with the mist still descending, Lieutenant Baylor called another halt.

"Twenty miles to Crow Spring, men," he said, wincing as he stuck a fist in the small of his back. "Let's feed the animals and ourselves, work a few of the kinks out of our backs and legs, and get ready for the final run."

Dismounting in silence, several Rangers stretched out straightaway on the ground, pulling their hats down to cover their faces. Others tended the horses and mules.

"If they don't come for us before dark, we may at least win clear to the old station," Gillett said to Andrews. "As a general rule, the Apaches don't like to fight at night. Or in the rain."

"Well, then we've got darkness and damp in our favor," Andrews said, trying to shelter his biscuit from the precipitation.

"Why don't you try to get a little rest, Sergeant?" Wiswall said. "I'll see about your horse."

Gillett hesitated a moment, then handed his reins to Wiswall. "I'd be much obliged." He walked off a few paces and stretched himself beneath the bare branches of a cenizo bush.

An hour later, with Simon Olguin riding point, they set out again. Dark had fallen, but still they pressed ahead.

At the last fading of the light, one of the men said he counted thirty Apaches in all, about the same number shadowing them to the north as to the south.

"They'll still be out there, even in the dark," Gillett said.

"Well, I'd just as soon not have to look at them, anyhow," one of the men said.

"I just hope we don't have to see them up close," said Wiswall.

Andrews found himself riding beside Lieutenant Baylor, both of them following the barely visible hindquarters of Simon Olguin's pony.

"Unbeknownst to you, Mr. Andrews," Baylor said, "you and your partner picked the very spot for your overnight stay that Victorio and his people know the best. We've realized for a while now that they use the old Crow Spring station on their way south from the Guadalupes toward the country around Fort Davis. It's far enough east, and sufficiently isolated that they don't usually have to worry about being disturbed when they stop there for water."

"Well, I assure you, we had no intention of becoming part of his plans."

Baylor gave a low chuckle. "I expect they were delighted to find fresh horses just outside the station walls."

"I tell you the truth, Lieutenant, they made off with our horses as handily as you please. The hobbles didn't seem much of a deterrent."

"Oh, there's not a thing about stealing horses that anybody can teach the Mescaleros," Baylor said. "It's how they've done business for many a year. They are past masters at the art."

"Their skill was certainly in evidence, much to our disgust. Tell me truthfully, Lieutenant," Andrews continued in a lower voice, "how much danger are we in?"

Baylor rode for some moments without replying. "They seem to be gathering up on our flanks at a great pace," he said finally. "But now at least we have the concealment of darkness—though the noise of our passing tells them a great deal, no doubt. We'll come to the station all right, I calculate. And I hope with all my heart that we find Shep there, waiting for us."

"Yes, as do I, but . . . It's a long way back to Ysleta, isn't it?"

There was another long pause. "That is a problem for another day," Baylor said at last.

After they had ridden another quarter-mile, Baylor tugged his slicker about him. "The mist has let up, but do you feel how the temperature is dropping, now? It may get mighty cold tonight, especially if the sky clears off. I hope Shep has been able to keep warm enough."

"Well, we left every blanket we could spare in the ambulance and made sure he could get in there if he wanted to."

Baylor nodded. "I expect he'll be all right, then."

"That is my deepest hope right now," Andrews said. He tugged his hat down, turned up the collar of his woolen coat, and said another silent prayer for the dog that he hoped was waiting for them, somewhere in the darkness ahead.

Chapter Eighteen

Farther back down the line of riders, Wiswall asked Gillett how much farther he reckoned it was until they reached Crow Spring station.

"If we've stayed on course—and with Simon Olguin leading us, I fully expect we have—we ought to get there within the hour."

The night sky had cleared sufficiently that now, they could discern the indistinct, cottony shapes of clouds tumbling away toward the southeast, shoved along by a cold wind driving down from the Sacramento Mountains, behind them. Now and then, a patch of moonlight swept across the terrain. The moisture that had been drifting down on them all day, since their departure from Hueco Tanks before dawn, was now freezing on loose-hanging tack and in the horses' manes and tails.

"I never thought I'd be sorry to see it quit raining on me along the trail," Gillett said, "but if it clears off tonight, it will be mighty chilly sleeping weather."

"Not that we'll be doing much sleeping," Wiswall said. "The way it's looking, we may have half of the Apaches in Texas and the New Mexico Territory paying us a visit."

"There is that to consider," Gillett said. "Maybe we can leave again in darkness and be back on the trail to Hueco before our friends out there in the dark realize what we're about."

Wiswall greeted this assessment with a silence that spoke volumes.

"What was that?" Gillett said, suddenly. He sat up straight in his saddle and cocked his head sideways, listening.

"What did it sound like?" Wiswall said. "I wasn't paying—"

The noise came down the wind, faint and intermittent, but present, at the very limit of hearing: a dog barking.

"Shep!" Wiswall spurred his horse forward into a canter, quickly passing the others in the column. He tore past Baylor and Andrews; their surprised faces barely registered as he went by. He quickly bore down on Simon Olguin and then passed him, bearing straight along the line of travel, toward the far-off tumble of the abandoned stage station, barely visible in the intermittent washes of moonlight coming through the scudding clouds.

"That damn fool is liable to get us all killed!" one of the men yelled, just as Andrews kicked his horse forward.

"Shep! I hear you, boy!" Wiswall shouted, urging his laboring mount forward. He heard hoofbeats coming up on his right flank.

"What are you doing?" Andrews shouted, closing to within a few yards of Wiswall and his galloping mount.

"I heard him!" Wiswall called over his shoulder. "Shep! Sergeant Gillett heard him, too!"

"We ought to stay with the others," Andrews hollered.

"You can stay with them if you want; I'm going to get our dog!"

They made all the haste they could squeeze from their nearly spent horses, but the ruined station walls crawled toward them at an agonizingly slow pace. Andrews peered out at the desert landscape as best he could from the back of a galloping horse; if the Apaches were coming after them, he couldn't see any evidence. He hoped his senses were telling him the truth.

When they had nearly halved the distance between themselves and the Crow Spring station, they could plainly hear Shep barking. Despite their fatigue and the bitterly cold wind crawling down their necks, Andrews and Wiswall started laughing.

"Shep, you old rascal!" Andrews crowed in delight.

"Did you save us any bacon, Shep?" Wiswall yelled.

By the time they were a hundred yards away they could see him clearly, perched on the broken wall of the station, jumping up and down on his front legs and barking for all he was worth. After days and days in a desolate, abandoned place—most of it spent with only himself and the lurking coyotes for company—Shep was still there, still waiting for them, still standing watch over the ambulance and the supplies they had left there.

The partners reined their mounts to a stop in the crumbling doorway of the station and clambered down out of their saddles, their cold hands and cramped legs temporarily forgotten. Shep bounded up to them, whining and licking and wriggling like a new puppy. The two men fell on the dog, both exclaiming over him, petting him, rubbing his muzzle and head, his back, his belly.

"He's thinner," Andrews said.

"But he still has some pep," Wiswall said. "If he was in a really poor way, he wouldn't be acting so happy to see us." Shep had not stopped thrusting his nose toward the two men's faces, licking their hands, their cheeks. His tail rotated like a windmill.

A few minutes later, Simon Olguin rode up, with Baylor beside him. They dismounted and stood, watching the joyous reunion of the two men and their canine amigo. Before long, the rest of the Rangers had gathered up and begun dismounting and leading their horses inside the old station walls. Not a one passed by who didn't grin through his weariness—including the impassive Simon Olguin.

"Well, gentlemen, it looks like your sentinel stood to his post, just as you asked," Baylor said. "You couldn't ask for more faithful duty than that."

"I am sure enough glad to see this old cuss," Andrews said. He couldn't take his eyes off the dog, couldn't stop patting him; neither could Wiswall.

"All right, boys," Baylor called out, "since we have the dog, the Apaches be damned—at least for the next few hours. Let's get the animals hobbled and picketed and get a fire going. The Mescaleros know where we are, so there's no sense in a cold camp tonight."

Andrews and Wiswall, with Shep padding along between them, led their horses inside the walls of the station. The ambulance was still there and appeared undisturbed. On the ground underneath the wagon, a very small morsel of the side of bacon they had left with Shep was still visible. The sack of corn was mostly depleted.

"Coyote sign all around," Simon Olguin said, peering at the ground. "Dog kept them away."

"This old soldier had his work cut out for him, that's certain," Gillett said, scratching Shep between the ears. "I declare, it's a marvel, though; you told him to wait, and by gum, he waited!"

"Listen to him!" Baylor said as Shep whined and yipped, still fawning over his owners. "I don't believe I've ever heard a dog utter such sounds before. Fellows, that dog is talking to you as plainly as any animal ever spoke with a human, I do believe."

Some of the men had gathered enough wood for a good-sized fire and enough dry kindling to get it started; it was beginning to lick up from the center now, crackling and popping as the larger twigs and branches began to blaze. Someone filled the large, tin coffee pot with water from the station tank and set it to heat.

"Put the pack loads in the ambulance," Baylor said. "We'll hitch the mules to it in the morning."

Baylor and Gillett set the watches: three men in two-hour shifts, throughout the night. After a while, bacon sizzled in a pan over the fire. Somehow, the sound and the aroma made the night wind feel less chilly, allowed the still-present danger to recede from the men's minds, ever so slightly.

As the men and animals ate, Baylor reminded every-one to sleep with loaded rifles at their sides. "The Apaches don't usually attack at night, but we can ill afford a sur-prise," he said.

"Wonder how many of them are out there, now?" one of the men said.

"Reckon we'll know in the morning," another muttered.

Over the next half-hour, most of the clouds disap-peared; the moon glowed silver in a sky dusted with stars. Baylor, Gillett, Andrews, and Wiswall hunkered near the fire, huddled in their coats. The two Coloradoans fed Shep from their plates as the dog lay between them.

Wiswall, sipping on his third cup of coffee, said, "Lieu-tenant, I don't know how we can ever thank you enough."

"Let's wait until we're all back in Ysleta before we start passing out laurels," Baylor said.

Andrews stared around at what he could see of the deserted station by the moonlight. What little remained of the adobe walls was cracked and weathered from top to bot-tom. The whole place gave the impression that a few solid shoves would topple what structure remained. But if it came to a fight with Victorio in the morning, these crumbling walls would be better than no cover at all.

"What is the history behind this godforsaken place, anyway?" Wiswall asked.

"Well, from what I understand, this station was built about six months after the ones over at Cornudas de los Alamos and Ojos de los Alamos," Baylor said. "The stage line started using them in early 1858. Then, when they switched the route farther south in August of the next year, none of these continued in regular use. Over the next ten or so years, Cornudas and Ojos just about fell to the ground, and the only building left here at Crow Spring was a single structure within this little four-sided enclosure."

A while later, Wiswall said, "Lieutenant, how do you reckon we'll get out of here in the morning? Making the assumption that our escort is still out there, watching, won't it be obvious when we try to leave?"

"Maybe there'll be a fog or a mist to cover our retreat," Baylor said.

Wiswall tipped his head back and studied the jeweled sky, lit by the moon, still riding almost halfway up the western sky. "Fog will have to hurry, I'm thinking," he said.

"Do you know anything about Victorio's history?" Andrews said. "All we know about him is what we've heard along the trail and from you, and none of it has been good. Where did he come from? How did he come to be such a formidable foe?"

Baylor stared at the fire, starting to gutter lower and fall into red coals. "He was born Bidu-ya, I'm told," the Ranger commander said at last. "Supposedly that means 'He who checks his horse.' But as long as I've been out in this part of the country, no one has called him anything but Victorio. From what we can gather, he's old, in his 70s by now."

"Impressive that a man can live to be that old, given his history," Wiswall said in a musing voice.

"He has learned from some of the best," Baylor said. "As a young man, he rode with the war band of Mangas Coloradas, who terrorized much of northwestern Mexico from the 1820s to nearly 1840. Well before the Civil War, Victorio was known to the cavalry and every Indian throughout the southwest as a segundo: second-in-command of the Warm Springs band. Later, he gathered a large number of Mimbreños and Mescaleros under his leadership. With Cochise and Geronimo, the main Apache chiefs just about ruled this country during the Civil War, when so many troops were withdrawn back east."

"Have you ever seen him in person?" Wiswall asked.

Baylor shook his head. "Only the effects of his passing, I'm afraid. The few whites I've been able to speak with who have observed him up close described him as having a certain gallant air. And I am told that he can be generous and even solicitous with his own people. I'm afraid that I have not observed any evidence of such, however."

A long silence crept past, punctuated by soft pops and crackles from the fading fire. "Well, I suppose we'll know more of his disposition in the morning," Andrews said.

"Something tells me that he'll be here," Baylor said, nodding.

By now, the men not standing sentinel were finding their bedrolls. Andrews stood and went to the Coolidge, where he had placed his Sharps upon arriving at the station. "Make sure your ammunition is dry and at hand, partner," he said to Wiswall, who still sat on the ground, leaning against a wheel of the ambulance as he rubbed a hand up and down Shep's back. "It's likely that we'll have call for it in the morning."

The two partners rolled out their blankets on the ground underneath the ambulance, since the interior was filled with the contents of the mule packs. They made themselves as comfortable as they could; Shep curled up near their feet. Within the space of a half-hour, the Ranger camp was silent and motionless, except for the ceaselessly roving eyes of the sentries.

Andrews woke from a fitful sleep to hear a low voice muttering words in a strange tongue, near the place where Shep was lying. He opened his eyes and, moving his head as slightly as he could, he saw the huddled figure of Simon Olguin, squatted on the ground beside Shep, gently scratching the dog's neck and speaking half-whispered words in what Andrews assumed was the Tigua language.

As he watched, Simon's head moved; he was looking at Andrews. As quietly as he could, Andrews eased out from under the wagon and went over to sit on the ground beside Olguin. The Indian's hand never stopped stroking Shep's neck; the dog lay with his muzzle resting on his front paws, his eyes closed. He was clearly relishing the attentions of the Tigua scout.

"Sergeant Olguin, may I ask what you were saying to him?" Andrews said, after a while. "Were you speaking to him in Tigua?"

Olguin nodded, his eyes never leaving Shep. "I tell him a story of his ancestors."

Andrews smiled. "I expect he was glad to hear it. He's likely tired of the nonsense that Wiswall and I chatter to him about, day in and day out."

"I tell him about Coyote, who brings luck for the hunt."

"You hear that, old fellow?" Andrews said, running a palm along Shep's backbone. "You come from lucky ancestors. I'll warrant you've been wondering where your luck got off to, these last few days here, by yourself."

"Many coyotes have been here," Simon said, gesturing about the abandoned station yard. "They could have taken the dog's food. They could have killed the dog, if they wanted to. But they did not.

"They saw that he was their brother. They saw that he was strong-hearted and not afraid. And so they left him alone."

Andrews peered out at the yard, trying to imagine it full of coyotes—watching Shep, smelling the bacon, but not attacking.

"Dog has the luck of Coyote," Olguin said after a few moments. "It keeps him alive." For the first time, the Tigua looked directly at Andrews. "Keeps us alive."

Andrews stared into the scout's eyes for several seconds. Then both of them turned to look at Shep, who still lay as he had, except that now, his eyes were open, flickering back and forth between the two men.

After a while, Andrews returned to his bedroll under the ambulance. Simon Olguin's words were going round and round in his head: Dog has the luck of Coyote . . . keeps us alive . . .

Eventually, he slid into a fitful sleep interrupted by dreams of coyotes . . . circling, circling.

A few hours later, when Andrews woke, he felt that something was amiss. There was plenty enough light to see, yet he heard no sounds of making ready for departure, nor even the sound of feet shuffling back and forth.

He looked beside him on the ground; Wiswall's blankets still lay there, but he was not in them. Shep was nowhere in sight.

Taking up his Sharps, he cautiously rolled out from under the Coolidge and came up on his knees. The Rangers were all peering out over the tumbled walls of the station. Baylor stood in the center, staring fixedly out past what was left of the station gate.

What was everyone looking at so intently?

With a chill tightening about his entrails, Andrews stood, very slowly, his finger on the trigger of the loaded Sharps rifle.

The station was completely ringed about with Apaches.

And standing in front of the ring closest to the station, plainly visible through the ruined gate, was a man who could only be Victorio.

Chapter Nineteen

For a moment, Andrews wondered if he might still be asleep and dreaming. No one was moving; there were no voices. Each Apache fighter stared fixedly at the station and the Rangers inside, and the Rangers looked at the small army surrounding them, and all was motionless. Even Shep, who sat on the ground beside Wiswall, was as still as if he were a statue of a dog.

Wiswall was standing near Baylor and Gillett, who occupied the near-center of the station yard. Moving as deliberately as he knew how, Andrews went over to them.

"They gathered up before it got light," Wiswall said in answer to his unspoken question. "By the time the sun came up, they were already there. And they haven't moved since—neither has Victorio."

"So . . . that is Victorio, then?"

Baylor nodded. "Has to be. The only place any of those braves are looking, other than at us, is at him. He could flick a finger right now, and we'd all be pincushions."

"What do you imagine he intends?" Andrews said. "If he wanted to slaughter us—"

"We'd already be dead," Gillett said quietly. "I have considerable curiosity about his intentions, that's sure."

"Simon? What do you make of this?" Baylor said to the Tigua scout, who stood a few feet away.

"He is watching," Olguin said. "He is thinking."

After a few seconds, Wiswall said, "Let me go out and talk to him."

Baylor whipped around to stare at the stocky Coloradoan. "What are you talking about?"

"Will he recognize a flag of truce?" Wiswall said, already

walking slowly, with his hands in plain view, toward the ambulance. "I will go and talk to him. And Shep will go with me."

Now Andrews joined his voice to Baylor's. "Partner? Are you quite sure of your purpose? And your mind?"

Wiswall leaned inside the ambulance, and they could hear the sound of his knife ripping through one of the muslin bags that contained the rations carried on the mules. He sawed off a rough square and fixed it to a long stir-stick from the cooking kit. He stepped out from the ambulance and, in plain view of all the Rangers and the encircling Apaches, he removed his Colt revolver from his holster and laid it on the ground.

"Shep, come here," he said, and the dog, as if he had been waiting for just this word, rose up and padded to stand beside Wiswall.

"Mr. Wiswall, I cannot permit you to do this," Baylor said in a stern voice.

"Respectfully, Lieutenant, I am not asking your permission," Wiswall said. "The only one who can keep me safe right now is the Almighty, and I believe he outranks even yourself. Sergeant Olguin, are you willing to help me speak to Victorio?"

If the Tigua was surprised by this request, it didn't show on his face. He simply walked over to stand beside Shep, facing toward the waiting Apache chief.

"God go with you, William," Andrews said quietly.

Wiswall nodded. He turned toward Victorio, held his white flag high above his head, and walked forward, through the station gate. Shep and Olguin paced him, step for step.

As he walked toward the dour Apache chief, Wiswall told himself to look directly into Victorio's eyes and to show no fear. He had the fleeting thought that it would also be handy to know exactly what he intended to say. God will provide, he thought. And then, he, Shep, and Simon Olguin were standing in front of Victorio.

The chief was broad chested, but not tall—much like Wiswall himself, though less stout. In fact, as Wiswall looked at the older man, he guessed that nothing in Victorio's life would have lent itself to the accumulation of extra body weight. The chief looked like the plants of the surrounding desert: tough, hardy, able to survive where little else could.

His mouth was wide and full; it was set now in a straight line as he looked first at Wiswall, then at Olguin, and finally, for a long moment, at Shep, standing attentively between the two men. Victorio's hair was thick and dark, falling in long, loose locks on either side of his weather-creased face. A red, well-used bandanna circled his head. He wore a simple cotton shirt with a plain front and no collar, and his threadbare, homespun breeches were tucked into leather moccasins with attached leggings that came halfway up his calves.

Wiswall realized suddenly that Victorio carried no weapon other than the long knife in his belt. Of course, the scores of warriors surrounding them were armed with an assortment of bows—each with an arrow nocked to the string and ready to pull—and old Springfield and Enfield rifles. A few brandished ancient-looking Colt Navy model revolvers.

Victorio was speaking. He paused, and Simon Olguin said, "He says you are one of the men from the wagon who came here alone, with this dog."

Wiswall nodded, keeping his eyes on Victorio.

Victorio spoke again, and Olguin translated, "He says his braves watched you from the time you left Hueco Tanks until you came here. You were not careful with your horses."

Wiswall nodded again. He realized that he was fighting the urge to smile. Keep your tongue in your head until you have something to say, Wiswall, he thought. None of your brash foolishness. Still, the notion that an Apache chief who was, by all accounts, one of the most ruthless enemies the US Army and the Texas Rangers had ever encountered would take the time to lecture him about taking better care of his livestock was so unexpected that Wiswall found himself amused, even though he might not live long enough to walk back to his companions.

More terse words from Victorio. "He wants to know why you have come back," Olguin said.

Slowly, deliberately, Wiswall looked away from Victorio then, kneeling down to pat Shep's withers. "Tell him we came here to get the dog."

When Victorio heard Simon's translation, his eyes widened slightly. He didn't move, but even such a slight variation was notable in such an otherwise stoic face. He said something short, and Olguin repeated it back, nodding once. He said something else, and Olguin said, "He says that he has never seen a white-eye who would do such a thing. He says you must have great power, to make these others risk death for a dog."

"Tell him that everyone who came with me did so by his own choice," Wiswall said, standing up again. "And then, ask him why he thinks it is strange that people like us would show kindness to an animal."

Olguin spoke, and as he did, Victorio's face hardened. Almost before Olguin had finished, the chief was speaking. The words went on and on, and as Wiswall watched Victorio's face, he fancied he could understand the chief's meaning, though the words themselves were incomprehensible. Finally Victorio stopped and looked at Olguin.

"He says that it was white-eyes who took away the land at Ojo Caliente that was promised to him and to his people," Olguin said. "It was white-eyes who lied to him and who would not listen when his women and children were hungry. It was white-eyes who told him he had to leave his crops half-grown in the fields and go to a place far to the west where he had to make his wikiup in the middle of his enemies. It was white-eyes who killed Mangas Coloradas, even though he came to them under a flag of truce like the one you hold.

"He says that most of the white-eyes he has known have hearts that are black, like meat left too long in the sun. They care nothing for the land, for the other living things, or for the people—only for their bellies. He wants to know what it is about this dog that makes a white-eye think he is worth dying for."

Wiswall stared at Victorio for a long time. The sun was well up by now, and though the air was cold, it did not have the sharp bite that it had held through the bitter night. The breeze had shifted around to the south, and it played around them now, shifting the locks of Victorio's hair and gently stirring the branches of the cenizo bushes nearby. The breeze felt good. Perhaps because he was standing in the shadow of death, Wiswall felt intensely glad to be alive.

"Tell him that the same heart that beats in the Mescalero beats in me and in the rest of my companions," Wiswall said finally. "Tell him that we know what it means to love something enough to risk death. Tell him that this dog is loyal to me, and that means that I am loyal to him: that just as Victorio cares for his people, I care for this dog. And . . . tell him that if I die because of that, it will be a good death."

Simon Olguin turned to look at Wiswall, and Wiswall nodded. "Tell him. Everything I just said."

The Tigua translated; Victorio's eyes shifted back and forth between Wiswall and Shep. When Olguin finished speaking, it was Victorio's turn to stand silent, carefully studying the face of this man who was saying things that surprised his ears.

Shep chose that moment to step forward slowly, sniff carefully at Victorio's hand, and lick it gently once, then again.

Wiswall would later swear that one corner of Victorio's straight, severe mouth had twitched upward in something that wanted to be a smile. Then he spoke.

"He says that you may die very soon, but it will not be today," Simon Olguin said. "For the sake of this dog, he and his men will let you and the rest of us pass. He says that he is still at war with all white-eyes, but maybe he will not have to kill you or the others who came here with you."

Wiswall sternly counseled himself to keep his relief off his face. "Tell Chief Victorio that I thank him, for myself and my friends. Tell him that I wish there could be peace between us, more than just today. Tell him that I wish that his women and children did not have to find their food in the desert."

When Olguin translated, Victorio spoke again.

"He says that your wishes will not fill the bellies of his people."

Wiswall nodded.

Victorio turned around and walked away a few steps, until he was standing in line with the nearest of his braves. "Enough," he said in English. "You go now."

Chapter Twenty

Wiswall walked back toward the station, where the others waited. He heard Simon Olguin's soft footfalls behind him, and Shep padded along beside. He did not look back. Despite what Victorio had said, his back tingled between his shoulder blades, anticipating an arrow or a bullet from an Enfield.

But neither arrow nor bullet came. He walked back into the station yard, every eye fixed on him. He went up to Baylor and said, "Victorio says we can go. He will not hinder us."

"Is this some sort of joke?" the Ranger commander said.

"It is true," Simon Olguin said, standing just behind Wiswall's left shoulder. "No fight. Because of dog."

Baylor looked out toward the surrounding Apaches, and indeed, they were walking away, Victorio at their head—as if they had seen all they came to see and now had no further interest in what happened. The line of them was angled away toward the place, just on the other side of the old Butterfield trail, where some younger boys waited with the band's ponies. Only a handful of warriors remained in place, observing the Rangers.

"By God, I reckon I can take him down," someone said. Wiswall looked, and one of the younger men was leveling a rifle at the departing back of the Apache chief. He sprang toward the man and slammed the muzzle toward the ground, just as Sergeant Gillett grabbed the Ranger from behind.

"You damned fool! He's letting us go," Wiswall said. "Don't make him change his mind."

"He's right, Allen," Gillett said. "You'd best listen to him."

The man struggled for a moment, but then he relented. He looked around the group, and when his eyes found

those of Lieutenant Baylor, staring at him like a hawk studying a rabbit, he ducked away. "All right," he muttered, looking at the ground. "I'm all right, now."

For perhaps two full minutes, the men in the abandoned station watched the astonishing procession in disbelief. Then, as if coming out of a trance, Baylor began giving
orders.

"Let's hitch the mules to the ambulance. See that all
your gear is in order, and keep your rifles close to hand."
Now he aimed a pointed look at Allen. "But do not show them
openly or point them in the direction of the Indians; if they
truly mean to let us go on our way, we will show them no
reason to reconsider."

"What in the name of all that is holy did you say to
Victorio?" Andrews said to Wiswall as they gathered their
tack and made ready to hitch the mules to the Coolidge.

"Mostly, I listened," Wiswall said, a faraway look on
his face. "Shep was the one who presented the majority of
our case."

Andrews studied his partner's face, then peered at the
dog, who had not left Wiswall's side. "If I didn't know about
your gift of blarney," he said, "I'd have more than half a mind
to believe you."

Wiswall gave a little smile. "Sometimes a man just
needs to say what is on his mind, partner. And then it's a
little easier for him to let the other fellow do the same."

"You'll be lecturing in the halls of Congress next, I
calculate."

"Oh, no. My gifts of persuasion are wasted on such
unrepentant blackguards as those."

Andrews laughed, and it felt good. It was the first time
he had laughed out loud since first laying eyes on Shep, the
night before.

"We leave immediately, men," Baylor announced. "If
we reach the Tanks tonight, we'll break out the fiddles for
some refreshing music." He walked over and put his hand
on Wiswall's shoulder. "Just about now I confess to feeling a
little lightheaded, free for the first time in days from fear and
anxiety. I would deeply appreciate your company on at least
part of today's ride, Mr. Wiswall, so that you can inform me
what witchery you employed to secure our free passage."

"I am happy to ride with you any time, Lieutenant," Wiswall said with a smile. "But I don't know how much my explanation will enlighten you. I'm not certain I understand myself everything that just happened—and I was there."

"I will make you one guarantee, Lieutenant," Andrews said, grinning. "Wiswall can throw a lasso of words around you that will have your head spinning even faster than it is right now. I predict that by the time we've ridden five miles, you will be begging for mercy."

The men saddled their mounts and rigged their gear. Andrews and Wiswall hitched the mules to the Coolidge, now full of the provisions they had brought for the expedition. Smiles and good-natured jest were much in evidence; the dark cloud of danger that had hovered over them all was now lifted. The last Mescalero watchmen, apparently satisfied with the Rangers' intention to leave, plodded away across the desert to their waiting mounts; the single-file line of riders in the main Apache band wound behind a small rise and out of sight, no doubt headed back toward the concealing crags and ravines of the Guadalupes.

"Any objection to taking our breakfast along the way?" Gillett called out.

"Hell, no, Sergeant!" one of the men shouted. "Excuse the cussing, but the sooner we put this damned old place at our backs, the better I'll like it!"

Several of the men chuckled at this. Baylor swung into his saddle, looked around for a moment or two, and pointed out the gate and across the desert, in the direction of Hueco Tanks. He clicked his tongue and put his heels to his mount, and the return journey was underway.

Simon Olguin, as always, took his place well out in front of the rest, and Shep went out to join him, pacing along a few feet in front of Olguin's pony. From his seat on the Coolidge, Andrews grinned and pointed. "Shep always takes point. I hope Sergeant Olguin doesn't mind the company." Gillett, riding beside Andrews, chuckled at the sight.

"Well, sir, I tell you the truth, that was a nervy few minutes back there," Ranger Cloyes said, riding on the other side of the ambulance. "I don't know what your partner said to old Victorio, mister, but I'm sure enough glad he said it."

Gillett, who had just reached for his canteen, now

held it aloft. "A toast, my friends," he said, raising his voice to carry all along the line of riders. "To Shep, our savior, and to our two new friends!"

"And a toast to no more of them Mescaleros ready to fill our hides full of arrows!" Cloyes shouted. Everyone within earshot laughed aloud.

With the danger and urgency past, they set a more leisurely pace for the horses, ambling along at a steady walk across the nearly bare, gray terrain of the flats. They had the western Guadalupes at their backs and were aimed toward the distant Cornudas range. The sun's rays were brilliant; an easy south wind fanned them from behind.

By noon, the indistinct, brown outline of a mountain range began to rise on the western horizon, smudged against the crystalline blue sky. "About five or six more hours, I calculate," Gillett said, "and I don't think we'll make Hueco by nightfall. But we can find a likely enough spot for camp in the Cornudas, I'm thinking."

"We're under the wing of old Victorio now, boys," another Ranger said. "No one is going to hurt us. Day after tomorrow, we'll be home."

By the end of the afternoon, they rode into a splendid sunset, arriving in a ravine that cut through the middle of an outlying knoll of the Cornudas. They set quickly about setting up camp and staking the horses and mules, under the watchful eyes of three of the Rangers, to graze for an hour or so among the sparse, curly grass clinging to the chert slopes. Dusk purpled into night as they cooked and ate their travel rations and drank their coffee, taking this meal in considerably more ease than any they had consumed since setting out from Ysleta, days before.

With supper eaten, plates scraped into the fire and wiped with bandanna or shirttail, and smoke from cigarettes and pipes drifting slowly upward in the chilly air, all eyes gradually turned toward Wiswall, sitting cross-legged on the ground between Baylor and Andrews. Shep, of course, was splayed at the feet of the three men.

"Would you favor the men with what you told me on today's ride?" Baylor said into the thoughtful silence. "I believe everyone here would like to know whatever you would care to tell, and for my part, I would certainly not mind hearing the telling at least once more. I suspect this is a story we'll all be telling ourselves and anyone else who will listen, for the rest of our lives, maybe."

Wiswall stared into the fire for the space of perhaps ten breaths, then down at Shep. He reached down and thoughtfully rubbed the shepherd's jaw; Shep's tail thumped slowly on the ground—otherwise, he was motionless.

"I am afraid I can't exactly explain what came over me," he started slowly, sounding like someone telling himself a story he had never heard before. "I was there with the rest of you, looking out there at all those Apaches, every one of them armed and ready for trouble, and a damn sight more of them than there were of us."

"Nothing wrong with your arithmetic, then," one of the men said with a grin. A few low chuckles greeted this remark.

"All of a sudden, the notion came to my mind—from where, I still can't tell you—that for all his cruelty and cunning, Victorio was a man of flesh and blood, just like me . . . like Lieutenant Baylor, like every one of you.

"I studied on that thought for a bit, and then the notion hit me that I might as well try and talk to him, man to man. He might kill me on the spot, in which case I would have been on hand to hold open the Pearly Gates for the rest of you."

A little more rueful laughter came at this; the men looked at each other and nodded knowingly.

"So, with nothing to lose, more or less, I decided to just walk out there and talk to him. And then, it came to me that I ought to take Shep. After all, he was the reason I was there in the first place, and likely the reason for the rest of you coming along."

"It sure wasn't to save your mangy hide, partner," Andrews said. More laughter erupted.

"So the three of us went out there, while the rest of you watched, likely thinking I'd lost what little was left of my judgment."

"Amen," said Andrews.

"And I wish I could tell you that I knew exactly what I was going to say when I got to Victorio, but that would be a lie. I stood face to face with a man whom I knew could lift a single finger and end my life instantly, and I didn't know what I would say to him—until he asked me why I had come back.

"And that was when I decided to just tell him the truth. We all came back for this fellow, right here." He leaned forward to pat Shep again. "He has been the constant companion of Andrews and me since the day we found him, and we could no more leave him behind than one of you would leave a fellow Ranger. We had to come back for him; that was all there was to it."

No wisecracks greeted Wiswall's pause: only thoughtful looks, deep draughts on smokes, and a few nodding heads.

"And as soon as that thought came clear in my mind, I realized that if anything could change Victorio's mind about whether or not we deserved to live, it was that. Caring enough about a fellow being to put your life on the line . . . that was something he respected—something he understood.

"I knew he understood that, because that is the same thing he has done."

At this last, a few surprised expressions appeared around the campfire.

"Now, men, don't take me wrong," Wiswall continued. "You are Texas Rangers, and you are sworn to uphold the laws of the state and to protect its people. You don't have much choice about that, and if you weren't willing to do it, you ought not to wear the star.

"But don't you see? Time and the tide of history have put Victorio and his people in a bad pinch. They've been forced off their land and made to move from pillar to post. He's got hungry children that he is responsible for—women who aren't getting enough to eat. I keep asking myself: 'What would I do if my back were to the wall like that?' I think I might be fighting mad all the time, too."

Unnoticed, Simon Olguin had drifted into the far reaches of the flickering firelight. Andrews saw his dim form, standing as still as stone. His face was fixed intently in Wiswall's direction.

"Anyhow, when I told Victorio that I came for the dog—that each one of you came of your own free will, out of sympathy for a good, loyal animal—something changed. I could tell he wasn't expecting to hear that.

"Oh, he's still on the warpath, no question about that," Wiswall said. "If you ride out on his trail next week, it will be 'kill or be killed' when you meet. His anger at his situation is not abated, not in the least.

"But just for today, he saw me—saw each one of you—as men, the same as he is. He saw that some of us white-eyes, at least, have hearts capable of caring for something. And just for today—I'm still not sure why—he decided to let things be different. And that is as much as I can tell you about why we're sitting here right now, smoking our pipes, instead of lying dead or dying back at Crow Spring station."

Andrews looked out toward the place Simon Olguin had appeared. He was still there, but now, barely visible at the edge of the unsteady glow from the campfire, he raised one hand, palm out. It was a salute; Andrews wasn't sure if it was intended for Wiswall or Shep. Maybe it didn't matter.

As he continued to watch, Olguin faded back into the darkness of the desert night.

Chapter Twenty-One

By four o'clock the next morning, clouds began rolling in from New Mexico, gradually erasing the glittering stars and dimming the light of the moon that had bathed the Ranger campsite after the fire was coals and ash. By six a.m., the growling of distant thunder was enough to arouse the men, though they were sleeping more soundly than they had since leaving their bunks in Ysleta.

"I knew yesterday's weather was too good to hold," Wiswall grouched, rolling up his blankets and stowing them in the ambulance. "But it would have sure been nice to get back home, at least, before getting drenched again."

"So El Paso is home now, is it?" Andrews said, giving his partner a sly smile. "I thought you had a fiancée you were anxious to get back to."

"You know what I mean."

By the time they had doused the breakfast fire and climbed back into saddles and onto the Cooldige, a slow rain was pattering down. They lined out on the trail, hiding from the shower in their slickers as best they could.

By midday, the worst of the storm had passed; only intermittent drops fell on them as they rode through the afternoon toward Hueco Tanks. They made camp there that night, and despite the damp and cold, the men were cheerful, knowing that they would be back in Ysleta by the end of the next day.

Bernardo, Ponciano, Francisco, and Domingo—Simon Olguin's brothers and nephew—were at the Tanks, waiting for them when they rode in. Baylor greeted them with glad words. "Your brother can tell you about all that has happened to us in the last two days," he said. "It will make quite a story. And I will swear to the truth of every word." Later, Andrews and Wiswall saw the Tiguas huddled in a group, the four listening intently as Simon spoke and gesticulated. From time to time, one or all of them would look over in their direction. Andrews and Wiswall weren't sure if they were studying Wiswall or Shep, who lay on the ground beside them.

"Simon told me a while ago that three Mescaleros were trailing us all day, yesterday," Gillett told them as they sipped coffee by the fire, after supper. "They only turned back when we got here, to the Tanks. He says they were watching us."

"We sure didn't see them," Andrews said.

Gillett shook his head. "I reckon they wanted us to see them on the way out. On the way back, they didn't."

They broke camp at first light the next morning, the men chattering with uncharacteristic animation at the prospect of sleeping in a real bed that night. Toward midday the Ranger party began encountering people working in large, flooded fields, vaqueros moving cattle or horses, loaded ox-carts, and other evidences of the proximity of the town and its comforts.

Near noon, they made a brief halt beside an acequia for a quick lunch from their saddlebags and a chance for the horses and mules to rest and drink. A lone horseman came upon them and halted, staring.

"What is the matter, friend?" Baylor called to him.

"Are you Lieutenant Baylor and the Rangers who went after that dog out at Crow Spring?" the man said, still staring.

"The same, now returning with that valiant dog and the property he faithfully guarded for his owners," Baylor said.

The rider shook his head. "Everyone in town thinks you were all slaughtered. It's all the talk, up and down the street."

A couple of the Rangers started chuckling. "Well, you may assure them that we are not only alive, but almost back home," Baylor said with a big smile. The man rode off toward El Paso, still shaking his head.

"I've always wanted to witness a resurrection," Wiswall said. "I guess that participating in one is even better."

"What do you think, Shep, old fellow?" Andrews said, briskly rubbing the dog's neck. "We've come back from the dead!"

As they resumed their ride after eating, Gillett said, "Lieutenant, when we ride into town, we ought to set Shep up on the wagon seat, so everyone can see him."

"Capital idea," Baylor said. "What do you say, Mr. Andrews?"

"As long as Wiswall doesn't mind either driving the honoree or being his outrider, that suits me fine, Lieutenant."

"It's settled, then," Baylor said. "We'll organize a little parade, in honor of Shep's homecoming. We can even stop at the Osguedo rancho, just down the trail a ways, and paint a sign to hang on the ambulance. 'Faithful Shep,' it ought to say."

And so it was that by early afternoon the troop arrived at the Rancho Osgueda, less than five miles from downtown El Paso. Don Ygnacio himself met them at the front gate of his hacienda.

"Bienvenidos, Capitan! Only yesterday we heard to our deep sorrow that all of you had perished in the desert! And, now, as God wills, here you are, mi compadre! Come and rest, all of you. And especially this perro valiente, who is the cause of such a great adventure!"

Baylor explained that, regrettably, they could not stay long. But Don Ygnacio was only too delighted to have a board and some paint brought from his workshop. Very soon, the Coolidge was adorned with a sparkling white sign with bold red lettering, announcing the presence of Shep, the redoubtable sentinel dog.

Don Ygnacio even insisted on sending along with the party a wagon to carry musicians. "There cannot be a homecoming parade without music," he said. "The bajo sexto and the violín will go with you to announce to the town the return of the heroic dog and his compañeros."

Before much longer, they were on the outskirts of the town. News of their return had preceded them; more and more people were arriving, lining the muddy route, then joining the entourage. Shep rode on the wagon seat beside Wiswall, who drove, and Andrews rode behind the Coolidge. Led by Baylor, the Rangers came immediately after, trailed by the musicians; by now, they were busily strumming, bowing, and singing. Andrews thought he recognized the sound of "Trigueña Hermosa," a song popular with the Mexican mine workers back in Colorado. But the words didn't sound the same, somehow. Maybe the singers were changing the lyrics to fit the occasion.

The growing column entered El Paso like a triumphal procession, by now augmented by several dozen children and at least half as many stray dogs. Though the winter sun was already more than halfway down the western sky, Baylor directed his cavalcade past the canal leading down to the Rio Grande, then left, toward the plaza at the town's center.

People poured out of the buildings on both sides of the muddy streets to see the display. The doors of business establishments opened, and customers, clerks, and owners jostled out, some elbowing each other for a better view and all giving the appearance of wanting to know what the hell was going on.

Once within the large plaza, Baylor led the procession directly to the center; at his urging, Wiswall drove the ambulance right up next to the small pergola, built in a fit of civic pride but now with its paint peeling and a here and there a slat that needed to be nailed down again. The lieutenant dismounted and walked up the steps to the bandstand, then he motioned for Wiswall, Andrews, and Shep to join him there.

Just then, the gathering crowd parted to reveal Sallie Baylor, followed closely by her two daughters. Lieutenant Baylor met them at the base of the pergola steps, and the next several minutes were spent in enthusiastic hugs, tearful greetings, and manly reassurances.

Ascending the steps again, Baylor turned toward the crowd. "Friends, thank you for such a wonderful welcome. These men have ridden far in pursuit of an honorable ideal, and they have come home safely from insurmountable danger. And all of it is because of this dog that you see here, beside me."

He told them the story of how Andrews and Wiswall, unwilling to leave their faithful companion to his fate, implored Baylor for his help. He told about the cold, wet ride to the abandoned station at Crow Spring. And he told of the confrontation with Victorio and its astounding outcome.

"I make no claim to understand the workings of fate or

the will of the Divine," he said. "But I do understand faithfulness and courage, and I say to all of you here that this dog, Shep, ought to be known as an honorary Texas Ranger."

The crowd cheered wildly. Andrews and Wiswall looked at each other, grinning like schoolboys.

"I wish we could build a monument to this dog, right here in the plaza," Baylor said. "Such a memorial ought to be inscribed, 'Faithful Shep: a salute to a valiant, noble warrior who leaped into our hearts, and whose blood flows forever with our own.'"

The crowd cheered again, the musicians broke into a joyful cancion, and most everyone in the crowd came up to shake the hands of one or more of the Rangers.

Shep watched it all from his vantage point on the bandstand, his tail wagging vigorously.

Epilogue

Andrews hauled back on the lines, and the horses stopped by the gate of the Ranger station. He looked across at Wiswall. "Well, we're here."

"I can't say I'm looking forward to this."

"We can't just leave without saying goodbye."

Wiswall shook his head and climbed down from the Coolidge. Andrews reached behind him and picked up the Springfield he had brought. Shep hopped down and walked between them as they trudged across the yard toward Baylor's house. They walked up the steps onto the broad porch and knocked on the door. The Mexican housemaid opened the door and motioned them inside.

"Yes, you too," Wiswall said to Shep, who hesitated on the threshold.

"Sí, sí," the housemaid said, smiling down at Shep. "El perro es muy bienvenido, todos los días."

"Well, you heard her," Andrews said, grinning at the dog. "Say 'Gracias,' like a gentleman."

"So you're on your way, then?" It was Baylor's voice. The lieutenant was striding toward them, coming from the direction of his study.

"Yes, we'd best be getting on," Andrews said. "But we wanted to be sure to stop by and thank you for . . . well, for everything."

"I believe I ought to thank you," Baylor said, shaking their hands in turn. "If not for you, I would never have had the honor of meeting this fellow." He kneeled down and took Shep's head in both his hands. "Now, Shep, you take good care of these two, all right? Don't let them go getting into any more trouble." He stood. "I hope you'll take the southern route, this time."

"Oh, yes! Across to Fort Davis, and then back north," Andrews said. "I think we've learned our lesson about taking shortcuts in this part of the country."

Baylor smiled. "And you're sure you won't consider my offer?"

"Lieutenant, I hope you know how honored we both are that you would consider us worthy of joining the Rangers. But I think I can speak for Mr. Wiswall and myself when I say that we have been too long away from our lives and livelihood, up in Ouray County. We didn't succeed in our attempt at brokering burros, but we have had an adventure that nothing else in our experience is ever likely to match. And now, we feel the need of going home."

Baylor nodded. "I can certainly understand that need."

Now Andrews brought forward the Springfield he had fetched in from the wagon. "Lieutenant, it would be impossible for us to adequately thank you for your courageous assistance to us in our time of need. But as a poor substitute, I want you to take this Springfield rifle. It is in top-notch condition, I assure you; I believe it will give you good service."

Baylor's eyes glowed with pleasure as he took the rifle and examined it. "This is indeed a fine weapon," he said. Then he offered it back to Andrews. "But I couldn't possibly accept this. My men and I were only doing our duty."

"No, sir, I must insist," Andrews said, pressing the rifle back toward Baylor, "you did considerably more than that. You rode into certain danger of your own free will, as did the others. Please, Lieutenant; do not dim my pleasure in this gift by protesting it."

Baylor looked again at the rifle. "Well, Mr. Andrews, if you are certain . . . This is certainly a generous gesture."

"Yet one that has been well earned, in my estimation," Andrews said.

Baylor shook their hands again. "Well, if you ever have occasion to be back in Texas, you'll always have a place here. And you too," he said, leaning down to pet Shep. The dog licked Baylor's hand and wagged his tail.

When they turned to go, Sergeant Gillett was standing in the doorway. "I heard you were hitting the trail today. I wanted to say my good-byes and see this old fellow here, one more time." He smiled down at Shep. "I wish your partners would leave you with us, Shep."

Shep went over to Gillett and received a vigorous petting. He clearly reveled in it, reaching upward with his snout to lick at Gillett's face. Gillett stood and came over to Andrews and Wiswall. He shook each man's hand. "I don't expect I'll ever forget the events we've been through together," he said. "If I ever write my memoirs, I will mention our adventures."

Andrews smiled. "Well, Sergeant, you're welcome to make any use of it you wish. I won't ever say anything to contradict or take away from anything you write."

They went outside and walked back to the Coolidge. A knot of men had gathered in the yard, most of them from the party that had ridden to Shep's rescue. Andrews and Wiswall had to slow their progress; each man in the group wanted to kneel down in front of Shep, scratch him behind the ears or along his neck, and say a few words of parting. One or two of the most hardened among them, to Andrews and Wiswall's amazement, even appeared to be choking on their words, swallowing and blinking as they bade farewell to their canine compadre.

Finally, they were back on the ambulance and pulling away from the station. Both men shared the seat, with Shep perched in between.

"I'm going to miss those fellows," Wiswall said, after they had driven perhaps two miles.

"As will I. And yet, I have the feeling that our affairs will bring us back to Texas, one day. At least, I hope they will."

"Next time, let's pay better heed to the travel warnings we receive along the way."

Andrews laughed.

A slight rise angled upward ahead of them, and they noticed two figures standing motionless at its crest. As the wagon approached, they did not move; it appeared as though they were actually waiting for the travelers. The nearer Andrews and Wiswall came, the higher their curiosity mounted.

"I wouldn't think that highwaymen would stand out in the open, so bold, and announce their presence," Andrews said.

"But just in case," Wiswall said, "I'll have my hand on my Colt, and I'd advise you to do the same."

"I am ahead of you, partner."

And then, Shep's ears flicked forward. His eyes fixed on the two men—as it now became clear that was what they were—and his nose worked busily, sieving the air for their scent. Next, he stood up on the seat, and his tail began to wag, slapping at Andrews and Wiswall, seated on either side of him.

"Well, Shep finds nothing to fear," Wiswall said.

Andrews peered ahead. "By heaven, Wiswall, that is Simon Olguin, standing there! And another Indian with him—one I don't recognize."

The Tigua scout and his companion were as still as statues while Andrews and Wiswall drove toward them. "Hello, Sergeant Olguin," he said when he pulled the team to a halt. "I am glad that we can see you one more time, before we go back to our home."

"This is Itza-chu. He comes from Victorio."

Andrews felt his eyes go wide. One of Victorio's warriors? This close to Ysleta, the army, and the Rangers?

Wiswall found his tongue first. "We are honored that he has come."

"Victorio sent him here under truce to say good-bye to the spirit brother of Coyote, who rides with you."

Andrews and Wiswall stared at each other, then at Shep. Finally, Wiswall said, "Well, Shep. This man has something he wants to say to you. You'd better go talk to him."

The dog peered up at Wiswall and Andrews. "Go on," Andrews said, gesturing with a forefinger.

Carefully, Shep hopped down from the wagon seat. He padded over to the two Indians, first going to Simon Olguin. The Tigua leaned over and caressed Shep's snout, muttering to him in what Andrews and Wiswall guessed was Tigua.

Then Shep turned toward the Mescalero. Itza-chu went down on one knee. He did not touch Shep; instead, he peered intently into Shep's eyes for what seemed like several minutes. Shep stood stock-still, returning the warrior's gaze. Then, Itza-chu laid the tips of his fingers on the top of Shep's head and said a half-dozen words that neither Andrews nor Wiswall understood. He stood and backed up a couple of steps.

Shep, as if on signal, turned and padded back to the

ambulance. He climbed back up onto the seat and settled in between Andrews and Wiswall.

"What do you reckon he just said to Shep?" Wiswall said.

"I don't believe we're supposed to know."

Simon Olguin raised a hand; Andrews and Wiswall returned the gesture. Andrews shook the reins and clicked his tongue, and the team leaned into their collars. The ambulance rolled forward.

"Well, that just about beats all," Andrews said, several minutes later.

"Yes, partner. I believe it does."

Afterword

Since the story you have just read is an effort at commingling fictional action and dialogue with historical fact and geography, it is imperative the author reassure his reader as to which personalities and events are the product of history, and which arise solely from the author's imagination.

First, all the characters presented here are based on people (and animals) who actually lived; careful research substantiates their veracity. Indeed, the following novel emanates from three paragraphs, a sketch in less than 300 words, reanimating a long-forgotten incident described, among other places, on pages 398–399 in Walter Prescott Webb's classic history, *The Texas Rangers: A Century of Frontier Defense*, published in 1935.

Years later, speaking of the events from which this story is drawn, Ranger George Lloyd insisted that the survival of the Baylor rescue party was due to "divine grace." Pvt. Oscar Burnes, another Ranger volunteer who usually rode point for the group, claimed the week-long encounter blended, then ignited, an "astonishing human activity between Mescalero Apache Chief Victorio, Captain Baylor, us Rangers, and dog Shep that transcended all credibility." The exact meaning of Burnes's somewhat cryptic description is now impossible to verify, but his words stayed in the author's mind, producing the stream of conjecture that served as the source for this work of fiction.

Such recollections demanded from this writer further explanation, and, if deemed fortuitous, exhumation of as many facts as possible for the story's expansion. Following the first faith, first belief, and first lesson of the first writers of the frontier fiction—". . .invented stories, fictitious literature, and figments of imagination can easily have happened in the way you dream them to have happened"—I created a series of chapters endowed with actual personalities in figurative chats and conversations during a special time frame, the intention being to share a noble moment in the long history of other noble Ranger moments.

This story is about larger-than-life heroes: larger-than-life because, as ordinary and unremarkable men hanging around their Ranger post in Ysleta, they in actuality possessed the most admirable of all human traits—the self-sacrificing courage to risk their lives for that of another being, albeit a dog, by entering the heart of Mescalero country during the coldest, windiest, wettest week in West Texas history to fetch and bring home that stranded, hungry animal.

The reader should know that I can find no historical evidence that Victorio and the Rangers ever had the type of confrontation and conversation depicted in the central scene of this book. Nevertheless, I have taken the liberty of supplying it in the interest of the yarn and in the hope that the words exchanged in this imaginary interview might represent some semblance of what these characters would have said in real life, had circumstances been different. I hope that the reader will not only forgive, but actually enjoy, this flight of fancy on my part.

Because of men like J. W. Seaburn, John Thomas, J. P. Miller, George Lloyd, R. M. Head, J. N. Garcia, D. B. Fitch, A. J. Cloyes, Oscar Burnes, J. L. Allen, J. B. Gillett, G. W. Baylor, J. W. Andrews, W. P. Wiswall, and Tigua Indian scout Simon Olguin with his three brothers and nephew, Shep still lives. He is everywhere, in every dog. Just look into the eyes of your own, and you'll see him.

Baylor Manuscript for *El Paso News*

The following pages are reproduced from George Wythe Baylor's February 3, 1900 article for the *El Paso News*. The article gives an account of the incident that inspired this book.

949 514 5319

George Wythe Baylor.
El Paso Herald.
Feb. 3, 1900.
P3 C4,5,6.

EXCITING ADVENTURE

Of Two Young Men at Crow Flat and
Guadaloupe Peak With a Band of A-
pache Indians.

By Geo. Wythe Baylor.

In the spring of 1880 two young men named Andrews and
Wiswall, of Denver, Colorado, came west to grow up with the country. After looking over the valley of the Rio Grande, and an
insignificant little dirt daubed placed called El Paso, Franklin, or Magoffinsville, according to one's taste, they concluded to try Black River, or Seven Rivers in the Pecos valley.
Getting an ambulance with a good pair of horses, plenty of grub
and an outfit for camping, they started on the old Butterfield
overland stage road. ——SPRING
At Crow Flat they stopped for dinner at the old deserted
station. They had hobbled their horses and were soon busy with
baking bread, frying meat and boiling coffee, not dreaming there
was an Indian in the country, though they had been warned to look
out for them. It is an open county with some few trees and tules
around the water holes and sand hills. When they had commenced
eating - like all men traveling in that country, they had the
appetities of coyotes and became deeply absorbed in stowing a-
way rations - the horses had grazed off about a hundred yards,
and the first thing they knew they heard a yelling and trampling
of horses' feet, and looking up they saw four or five Indians
driving off their horses. Grabbing their guns they started after
the Indians at top speed, both being western men and good shots.
They hoped to get near enough to the Indians to prevent them
from taking the hobbles off of the horses by opening fire on
them, with their Winchesters. But the Apaches can't be taught
anything about stealing horses. So some of the Indians stopped
and began shooting at the boys, who returned their fire. But
the boys, who returned their fire. But the horses made about
as good time as though they were foot loose. This fact was well
known to the Texas Rangers, who hobbled and side-lined also,
and even then their horses when stampeded would run as fast
as the guards could run on foot for a considerable distance.
The boys kept advancing and firing, but it was no use. The danger was that the Apaches might make a circuit and beat them back
to the ambulance, thus setting them afoot without grub or blankets which would be a bad fix to be in during January in that
country. So they could only return to their camp feeling very
blue indeed.

94396

(2)

A council of war was held and they were undetermined as to the best course to pursue. To walk back 100 miles to El Paso, packing grub and blankets, was no picnic. On the other hand it was at least 40 or 50 miles to the first ranch on Black River. But they finally decided to take the shortest way to assistance, which proved the traditional longest way. They determined to stay within the friendly adobe walls of the old stage stand until night. To keep up appearances they made two dummy sentinels and put them on guard, and got their ambulance inside. They had no fear of an attack at night, especially as they had a spendid Mexican shepherd dog to keep watch. As usual after going to sleep they overslept themselves and did not get away until after midnight. Shep, the dog, wanted to go too, but they put a sack of corn and a middle of bacon under the ambulance and give him to understand he was to guard it.

By daybreak they were well on their way to San Martin Springs at the foot of Guadalupe Peak. The road is a horrible one, mostly deep sand, and when they arrived at San Martin they were pretty well worn out. But after a cup, or rather two or three cups of strong coffee, some old ned and camp bread they w were ready for the road again.

The old stage road here turns to the right, and gradually winds around the mountains to get on the mesa land. It makes quite a circuit before getting to the next water, Pine Springs, but there is an old Indian trail that leads up a canyon and straight through. As they were afoot, and taking all short cuts, they took this trail. It was nearly sunset when in a sudden bend of the trail they came in full view of an entire village of Indians coming towards them, taking the near cut also. The Indians were three or four hundred yards off, and had discovered them also. Under such circumstances, the frontiersman has to think quick and act accordingly. They determined there was only one chance for their lives. There was no use running. The Indians, most of them, were mounted, and they themselves were pretty well worn out. Fortunately to the south of the trail there was a sharp sugar loaf peak, and for this they made with all their speed. Getting on top the, hastily threw up a breast works with the loose rocks, and as soon as the Indians came in sight they opened fire on them. The Indians began firing too, but soon discovered it was a waste of ammunition and ceased firing. The boys were suspicious of some trick and kept a sharp lookout. They soon discovered that the Indians were crawling and pushing boulders ahead of them large enough to shelter their bodies, and were gradually nearing the top of the hill. The boys then decided to keep perfectly still, one on each side, and watch for a chance to kill an Indian, run over him and dash down the hill, trusting to their heels.

(3)

The one on the west side, where the fading light still
enabled him to see say a black mop of hair rise cautiously over
the rock he was rolling, and fired. The head disappeared and
the boulder went thundering down the hill, with the two men after
it running over the Indian who was kicking around on the ground
like a chicken with its head cut off. As good luck would have
it most of the Apaches were on the east side, taking it for
granted the men would try and escape in that direction. Before
the astonished Indians could make out just what was occuring
the boys were running like old black-tail bucks and were soon
out of hearing, while night spread her dark mantle over them
in kindness. Keeping clear of the road and being good woodsmen,
they had no trouble in shaping their course for Crow Flat again.
Worn out and weary they made the old stage stand, and found their
dummy sentinels still on guard, with the faithful shepherd dog
at his post and overjoyed at their return.

At the old adobe they were in a measure safe, having grub
and water, while the walls of the old house were about five feet
high and would shelter them. The fact that no attempt had been
made to kill the dog, or rob the ambulance, satisfied them that
the Apaches, after getting their horses, had kept on their way
to the Mescalero Agency near Tularosa. This was the highway of
these Murderous, thieving rascals, who were constantly raiding
Texas and Chihuahua. In the raids they had made a great deep
trail leading north from the Crow Flat Springs towards the Sacramento Mountains. After they had cooked and rested the two
boys decided they would pull out after dark, and hoof it for El
Paso. Again giving Shep his orders, with heavy hearts and sore
feet they turned their faces to the Cornudas Mountains, the next
stage station, and made it through safely. Amongst its shady x
nooks they found sweet, cold water and rest. After several days
they dragged their weary bodies into El Paso, and went to the
commanding officer at Fort Bliss. But as he had only infantry
he refused to go after their ambulance. They then went to the
Ranger camp at Ysleta, and asked me if we would go. As I had
promised the old alcalde to "represent the honor and dignity of
grand old Texas" we began preparations at once. Leaving two men
in camp, I took eight rangers and one Pueblo Indian, and with
Andrews and Wiswall we had a dozen in our crowd. We started out,
not to find the North Pole, but to see if the pole of the ambulance left by Wiswall was safe.

The first day we made the Hueco Tanks, so called. But
hueco in Spanish means tank, and in early days travelers spelled
it Waco Tanks. Senor Juan Armendariz has now utilized the immense pile of granite rock, which is equal to a tiled rock, in
filling reservoirs of water of his stock. And a splendid ranch
it is too, while Don Juan is one of the most progressive men of
the Rio Grande Valley.

(4)

many wild adventures have occurred at these tanks - fights between the Mexicans and Comanche Indians. During the gold excitement it was the main emigrant route to California. Here, too, the old Overland Stage company had a stand. The names of Marcy, General Lee, and thousands of others could be seen cut or written on the rocks. The Indians had made many rude pictures, one of which was quite artistic, being a huge rattlesnake on the rock under the cave, near the old stage stand, on the eastern side of Hueco. Old man Hart was the vandal who destroyed it, and hundreds of names, by camping under the cave and building a fire against the wall. He was punished for it by the hand of fate. Once going on a scout to the Sacramentos to look after the Indians with my rangers, and being anxious to know about water at the Jarillas, in a tank made by Hart, we met an old dusty, tired prospector driving his burros. I asked him if he knew whether we could get water at the Jarillas. "Not unless you got plenty seeds," he replied. "Do you know old Hart?" I asked. He looked at me without cracking a smile. "Yes, I licked him this morning."

Our next halt was at the Alamos across the beautiful plains at that time covered with antelope, that could be seen scudding away with their swift change of direction, looking like a flock of white Birds. At the Alamos we found some Indian sign on the flat above the spring. But it was old. At the Cornudas we again saw old sign of the Apaches. This was a favorite watering place with the Tularosa Agency Indians on their raids into Texas. The rangers under Lieutenant Tays had quite a battle with them here. One ranger, said to be a Russian nobleman and nibilist who had joined the rangers, was killed in the fight, and for many years a head board was placed where he was buried. But the Indians had defaced it. He stood up straight, though he could have had splendid cover, according to the etiquette prevailing amongst British officers in the Transvaal, and was shot through the brain, but not until he had killed an Indian. We saw the Indian's blood on the rocks long afterwards.

From Cornudas to Crow Flat is a long, monotonous tramp of some 36 miles, and we arrived in the night and were challenged by the faithful sentinel, old Shep. But when he heard his master's voice he went wild with joy, barked, rolled over, stood on his head, and came as near talking as any African monkey or gorilla could, and we gave him a cheer. He had been there alone for fifteen days. His side of bacon was eaten, and the sack of corn getting very low. The rangers were as much delighted as if it had been a human being they had rescued. He had worn the top of the wall of the old stage stand perfectly smooth, standing off the sneaking coyotes. Tracks of the latter were thick all around the place, but Shep had held the fort with the assistance of the dummy sentinels.

(5)

We found every thing just as the boys had left it. The Indians probably were on their way to the reservation, and never came back. This was on their main trail when they raided Texas and Chihuahua, and the broad deep trail showed thousands of head of cattle and horses had been driven over it by these government pets.

We arrived safely in camp, having made the two hundred miles in a week, Andrews and Wiswall wanted to post the commander at Fort Bliss, Major Osborne, for cowardice, but I told them I knew him personally and he was both a gentleman and soldier. He could hardly be expected to tramp infantry two hundred miles for an ambulance and dog, with the probability that neither would be found. We found that news had beaten us back to Ysleta, and that according to the "reliable gentleman or intelligent contraband" our entire party had been massacred. This was quite a probability, as three hundred Apaches were reported by Wiswall, and our little band would have had a tight old squeeze to get through. I don't know if Wiswall and Andrews are alive, but that Mexican shepherd dog is entitled to a monument in the El Paso plaza instead of those eagles and rabbits.

Geo. Wythe Baylor.

February 3, 1900

FŽ C4,5,6

El Paso Herald

Baylor Comes to El Paso

Excerpted from *Six Years with the Texas Rangers*, by James B. Gillett,

published by Yale University Press in 1925

Early on the morning of August 2, 1879, our tiny detachment left San Antonio on our long journey. One wagon
carried a heavy, old-fashioned square piano, and on top of
this was loaded the lieutenant's household goods. At the rear
of the wagon was a coop of game chickens, four hens and a
cock, for Lieutenant Baylor was fond of game chickens as
a table delicacy, though he never fought them. His family
consisted of Mrs. Baylor, two daughters—Helen, aged fourteen, and Mary, a child of four or five years—and Miss Kate
Sydnor, sister of Mrs. Baylor. The children and ladies traveled in a large hack drawn by a pair of mules. Rations for
men and horses were hauled in a two-mule wagon, while the
Rangers rode on horseback in advance of the hack and wagons. Two men traveling to New Mexico in a two-wheeled cart
asked permission to travel with us for protection. Naturally, we made slow progress with this unique combination. As
well as I can remember, 1879 was a rather dry year, for not
a drop of rain fell during this seven-hundred-mile journey.
When we passed Fort Clark, in Kinney County, and reached
Devils River we were on the real frontier and liable to attack
by Indians at any time. It was necessary, therefore to keep a
strong guard posted at all times.

Around our campfires at night Lieutenant Baylor en-
tertained us with accounts of early days on the frontier. He
was born August 24, 1832, at old Fort Gibson in the Cherokee
nation, now the state of Oklahoma. His father, John Walker
Baylor, was a surgeon in the United States army. Lieutenant

Baylor was a soldier by training and by inheritance. In 1879 he was in his forty-seventh year and stood six feet two inches tall, a perfect specimen of a hardy frontiersman. He was highly educated, wrote much for papers and magazines, was a fluent speaker, and a very interesting talker and storyteller. He was less reserved than any other captain under whom I ever served. He had taken part in many Indian fights on the frontier of Texas, and his descriptions of some of his experiences were thrilling. Lieutenant Baylor was a high-minded Christian gentleman and had been a member of the Episcopal Church from childhood. In all the months I served with him I never heard him utter an oath or tell a smutty yarn. He neither drank whiskey nor used tobacco. Had he written a history of his operations on the frontier and a biography of himself, it would have been one of the strangest and most interesting books ever written.

I have not the power of language to describe Lieutenant Baylor's bravery, because he was as brave as it is possible for man to be. He thought everyone else should be the same . . . He was as tenderhearted as a child and would listen to any tale of woe. He frequently took men into the service and stood good for their equipment, and often he had to pay the bill out of his own pocket. All men looked alike to him, and he would enlist anyone when there was a vacancy in the company. The result was that some of the worst San Simon Valley rustlers got into the command and gave us no end of trouble, nearly causing one or two killings in our camp. . . .

Another peculiarity of this wonderful man was his indifference to time. He would strike an Indian trail, take his time, and follow it to the jumping-off place. He would say. "There is no use to hurry, boys. We will catch them after a while." For instance, the stage driver and passenger killed in Quitman Canyon in January 1880 had been dead two weeks before the lieutenant returned from a scout out in the Guadalupe Mountains. He at once directed me to make a detail of all except three men in camp, issue ten days rations, and have the men ready to move early next morning. An orderly or first sergeant is hardly ever called upon to scout unless he so desires, but the lieutenant said: "You had better come along, Sergeant. . . ."

Baylor was one of the best shots with firearms I ever

saw. He killed more game than almost the entire company put together. When we first went out to El Paso he used a Winchester rifle, but after the first Indian fight he concluded it was too light and discarded it for a .45-70 Springfield sporting rifle. He always used what he called rest sticks; that is, two sticks about three feet long the size of one's little finger. These were tied together about four or five inches from one end with a buckskin thong. In shooting he would squat down, extend the sticks an arm's length out in front of him with the longer ends spread out tripod fashion on the ground. With his gun resting in the fork he had a perfect rest and could make close shots at long range. He always carried these sticks in his hand and used them on his horse as a quirt. In those days I used to pride myself on my shooting with a Winchester, but I soon found that Lieutenant Baylor had me skinned a mile when it came to killing game at long distance. I never could use rest sticks, for I always forgot them and shot offhand.

I cannot close this description of Lieutenant Baylor without mentioning his excellent wife, who made the long, tedious journey from San Antonio to El Paso County with us. She was Sallie Garland Sydnor, born February 11, 1842. Her father was a wholesale merchant at Galveston, and at one time mayor of that city. Mrs. Baylor was a very refined woman, highly educated, and a skillful performer on the piano. Her bright, sunny disposition and kind heart won her friends among the Rangers at once.

When we had passed Pecan Springs on Devils River there was not another cattle, sheep, or goat ranch until we reached Fort Stockton, two hundred miles to the west. It was just one vast uninhabited country. Today it is all fenced and thousands of fine cattle, sheep, and goats roam the hills. The Old Spanish Trail traverses most of this section, and in traveling over it today one will meet hundreds of people in high-powered automobiles where forty years ago it was dangerous for a small party of well armed men to journey. While ascending Devils River I learned that Lieutenant Baylor was not only a good hunter, but a first class fisherman as well, for he kept the entire camp supplied with fine bass and perch, some of the latter being as large as saucers. Forty miles west of Beaver Lake we reached Howard's Well, situated in Howard's Draw, a tributary of the Pecos River. Here we saw the ruins of a wagon train that bad been attacked by Indians a few months before. All the mules had been captured, the teamsters killed, and the train of sixteen big wagons burned. Had the same Indians encountered our little party of ten men, two women, and two children we would all have been massacred.

Finally, we reached old Fort Lancaster, an abandoned government post, situated on the east bank of Live Oak Creek, just above the point where this beautiful stream empties into the Pecos. We camped here and rested under the shade of the big live oak trees for several days. From this camp we turned north up the Pecos, one of the most curious rivers in Texas. That time, before its waters were much used for irrigation in New Mexico, the Pecos ran bank full of muddy, brackish water almost the year round. Not more than thirty or forty feet wide, it is the crookedest stream in the world, and though only from three to ten feet deep, was so swift and treacherous that it was most difficult to ford. However, it had one real virtue; it was the best stream in Texas for both blue and yellow catfish that ranged in weight from five to forty pounds. We were several days traveling up this river to the pontoon crossing, and we feasted on fish.

At Pontoon Crossing on the Pecos we intercepted the overland mail route leading from San Antonio to El Paso by way of Fredericksburg, Fort Mason, Menard, Fort McKavett, Fort Concho, Fort Stockton, and Fort Davis, thence west by Eagle Springs through Quitman Canyon, where more tragedies and foul murders have been committed by Indians than at any other point on the route. Ben Fricklin was the mail contractor. The stage stands were built of adobe and on the same unchanging plan. On each side of the entrance was a large room. The gateway opened into a passageway, which was roofed, and extended from one room to the other. In the rear of the rooms was the corral, the walls of which were six to eight feet high and two feet thick, also of sun dried brick. One room was used for cooking and eating and the other for sleeping quarters and storage. The stage company furnished the stage tender with supplies and he cooked for the passengers, when there were such, charging them fifty cents per meal, which he was allowed to retain for his compensation.

When the stage rolled into the station the tender swung open the gates and the teams, small Spanish mules, dashed into the corral. The animals were gentle enough when once in the enclosure, but mean and as wild as deer when on the road. The stage company would buy these little mules in lots of fifty to a hundred in Mexico and distribute them along the route. The tiny animals were unbroken bronchos right off the range. They were tied up, or tied down, as the case might be and harnessed by force. When they had been hitched to the stagecoach or buckboard the gates to the corral were opened and the team left on the run. The intelligent mules soon learned that all they had to do was to run from one station to the next, and they could not be stopped between posts no matter what happened. Whenever they saw a wagon or a man on horseback approaching along the road they would shy around the stranger, and the harder the driver held them the faster they ran.

On our way out, our teams were pretty well fagged out, and often Lieutenant Baylor would camp within a few yards of the road. The Spanish stage mules would see our camp and go around us on the run, while their drivers would curse and call us all the vile names they could lay their tongues to for camping in the road. When we camped at a station it was amusing to me to watch the stage attendants harness these wary little animals. The stage or buckboard was always turned round in the corral and headed toward the next station, and the passengers seated themselves before the mules were hitched. When all was ready and the team harnessed the driver gave the word, the station keeper threw open the gates, and the stage was off on a dead run.

There should be a monument erected to the memory of those old stage drivers somewhere along this overland route, for they were certainly the bravest of the brave. It took a man with lots of nerve and strength to be a stage driver in the Indian days, and many of them were killed. The very last year the stage line was kept up (1880) several drivers were killed between Fort Davis and El Paso. Several quit the stage company and joined Lieutenant Baylor's company, and all of them made excellent Rangers.

From Pontoon Crossing we turned due west and traveled the stage route the remainder of the way to El Paso

County. At Fort Stockton we secured supplies for ourselves and feed for our horses, the first place at which rations could be secured since leaving Fort Clark. Fort Stockton was a large military post and was quite lively, especially at night, when the saloons and gambling halls were crowded with soldiers and citizen contractors. At Leon Holes, ten miles west of Fort Stockton, we were delayed a week because of Mrs. Baylor's becoming suddenly ill. Passing through Wild Rose Pass and up Limpia Canyon we suffered very much from the cold, though it was only the last of August. Coming from a lower to a higher altitude we felt the change at night keenly. That was the first cold weather I had experienced in the summer.

Finally, on September 12, 1879, we landed safe and sound in the old town of Ysleta, El Paso County, after forty-two days of travel from San Antonio. Here we met nine men, the remnant of Lieutenant Tays's company of Rangers. The first few days after our arrival were spent in securing quarters for Lieutenant Baylor's family and in reorganizing the company. Sergeant Ludwick was discharged at his own request, and I was made first sergeant, Tom Swilling second sergeant, John Seaborn first corporal, and George Lloyd second corporal. The company was now recruited up to its limit of twenty men.

Before winter Lieutenant Baylor bought a fine home and fifteen or twenty acres of land from a Mr. Blanchard. The Rangers were quartered comfortably in some adobe buildings with fine corrals near by and within easy distance of the lieutenant's residence. We were now ready for adventure on the border. Though the Salt Lake War was over, new and adventurous action was in store for us, and within less than a month after our arrival in Ysleta we had our first brush with the Apaches, a tribe of Indians I had never before met in battle. . . .

Acknowledgments

Faithful Shep was written as an encomium to great daring, bred in bravery, when saving life.

It is dedicated to all who revive, then ennoble, with loving care, the warmhearted animal in distress, pain, and abandonment. Hopefully, this story of a stranded, starving, yet courageous dog, retrieved by ordinary men trekking a hundred miles into the Mescalero Apache wilderness during the dead of winter, will not only serve as an inspiration of resolve, but also an unflinching, unshakable reverence for life.

With singular appreciation, I acknowledge half the population of Texas for allowing relentless pestering while researching El Paso and Rio Grande milieus, as well as endurance in west Texas geographical settings, from letters of ancestors, official Ranger records, documents, correspondences, and newspaper clippings. University researchers and reference librarians, as well as state archivists, where especially kind and helpful. Too numerous to name, all know who they are, and how each helped a hero dog live again.

Two names, however, must be avowed openly, indeed, whose names should have appeared on the title page: Paul Ruffin (1941-2016), publisher and editor of Texas Review Press, who believed in Shep more than the author; and Thom Lemmons, a nonpareil copy editor, who cheerfully metamorphosed 200 pages of thin, vague writing into a readable, quality narrative.

How is such gratefulness expressed? Indebtedness paid?

Don DeNevi

"Thirty years ago, those sterling-silver Company C Rangers of mine who volunteered to retrieve Shep set a new standard for courage. I still see the radiance flaring from the glint off their glory and honor—offering their blood for a cold, lonely, hungry dog. Death would never have been more gallant for those of us who went. That rainy week, God observed their nobility of Spirit, and their reverence for the sanctity and inviolability of life. Most of all, He saw the simple love between ordinary humans and an animal who worshiped them back—God had to have smiled."

Although with no proof, a quote the author is certain, George Wythe Baylor, Captain (Ret.), Company C, Frontier Battalion, made with pride while addressing church groups in 1910

CPSIA information can be obtained
at www.ICGtesting.com
Printed in the USA
LVOW08s0413230317
528145LV00002B/6/P

AMERICAN MIXED RACE

AMERICAN MIXED RACE

The Culture of Microdiversity

Edited by
Naomi Zack

Rowman & Littlefield Publishers, Inc.

ROWMAN & LITTLEFIELD PUBLISHERS, INC.

Published in the United States of America
by Rowman & Littlefield Publishers, Inc.
4720 Boston Way, Lanham, Maryland 20706

3 Henrietta Street
London WC2E 8LU, England

British Cataloging in Publication Information Available

Library of Congress Cataloging-in-Publication Data

American mixed race : the culture of microdiversity / edited
by Naomi Zack.
p. cm.
Includes bibliographical references and index.
1. Racially mixed people—United States. 2. United States—Race
relations. 3. United States—Ethnic relations. I. Zack, Naomi.

E184.A1A6363   1995   305.8'00973—dc20   94–38408   CIP

ISBN 0-8476–8012–6 (cloth: alk. paper)
ISBN 0-8476–8013–4 (pbk.: alk. paper)

Printed in the United States of America

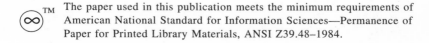

This collection is dedicated to
the upcoming generation of mixed-race Americans,
and to each succeeding generation thereof,
until the problems of American racial categories
are resolved.

Go to, let us go down, and there confound
their language, that they may not understand
one another's speech.

Genesis 11:7

Contents

Preface

In present academic culture, "diversity" is sometimes a euphemism for "racial difference." The title of this collection is meant to confront a comfortable nuance of that code. Those in favor of diversity, or its synonym, "multiculturalism," support the increased presence of racially nonwhite students, faculty, and staff on American college campuses; they are usually also interested in the critiques of traditional disciplines that the "representatives of under-represented groups" may bring to the classroom and, more formally, to scholarly research and publication. Those opposed to diversity or multiculturalism rarely say that they intend to exclude nonwhite groups from American college life or to restrict the curriculum; rather they express concern that affirmative action is "reverse discrimination" and scholarly multiculturalism is a subversion of the Western canon. The task, here, is to deepen the discussion by questioning the parameters that pertain to race. The term *diversity* is normally used on the assumption that there are different racial groups that can be added to the academic situation as groups through representation by their individual members. The purpose of this collection is to underscore the point that in American life the picture of monolithic racial identity that differs only across groups is a model that does violence to the identity and experience of many individuals. In fairness to individuals who not only differ from other members of the groups of which they are designated members, but who fail to fit into any designated group, discussion of diversity ought to include *microdiversity*. Microdiversity refers to the reality and scholarship of racial difference within single individuals. A focus on microdiversity considers individuals, as well as groups, as the subjects of diversity. The number of groups of racially mixed individuals who have common racial characteristics as racially mixed, is much greater than the number of presumably racially pure groups. Given the complicated possibilities for racial mixture over generations, there may also be individuals who are racially unique.

As a contributor to this volume, I am pessimistic about the long-term success of any intellectual (or practical) project of microdiversity because I think that current ideas of diversity (or racial difference) are based on outdated pseudoscientific beliefs about race; and the Balkanization of a bad idea, no matter how well-enshrined that idea is historically, can only lead to more trouble. But, also in the long run, the trouble will have been a necessary catharsis toward the ultimate racial harmony that can result only from a complete dissolution of the American concept of race as a social construction rooted in colonialization, exploitation, and slavery. The reality of mixed race needs to be written and talked out before the illusion of race itself can be dispelled. And that is why I have assembled the collection that follows.

I'll now try to explain the intellectual origins of this anthology and where it fits into the general framework of the emerging multidisciplinary field of racial theory. In 1993, I published a monograph, *Race and Mixed Race*, that was the first book-length philosophical analysis and critique of American categories of black and white race.[1] This work came out of an intersection of autobiographical experience with a return to academia after a twenty-year absence. I pointed out the difficulties with any concept of race in view of widely accepted scientific data, and argued that there is no empirical foundation for the ordinary concepts of black and white race in the United States, especially insofar as the black–white racial distinction rests on the social value of whiteness. The main problem with the American categories of black and white race surfaces with the existence of mixed-race individuals. Mixed black and white Americans have always been designated black, according to the so-called "one-drop rule," and they have never been allowed to develop a racial identity that includes their complete heritage—white ancestors are ignored, or else black ancestors are concealed if the mixed-race person passes for white.

Given the flimsiness of any concept of race in general and American black and white categories in particular, I wanted to conclude *Race and Mixed Race* with a strong repudiation of all racial identity—black, white, and even mixed race. But I hesitated to do this because I thought that more discussion was necessary before anyone could fairly come to such a conclusion. I also thought that many mixed-race individuals might place a high value on mixed-race identity if they had the opportunity to develop it.[2]

While *Race and Mixed Race* was in press, I realized that my reservations were appropriate. I read *Who is Black?* by F. James

Davis, and Maria P. P. Root's ground-breaking anthology, *Racially Mixed People in America*.[3] I also became aware of two "grassroots" organizations, the Association of MultiEthnic Americans (AMEA) and Project RACE (Reclassify All Children Equally), and their newsletters and activities to change public racial categories to include mixed-race designations. More broadly, I became aware of an emerging body of new work on racial identity in sociology, social psychology, public policy, and literature that directly addresses the subject of mixed race in terms of individual experience and academic study. Much of that work is by younger researchers and scholars who are mixed race and who grew up after the egalitarian principles of the Civil Rights Movement became part of public consciousness. I think that despite backlash, and limited group interests, social justice in the area of race is now a fundamental given in American conscience.

That broad sense of social justice had to become entrenched before a new generation could move to the next stage in the American racial story, the stage of questioning the parameters of race itself. And the logic of emancipatory theory, as a progression of ideas in time, is now precisely at that point. The fact that many of the young scholars and researchers on the subject of mixed race are themselves of mixed race informs their work with motives and experience in a way that is now recognized to be necessary for the advancement of a discussion within an emancipatory tradition.

What I am generally calling racial theory is the ground on which racial identity is constructed in the sciences, ordinary life, and academic letters, as well as the forum in which racial identities can be studied and criticized. Mixed race, or in this context, microdiversity, is a subject, as well as the source of a point of view, within racial theory. It should also be noted that racial theory and microdiversity go beyond ethnic studies, black studies, or any empirical studies of culture. Racial theory and microdiversity make room for questions about how people come to be classified into the categories that can be investigated by those empirical studies. This allows for criticism of systematic work that has been done on the assumption that racial categories are real.

Acknowledgments

I want to begin with a note of thanks to Jane Cullen.

The collection would have taken much longer to prepare for publication if not for the Faculty Research Award Program at the University at Albany from which I was awarded funds for study and manuscript preparation during the summers of 1993 and 1994. Specific thanks to Thomas Reynolds for his diligent clerical assistance, during the summer of 1994, in "file management" and other amazingly complicated details of the penultimate copy of a manuscript that involved over 600 double-spaced typed pages and twenty-two contributors.

My main substantive debt is to the contributors to this work. Their scholarship, life experience, insight, and enthusiasm for the project gave it a life of its own almost as soon as I got the idea for it. Working with them has given me the support of intellectual community behind what would otherwise be solitary progress through the subject of racial theory.

At the University at Albany, I am grateful to President H. Patrick Swygert and to Dr. Gloria DeSole, Director of Affirmative Action, as well as my colleagues in the Department of Philosophy, for continued encouragement of my work in racial theory.

The final preparation of the manuscript that included recording all changes "to disk" was in my hands during November, 1994. I appreciate managing editor Julie E. Kirsch's efficiency during that time. Beth Mitchell was conscientious and thorough as copyeditor. Of course, the book would not have emerged in its present form without Jennifer Ruark's efforts as acquisitions editor at Rowman & Littlefield, and I am grateful for her suggestions and those of the external reviewer.

Introduction

Microdiversity vs. Purity

As contributors, we all agree that American racial categories are too rigid, because they unfairly and, at times, brutally have imposed identities on individuals that do not fit them. We believe that everyone ought to be allowed to self-identify racially. However, we are of different minds about how mixed-race individuals ought to identify and whether the concept of race ought to be dispensed with as a human category.

It might be helpful to explain the points of agreement. I will therefore state the ordinary American concept of race, briefly explain what is wrong with it on its own terms, and then describe how this idea of race is related to myths of racial purity.

The ordinary concept of race usually entails that there are three main human racial groups: white, black, and Asian. These races are not as distinct as species because interbreeding is possible; they are held to be something like breeds, because they seem to be natural biological groupings of human beings into which all individuals can be sorted, based on traits such as skin color, hair texture, and body structure. Although different races have different histories and cultures, their histories and cultures are not part of the biological foundation of racial differences because they are not physically inherited. Racial cultures are learned and taught over generations.[1] Most Americans assume that the biological foundation of race has value-neutral or factual support from science. Therefore, they believe that if a racial term is attributed to a person, then something factual or objective is said about that person. In other words, according to received opinion, the term *race* refers to something real, even though racial prejudice and discrimination are unjust.[2]

The main problem with this ordinary concept of race is that it is supposed to be based on scientific information, but the facts do not

support it. In contemporary science, race is at best a loose description of isolated breeding populations that have rarely been sufficiently
isolated so that all of their members have more physical traits in common
with each other than with any members of other races. A classic example is the case of American blacks: more than 75 percent are estimated to have white racial genes, and the designated American black
population shares 30 percent of its genes with the designated white
population.[3] But, although the American black population is largely
racially mixed, the mixture is not taken into account because all individuals with at least one (known) black ancestor are automatically
designated black.[4]

Another aspect of the scientific problem with this ordinary concept of race is that the biological sciences yield no genetic information on racial traits, per se. Contrary to "common sense," there are
no guidelines for identifying such traits on any general level that can
be used to predict either the presence of other racial traits in the same
individual or nonracial traits that always occur with the racial traits.
This means that there is no scientific way to identify human racial
traits as opposed to other human physical traits. Race is unlike sex,
for example, which has the chromosomal markers of XX and XY. There
are no general genetic markers for race.[5]

The idea of racial inheritance is based on nineteenth-century
pseudoscientific speculations about racial essences and the fractional
inheritance of particular types of racial "blood." In fact, human blood
groups are not distinguished by race, and there is no evidence that
individuals of mixed race inherit predictable fractions of their forebears' racial characteristics. For example, if I have a black grandparent, it means little, if anything, in biological terms to say that I am
"one-quarter black."[6]

Racial traits, and their underlying genes, are simply physical traits
that have historically been picked out as racial traits in biologically
arbitrary ways. They have been selected to rationalize the oppression
of groups of people who happened to have had those traits in the
past. The modern concept of race was invented during the most intense periods of colonial exploitation, which included chattel slavery
in the eighteenth and nineteenth centuries; and there are no analogues
to that concept within the "native" populations that became so oppressed. Native Americans and traditional Africans, for example, did
not have an idea of race as we know it.

Finally, the ordinary concept of race has dialectically ridden on an
assumption of racial purity that has been used to racialize dominated
groups as it suited dominant interests. That is, individual racial designation depends on assignment to a racial group, and the race of the

group is a reflection of its past and present position in the wider power structure. For example, after it became illegal to import new slaves, and the cotton gin led to an increased demand for slave labor, it was necessary to breed slaves in the American South. For the breeding of slaves to pay off, the children of slave women had to be born slaves, regardless of their biological racial origins. Because only Negroes could legally be enslaved, these children had to be *born* Negroes and so they were, regardless of how many white ancestors they had through the families of their white fathers, or through the families of their mixed-race mothers, if miscegenation had occurred in an earlier generation.[7]

This one-drop rule of social *hypodescent*, or the inheritance of only the lowest status racial category of one's ancestors, first served the property interests of slaveowners. But it has survived slavery to this day, partly because it was taken up by black Americans themselves during the Harlem Renaissance of the 1920s and partly because it reinforces both black and white myths of white racial purity: to be white, an American need have no known nonwhite ancestor, which is to say that to be white one must be purely white.[8]

A kind of reverse one-drop rule is at work in mixed-race American Indian designation. Legally, Indians have been privileged by their property entitlements according to treaty obligations, although these have rarely been fulfilled by the U.S. government. Because only Indians can claim the relevant entitlements, it has always been in the property interests of those with non-Indian as well as Indian ancestry to be designated Indians. But, it is in the conflicting property interests of the government and white citizens that as few mixed-race Indians be racially designated Indian as possible. Therefore, the notion of "blood quantum" was invented and one result has been that not all individuals who are recognized as Indians by their tribes are so recognized by the federal government.[9] Thus, in contrast to black and white racial designation, designations of racial purity have been preserved for Indians by white property owners. This contrast between black designation for mixed black and white people and non-Indian designation for mixed-race Indians shows that ideas of racial purity work against oppressed groups, regardless of whether the purity of the oppressor or the purity of the oppressed is at issue.

Given the equivocal force of the idea of racial purity, it is easy to dismiss that notion as a mere rationalization for bad behavior in race relations. However, it is not clear that it is possible to talk about race at all without some assumptions about the sameness of physical traits that have been racialized by society. That is, the concept of race seems to rest on an assumption of homogeneity over time, and any attempt to sort people into groups on that basis is conceptually close to an idea of racial purity within those groups. If one speaks of race in the terms of mixed race, as the writers in this book do, then one needs to hold some false idea of race constant to construct mixed-race identity or reconstruct the concept of race.

A reader who systematically goes through this book will notice a wide range of positions on the issue of retaining or dispensing with the concept of race. If this is confusing, no one is in a position to apologize for it and no one has the right to override the racial experiences of others, in the interests of "clarity." The confusion is not the result of intellectual error but a consequence of the contradictions inherent in the social and historical reality of race.

Summary of Contents

These articles could have been presented in different ways because this book and many of the articles are multidisciplinary. The subject of mixed race is itself constituted across the prevalent categories of ethnic or racial studies in contemporary scholarly culture, so it would go against that constitution to divide the work according to racial categories. Still, many writers who work in mixed black and white race, Native American mixed race or Asian mixed race, have not considered giving up the particularity of their own racial parameters to identify in a broad sense, as racially mixed.

I have divided the collection into the academic disciplines that seem to best characterize individual pieces, in an order of increasing abstractness: Autobiography, Art, Social Science, Public Policy, and Identity Theory. Although I am not sure that public policy is more "abstract" than social science, it would seem to be based on the empirical findings of social science. And although autobiographical writing might be as much a theoretical exercise as identity theory, and identity theory, here, is informed by personal experience, identity theory need not explicitly refer to the writer's specific history, whereas autobiography always does. Insofar as art deals with the subjective (in the sense of feeling) aspects of experience, its ability to inform is descriptive, which is why it comes right after autobiography, although, as a distillation and reflection of every conceivable human category and an expression of value concerns, it could be anywhere.

The following summary is a sketch of the chapters in the order they appear, but any one part, and any one article, can stand on its own, depending on the reader's interests.

Part I, Autobiography

The book begins with "Five Arrows" by Susan Clements, which is a family story that branches into reflections on the problems of feeling whole for Indian and "mixed" Indian residents of Turtle Island (the United States). Resistance to white racism and artificial culture finds a self-destructive outlet that nonetheless remains true to a "wildfire of the spirit." Clements dreams of a future unity of all human beings, beyond "the tragic absurdity of defining people by 'blood.'"

In "Color Fades Over Time," Brunetta Wolfman recounts the racial identities of six generations of her American black and white family, over 130 years. She relates how, from her great-grandparents to her own grandchildren, racial "color" has become less pronounced and racially mixed individuals have gained more freedom in their choice of racial identity. Her optimism, however, is tempered with the knowledge that social class, education, and economic advantage make it easier for her grandchildren of mixed black and white race not to feel as pressured and defined by the racial differences in their backgrounds, as were their counterparts before the Civil Rights Movement.

Cecile Ann Lawrence, who was born and raised in Jamaica, comments indignantly on the American biracial system in which the words *black* and *white* have little relation to individual appearance. Her perspective in "Racelessness" is firmly aracial and her accounts of the derogatory ways in which Americans have identified her racially, because of her "nonwhite" appearance, become increasingly startling as the reader understands that in contrast to this society, mixed race is the visual and cultural norm in Jamaica. Lawrence indicates the difficulty for many immigrants from the Caribbean to even conceive of how the American assumptions about racial purity could be possible.

Zena Moore's reflections on the contrast in her racial identification from Trinidad to the United States are a discursive analysis of the ways in which class intersects with race in both cultures. In "'Check the Box that Best Describes You'," Moore relates how it was only after leaving home that she realized she had been brought up in a "China Town"; only outside of her family did her mother's Guarajun Indian heritage give her the label, *Black Chinee*; and how only in the United States, does physical appearance determine racial category, which conclusively defines social status.

The title, "What are they?" by Stephen Satris, refers to a question strangers have asked him about his two daughters. Because Satris's ancestry is European and their mother's is Japanese, he knows that there is no answer to this demand for a short response of one racial category. From that starting point, Satris examines the different emphases on ancestry and appearance in American racial sorting. He suggests that if Asians, who are now classified based on appearance, are to become fully assimilated Americans, then it is the predominant Anglo-Saxon visual image of race that will have to "melt."

Part II, Art

Freda Scott Giles provides a comprehensive history of the tragic mulatto as a character type in "From Melodrama to the Movies." Beginning with minstrelsy in the nineteenth century and concluding with contemporary film and television portrayals of mixed black and white race in the United States, Giles summarizes a wide panorama of plots and depictions by both black and white writers. Her compendium supports her interpretation of the irretrievably tragic stereotype of the mulatto as a symbol of American racial problems who has often been dramatized with deference to the ignorance and prejudice of white audiences. The doomed mulatto character is a scapegoat for the sins of her parents and the problems in society, while those sins and problems remain behind the scenes of dramatic action.

In "Theater of Identity," Teresa Williams begins her analysis of Eurasians and Afroasians on the American stage and screen and in the fashion industry, by autobiographically situating herself as Eurasian. Through many examples, including Bruce Lee martial arts movies, the 1990 casting controversy surrounding the musical *Miss Saigon*, and *Map of the Human Heart*, the 1993 film about mixed-race Eskimos, Williams argues that the appearances of the actors who are cast to portray mixed-race Asian characters reflect dichotomous cultural stereotypes of race. Thus, a mixed-race character may be played by an individual who looks predominantly white, which would preserve white aesthetic ideals, or who looks predominantly of the relevant non-white racial category, so as to uphold a "one-drop" rule through visual perception.

Carol Roh Spaulding considers mixed-race characters in twentieth-century American literature as a trope for the conceptual problems of biracialism. In "The Go-Between People," she develops the idea of mixed race as a way of *reading* race, which, in literary theory, can be a starting point for identities of racelessness. Although racelessness resembles universalism, and Spaulding suggests that it does not matter what the racial components of any particular character's racelessness are, nevertheless, the great diversities within characters who are mixed raced, and thereby not-raced in a biracial system, would hold promise for better understanding the power relations that are predicated on pure race.

Part III, Social Science

F. James Davis's article, "The Hawaiian Alternative to the One-Drop Rule," begins with a definitive survey of different cultural practices and rules concerning mixed-race populations. At one extreme is the one-drop rule of hypodescent (whereby children inherit the race of lower status given mixed-race ancestry) in the mainland United States, while, ironically, the other extreme can be seen in the self-consciously pluralistic multiracial society of the state of Hawaii. Davis discusses how several Latin American cultures allow racial categories to be negotiated, depending on other marks of status, and how even a society as historically repressive towards blacks as South Africa, recognizes the existence of mixed black and white individuals. Davis upholds the Hawaiian pluralistic tradition as an egalitarian ideal, and he speculates that if present trends toward multiracial identity continue on the American mainland, and are able to gain recognition over both black and white majority insistence on hypodescent, "this tail [might] eventually wag the dog."

In "Some Kind of Indian," M. Annette Jaimes examines how the terms *race, full-blood, mixed-blood*, and *halfbreed* have different meanings for North American natives and nonnatives. Jaimes shows how traditional tribal criteria for membership have been distorted by U.S. federal mandates and policies and how Indian identities have been affected by European property acquisition and indigenous entitlements. So-called mixed-race American Indians have been denied both native identity and nonnative rights by tribal partisan politics as well as by ongoing EuroAmerican colonialization. Jaimes argues for the self-determination of Indian identities, which would include exogamy, naturalization, and adoption, in addition to matrilineal or patrilineal ancestral lineage—all of which have been recognized by native tribes, both off and on reservation-based areas.

Abby Ferber discusses how belief in fixed racial categories has shaped sociological studies of interracial relationships. In "Exploring the Social Construction of Race," Ferber explains how pluralist and assimilationist theories of social interaction, which were originally developed to deal with ethnic differences, reinforce the belief that races are natural, biological categories, even though social scientists themselves may disclaim such beliefs. She suggests that racial identities make human beings "culturally intelligible," and claims that social scientists need to explore the ways in which their own discourses are "imbedded in relations of power." Ferber argues that racial subjects and race itself are constructed in the process of establishing boundaries between races, and she applies this analysis to white supremacist literature against interracial heterosexual relationships.

Helena Hershel's chapter, "Therapeutic Perspectives on Biracial Identity Formation and Internalized Oppression," combines psychological theory and clinical practice to analyze the need for recognition of mixed-race identity. Hershel discusses the importance of *belonging* for psychological wellness in the development of selfhood, and she explains how exclusion and censorship from the immediate family and wider community may lead to internal conflict that is not originally due to psychological problems in the biracial individual. Because pathologies of race can lead to internalized oppression for a biracial person, Hershel advises that prevention is essential in protecting the development of self-esteem and sense of self in biracial children. Parents can prepare children for external questions about their identity and assist their self-understanding by explaining and supporting their difference from other members of their families. Insofar as positive self-development and self-understanding are furthered by in-depth psychotherapy, the therapist, also, can assist in repairing the alienation of a biracial individual by "reconnecting" her through a relationship based on understanding and trust.

Part IV, Public Policy

The first two chapters in this section are written testimony by Susan Graham and Carlos Fernández, concerning the inclusion of multiracial categories in federal census forms, which was submitted to the United States House of Representatives in June 1993. In "Grassroots Advocacy," Susan R. Graham, a mother of multiracial children, relates how her experience in Georgia, of not having an official racial category for her children on school registration forms, is shared by parents of multiracial children, nationwide. She argues that this omission is a form of discrimination, contrary to the provisions of the Civil Rights Act of 1964, and that recognized identity for multiracial children is necessary for their well being.

Carlos Fernández, in "Testimony of the Association of MultiEthnic Americans," claims that his organization represents one of the fastest growing populations in the United States. Fernández presents this population as an embodiment of racial and ethnic harmony in a society and a world rife with racial and ethnic conflict. He emphasizes the importance of promoting a positive awareness of interracial and multiethnic identity and argues that the federal government cannot make the relevant public policy decisions in education, public health, or social services generally, unless it amends the Office of Management and Budget Statistical Policy Directive 15 to include a "multiracial/ethnic" category.

Jennifer Clancy claims that the presence of mixed-race people does not in itself change prevailing social paradigms of race. In "Multiracial Identity Assertion in the Sociopolitical Context of Primary Education," Clancy points out the limits of examining multiracial identity choice through a framework that focuses on multiracial individuals and their immediate families and community, and she argues that such a choice needs to be understood as a wider institutional decision. Clancy suggests that the classroom, as a representation of the larger culture, can be used as a site for renegotiations of racial identity, through changes in curricula and student participation and empowerment, that include mixed race.

Mariella Squire-Hakey documents the historical denial of the existence of the Abenaki Indians in Vermont by the white majority, in "Yankee Imperialism and Imperialist Nostalgia." The ways in which these "Yankees," many of whom had Abenaki ancestry themselves, taught school children that the Abenaki were extinct and that local migrant farm workers, who were (and are) Abenaki, were "gypsies," is unpacked in the layers of Squire-Hakey's historiographical analysis. Her criticism of the Yankee idealization of Indian "spirituality" that was concurrent with ethnocide, when not genocide, has a bitter irony reproduced in her own experience: In grade school and high school, Squire-Hakey's Indian features did not permit her to be accepted as white; but, in college and graduate school, although welcomed as a living relic by anthropologists who "handed her over to folklorists like a piece of lost luggage," her Indian identity was at the same time questioned by white academics because she has blue eyes and fair skin.

Part V, Identity Theory

Maria Root's article, "The Multicultural Contribution to the Psychological Browning of America," combines an answer to the question of how others determine where a mixed-race person lands in the choice of racial identity with positive reasons for affirming traditional rules of hypodescent. Many multiracial individuals who now choose to identify with their relatives of color may be motivated by family acceptance and a better known family history, as well as rejection from white relatives. The sense of belonging that accompanies present choices of hypodescent may be preferable to the isolation and alienation that could accompany insistence on white identity, mixed identity, or no racial identity.

In "Made in the USA," David Goldberg explores how the overriding American racializing project might appropriate categories of mixed race as a new way of reifying and packaging the old idea of race for popular consumption. He analyzes how the American category of "Hispanic" was manufactured to cut across racial designations, with exploitative and divisive results for people "of color"; how the South African category of "Coloured" reproduces race to shift and control social status in nonracial senses; and how present racial restrictions on adoption in the United States solidify false ideas of race while at the same time purporting to correct racial bias. Goldberg suggests that a conceptual fluidity about racial categories, which acknowledges cultural heterogeneity, can be used to construct new identities and at the same time *undo* old ideas of race. This fluidity would at the same time undermine a reification of "race" in mixed-race.

In "Mestizo Identity," Linda Alcoff aims to contribute to new thinking about racial identity without purity. She relates how her mestizo identity that was normal in Panama became a source of pain when she moved to central Florida in the 1950s. Alcoff suggests that foundational Western concepts of the self and identity are linked to ideas of purity, wholeness, and coherence that are withheld from the public and subjective experience of multiracial individuals. She argues for a norm of assimilation, away from (Northern) Anglo dominance and toward (Southern) non-xenophobic mixed-race identity. Alcoff thinks that a rejection of all racial identity could lead to new forms of alienation and exploitation in a capitalistic system and she begins to develop a concept of the mixed-race individual as a cultural negotiator and traveler, who embodies "the organic integration of a new human blend such as the world has never seen."

Debra Barrath analyzes her lack of cultural situatedness as a "Coloured" woman in South Africa, from her present location in Canada. In "Race and Racism," she points out that within the margins of white society, people of mixed race are further marginalized because their lack of monoracial identification, in-between class status, and cultural heterogeneity deprive them of cohesive identity. Barrath calls for mixed-race women, as well as monoracial women, to find common cause on the basis of gender, not because gender is a privileged difference but because it can represent a progressive cross-section of complex society, especially in South Africa.

Laurie Shrage examines the problematic aspects of cultural assimilation and difference through the meaning of Jewish identity in contemporary American society. In "Ethnic Transgressions: Confessions of an Assimilated Jew," she considers the possibilities for claiming mixed or hybridized and multiple racial and ethnic identities and also explores the political value of socially transgressive racial and ethnic performances and classifications.

I contribute the final article in this collection, after the advantage of having considered the foregoing pieces for some time now. But I cannot claim an editor's vantage point for "Life After Race," because I doubt that many of the writers here would agree with me. First, I try to relate theoretical identities of mixed race to contemporary American intellectual life. I then offer a philosophical test of the meaning of 'race' and conclude that this concept ought to be let go. Finally, I suggest that we look for clues to how to live without it, by historically analyzing the motives for it in the seventeenth century, before the modern racial paradigm was constructed.

Part I
Autobiography

1

Five Arrows

Susan Clements

There was a story told to me by my sister, with an image branded into the core of the story that I shall never forget. The story revolved around a male cousin who went drinking one Saturday night in a Catskill bar called THE BLUEROOM, a mountain dive that once doubled as the stage for passions generally kept hidden behind the daytime quarter-smiles and "Do you think it might rain?" talk of mountain people, a Dreamtime dive that has long since been fired down to unseen rubble beneath grass. When I make one of my infrequent forays back to Livingston Manor, the increasingly sad and seedy upstate-New York town I grew up in, I can never stop myself from remembering the story as I pick my way down Main Street's cracked sidewalk past the grass concealing the lost blue room of dreams. Now the grass has been decreed a park by the town's "fathers" and "mothers," an Earthly Paradise in the town's center stretching to the banks of the Willowemoc River. But, really, it is a jumbled collage of emptied beer cans, Thunderbird bottles, used condoms, alley cats, candy wrappers, and urine stains. It is the perfect burial ground for the story about my cousin, for stories about other relatives, and for the untold or soon-to-be-forgotten stories of all the mountain people who used to make their night migrations to this patch of earth formerly lit by blue neon and faces given the courage to shine by beer and whiskey. As I stumble down Main Street—the old child-chant "Don't step on the crack, you'll break your mother's back" needling the memory-grooves of my brain—I know this intended paradise is the perfect burial ground for my story/my stery, too.

3

When my sister began spinning the story, I imagined something fierce, wild, and probably crazy was going to happen because our cousin is connected to us through our mother's side of the family, the Indian side, the Hendricksons. Like us, our cousin is Blackfoot, Mohawk, Seneca, and several whiter shades of Pale. We are what some people would like to capture inside the labels of "mixed-bloods" or "breeds," but we grew up feeling ourselves to be Indian while also recognizing and affirming our white "blood"—English, Irish, Swiss, Austrian, and Czech. We could be considered the flesh-and-blood embodiments of the history of the United States, both conquerors and conquered, but no one in my family has ever, finally, felt conquered, nor have they surrendered themselves or their dreaming hearts to a government that is only at its best where it was influenced by the Iroquois, or Haudenosaunee (People of the Longhouse). We are still very much Turtle Island people, and it may be said that the white people who married in with the Indian did so because they felt a closeness to Indian ways of seeing and doing, ways similar to those of mystics and poets.

So in the story where my cousin went drinking, I sensed it might turn out strange. When people like ourselves partake of the proverbial firewater, it is as if we are fused in a crucible that transforms us back into our Indian ancestors before Columbus invaded Turtle Island, before the entire tragic history of genocide, culture-ocide, and the Great Death by disease began to shock-wave across five shameful centuries. We become wholly Indian again, and the conflagration of hurt that has flamed inside us for so many years because of all the lies we have heard hissed about us, all the names we have been called, all the knowledge we've been robbed of— that wildfire of the spirit burns brighter with the fuel of alcohol. And our resilient pride, deep love, and warrior spirits blaze brighter, too.

In the story my sister told, our cousin was drinking whiskey from a bottle, listening to Hank Williams, George Jones, and Patsy Cline on the jukebox, in between drinks slow dancing through the smoke with a green-eyed, red-haired, other-side-of-the-tracks white girl who grew more and more beautiful to him the more he drank. She was one of those Frito-Lay-and-corn-chip-fed mountain girls who never quite get their bellies filled except by babies. But before the babies come, such girls can be startling in their beauty and hunger, their effect on men that of a false and too early spring. So our cousin was affected, to the point where his heart burned to break-

ing for the green-eyed girl and her doomed, too early flowering.
He asked her to love him, make love to him, marry him. But, like
the winter flower she truly was, she shrunk back from his hot requests. A heart-and-dagger tattooed, tobacco-chewing redneck, half-
humped against the bar, sneered John Wayne-style, "That's right,
you dirty redskin, leave the little lady alone. She don't want no
animal like you." Then our cousin did break, grabbing his whiskey
bottle, smashing it into his forehead, over and over again. As he
hit himself, he cried, "I am a half-breed, nothing can hurt me, nothing,
nothing, nothing," until the bottle shattered, leaving myriad glass
shards arrowed into his skin. Blood streaming into his eyes and
down his face with its high ledge of cheekbones, he stood, unseeing, inside the four square walls of THE BLUEROOM.

In the story told to me by my sister, with its core image of our
cousin smashing a whiskey bottle into his skull, I realized it could
have been me, it could have been her, it could have been any so-
called "breed." In the communality of storytelling, we both remembered without saying so our own neon-lit nights in THE BLUEROOM
and other bars, those times when we behaved like desperados wondering if there were any goddamn men left in the world whose bodies
were all passionate, crying, ecstatic heart, instead of those rinky-
dink, urban landscape, watered-down Perrier men who talk through
their assholes, as mountain people put it, men not courageous enough
to love up close but cowardly enough to kill from a distance. My
sister and I could still see the flickering neon in each other's eyes,
the firewater and the fire, and we knew what our cousin did summed
up the pain and confusion of what it's like to grow up as a "half-
breed" or a "mixed-blood." We also knew that he had made a stand.
We understood what the people who would call our cousin an
idiot-redskin, and worse, could never understand, that he had drunk
and loved and burned and cut himself back into the primordial forest
of real existence. That night, in his own way, he had let everyone
know that he wasn't a vanishing Indian, or a wooden Indian, that
they were not going to hurt him anymore. My sister and I knew he
had made a stand, all right, the kind of stand that can end in a
suicide.

The suicide rate among Indian teenagers in what is called the
United States is four times the national average, and I doubt that
chilling statistic includes the suicides committed by Indian children not officially enrolled in tribes. The U.S. government has long
manipulated numbers in such a way as to abstract out as much misery

as it possibly can on the part of American Indians. It just so happens there may be 15 million human beings now living on Turtle Island who have Indian "blood" flowing in their veins, Indians who are not certified as belonging to any particular tribe or nation, people who are not papered like dogs and don't wish to be, but who are fiercely proud of being Indian.

Unfortunately, the U.S. government's policy on what it is that makes an Indian an Indian is a divide-and-conquer policy that involves blood quantum and whether or not a person is listed on tribal rolls. It is a policy that would make any Nazi feel he had finally goose-stepped his way to Wagnerian glory. It is a policy that pointedly ignores the tragic history of Turtle Island and why so many Indians are mixed-bloods, especially on the East Coast. For instance, consider that in the late seventeenth century the Mohawk Nation was so nearly destroyed by disease and murder, a holocaust compounded by suicides and abortions, that what few warriors were left began raiding Hurons and Whites to incorporate them into the Nation and so save the Mohawk people from total extermination.

Obviously, my ancestors' understanding of what it means to be a Mohawk wasn't solely a "blood thing." It is a Government policy that pretends not to know there are clusters of Indian families such as mine, the Hendricksons, who sought sanctuary in hidden mountain places as a strategy for remaining freer than those families corralled onto reservations. And, most sadly, it is a policy that certain certified Indians (certified what? Crazy?) have embraced as one might a poisonous snake, copping an "I'm more Indian than thou" attitude right out of Christian missionary land. As my oldest brother so eloquently put it this past November when my husband and I had him to our house to celebrate his birthday, "I never even heard about this certified shit until last year." Indeed, when he, my other brothers, my sister, and I were growing up in the 1950s and 1960s, we only had to contend with the pain caused to us by white racists. In the small constellation of Indian families starring that part of the Catskill Mountains I was born to, an unspoken bond always existed among us, a quiet but fiery pattern that said, "We are still here, shining in our aliveness, and we are something beautiful whether non-Indians can see it, or not." All our friends happened to be mixed-blood Indians, although I don't think that they were friends based on "blood," but because they were possessed of a certain vision of the world that happened to be Indian, rather than white at its most destructive.

In the story my sister told, our cousin smashed a whiskey bottle into his forehead until it broke. In our lives, far inside our hearts, many of us Indians, mixed-blood or otherwise, stand inside the four square walls of a blue room, blood and tears in our eyes. We stand, unseeing, longing to get back to the forest, the prairie, the mesa, to an incomparable love and freedom, to not feeling hurt anymore. So I remember another story, one given to me by my mother, in which I learned the last word my Indian grandfather ever said, cried, when he was dying, was "Mother." I used to hear that cry as a call to his mother who, ice-fishing one winter in the Willowemoc River not far from her cabin, crashed through the ice and died soon after from pneumonia. That winter my grandfather was nine. Following his mother's death, he, his sisters, and brothers were sent to an orphanage in Binghamton, New York, from where children very often were packed off to farms and used not much better than slaves.

As I have grown older, I have considered further how my great-grandmother, Lillian Hendrickson, died, how my nine-year-old grandfather was taken to the orphanage against his will, how he and his sister Grace kept running away until they finally made their way back to the mountains for good. So considering, I have come to hear my grandfather's cry to his mother better. That cry has grown louder and clearer inside the spirals of my inner ear, has radiated out inside the interior of my body until I now hear it as not just a cry to the individual mother who gave birth to my grandfather, but as a cry to Mother Earth, as well. It must have been horrible for my grandfather to have been driven against his will to a city, locked inside an orphanage, handed over to a succession of farmers who couldn't keep, tame, or shame him. I always smile a little when I envision my grandfather with his black, other-side-of-the-moon hair and sharp cheekbones running away from the orphanage and the farms. I used to run away when I was young, too, and I know that bold, heady, hair-flying, "wild-wild-horses" feeling that accompanies such running. I used to feel that if I could just run fast enough and far enough I could race right out of the surreal techno-scape of superhighways, skyscrapers, factories, walled schools, missile silos, barbed wire, posted property, automobiles, air pollution, shopping malls, TVs, and too many over-populating, hate-filled human beings trapped inside windowless halls of misery-mirrors. I liked feeling the way my grandfather must have felt when he ran away; I hope he got to where he wanted to go.

In the late twentieth century perhaps it is even harder to get there, that "there" being, more than anything else, a balance and wholeness in the human spirit. It is difficult to remain sane when one knows one's Mother is daily being raped, and when it is nearly impossible to extricate oneself from the process of her destruction. This is devastating for many people. For American Indians it really can be beyond bearing. So we get my cousin shattering a whiskey bottle against his head, or an Indian artist's son slitting his entire left arm open, or an old mixed-blood friend's sister destroying her God-gift for painting with a mixed-drug ingestion of alcohol, cocaine, speed, acid, chill pills and percodan. Any Indian knows that it is not possible to be sane unless a person lives close to the Earth, thereby experiencing everything as vibrantly alive and interconnected, a matrix of music that pulls all hearts together into one Heart, one dance.

In the clock-time years that I grew up in, the fifties and sixties, it could be very painful for children like myself, and even more painful for reservation Indians, to see our people repeatedly portrayed by whites as unredeemable savages bereft of intelligence, as "redskins" inferior beyond belief, with no culture, religion, or system of government worth preserving. For decades the old religious traditions, the sacred songs and dances, the visions, the ecstasy, love, and exuberance had been suppressed or driven underground. The reservation children were forcefully exiled to boarding schools where they were beaten for speaking their native languages or refusing to have their flowing long hair cut, for trying to maintain the old ways in *any* way. Mixed-blood children like myself daydreamed through grade after grade of public school being told that Manifest Destiny was right, that Christianity was the best thing that ever happened to the heathen Indians, that Indian killers such as General Sheridan, Kit Carson, Andrew Jackson, and George Armstrong Custer were great Indian fighters and heroes. Innocent, we sat through countless cowboy-and-Indian matinees with all the other kids, seeing the Indians, played by Mexicans and Italians, depicted as the dark-eyed bad guys. We watched "The Wizard of Oz" every Christmas without ever knowing that its creator had once called for the absolute, total extermination of Indians, a race, in his view, too shamed and beaten to be allowed to live. It could be said that we were silenced before we even knew we were being silenced, because how can a small child realize at first that she, or he, is being lied to by adults who are looked up to and trusted?

I used to wonder, wandering through those long and labyrinthine years of lies all around me, what it would have been like had I just been born white and solely of one race? Or what would it have been like if I had been born a "full-blooded" Indian, a reservation girl? I wondered if it would have provided me with a greater simplicity of spirit, and if life would have been easier for me. But through the years I have come to feel gratitude for containing what Walt Whitman might have referred to as "multitudes." Such abundance taught me early on to question the surfaces of words, to discern that the books I loved could sometimes contain unforgivable lies, to learn how to scry the radiance, or lack thereof, in people's faces. It taught me that there are many different ways of coming at the world, and that I could take all the entangled flora and fauna of my heart and transform it into a daily celebration, into poetry.

In the Silver Covenant Chain that was forged between the Haudenosaunee and the Europeans, the Indian pointed out that the white man travels on the Creator's waters in his boats and the Indian travels on those same sacred waters in his boats. But someday there might be people who try to keep one foot in the white man's boat and one foot in the Indian's boat, one foot, in other words, inside two different ways of journeying through life. And if a strong wind gusts up, the boats will whirl apart and the person with a foot in each vessel will tumble into the water, be swept away and lost forever. I have often meditated on this section of the Silver Covenant Chain, on what might be viewed as a cautionary tale for anyone who is of mixed Indian–white heritage and who lives on Turtle Island. I more and more wonder why any human being should be confined to just one vessel and just one trip; I like to laugh and say that if a person is balanced enough nothing can buck her off those boats into certain death by drowning. I have asked myself which boat it is that I have chosen, and I feel in my heart that through my poetry my feet are moving more inside the Indian boat. But there is so much culture overlap that a lot of whites are making canoes these days, so who ever knows what one might be stepping into?

In the story my sister told, our cousin went drinking and drummed a bottle into his head. This is a scene that never could have happened if other human beings hadn't already tried to break him into pieces as much as he broke that bottle into bits. I always hated people trying to grate me down into fractions. Fractions always made me feel fractious in the math classes I was forced to take in school, and having my entire being viewed as disconnected parts by flesh-and-blood paragons of human insensitivity makes me very irrita-

ble, indeed. The real tragedy in Indian Country these days, after
the initial flowering of renewed Indian pride and the start of showing American Indians as complicated human beings in books, movies, paintings, and music (still a long way to go), is how some Indians
have been attacking other Indians, accusing their brothers and sisters of not being Indian because they are not on tribal rolls, or because
they don't meet someone's arbitrary standard of right blood quantum, or because they can't prove through birth certificates or past
tribal rolls that they are Indian. Or, hey, maybe they just don't look
Indian—don't have high cheekbones, or swarthy skin like those
Italians and Mexicans playing Indians in the old movies. I've met
more than one Indian who who has worked up a whole Cyrano-de-
Bergerac-type routine to handle the "That's funny, you don't look
Indian" ignoramuses of whatever race: "Oh, really? That's funny,
you don't look rude." "Oh, that's funny, you look as if you could
pass for a human being." "Oh, that's funny, you don't look as if
you could say something so unfunny." And so it goes.

What I happen to find most unfunny is that after all the centuries of white oppression of Indians is that Indians themselves are,
as I noted earlier, playing into the divide-and-conquer policies of
the United States Government and the Bureau of Indian Affairs,
turning against and hurting their own. I never could have imagined
when I was a girl trying to figure out how to deal with white racism that there would ever be a creature as distasteful and mon-
strous as an Aryan Indian. I can still hear what Zack Brown Bear,
a Cherokee artist who makes Four Directions Feather Pieces, once
said to my husband and me: "Finally I am not part Indian or part
White, part this or part that; I am a whole human being." He spoke
aloud what already resided in my heart in silence, and what I believe resides in a lot of people's hearts. Most people I speak to of
whatever background are weary of racial division and people being pitted against each other because of skin color and "blood."
As any true Indian knows, as anyone with an Indian heart knows,
we are responsible to our children, *all* children, down to the seventh generation. Trying to deny people their identity and wholeness of spirit is not being responsible, nor is hating each other because
of race. How many broken bottles, slit arms, lost gifts, and suicides is it going to take before people remember what their responsibility is and where their love must lie?

When the Peacemaker arrived among the Haudenosaunee in a
time before clocks and helped them to create the original great

Confederacy of Five Nations, the Seneca, Cayuga, Onondaga, Oneida, and Mohawk, he took up one arrow in his hands and said, "If you take one arrow alone and try to break it, you can easily do so." And he snapped the arrow in half. Then he took up five arrows in his hands and bound them together and said, "If you take five arrows bound together and try to break them, you can never do so." And he tried as hard as he could to break those five arrows, and even let others try, but no one could break those arrows bound together. "So," the Peacemaker said, "if you five nations are bound together into one confederacy, no one can ever break you."

Despite the mistaken notions that many Americans have about Indians, including that there are only about ten little Indians left in the entire country, the Iroquois Confederacy (which now also embraces a sixth nation, the Tuscarora) still exists. And the Great Tree of Peace with its white roots extending out in four directions, inviting all people to follow them back in order to live inside the law and ways of the Confederacy, still exists. How many years will it be, yet, before all the nations of the earth can envision themselves as being like those five bound arrows in the Peacemaker's hands, before too many human hearts are Balkanized and broken because of the tragic absurdity of defining people by "blood"? And how many years will it be before Mother Earth is totally destroyed if all those nations continue to exist each as a single arrow, easily snapped in two?

My sister told me a story. There was an image branded into the core of the story that I shall never forget.

2

Color Fades Over Time

Brunetta R. Wolfman

"Girl, git out of the sun so you won't be any blacker than you are now." I heard that admonition hundreds of times during my girlhood, and perhaps because and in spite of it, I love the sun's rays and the darkening of my normally tan-colored skin. My ivory-colored, wavy-haired, green-eyed mother was not only sensitive to the sun but very sensitive about my dark coloring and "nappy" hair, though she loved my green eyes. I mention hair because African Americans almost always associate hair texture, ranging from straight to kinky, with skin color. In the years since my childhood, the civil rights movement, the talk of "Black is Beautiful," and racial pride have done little to erase the obsessive concerns of African Americans with their appearance—they still measure themselves by European beauty standards.

Color and hair characteristics were constant topics of discussion in my family and in my younger life because they were so frequently equated with race and status in America. Perhaps because of our marginal sociopolitical position, we continually used descriptions of hair texture and skin color as the most distinguishing characteristic of a family member or friend. This is one of those off-limits topics in the company of Caucasians. Of course, the intimate details of race identification are murky, controversial, and unexplored across racial lines in American life. Intraracial discussions are more common than are interracial discussions though the latter are usually motivated by changes in social policy rather than desires to understand people across the racial divide. Changes in legal stat-

utes and social policy have expanded opportunities, provided more
protection for minority citizens, redefined American society, and
resulted in changed attitudes and behaviors on the part of the majority. The end of restrictive miscegenation statutes allowed greater freedom in choosing marriage partners and raising children and
affected perceptions of color and race. This is what I will explore
in this chapter, focusing on my family over six generations.

My mother's family has been the dominant familial influence in
my life since she and my father separated when I was a toddler,
and I never knew my paternal relatives. It was a marriage under-
taken without the blessings of either family; in fact, the relationship seemed to have been cursed by familial disapprovals. Curiosity
has never motivated me to explore my paternal origins because I
have dim memories of living in an icy cold house in Memphis, Ten-
nessee, with a remote unloving dark brown skinned grandmother
hovering in the background of those memories.

Soon after the Civil War, the first generation of which I am aware
settled on a homestead in a rural Louisiana parish bordering Mississippi, about 1866, seeking respite from oppressive conditions.[1]
They may have journeyed across the Pearl River from a nearby
plantation in Mississippi, maintaining relationships with other former
slave families because census records show the family's marriages
to spouses born in close proximity. This intact family joined with
other freedmen to quickly establish a Methodist church,[2] probably
continuing an institutional form familiar to them; that church, Wesley
Chapel, is still functioning as a religious and social center for their
descendants in a hamlet in Washington Parish. This first generation farmed, worked hard, and built a viable community although
the family heads were in their late teens and early twenties.

My mother's maternal grandmother who was dark brown gave
birth to four children by her first husband and then had three others fathered by a man who has receded into the shadows of family
memory. This second relationship was probably an interracial liaison, outside the law, but sufficiently accepted so that the children
were given the father's last name. The community mores were
patriarchal, and paternal recognition of children gave them a place
in the community and the protective cover needed to survive in a
dangerously repressive society. This was fairly common practice
in Louisiana and other southern states.[3] My great-grandmother's
marriage to the first husband also may not have been sanctioned

by law; it could have been a slave marriage condoned by the community and perhaps by their church. When I tried, as an adult, to learn more about my mother's maternal grandparents, the remaining children of the matriarch were reluctant to say more than that she had two families, and they would give me no information about the father of the second family. Their hesitation may have been derived from habits of circumspection caused by living life in a segregated society or not wishing to cast aspersions upon a mother whom they adored. Nevertheless, both relationships appeared to have been monogamous. There was a great difference in the skin shading of the those two sets of children; the first were dark brown with long faces and features, while the second set had cafe au lait coloring, wavy hair, light brown or green eyes with slightly elongated faces and noses. My maternal grandmother was the youngest of the brood, reputed to have been babied and pampered by her mother and siblings and only reluctantly given in marriage to a good prospect, an older man, a college graduate and teacher.

My maternal grandfather was born around 1866, raised in a three-generation household in rural Mississippi, possibly also on a homestead; his grandfather who was head of the family was born in Africa and married to a woman born in Virginia. My toffee-colored grandfather's brown eyes had strong yellow tints in them, and his hair was medium kinky. He and my grandmother produced one child, my mother.

The two generations, so close to slavery and the Civil War, accepted "color," which defined their status in that repressive Southern society and circumscribed their lives. They did not rail against the social conditions, but persevered, putting their faith in God, education, and hard work with a conviction that life would be better for their child and grandchildren. They led upright Christian lives using the Bible as a guide for their daily lives and separated themselves from the uneducated poor by their temperance, restrained devotion, and good works. They never abandoned the hopes and aspirations that came with the end of the Civil War and homesteading, not even in the bleakness of the end of the nineteenth century, a hard time for African Americans in Louisiana and Mississippi. If they had questioned their racial identity or sought to deny it, they might have faced death; therefore, they needed the protection of the Black community and Black identity where there was security and few questions about identity. In fact in the United States there has always been security in assuming a lower status role and identity that does not threaten the hegemony of the white dominant class.

Some of Grandfather's generation left quietly, telling family members in hushed tones that they were going north or west, as did Grandfather's brother, but most stayed in the South until after World War I. Those two generations had an unambiguous sense of identity, clearly defined by the Jim Crow laws and social customs. They valued education, were aware of and took sides in the controversies of Black intellectuals of their time, led active community-focused lives, lectured at and raised a restless generation that would abandon "down home" for better prospects "up north."

My mother, born in 1913, was my grandfather's second child. A half-brother from a prior relationship was sufficiently older to have been considered a man when she was born. He was a tan-colored working man who settled in Alaska after World War I, raising a family there. My mother was a mass of conflicts and contradictions about racial coloring and identity, just as she was always in conflict about what she was. She was born and grew up in strictly segregated Southern small towns, in a privileged family headed by a teacher, a high status position. She was always restless, yearning for something better than dirt streets and Sundays spent in church or summer vacations working for white women. Her father strongly believed that there should be no leisure time. The everyday etiquette of Southern living was emotionally tiring—being subservient, stepping off the sidewalk to make way if a white person walked by, riding in the back of the bus, and so on.

Mother's ivory skin coloring, long wavy braids, and green eyes ensured her popularity with teachers, neighbors, and boys, and often, a second look from Caucasians to determine her race. As an adult, she could have "passed," but it would have meant denying her family and child, none of whom were as light colored as she. Her short marriage to my father was probably an impetuous act of rebellion. She dropped out of college and married a very dark skinned eighteen-year-old penniless musician. After the end of the relationship, she sought refuge for herself and me with her aunt, her mother's oldest sister, the surrogate mother whose warmth, loving nature, and wry humor had long given Mother relief from Grandfather's strict home and his second wife whose energies were focused on her own four children.

My great aunt was the preeminent seamstress to the wives of the white gentry in the small Louisiana sawmill town. She was a childless widow who loved providing a home for my mother and me and intermittently for her brother's daughter, the only other child of the third generation. This cousin was also tan, the progeny of a very dark woman and Grandmother's only brother, a fair-skinned rogue with wavy brown hair and green eyes. My great aunt knew everyone in town and seemed to be related to many in the parish, black, white, and Indian, something that everyone seemed to know and acknowledge.

There was little work in those Depression years for young black women, so they sought work in New Orleans and later in Chicago. My mother lived with family friends in New Orleans and worked in a dress shop; the light-colored, broad-featured husband of the family was a professor at a local black college and had a loving marriage to a Caucasian woman who passed as black. My mother enjoyed the intellectual stimulation of their home, the cosmopolitan city, and the freedom of movement afforded by her color in that creole community. It was during that period of time that she often attended Roman Catholic church services where even though she sat in the back pews, she felt more entitled as a human being. She chafed at the restrictive nature of segregated life in the small town when she returned to visit my great aunt and me. Eventually, Mother followed her cousin to Chicago where they worked in the same exclusive dress shop, alongside immigrant Jewish seamstresses. She boarded with a brown-skinned Jackson, Mississippi, woman whose family was acquainted with Grandfather; when I moved to Chicago to be with my mother and go to a better school than that in Bogalusa, Louisiana, I was still the only child in the household and pampered. I was the only child in the fourth generation of my mother's immediate family.

Mother tortured my childhood years by pulling at my hair trying to make it straighter, yelling at me to stay out of the sun, and pushing me to behave like a "white child." There was no rational reason for her color anxiety because the skin hues in her family ranged from African dark brown to ivory; her neurotic concern with color was perhaps a reflection of the national obsession with color and separation based on race. She somehow embodied many of the white American ideas and foibles about racial colors. In some ways, she wanted to be white and disliked many of the African-derived physical characteristics of the Negroes. However, her marriages and romantic liaisons for most of her life were with men who were dark brown and adoring; it was and perhaps still is considered a mark of status for an African-American man to marry a light skinned woman. Though she was ambivalent about color, my mother was proud of the historic struggle for equality and accomplishments of African Americans and made sure that I understood and appreciated my heritage. Some of this was in deference to my grandfather's scholarly interests and race pride, and some was to prepare me so that I could succeed in spite of society's strictures. She transmitted my grandfather's legacy that color should not be an obstacle nor a crutch and that we had a proud heritage on which to build.

Our family friends and extended family were of all shades, so my mother never attempted to impose a color line on our social contacts nor did she encourage me to associate only with "light-colored" friends. She often lectured me that color was irrelevant because character was a much more important quality in choosing friends and associates. Her relationships at work always seemed comfortable and equitable, perhaps because all of the seamstresses were either immigrants from Europe or black women from the American South, and the European women had few of the innate prejudices of native-born Caucasians.

Mother and the family in the South were concerned about the conditions of life in Chicago's South Side where the immigrants of the Great Migration from the South had settled. I was sent back to the South each summer and often at Christmas to be out of harm's way and to maintain contact with the family. It seems that the family had prevailed on my mother to get me out of the growing black Chicago ghetto by having her marry the second oldest son of her stepmother. We moved to Los Angeles where my new father, brown skinned, was the gardener and chauffeur on the estate of a wealthy white family in Hollywood. We lived on the estate, and I attended the local schools where I was a prized oddity, benefitting from the attention and praise.

I quickly made friends with the Caucasian children in school, went to Sunday School at the local Episcopal church, did extensive borrowing of books at the little nearby public library. I was popular with my peers but I missed the dark homogeneity of Chicago's South Side. My mother was sometimes suspicious of my white classmates and friends, afraid that they would hurt my feelings with unintended snubs or conscious acts of white superiority. She pushed me to succeed in school by being a better student than my classmates, holding up to me the importance of education, teaching me to be self-sufficient and to achieve more than had she and the rest of the family. Though she was proud of my academic and extracurricular accomplishments, she was afraid and reluctant to attend school functions, pretending that she could not get time off from work or was too tired at night. I think that race and the dread of being insulted or patronized were the real inhibiting factors.

I then attended all-white schools from the fourth grade through college, because my parents wanted me to have the best possible education. At the time that I started high school, I desperately wanted a more active social life and contact with peers of color, but my parents would not agree to petitioning for a transfer to an integrated high school because it would have meant a three-hour daily commute. They also would not consider sending me to Howard University on graduation from high school. Their reasons were the travel expense to and from the East Coast and their conviction that the education would not be as good as that at the University of California at Berkeley.

Mother was most unhappy when I brought home the man whom I was to marry; it is still not clear to us if her unhappiness was because he was Caucasian or Jewish, the son of Russian Jewish immigrants. My parents were very chauvinistic American patriots. Mother had tolerated the immigrants with whom she worked in the garment business, but having a son of immigrants in her immediate family tested her patriotism.

Our children, her grandchildren, delighted her because they were good looking, one with Mediterranean coloring, black wavy hair and olive complexion and one with her ivory coloring. Her granddaughter inherited her sensitivity to the sun and has to be protected from over exposure to the sun, and her grandson had her somewhat aquiline nose. She was fond of her grandchildren and grew quite fond of her Caucasian son-in-law.

She divorced my stepfather, had a brief liaison with an extremely dark, almost jet black, man, and subsequently had relationships only with Caucasian men. She crossed over the color line in her fifties although she never verbalized what she had done. Our conversations about her men friends conveyed her uneasiness and concern that she would be "found out." Though my marriage to a Caucasian seemed to liberate her enough to have interracial relationships, she and her partners were victims of their generation's racial perceptions and fears, and I met only two of her many white male friends. My husband and I were relieved in some respects, because

my mother and her friends drank excessively and set poor examples for our children. She attempted to drown her anxieties and
ambiguities in alcohol and prematurely was committed to a nursing home. Once she had the security of total care, she freed herself
of the past by rejecting us and reveling in the attention of the other
patients and staff. They saw my mother as a quaint, cute Southern-
born Caucasian woman with a distant family. She refused our offers to move her back to the family in Louisiana, because she didn't
want to live with all those "colored folks." I regret that my children did not have an opportunity to know the woman whose drive
and aspirations created me, but that woman had disappeared by the
time that they were in elementary school.

This fifth generation, my mother's grandchildren, grew up during the period of the civil rights movement and Black Power activism; race was always an oppressive factor in their lives. In many
respects, my husband and I tried to protect our children from racial discrimination and color bigotry while keeping them from being obsessed with blackness as I had been or stigmatized by color
as their grandmother had been. Because they grew up in somewhat
racially integrated academic communities with politely enlightened
neighbors, they had to learn how to handle racial problems when
necessary, often with our guidance and assistance. They have learned
to live with greater confidence than my own or my mother's generation, without hiding or denying their origins. They were raised
with the concept of the "powerful drop," so they were aware that
"blackness" would always be a part of their lives. They were put
on the spot many times during the 1960s and 1970s, having to explain
who they were and to what group their loyalties belonged. Both
children experienced the racial rages of the era, participated in civil
rights marches, protested in administrators' offices, and attended
endless student meetings trying to change the attitudes and behaviors of their teachers and white peers.

In the late 1960s, our son decided that he had to have an Afro
hair style so that there would be fewer questions about who he was.
The Afro was a symbol synonymous with Black Power, and the
wearer was instantly recognizable as a "Brother." Unfortunately,
our son's hair was not coarse enough to stand up, so he had to get
permanents to make his hair curly and coarse enough to simulate
an Afro. He then felt that he was relieved of the necessity of explaining who he was. Two decades later, he and his sister convinced
me that I should stop straightening my hair because my natural

curliness and texture were fashionable, and I did not need to rely on the beautician's chemicals. They were right, and I still lament the day that my mother dragged me to the beauty shop to get my hair "pressed," so it would be easier for her to comb.

Both of my children identify themselves as black or African American even though there are other options in the 1990s; they were born in the 1950s when those options were not available. They are both well educated with degrees from selective institutions and are competent professionals who are employable without being racially categorized but surprisingly, both feel that it is to their advantage to be identified as black for affirmative action reasons. Neither was hired because of race, rather in spite of race although affirmative action policies may have helped them gain initial consideration. My children seem to feel that their employment is more secure if they are entered in the statistics as black because there are few blacks in their organizations and professions. It is not clear if their employment has helped their organizations fulfill affirmative action timetables or goals.[4] Though their rationale for racial identification may be disappointing to me, their actions may be less opportunistic than realistic. Both children grew up during a period when they had no options other than being categorized as Negro and later as black.

After many dating relationships with Caucasian and African Americans, our children chose marriage partners who were Caucasian, cosmopolitan, and from permissively accepting families; their spouses are of Irish–Italian and WASP backgrounds. The four boys of those unions are an amalgam, one with very tight kinky blonde hair, one with straight dark hair, one dark blonde with curls becoming wavy, one with short hair beginning to curl, and with skin colors ranging from ivory to Celtic, brownish hazel eyes, blue eyes and features that look vaguely familiar but not characteristic of any particular racial group. They are truly representative of mixed race.

The oldest boy used to say that he was white, because his father is white and his earliest neighbors and babysitter described him as white; now that he is in the upper elementary grades, he will describe himself as half African American though he is only one-quarter or to use an old fashioned word, quadroon. His brother, five years younger, has never described himself in racial terms. These boys attend interracial schools and have playmates and teachers from all racial groups. Though they recognize differences in color shadings, in the family and school, they rarely identify persons by race or color, nor do they discuss race as a problem or topic. They have never been heard to use any racial epithets or negative descriptors of anyone's race or color. It may be that race as a problem or identifier is seldom discussed in their household because their patriarchal family is headed by a white man not bothered about racial identity, who has the self assurance that comes of being WASP.

My son's children have a Caucasian mother and are classified by their parents as interracial, multiracial, and interfaith; the older boy in this family is listed in his preschool register as interracial. Their home has many books and toys with multiracial, multicultural themes, and the three-year-old seems rather aware of differences in skin color and hair textures. He notices and mentions brown skin and curly hair like his own, but calls his father's wavy hair, "bumpy." Skin color and hair texture have no negative connotations to them, and they are friendly to people of all shades. This family is also patriarchal, but headed by a black father and a mother who grew up in a close-knit ethnic clan and values ethnicity and identification, so the children will probably be raised with a strong sense of identity.

This youngest generation appears to have an acceptance of peoples of all colors and a lack of self-consciousness about color. In fact, one might say that they lack an awareness of color as a distinctive aspect of a person's definition. When they are asked to describe someone color is rarely used as a definitive characteristic.

Racial identity, in this family, has always been that of the colored, Negro, black, African-American group until the children of the sixth generation. Earlier generations did not question their place in the American society because it was easier to be a part of and treated as a lower caste person than to defy the society's visual identification. In traditional African-American communities and families, it has always been the woman and mother who has protected the sanctity of the race and shielded her family and community by not alienating the dominant community by trying to become a part of that community. It was the women who kept the traditions, built the social organizations, and established the moral standards of the homes and communities. Those principles would have been compromised and threatened by close association with whites who represented evil and corruption as evidenced by the practice of slavery and white supremacy. Therefore, being black meant being held to a higher moral standard and greater favor in the eyes of

God. In my family, the female relatives upheld righteousness, decency, and self-respect and viewed these characteristics as synonymous with membership in a racial group subordinated by color. In many ways, they and my male relatives thrived on tales of quiet superiority and triumphs over the evils of prejudice and bigotry. If any of them had chosen to identify with whites, they would have abrogated their moral positions and self-respect and would have had to confront the insecurity and dangers of "passing."

It is reassuring and paradoxical to observe the changes in American mores so that the Census Bureau may establish a category designating "other" or "biracial," recognizing the changing racial mixture of the population. Perhaps, this began with the recognition that classification of Hispanics was not a simple matter because they could be "of any race." It may also be attributed to the quiet reasoning of young parents like my son and daughter-in-law who wish to have their children recognize both parents, rejecting neither on the basis of an arbitrary descriptor of race.

As I have discussed my own family, the one into which I was born and the one that I have created, it becomes apparent that color has faded, in reality and as a fearful and stigmatizing concept. In the 1990s, there appear to be choices about racial identity, particularly when one is cushioned by social class and income. This does not mean that racial discrimination and bigotry are disappearing in the United States; to the contrary, instances of racial hatred and intolerance seem to be increasing, perhaps indicating greater insecurity on the part of the perpetrators. What seems to have happened in the past 130 years, from my great-grandparents' era to my grandchildren's, is that there are greater degrees of personal freedom to choose mates and determine one's racial identification. Today, income and education are more likely to splinter families than racial designations. The new autonomy opens the way for Americans to begin to discard old arbitrary racial labels and more reasons to begin a rational dialogue to better understand the true nature of this country.

3

Racelessness

Cecile Ann Lawrence

Jamaicans who move to the United States, even those of the darkest skin color, often face a wrenching dilemma. Americans, the U.S. government and its agents, and other Caribbean people and West Indians, including Jamaicans who have lived in the United States a long time, insistently inform these new arrivals that their thinking about themselves and their identities is all wrong. New arrivals look around and see that prominent American-raised children of Jamaican parents are designated as "black" or "African-American." Examples include Colin Powell (former Chief of Staff of the U.S. Armed Forces) and Vanessa Williams (former Miss America). Calling an immigrant from the Caribbean an African-American is as or even more ridiculous, pernicious, and destructive to self-concept than when the term is applied to "dark-skinned" people born in the United States of American parents.

What happened to the island of origin to make it disappear? Even more importantly, what happened to the other parent, the other ancestors? Must we be forced to hold grudges against them, grudges that we did not originally have? Must we be forced to deny the existence of that ancestor who gave me my green eyes or contributed to the color of my skin? Why? This is the insanity that allows a person like Lani Guinier, President Bill Clinton's nominee for a Civil Rights position, to be categorized as black, completely ignoring the reality of her Jewish mother, that requires a woman like Lani Guinier to affix the political label "black" to her presence. This is the confusion that requires that racial label "black" for the "mixed-race" people being marketed by politicians as the first "black" this or that, whether it be a Surgeon General (Joycelyn Elders), a Secretary of the Department of Energy (Hazel O'Leary), or a Secretary of Commerce (Ron Brown). Where is the black hole into which the non-"black" ancestors of these people get sucked?

I should make clear now that in this chapter when I use words of color as a Jamaican would use them I mean them to communicate colors of the palette and nothing more. When I use the terms of color "black" and "white" as an American would use them, I mean them to communicate as an American would mean them to communicate, that is, not simply as terms of colors of the palette, but politically charged terms with no basis in optical reality. When I use the terms "dark-skinned" or "light-skinned" or "pale-skinned" I mean them to communicate optical perceptions with no political connotations.

Labeling as black, persons whose skin color is clearly not as dark as human skin color can be, violates the self-concepts with which they grew up, if they grew up in places other than the United States, such as the Caribbean, and begins to impose on them an obsession, a burden, a questioning, a constant companion that they did not have before. This is the constant companion that persons categorized as non-white in the United States carry with them on their backs. Could it be that this is one of the reasons why, compared with any other racially labeled group, hypertension rates are higher among people categorized in the United States as black, because when they look in the mirror and do not see the palette color black they have to deal with perceptual dissonance every single day of their lives?

This new burden for Caribbean newcomers to the United States was recognized by a writer on immigration to the United States who noted that in "the West Indies status had been determined only in part by color and many West Indians, unaccustomed to broad discrimination on a racial basis, found it galling to have to adjust to America's biracial [either/or] pattern."[1] Worse is the fact that passing off mixed-race people as "black" allows the "white" power structure to pat itself on the back for "allowing" "black" people into positions of power, when what they really are doing is letting in mixed-race people whose physical appearance is more acceptable culturally than very dark-skinned people. Look at the early Bill Cosby television shows and you can see that the children, especially the females, were clearly mixed race and genetically, except for the son, not likely to have been produced by a couple such as those two parents. But the culture at that time required that for "black" females to be acceptable, they really had to be mixed race and with as much "white" in them as possible. Notice that the one male child was darker than all the females. Was it because the show's producers felt a darker colored male child would be acceptable because of the dark skin of the star of the show, whose outstanding talent was almost, but not quite, enough to overcome objection to the color of his skin? As the years passed, the youngest child arrived darker than her female television siblings, and the new extended family relatives were allowed to be darker, including the females. But even then they mostly were mixed race, all busily denying the existence of their other ancestors.

Apart from the argument or custom handed down from slavery, based on the one-drop rule, that a single drop of black "blood" is so terrible or all-pervasive that the holder must be labeled "black," other arguments have been given for referring to mixed-race people as black. One is that during and shortly after the existence of slavery, mixed-race people, specifically "black" with "white," were produced as a result of rape of a "black" woman by a "white" man. Therefore, subsequent generations must repudiate this part of their ancestry. But this results in an additional basis for self-hatred or at least low self-esteem as a victim because the reality is that the existence of that ancestry cannot be argued away. So a "black" person is taught to hate himself because his ancestors were slaves and has the burden of fighting against that teaching. And a "black" person who is really mixed race has that burden also, and in addition, has the burden of fighting against the hatred of that part of himself that descends from a rapist. The mixed race person is doubly burdened with the messages that say he is less than ideal because an ancestor was a slave and, also, he is less than ideal because an ancestor was a rapist. Of course, that is always the assumption, forgetting about the possibility of willing unions between "black" and "white." Let's get rid of both pieces of self-hatred by accepting equally all parts of a person's ancestry. Of course, the crux would be for everyone to truly accept that all "races" are equal. The liberal "white" person also perpetuates this perception of inequality by refusing to acknowledge that part of his "white race" that is in the mixed-race person, even in the very act of offering him a position or lauding him as the first "black" whatever.

Another argument holds that "black" Americans have had to suffer such an enormous amount of injustice and abuse that, as a minority in numbers, the term "black Americans" should include as many people as possible to increase the amount of power that the group may acquire. This is especially true because the dominant culture has been more accepting of people with "lighter" skin color than with "darker" skin color, preferring "lighter" people to act as spokespersons for the "race." (A good example is Adam Clayton Powell, Jr., clearly a mixed-race person.)

Mixed-race people have been less threatening to the dominant culture, and the dominated culture has allowed the dominant culture to get away with this two-faced hypocrisy. Why is it two-faced hypocrisy? On the one hand, the dominant culture says you are less than ideal because you have a drop of "black" in you, or a "touch of the tar brush" in your ancestry, and no amount of "white" blood is good or strong enough to outweigh that stain. On the other hand, that same dominant culture also says that the more "white" blood you have in you, the closer to the "white" ideal you are, the more we will let you into positions and maybe our houses, but you and your progeny can never attain ideal status of "white-ness." This is really confused thinking. The only way to prove that a "white" person is truly not racist, no matter how liberal that person avows herself to be, is to ask that person if she would object to procreating or allowing her son or daughter to procreate with a non-"white" person. Racism may be solved only in acceptance of willing sexual relationships.

Africans who come to the United States are sometimes amused, but mostly frustrated by the American obsession with racial categorization. A student from Sierra Leone with an African father and a Chinese mother told me of her anger and sorrow at the insistence of "black" Americans that she call herself "black" because they were forcing her to deny the existence of her mother. She socialized mostly with students from the Caribbean because she found them more able to understand and agree with her perspective of "many in one."

Allowing or requiring mixed-race people to "pass" for "black" in U.S. terms also has the pernicious effect of keeping the darkest skinned people at the bottom of the opportunity pile. This creates divisions within the native "black" population in U.S. terms, as well as divisions between "black" Americans and "dark-skinned" or mixed-race people from the Caribbean. In the nature of the event of immigration, it is the more assertive, more educated, more creative people of a population who tend to leave their home and move to another. They therefore will tend to fare well economically in their new country. As Maldwyn Allen Jones notes, "by the 1930's, a high proportion of New York's Negro physicians, dentists, and lawyers were immigrants from the British West Indies."[2] She goes on further to note that immigrants from the West Indies were hostile towards native American "black" people and the hostility was returned because the

> bulk of the latter [West Indian "Negroes"] were generally better educated than American Negroes, their religious affiliation was Episcopalian rather than Baptist or Methodist, and, as a result of their contact with British culture, they had a predominantly European attitude toward the role of the family. Looking down upon American Negroes for their alleged ignorance and supineness, the newcomers were cordially disliked in return for their supposed aloofness and aggressiveness.[3]

Combining this situation with the fact that many of the newcomers, coming from a mixed-race culture, tended to have lighter colored skins than native "black" Americans, the practice of categorizing "non-white" people as "black," in U.S. terms, served furthermore to keep at the bottom the very people most in need of redress for past grievances—the darkest skinned, the most discriminated against descendants of slaves in America. There may be some hope of sanity in a former mayor of New York City referring to immigrants from the Caribbean as Caribbean-Americans. Although it still is labeling and my argument is against labeling, at least it is not a baseless, nonsensical, and racist labeling as is the U.S. use of "white" and "black."

An early event on a sidewalk in New York City slapped me into awareness. Scurrying my way to a subway entrance one evening after work, a man behind me growled "Outa my way, spick [or spik or spic]," and when I looked around there was no one else in the immediate vicinity but me. Puzzled, I went back to my family's apartment and received an education from relatives who had not just arrived in the United States, as I had.

Several points about the incident were disturbing. I came to understand that the word "spick" was an American derogatory term for Spanish-speaking people in the United States, usually those from Puerto Rico and sometimes Mexico. Now, because I did not speak any Spanish other than what I had learned in school and college

how could that term be used in reference to me, especially because
there had been no conversation between the man and myself? So
then, he had used the term solely on the basis of something in my
appearance that communicated to him that I must be of the group
of people labeled Puerto Rican or Hispanic.

But then it became really confusing. That is the most heterogeneous of the labels that the U.S. has come up with because it includes anybody under the sun regardless of skin color or
background—the person could be "white," "black," or mixed. The
concept however begins to fall apart when faced with a Chinese-
looking Spanish-speaking person, for example—as long as that person
or one or both of his parents, comes or came from or grew up or
was born in an area outside of the mainland United States where
the accepted language is Spanish, and sometimes also the person
must have a last name that looks "Hispanic." What does one do
with an Argentinean with a German-looking last name? In spite of
all this, supposedly, there is a typical or stereotypical "Hispanic"
look. One of the most amusing—if it were not so destructive—bits
of behavior in this culture is the practice of data gatherers such as
college admissions offices stating that students who label themselves
"other" are really Hispanic—insinuating that these people are confused, uncooperative, subversive, or all of the above.

But, at bottom, in this experience of being called a "spick," it
wasn't so much the word, but the emotion with which he said it
that was new and frightening to me. Later, in upstate New York,
sitting one afternoon in a graduate dormitory lounge, a dark-skinned
student engaged me in conversation, offering that he was from the
South. In short order, he had my hand in his as he scrutinized my
fingernails for some mark unknown to me that would reveal me as
a "black" person. He never told me whether he found it or not. It
was a really strange, almost surreal, experience. I could not understand why he had this burning need to know this "fact." It takes a
lot of energy and time for people to worry about what a person is
racially—time and energy that could be spent more productively
elsewhere, such as in getting to know each other as individual human
beings.

At a state government office, my first day on the job as a secretary, the assistant director, a young pale-skinned man, informed me
that he was really "ticked" that I had gotten the position instead of
his friend, especially because I had gotten it because I was "black."
My thinking had been completely different, because I thought that

with an M.A., I was really overqualified for that secretarial position. But, again, it was clear that my thinking was "wrong."

I recall a dark-skinned twelve-year-old in a classroom in Buffalo, New York, saying to me in true puzzlement and with some anxiety as if my very existence had violated some truth, some given,
"Are you black or are you white?" When I answered, "Neither," I
could see that she had difficulty comprehending my answer. On
the walls of the classroom were posters of "black" notables in
American history and clearly the majority of them were neither truly
"black" nor "white."

Moving to another city for another position, sitting at the table
filling out papers for the personnel office, the professional making
sure I was completing them as required was puzzled when I balked
at the question on "racial" category, drew a little box, wrote next
to it "Other," and checked the box I had made. He insinuated that
that was an uncooperative act and would cause problems for me
and in their record-keeping. In this job, I later found out to my
chagrin, that it was assumed that I would have a special interest in
"black" students above my interest in students in general, that I
would attend "black" functions, and that, unlike my "white" colleagues, I would be invited to join and expected to join all-"black"
social groups. The "problem" is that my comfort level is highest
when I am in a group that is very mixed.

I recall attending a lecture about racism and after the presentation, a discussion ensued about race-specific groups, such as the
Society of Black Accountants. The lecturer insisted that all people
have a racial identity. I offered a different perspective, of lack of
racial identity. She responded with disbelief and some anger. I was
encouraged when one or two others in the audience then spoke up
as coming from backgrounds with parents of different "races" and
colors and even religions (say, a Jewish mother and a Roman Catholic father) and the difficulties that caused them in living in this
either/or culture. They did not want to be forced to deny the existence of one part of their backgrounds, but they were forced to
struggle with it every single day.

I met an American whose mother was probably "white" and who
somewhat reluctantly admitted to having a father labeled Cheyenne.
I thought it was good or at least cool to have such an interesting
background. It was something new, not among the possibilities in
Jamaica because the Jamaican "Native Americans," the Arawaks,
had been exterminated. I was intrigued, enthusiastic; I bought, framed,

and hung poster reproductions of paintings of proud Indians. His feelings about it were colored by the clearly hurtful memory of being forced by teachers as a boy in elementary school to dance with the "black" girls because of his lightly swarthy skin color and the resentment he carried from that experience. He never had anything to do with Indians, that I knew of, except to categorize "them" in statistical reports he prepared. His grandmother wrote in her diary, before she met me, of the horror and heartbreak of her grandson taking up with a "black" woman from Jamaica. The family rarely spoke of their Native American familial connections, except behind one another's backs.

It became increasingly difficult to hold on to the beliefs about myself that I had brought with me from my home which now seemed so far away as to be on another planet. I looked in the mirror and still saw just me. I did not see a "race," no matter how hard I tried. But I began to give in and refer to myself as "a person of color," not really having any good idea what I meant by that. Sometimes, I would get obsessed with scrutinizing little physical details to determine whether this or that was a "racial" characteristic and, if so, of what "race." I began to think that, after all, perhaps I was wrong to hold onto these beliefs about myself that so many around me rejected and which had affected my relationships with others in personal as well as professional situations.

It became more confusing and crucial as my son grew older and became more conscious of the possibility of a racial self. He had always known that his mother was Jamaican and that was the limit of the cultural, racial, ethnic self-identification I had given him; and his father was half Cheyenne, and as far as I was concerned, that was an interesting background item, equal with the other background items. I had reared him with the terminology of "dark-skinned" and "light-skinned" to use when describing people if one really was forced to use skin color to describe them, avoiding the terms "black" and "white" because they were nonsensical and meaningless. But the messages from outside, from the culture in which we lived, shouted above my words for his attention and allegiance. So many experiences served to confuse him. A Cuban physician in Florida labeled him "Caucasian" on his medical forms. We moved back to the northeast United States and he continued his schooling in the suburb of a small city. He told me that after a few months the students around him wondered at the change in his skin color from darker to paler, almost as if he had changed race, asking him how come, almost demanding that he give an accounting of his behavior! When he fills out forms that ask that the respondent choose a racial/ethnic label, he checks all of the boxes, including the box for "other" if there is one. I wonder what their computers make of that kind of response.

Then my body brought me to my senses. When the issue of "race" became a medical one, I decided that I had no choice but to center on what I had truly believed all along about my identity, who I am, which is, an individual, not a member of a "color" or a "racial" category. In the process of getting diagnosed and obtaining treatment, I found to my horror that the political uses of baseless terms like "black" and "white" to refer to people were being used as the basis of treatment and in the description of the occurrence of the ailment in the population. I had to go back to my roots, my belief in the essence of who I am, which is raceless, simply an individual, a one of many, back to the beginning of time.

Having grown up in Jamaica, the recollection I have is that on the rare occasions when the topic of the color of a person came up, usually when a story was being related and someone needed to be identified, most often a palette color word was used, such as "brown," or "chocolate," or "tan," and there was a special term "red," meaning pale-skinned enough to burn easily in the sun, but not used in reference to a "white" foreigner, with the emphasis on foreigner. Rarely were the terms "black" or "white" used because the palette colors of black and white do not exist on human skin, so therefore the terms "black" and "white" as used in the United States were rarely used. With the spread of American culture, that has been changing, unfortunately.

My father, a man who in American terms could "pass" for "white," described himself as "red," but I am fairly sure that in some parts of the United States, using finely tuned criteria still beyond my understanding, perhaps texture of hair or contour of face, some Americans would categorize him "racially" as "black." This is how insane this topic can get.

While by no means was it a perfectly color-conscious-free society, my memory of Jamaican culture, at the time I was growing up, is that there was not a constant harping on what color or "racial"-category label to pin on a person or on oneself. Everyone knew that people around, friends, relatives, in addition to oneself, could not really "racially" identify who they were, and saying one was "mixed race" seemed a bit lame. Mostly, we were simply Jamaicans, and then the topic was usually dropped as being trivial, after it had been brought up, usually by someone not from the Caribbean. What little categorization there was, tended to develop in layers based on the geographic region. First, one may be from the Caribbean, which includes all the people from all the islands and perhaps even the Guyanas and includes different languages. Then, if one is from an English-speaking island, one may be a West Indian, as a subcategory. Then, finally, in the last layer of subcategory, one goes to the island of origin; one, at bottom, could be a Jamaican, or a Barbadian, or a Trinidadian. And there the matter usually ends.

By United States either/or biracial standards, I understand that I am perceived often as "racially black," perhaps because of the shape of my nose or the appearance of my lips, or the texture of my hair. I say "understand" because no matter how hard I try, I am unable to internally comprehend this perception. No matter how far back I go, I have no knowledge of any one particular customarily labeled "racial" category in my ancestry, except for a great grandmother alleged to have been Indian (Asian). And we don't know whether this Indian ancestor was from the south of India (dark-skinned) or the north of India (pale-skinned). And, to be honest, we really don't care.

In Jamaica, when forced to attempt an accounting, even if our skin color is clearly the darkest you have ever seen, we engage in a process of elimination. From writings of earlier inhabitants of the island and neighboring islands, we learn that the original people, the Arawak Indians, were abused and sickened and eventually exterminated as a result of the arrival of the Spaniards, so we can exclude them from our backgrounds. We learn that once England wrested Jamaica from Spain, the settlers imported huge amounts of slaves from Africa, so we can exclude early Spaniards from our backgrounds and include the possibility of dark-skinned peoples from the slave-exporting areas of Africa in our backgrounds.[4] We are told that, increasingly, newcomers came from Ireland, Scotland, and Wales, as well as from England, and that each of those groups had groupings of separate physical characteristics that could account for some of the appearance of current Jamaicans, but who could really tell? We know that later settlers arrived from Germany, from other parts of Western Europe; Jews came from Spain and Lebanon; indentured servants came from China and India. In the culture of that small island they all blended with each other from the start.

No simple division between master and servant or white and black
was ever made. From the beginning of English settlement there were
indentured white servants whose conditions were very close to
slavery: on the other hand many blacks earned or were granted their
freedom. The position of the individual in the scheme of things was
more important than his colour. There was no "simple division between
master and servant or white and black."[5]

So the result has been several generations of different combinations of mixing of peoples from different areas. At first, there
was some attempt at subcategories such as "coolie-royal" (or *rial*)
to denote the offspring of an Indian (Asian) father and a Chinese
mother, or "chinee-royal" (or *rial*) to denote the offspring of a Chinese
father and an Indian (Asian) mother (note the Anglicized patriar-
chical focus on the father's "race"), but pretty soon, as they mixed,
then mixed again and again in subsequent generations, the labeling
had to be given up as a fruitless activity.[6] These terms were originally neutral in connotation. This neutral, if not positive, attitude
toward mixing is contrary to deep-rooted American notions about
miscegenation. However, now these terms are considered insult-
ing.[7]

As a result of this generation-after-generation of mixing, much
of the Jamaican population is "mixed" including those categorized
by outsiders as "black." This is contrary to the commonly held notions
by Americans that the Caribbean islands are populated by "black"
people and that the cultures of the Caribbean islands are "black"
cultures. The only thing that could be as far from the truth is if the
cultures of the Caribbean islands were to be called "white" cultures. One result is that, pushed by an anxious student in a New
York City classroom to label herself "racially," my mother has responded "Heinz 57 varieties," and not a bit facetiously.

Faced with an assortment of medical personnel who were ready
to prescribe medication for me that studies showed was allegedly
more efficacious for "black" people than another type of medication, I began to educate myself on medical issues and to educate
the medical people whom I dealt with about the fact of mixed race,
multirace, individualism. I was told that I must be tested for sickle
cell anemia, in spite of my protests that I did not have the symptoms that the learned doctor hurriedly assumed I had. I refused.
Once he perceived me as a member of one side of the either/or
categorizing, then, of course, I must be mistaken in telling him that
I had none of the symptoms correlated with that ailment. Again,

my perception of reality was "wrong." However, I am encouraged by the recommendation of the Agency for Health Care Policy and Research (AHCPR) that sickle cell disease be among the diseases for which there is universal screening.[8] Although the author of the report in the *Journal of the American Medical Association* does fall into the usual simplistic behavior of confusing geographic origin with a politically charged label such as "African-American," he does state that the AHCPR's recommendation for universal screening is based on the "novel" position that "it is not possible to determine reliably an individual's racial or ethnic background by physical appearance, surname, presumed racial heritage, or self-report."[9] Halleluia!

When I was diagnosed with another ailment, which statistical studies claimed to be found primarily in "whites," I encountered some amusing results. Attending a conference dealing with that ailment, another victim of the ailment came up to me and told me in marked surprise that I "must" have some "white" ancestors because this was an ailment found almost exclusively in "whites." Well, although clearly this was news to her, I have lived with it and been struggling to be allowed to acknowledge it or, much more preferably, move beyond it, all my life in the United States.

The either/or dichotomy also played a part in the reaction of some medical people to my obvious intelligence, knowledge, and capacity to understand the terminology, the treatment options, and even the discussion. I brought medical articles; I questioned. I learned to use the reaction of the physician to this behavior as a litmus test as to whether I could work with this person or not. I especially used this as a test after I noted that a friend who is on the other side of the American either/or racial dichotomy, in other words "white," got much more cordial responses than I did from the same physician. However, this could have been complicated by my friend being a male, in contrast to my clear femaleness. This experience brought home to me how crucial it is for my physical health as well as for my sanity, that I center on my individuality, on my uniqueness as a human being, as each and every other human being is unique. More and more we learn that every individual responds to medication differently, no matter how many studies may purport to show "racial" tendencies, especially as those studies label as "black," people who really are mixed of an enormous variety of gene pools, making their genetic backgrounds much more hetero-

geneous than the also very mixed gene pools of the "white" populations.

Earlier I referred to an experience at a lecture on racism. I only
wish that more of the people like those in the audience at this lecture would speak out and talk so that our voices eventually would
shout above those in the culture who would hold on to a meaningless, racist system of biracial categorization. Only then would the
United States truly be able to call itself the first global nation.

One person at a time, I have pledged to change the thinking of
people with whom I come in contact about this crazy biracial system. So new or different is this way of thinking to many I have
met that it seems almost as if a major rewiring of some part of the
brain needs to be done. It takes time and patience.

4

"Check the Box that Best Describes You"

Zena Moore

[ ] WHITE   [ ] BLACK
[ ] HISPANIC (NOT MEXICAN)   [ ] HISPANIC
[ ] ASIAN/PACIFIC ISLANDER   [ ] NATIVE AMERICAN/ALASKAN

I propose that race, like gender, privilege, and class, is not monolithic. Race is socially and economically constructed to serve the interests of the privileged, whoever they may be. When race is viewed in combination with gender, religion, and class, attempts to discuss these issues become even more complex and confusing.

Here I narrate some of my own experiences that show that women not only have different gender experiences within their own culture, but experience cross-cultural conflicts with other women from other cultures, particularly from Western cultures where privilege is defined as largely a "white-male thing."

I will position myself in context: first, as a member of a majority group in my country of birth; second, as a designated member of a minority group in the country where I work and reside; third, as a brown-skinned upper-class woman of non-African descent in my country of birth; and fourth, as a "black" woman belonging to the race defined as "other" in the country of residence. These multipositions allow me to present what bell hooks[1] refers to as the view from the margins. This advantaged position (privilege) underscores Sandra Harding's[2] emphasis on "importance of using women's experiences as resources for social analysis."

Chinee, Chinee never die
Flat nose and chinky eye[3]

Some thirty-five years after I was born, I read that the neighbor-hood where I was brought up, "socialized," so to speak, was really a China Town. I had always associated this nomenclature with the United States, where the term was and still is used to describe the ethnic enclaves of Asians (Chinese, mainly but not solely). For the average white American, the term evokes places of interest where one can get inexpensive exotic Far Eastern goods and authentic Oriental cuisine. As children we never referred to our neighbour-hood as China Town. I guess we never felt that we had to use this ethnic identifier to describe a place that was obviously populated by Chinese.

It never occurred to us to use such descriptors as Portuguese Town, or Syrian–Lebanese Town, or French Creole Town to de-scribe the other neighborhoods. So why should this one be singled out for attention? In 1993 when a Trinidadian journalist[4] writing about the Chinese in Trinidad borrowed the U.S. street sign and used it to identify the community in which I grew up, images of Spike Lee's opening sequence to *Jungle Fever* flashed before my eyes, and I could not help but smile wryly. Like so many things borrowed from the United States, this label was for me a cross-cultural misapplication. We did not share with Americans the im-portance in identifying neighborhoods by ethnic roots. For one thing, many of us would have problems determining our ethnic origins and for another we would have to select one ethnic group out of many, and some like me would have to split ourselves into two. "China Town" conjured up in my mind pictures of San Francisco with tourists consuming whatever there was to be consumed. Or side walk vendors underselling each other in Soho. No, the label China Town was not a fit descriptor for the neighbourhood where I grew up.

My child-eyes (chinky though they were) saw nothing exotic around me. The dirty streets stretching from Charlotte Street down to Marine Square, extending across Queen Street onto Henry Street, from the 1940s well into the 1970s housed the 500 grocery stores, the 15 supermarkets, and the 70 laundries of the 8,000 Chinese who came to Trinidad, according to Trevor Millette.[5] They came either as indentured laborers, or ambitious businessmen who heard through the Chinese network that the island had the potential for success in business, or the highly educated upper classes who were probably the last set of Chinese immigrants to arrive on the island. No, this was not an exotic tourist spot where visitors flocked to buy T-shirts, ivory chopsticks, and soup bowls to take back as evidence of having traveled.

This was my home, the home of a curious breed of small-figured, fast-walking Chinese people, whose adults spoke their Hakka language only among their peers. I vividly remember my sense of shock on hearing my father speaking this Cantonese dialect with the mother of one of my friends. I had no idea that they even knew each other. He had never indicated to me that he knew the family, nor did my friend ever cue me to the fact that she knew my father.

One of the few Hakka words I did learn sounded like "Haquai," which I figured from the context in which it was always used meant Negro People. At least that was what it meant to me, because it was always used in reference to the African-Trinidadian friends who came to our home. My "Haquai friends" were my "black friends." The word, however badly spelled by me, belonged to the vocabulary of my father, and I had no interest in learning his language. Not when so many of my friends made fun of the children who bore names like Sing Lee, Tang Pong, Lue Qui, and Ng Wai, obvious identifiers of these "chinky eye," "stingy" people.

My father's people certainly were not the poor people of the country, although they were the butt of many an ethnic joke. They were the sole proprietors of laundries and bakeries. They may have chosen to engage in these commercial enterprises because they obliged them to speak the minimum of English in their daily transactions. In addition these basic services required little or no advertisement, thus no economic urgency for learning the English language. So they developed functional competence, learning words and phrases from their clients.

Their language was a deliberate barrier that they built around their community both for protection and for solidarity. Being a product of that environment, how I could I avoid its cultural effect? I lived for years under the impression that every Trinidadian had either sweet or sour pows for breakfast, ate lots of white rice, and drank Hong Kong tea because the (Hong Kong) coffee was for adults, and coffee according to my father "was not good for the brains." When I was thirteen years old I was invited, with several other friends, to one of the "gang's" home. There I feasted on food I had never seen or tasted before. There was baked chicken, baked beans (from cans), potato–mayonnaise salad, and macaroni pie, typical Trinidadian Creole dishes, I later learned.

My father was 43 when he married my teen-aged mother who was then 16. He attempted to teach neither her nor us his language. On the contrary, he placed extreme emphasis on our acquiring the "Queen's language." For this reason, he had us enrolled in the best elementary schools, those run by the Roman Catholic Sisters, "because they know what discipline is." My father considered education the most important asset in life. He made a ritual of "joining us in the Public Library," as soon as we reached membership age of five.

For years my father would arrange dentist appointments for us with one Dr. Tam Loon, who, I learned, only as an adult, was my cousin. (That is why we never paid him, I realize even now as I write.) For years we did all our shopping using credit from Mr. Chan Pong. Our daily bread we bought from Lee's bakery and our prescriptions were filled out in Ling's pharmacy. Why did the Chinese community cling together so tightly? Why did they distance themselves from the cultural activities of the average Trinidadian?

I had been to the North American China Towns several times and was always struck by the familiar sights that had for the first 21 years of my life been my neighborhood, my community. I never found these neighborhood stores with their over-packed shelves, their soup bowls and delicate soup spoons wrapped in newspaper to protect them, and their finely sculptured, big-belly Buddhas, exotic. They were untidy, badly crowded, dingy, smelly one-door shops whose owners could not speak English even after many years in an English-speaking country.

Yet, I felt no shame for my neighborhood until I moved out of the community (distanced myself) to attend the "most prestigious" school on the island, St. Joseph's Convent.[6] There it was that I first heard the word "slums" as a referent to my neighborhood. The shame that I was made to feel as a teenager was a response to a group of people designating my community, my family and friends as people in "the margins," not belonging to the mainstream.

That was probably when I realized that class, ethnicity, color, language, and education were intricately linked together. Attendance at the more prestigious schools was interrelated with class and color. Students who attended the less prestigious schools were mainly from the lower classes, which invariably meant economically poor and black. My situation was a little complicated. Clearly I was not white.

Neither was I black, because I had no African heritage. My Chinese and South American mixture placed me in a category somewhere along a spectrum of colors between the two extremes, black and white; and privilege and status were given to those who occupied the spaces nearer the white pole. Because the majority of the population were of various shades of brown, other categories were created to differentiate between peoples. Education, economic status, religious affiliation, and political connections were more powerful forces than race and color.

"Yuh sure you're Trinidadian?"

Years after I had "grown into my own woman" and left China Town, a friend of mine, from the eastern part of the island, was amazed that I had never been advised by my mother to walk with "vex money,"[7] that I did not know that "baigan"[8] was the native word for spinach, that I did not know "grammichel" was the way the natives pronounced "Gros Michel,"[9] the name of the sweetest banana grown on the island, and that I had never gone shopping in the market and so had never learnt "the language of the market"— in short that I was ignorant of the Trinidadian culture and dialect. "Yuh sure you're Trinidadian?" was the constant query.

I spoke a variation of a dialect I call "Convent dialect." It is a dialect with its own intonation and accent that mark the speakers as clearly middle class. I remember after my first day in Convent, when I returned home, I stood, in privacy, in front of the mirror in my bedroom, and practised for hours to say "Hi" as the other Convent girls (we refer to the school as "the Convent" and every Trinidadian understands the significance of being a Convent girl). "Hi" was not a word in my family vocabulary. You simply greeted friends and neighbors with "good morning," "good afternoon," "good evening," and "good night." So "Hi" was a word in a foreign language, spoken by a foreign group of people, people who all were white-skinned, with brown or blond hair, and blue, green, grey, or brown eyes (certainly not black chinky eyes).

My community was made up of "stingy-flat-nosed, fast-walking Chinee people," who ate cats and bowls of plain white "lice" (rice) every day with deft handling of chopsticks. I learned to disassociate myself from the ethnic jokes that were abundant, but later learned to prefer ethnic jokes about Chinese to those about "niggers," another term borrowed from the United States to describe the African Trinidadians. Thank God, that my eyes weren't so chinkee and my nose was not so flat. Besides I was blessed with "good" skin texture and my legs were hairless, features that were marks of physical attractiveness in the culture. In addition my hair was straight. So the racist remarks made by the nuns in the Convent to my less-fortunate friends left me unaffected. Or so I naively believed.

Who is Zena Aqui??
Mother Helen wants her for the singing test.

This announcement came like the heralding of some honor to be bestowed upon some lucky few. Usually it was for the selected light-skinned girls who formed the Convent choir. When I entered the Music room, however, it was clear that someone had played a trick on Mother Helen. She was not expecting a dark-skinned girl with the same Chinese name as two others of her lighter skinned choir members who, I later learned at my father's funeral, were my cousins. Her embarrassment at my physical appearance was increased by the fact that I had a good singing voice, which she adjudicated "had a quality better suited for the radio." I discovered a few weeks later through one of her pet students, a white friend from a French Creole family, that I had actually scored in the highest percentile in the singing test. Joanne (bless her heart) failed to understand why I was not chosen to be a choir member. The racist comments, actions, innuendos, and open insults sometimes flew over my head; other times they gnawed and buried themselves deep into forgetfulness, or angered me. There was the other side, you see. Those who said

You so lucky to have Chinee blood.
Chinee blood can't hide.
You could always tell it by the skin and the hair.

But my hair bothered me. I wanted curly hair that could be styled in different ways. This thick black straight hair that "stood up like porcupine" whenever it was cut too short was something I always wanted to change for brown-colored, soft "white people hair," or wavy hair. Did all girls like me wish for "white-people hair"? Adopting their dialect was not so difficult. I imitated the accents and the intonation well enough. I even learned how to throw back my long hair with the casual gesture of the American filmstars.

While I longed for just a few waves to break the ugly monotony of the straight blackness, some of my friends went through the pain of straightening their hair with chemicals. They pressed and greased their hair into straight tresses. This made their hair more manageable, they argued, and more versatile. What confused teenagers we were! Some of us spent hours in the sun getting tanned to acquire a more romantic-looking complexion, while others pressed, straightened, and bleached their hair to look white.

I could not hide my racial mixture. The tell-tale signs were there. My confusion, however, was further increased, because I was not yellow skinned. My grandmother's blood from my mother's side flowed strong in my veins. I looked like the Guarajun Indians of South America.

You look just like your Venezuelan grandmother.
A real Guarajun Indian.

The word Guarajun I could not spell for years. All I knew was I did not want to look like those "uncivilized, primitive Indians from the Main."[10] The Guarajun blood gave my skin a hue that was a "little shade too dark." "Black-Chinee," in the opinion of my Indian-Trinidadian university colleagues, was a more precise appellation. Clearly, to their eyes I was not East Indian, although I shared many of their physical characteristics. Culturally, I was not East Indian. So, I was given yet another ethnic descriptor. A term that actually I preferred. It was quite flattering because to be a Chinee in Trinidad was somewhat a privilege, if only because of their economic prosperity. There was, of course, the racial factor. The complexion of the Chinese, it is argued even today in the United States, is just a shade different from the white skin. Added to that, they were "bright." And I too was bright! Mine were a people who valued academic success. I often wondered whether Trinidadians could tolerate a Prime Minister with Ronald Reagan's background or Dan Quayle's intellect.

My father's race actually protected me from the fierce, direct racist comments constantly made by the Roman Catholic European nuns who schooled me from elementary through high school, and who ran the "best" and most prestigious schools throughout the island. I was neither "black" nor "white" in St. Joseph's Convent. I was a "brown-skin" girl, who escaped many, but not all, racist statements about length of hair and bodily odors, statements made to many of my "Haquai" friends. So although my skin was dark, it was the darkness of another exotic tribe. Those *pañol* people from the Main.

The language of my mother was Spanish, for want of a more accurate linguistic code for what the people speak in Venezuela. She came from a Venezuelan family who lived sporadically in Trinidad, while they traded and conducted business. She was brought up in what may be called Spanish Town, on the southeast side of the city, a community that housed another marginalized group of foreign language speakers, of similar hue and complexion to the ruling upper-class, light-skinned French Creole plantation owners. But their language set them apart.

Don't speak that language in this class.
That is not good Spanish!

I knew quite a bit of Spanish before I entered Convent. The other half of my cultural existence was the shameful *locura*[11] of my mother's relatives, or so my father described them. My uncle Francisco was a lover of music, alcohol, women, and good times. I learned to enjoy the weekly *parandas*[12] which marked the coming of Christmas. Tío Francisco would always bring the *paranderos* to our house, much to my father's irate disapproval. These frequent interactions and the fact that Latin American music was always popular with Trinidadians helped me develop a close-to-native accent and an understanding of the Venezuelan language. Imagine my chagrin and embarrassment when I was chided by Madre María, my Spanish teacher from Madrid, that I was not to speak "that language." I reasoned later that it lacked the haughty lisp of the Castilian monarch. But in my immature insensitivity, I stormed into the kitchen that afternoon informing my mother that she was not to speak to me in that language, because it was not "good Spanish."

So, on the one hand I denied my mother's first language, but on the other I was never taught my father's first language, and I learned, not standard English, as many of my friends would like to believe, but a standard Trinidadian English. I learned Keats, Byron, Shelley, and all the other Romantics. I studied Latin and two other Romance languages. In short I followed the curriculum designed for the students at Oxford and Cambridge.[13]

If you're white step right up.
If you're black stay back.
If you're brown, hang around.

I guess that I was one of those who were fortunate enough to be allowed to "hang around." This was postcolonial Trinidad, after all. The "negroes" were from "behind the bridge," what the French Creoles called *le diametre* (pronounced in Creole "jammette.)"[14] The generous kind-hearted Cluny sisters allowed some of them passage into the Convent, if they were bright enough, or if their parents had enough money to pay the school fees. That, of course, eliminated most of the Negroes, who then had no other recourse than to seek admission to the less prestigious schools. Most of the people from behind the bridge were poor and black.

Many Trinidadian dialect expressions are difficult to understand without a knowledge of the sociocultural factors operating in the communities from which these expressions emerge. Therefore, to understand the expression "to come from behind the bridge," one has to understand the historic divisiveness of the Trinidad society in postcolonial times. When the first steel pan was invented by a man from behind the bridge, and when the steelbandsmen came from this same location, the racist attitudes and the scorn leveled at the artists were transferred to the artform. Jammette behavior, the descriptor for loose behavior, such as was exhibited by people of this lower class, was associated with the steelbandsmen and steelband music, and by extension, the calypso. The expression "behind the bridge"[15] carried with it notions of race, color, economic status, religious values, and level of education. One of the most effective ways of bringing shame to and threatening the values of upward-bound middle-class families in the early 1950s and in the 1960s was to form an alliance with one who was marginalized.

Girl you have no ambition? A steelbandsman!
You, a Convent girl! That is all the taste you have?
He never even went to College!

I experienced the prejudice and racism meted out to the "marginalized" when, as a romantic teenager, I fell in love with a steelbandsman. He was not from behind the bridge though. He was from Belmont, a suburb of Port of Spain, where many light-colored families elected to live. Belmont was adjacent to the site of the governor's house and within walking distance to St. Clair, the wealthy neighborhood of the French Creoles and other white Trinidadians. Mario was racially mixed, of light skin with obvious negro hair. His physical appearance, being light-skinned (my friends called him "Red-Nigger") in spite of the fact that his family lived in a suburb, was somehow not powerful enough to override the lowly ambition of wanting to be a steelbandsman. I paid for this love with many a blow and many a ban. My mother's disapproval fired my rebelliousness, which in turn magnified my love for Mario. He was my Marlon Brando; he walked and dressed like Marlon Brando. How could any romantic, uninformed teenager, lost in a quest for her own identity, not fall in love with the American hero of the Waterfront, both images capturing the distant and the dangerous?

Race then was tied up with education, with language, with color, with religion, with politics, and with culture. The artforms of those from the ghetto, from behind the bridge, from the margins, suffered the prejudices and legal biases of those who regarded anything from Africa, the Dark Continent, as evil and debased, very much like the attitudes to American Blues and jazz, with their roots deeply fixed in West African rhythms. All through my childhood the calypso and the steelband[16] were considered sinful indulgences. They were banned from the radio during the season of Lent.[17] I remember the many confessions I made, for I was an ardent Roman Catholic, as was 90 percent of the population.

> *"Bless me father, for I have sinned.*
> *It is one week since my last confession.*
> *I listened to and sang calypsoes four times during Lent."*

My friendship with Mario carried all these nuances. He did not go to high school, he played steelband, and he had Negro blood in his veins. To crown it all, his mother was not even married to his father.

When I did marry, a light-skin (could pass for white), bright, product of the most prestigious boys' college in the island, a Roman Catholic, son of a Belmont family with an English last name, the match was well received. I could not have chosen better. As I grew closer to this family, I realized that I was giving up my own family ties and that I was developing a preference for the "other."

I was fascinated with the "foreign" culture of my in-laws. Their family sat down to every meal together. The Pater began by leading the family in saying the "Grace Before and After Meals" and then was served by the Mater who gave due honor to the patriarch of the family by offering him the juiciest piece of the chicken. She in turn received her due by the chorus of sibling voices raised in constant emphatic declaration and affirmation—their mother was the best cook on the island.

Such strange discussions. Why was it important for these people to try to claim excellence in this culinary art? Was this competence a sign of identity with the European (white) culture? Why was it important to be forever reinforcing in their discussions the importance and prestige of the family name? What sort of insecurity existed among this almost-white middle-class family? Were they measuring their life style against one of which I was totally ignorant? What small, petty prejudices and insecurities existed among families like this in postcolonial times? The film *Wide Sargasso Sea* with its eerie quality and erotic scenery hints at this confusion and tension of being white-skinned but not white. Of being viewed as only native by the European. Of the psychotic anxieties that may be the result of the struggle for identity. I have many friends who came back from studying in Europe and the United States completely devastated from similar experiences. My Brazilian friend Claudia expressed it so vividly when she said in exasperation one day:

> I can take it no more. I am going home. I do not belong here. In my country I am considered white, and here in this country I am an alien, a Third World person, of colored parentage, and even referred to as black. This is so humiliating. In my country I am white, here in this country I am black.

The oldest sister of my in-law family was the one most obsessed with the family name, the prestige of being called the best cook, and so forth. She once described her three nephews as white–brown, red–brown, and black–brown. Through her experiences, her eyes were trained to see subtle differences in hues and shades of brown. Many white Americans have not developed this sharp ability of telling people of color apart. Their culture has not taught them to differentiate between shades of brown. For them black is black is black. Brown is nonexistent, and white many times has the preferred meaning of "blond with blue eyes." The obsession that my sister-in-law had with shades of complexion was tied up more with status, class, and social acceptance.

I had grown up a privileged female child although I had come to realize that my older sister was the preferred female sibling. She was fair skinned and had the features of my Chinese relatives. She was the favorite of my aunts and uncles. I, although darker skinned, was brighter and attended the most prestigious school. These seemed to compensate for what I lacked in complexion. Moreover, as a Convent girl I had role models of strong women educators, strong leaders. We were encouraged, as young women, to develop leadership qualities, to be ambitious and successful, to compete with the male scholars in the classroom and on the sports field. I was not only a "special" student as far as academics were concerned, I was also a sports captain, and represented my school in many sporting events. So when I was not chosen to be a choir member, I had already been forewarned that Mother Helen preferred "white girls." The students knew which nuns were "color prejudiced," as we referred to this bias; and because some honestly tried to develop a true Christian love of all people, we learned from their example that racist attitudes were not entrenched nor institutionalised.

When I came to the United States to do my doctorate, it was like reliving my teenage years in high school. Reruns of prejudice, racial bias, and open racist statements, which I had experienced in high school, played over and over. This time they were not from white Irish Catholic or French Catholic nuns. Here, they were from everyone who was white. Here, I learned that one is judged not so much by achievement, academic success, or status in society, which in my culture allowed one to cross social barriers, but more by color and race. It was, and still is, extremely difficult to deal with the sacker in the supermarket who looks at you with the unspoken questions on her lips: *"Can you afford this? Do you have food stamps to cover this?"* or the open statement *"I have to check with the manager to see if we can honor this check."*

Here race is institutionalized. You are categorized by the color of your skin. The official documents demand that you say to what ethnic group you belong, these ethnic groups having been determined by the white majority in authority. Whenever I have to fill out these forms, I do one of two things. I either mark the box "OTHER" or create a box and call it "OTHER." This is my method of defiance. And yet it is the truth. I belong to none of the ethnic groups described here. What does black mean? What are the referents associated with the term? Can I honestly claim a heritage and a history that I do not have? If I were to select Asian, because my father is Chinese, does that deny my South American Indian ancestry, and consequently the other half of my being? I find myself forced to make ridiculous choices where I never had to before. At home you are either Trinidadian of East Indian descent, Trinidadian of African descent, or Trinidadian of mixed parentage. In my culture the word black does not have the same meaning as here in the United States. Here the obvious meaning is nonwhite. But what does white mean?

That does not negate the current racist attitudes or presence of color preference in my culture. Few African-Trinidadians are of pure African blood, and a sizeable portion of the population is *Dougla*, a term coined to describe persons with both African and Indian Trinidadian parentage. These are the two ethnic groups who become the instruments for political rivalry. The racist monster feeding on the tension between these two marginalized groups raises its head every election year. And although this tension between these two ethnic groups must have begun somewhere in the early 1950s, it is more evident in the rural regions of the island. My upbringing was a city child's experience and so I did not have first-hand experience of this rural reality.

In the United States, by contrast, black means not white. This assignment of people to categories based on color becomes more ridiculous when one considers that South Americans of European parentage are classified as Hispanic, or nonwhite, whereas European Spaniards are classified as white. All of this supports the belief that race is an ideological construct. It is an arbitrary categorization that attempts to divide a people with the intention of retaining power in the hands of a few. In cultures where race is not applicable, other forms of categorization are created, be it clan superiority, caste inferiority, or royal blood. The intention is always the same, the maintenance of status and power.

5

"What Are They?"

Stephen Satris

Much of the discussion about people of so-called mixed race is scientifically defective and literally confused. Most race talk is itself quite unscientific anyway (although it often pretends to have scientific support), and mixed-race talk is even more obviously strange. If people always fell into definite racial categories, then we could have clear cases of racial mixtures and individuals of mixed race. Presumably, it would be possible to keep track of these things for several, perhaps many, generations. Of course, after some time, one of our original assumptions (namely, that people always fell into definite racial categories) would not be true. But racial categorization is far less quantitatively and scientifically determined, and far more socially determined, than is generally admitted.[1]

In this country—due to social forces, not science—most people of mixed black and white racial ancestry have been classified and treated as black, and most continue to be so. This is easy on the minds of (those who think of themselves as) white Americans in a number of ways. First, such people can continue to use the same simple, dualistic racial categories that they have already been using; second, they can be assured that "white" (their own category) implies a certain "purity" such that even a slight nonwhite ancestry can defeat a claim to a white racial classification—as Plessy found out in Louisiana.[2]

This racial system is not a matter of classifying people according to their predominant ancestry but rather a matter of screening the population for those who will be admitted into an exclusive "white" group. All other people—nonwhite people—are classified as belonging to the "colored" racial category. On this view, everyone must fall into one of the two categories; in particular, there can be no racially mixed people.

But there are racially mixed people. And one result of acknowledging this is that much of the senselessness of racism and related phenomena becomes more obvious than it already is. This senselessness becomes more obvious both to the individuals who are racially mixed and to third parties such as their friends and relations. The existence of racially mixed people causes trouble not only for Plessy-style segregation, but for very many racist practices. Racism requires fairly rigid racial categories; but, ironically, once these racial categories are established, there is the possibility (and often the actuality) of racial mixtures.

A whole host of social activities cannot be carried out unless many people (including, generally, all those most directly involved) are classified into racial categories. The most serious classification—the one with the most serious social consequences in this country—has traditionally been the classification as "white" or "black." One way in which such racial classification can be upset is described by Bill Hosokawa in his book *Nisei: The Quiet Americans.* Speaking of the Japanese Americans who were sent to internment camps during World War II, he recounts their experiences in Arkansas, where white people had long made a distinction between the white race and the black race and clearly separated them. The Japanese Americans were encouraged by the whites to sit in the front of the bus, and to drink from the white water fountain. They were also regarded by the blacks as their colored brethren and were expected to take that role and stand together with them against the whites.[3]

One response to this situation is to say that a black–white racial scheme is simply too limited to handle the cases presented by Japanese Americans. The remedy is to expand the classificatory system. An expanded system could include categories for blacks, whites, Asians—and we could even expand the system further and add categories for Hispanics, Native Americans, Polynesians, Aleuts, and other groups and subgroups. But no matter how many categories we add (apparently trying to accommodate more and more people or make finer and finer distinctions), so long as it is assumed that each person will fall into one and only one category, people of mixed race will frustrate the system. The system is supposed to enable its users to pigeonhole people, to have a handy set of categories (and perhaps stereotypes) to relate them to. Mixed-race people will cause anxiety among those for whom it is important to establish a one-category classification for everyone.

Even the plan to send Japanese Americans to the internment camps in World War II was complicated by intermarriage and miscegenation. Special rules dealt with women of Japanese descent who married Caucasian men, men of Japanese descent who married Caucasian women, children of such marriages, widows whose deceased husbands were of a different race, and orphaned children of Japanese descent who were being raised by Caucasian parents.[4] And who were Japanese Americans anyway? One formula counted anyone living in the United States who was one-sixteenth Japanese as Japanese American; however, because fewer than one hundred years had elapsed since formerly isolated Japan was opened to limited exchange with the West, the existence of a person who counted as one-sixteenth Japanese, although perhaps a mathematical possibility, was highly unlikely.

Although, so far as I know, I myself have only European ancestors, my children have Japanese and European ancestors. Thus, although I am readily placed in a common racial category, the situation regarding my children is more complicated. I have witnessed some of the confusion and difficulty experienced by people who want to classify them racially. People have expressed their confusion to me, especially when the children were younger. Moreover, when I am alone and it seems to be assumed that my family is monoracial, people sometimes say things to me that they would not otherwise say.

My own experience of contemporary racism in this country indicates that there are at least two major types. First, there is the white–black kind, which is basically antiblack. When one of my daughters came home from school with her race identified on paper as white, my reading of this was that there had been an identification of some people as black, and she was not included. She did not have what Plessy had—some amount of black ancestry—and she was able to escape the first form of racism, the anti-black kind, which is really quite powerful. This white–black divide is, of course, the big racial divide.

The second form of racism is less focused on blacks as a target. In this case the divide is between whites and everyone else. The idea here is not so much to target African Americans (although they are of course included), but to privilege whites. As in the Plessy case, "white" is narrowly construed and no special qualifications are required on the part of those who determine such racial categorizations.[5] But, in contrast with the considerations that were operative in *Plessy*, this way of drawing a dividing line acknowledges that the nonwhite side of the dividing line contains people who are of a variety of racial backgrounds.

Now is the time for me to use a terminology that I find particularly problematic. According to the line between whites and everyone else, we refer to those of the first group as whites and those of the second group as people "of color." The idea seems to be that people can be divided into those who are white and thus have no color and those who are "of color." It seems to be further suggested that those who have no color have no race (they are free of that), while those "of color" have a race, although it is not thought to be important what precise race an individual person "of color" might have.

I think this way of describing the situation is extremely problematic. In particular, white people are not race-free—as this sort of terminology encourages us to think. I think the "white or of color" dichotomy is another of the simplistic, dualistic models that is inadequate to reality. It is, in fact, surprisingly like the simple classificatory scheme in *Plessy*. But it seems to me that people often desire simple models and systems.[6]

Even more complex categorical schemes are used simplistically when it is assumed that everyone will fall into one and only one category. Once, in a public place, after my children had gone into another room, someone asked me "What are they?" Many truthful answers could have been given to this question (e.g., "My children," "Two girls") but I understood the question to be about their racial background. Such a question need not express racism on the part of the person who asks it. I take racism to include a belief claiming the inferiority or superiority of a race. I took this particular question as an innocent and naive one; I also took it as one that anticipated a very short (and possibly one-word) answer. Because I was obviously Caucasian, perhaps—and I suspect this was actually the case—the questioner thought that I had adopted these children. If that thought had been true, and I had said "Japanese," the questioner would have been enabled to place the children in the "Asian" or "oriental" racial category.[7]

In any case, the questioner wanted to know how to classify these people racially, and she seemed to think that a short answer would do. But there is no such short answer. Instead, I wonder what the point of the question is. What hinges on such a question?

The "What are they?" question is based on a false assumption. The false assumption is that they—and, apparently, everyone else—belong to one and only one race.

Many times I too have been asked a question that is based on a false assumption: "Where are you from?" I have lived in numerous states and several countries. Even while growing up, from birth to age eighteen, I had lived in several different states. The details are unimportant. But most of the askers of this question (i.e., those who fancy themselves to be asking about the name of a certain place, the place that I am from) do not want to ask about *this*. We both regard my longwinded response not so much as an answer to their question, but as an explanation of why the question does not apply. Usually, this bothers the asker. Recently, an asker of this question was very bothered and very persistent, although she seemed satisfied when I stated that I was born in New York City (although, as I told her, in a few months my family moved to another state). "Where are you from?" does not ask for a retracing of the road that led me here; rather, it presupposes that there is some one specifiable location that I am from. Naming a series of places where I have lived is not construed as an answer to that question.

Similarly, the "What are they?" question is not to be answered with a multiracial story. Such a story, if given, shows why the original question cannot go through. That question is based on a false monoracial assumption.

But the situation is worse with respect to the "What are they?" question than with the "Where are you from?" question. (Indeed, it is so obviously worse that I can imagine many people will think that the questions are not comparable at all.)

What hinges on such questions? The "Where are you from?" question might lead to connections being drawn or acknowledged. For example, suppose a person answers "Minnesota." The questioner might make a statement like "Oh, that's a beautiful part of the country" and go on to talk about time spent there, or "My next door neighbor is from Minnesota! I wonder if you know where St. Peter, Minnesota, is" or "My best friend in elementary school moved to our area from Minnesota." Such statements affirm connections and may bring the questioner and the Minnesotan together.

The "What are they?" question does not play this role. It does not lead to connection-drawing but often to a conversational dead end.

The questioner demands an answer in his or her own terms. The questioner makes an assumption that everyone falls into some (one) racial–ethnic category, and the "What are they?" question aims for the identification of the category that these people fall into. But one response here might be one of unwillingness to use the questioner's categories. Is the person who is questioned bound to use the categories of the person who questions? In addition to the use of categories, the one who is questioned might also wonder about the use that an answer will be put to. Are stereotypes going to be imposed? Is some form of racism in the offing? What difference will it make to the questioner whether the person being asked about is a member of this or that group?

Suppose we try to disregard the use that the racial categorization will be put to and simply try to determine a racial classification.

Unfortunately, there are discrepancies between the results of several ways of arriving at racial classifications. One method, seemingly scientific but often pseudoscientific, has to do with blood quantum, lines of descent, ancestry, and so forth. A second method of racial identification relies on looks. For example, the court records of the 1890s indicate that Plessy's looks did not exhibit any black ancestry. To judge by looks alone, Plessy was white. A third method relies on the perceptions and determinations of others. For example, in the Plessy case, others determined that Plessy was not white. A fourth method of racial identification relies on self-ascription. On this view, the best evidence that a person is of a particular race is that he or she says so. A fifth method of racial identification relies on cultural experience and assimilation. For example, two individuals, A and B, who would seem to fall into the identical racial class, Native American, according to the first method, would be categorized differently, depending on their cultural experiences. A speaks Navajo, lives on a Navajo reservation, knows much traditional Navajo lore, is a tribal leader, and represents Navajo interests to those outside of the group, but none of this is true of B, who does not think of himself as a Native American at all. According to this method, A is a Native American while B is not.

According to the most popular racial hierarchy, which is largely determined by whites and which places whites above blacks, Asians fall into a middle position, above blacks but below whites.

What has been called the principle of hypodescent—the principle that a person of mixed racial heritage must assume the racial identity of the lowest-ranking racial group of that heritage—has been thought to fall most heavily upon those who have some black heritage (even "one drop" of "black blood") because the black racial group occupies the lowest position on the social hierarchy of races. I do not wish to deny this.

However, there is an analogue of the "one-drop rule" for Asians. The social determination of who is Asian is largely a matter of looks. In the Plessy case for example, the court records show that Plessy did not look black, but it was pointed out that he had a great-grandparent who was black and so Plessy "really" was black and could not ride in the white railroad car. A person is often categorized as "really" Asian precisely because of looks.

What does this mean for the future? Most marriages of Japanese Americans are now to non-Japanese Americans, and it seems that this is one racial group that could achieve full melting in the melting pot. But, because Asian looks are so important, the offspring of such unions (and their offspring) who look Asian will be thought of by others as Asian—and melting will not have occurred. So, it seems that we have a group that is fully assimiliating into the mainstream. But, if looks continue to play the role that they have, full assimilation will be impossible.

Moreover, looks will do so in a remarkable way. Consider a group of people who have biracial backgrounds that include Caucasian and Asian elements. Imagine a range of looks, from "very Asian," say, to "not Asian at all." Imagine also that there is spectrum of self-identifications according to which the individuals in question will identify and think of themselves as Asians or whites. Now, from what has been said so far, there is no reason to think that looks will correlate with self-identifications. Yet looks are what others see and could be cues for others to identify someone as Asian or white. On this view, anyone with any discernable Asian features will be classified as an Asian.

Perhaps, in the future, an American will say (e.g., in answer to some inquiry based upon looks), "My great-great-grandfather came to this country from Japan" and will hear in response, "I thought you were Asian!" Perhaps, the concept of general American identity will be more inclusive than it now seems to be. This will require some "melting," but it is the Anglo-Saxon image—an image that has proven resistant to melting—that will have to melt so that general American identity will be more inclusive.

Part II
Art

6

From Melodrama to the Movies: The Tragic Mulatto as a Type Character

Freda Scott Giles

That is the uneffaceable curse of Cain . . . Of the blood that feeds my heart, one drop in eight is black . . . that one drop poisons all the flood . . . for I'm an unclean thing—forbidden by the laws.

—from *The Octoroon* by Dion Boucicault

You're nothing but wannabees; wanna be better than me.

—from *School Daze* by Spike Lee

"[H]e . . . was a complex, multilayered . . . character whose basic inner turmoil and unalterably alien presence could provide a strong focal point for any number of dramatic possibilities."[1] This description of Spock, the interplanetary tragic mulatto character created for the science fiction television series *Star Trek*, is an apt description of the stock mulatto character originally created for minstrelsy and melodrama[2] that has persisted through the entire epoch of American theatre history. Whether mulatto, octoroon, quadroon,[3] or other mixture of African-American and European-American genes, this child born of miscegenation has served as a readily identifiable symbol of racial conflict, alienation, and insurmountable struggle against an untenable position in American society. The mingling of colors and features made American apartheid that much more dif-

63

ficult to enforce and threatened the security offered by the fantasy of racial purity. The mulatto could be identified with and pitied as the victim of the miscegenation taboo while at the same time be feared as the despised other lurking within who had to be punished, either for trying to sneak into the white world as an imposter or for reminding the black world of the mark of the oppressor. The inexorable destruction that dramatic fate decreed, whether or not the character was drawn as deserving it, was viewed as a form of poetic justice. Only in very few exceptions, in the hands of either a white or a black playwright, could the mulatto be granted a happy ending.

The Nineteenth Century: The Pattern is Set

The tragic mulatto was usually depicted as female to amplify her vulnerability and impotence. In minstrelsy, where white men recreated black people in the images of their fantasies, she was personified as the "yaller gal." Unlike the dark mammy, she could be depicted as virtuous, and when courted romantically, she could indicate the sexual component of race relations without offending white audiences (the song, "The Yellow Rose of Texas" serves as one example):

> Considering whites' preference for light-skinned Negroes and the large number of mulattoes in America, minstrels' creation of the yellow girl for their romantic love songs is not surprising. . . .What is surprising is that there were no yellow men in minstrelsy.[4]

Even as a joke, an image of black male sexual potency would prove too threatening, but the mulatto woman became a staple minstrel character, and a number of white men became famous for their drag impersonations of her, even after the admission of women to their ranks.

The most widely known racially mixed characters on the nineteenth century stage were probably George and Eliza of *Uncle Tom's Cabin*,[5] followed by Zoe, the title character of *The Octoroon* (1859) by Dion Boucicault. The two plays illustrate the standard tragic mulatto formula with some variations that occurred in abolitionist dramas.[6]

Zoe follows the traditional pattern of the tragic mulatto created for the commercial stage that catered to the mores and prejudices of the white middle-class audience. For Boucicault, a master of the melodrama form, this also meant pleasing northern and southern whites. Despite the fact that Zoe's father, "the Judge," was a dissolute slaveowner who died leaving the plantation in a state of disarray and Zoe, who he was reputed to love, remained a slave, he was never criticized by the other characters, including Zoe, who accepted her status and despised her unfortunate "contamination." As was often the case, contact with either the black or white parent during the action of the play was kept minimal. Zoe's mother's absence was left unexplained, so the relationship between her parents could be effectively ignored. The Judge had died before the action of the play, leaving Zoe in the care of his loving and forgiving wife.

Much of the plot revolves around the efforts of the hero, the Judge's nephew, to save the plantation, and those of the villain, the overseer, to steal it. Zoe, as a valuable piece of property, was placed on the auction block; one of the major scenes of the play involves the bidding war over her, which the villain wins. Like most melodrama victims placed in jeopardy, Zoe is eventually saved; however, because she is not totally white, she and the Judge's nephew cannot realize their love for each other. Zoe commits suicide to clear the path for a worthy white wife for her lover. She is pitied for her suffering. Tears, the end result of melodrama catharsis,[7] are shed.

As with the minstrels before the 1850s, the actors who portrayed African Americans on the stage were whites pretending to be black (at least as far as the audience knew). There could be the element of pretense without danger and the acting out without consequence that permitted the audience to empathize with the black or mixed-race character without having to deal with the reality of an authentic African American being placed before them. Even an African-American Uncle Tom did not appear on mainstream commercial stages until the 1870s.

The George Aiken version of *Uncle Tom's Cabin* was first produced in 1852. Because it was based on Harriet Beecher Stowe's abolitionist novel, it varied a bit from the standard tragic mulatto formula. The noble, resourceful slave of mixed race was a staple of abolitionist literature. The closer the slave to Caucasian skin tone and features, the more cogent the case for freedom. This, combined with another major theme, the immorality of the separation of families, assisted the white audience in being more sympathetic with George and Eliza's efforts. George and Eliza, who do not seek to step outside the boundaries of race, except as a means of disguise during escape, but to live together within those boundaries as a free, intact family, are allowed to find safe haven in Canada. Uncle Tom serves as the tragic hero, while Eliza provides the "sensation scene," a spectacular visual effect, through her escape across an icy river, bearing her child in her arms.

A supporting character of mixed race, Cassy, former mistress of the villain Simon Legree, subtly indicates that sexual exploitation was a component of slavery, but the issue is never overtly explored. Among the slaves it is Cassy who speaks most freely to Legree and brings out whatever humanity is left in him. Nothing is said of her fate after the death of Legree.

During the nineteenth century there were few places where interracial marriages or children of mixed race were acknowledged and accepted,[8] though the fact that interracial relationships and children existed could not be denied. The commercial theatre attempted to present the character of mixed race without offending the white audience by reminding it where the character came from; if parents were mentioned at all, there was a white father and a black mother, who was herself usually presented as being of mixed race, and they were for the most part excluded from the action of the play. The child invariably served as a scapegoat, made to pay for the sins of the parents.

William Wells Brown sought to expose issues glossed over by white playwrights in his abolitionist melodrama, the first published by an African-American author in the United States, *The Escape, or A Leap to Freedom.*[9] Brown began giving public readings of his play in 1857, the year the Supreme Court handed down the Dred Scott decision. His mixed-raced protagonists, Glen and Melinda, are frequently endangered by their outspoken resistance to maltreatment by their owners. Secretly married, they must escape the threats of sexual coercion by Dr. Gaines, Melinda's owner, and the overt jealousy of Mrs. Gaines, who at one point threatens Melinda's life. Abolitionists assist them, but Glen and Melinda work actively to shape their own destiny. They contribute to their escape through resourcefulness and courage and fight for their freedom when necessary.

Another mulatto character in the play is Sampey, who is drawn from Brown's real-life experience. A house slave, Sampey is brutally punished for being mistaken for the master's son; although he does not escape, he assists Glen in his efforts. Brown often spoke of the abuse he suffered for being mistaken for a child of his owner, who was his white father's cousin.

The tragic mulatto entered the twentieth century with very few variations on the formula. A partial list of successful plays includes *Moorcraft* (1874) by Bronson Howard, in which the protagonist is led to believe he is a mulatto and is sold as a slave but is saved when he turns out to be all white; *The Nigger* (1909) by Edward Sheldon, in which a man who thought he was white is discovered to be of mixed race and watches his promising political career go down the drain; and *White Cargo* (1923) by Leon Gordon, in which the smoldering sensuality of the "half-caste" Tondelayo sends a white man to the depths of dissolution. Eugene O'Neill's experimentation with African-American characters, better known in *The Emperor Jones* (1920) and *All God's Chillun Got Wings* (1924), was also apparent in his earlier sea plays. One of the three characters in *Thirst* (1916) is a murderous mulatto sailor.

On the eve of the entrance of the United States into World War I, *Three Plays for a Negro Theatre*, an evening of one-acts by Ridgeley Torrence, opened on Broadway. One of the plays, *Granny Maumee*, was about a woman, very proud of her pure African blood, who comes close to killing the father of the mulatto child her daughter has brought home. Instead, her heart breaks and she dies. *Danse Calinda*, written by Torrence in 1919, tells in pantomime the story of two Creoles (of mixed French or Spanish, and African ancestry) who sneak into a Mardi Gras ball, are unmasked, and ejected. The critical success of Torrence's plays foreshadowed a "discovery" of the African American by white American playwrights, as part of their search for indigenous American material for the theatre. The new generation of emerging playwrights frequently experimented with the subject of race, but were seldom successful in depicting the "authentic" experiences they sought.

In 1931, DuBose and Dorothy Heyward, more widely known for the highly successful 1927 production of *Porgy* (Porgy's love, Bess, is not directly identified as mulatto, but shares much with the tragic mulatto), staged a less successful play, *Brass Ankle*. The plot depicts events leading to the death of a woman who passed for white, married a white man, but bore a "throwback" child who revealed her mixed African, Native American, and Caucasian racial heritage. To protect her other child, who is blond and blue-eyed, she leads her husband to believe she has had an affair with a black man; her enraged husband strangles her. The mixed-race character unmasked by the birth of a "throwback" to the "savage black" was another popular plot device for plays about mixed race. *The Pride of Race* by Michael H. Landmon (1916) and *White Man* (1936) by Samson Rapahelson followed similar story lines.

Julie, a featured character in the Jerome Kern–Oscar Hammerstein musical adaptation of Edna Ferber's novel, *Showboat* (1927), is also a typical tragic mulatto. Oscar Hammerstein's adaptation of Bizet's opera, *Carmen*, turned the gypsy Carmen into the tragic mulatto Carmen Jones (1943). Richard Rodgers and Hammerstein would later adapt characteristics of the tragic mulatto to the south seas setting of *South Pacific* (1949). E. Y. Harburg and Fred Zaidy created a variation on the character in the satiric *Finian's Rainbow* (1947) by having a white bigot magically transformed into a black man.

African-American Playwrights and the Tragic Mulatto

A substantive body of work by African-American playwrights was not developed until the post–World War I period known as the Harlem (or Negro) Renaissance, a period in which artists, writers, and persons of letters gained an unprecedented amount of recognition for their works, partially because of the great migration of African Americans to urban centers and the quickened tempo of the Civil Rights Movement that followed the Great War. In the theater, opportunities for the black performer increased, while black dramatists struggled to create a place for themselves. African-American actors had been performing on the mainstream commercial stage for some time, as well as in theaters in African-American communities, but there were few opportunities for African-American playwrights to find employment or publication outlets. A small but dedicated cadre of African-American playwrights formed to develop a body of work for a theatre of African-American experience, and the character of "mixed blood" figured in a number of plays.

Two plays written by Georgia Douglas Johnson during the 1920s, *Blue Blood* and *Blue-eyed Black Boy*, provide examples of themes explored by African-American playwrights of the period. In *Blue-eyed Black Boy*, Johnson attacks lynching through the story of an unseen mulatto character saved from a horrible injustice when his mother manages to get a coded message to his father, the governor of the state, who seeks to keep his patrimony secret. A significant number of plays from this period focus on the heroic efforts of mothers to shield their mixed-race children. In *Blue Blood*, a half-brother and sister are saved from an incestuous marriage when the mothers of the bride and groom discover that their children were fathered by the same prominent white citizen (one of the children was conceived by rape). The bride elopes with a dark-skinned man, and the truth is hidden from the groom to prevent him from seeking revenge against his biological father.

This plot device of potential incest between an unwitting brother and sister as a result of the clandestine relationship between a black and white parent was not new, and it was explored by white playwrights such as Paul Green, author of *White Dresses*, which was produced during the same period. In *Blue Blood* and *White Dresses*, the mother of the mixed-raced child plays a prominent role in the action of the play, and the white father is kept offstage. However, Johnson's play touches upon the ambivalence toward light skin and Caucasian features in the African-American community. "Blue veins" and Caucasian features heighten social status and are envied, even coveted, and the stratification and alienation that result in the community can prove highly detrimental. Zora Neale Hurston attacks this issue in *Color Struck* (1925), a play about a woman who hates her own color so much that she alienates the man who loves her, bears a mulatto child, and, in a jealous rage, allows the child to die. Lesser known dramas by African-American playwrights that feature tragic mulatto characters include *Holiday* by Ottie Graham (1923), in which a mulatto mother reveals herself to the brown-skinned daughter she deserted in order to pass for white,[10] and *Help Wanted* by Joseph S. Mitchell, in which the protagonist is forced to pass for white to obtain a decent job.[11]

The first nonmusical plays by African-American playwrights to reach Broadway did so during the 1920s. The first full-length play of this kind, *Appearances* by Garland Anderson, was produced in 1925 and featured a mulatto character, portrayed by a white actress, who, passing for white, is paid to falsely accuse the hero, a black bellhop, of rape. When her racial background is revealed, her credibility is destroyed. Mixed race was not a central issue, but the nature of the character reinforced a negative image, and the imposter was duly punished. The presentation of the mulatto as a devious miscreant was also a popular approach. In 1927 Burns Mantle selected *Black Boy* by white authors Frank Dazey and Jim Tully as one of the best plays of the 1926–1927 Broadway season. Paul Robeson portrayed a boxer who rejects his lover after finding out she is not actually a white woman.

African-American playwright Hughes Allison's *The Trial of Dr. Beck* was produced by the Federal Theatre Project in 1937. In this courtroom melodrama, Dr. Beck, a light-skinned mulatto, is accused of murdering his wealthy, dark-skinned wife to free himself for marriage to his light-skinned mistress. Dr. Beck is also the author of a treatise that urges superior dark men to marry only light-skinned women to lighten the race and make blacks more acceptable to whites. The real murderer turns out to be his wife's sister, whose hatred of her dark skin, combined with her love for Dr. Beck, drove her to desperation. The revival of this play at the New Federal Theater in the early 1980s engendered controversy and passionate discussion of the role of color in the stratification of the African-American community.

Langston Hughes was the first African-American playwright to have a play produced commercially in which the tragic mulatto was a central character. The producers of *Mulatto*, written in 1930 and staged in 1935, made alterations in the play that were objectionable to Hughes,[12] but a different dimension of the mulatto character was preserved. A comparison of *Mulatto* with another successful Broadway play, *In Abraham's Bosom*, for which Paul Green was awarded the Pulitzer Prize in 1927, shows some marked differences in conception and perception.

For the most part, Paul Green follows the tragic mulatto formula through the character of Abraham (the title is an ironic reference), who is desperate to fulfill a vague dream of doing great things for his people, but doomed by his black blood to fail at everything he tries. His tragic flaw lies in trying to reach beyond his racial limitations. The black community is depicted as being highly critical of his aspirations:

> De white blood in him comin' to de top. Dat make him want to climb up and be sump'in. Nigger gwine hol' him down dough. . . . Give a nigger a book and you might as well shoot him.[13]

Eventually Abraham confronts his white father, who has shown some sympathy for him but eventually brushes him off. Driven to madness by his inability to realize his dreams, Abraham ends up killing the white brother whose sadistic taunting he can no longer tolerate. Abraham flees into the turpentine-country forest where he will be hunted down and killed by a lynch mob.

A similar fate awaits Robert, the tragic mulatto of Hughes's play. In a fit of rage, he strangles his white father, but he shoots himself before the lynch mob can reach him. *Mulatto*, like *In Abraham's Bosom*, is set in the post–Civil War South. Hughes's goal, rather than to present the usual mulatto tragedy, is to protest the economic, social, and sexual exploitation of African Americans. Robert's mother, having long before accepted her position as housekeeper and concubine, manipulates Colonel Norwood, the plantation owner, as much as she can to benefit her children. She has gotten most of them off the plantation and shipped them North to be educated for professions the Colonel would not approve. Robert, home for summer vacation, "resenting his blood and circumstances of his birth,"[14] rebels against the racist social structure that denies him his right to equal treatment, just as he rebels against his father's denial of his birthright. He takes every opportunity to act against the system by refusing to submit to the customs of subservience the system dictates, antagonizing the white citizenry, and driving his father to a fatal confrontation. At the root of their estrangement is a vicious beating Norwood delivered to Robert as a child for calling him "father" in public. Robert is in conflict about his identity and is doomed, but not by his African-American blood; he is doomed by racism. His efforts to fight back fail because he fights alone. From this tragedy, his mother divines meaning, which she relates to the dead Colonel:

> White mens and colored womens and little bastard chilluns—that's de old way of de South—but it's ending now. Three of your yellow brothers yo' father had by Aunt Sallie Deal—what had to come and do your laundry to make her livin—you got colored relatives all over this country. Them de ways o' de South. . . .[15]

The next major treatment of the tragic mulatto by an African-American playwright came nearly thirty years later, in *The Slave* (1964) by Amiri Baraka (LeRoi Jones), who called this play the last in which he tried to talk with blacks and whites—afterward he created theater exclusively for black audiences.[16] The unseen presence of the children of an African-American father and Caucasian

mother and the suspense concerning their fate dominate the action
of the play. The premise of the action is that a racial war has broken out, and Walker Vessels, a black revolutionary leader, has crossed
enemy lines to confront his former wife, Grace, and claim their
daughters. The confrontation turns into a fight to the death with
Grace's present husband, as shells explode close to the crumbling
house. A wall collapses on Grace, and as she dies, Walker tells her
he has killed the children; throughout they have remained unseen
and ominously silent. Just after Walker leaves, the cry of a child is
heard. The ambiguity of the children's fate reflects the unresolved
emotions Walker has toward them, which bind him as a slave to his
past. In general, the theater of black nationalism that emerged during the 1960s viewed the search for identity as movement away
from any identifications with whites or their institutions.

In 1992 Lisa Jones, one of Baraka's daughters from his first,
interracial marriage, wrote *Combination Skin*, a play that incisive-
ly examines the ambiguity of the position of the mixed-race child
from the child's point of view. Jones combines realism with surre-
alism to show several scenes from the life of a young woman of
mixed parentage. In one scene, the woman becomes a reluctant
contestant on a game show, a kind of wheel of fortune where mulattoes attempt to select their fates. In a climactic scene, the woman desperately seeks affection or some form of affirmation of her
existence from her African-American father, a famous jazz musician. She has done everything in her power to renounce the Caucasian portion of her background and to devote herself to him to no
avail; he remains indifferent. The mixed-race child is denied the
right to claim both heritages and is forced to choose; even then,
she is not guaranteed acceptance of her choice.

Adrienne Kennedy carried the alienation of the tragic mulatto
across the surreal, symbolic, suppressed dreamscape of the sub-
conscious in *Funnyhouse of a Negro* (1964), *The Owl Answers* (1965),
A Rat's Mass (1967), and *A Beast's Story* (1969). Each play reveals a fragmented identity searching for wholeness. In *Funnyhouse
of a Negro*, Negro-Sarah, child of a black father and a white, or
very light black, mother, faces herselves as the Duchess of Haps-
burg, Queen Victoria Regina, Jesus, and Patrice Lumumba. In *The
Owl Answers*, SHE, who is CLARA PASSMORE (a surname that
suggests the idea of passing for white or disguising a part of the
self), who is the VIRGIN MARY, who is the BASTARD, who is
the OWL, confronts herself through BASTARD'S BLACK MOTH-

ER, who is the REVEREND's WIFE, who is ANNE BOLEYN; GODDAM FATHER, who is the RICHEST WHITE MAN IN THE TOWN, who is the DEAD WHITE FATHER, who is REVEREND PASSMORE; THE WHITE BIRD, who is REVEREND PASSMORE'S CANARY, who is GOD'S DOVE; THE NEGRO MAN; and SHAKESPEARE/CHAUCER/WILLIAM THE CONQUEROR.

Racial, religious, and cultural symbols mixed with personal and psychological symbols conflict and recur in these plays. The central character is a displaced person rendered dysfunctional by the unresolved fragmentation of her identity. Negro-Sarah is about to commit suicide and Clara Passmore is traveling to an unknown destination on a subway car. Images of the owl, which may portend death or an ill-omened life, kinky hair and silky hair, and birds, which may be messengers, are among those seen again and again. The symbolism of the images allows the idea of the tragic mulatto to be expanded to a crisis of identity for any African American seeking to reconcile disparate cultural and psychological identifications in a hostile environment. Because every American lives within a not-always compatible combination of cultures as well as racial identities (it has been estimated that 70 to 90 percent of European Americans have some percentage of black ancestry and 80 percent of black Americans have some white ancestry),[17] nearly everyone in the United States is potentially a tragic mulatto.

The first African-American playwright to be awarded the Pulitzer Prize, Charles Gordone, included a form of the tragic mulatto character in *No Place to Be Somebody* (1969). Gabe Gabriel, who frames the thematic and philosophic themes of the play, identifies himself as an African American, but, because of his near-white appearance, has trouble convincing others that he is black enough. He is often placed in the position of having to prove his blackness. Gabe is forced to kill his best friend, a dark man who has caught the "Charlie fever" and seeks to out-oppress the oppressor. Gabe is seen in symbolic mourning at the end of the play, but his fate is left open:

> I will mourn the passing . . . of a people dying into a new life. A people whose identity could only be measured by the struggle, the dehumanization, the degradation they suffered. . . .[18]

The tragic mulatto is still of interest on the stage, though in recent years has been more frequently seen in the more powerful mass medium, film. A recently produced play by African-American play-wright Eugene Lee, *East Texas Hot Links* (1994) is an explosive drama in which the hidden motivation for horrific racial violence is revealed to be the unwitting racially mixed offspring of a Ku Klux Klan member.[19]

Variations on the Tragic Mulatto in Film and Television

Film historian Donald Bogle has traced the tragic mulatto back to the silent film era in his book, *Toms, Coons, Mulattoes, Mammies, and Bucks*. A surprisingly long list of films are concerned with this character, in a number of permutations.

The most widely known modern treatment of the standard tragic mulatto formula in film is most likely the 1934 production of *Imitation of Life* and its 1959 remake. The very light daughter of a darker mother, desperately dissatisfied and unfulfilled, attempts to pass for white. To do so, she must break all ties with her mother, which breaks her mother's heart. She is returned to the black community at her mother's funeral, distraught with remorse. Her future fate is left unknown. It should be noted that in the 1934 film, Fredi Washington, an African-American actress, portrayed the tragic mulatto character. Because she was identified as black, any suggestion of possible miscegenation was avoided.[20] Susan Kohner, a white actress, portrayed the character in the remake and was allowed to have a white boyfriend, who was allowed to slap her around when he found out about her racial background. The convention of reserving "interracial" sexual contact with whites for white actors only pretending to be black remained stable in Hollywood films until very recent years.

Explorations of the tragic mulatto character can be found in *Hallelujah* (1929), *Pinky* (1949), and *Kings Go Forth* (1958). The most successful, and, in its time, controversial of these films was *Pinky*. The title character was portrayed by Jeanne Crain, who played a nurse who returns to the South after passing for white in the North. Persuaded by her black grandmother (Ethel Waters) and a white mentor (Ethel Barrymore) to stay on and help her people, she overcomes white opposition and opens a school for black nurses. The price she must pay for rediscovery of her identity is the loss of her relationship with her Northern fiance, a white doctor.

Before Spike Lee, the main black filmmaker to explore the issue was Oscar Micheux in his 1937 feature, *God's Stepchildren*, in which a mulatto woman was ultimately punished for passing for white. Its formulaic treatment was generally considered outdated and reactionary by the black audience. Mixed race was either a direct or indirect issue in the 1960s and 1970s films *Mandingo, Cinderella Liberty, Guess Who's Coming to Dinner,* and *The Landlord.*

The retrogression of black–white relations during the 1980s precipitated a significant resurgence of interest in the mulatto character. In *Purple Rain* (1984) and *Under the Cherry Moon* (1986), the rock star formerly known as Prince placed the character in a musical context. *The Cotton Club* (1984), *The Brother from Another Planet* (1984), and even the remake of *Brewster's Millions* starring Richard Pryor (1985) dealt with some facet of the character.

African-American auteur Spike Lee gave two different insights into the tragic mulatto in *School Daze* (1987) and *Jungle Fever* (1991). *School Daze* looked frankly into the destructive impact of color consciousness on the African-American community by presenting the microcosmic world of a black college campus. A confrontation between dark-skinned women, who are called "jiggerboos," and light-skinned women, called wannabees, is set as a musical number on a symbolic battle ground, the beauty parlor. One of the major plot threads involves the role of color consciousness in twisting the relationships of the light-skinned sorority sisters and fraternity brothers. In *Jungle Fever*, the protagonist, Flipper, enters into an affair with his Italian-American secretary. The effect on his marriage is devastating, not only because of his adultery, but also for the emotional toll it takes on his racially mixed wife, who has been engaged in a lifelong struggle with her own identity.

For eleven television seasons (1975–1985), George Jefferson, African-American father-in-law of racially mixed Jenny, referred to her and her brother as "zebras" and mercilessly taunted Jenny's parents, the Willises, a happily married white father and black mother. Though its goal was to satirize bigotry, *The Jeffersons*, a spinoff of *All in the Family* which enjoyed immense popularity for a time, rendered racial antagonism more palatable by casting the most bigoted character as black.

One subcategory of the tragic mulatto character is the "unwitting mulatto," who must come to grips with the discovery of a mixed heritage. *Lost Boundaries* (1949), the seminal film in this category, tells the story of a mulatto couple who have hidden their mixed heritage from their children. When the children find out, extreme identity crises ensue. In the Civil War melodrama *Band of Angels* (1957), Yvonne de Carlo is sold into slavery after learning of her racial past, but is eventually rescued by Clark Gable. Most recently, *Made in America* (1993) attempted to explore this issue comedically on the premise that the character played by Whoopi Goldberg may have conceived her daughter through artificial insemination by the character played by Ted Danson. The daughter is tormented by her desire for a father figure and tries to make one out of the reluctant sperm donor. Because this is a comedy, all ends happily.

An offshoot of the unwitting mulatto is the "suspected" mulatto, as illustrated in the films *Raintree County* and *Island in the Sun*, in which white characters are placed in crisis because it is possible they have African-American blood in their backgrounds.

The fear of exposure, especially through the potential birth of a "throwback" child, figures prominently in *Night of the Quarter Moon* (1959) and *I Passed for White* (1960). In both films, a woman passing for white (in each case portrayed by a Caucasian actress) suffers temporary or permanent estrangement from her white husband when the inevitable truth is revealed.

The history of *Birth of a Nation* (1915) as both a leap forward in filmmaking and a paean to the Ku Klux Klan is well known. In this film, D. W. Griffith portrayed the mulatto as a brute, another potential rapist of white women. The opposite of this character might be described as the militant mulatto, the male mulatto figure who is aggressively black. The leading character in the 1960s exploitation film, *Trick Baby*, looks white (and was portrayed by a white actor), but uses his looks against whites for the benefit of blacks. In *Buck and the Preacher* (1972), Harry Belafonte portrayed a man of mixed race who lived at the margin of the law, who became a hero to the black settlers he helped, and who, in his past, had extracted a terrible revenge on his brutal white father.

When portrayed by a dark-skinned black actor, the racially mixed character presents little or no ambivalence about his heritage. In the television miniseries based on Alex Haley's *Roots* (1977–1979), Chicken George, son of a slave and a plantation owner, portrayed by Ben Vereen and Avon Long, became a pillar of the black community. (In *Queen*, another Haley family saga made into a miniseries, the mixed-race heroine suffered more of the mulatto angst.) In a later film, *Carbon Copy* (1981), Denzel Washington portrayed a mulatto who sought out his white father. A bond was formed, but it was not Washington's character who suffered the tragic mulatto's fate—it was his white father who lost his career and status in the community when the relationship became known. A serious treatment of this loss was seen in the 1964 film, *One Potato, Two Potato*, which showed an intact, happy mixed family with a black father and white mother; the couple were forced to yield custody of the woman's white child from a previous marriage to the child's white father.

Another version of the tragic mulatto character might be called the metaphoric mulatto, where black and white are internally linked some way other than by birth. In *Black Like Me* (1964), based on a true story, a white man travels through the South made up as a black man to expose the realities of racism. A much less serious effort, *A Change of Mind* (1969), explores the ramifications when a white man's brain is placed in a black man's body. *Watermelon Man* (1970) starred Godfrey Cambridge, a black man, in a satire in which a white man suddenly, inexplicably, is turned black. Again, the 1980s witnessed a return to this form of exploration of racial conflict. In *Soul Man*, a white college freshman disguises himself as an African American to get a scholarship. In *Heart Condition*, a murdered black man's heart is transplanted into a white man's body, and a psychic bond is formed that leads the white man to capture the murderer. The usual premise is that the white man is bigoted until he learns what it is like to be black.

The Submerged Other

Toni Morrison, in her collection of essays on the effect of the African-American presence on the Euro-American literary imagination, lists "common linguistic strategies employed in fiction to engage the serious consequences of blacks." Economy of stereotype and metonymic displacement (color and physical trait coding) are included on this list, as well as fetishization:

> This is especially useful in evoking erotic fears or desires and establishing fixed and major difference where difference does not exist or is minimal. Blood, for example, is a pervasive fetish: black blood, white blood, the purity of blood; the purity of white female sexuality, the pollution of African blood and sex. Fetishization is a strategy often used to assert the categorical absolutism of civilization and savagery.[21]

Morrison's dissection of the semiotics of Euro-American literature could also be applied to American drama and theatre. The tragic
mulatto is a complex symbol read as the submerged other that cannot be kept completely hidden, the object of attraction and repulsion that cannot be exorcised, the taboo that has been breached,
resulting in a divided consciousness. In the hands of the white playwright, the other is bestial sensuality, the enemy of civilization. In
the hands of the black playwright, the other is the continual reminder of what in this country connotes power and what connotes
powerlessness.

The perceived race of the actor playing the character adds another layer of meaning, and a set of conventions was developed
concerning the race of the actor to allay the fears of the predom-
inately white audience. An anecdote related by Lena Horne that
describes how she was cast as Julie in the 1951 remake of the filmed
version of *Showboat* only to lose the role (and her specially blended make-up) to Ava Gardner serves as one example.[22] Despite the
fact that interracial relationships are shown more frequently in the
mass media, a shock value is still attached to them. Even in the
land of MTV, there was an outcry when Madonna embraced a se-
pia Christ figure in her "Like a Prayer" video.

The mulatto character has not escaped being cast as a pariah, a
marginalized person. Seldom is the character shown within an intact, two-parent family. Seldom is the character permitted a choice
or merger of identities. Identity is determined by appearance. Sig-
mund Freud's observation that anatomy is destiny holds very strongly
when applied to racial relationships. In most commercial theatre
and film, the mulatto character is caught attempting to escape the
dark (or more recently, the white) "other," which cannot be escaped.
The tragic flaw, the element within that combines with fate as a
harbinger of doom is not character, but blood. The consciousness
remains ever divided, because the blood is always at war. In the
ebb and flow of attitudes toward race and issues of race, in the
evolution of racial imagery, the view of the mixed-race character
appears to have remained remarkably constant. This seems most
ironic in a nation that is probably more racially mixed, under the
traditional definition of race, than any other in the world.

7

The Theater of Identity: (Multi-)Race and Representation of Eurasians and Afroasians

Teresa Kay Williams

As a person who is more often than not racially and culturally misidentified, I acquired a heightened awareness of racial appearance or phenotype and, thus, learned to question the rigidity of racial membership rules and their application to one's social roles and identity at an early age. The Japanese and U.S. media, respectively, became the sites where I could explore the creation and re-creation of race,[1] and also apply visions and names for the racial and phenotypical contradictions that I saw and felt as a biracial, bicultural, bilingual, and binational person. Nowhere else is one's phenotype so powerfully presented as in the entertainment industry in which "looks" are one's commodified asset. Thus, in this chapter, I shall explore racial images and representations[2] of biracial[3] Eurasians and Afroasians in the American entertainment media in which the articulation and presentation of self and group identity have raised questions of inclusion and exclusion by way of racial appropriateness and phenotypical acceptability. My own biracial, binational Japanese-European-American experiences serve as the backdrop of my analytical thinking. Finally, I deconstruct the notion that races are rigid, unequal, and oppositional and argue that biracial identity can only be understood as structurally fluid, complex, dynamic, and ever-transforming.[4]

Misidentification, Affirmation, and Identity

Affirmation of self and group identity and assertion of one's life experiences are political acts in themselves. Therefore, I respect and honor a person's expression of a monoethnic identity, even though the imprint of "biracial" is often written on the face and spelled out in his or her consciousness. Although my identification with a monoethnically identified person on the basis of our multiple racial and cultural ancestries is often censored or silenced, I accept the personal and political importance of one's articulated identity.[5] So many people I have known and loved as my multiethnic heroes in this society are most often monoracially and monoculturally identified[6] by reactionaries *and* progressives alike, who have espoused or internalized the racist invention of "race" and uncritically adopted America's rule of hypodescent or the "one-drop rule."[7]

I learned at a very early age that although I may share phenotypical ambiguity or multicultural expressions with the biracially identified like *haafu*, Amerasians, Eurasians, Afroasians, mestizos, mulattos, metis, etc.,[8] I should never assume he or she may share my multiethnic identity—especially in the case of African ancestry. At age eight when I innocently asked an African-American boy why his family did not look "black," although everyone else called them "black," my embarrassed mother scolded me and said, *"Soo yuu koto wa shitsurei dakara kuchi ni shite wa ikemasen!"* (Those kinds of topics are impolite so you mustn't speak of them!) Even my Japanese mother, who had only lived in the United States for four years, could articulate the "one-drop rule" as if it were a simple matter of mathematical logic. From that moment on, I explicitly understood that I was never to question people who possessed any amount of "black blood" about their racial history and identity. What my little eight-year-old self, still somewhat untainted by racial taboos, saw and felt went against America's racial contract. Although consciously silencing myself on matters of race, I continued to search for words that expressed what I saw, heard, and felt. It was not a colonial fascination with the African-American "Other" that drove me to defy America's long-held racial contract, but rather it was the search for my own social location in American society that had denied my hybridity. Understanding black and brown America's cultural, racial, and phenotypical multiplicity seemed to hold the key to my own self-expression and identity.

My father is European American, the son of a coalminer from

Beckley, West Virginia. My mother is Japanese, the daughter of a successful entrepreneur from Tokyo, Japan. My Japanese and European American grandfathers were both hard-working and self-sacrificing. My Japanese and European-American grandmothers were loving and caring child-bearers, dedicated housewives, supporters of their husbands' work, and the lifeline of the Suzuki and Williams families, respectively. My father's family was poor, (white) American, and Christian, whereas my mother's family was wealthy, Japanese, and polytheistic. I grew up during the mid-1960s, 1970s, and early 1980s in Japan—a nation that has long prided itself for its so-called monoethnic uniformity and harmony. Many Japanologists have made reference to the famous proverb "Hammer down the nail that sticks out" as summing up Japanese society. I grew accustomed to standing out as a *gaijin* (foreigner) and *haafu* (half) among the Japanese. Being the nail that sticks out had its rewards and punishments. I enjoyed special treatment, but experienced loneliness because I could not fully belong regardless of my partial Japanese lineage and full cultural comprehension. Had I been a visitor to Japan, I would have thoroughly enjoyed being pampered, but being a resident who had no plans of leaving my motherland, I longed to be fully accepted as a legitimate member of Japanese society. In a self-proclaimed, male-dominated, male-centered, patriarchal society infused and overcome with Western ideology, perhaps I was seen as less threatening than my brother as long as I played the roles assigned to little girls and young women in Japan: to be a cute, petite, and silent *burriko*.

I was born in Sacramento, California, one year before the 1964 Tokyo Olympics, a time when Japan was still socially and economically recovering from a devastating World War. My parents met and fell in love after the seven-year U.S. military occupation had ended during the Korean War. In the early 1960s when my parents married against my Japanese grandfather's wishes, my Japanese relatives had just begun enjoying the fruits of their labor from rebuilding the family business, the *Waraku* Corporation Inc. (which literally means "Harmony and Comfort"). My grandfather's pride and joy, *Waraku*, had burned to the ground during the Tokyo bombings that killed millions of Japanese civilians and left the capital city an urban wasteland or *yake-nohara*. At about this same time, the Japanese media had become fascinated with thousands of "Amerasian" children being born to U.S. servicemen and Japanese women and began a love affair with them—especially those who were Japanese and

European American or Eurasians—while the society at large assigned them a pariah status.[9] A *Konketsu buumu* (Mixed-Blood Boom) had swept Japanese popular culture with the likes of Afroasian blues singer, Michi Aoyama, and Eurasian singer, Linda Yamamoto and the group, "The Golden Half," in which five Eurasian women bilingually sang American, Caribbean, and Japanese remakes.[10] The Japanese media was filled with Eurasian singers, models, and actors with whom I could identify; they too were either placed on pedestals of hybrid vigor or deemed perpetual outsiders doomed to sad, unfulfilled, in-between lives of mixed-bloodedness, even though like myself, the *haafu* were cultural insiders. And thus, my life-long love–hate relationship began with my motherland, which at once adored and despised my dual realities. The Japanese and European-American "mixed-blood" represented this love-hate pendulum that Japan had been swinging back and forth on the West since the era of the 1868 Meiji Restoration. Certainly as products of their environment, my Japanese relatives sometimes responded to my mother, my father, my brother, and myself in this love–hate fashion. However, they were the ones who often protected, loved, and nurtured my interracial family when Japanese society shunned us. When Japanese children would tease me and question my mother's moral character for having married a *gaijin*, my *Obaachama* (grandmother) would sit me on her lap, warmly hold me, and softly sing, *"Aoi me no Oningyo"* (Blue-eyed Doll)—about a blue-eyed doll left behind during the prewar years, crying tears of sadness and longing to return to her American homeland. My *Obaachama* was often the only one who understood the depth of my alienation.

My relationship with my European-American family has always been warm and loving, yet geographically distant. Because Japanese society clearly let it be known that I could never be a true Japanese, I cultivated an "American" identity—at times refusing to admit I even spoke or understood Japanese. I longed to share in the realities of *The Brady Bunch, Bewitched,*[11] and other American sitcoms that I grew up watching in dubbed Japanese. However, on my third visit to West Virginia with my European-American relatives at age ten, I learned that poverty, alcoholism, born-again Christianity, and despair filled their hard-working, coal-stained lives. Many of the stereotypical, fictional images I had formulated in my mind often meshed with reality. Most of my West Virginian white peers spoke funny English and listened to lively music called "country" and "hillbilly." Winters were brutally cold and summers uncomfortably humid, yet the rural beauty of Appalachia and the kindness of the locals could momentarily soothe any unhappiness caused by worldly temptations.

I soon realized that although my European-American relatives possess racial privilege to which I was not fully privy, my father's humble but stable military career allowed for his family's middle-class status to concretize. Unlike my European-American relatives, my blended Japanese and European American family enjoyed class privilege. As "white people" in America, my relatives certainly have accepted supremacist notions of whiteness, yet many of them have been considered "poor white trash" and excluded by the very social system they have embraced as their own. In their social reality, the racial lines of demarcation between black and white are rigid, clear, and pure. When one of my cousins ardently put forth that she "could never marry a Puerto Rican" because Puerto Ricans are really "black people in disguise," I asked her what she thought about my father marrying my mother. As my cousin tried to clarify why my family was not "truly" an interracial one, my other cousins joined in to help her explain that unless one fit into the black–white realm of interraciality, then it did not actually count. Although my interracial family and biracial personhood were never totally absent in their eyes, they found my family and me acceptable—that is, "almost white." Over the years, I have become more intimate with my European-American relatives in ways I have always been with my Japanese relatives. I have begun to share meaningful family moments with them and have come to appreciate their difficult lives as poor, working-class European-Americans. I do not fault them for their acceptance of white racism just as I do not fault my Japanese relatives for their notions of superiority. In many ways, they can only deal with my biraciality as tolerable (perhaps even desirable) if they view it as an embodiment of two "races" they deem genetically and phenotypically close and socially acceptable. Their solution for understanding my biraciality has been to attribute the best-of-both-worlds explanation. Across the globe, both sets of my relatives have internalized and perpetuated the United States's unequal, hegemonic, binary black–white schism and have placed me in an acceptable racial location within it.

As a Japanese–European American, these are the paradoxes and contradictions within myself, within my families, and within my homelands I must synthesize and integrate into the construction of my personal and political identities. As more and more interracial families emerge and biracial offspring come of age and demand their rightful place in American society, we hear the old oppositional and binary race relations paradigms often being rearticulated because they are familiar, comfortable, and identifiable. Despite the rhetoric of inclusion and multiplicity, the larger trend of the multiracial movement has been anchored in (single) identity politics—especially among those who advocate a multiracial census category. Many biracial individuals have been unable to understand that the denial and reduction of multiplicity are not limited to the realm of the racial. Many have not critically interrogated the systems of stratification as they continue to measure their likeness to the people who run these systems. As biracial people fight for their freedom of expression in the racial and sexual arenas, they must simultaneously reject these coexisting hierarchies. If biracials are affirming biraciality to escape a part of their heritage that is identified as the devalued one, or to draw a sexual parallel, if bisexuals are claiming bisexuality to hide gay and lesbian sexuality, they are in fact destructively rejecting themselves and contributing to the perpetuation of oppressive systems of stratification. My challenge as a Japanese–European-American woman is to love and affirm the totality of my overlapping, intersecting, and multiple selves without demeaning or hating others. For this to be actualized and perfected, this existing system must cease to exist.

Theater of Identity

Theater is often described as the suspension of reality. However, sociologist Erving Goffman has provided a dramaturgical analysis in which he compared everyday life to the theater setting.[12] As the saying goes, "All the world's a stage and all men and women merely players." Within this framework, people play a variety of roles, and foster particular impressions, while concealing others and staging their social encounters. Actors on the stage of life participate in the manipulation and manufacturing of their "selves." For phenotypically ambiguous (and therefore racially ambiguous) biracial people, certain settings in which their racial codes cannot be read or broken can suspend their racial and ethnic realities and effect unpredictable interactional outcomes. The presentation of their outward racial selves therefore is not something biracial people necessarily manipulate, but rather something that is viewed by and responded to contextually by their audiences. Sociologists Michael Omi and Howard Winant explain that "One of the first things we notice about people when we meet them (along with their sex) is their race. We utilize race to provide clues about who a person is. The fact is made painfully obvious when we encounter someone whom we cannot conveniently racially categorize—someone who is, for example, racially 'mixed.'"[13] They go on to state, "Such an encounter becomes a source of discomfort and momentarily a crisis of racial meaning." Therefore, one's phenotype becomes an important clue as to how one is to be racially responded to and socially placed. Although Eurasians and Afroasians possess a variety of phenotypes and make an array of complex identity choices within their structural limitations, racial images that uphold the binary either/or racial system and reinforce the social–psychological underpinnings about race, color, sex, and race-mixing in America are the ones powerfully represented in the mass media and entertainment field.

Eurasians

In 1990, the theater world became the battleground for Asian Americans, mixed-race Amerasians, and the white producers and directors when a European actor was cast to play the Eurasian character in the musical, *Miss Saigon*. The *Saigon* controversy of casting a Welsh actor (with prosthetics to make his eyes appear Asian) in the role of a Eurasian pimp sparked Asian-American protest. Los Angeles School Board member Warren Furutani publicly expressed his disapproval of casting a white actor for an "Asian" role. He pointed out that the role of the Engineer is an Asian one and attacked Hollywood for historically using the Eurasian as a "buffer zone."[14] Conservative columnist, George Will, on the other hand, argued that the role of Engineer is not an Asian one.[15] Both Eurasian actresses, Mari Sunaida and Amy Hill, whose respective one-woman shows, *Hybrid Vigor* and *Besides Myself,* are about the trials and tribulations of being Japanese and European-American in both homelands, supported the Asian-American position, whereas Afroasian playwright Velina Houston said,

. . . the "Saigon" situation . . . is not either/or (that is to say, white or Asian). It is difficult for me to listen to arguments about something being red or blue, when that something is actually violet. The role of the Engineer is neither Caucasian nor Asian; it is Eurasian— half Caucasian and half Asian. . . . It's sadly ironic that such a musical has led to a public battle about race—a battle where both sides ignore the fact that the character in question is biracial.[16]

In the end, all were losers because representatives from each camp were arguing over roles that demean, devalue, and objectify women and men of Asian descent.

The *Miss Saigon* controversy notwithstanding, Hollywood has tended to cast Asians in Eurasian roles and Eurasians in Asian ones. By casting Eurasians as Asian, Hollywood is proclaiming that the "more Caucasian-looking Asian" is the more acceptable one, while casting "unmixed" Asians in Eurasian roles states that Eurasians are perceived as "a kind of Asian." Like the silver screen's love affair with the Vietnam war, several prime-time television shows (including a sitcom called *Emergency Room*) capitalized on the Vietnamese–Amerasian in search of the American father or conversely the American father in search of his Amerasian child. In most of these comedic and dramatic portrayals of Vietnamese–Amerasians, monoracial Asian-American actors were cast to play the Amerasian parts. In either case of Eurasians playing Asian roles or Asians being cast as Eurasians, the rule of hypodescent has been assigned, maintaining a racial order in which white and Asian, as manifested in these phenotypical media representations, are treated as clearly separate groups in which their racial blending has been denied.

Many of the leading "Asian-American" actors and actresses (or those who are "passing" as Asian) are allegedly "Eurasian" or those who possess various "blood quantities" of European and Asian ancestries: Russell Wong from *New Jack City*, John Lone from *The Last Emperor*, Brandon Lee from *Rapid Fire*, Susan Pai from *Little Trouble in Big China*, Lindsey Price from *All My Children*, Ariane Mitsuye Koisumi in *The Year of the Dragon*, and both leading male and female actors in *China Cry*. A few alleged "Eurasians" have played strictly "nonracial" or "white" roles, as well as projected a non-racial or "white" public persona: Meg Tilly, Phoebe Cates, Keanu Reeves, and the new Superman, Dean Cain, who was characterized as "vaguely ethnic" in one of the reviews of the new ABC series,

Lois and Clark. Then, there are those who have been cast in a variety of ethnic roles, ranging from Latino to Eskimo to European American (e.g., Lou Diamond Phillips from *La Bamba* and Jennifer Tilly in *Made in America*).

Eurasian characters are often depicted by monoracial actors because ambiguity and intermediacy strongly defy the fixed either/ or social order on which the entertainment community thrives. The complexities of multiple racial identities cannot be imaginatively portrayed in a world where caricatures define reality. Most portrayals of Eurasians have been one-dimensional stereotypes wrought with racial, sexual myths about their parent groups. Rarely do Eurasians play themselves—reminiscent of a time when whites played African-American, Native American, Asian, Chicano, and Latino characters.

In *Dragon: The Bruce Lee Story* (1993) the different babies and young boys who depicted Bruce Lee's Eurasian son, Brandon, phenotypically switched back and forth from appearing fully Caucasian at one age to completely Asian at another. By the end of the movie, Brandon Lee was played by a more "Eurasian-looking" actor. The real-life Brandon Lee phenotypically leans toward appearing more European American, although unlike other Eurasian stars, his Asian ancestry was never publically concealed or minimized. The movie's alternating phenotypical depictions of Brandon Lee initially seemed bothersome. As I thought of my own phenotypical changes not only through the natural course of my lifetime (as a baby, a toddler, preadolescent, teenager, etc.) but also depending upon the way I wear my hair or apply make-up, I realized that it is not uncommon for biracials, to shift their phenotypical appearances in which their racial coding could be affected and thus, their social status shifted from one race to another. For example, through natural or artificial processes, people lose their youthful looks, their skin complexion tans or loses a tan, their hair color lightens, darkens, straightens, and so on. These slight changes in phenotype can substantially alter a biracial person's appearance, which is often already racially ambiguous.

A popular theme in "forbidden" romance films is that grandchildren become the symbol of parents' forgiveness of their child's decision to cross taboo barriers in marriage. In *Dragon,* Bruce Lee's white mother-in-law finally accepts her daughter's marriage to a Chinese American when their Eurasian son is born. Likewise, in *Come See the Paradise* (1990), the Eurasian granddaughter becomes the source of reunification for Lily Kawamura (Tamlyn Tomita) and her *issei* (first-generation) parents who disowned her for marrying Jack McGurn (Dennis Quaid), an Irish-American labor organizer.

Because of community scrutiny and input, the casting of the Japanese and the Eurasian characters in Alan Parker's *Come See the Paradise* was more sensitively handled than in Parker's previous film, *Mississippi Burning*. All the actresses who played Lily's and Jack's biracial daughter throughout the different ages of her childhood were Eurasian. The actress who played the Eurasian girl during her preadolescent period spoke Japanese with native command, unlike some of the awkward Japanese spoken by many of the monoracial Asian-American actors and actresses. The heightening racism against people of Japanese ancestry and adherence to the one-drop rule as it applied to biracial persons of Japanese ancestry, which ultimately led to their unjust imprisonment during World War II, is captured in a scene in which Quaid's character takes his biracial daughter to visit Santa Claus at a toy store during December 1941. When the Eurasian girl goes to sit on Santa's lap, he rejects her because she is a "Jap." Racist hysteria blinds Santa so that he cannot see her white father and therefore ignores her European ancestry.

Map of the Human Heart (1993) is a story about two biracial individuals with similar genetic make-up and similar identity struggles as "half-breeds." Yet, their different phenotypical appearances place them in oppositional social locations within the Euro-North American colonial context. The movie is not really about "Eurasians," yet it is interesting to note that a monoracial Asian American, Jason Scott Lee, was cast to play the biracial Eskimo–European man, Avik, who can *not* physically pass for white. A monoracial white European woman was cast to play the role of the biracial Native American Indian and French metis, Albertine. They meet in a Canadian orphanage in the 1930s. Albertine, unlike Avik, can phenotypically pass for white. Longing to see her white father, she sings a French song that states, "He's a half-breed man. He leaves his wife searching for gold. He dies. But they will love one another in heaven." Avik asks her if it is a happy song. Albertine answers, "Yes, because they meet in heaven."

Avik and Albertine quickly learn the social significance of their biraciality and phenotypical appearances. As long as Albertine can conceal her non-European ancestry, she can have full access to white privilege. She is then forcibly taken from the orphanage to be "bred" and made to lead the life of a white woman. When Avik meets Albertine again in the 1940s, she tells him, "I'm not that half-breed girl anymore." Avik and the white man, who had assisted Avik's entry into the white world as his father figure, compete for Albertine. Although Albertine marries the white man, who provides her with material comfort and status, it is Avik whom she loves and bonds to emotionally and sexually.

Both biracial characters are played by monoracial people, rather than Eurasians or other biracial individuals who may have fit the descriptions and phenotypical realities of the characters. Certainly, a Eurasian's appearance and identity can be completely Asian or completely European. The phenotypical outcome of any offspring does not always match its genotypical make-up. Cultural affinity toward one group or the other could develop based upon a variety of social and environmental factors. Moreover, a Eurasian individual can possess every intermediate look and identity possible. The two characters in *Map* represent opposite ends of the social, cultural, racial, and phenotypical continuum of biraciality. Perhaps, the same story could have been told with actual biracial Eurasian or metis actors whose phenotypes varied.

Regardless of their racial appearance and intermediate phenotypical variety, biracial individuals are affected deeply by the same identity questions with which Avik and Albertine grappled. They are both handsome, beautiful, charming, and playful. As children, they enjoy their freedom from the rigidity of Western civilization. They are more fortunate than their monoracial Eskimo and Native American counterparts, but not as fortunate as monoracial Europeans. Life as a mixed-blood breeds tragedy and failure. This is why Albertine chooses to pass as white and leave behind her barefooted, savage, half-breedness. As a result, they cannot forge a "legitimate" love, although it is genuine and produces a daughter. Avik, who succumbs to alcoholism in the face of western colonial encroachment, can only be with Albertine in death as the French song states. The "hybrid degeneracy" theory puts forth that race-mixing produces genetically inferior, unnatural, and disharmonious offspring. Avik and Albertine embody the social, psychological, and physical consequences of a forbidden and unnatural union. They are portrayed as physically, mentally, emotionally, and morally weak (childlike, compared with Europeans). According to the hybrid degeneracy explanation, if they do not die early from their biological inadequacies, and psychological weaknesses, then they will surely succumb to mental disorders or to immoral temptations or to both. Perhaps, the hope lies in the daughter born to Avik and Albertine. Her racial appearance represents the "intermediate phenotype" of a multiracial person. Moreover, she is determined to search for her father, Avik, suggesting the cultural affirmation of her Eskimo heritage.

The Eurasian, like the mulatta or mestiza, represents the dangerous, yet exciting blend of purity and sin. The popular soap opera, *General Hospital*, temporarily featured "Desiree," a Eurasian seductress, played by multiracial actress, Chien Telemaque, who used her exotic beauty to allure, enamor, and seduce. Ethnohistorian Paul Spickard has noted, "One type of Asian—the Eurasian—was singled out as especially sexy. The very thought of a woman whose parents had dared cross racial boundaries for love or sex set American male hearts atingle with erotic anticipation."[17] He presents an array of Eurasian images portrayed in pornographic books and movies.

Eric Amber's otherwise admirable 1956 thriller, *State of Seige*, depicted Eurasian women as remote, inscrutable. . . . One of the hottest of the pornographic movies of 1975 was *Erotic Fantasies of a Eurasian Nymph*, "She's a new breed of woman. Part Oriental part European. She'll jolt you right out of your seat!". . . . Gillian Stone's *Land of Golden Mountains* was not the only pulp novel to caste a Eurasian woman in a hotly sexual role. The back cover read, "She was the child of the savage coupling of her beautiful Chinese mother and her handsome American father. She had her first lesson in life and love in the most elegant and depraved brothel in the Far East— and learned of passion in the arms of a lawless and forbidden lover. She came to America to be sold into an ultimate hell of degradation—and began her climb toward wealth and power man by man, selling her irresistible flesh to feed her insatiable ambition."[18]

Psychologist Carla Bradshaw has also put forth the two primary representations of multiracial peoples, "the beauty" and "the beast." She has written

"What are you?" the multiracial person is often asked. Though this question is often innocently intended, it reveals an awareness of unfamiliarity due to variances in physical features; underlying this question is the assumption of the multiracial person's foreignness or non-belonging. Thus, the multiracial person experiences exaggerated emphasis on physical appearance, is often treated as an unfamiliar, one to be correctly racially categorized. This increased attention to physical appearance is expressed in such labels as exotic, beautiful or fascinating (the Beauty). . . . Obstacles to claiming racial belonging unambiguously leave the individual constantly vulnerable to rejection and identification as the Other (the Beast).[19]

Tina Chow, born Bettina Lutz, became internationally known for her Eurasian beauty and high-fashion sense. In the April 1993 *Vanity Fair* article, "Ciao, Tina," Maureen Orth traced the much too short, but celebrated life of Tina Chow, who had become one of the first celebrity women to fall to AIDS. A London decorator, Nicky Haslam, said that, "She (Chow) wasn't like a woman but an *objet* dressed."[20] Characterized as "the stylish enchantress," Orth wrote, "Tina Chow was known for both her star quality and her heart; she was an unjaded, upbeat, enthusiastic half-Japanese, half-American jewel set loose among mannered aesthetes. They worshiped her androgynous angularity." There is a resemblance to this characterization of Chow with Albertine in *Map of the Human Heart.* Chow was described by Paige Powell, Orth continued, as possessing a "Zen-like" duality: having serenity and allure; yet, being regal and removed.[21]

In 1990, Vietnamese–Amerasian model Mary Ngyuen was selected as "Revlon's Most Unforgettable Woman of the Year." In her essay, Ngyuen had written

I am unforgettable woman because I possess an inner beauty that along with my striking appearance captures the heart of all who encounter me. Growing up as an Amerasian in Viet Nam, I had to accept that I was considered a dishonor to my country: a child of the dust. I painfully learned that in order for me to overcome this obstacle, I had to develop a stronger sense of myself. One cannot rely on looks alone.[22]

Ngyuen is torn between accepting a pariah status (child of the dust) or what Bradshaw named beast, or embracing and even capitalizing on her "striking appearance" or what Bradshaw called beauty. Although she recognizes that she cannot rely on her looks alone, it is ironic that this is the essay that she submitted to win one of the biggest cosmetic company's "Woman of the Year" contest. Like Chow, Ngyuen's womanhood is summed up by a paradoxical duality in which physical appearance is at the center, with degrees of ambiguity and multiple otherness concentrically enveloping it.

It is no wonder that biracial peoples have often been overrepresented in the fashion industry, beauty pageants, and the entertainment field where physical appearances are the prized commodity. When an English and Japanese bilingual Eurasian woman, who had spent time in Japan, won the Miss Nisei Week Queen in the early 1980s, Japanese-American readers of the *Rafu Shimpo* wrote in questioning why a Eurasian (who was obviously more Caucasian-looking than "unmixed" Japanese Americans) was selected to represent Japanese beauty. This discourse perhaps was similar to the questions raised about why the first Miss America of African descent possessed such phenotypical likeness to European Americans, when Vanessa Williams was crowned Miss America in 1984. Many male and female Asian-American beauty pageant contestants have in fact been Eurasian, while very few have been Asian-Latino and Afroasian. The notion of "best of both worlds" is often used to objectify the biracial person and exotify mixed-race physical appearances. Ordinary biracials are neither the beauty nor the beast, yet these assumptions about mixed-race people expect them to have narrowly defined appearances, behaviors, identities, and social status.

Afroasian

The most visible Afroasian depiction in American pop culture which unfortunately has fallen victim to the stereotypical depictions is *Kinu* (which means silk in Japanese) on the hit series, *A Different World*. Kinu goofily spouts off phrases like, "I love to rub and tickle your feet, Dwayne-*san*" in her awkwardly accented Japanese and slides around in baby steps as if her feet were bound. In addition to being sensuous and geisha-like, she is also physically slender and academically intelligent. Perhaps, Kinu is a safe and acceptable "Asian" female substitute in a predominantly all–African-American cast because she is also half African American. The writers and producers of *A Different World* have generally been socially conscious and politically sensitive with their character depictions and storylines. However, when including Kinu, the Afroasian love interest of Dwayne (Kadeem Hardison) and love rival of Whitley (Jasmine Guy), they were as insensitive and stereotypical as most white writers and producers are with ethnic minority characters. Although characterized as sociable, likeable, friendly, outgoing, attractive, and intelligent, Kinu was still seen as an "outsider" from most of the African-American characters. In many ways, she was depicted as the "Oriental *but part-black* Other." In the controversial film, *The Rising Sun*, Tia Carrere plays an Afroasian character who is beautiful, successful, intelligent, and self-assured. Although Jingo in *The Rising Sun* is similar to Kinu in *A Different World*, *Rafu Shimpo*'s English editor and Asian-American critic Naomi Hirahara, has observed, "Tia Carrere, transformed in appearance by crimped hair and dark makeup, makes a minor appearance as Jingo Asakuma, an African-American-Japanese computer whiz with a deformed hand. There's a bashing rhetoric."[23] As part of an elaborate ideology of scientific racism and the eugenics movement, miscegenation or race-mixing was often thought to produce physically deformed, genetically degenerate, and culturally mediocre offspring.[24] Hirahara reminds her readers that the character of Jingo Asakuma is reminiscent of these racist principles upon which American race relations have rested.

On the other hand, in the wake of the Rodney King trial and the Los Angeles urban rebellion, it is interesting to see how the "Afroasian" has become one of the Los Angeles Police Department's icons for interethnic unity and ethnic recruitment for the police force. The LAPD has featured a woman who is "actually half Asian, half African-American, but looks Latina or even Native American" in its recruitment advertisements. The billboard reads, "Join your LAPD. It's not as uniform as you might think."[25]

The visibility of Afroasian images—positive or negative—has been virtually nonexistent until recently because, for the most part, the national discourse on race has been framed as white versus black and dominant versus subordinate. Relationships between groups of color have often been sabotaged by white representations of them. Thus, people of color often view each other through the dominant European-American lens or what W. E .B. Dubois called, "the veil."[26] Each group of color has referenced itself to the European American in its attempts to gain personal and political liberation. Thus, race mixing is only fascinating and titillating when socially constructed boundaries are being crossed in taboo form. Most antimiscegenation laws, for example, were written to prevent whites and nonwhites, specifically, from marrying; they were not really concerned with Native Americans marrying African Americans or Asian Americans marrying Latinos, and so on.

In *Chinese American Portraits* (1988), Chien Telemaque told how her Asian and African biraciality defies Hollywood's neatly fitted

racial typecasts. She explained, "At calls for black actresses I'm
not 'black' enough and at Asian calls I'm not 'Asian' enough."[27]
In 1991, Telemaque starred as Akemi, a Japanese and African-
American young woman, in Velina Hasu Houston's "pan-Amerasian"
play, *Broken English*, which explored race, gender, nationality,
language, community, family, and identity. Voices of those like
Japanese, Native American, African-American playwright Houston,
whose works are informed by her "triple racial minority" experiences,
and Eurasian artist Nobuko Miyamoto, founder of Great Leap Inc.,
have altered the Asian-American community's idea that the only
legitimate *hapas* are Eurasian.[28] While arguably the theater is about
the suspension of reality and the manipulation of self, it creates,
projects, and represents. There was a time when people of color,
including biracial people, were systematically not allowed to represent
themselves on television, in the movies, and on stage. Biracial
individuals and characters have often been manipulated by European
Americans and groups of color to justify their political representations.
In a social reality where race accompanies layers of meaning and
myths about material wealth, beauty, intelligence, physical capacities,
sexuality, femininity, masculinity, group allegiances, and so on, it
is important to examine critically the Eurasian and Afroasian images
that are being manufactured and presented.

Conclusion

In this struggle for naming one's identity in a society that demands thorough disassociation of one from one's total self, biracial individuals often seek self-affirmation without questioning the
unequal relationship between their two parent groups. Eurasians claim
their Asian ancestry at the expense of the European because they
have bought into the larger society's notion of the one-drop rule or
more recently the dominant society's cooptation of "racial correct-
ness." Afroasians embrace their Asian ancestry to the exclusion of
the African because, as playwright Velina Hasu Houston has said,
"it's now L.A. cool!" to be Asian. The monoracially identified Asian
Americans raised in the United States ironically distance themselves
from any connection to Asia as a challenge to a racist social order
that denies them Americanness and grants them perpetual foreigner status. African Americans with Native American ancestry fail to
bond with their Native American past because of their sole alle-

giance to the politicization of blackness in the onslaught of whiteness. However, we must begin to recognize where each of us is socially situated and join struggles to integrate our multiple realities. New ways of examining racial and ethnic identity that do not reproduce the dominant racist discourse need to be articulated more than ever before. Indeed, many writers have been putting forth new models for understanding, processing, and manufacturing multiple identities despite a racist social context. W. E. B. Du Bois's *Souls of Black Folk* passionately conveyed the gift of the second sight, the ever twoness, the double-consciousness, and the two warring ideals that make up the souls of black folks—by definition a multiethnic group.[29] Sociologist Michael Thornton applied Du Bois's insights to the multiple struggles of Afroasians in America by explaining how the Afroasians have three warring ideals, possessing one black, one Asian, and one American. He argued that it is crucial for Afroasians to understand and cherish all three, especially emphasizing the ancestries that are less valued if they are going to achieve a truly positive identity.[30]

Gloria Anzaldua's "new mestiza" has also provided a framework from which to deconstruct binary either-or identities and reconstruct a truly multiethnic self, transforming ambivalence into something positive. This new mestiza is one who "copes by developing a tolerance for contradictions, a tolerance for ambiguity. . . . learns to juggle cultures. . . . operates in a plualistic mode—nothing is thrust out, the good, the bad, and the ugly, nothing rejected, nothing abandoned."[31] Anzaldua's model opens up the possibility for a Japanese–European-American woman like myself to cross all lines of demarcation between my parent groups, tear down the barriers of oppositional, binary structures upon which the subject–object dichotomies such as white–nonwhite, male–female, heterosexual–gay, Christian–non-Christian are founded, and to develop new and creative ways of understanding and appreciating myself and others.[32]

The struggle for identity should neither be contingent solely upon presenting only the socially desirable "best of both worlds" aspects of the biracial self, as Irving Goffman's dramaturgical analysis may imply or Carla Bradshaw's notion of the beauty states, nor putting forth only the tragic worst of both worlds' characteristics of biraciality or Bradshaw's notion of the beast or the other. Rather, the struggle for identity must necessarily interrogate the unequal relationships between and among one's multiple ancestries and must encompass how one can transgress racial, class, gender, and sexual boundaries as Anzaldua has posited. Why must affirming a Eurasian identity be framed as antithetical to the liberation struggles of Asian Americans or European Americans in Appalachia? Why must celebrating an Afroasian identity be seen as standing in direct opposition to black liberation or the liberation struggles of peoples of color in general? Why must we assert our multiraciality to the exclusion of our age, gender, class, sexuality, physical abilities, or documented status in a country? As the biracial population continues to grow and a biracial–multiracial consciousness is heightened, these questions and the need for their solutions become more stubbornly pertinent.

8

The Go-Between People: Representations of Mixed Race in Twentieth-Century American Literature

Carol Roh Spaulding

> Since the contact of races in the modern age has rarely been smooth and harmonious, there is something universal in the problem of racial hybrids.
>
> —Everett R. Stonequist, *Marginal Man*, 1937

Just as it is true that people of mixed race have always existed in the United States, so it is also true that literary representations of mixed race have appeared throughout American narratives, from Washington Irving's depiction of the half-blood, Pierre Beattie, in *A Tour on the Prairies,*[1] to William Faulkner's tragic mulatto, Joe Christmas, in *Light in August,*[2] to the three young Eurasians in Diana Chang's *Frontiers of Love,*[3] to the "breed" Pauline, in Louise Erdrich's *Tracks.*[4] By the same token, just as Americans of mixed race lack a collective identity, so has the "mixed blood" commanded little attention in literary studies. Judith Berzon's *Neither Black Nor White,*[5] William J. Scheik's *The Half Blood,*[6] and one chapter in Amy Ling's *Between Worlds: Women Writers of Chinese Ancestry*[7] examine the mulatto–muletta, the half-blood Indian, and the Eurasian in literature; but studies such as these are confined within the bounds of their individual ethnic fields. Irrespective of their ethnic particularities, mixed bloods in American literature share important commonalities that traverse current racial and ethnic formations called African-

97

American, Asian-American, Latino–Latina, and American Indian literature.

This chapter examines the mixed blood as a literary trope in selected twentieth-century narratives with the goal of emphasizing its cross-ethnic and cross-racial commonalities.[8] Although the literary portrayals have many variables, they share several important common denominators. First, mixed race is founded in the experience of marginality; second, mixed-race characters are always negatively defined (neither "white" nor "raced"); third, the characters serve a kind of barometric function, revealing the racial tensions embedded in the text; and, last, mixed-race protagonists come to a crisis point in the narrative when they are forced to confront in some manner their indeterminate racial status. The literary mixed blood exists because racial distinctions exist in American literature and because those distinctions have been portrayed as somehow inadequate to mixed-blood identity. Because the portrayal of mixed race from the turn of the century to the 1990s essentially involves some critique of the racial distinctions depicted in the narratives, the study of mixed race offers a unique perspective for what Henry Louis Gates, Jr., calls "reading race" in American literature.[9]

A truly comprehensive examination of literary depictions of the mixed blood, which most often includes the mulatto and mulatta, the Eurasian, the half-blood Indian, the mestizo and mestiza, and those who identify themselves as part Jewish, is impossible in a brief survey. This chapter also leaves aside (but does not discount) other organizing principles that could prove useful; for example, future studies might focus on a more concentrated historical time period or on more specific designations of region, gender, and class. Nevertheless, I examine the mixed-blood character from several angles that can serve as an introduction to the study of mixed race in literature. I have concentrated on fiction and autobiography because these genres include most of the representations of mixed race in American literature. My taxonomic approach focuses on representations in literature as opposed to distinctions (which might be fruitfully drawn elsewhere) between "ethnic" and "canonical" authors or between "white" and "full-blood" authors and their works. The patterns discussed are intended as indicative rather than definitive.

In American literature of the twentieth century, the term "mixed race" almost invariably refers to individuals who are part "white" and part "raced." Like spokes on a wheel, the mulatto and muletta and mestizo and mestiza, the half-blood Indian, and the Eurasian are all defined by their relation to "whiteness." Adrienne Rich, who has written about the conflict she felt at being half-Jewish, has called it "split at the root."[10] Racial mixes that do not include "white" simply have not figured equally in the literary imagination. Therefore, this study focuses solely on mixed bloods who are part "white" and part "raced." What qualifies as "white" or "raced" in any given setting and period changes over time and has changed in literary depictions, as well.

"Whiteness" in literature has never really signified color so much as it has signified full legal, social, and economic personhood in the United States. For example, before the turn of the century, an Irish-American, Italian-American, or German-American character did not necessarily qualify as "white." Theodore Dreiser's *Jennie Gerhardt*, set in the 1890s, depicts a family of recent immigrants from Germany opposite the established "Americanized" Kane family. The relationship between Jennie Gerhardt and Lester Kane is a "mixed" marriage regarded by Boston high society as quite as unnatural as if the lovers had different skin color.[11] Similarly, many "white" characters of our time would not necessarily have been regarded as "white" during World War II, when having even some Japanese or Jewish ancestry called into question one's personhood. Certainly, the definition of "white" and "raced" will change again, and pose new threats (or revive old ones) to currently secure identities. What has not changed is the binary system of classification itself. One is designated "white" (or passes for "white"); one is designated "raced" (or passes for "raced"). The more creative or adventurous may play at one designation or another in various times or places, but the choice of either-or remains intact. No matter how mixed one's ancestry, racial identity in American literature is most influenced by a character's status in relation to how the narrative defines "whiteness."

In spite of—or perhaps because of—this trenchant binarism, the mixed blood in literature inhabits the space between an abstract notion of racial status and the lived consequences of racial being. This conflict has often captured the American literary imagination, especially during this century. Technically, the mixed blood should not exist at all; within a binary caste system, mixed blood is classified as "raced" along with "full blood" racial minorities—hence, the "one drop of black blood" rule. Yet the mixed blood does indeed exist in American literature as a product of—and a challenge to—biracial stratification. Defined by their racial indefinition, mixed-blood characters point to the limitations of the century's racial formations in which "raced" is as much a misnomer as "white." In this respect, the mulatta, Irene Redfield, from Nella Larsen's *Passing*[12] has as much in common with the Eurasian, Rosalie Chou, in Han Suyin's *The Crippled Tree*[13] or with the half-blood Indian, Tayo, in Leslie Silko's *Ceremony*[14] as she does with Larsen's other well-known mulatta heroine, Helga Crane, in *Quicksand*.[15]

Why has the study of literature not turned its attention to the mixed blood until recently? One answer might be found in Naomi Zack's *Race and Mixed Race,* where she argues that people of mixed race have almost no documented history. Only clearly delineated racial groups possess—in fact, depend on—the potentially liberating knowledge of their members' collective "roots."[16] Mixed bloods lack previousness and, by extension, the representations and examinations of mixed-blood characters in literature also lack a common history. Another answer is that racial and ethnic formations have had and continue to have great authority in the reading of race. A mulatta heroine belongs to African-American literature. A Eurasian to Asian-American literature. A half-blood to American Indian literature, and so on. By the same token, these distinctions have great political and social importance to these ethnic literatures, and I do not mean to suggest that they be discarded; but neither should they preclude other ways of reading race.

Here I examine three major variations of the mixed blood figure, which I have called abjection, secession, and prospection. These categories reflect not a chronological but a thematic progression. Each section contains a survey of texts that illustrate the thematic concept presented, a specific examination of selected portrayals of mixed-blood protagonists, and a discussion of the racial views that unify the texts.

Abjection:
Joe Christmas's "Impossible" Self

In her psychoanalytic study, *The Powers of Horror: An Essay on Abjection,* Julia Kristeva describes the abject as ". . . what disturbs identity, system, order. What does not respect borders, positions, rules. The in-between, the ambiguous, the composite."[17] This is a particularly apt description of certain mixed-blood characters, es-

pecially those who inspire fear, repulsion, or awe. In Winnifred
Eaton's "Japanese" romance, *Tama* (1910), the "enchanted Fox
Woman" of the province of Fukui is none other than the blind daughter
of a departed sailor and a deceased Japanese nun-gone-wrong, who
wanders the redwood forests, as an outcast. The citizens of Fukui
believe that "no clean being may look upon or touch her," bewitched
as they are by her "unnatural" blue eyes and golden hair.[18] In Lanford Wilson's play *The Redwood Curtain* (1993), the Eurasian heroine, Mimi, also wanders the redwood forests, but she is on this
side of the Pacific in search of her long-lost Vietnam Vet father.
Mimi has the power to make the sun go out and to make the clouds
gather, and she uses these powers in her search.[19] Most often, the
character is simply reviled for her racial indistinction. Charles W.
Chesnutt's Rowena Warwick in *The House Behind the Cedars* causes
repulsion in her rich white suitor when he first discovers the truth
about her racial background.[20] Walt Whitman's character, Boddo,
in "The Half-Breed" is grotesquely physically misshapen, loves to
frighten young children, and sports a "malignant peevishness, dwelling
on every feature of his countenance."[21] And the conniving mulatta
of Thomas Dixon's *The Clansman* lurks behind chamber doors,
plotting to overthrow the U.S. government.[22] Whether or not their
acts are wicked, these characters inspire dread not so much because of what they do as because of what they are. Their bodies
are read as signs of their power to disrupt racial—and by extension social—order. Their mere existence is itself the sign of degeneracy or danger, for they have proven themselves to be beyond
classification.

In some ways, Faulkner's Joe Christmas in *Light in August* comes
closest to a paradigmatic mixed-blood figure—the tragic mulatto—
and is therefore the focus of this section. Kristeva's definition of
the abject as it applies to individuals might best describe this figure: the self "finds the impossible within; when it finds that the
impossible constitutes its very *being,* that it *is* none other than
abject."[23] Intensely alienated from all he encounters, Christmas
wanders the South the same number of years as Jesus Christ lived,
questioning and testing his racial indistinction at every turn, trying
on "blackness," and alternating with "passing" for white (even when
he's not sure he's *not* white) until, eventually, he suffers a dubious
martyrdom at the hands of that upholder of early-century, Southern
racial divisions, Percy Grimm. Yet in another sense, Christmas makes
a questionable tragic mulatto because he's never sure he really *is*

mulatto. Because he has no phenotypical signs of being black, he actually has to choose racial ambiguity. Donald M. Kartiganer notes, "The only identity that will satisfy him is the one which, in Faulkner's South, is no identity at all, but rather an image of disorder."[24] When Christmas realizes that the impossible is within, then he insists on his doubleness. Thus, his self-definition alone—no matter what other ways Joe Christmas breaks the law—is the fundamental threat to the social order. It is his first crime. As the black janitor at the orphanage of Christmas's childhood predicted, "You don't know what you are. And more than that, you won't never know. You'll live and you'll die and you won't never know."[25]

Abjection includes other characteristics that seem particularly suited to the discussion of mixed blood, especially in the case of Joe Christmas. The abject inhabits a "land of oblivion," Kristeva tells us, like Christmas's "exile" within the community of Jefferson.[26] Abjection is, she continues, perverse, in that it "neither gives up nor assumes a prohibition, a rule, or a law; but turns them aside, misleads, corrupts; uses them, takes advantage of them, the better to deny them."[27] Appropriately, almost every action Christmas takes in Jefferson is that of an "outlaw"—his bootlegging, his taking a white woman for a lover, his murder of his lover.

Finally, Kristeva's abjection is "edged with the sublime." Christmas's death scene has a similar quality of rapturous uncontainability:

> Then his face, body, all, seemed to collapse, to fall in upon itself, and from out the slashed garments about his hips and loins the pent black blood seemed to rush like a released breath. It seemed to rush out of his pale body like the rush of sparks from a rising rocket; upon that black blast the man seemed to rise soaring into their memories forever and ever.[28]

Here, blood merges into the imagery of fire and flight, and the memory of Joe Christmas is sent into peaceful, eternal orbit in the minds of the community. Blood is then transfigured yet again in the closing sentences, from memory into a ghostlike or muselike presence, into a piercing sound that crescendos into oblivion and unnamability.

The abject figure is probably even now the most common and the most potent form of the trope of mixed race in American literature. What J. M. Coetzee has written about South African literature seems applicable today: "There is an essential flaw in the fact of being a racial hybrid."[29] In other words, because only the degenerate would commit miscegenation, racial hybridity is essentially malign. In the popular imagination this view has thrived in the United States in the form of legislation that prohibited intermarriage until as recently as 1967. And in literature, portrayals from as early as William Gilmore Simms's *The Partisan* (1835) in which the vicious Goggle is depicted as physically and morally corrupt,[30] to Mark Twain's unregenerate mulatta "heroine" Roxy,[31] to Toni Morrison's unsympathetically portrayed mixed-blood Elihue Whitcomb,[32] the idea of the essential flaw lives on.

Secession:
The "Diminutive World" of the Mixed Blood

Abjection and self-destruction are not the only fate possible for the mixed-blood character. In some portrayals of mixed race, the characters achieve a kind of "symbolic exile."[33] These mixed bloods are also outcasts, but they are not ruined. They choose a way out of their conflict by finding a way out of their culture.

In her provocative discussion, "National Brands, National Body," Lauren Berlant argues that the notions of "embodiment" versus "abstraction" are relevant to discussions about race, and that these are bound up with distinctions of sex and nationality, as well. According to Berlant, real authority as an American citizen resides in the power to suppress the body and to "abstract" oneself as a national subject, thereby achieving a "prosthetic" identity. Historically, self-abstraction has been most available to white, male landowners. Any form of public embodiment—for example, being poor, being female, being "raced"—is "a sign of inadequacy to proper citizenship."[34]

If cultural legitimacy lies in self-abstraction the mixed blood has no such recourse. He or she is disembodied and yet remains indestructible. This condition is potentially liberating, but it is not automatically treated as such in literature. Depending on how his or her body is read by the culture, the mixed blood may be able to pass in either direction. Passing is one form (albeit an imperfect one) of bodily suppression similar to self-abstraction; however, literary depictions almost always show that passing is far from an ideal solution. It requires constant performance, internal estrangement, and the danger that the body will reveal itself or be revealed at every turn. Whereas in narratives of the abject, the mixed blood finds no solution to indestructibility or disembodiment, and thus ends in doom, other narratives suggest a different solution. Those whose racial questionableness leads to their questionableness as citizens choose an affirmative, if self-marginalizing solution: secession. That is, they form a territory unto themselves—their own "nation," in a manner of speaking.

Winnifred Eaton's "Japanese" romance novel, *The Heart of Hyacinth*,[35] offers such a solution. Hyacinth, Eaton's heroine, is raised by a Japanese surrogate mother. Her brother Koma (of different parentage) is also Eurasian. The two pass an idyllic country childhood together, but when Koma comes of age, the two are repeatedly separated for years at a time by Koma's British schooling. Alone, neither Koma nor Hyacinth can face the difficulties of being cultural and racial misfits. They want only to be together and to have the right to call themselves Japanese, even though the Japanese do not accept them as countrymen. In the penultimate scene of the book, Koma and Hyacinth drift aimlessly in a rowboat far out on the water, dreading what is to be their final separation. The image of the boy and girl floating out beyond their troubles, which means, also, beyond civilization and home, is a telling one in light of their solution. "I am afraid . . . to leave the land of gods and go out into the unknown," says Hyacinth. Nevertheless, Koma persuades her to steal away with him at night, into self-imposed exile. They escape to a forgotten Buddhist temple, where they take the only course of action that will allow them to remain together—they marry. This solution is significant because it is the marriage of two people whose identity has been made ambiguous and troublesome because of cultural forces beyond their control. Furthermore, the incestuous overtones suggest that the racial hybrid is a kind of exotic species that can only reproduce among its own kind, echoing ironically, perhaps, the nineteenth-century belief in the sterility of the mulatto.

While the novel's resolution celebrates the triumph of romantic love more readily than it does the right to self-determination, its provisional remedy does offer an alternative to the dichotomy of embodiment and abstraction as the only legitimate avenues of citizenship. That is exile. But this exile is not without possibility. Koma and Hyacinth can be regarded as edenic figures, the progenitors of a "new people," to echo Joel Williamson's term for mixed bloods.[36] Rather than capitulate to racial designations, Koma and Hyacinth escape from them—a diaspora of two. This solution is similar to Homi Bhabha's concept of the "Third Space," that alien territory that makes possible an alternative identity beyond the concept of margin and center and beyond the concept of pure or essential racial types.[37]

Mourning Dove's *Cogewea, the Half Blood*[38] provides a strikingly similar conflict and resolution compared with Eaton's earlier novel. Cogewea is raised by her Indian grandmother and, like Hyacinth, she enjoys an idyllic childhood, in this case on the Horseshoe Brand Ranch of the North American plains. Also like Hyacinth, Cogewea has a brotherly lover of mixed race in the half-breed Indian, Jim, an unrefined, but good-hearted ranch hand. But our heroine falls for the unscrupulous attentions of the city boy, Densmore, who cuts an impressive figure in the eyes of this sexually maturing Cogewea.

Densmore is successful in winning Cogewea's affection for several reasons. He speaks to the part of her that cannot completely accept her full-blood grandmother's traditional ways, even though she respects them greatly. Furthermore, as a strong-headed young woman, Cogewea sees the difference between herself and her grandmother not only as racial but as generational. Finally, Densmore's appeal seems to rest, in part, on his cosmopolitanism—his ability to traverse borders of class, race, and landscape with seeming ease. Cogewea makes several references of sorts throughout the novel to the enclosure of "breeds" in their own territory. For example, she says they are "just a go-between people, shut within their own diminutive world."[39] In another instance, she states, "We breeds are half and half—American and Caucasian—and in a separate corral."[40] Later, on a more positive note, she defends her "double vision" to Densmore, insisting, "But why not stay in my own class, the mixed-blood?"[41] For the most part, however, this separate class of citizens is contained, if not entrapped, within boundaries that are not, to Cogewea's mind, of her own making. Small wonder that the urbane, mobile Densmore sweeps her off her feet. Yet, as everyone but Cogewea herself predicts, Densmore betrays her.

Interestingly, Cogewea does not, as a result of Densmore's betrayal, revert to the thinking of her traditional full-blood grandmother, who had warned her all along about the deceptiveness of the "Shoyahpee" (whites). Rather, she accepts Jim's hand in marriage and avoids the impossible choice between a full-blooded tradition on one hand, which she cannot accept as her own, and marriage into a society that will not fully accept her as its own. At the end of the novel, Cogewea still smarts from her recent emotional wounds and complains, "We despised *breeds* are in a zone of our own and when we break from the corral erected about us we meet up with trouble."[42] This is a near-retreat into bitterness, which her new lover manages to turn to good. Just as Hyacinth fears her exile but becomes convinced by Koma that it is their only reasonable alternative, so Cogewea fears entrapment and yet Jim convinces her that the "separate corral" is not a prisonhouse, but a haven. "S'pose we remain together in that there corral you spoke of as bein' built 'round us by the Shoyahpee?" he suggests.[43] Significantly, this corral is not merely a reservation within the confines of an Indian reservation. It is a freely chosen space beyond the reservation and the white man's world. Their voluntary exile is a creative act of survival, like Koma's and Hyacinth's, and suggests the possibility of reinterpreting racial designations through the racially mixed offspring to come. Both of these marriages ironically recombine the "white" and "raced" division that caused their marginal status to begin with. (Koma and Hyacinth are Eurasians; Cogewea and Jim are half bloods.) Genetically, their offspring will be more "pure" than their parents; thus, their "miscegenous" union mocks the idea of racial purity.

Other mixed bloods, as well, might be said to inhabit their own "diminutive worlds." The half-blood Pauline, in Louise Erdrich's *Tracks* resorts to madness as a response to the conflict she experiences between ancient Chippewa beliefs and the pull of Christianity. Although insanity might more appropriately be termed a form of abjection and is certainly an imperfect solution, it is, nevertheless, significant that Pauline creates a psychic territory for herself rather than capitulate either to Western or Native religion.[44] In Silko's *Ceremony*[45] the mixed-blood characters Tayo, old Betonie, and the Night Swan create what Patricia Riley calls a "contemporary mythic space" in which they are able to achieve "the kind of adaptation that is necessary for survival in the face of contemporary reality."[46] Finally, Ana Castillo's *Sapogonia* takes the concept of the Third Space (to return to Bhabha's term) to its furthest extension. Castillo invents an imaginary territory "not identified by modern boundaries" in which all mestizos reside. Sapogonia is not a geographical location, but a state of mind wherein the consciousness of a past weighted with the encounter between colonial and indigenous peoples continues to dominate one's worldview. For the protagonist, Maxmillian, Sapogonia is the "place" where he feels a connection to all other mestizos.[47]

The liminal condition of mixed bloods discussed is significantly different from abjection, in which the mixed-blood figure is often destroyed by the weight of racial tensions embedded in the narrative. Here, if the characters have not discovered a perfect solution to Joe Christmas's "impossible" condition, they have at least discovered one that avoids their own destruction. They are suspended beyond impossible racial formations and suggestive of new ones.

Prescription:
Toward "Racelessless" in Literature

In the novel *Le chinois vert d'afrique* (The Green Chinese from Africa), Franco-Algerian writer Leila Sebbar creates the character of young Momo, a French boy who is part Algerian, part Vietnamese, and part Turkish. Momo lives in the public gardens of greater Paris, a runaway from a family with a past so fragmented by the crossing of cultures that he lacks any national, racial, or ethnic sense of himself. Although Momo feels a certain contentment in the life he has made for himself—adding to his meticulously organized assortment of junk odds and ends and befriending other neighborhood outcasts—his own dubious freedom from categories keeps him in constant danger. In almost every scene in the book, Momo can be seen running—not running to or from anything in particular, just moving, as though stasis were dangerous. Sebbar gives a humorous portrait of the ridiculous French police, who busy themselves trying to catch this child-on-the-lam. They don't catch Momo, but they do confiscate his things, box them, label them, and put them away in some government office. Momo must be caught, not because he has violated any specific law, but because, like the treasures in his garden hideout, he must submit to classification. His danger lies in his unclassifiability, his buzzing around legal and social borders. And his condition is permanent.[48]

This example from world literature is relevant to the discussion of mixed race in American literature because it highlights a response to racial indeterminacy that has rarely been discussed in the United States. Momo is not an abject figure nor is he safe in his own diminutive world. He has neither capitulated to nor retreated from racial designations. Instead, he practices what Sebbar has called "permanent disequilibrium," in which identity is multifocal, dynamic, provisional—not a consequence, but a process.[49] Far from being diminishing or containing, *metissage* is fruitful. At the heart of constructive racial imbalance is a refusal of biologically and culturally based designations altogether—and an acceptance of the lived consequences of this deliberate practice.

In American racial discourse, Naomi Zack's term *racelessness* probably comes closest to this concept. The "impossible" identity of the mixed-blood figure is similar to racelessness, except that the latter term envisions a potentially constructive rather than a decidedly destructive identity. "It would have to be an identity that looks to the future rather than to the past," argues Zack, "an identity founded on freedom and resistance to oppression rather than immanence and acceptance of tradition."[50] Sebbar's Momo provides one example of such an identity and its consequent provisionality and imbalance. Yet, American literature of the twentieth century offers no quintessential raceless figure. Certainly, whiteness in literature is never actually raceless, although it has almost always masqueraded as such. The raceless figure appears only in glimpses throughout the century.

One such glimpse is offered in the early part of the century by the Eurasian writer, Edith Maud Eaton, the Canadian-born daughter of an English father and Chinese mother, who wrote under the pen name Sui Sin Far. The older sister of the "Japanese" romance novelist, Winnifred Eaton *(The Heart of Hyacinth),* Sui Sin Far chose to write from the perspective of the Chinese and Chinese Americans on the West Coast around the turn of the century. Her collection of short stories, *Mrs. Spring Fragrance,*[51] portrays the difficulties of immigrant life in Chinatown and the conflicts between white America and Chinese America. She is less well-known for her autobiographical piece, "Leaves from the Mental Portfolio of an Eurasian," which details her experience as a mixed blood.[52]

Probably the most remarkable aspect of "Leaves" is its emphatic rendering of Eurasian experience as difficult, even though the narrator is normally regarded as white. As a child, the narrator discovers that she is "Chinese" because her mother is Chinese, and, soon, that Chinese people are reviled—she along with them. She is taunted with "yellow-face, pig-tail, rat-eater"[53] and most often simply by the word "Chinese," as though its utterance alone is sufficient insult. In one scene, nervous sickness resulting from her sense of racial aberrance leads her to a comparison with Jesus Christ's burden: she exclaims that "the cross of the Eurasian bore too heavily upon my childish shoulders."[54] And she concludes the piece with the observation that, although prejudice seems to be diminishing, "My experiences as an Eurasian never cease."[55]

Eurasian experience is portrayed as a struggle quite on par with that of other mixed-race portrayals of Sui Sin Far's time, or before. Washington Irving's *A Tour of the Prairies,* William Dean Howells's *An Imperative Duty,*[56] or W. E. B. DuBois's *The Souls of Black Folk*[57] all include portrayals of mixed race that may have been familiar to Eaton. In comparison to these other narratives, this narrator's family background is never questioned once she reaches adulthood, nor does her appearance betray any sign of racial ambiguity. Nevertheless, much like Joe Christmas, young Sui Sin Far insists on her doubleness, on her identity as a Eurasian, even when she could easily pass for white. In social situations involving white people who defame the Chinese, she boldly announces that she, herself, is Chinese. Sui Sin Far declares herself to be a racial "pioneer," adding that "a pioneer should glory in suffering."[58] She consciously embraces a racial identity far more difficult than the default position of whiteness that is available to her. For Sui Sin Far, racial status is more than phenotypical signs; it is a moral stance—one that allows for self-definition. She *must* define herself as Eurasian, because she cannot bear to be mistaken as the persecutor of her mother's people. In doing so, Sui Sin Far opts for a life like Sebbar's Momo—one of permanent disequilibrium. "So I roam backward and forward across the continent," she writes. "When I am East, my heart is West. When I am West, my heart is East."[59]

Sui Sin Far's narrator comes closest to being a prototypical "raceless" figure in American literature. Even though she seems to embrace her Chinese identity, she does so not because she desires a single ethnic identity but because her proclamation counteracts the assumption that she is only "white." However, she stops short of racelessness in one crucial respect. Although the narrator does refuse the racial designations of her time and place, when she imagines a future in which such designations disappear, she falls into a vision of cultural homogeneity rather than a vision of mixed bloods as "new" people. The narrator muses, "Only when the whole world becomes as one family will human beings be able to see clearly and hear distinctly."[60] This distinction is crucial because the idealized view of difference as insignificant ("we're all the same") never addresses the ways in which constructions of difference underscore an imbalance of power. Still, as a pioneer of mixed race, the Eurasian Sui Sin Far opts for the risks of a provisional identity lived

out on the symbolic frontier where "individuality is more than
nationality." A racial "outlaw" cannot take such risks lightly. In
her final statement, Sui Sin Far leaves us with the image of her
own racial body as the locus of opposing forces: "I give my right
hand to the Occidentals and my left to the Orientals," she tells us,
"hoping that between them they will not utterly destroy the insignificant 'connecting link.'"[61]

A further step toward a sense of mixed race as prescriptive rather
than merely descriptive is portrayed in Jessie Redmon Fauset's *There
is Confusion*.[62] The mixed blood, Philip, offers his version of constructive racial irresolution, one that recognizes both the battle and
the hope implied by this risky alternative. "Happy Warriors," he
calls them, "That's the ideal for us."[63] If we take happy warriors to
refer to not only mulattoes but all mixed bloods, then they can be
found in every major type of ethnic American literature. But the
truly raceless figure cannot occur within current racial formations.

Contemporary mestizo literature offers a variation of a raceless
future—arguably a uniquely American one—in the concept of the
"fifth race" or the "cosmic race," but in the end it risks becoming
another version of biological homogeneity.[64] In his essay, "Mixed
Blood: A World Made *Mestizo*," Richard Rodriguez playfully re-
vises the notion of conquest, arguing that, far from having been
vanquished, the Indians ensured their survival into the twenty-first
century by using a strategy that consumed the Spanish colonizers,
even as the Indians, themselves, were consumed. They achieved
their own renewal through miscegenation. "Mexico," Rodriguez tells
us, "carries the idea of a round world to its biological conclusion."[65]
That is, the world made mestizo.

Mestiza writer Gloria Anzaldua repeats the theme of *mestizaje*
in her book *Borderlands/La Frontera*, in which the mixing of "bloods"
and cultures will create a new consciousness, a "cosmic race."[66]
Like other writers on mixed race, Anzaldua describes the constantly shifting, thoroughly dynamic process of racial identity, calling it
"mental nepantilism," which coins the Aztec concept of being torn
between two ways.[67] Like these other writers, she stresses the necessity of tolerating ambiguity and pushes toward an embrace of
that provisional self—difficult and painful as this may be. Similar
to Ana Castillo's imaginary territory of mestizo–mestiza exile, Sapogonia, Anzaldua's borderlands are transformed from the actual
geographical locus of in-betweenness into the symbolic region where
"the squint-eyed, the perverse, the queer, the troublesome, the

mongrel, the mulatto, the half-breed, the half-dead" reside.[68] Mixed-race autobiographer, Cherrie Moraga, as well, takes up the concept of borderlands to discuss her identity as both a mixed-blood Chicana and a lesbian in *Loving in the War Years*.[69] Anzaldua writes:

> We are the people who leap in the dark, we are the people on the knees of the gods. In our very flesh, (r)evolution works out the clash of cultures. It makes us crazy constantly, but if the center holds, we've made some kind of evolutionary step forward.[70]

Here, the idea of nepantilism becomes the constant struggle toward a spiritual mix of peoples.

Mestizo–mestiza literature offers some of the most striking depictions of individuals who respond creatively and affirmatively to the conflict of being mestizaje. It is, after all, the oldest mix in the Americas, and the "borderlands" is essential to the study of mixed race. One problem with the concept of the cosmic race is that its universalizing tendency ("we're all one blood") may camouflage rather than call into question the racial designations that create the mixed-blood character in the first place. Is not "cosmic race" simply a more fanciful description of the "browning of America"? Is reading mixed race in literature nothing more than the search for a politically correct form of a revamped melting pot? Universalism is really only multiculturalism at its logical extreme: When everybody gets to be ethnic, then nobody gets to be anything. Just as ethnicity is leveled to meaninglessness, so does the danger exist for a similar leveling to occur with the concept of the browning of America. But why shouldn't Americans look forward to brownness as the "biological conclusion" to "race?" Why shouldn't "race" (as a biological fiction and a cultural construction) become obsolete?

Indeed, such predictions are ideals, and they are not yet realities. Something gets lost in the shuffle between the individualist and democratic impulses, here—some important questions about differences in history, cultural status, and future prospects between supposedly equally tolerated or "celebrated" identities. Although it may be hopeful to imagine that "race" will one day lose its signifying privilege, difference, itself, will find some (most likely equally essentialized) signifier. This is why it's a suspicious notion that centuries of a binary model of racial difference can vanish into thin air through the magic of universalism. Universalism doesn't really undo racial dichotomy at all; it camouflages it, leaving "raced" and "nonraced" intact at either end and allowing a proliferation of *contingent* alternatives between. A quadroon, for example, is a term that only has meaning given the idea of "pure black" and "pure white." The many Americans who boast of being, say, one-sixteenth American Indian, derive meaning from their family heritage precisely because such gradations of blood range from 0 to 100 percent. This may help to explain why the figure of the mixed blood persists despite changing racial ideologies; why the mixed blood is mentally unstable, is physically disfigured or degenerate, is sterile, is invested with magical powers, is corrupt, perverse, an outcast exile, is the embodiment of and a challenge to current racial designations and a projection of a future without them. In literature, the octoroon, the 'breed, the mulatress, the Amerasian, the 'blood, the mongrel, the mutt—all bear the metaphorical weight of binary racial stratification.

There is, of course, nothing natural about reading "race" as a meaningful articulation of difference. But in the United States, and in twentieth-century literature, "race" is the Great American Difference. Racial identity does a lot of work not only for racists but for individuals who have, historically, been assigned the culture's racial designations. In other words, racial identity is as meaningful to Black Nationalists as it is to Grand Dragons. Although it is certainly true that the relations of power these groups seek are very different, it is also true that the racial designations that would found those power relations will not disappear as long as individuals find them useful. Neither will the concept or condition of mixed race disappear. It would seem that it is not as important to eliminate "race" as the marker of difference as it is to understand *how* it differentiates and to what ends, and then to interrogate this privileged signifier from as many angles as possible. Difference cannot be made to disappear, but it can be continually refigured. Meanwhile, reading mixed race in literature can teach us much about the "benign possibilities and malign probabilities" (to borrow a phrase from William J. Scheik's discussion of the half-blood)[71] in that peculiar condition of being a go-between.

Part III
Social Science

9

The Hawaiian Alternative to the One-Drop Rule

F. James Davis

The Contrast: The Mainland versus Hawaii

In colonial America and later in the United States, the dominant rule that developed during slavery for black–white miscegenation was the hypodescent or "one-drop" rule. In accordance with this rule, a mixed child and all his or her descendants were defined as black and assigned the slave status. Thus "whiteness is nothing more than the absence of any black forbears, and blackness is nothing more than the presence of one black forbear."[1] Whites applied the same rule to the mixed children of blacks and Native Americans and to those with triracial ancestry. One black ancestor (or "one drop of black blood") made the person black, regardless of the proportion of black ancestry or the person's physical appearance.[2]

The hypodescent rule did not die with slavery but rather was strengthened by the Civil War and subsequent developments in the nineteenth and twentieth centuries. The rule has received legislative support in many states and has been legitimized by state and federal courts. In 1986, in a case involving a woman who looks white, who said she had always thought she was white, and whose ancestry is apparently 3/32 African black,[3] neither the Louisiana Supreme Court nor the United States Supreme Court saw any reason to disturb the application of the one-drop rule.[4]

The Hawaiian Islands became subject to the laws of the United States in 1900, when Hawaii was annexed as a territory, long before Hawaii became a state in 1959. However, the history of race relations since Haoles (non-Polynesians) first arrived in the islands has been very different from that of the mainland. Interracial and interethnic marriages have been common in Hawaii, whereas most of the black–white miscegenation on the mainland has been coercive and outside of marriage. Racially mixed people in Hawaii, rather than being assigned membership in any parent group, are perceived and respected as persons with roots in two or more ancestral groups.[5] The implicit rule has been that mixed-race persons are to be accepted as such and treated as equals by all racial and ethnic groups.[6] The practice has been the same for the small proportion of persons with African forbears as it has for those with other ancestries.[7]

Since abandoning the effort to count mulattoes in 1920, the U.S. Bureau of the Census has required each individual to be identified as a member of a single race, with no provision for mixed-race ancestries. When Hawaii became a state, this bureau system of monoracial classification replaced the island practice of recording racial mixtures.[8] There was no mixed-raced or multiracial category to select in the 1980 census enumeration and, apparently for several reasons, two-thirds of the people of Hawaii designated "other" as their racial identity. By 1989, racially and ethnically mixed people were the largest segment of the Hawaiian population, at least one-third. The current rate of intermarriage among the ethnic groups is 45 percent, suggesting that unmixed persons, ethnically and racially, will be rare in a few more generations.[9]

Other Patterns, Other Rules

Before probing further into the contrast between the Hawaiian and one-drop rules, we need some additional cross-cultural perspective. With the exception of the one-drop rule, racially mixed progeny are identified everywhere in the world as mixed people rather than as members of either (or any) parent group. However, there are great variations in the statuses to which mixed-race people are assigned. Let us note five other rules for mixed-race populations in addition to the Hawaiian and hypodescent rules, one of the five for non-black groups in the United States.[10]

A third rule decrees that a mixed-race population is a separate people with a lower status than that of either parent group. For example, this is the case with mixed children fathered by American soldiers, white or black, in Vietnam.[11] The children of American soldiers in Korea also have been subjected to contempt and severe discrimination. A child's identity and citizenship derive from the father in Korea and Vietnam. Except in rare cases where a valid marriage can be proven, the mixed children have no citizenship either in their native countries or in the United States. The Ganda peoples of Uganda in East Africa provide a similar example. They regard mulattoes with contempt and, during the British colonial occupation, both parent groups seriously considered removing all the mixed-race people to an island in Lake Victoria.[12]

The métis of Canada (progeny of whites and Canadian Indians) further illustrate the bottom-of-the-ladder outcome; although for a time they had an in-between status, the métis were despised and rejected by the Indian tribes and also by the British and French. In 1884, after their second rebellion, the métis were crushed by British troops and scattered throughout the wilderness of the Canadian West. Today there are more métis than full Indians in Canada. Many still live as isolated outcasts; those who have moved to the cities are a poor, demoralized underclass. Although "mixed-bloods" in the United States have generally been perceived by the tribes as less worthy than full Indians, they have fared far better than have the métis in Canada. In the United States, tribal definitions of eligibility for membership vary from extremely small fractions of tribal ancestry to one-half, whereas the federal government's position generally has been that a person must have one-fourth Indian ancestry to be classed as "Indian."[13]

Following a fourth rule, a mixed-race population is defined as a separate people but accorded a status higher than that of either parent group. This occurred in Haiti after a long rebellion ended French control in 1804. The mulattoes, who had been an in-between group before independence, became dominant over the far larger population of unmixed blacks. They became political and economic elites who looked down on whites as well as blacks and prevented intermarriage with both parent groups.[14] The mulattoes' political monopoly ended in 1957 with the coming of the first Duvalier regime, although they still vie for power. Mulattoes also became dominant elites in the African societies of Liberia and Namibia.

The political ascendance of the mestizos in Mexico since 1821 further illustrates the fourth rule. During the three centuries of Spanish rule, there was large-scale miscegenation between the Spanish and the Indian peoples. During this period the mixed-race people, the mestizos, had an in-between status. After the success of the revolution against the Spanish in 1821, the mestizos became politically dominant over the Spanish and Indian (and small black) populations. Although the Spanish and other presumably unmixed whites continue to have considerable wealth and influence, mestizos—by far the largest population group—hold the balance of political power.

The fifth rule defines racially mixed progeny as a separate people who occupy an in-between status position. Some such people identify more with one of the parent groups than the other, although this allegiance may shift with changing circumstances. Some develop a firm identity of their own, such as the mixed children living on military bases in Japan—half Japanese and half American white or black.[15] In-between groups provide a buffer between the parent groups and are often liaison agents between the two. Sometimes they develop specialized economic tasks, doing necessary work the dominant group does not want to do, in which case they become middlemen or simply middle minorities.

Politically, whether racially mixed or not, middle minorities are relatively powerless and their status is uncertain and volatile. In crisis situations the dominant group does not protect the middle minority from resentful lower status groups.[16] For a long time, the métis of Canada had a strong group identity and were proud of their special occupations—transporting goods by canoe and a special cart, hunting buffalo, and acting as interpreters for Indians and whites. The building of railroads and the rapid settlement of the Canadian frontier brought an end to the special occupations of the métis and precipitated their rebellion and disastrous fall from the middle status.

In the Republic of South Africa, the Coloureds and the Asians have been buffer groups between the whites and blacks. The rule for the Coloureds, particularly explicit during the apartheid era, has been that they shall have a separate identity and a status between that of unmixed blacks and whites. The Coloureds would be defined as blacks in the United States. Clearly there has been no one-drop rule in the Republic of South Africa.

The fourfold system of segregation under the apartheid laws was designed to keep what are called the "four races" apart to prevent further black–white miscegenation, to maintain the two buffer groups between whites and blacks, and thus to perpetuate white control of blacks. Passing as white has occurred but it has been open, following official administrative procedures for changing one's identity from Coloured to white. By contrast, passing has had to be secret in the United States to get around the one-drop rule. The establishment of the Apartheid system in 1948 forced large numbers of Coloureds to move to designated areas and imposed other hardships and status losses on them. As a result, the Coloureds have identified less and less with the whites and have increasingly supported the black protests.

A sixth rule is followed in lowland Latin America south of Mexico and in the Caribbean. The rule says that the status of all mixed-race persons may vary all the way from quite low to quite high, depending on the individual's lifestyle, mainly on economic and educational achievements. Whites are at the top of these class structures and unmixed blacks and Indians on the bottom. Blacks are defined as only those of unmixed African descent. Although the many rungs on the long status ladder are indicated by terms that describe the highly variable physical appearance of mulatto and mestizo individuals, this racial terminology can be quite misleading. These are actually class systems in which lifestyle is much more important than racial ancestry or physical traits.[17] "Money whitens," as the phrase goes, and a person who rises in educational and economic status is identified by whiter racial designations.[18] Persons with some obvious African or Indian traits may even be accepted as white, if they are quite prosperous and well educated.[19]

The above pattern pertains in the Iberian or Spanish-speaking islands in the Caribbean, where high status enables light mulattoes and mestizos with visible African or Indian traits to marry whites. On the British and other Northwest European islands in the Caribbean, persons with known African or Indian ancestry are also accepted for marriage with whites but only if they appear white.[20] Secret passing is unnecessary because there is no one-drop rule on either the Iberian or the northwest European islands. The rule for the latter islands seems to be followed generally in Northern Europe, whereas the Iberian variant is generally followed in Southern Europe.

In Puerto Rico, as in lowland Latin America and elsewhere in the Caribbean, racial terms of reference for mixed-race people have uncertain meanings, class criteria outweigh physical traits, and racial identity is a negotiable entity.[21] Approximately three-fifths of all Puerto Rican migrants to the United States have had some visible African ancestry and have therefore been perceived on the mainland as blacks. However, most of these migrants were known on the island by one of the many designations for mixed-race people, not as blacks, and many of them were classed as whites. Some migrants who do not look too black or Indian succeed in emphasizing their Spanish heritage and in becoming known as Hispanics or Latinos, cultural rather than racial designations. The darker migrants tend to pressure their youth to marry light mulattoes or whites to "whiten" the family and promote upward social mobility.[22] This strategy creates cultural misunderstanding and antagonizes the American black community, which sees it as disloyalty—as "denying their color."

The seventh rule assigns the status of an assimilating minority to mixed-race people. This rule is implicit in the treatment of all racial minorities other than African blacks in the United States—of East Asians, Native Americans, and others. Persons who are half white and half Chinese or Filipino, for instance, are usually considered marginal to both parent groups and they have an ambiguous status. In some situations the hypodescent tendency predominates—to treat such persons as members of the lower status group—but no one-drop rule is invoked. When further miscegenation occurs, however, children whose ancestry is one-fourth or less from such a group are generally able to marry whites if they wish to and become fully assimilated into Anglo-American life. These assimilating individuals, like European immigrants, may be proud of being one-fourth or less Japanese or Korean, three-eighths Irish, and so on, and do not have to pass secretly into the dominant community to receive full acceptance and equal opportunity. This largely one-way assimilation in the United States contrasts with what is more nearly a melting-pot process in the Hawaiian Islands. Also, despite some similarities, it differs from the process in Latin America and with both variants in the Caribbean.

The History of the One-Drop Rule

Black–white miscegenation began in Colonial America when slaves from Africa were introduced more than 350 years ago. The first widespread mixing occurred in the Chesapeake Bay area.[23] Despite legal uncertainties, the one-drop rule had become the social or customary definition of who was black in the upper South by the early 1700s. Virginia drew a genetic line by statute in 1785, defining a Negro as anyone with one-fourth or more African ancestry, a legal rule adopted generally in the upper South at that time.[24] Such laws defined as white a large number of persons with known, and often visible, black ancestry. This conflict between the social and legal definitions persisted for decades.

The one-drop rule was initially neither the legal nor the social rule in parts of the lower South. Especially in areas around New Orleans and Charleston, South Carolina, many of the early mulattoes were freed and became a class with their own identity and a middle minority status between that of blacks and whites. South Carolina's courts rejected the one-drop rule explicitly.[25] Until the 1840s in South Carolina, known and visible mulattoes could marry into white families. The early Black Creoles in southern Louisiana were prevented by law from marrying either blacks or whites, although some did so,[26] and they successfully avoided the one-drop rule until the 1850s.[27]

During the plantation era, white males often obtained sexual access to slave girls and women by threats of violence or other punishments.[28] The all-pervasive master–slave "etiquette" allowed white males to gain this physical intimacy but still to remain in total control of the slaves. Sexual contact between black men and white women, however, was absolutely forbidden. Another mixed child in the slave quarters was an economic asset, but a mulatto child in the big house would threaten the system. White men thus enslaved their own children and grandchildren.[29] Mulatto–unmixed black sexual contacts accelerated the "whitening" of the slave population and mulatto–mulatto unions continued the interracial mixing of the genes.

By 1850 the discrepancy between the social and legal definitions of who was black became a bitter conflict. White fears of slave rebellions and of the end of slavery fanned hostility toward mulattoes throughout the South.[30] Support for the rule that mulattoes were an in-between group rather than blacks declined rapidly, even in South Carolina and Louisiana.[31] The more the whites rejected the tie with mulattoes, the more the latter were compelled to see themselves as Negroes rather than as "almost whites." As the South braced itself to defend slavery, the one-drop rule became more nearly universal.

The net effect of the Civil War and its aftermath was to strengthen support for the one-drop rule among whites and blacks, including mulattoes. During the Reconstruction years in the devastated South, the legislatures and courts of South Carolina, Louisiana, and some other states limited the definition of black persons to those with one-fourth, one-eighth, or some other fraction of black ancestry. In cases of doubt, however, the one-drop rule increasingly prevailed.[32] The war accelerated the alienation of whites from mulattoes and the latter emerged as Negro leaders in the South. Black–white sexual contacts were probably at a low point because of heightened racial animosity and the relative lack of interracial proximity in the new sharecropping system.[33]

Developments after Reconstruction in the South further undergirded the one-drop rule. Working-class whites led the passage of segregation statutes, voting restrictions, and other legal devices designed to reduce blacks to a near-slave status. This Restoration movement was legitimized by a United States Supreme Court decision in 1883[34] and in the 1896 separate-but-equal precedent case of *Plessy v. Ferguson*.[35] Homer Plessy, who was one-eighth African black and looked white, challenged the Louisiana statute requiring racially segregated seating on trains. The Supreme Court briefly took judicial notice of the definition of a Negro as a person with any known black ancestry. The case shows how the one-drop rule was used to strengthen white domination of blacks.[36]

By 1910 the Jim Crow system of segregation was well established. To enforce the antimiscegenation laws that were included in the flood of Jim Crow legislation, the concerned states had to define a Negro. Some states specified small fractions of black ancestry and others explicitly stated the one-drop rule. By 1915 the one-drop rule had become universally backed by whites, in the South and North.[37]

During the building of the Jim Crow system, white animosity toward mulattoes was strong, and there was much fear of "invisible black blood." The oppression of blacks was notably violent during this period, and lynching reached its peak between 1890 and 1910.[38] It was at this time that W. E. B. DuBois and other mulatto leaders began their long struggle for civil rights, especially to bring the Jim Crow system down. Many of the lightest mulattoes took the drastic and painful step of passing as white to escape the racial obstacles to achievement. The peak years of passing were probably from 1880 to 1925.

Black migration to Northern cities was accelerated by World War I. In the 1920s, laws blocking immigration from southern and eastern Europe, Asia, and Africa opened up low-cost housing in the inner cities for large numbers of Southern blacks and Hispanic migrants. Mulattoes in New York's Harlem and other cities led the Black Renaissance of the 1920s, celebrating a black identity and a black culture rooted both in African and American experiences. By 1925 the American black community, including most mulattoes, firmly supported the one-drop rule.[39]

Most of the Jim Crow laws required racial segregation in public facilities, including schools, but some pertained to miscegenation and others to political, legal, or economic life.[40] The primary means of ensuring white control in black–white personal contacts was the master–servant behavior known as the racial etiquette. Blacks had to act out their subordinate position to avoid being accused of getting out of "their place." Black violations of the etiquette or other challenges to the system resulted in warnings, threats of violence, and acts of terrorism, including lynching.[41]

The one-drop rule and the symbol of white womanhood, which meant no sexual contacts between white females and black males, were crucial to the perpetuation of the Jim Crow system. Many of the same white males who used strong rhetoric about the dangers of "mongrelization" also used threats of violence or other punishments to gain sexual access to black women and girls. The resulting children, in accordance with the one-drop rule and the expectation that a child stays with its mother, lived in black homes and thus posed no danger to the Jim Crow system. Mixed-race children in white homes were not tolerated because, as under slavery, they threatened the system.

Although not required by law, except for some antimiscegenation statutes, systematic segregation also prevailed in the North in public facilities, jobs, and housing. This northern pattern was widely supported by public opinion, threats, the Ku Klux Klan, and sometimes by violence. Black–white sexual contacts were limited, usually occurred outside of marriage, involved black males more than in the South, and were generally less coercive of black women.

The Civil Rights Movement of the 1950s and 1960s ended the Jim Crow system and achieved other gains, but the one-drop rule emerged stronger than before. The years of delay and white backlash against desegregation fueled the Soul Movement, a second black renaissance emphasizing black pride and political power. Black pride united lighter mulattoes with blacks in general more closely than ever. However, the intense focus on blackness often put light blacks on the defensive, and they have felt pressure to affirm their African roots, their black pride, their loyalty, and thus the one-drop rule.[42] The prestige of lightness in the black community had been devalued considerably by the mid-1970s.[43]

The one-drop rule has become strongly self-perpetuating in the black community, as witnessed by intense black opposition to passing as white and the infrequency of passing by persons who could do so.[44] Black family and community hostility is often great when a white-appearing "black" marries a white.[45] The message is that anyone with even the slightest trace of black ancestry who marries across the ethnic line is a traitor to the black community. Similarly, since 1972, the National Association of Black Social Workers has led opposition to the adoption by white parents of children with any black ancestry, on the ground that white parents are incapable of teaching the child the firm black identity needed to survive as a black.[46] By 1976, such adoptions were almost stopped and, by 1987, at least thirty-five states had a policy against "cross-racial" adoption.

From 75 to more than 90 percent of all members of the American black community have some white ancestry[47] and estimates of those with Native American forbears range from 30 to 70 percent.[48] Probably between one-fifth and one-fourth of the genes of African Americans have come from white ancestors.[49] The genes of peoples from Africa, Europe, Native America, and some from Asia have mingled to produce an extremely wide range of racial variation in the American population defined as black—all the way from persons who look African to others who look white, Native American, or even Asian.[50]

The American black community is composed of a "new people" in a sociocultural as well as a biological sense.[51] The one-drop rule has made soul brothers and sisters of people with widely varying physical traits. Sharing a culture based on a long history of oppression and other common experiences, African Americans are an ethnic group with a strong sense of group identity and pride. Although the one-drop rule provided crucial support for slavery and Jim Crow segregation, African Americans have taken it for granted for a very long time and now generally feel they have a vested interest in it. Ironically, the observation that the one-drop rule has been an arbitrary and racist social construction arouses fears that the black community will lose members, black political strength, and some valued leaders and role models.

There have been deviations from the one-drop rule on the mainland.[52] Those who have rejected or tried to avoid the rule include those who have passed as white, many white adoptive parents and their children, some intermarried couples and their children, many

Puerto Ricans and other Hispanic Americans, 200 or so small communities of American mestizos or Triracial Isolates in the East and South,[53] and Marcus Garvey and other proponents of black racial purity.[54] Such departures seem generally to have provoked affirmations of the rule and have reinforced it more than they have undermined it.

Strong reinforcement of the one-drop rule provides a firm black identity for most African Americans, but the rule has its costs. There are dilemmas and traumas over personal identity,[55] ambiguities and strains in everyday life, divisive conflicts over color in black families and communities,[56] collective hysteria about passing and about invisible blackness,[57] heavy pressure on light mulattoes to prove their blackness, administrative and legal problems of racial classification, misperceptions of the racial identities of huge populations in Asia and the Middle East, and failure to take miscegenation into proper account in scientific studies of African Americans.[58] These problems stem from the great physical diversity in the African American community, especially from classifying as black those persons whose ancestry is mostly non-African.

Mixed-Race Experience on the Islands

The original settlers in the Hawaiian Islands were Polynesians, a racially mixed people. Some 1,500 years ago they migrated to Hawaii from the Marquesas Islands and others came later from Tahiti.[59] The survivors of two Spanish ships wrecked in the sixteenth century found the Hawaiians friendly, tolerant, and accepting of sexual relations and marriage with Haoles. Captain Cook and his crew received the same hospitable treatment in 1778. The Hawaiians welcomed the first white settlers as equals and valued them as informants on the ways of outsiders.[60] The early traders and settlers reciprocated the equal treatment, being few and wanting economic benefits rather than military conquest or political rule.

Many of the early white settlers took Hawaiian wives, often the daughters of chiefs, and the first hapa-Haoles (half-outsiders) were accorded great respect. Still today it is prestigious to be part Hawaiian. The tradition of racial and ethnic tolerance, including treatment of racially mixed progeny as equals, was accepted by later arrivals. White newcomers to the islands, including Southern whites from the mainland, generally have accepted this cultural practice within a few months of their arrival.[61]

The native Hawaiians could not meet the rising demand for workers in the sugar cane fields in the 1850s, partly because they disliked field work, but mainly because their numbers had been decimated by diseases brought in from outside. The Haole planters first imported thousands of Chinese workers, next several thousand Portuguese and other Europeans, and then far greater numbers of Japanese. By 1900 the Japanese made up forty percent of the population, the largest ethnic group, while the Hawaiians and part Hawaiians constituted 25 percent.[62]

Several thousand Koreans and Puerto Ricans came after 1900, followed by more Portuguese, then by Filipinos.[63] Some of these Portuguese and probably more than half of the Puerto Ricans had some African ancestry, and they, along with other persons with African forbears, were defined in Hawaii as mixed-race persons and accepted as equals.[64] Many Pacific Islanders are themselves quite dark, although not because they have African ancestry. Since World War II, and especially since the abolition of the national origins quota laws in 1985, immigrants have come from many places, including the Pacific Islands, the Philippines, East Asia, South Asia, the U.S. mainland, Mexico, European nations, and the Middle East.

One reason mixed-race people in Hawaii have continued to receive egalitarian treatment is that there are so many of them and so many parent groups. Life on the islands has been characterized by the genetic mixing of the many different peoples. It is common to be able to identify ancestry in two or more groups and very bad manners to speak ill of miscegenation.[65] Except for the Japanese and Portuguese, most immigrants in the early twentieth century were young, single men, many of whom have intermarried with other groups. In the late twentieth century, women exceeded men as migrants to Hawaii.[66] Although ethnic in-group marriages are preferred, both ethnicity and race are usually less important in marital choice than personal qualities, education, and occupation. Racially mixed "locals" (islanders) are generally viewed as desirable marriage partners.[67]

The number of Hawaiians and part Hawaiians combined had declined to 38,547 by 1910, a disastrous drop from the 300,000 or so when Captain Cook arrived in 1778. There were more part-Hawaiians than unmixed ones by 1910 and almost nine times as many by 1960. By the mid-1970s, a health survey found 191,652 persons with one-eighth or more Hawaiian ancestry, 18.3 percent of the state's residents, the third largest population group after whites and Japanese. Some persons with native ancestry claim the Hawaiian identity while others do not. Many mixed-race islanders, not just part Hawaiians, change their ethnic identification as they move from one situation to another.[68]

The United States outmaneuvered Great Britain and Japan to become the "protector" of the Hawaiian Islands, and Queen Liliuokalani was eased out of power in 1893 by American economic interests. Sanford B. Dole headed the Republic established in 1894 and was the first governor when Hawaii became a U.S. territory in 1900. The native chiefs, who had made land concessions too cheaply and too often, continued to lose more land. As a result, some native and mixed Hawaiians have experienced unemployment, poverty, and disease. A revival of the traditional native culture in the 1970s produced charges that wealthy whites and other groups have been guilty of ethnic prejudice and discrimination against native Hawaiians and part-Hawaiians.

Although Haoles gradually seized economic and political power from the native Hawaiians, and despite the tensions that have often existed among ethnic groups, intergroup relations in Hawaii have not been racist. There has been considerable migration from the mainland in recent decades, but racial prejudice is still generally considered to be contemptible. Race has been unimportant in class competition, and there has been no systematic racial segregation or discrimination. Both individuals and entire ethnic groups, irrespective of racial traits, have moved upward in educational, economic, and political status.

In more theoretical terms, the history of Hawaii has been one of amicable relations among ethnic groups—cultural pluralism. It has also been one of extensive social participation within each ethnic community—structural pluralism. However, there has been a balance between pluralism and assimilation. Different ethnic traditions have merged to a considerable extent—melting-pot type cultural assimilation. Also, members of all ethnic groups interact in small groups and recreational activities as well as at school, work, and other public places—structural assimilation.

Although there are no racial communities as such, the Hawaiian practice is egalitarian pluralism—both cultural and structural—among the racial categories. The cultural pluralism and assimilation involved are that of the ethnic groups represented, and the structural assimilation often involves interracial dating and intermarriage—thus miscegenation. Racial identity by itself is not a significant factor in marital choice, occupational mobility, the professions, business management, or government. The tolerant, egalitarian balance between pluralism and assimilation applies also to racially mixed persons—including those with African ancestry—who may be found among successful professionals, leaders in education, business executives at all levels, or government officials.[69]

A brief comparison between the status of racially mixed people in Hawaii and in Latin America is instructive. Class placement of such persons hinges on education and economic attainment in both patterns and can range from very low to very high. However, in Hawaii the class position of mixed-race individuals is not affected by color or other racial traits as it is to some extent in Latin America and the Caribbean. The class ladder does not have a preferred color at the top as in Latin America, and the constant rhetoric about racial traits is absent.

If Not the One-Drop Rule, What?

The Hawaiian tradition of egalitarian pluralism for mixed-race people poses the sharpest contrast in the world to the hypodescent or one-drop rule. The histories of these two rules could hardly be more different—one grounded in tolerance and respect for racially mixed persons, the other in racist beliefs and designed to keep mixed progeny in the lower status group so as to perpetuate slavery and Jim Crow segregation. Will increasing discussion of the one-drop rule in the United States result in more pressure on Hawaii to comply with the mainland tradition concerning African ancestry, or might the tail eventually wag the dog?

By the 1970s, as we have seen, support for the one-drop rule had become at least as strong in the American black community as among whites. Until the 1990s, it had seemed unlikely that the rule would be seriously challenged in the foreseeable future. However, the movement to allow mixed-race persons to adopt a biracial or multiracial identity has recently developed considerable momentum and achieved some success. Rather than attacking the one-drop rule frontally, the emphasis in this movement is on the freedom to choose one's own racial identity and to affirm one's whole self by acknowledging all of one's ancestries. The movement helps mixed-race persons to resist the American pressure to identify with only one distinct racial category and instead to define an identity of their own.[70] It has been suggested that "this is the next logical step in the progression of civil rights."[71]

Multiracial experiences have been included in some multicultural studies programs since the latter 1970s, notably at the Berkeley and Los Angeles campuses of the University of California. More than thirty organizations that affirm a multiracial identity have sprung up since the early 1980s and are nationally coordinated.[72] In recent years, the *Interrace* and *New People* magazines have publicized personal experiences and supported the general recognition of a multiracial identity. Multiracial experiences have begun to receive considerable attention in articles in newspapers and general magazines, in books, and on radio and television talk shows.

The multiracial identity movement embraces all racial blends, not just those involving African black ancestry. Although neither Asian nor Native American ancestry has been subject to a one-drop rule, the rule for black ancestry has caused the multiracial identity option to be omitted from official lists of racial categories. PROJECT RACE (Reclassify All Children Equally), headquartered in Atlanta, has persuaded several state legislatures to consider requiring the multiracial category on all state forms where racial identity must be checked. Moreover, by June 1993, laws to this effect had been passed in Ohio and Illinois. Such legislation is pending in Georgia and Wisconsin. Also, some school districts in these two states, in North Carolina, and other states have added the multiracial category. If the current drive by Project RACE and other organizations to get the U.S. Congress to add the multiracial category on census forms succeeds, a significant dent will have been made in the one-drop rule. The NAACP has decided neither to endorse nor oppose the use of the multiracial category.

However, the multiracial identity movement will encounter formidable opposition if the strong support for the one-drop rule in the black community becomes effectively mobilized. Many whites who are sympathetic to the movement will probably not support it if there is determined black opposition. We have only to recall how effective the National Association of Black Social Workers was in the 1970s in stopping whites from adopting children with black ancestry. Many African Americans fear that whites who support the multiracial option want to divide the black community, coopt some of its members, weaken black political power, and undermine affirmative action and other civil rights remedies.[73] There is also fear that persons who want to affirm their European, Native American, or Asian roots are trying to deny their African ancestry.[74]

The one-drop rule has been so settled in state and federal case law that litigation of it has been rare since early in the twentieth century. When statutes mandating the multiracial category on official forms are tested in the courts, judges may invalidate them. Or, if they rule favorably, courts may well be reluctant to extend this precedent to other situations. However, if legislatures and courts eventually support a broader agenda to affirm a multiracial identity, what might replace the one-drop rule?

Neither American history nor current outlooks of both the white and the black communities would support the third and fourth rules as discussed above, whereby mixed-race people would occupy a separate status either below or above that of both (or all) ancestral groups. Might the fifth rule, which decrees a middle status for the racially mixed, reemerge from the decisive defeat it suffered in the South in the 1850s? African Americans in general now abhor such a rule, associating it with using light-colored Uncle Toms as a buffer group to help whites control blacks. The white and the black communities have become so polarized that a middle status for mixed-race persons seems most improbable.

The sixth rule emerged in Latin America where, as in the United States, miscegenation has produced the total range of racial traits from individuals who look black to those who look white or Native American. This rainbow of racial characteristics is found within the population defined as black in the United States, whereas mixed persons with black ancestry are not defined as blacks in Latin America. Fear has been expressed that our one-drop rule might be replaced by Latin American "colorism," a class system in which status is associated at least roughly with the lightness of one's skin.[75] However, the histories and current social structures of the two Americas are so different that the sixth rule would probably seem too alien to most North Americans, white and black alike. The northwest European Island variant in the Caribbean, which permits persons with known African ancestry to intermarry if they look white, might seem but a small step from the one-drop rule. However, in addition to the fact that all mixed-race people on those islands are defined as many degrees of colored and not as black, many North American whites still hold the irrational fear of "invisible blackness."

There is strong sentiment against applying the seventh rule to persons with black ancestry, in the American white community and the black. This implicit rule enables racial minorities other than blacks to intermarry and be fully accepted by whites if their minority ancestry is one-fourth or less. To most whites, widespread intermarriage with persons who are one-fourth or less black would be an intolerable departure from the ultimate barrier to the total assimilation of blacks, the one-drop rule. Blacks and whites take measures to limit informal contacts with members of the other group, and both are strongly opposed to the total assimilation of blacks by whites.

Perhaps the Hawaiian rule, different as it is from the one-drop rule, is the most feasible alternative after all. We have seen that mainlanders who move to Hawaii can accept the island pattern after a few months. Egalitarian pluralism for mixed-race people would avoid the aspects of the fifth and sixth rules feared by at least some supporters of the multiracial identity movement,[76] because race is not a factor in class placement in Hawaii. African Americans, Hispanic Americans, Asian Americans, and Native Americans have all moved in the direction of egalitarian pluralism in preference to total assimilation of their groups by Anglo-Americans. The Hawaiian pattern exemplifies a workable balance between egalitarian pluralism and assimilation. It also shows how the pluralistic trend on the mainland might be extended to mixed-race people.

Finally, the Hawaiian rule offers an alternative to the seventh rule for racially mixed persons of nonblack descent on the mainland. Such persons now have an ambiguous status if their ancestry is more than one-fourth Asian or Native American. Those with one-fourth or less such ancestry may prefer to retain a multiracial identity rather than to become fully assimilated Anglo-Americans. Thus the Hawaiian pattern of amicable relations among all ethnic groups would seem a desirable alternative for all mixed-race people on the mainland, not only those with African ancestry.

10

Some Kind of Indian: On Race, Eugenics, and Mixed-Bloods

M. Annette Jaimes

One "Red Race" of People

In this ahistorical era of heightened contradiction and controversy over American citizenry and national character, American Indian tribes have insisted persistently that they, and not the U.S. government, hold the right to define tribal membership and therefore Indian identification, as differentiated from their U.S. citizenship. Traditionally, most tribes have determined their members by cultural rather than political criteria, and as Native nationhoods. This is in contrast to any "scientific" approach with a racial construct used to determine "blood quantum" formulations. Actually, there is no factual evidence that indigenous peoples of the Americas, before the European conquest, applied a concept of race to their traditional membership, which, in fact, included "whites" as well as "mixed-bloods" via naturalization and adoption. After the conquest and forced assimilation, one does run across references in Indian dialogue that a particular group sees itself as a national entity, in terms of its communal conceptualization of nationhood as "a people." Yet, this is not the same as the perception and promotion of themselves as a distinct "race" of people that has come forth in federal Indian policy-making. A famous Shawnee leader Tecumseh, for example, did refer to a "red race" of Native people, and others used terms such as full-blood, mixed-blood, and halfbreed.[1] However, it is the position of this paper that such terms meant different things to the Natives and non-Natives.

Euroamericans designated all "New World" Indians as one sin-

133

gle "race," predicated on ideas of "purity of race" and culture. This ideal later resulted in a tropism of a race construct linked with ethnicity and nationality. A group of intellectual reformers, calling themselves "Friends of the Indians," in contrast to those among the military and government leaders who wanted to keep on killing Indians in the nineteenth century, went so far as to declare Indians "blank slates" in order to build a case for their "Americanization" as lower status citizens.[2] This Eurocentric preoccupation with and construction of "race" can be found in the nineteenth-century racial–racist doctrines that were based on prevailing pseudoscientific theories, especially at times in the mid-1800s when "white" scientists measured skulls of Natives, called *Crania Americana,* to compare and contrast with other racial types to justify "a case for Indian inferiority."[3] Such blatant pseudoscience was meant to establish a theoretical framework that ordered and explained human variety, as well as to distinguish superior races from inferior ones. In this racial hierarchy, Indians were in competition with African– Black Americans as the lowest "race of mankind," in what was referred to as "the great chain of being" by Eurocentric social scientists.[4] Such racist orthodoxy has since been soundly disputed as European pseudoscience, which the Euroamericans took to quite readily as a rationale for racial oppression of colonized peoples as "groups of color." It overlooked those eighteenth-century patriarchal ideals of the Enlightenment, among western Europeans, that espoused all humankind as one brotherhood. However, the biblical origin myths prevailed in espousing a "Christian-derived" parentage among them that envisioned a "white" Adam and Eve. In this chapter, I address the areas of traditional Native identity in contrast to the later U.S. colonization, eugenics coding that has contributed to American racisms, the status of "mixed-blood" identities in Indian–Tribal demographics, and I close with who is *Indigenous to the Americas.*

Traditional Native Identity and U.S. Colonization

"New World" Indians were considered "savages" and "heathens" by the Spanish, at the same time the Spaniards were burning "heretics" during the Inquisition, to justify their imperial aims. By the seventeenth century, entire peoples indigenous to this hemisphere had been wiped out, with their cultures for the most part destroyed. Such racistly based pogroms ignored the physical and cultural diversity that was evident among Native groups.

In pre-Columbian times, traditional Native peoples designated their societies, more often than not, on matrilineal descendancy, with few exceptions to patrilineal descendancy in tracing their ancestry. Both led to elaborate kinship traditions through clan structures or moieties. (These clans respected the plant and animal worlds as living and spirit entities, in what cultural anthropologists call "animism" and "totemism.")[5] Generally speaking, more indigenous cultures trace relationship through the mother than through the father. These communal societies also had spheres of matrifocal and/or patrifocal influence and decision making among their members; some spheres were designated by age as well as gender, especially delegating leadership and authority among senior members as elders. Women among the oldest Southwest tribes (i.e., Pimas/Maricopas, Hopis) had decision-making control in the education of the younger generations as well as in agrarian activities, whereas the men had more visible influence in religious ceremonies; all members participated in communal rituals. Yet, it is unlikely that traditional Native societies were matriarchies, as some feminists—Native as well as non-Native—attempt to claim;[6] the majority among them were matrilineal because it was much easier to trace a child from its mother. These kinship systems, consequently, allowed for much influence and power for decision making among the women in what are the closest models to egalitarianism among many Native societies.

In contemporary times, membership has been determined by some tribes to require birth on the reservation whereas some hold to a grandfather clause that accepts all identified as members before a certain date regardless of other factors. Assimilationist "policies," in contrast to traditional customs, have been influenced by mandated federal rules and regulations, which are primarily implemented by the Bureau of Indian Affairs (BIA).[7] Therefore, a variety of internally deduced cultural and kinship criteria are used to determine tribal membership. This may or may not coincide with the government's externally imposed policies of Indian identification process—primarily blanket-policies—implemented and regulated by several agencies of the federal government.

This conflict about identification has resulted in pressure for tribal councils to have "civil rights codes" written into their Indian Reorganization Act (IRA) constitutions (mandated by congressional legislation in 1934), and at times has intruded upon the exercise of tribal sovereignty in their internal affairs. The conflict becomes even more complex when, as in the case of *Santa Clara Pueblo v. Martinez* (436 US 49, 1978), a male-dominated leadership among a Pueblo society in New Mexico was able to take membership away from one of its women and her children because she had married a Navajo man outside of the tribe. This case reflects a "trickle-down patriarchy" as a result of IRA reorganization forced upon the Pueblo people by the U.S. government. The pre-IRA tradition of matrilineality that existed among the Santa Clara people, would have prevented this legal decision by a skewed male-dominated leadership on the Pueblo council.[8]

This usurpation of indigenous sovereignty in North America has a long history that involved European-spawned racial theories which led to federal Indian policy. The "blood quantum" stipulation first emerged from the interpretations of the General (Dawes) Allotment Act of 1887, which congressionally mandated the requirement that all eligible Indian individuals for allotments must be at least "one half or more Indian blood."[9] Such restrictive determination of who can identify as an "Indian" for federal entitlements has been fraught with inconsistencies and contradictions found in federal Indian policy throughout the twentieth century. These conflicts of policy have escalated during Republican administrations, particularly during the Reagan–Bush years.

> The blood-quantum mechanism most typically used by the federal government to assign identification to [Indian] individuals over the years is as racist as any conceivable policy. . . . The restriction of federal entitlement funds to cover only the relatively few Indians who meet quantum requirements, essentially a cost-cutting policy at its inception, has served to exacerbate tensions over the identity issue among Indians. . . . Thus, a bitter divisiveness has been built into Indian communities and national policies, sufficient to preclude achieving the internal unity necessary to offer any serious challenge to the status quo.[10]

The Allotment Act was designed to break up the communal land base of the particular tribes by dividing up land parcels among individual members. It was meant to coerce them into "white man's civilization" and rationalize their Christian salvation from "savagery." As a result of this act, there was even a campaign for non-Indian men to marry Indian women among the allotees, because the land-holdings would revert to the husband's control as patriarch of the family. In some cases, this led to the early death of the Indian wife, giving clear transfer of title to the "white" male spouse.[11] The hidden agenda in this legislation, which soon became apparent, was to coopt the land for non-Indian use and eventual ownership, as those Indians who "failed" as farmers and went into debt would either lease or sell their land parcels to non-Indians. This in turn led to the checkerboarding of non-Indian holdings among the Indian allotments; Cherokee communities in Oklahoma are a case in point. A drastic consequence of the allotment campaign in this forced assimilation, has cost Indian peoples at least two-thirds of their land base which has been expropriated by the federal government, under a "trusteeship" for the Indians, with cooperation from individual non-Indians. This has resulted in an estimated 100 out of 150 million acres being stolen by non-Indians with government complicity. Once all "blooded" Indians were "allotted," the federal government quickly opened up "surplus" land to non-Indian settlement; in addition, natural resources on Native lands were claimed by the federal government.[12]

Because of the imposed exclusion policy on Native Americans, most tribes today have succumbed to a required enrollment process and recordkeeping in order to insure federal recognition, as well as federal funding. These quasi-national entities may designate a different requirement of "blood quantum" than the BIA criteria of "quarter-blood," or none at all; the BIA reduced this standard from the "half-blood" quantum required in the Allotment Act as a result of the pressure to acknowledge the high degree of intermixing among American Indians. The Cherokees of Oklahoma are often represented as not requiring any "blood quantum" standard, which has contributed to their high membership population (240,000). The tribal registrar has indicated, however, that to apply for tribal membership, a person must first meet certain BIA criteria (as noted on the Cherokee membership application) that require a "Certificate of Degree of Indian Blood."[13] According to the latest data on American Indian tribes, Cherokees have recently surpassed the Navajo–Dine population (200,000) in numbers, but not in landbase.[14] Yet, the Cherokees are restricted to tracing their Indian descendancy through the controversial 1887 Dawes rolls (as listed in the Allotment Act), prepared by the federal government for designated allotments among "eligible" members on tribal rolls. As reported in the 1928 *Merriam Report*, these tribal rolls included many non-Indians who were listed as the result of the chicanery of "white" BIA commissioners. Marriages were arranged with "whites" causing Cherokee allotees to eventually lose their lands due to intermarriage. These practices led to the dispossession of traditional Indians from their homeland, as well as to the cultural deprivation of Oklahoma Cherokees.[15]

There are also the varying degrees of "blood quantum" requirements, to none-at-all among the Sioux (Lakotas, Dakotas, Hunkpapas, and Santees). The most recent tribe to remove the blood quantum requirement in its tribal constitution is the Osage in Oklahoma, but tribal enrollees have to have ancestors on the 1906 Osage rolls.[16]

Throughout the twentieth century, traditional kinship systems among Native cultures and their societies still survive, even if discreetly practiced, as can be attested to by cultural anthropologists and more recently sociologists, as well as by the tribal members themselves.[17] These kinship traditions are also in the context of what they hold in common as Native Nations with other indigenous peoples to the Americas, such as the Northwest fishing societies and the Pueblos of the Southwest, as well as *los Indios* of Central and South America. This is so even though a systemic and effective campaign has tried to diffuse and confuse these "Indian Identity" issues. At a 1969 congressional hearing, it was stated in testimony: "Questions of identity often trouble modern Indian youth, especially those of mixed Indian and white ancestry. Is being Indian a matter of adopted life-style and point of view, they wonder, or of physical appearance and the amount of genetic Indian-ness, which is traced by reconstructing a family tree ?"[18] Therefore, what contributes to the confusion are the various methods used to define and enumerate American Indians as a federal entitlement population in the United States. These include: legal definitions, such as enrollment in an American Indian tribe; self-declaration, as in more liberal U.S. census enumerations; community recognition, for example, by other Indians or tribal members; recognition by non-Indians; biological definitions, such as blood quantum (which is being condemned as a racist and genocidal policy by international human rights tribunals initiated by indigenous peoples); cultural definitions (which may include subjective determination, such as knowing one's native language or "acting" like an "Indian").[19]

Other systematic strategies in this colonization process are used to dispossess the Indians from their lands, and it was the allotment years that preceded a grander scheme of western expansionism. As illustration, the Allotment Act clearly demonstrates other economic determinants than the mere overflow of cash from the federal treasury into the use of blood quantum to negate Native individuals out of existence. The huge windfall of land expropriated by the United States, as a result of this act, was only the tip of the iceberg. For instance, in constricting the acknowledged size of Indian populations, the government could technically meet its obligations to reserve first rights to water usage for non-Indian agricultural, ranching, municipal, and industrial use in the arid West. The same principle pertains to the assignment of fishing quotas in the Pacific Northwest, a matter directly related to the development of a lucrative non-Indian fishing industry in that bioregion.[20]

Such racially constructed policy is indicative of an advanced stage of U.S. postmodernist colonization in the state of Native America. These race politics are succinctly stated by Rayna Green, curator of Native American Studies at the Smithsonian Institute: "There is a kind of 'ethnic cleansing' going on. . . ."[21] She was referring to the politics of "Indian Identity" over issues of who can or cannot claim to be "recognized" as a "legitimate" American Indian these days, which is interpreted from the amended Indian Arts and Crafts Act of 1990 (P.L. 101-644-1104 *Stat.* 4662) for self-serving ends. (This was actually her response to being targeted by "Indian Identity police," herself, for not being an "enrolled" Cherokee. However, the tribal chair of the Cherokee Nation, Wilma Mankiller, has come out in support of Green as a respected individual, regardless of her "unenrolled" Cherokee status, who has done much good for the Cherokee people.)

Individual attacks on nonfederally–recognized Indians, who have neither BIA certification nor tribal affiliation, are a kind of race-baiting with tragic consequences of ethno-racism and autogenocide among Native peoples, even though many of those targeted have documentation that traces their family trees to Native descendancy. Those who cannot "prove" they are Indian are also being accused of "ethnic fraud" by some self-serving Indian spokespersons and organizations.[22] Such charges seem to be underlined with neo-fascist tendencies and motives among the accusers. Questions arise as to whether or not a Native individual or group need be identified as Indian by geneology, as in kinship relations, and/or by culture. These identity questions come at a time when many Native cultures are under seige by mainstream society and their lifeways are threatened. This matter is not so much a problem among those who are trying to pass themselves off as "Indians," as it is among neoconservative tribal elite cultural brokers who are guilty of corruption brought on by Indian and tribal partisan politics. Hence, these campaigns to discredit Indians are based more on disinformation, rumormongering, and just plain mean-spiritedness that presume the person under attack is guilty until she or he can prove otherwise. Those individuals and families who are victimized in this way have decisions imposed upon them because they are out of favor with those in control, and these arbitrary decisions are often sanctioned by the BIA technocrats and federal authorities.

Eugenics Coding and American Racisms

Eugenics coding is not new to the Eurocentric historiography and the United States is no exception. Other groups of color and creed have been defined in racialist terms, for example, Africans were coded by "blood" to designate their ability to be "good" and "strong" slaves and to serve as "beasts of burden." Even after the Civil War and the emancipation of the African slaves in U.S. society, the "one-drop rule" still prevailed to determine if an individual was to be racially classified as a Negro. An attorney, Brian Begue, made this statement in an appellate court, "If you're a little bit white, you're black. If you're a little bit black, you're still black."[23]

This "one-drop rule" is the antithesis of how American Indians or Native Americans are determined, based on blood quantum formulations that require the minimum BIA standard of quarter-blood for federal recognition, and more recently tribal membership among some groups. In this process anything below that quantum disqualifies individuals from their Native ancestry and heritage. In 1972, intertribal organizations in the United States wrote a manifesto entitled *Twenty Points* that listed grievances as a result of U.S. colonization among disenfranchised and dispossessed Native Americans. One of these points denounced the BIA implementation of blood quantum criteria as a racist and genocidal policy to terminate the rights of Native peoples as individuals and tribal groups.[24] Some Native groups advocate that the blood quantum degree should be increased, from "quarter-blood" to "half-blood" (as called for in the 1887 Allotment Act); some tribal spokespersons now advocate a "racially pure" Indian people among their own tribes. This goes against current research on "genetic markers" which indicates a high degree of racial mixing among Native populations to North America, which was even evident in pre-Columbian times.[25] It would also violate traditional kinship taboos that prohibit incest while encouraging exogamy among Native Nations. Tribal entities with small population, such as the Turtle Mountain Chippewa tribe (in North Dakota), would be most affected with all the attendant health problems due to inbreeding. In the state of Hawaii, the 50 percent blood quantum has prevailed since its imposition by the United States authorities, to determine who are eligible to call themselves Native Hawaiian. A "People's Tribunal" on Native Hawaiian sovereignty was held in Hawaii in the summer of 1993. After hearing several days of testimony among the indigenous population of the Islands, nine notable international judges recommended that "Blood quantum standards of identification should be immediately suspended."[26] As Haunani Kay Trask states, "We [the Native Hawaiians] are the only population that are defined racially on the Islands. . . . We traditionally determined our membership by geneology that is connected with the land, and which is different then race."[27] These racist and genocidal polices had nothing to do with indigenous traditions and kinship structures of a land-based culture and nationhood that were manifested in Native spirituality until the coming of the racially preoccupied "white" Europeans.

This xenophobic perception of distinct and absolute races (those of Western European stock are deemed "superior" in contrast to "inferior" ones), which is predicated on skin color and other physical traits, has the underlying but unproven assumption of a "purity of racial blood." This assumption also was manifested in Nazi Germany with horrifying consequences and tragedy, to those who did not fit the ideal of the German "super race." In what he calls *The Nazi Connection*, Stefan Kuhl makes astonishing links with Nazi race policies and American eugenicists as collaborators in what is known as the International Eugenics Movement.[28] Historical analysis of Adolf Hitler's leadership has correlated the Fuerher's recorded interest in the earlier U.S. genocidal campaign that targeted early Native peoples as a model for his "Jewish Solution" during World War II.[29] Ward Churchill's treatise for "a functional definition of genocide" has laid out the premise that the containment policy in South Africa's Apartheid against the indigenous peoples in that country was also influenced by the United States–established reservation system.[30]

In the history of United States racism, the color lines were drawn on southern Europeans and Asian groups who were targeted for entry and citizenship restrictions by immigration quotas. These restrictions were invoked when large numbers of Asian-American immigrants posed a threat of the diffusion of "white" American citizens during this country's growth years.[31] U.S. miscegenation laws on the books discouraged Euroamericans from marrying persons of "color." These were officially struck down in 1968, as a result of civil rights legislation (of which some has been dismantled). But there is evidence that some states, especially in the South and more recently in the Pacific Northwest, covertly and illegally implement them.[32] During World War II and into the 1960s, America's Indians were mainly out of sight while contained on the reservations, or they were visible as alcoholics on skidrow only, especially the male population coming back from the war and suffering post-combat experiences.[33] Among the latter, many Indian veterans became recipients of federal programs in the 1960s, ironically to assist them in making the transition from reservation to urban life in the big cities, at the expense of relinquishing their tribal community status among their own peoples.

Postindustrial, high-tech modernization is an advanced stage of *institutional racism* that permeates the whole of American society. This is manifested in its salience as well as signification of race, gender, and class distinctions in hierarchical and elitist structures. In U.S. historiography, a strain of American racism unique to this country is predicated on Eurocentric myths interpreted from biblical scripture that a "chosen" people are meant to have dominion over nature and others as they subdue the Earth (Genesis 1: 28).[34] This can be called theological racism, but the Anglo-Americans who settled in this country called it their "manifest destiny," to justify the conquest and colonization of early indigenous peoples and their lands to the Americas, within the context of the arrogant "Doctrine of Discovery" of European imperialism. This "Christian nationalism" evolved to rationalize imperialism by a Protestant crusade in the United States.[35] A biological ideology to justify this race teleology was later extrapolated from Newtonian physics and Darwinian economics, but it has been debunked as pseudoscientism.

As a first-class power with Second and even Third World people among its "ethnic minorities," the United States is guilty in its mistreatment of all groups of people who do not meet "white" ideals of physical characteristics and "moral" character. In its mainstream xenophobia and racism against others the United States is also guilty of violating basic human rights; it has been particularly avaricious in targeting indigenous peoples with visible acts of genocide and ethnocide that can be correlated with ecocide.

There is an increasing amount of documentation on what is being calling *environmental racism*, because Indian lands have been targeted first for military sites, uranium mining, and toxic waste dumps. In the Southwest, the Four Corners area and Black Mesa, among the Dine and Hopi in Arizona, and Acoma and Laguna Pueblo in New Mexico were declared "national sacrifice areas" in the 1970s by the Nixon Administration,[36] and Native inhabitants were treated as expendable people on their own homelands. This game plan can also be linked with the *ecological racism* that denies Native groups their first-rights claims to water and other natural resources found on their designated landbases.[37] There is also the destruction by prodevelopment schemes, such as highway construction, that cause land erosion, stream deterioration and flooding of communities and sacred sites on Native lands.

At the same time, a prevailing Eurocentric mind-set laments the passing of traditional Native peoples and their cultures, as in bygone days, while proclaiming that these groups are participating in their own demise by getting in the way of "progress."[38] There is no other word for this than genocide, both cultural and biological. Indigenous peoples throughout the globe and especially in Third World countries find themselves under siege of prodevelopment agendas. Any indigenous group resisting its own destruction by the corporate domination and coercion of the prodevelopment technological paradigm is stigmatized as backward and primitive. This insidious prejudice negates Native peoples' environmental rights by referring to them as "ecological noble savages," a phrase inspired by romantic literati of the past and taken up by present-day satirists.[39]

Those tribal groups who succumb to prodevelopment schemes, which often involve Indian gaming, find they are denigrated for not behaving like "Indians" by environmental fundamentalists and others who do not want the competition. These tribal decisions are often made in order to build some kind of self-sufficiency after long years of poverty and colonization in the United States. On the other hand, there is a highly visible group of "cultural brokers" in the Indian world who have a record of opportunism, as well as "progressive" tribal leaders, who succumb to "economic bribery" at the expense of the well-being of their Native constituency. In one such recent scenario, the Mescalero Apache tribal council negotiated a nuclear dump site in their community, against the protests of their own people.[40] This is a Catch 22 that Native peoples face in the dialectics of their survival.

Currently, facts are coming to light that the United States is still on the path of imperialist designs for conquest and colonization, which first led to the subjugation of this hemisphere's original inhabitants in the formation of its race-conscious nationalism. As the only superpower in the world, the United States collaborates with transnational corporations and second- and third-rate world powers in super schemes (i.e., NAFTA [North American Free Trade Agreement] and the Trilateral Commission); the mainstream citizenry and well-being of this planet are threatened by its predatory pursuit of the profit motive.[41]

It is all too evident that American racisms are alive and well in U.S. social and political institutions. Even more insidious signs are on the horizon, as Native peoples in North America, among other indigenous peoples worldwide, are now being subjected to genetic research. This extension of the eugenics movement is being called the "Human Genome Diversity Project,"[42] as the latest form of racism on the globe. Selected Native groups are being targeted as intact biological, cultural, and land-based entities, and as "threatened" peoples; this means that such groups are soon-to-be extinct as biological and cultural gene pools. There are scientists who claim they are interested in preserving these groups for future study by soliciting DNA data sampling and collection from human subjects among their membership. At the same time, these same scientists do not seem concerned that these groups are facing their physical demise as distinct peoples and cultures. This kind of research is still predicated on the racist doctrines of *scientific racism*. This is a science of bigotry, that also has unethical aims because one of its major objectives is to patent the data accumulated as genetic resource data as the "intellectual property" of the geneticists.

The eugenics "experts" have already experimented with the genetic engineering of plants and animals,[43] which leads one to ponder what they have in store for humans. This is the "virtual reality" context from which genetic research is operating, and at the expense and exploitation of Native peoples as merely biological and cultural entities. Many Native human rights activists are concerned about this project which they call the "Vampire Project"[44] (because the best genetic sample is a subject's blood).

Indigenous delegations to the United Nations are beginning to suspect a new kind of racism that is continuing the genocide, ethnocide, and ecocide of these populations and their habitats. Some even suspect that the intent is to remove the Native peoples as final barriers to corporate development, which also includes land seizures and the intellectual property rights that indigenous peoples hold about agrarian and ecological knowledge.[45] The Human Genome Diversity Project is being initiated and backed by private transcorporate enterprises, and has been designated as a separate project from the larger Human Genome Project that is sampling the human species at large. Hence *genetic racism* is manifesting itself today under the guise of medical research to find cures for terminal diseases and to prolong human life. This is all happening in an era of human overpopulation and "endangered species," and yet there are predictions of human cloning and "designer babies" in the continuing search for the perfect human and ultimate immortality. A new eugenics is on the scene, but with more awareness from the past in raising questions as to *who* will have access to this data and power and *why,* and for *what* worthy or wicked purpose it will be eventually and inevitably used.

Mixed-Blood Identities

Miscegenation is a necessary topic in any discussion about race, especially because debates are often predicated on the strange Eurocentric assumption about the "purity" of the races. Miscegenation got the attention of the Spanish and Portuguese sovereigns when their own citizens persisted in intermixing with the Native population of the "New World." But those liaisons were often not recognized by the Roman Catholic authorities as legitimate marriages. Such indirectly sanctioned illegitimacy can be correlated with a pecking order in determining occupation that was to be used as a racist strategy for slave labor. This is documented in historical annals on the Spanish and other European social systems, which stratify the hierarchy of racial castes.[46] According to more modern prevailing attitudes on miscegenation, someone who is born of two diverse "races" is of marginal status and will therefore develop a marginal personality. It is assumed that these individuals will have difficulty in reconciling the two cultures from whence they come and that these difficulties will therefore contribute to their marginalization and even alienation.[47] The underlying presumption in this context is that "marginal" people have no ethics or moral conscience because they are not committed devotees, enthusiasts, or patriots of either social system. This presumption is also grounded in the presumed superiority of the national ideology referred to as the "Protestant Ethic" and Western Christianity in general, among Euroamerican immigrants to the United States.

In this racial–racist construction, it is also important to provide a context of how so-called mixed-bloods were perceived in pre-Columbian times. As noted before, there is no evidence that early indigenous peoples to this hemisphere based their membership on any construct of "race." The obsession with race was brought over with Eurocentric ideas that also subordinated women.

The Native cultures did acknowledge diversity in physical characteristics, but were more concerned with cultural differences between themselves and others. There was a strong sense of nationhood that can even be described as ethnocentrism among all Native Nations, but this was not predicated on any racial criteria. It was not until the importation of pseudoscientific ideas of race (with other Eurocentric ideas such as sexism), that racially designated sub-categories proliferated—mulattos, quadroons, mestizos, métis, creoles, half-breeds, and so forth—as hybrid categories. Among Native Americans, intermixing has led to mixed-blood categories, such as the Red–Black Indians among Cherokees, Lumbees, and other southeastern tribes, as well as the mestizo (of Spanish and Indian mixings) Indians of the Southwest and Mexico, and the metis (of French and Indian mixing, or Indian and white) among the northern Nations of the United States and Canada.

In analyzing "color, race, and caste in the evolution of Red–Black peoples," Jack Forbes quotes early Spanish and Portuguese sources on the origins of such biracial terms as mestizo and mulatto. Forbes also traces the growth of racism and disdain for "mixed-bloods," from simply describing status in occupation and citizenry to derogatory stereotypes.[48] The Spaniards were notorious for these racial classifications, and more than thirty categories were designated as interracial categories among their populace.[49] An ecclesiastical policy was even developed for how the church authorities determined who was biologically an ideal Christian, that included

being of "pure" race, which they called limpiezas de sangre (purity of blood).[50]

This xenophobia projected on "mixed-bloods" is confused with
a purity in culture as well as race, which is manifested in nationalist pride and other political ideologies. Such myths have led to
and even directly espouse "ethnic cleansing" in volatile parts of
the world today, as in the current Serbian war raging against the
Croatians in Eastern Europe.

The Lumbees of North Carolina have state recognition, but are
still in the process of pursuing federal recognition. For the first
time, tribal leaders among federally recognized groups have been
solicited to cast their votes in this process, and a majority voted
against the Lumbees. There are several theories as to what was behind
this and even talk of ethnoracism among the already-recognized
groups. And even though it looks like the Lumbees, among the Red–
Black Indians, might attain a pseudotribal status from the federal
government, they have been criticized for having too open an
enrollment policy in determining their tribal membership. In the
Southwest, several tribal peoples can rightfully claim a tricultural
description as a result of early missionization by the Spanish Roman
Catholics, and later the Protestant settlers. Among these Native
peoples are the Pimas, Apaches, Yaquis, and T'Ono O'dom (formerly
Papagos) in Arizona, as well as the Pueblo societies of New Mexico,
and the southern California Mission Band Rancherias.

Russell Thornton also has written about the high degree of intermarriage and miscegenation among American Indians since the
European conquest. He writes that this intermixing actually changed
the physical and genetic makeup of Indian populations. He states,
"In many if not most instances, mixing with nontribal or non-Indian populations was a result of the depopulation of American Indians, whereby the number of potential mates had been severely
restricted (such as epidemics)."[51] Thornton seems to have overlooked
the probability, which Forbes considers, that the indigenous peoples in some parts of the Americas had already been intermixing
with other "racial" and cultural groups, years before the European
invaders had reached their shores. This would then account for already
recognized physical diversity among Native populations, and what
some would refer to as racial strains or genetic markers.

Today, American Indians still have to deal with the Euroamerican treatment of "mixed-bloods" in the historiography, which still
has racist consequences. Traditionally, an individual could become

a member of a tribal society by kinship and intermarriage, or adoption and naturalization, no matter what the "racial" pedigree. Later, Euroamericans saw advantages to pitting "confused half-breeds" against the so-called fullbloods who were resisting the western expansion into Indian lands. There was even a period when "mixed-blood" leadership was handpicked by "white" Americans, to thwart the traditional leadership, because the thinking was that a "mixed-blood" was more likely than a "fullblood" to cooperate and assimilate to "white" men's ways. Actually, a solution to the "Indian problem" among liberal educators and policy makers, who called themselves "Friends of the Indians," encouraged intermarriage between Indians and whites to facilitate the assimilation of the latter.[52] But for the most part, and especially in recent times, "mixed-bloods" find themselves doubly marginalized in any society, because they are not fully accepted in any designated "race" or ethnic group. As Vine Deloria Jr., senior Native (Lakota) scholar, insightfully wrote in 1977: "No Indian tribe today can claim a pure blood stock as if this requirement necessarily guaranteed 'Indianness.'"[53] Deloria has since been working on a book about "Indian Treaty Making," that includes intertribal treaties made between Native Nations before those with the United States. He has noted that some treaties between Europeans and Indians had sections (some since removed) specific to the protection of "mixed-blood" members by the Indian leaders.[54]

There have been notable exceptions, however, to the thinking, based on racist assumptions, that "mixed-bloods" are easy assimilationists and that "fullbloods" are less able to be coopted. It can even be argued that what Indians meant by "fullbloods" was very different from what non-Indians meant because it had more to do with cultural criteria for determining tribal membership. Two historical cases are the famed Quanah Parker, a "half-breed" Comanche, and Captain Jack, a "mixed-blood" leader among the Modocs and Klamaths. Parker's mother was a "white" Protestant who was kidnapped by the Comanches when she was nine years old. She was later married to a prominent male leader in the tribal nation.[55] Both respected men used their leadership to resist European encroachment by negotiating for their people with the "whites." In modern times notable Native "mixed-bloods" have made their mark in Indian history. Among the more well-known were Will Rogers (Cherokee), the famed comic and satirist, and D'Arcy McNickle (Salish and Kootenai), a notable historical novelist. Both of these individuals were accorded full membership status among their respective tribal nations. But today we are witnessing a growing number of Native peoples with "mixed-blood" ancestry and heritage being denied their Indian identity by federal mandate via the BIA.

These divisive matters have now escalated to the point that many among the younger generations are denied federal services because of federal Indian policy that has closed their tribal rolls, terminated whole tribes, and even declared some extinct. This can happen to individuals even if they do meet blood quantum standards. Therefore, this can be perceived as discrimination against "mixed-bloods." Such issues also need to be put into the context that it has been estimated there is at least 50 percent intermarriage among Native Americans (with men slightly higher than women) who marry outside of their tribe, either other Indians (in intertribal relations) or "whites."[56] Intertribal relations have been in practice since pre-Columbian times, because exogamy was encouraged for political and biological reasons. Because these are highly politicized times, political motivations can determine, even among Indians themselves, why a particular group or an individual might not be "recognized" by the tribe and/or "certified" by the federal government.[57] Such decisions can be made for political expediency, that is at the expense of a tribe's or pueblo's cultural integrity, based on kinship traditions such as matrilineality (as in the legal case, *Martinez v. Santa Clara Pueblo, 1978*). Those with "mixed-blood identities" among Native Americans are hit even harder by this, because they do not fit into the rigid racial–racist categories in the census. This problematic situation is encouraging a growing trend among "mixed-blood" groups to challenge the imposed race categories.[58]

A contrast to U.S. Indian policy is Canadian government policy that recognizes its primarily landless métis populations and organizations, as having certain aboriginal rights. Métis, however, are considered a separate category that distinguishes them from Reserve Indians as tribal groups in Canada. In the province of Quebec, they are referred to as French métis because they speak a French patois and are Roman Catholics. (In the United States "mixed-blood" groups are lumped with other "ethnic minorities.") However, these same métis groups, especially the women, criticize the Canadian government because they are at a disadvantage when compared with land-based Reserve Indians.[59]

What also needs to be challenged in this arena is that the hybridization that exists among most of us is not negative or denigrating, but rather is an attribute we can take pride in as nonracist and universal in our affinity with biological and cultural diversity. The reality is, however, that a distinct "race" or a "pure" race of people cannot be proven, scientifically or otherwise. Therefore, the majority if not all of humanity at this time, are probably of "mixed-blood" descendancy as well as heritage, as a result of human inclination and capacity for intermixing and intermarriage.

Indigenous to the Americas

These intense years have brought American Indians through the twentieth century, to a mood of backslide toward reactionary politics. Even while the Clinton Administration proclaims a new day for Indians, new stratagems are at play for dispossessing Indians further, with colonial "identities" that are symptomatic of race and genetics that is correlated with nationalist issues and affairs. Indians are now being told to give up the last vestiges of their "Indianness," in order to compete like everyone else, for they have never fully had liberation from the European invasion. It is a fact of Indian life that the U.S. government still controls their homelands, and they are the most regulated and controlled population caught in a rat maze of federal and state bureaucracy. Indians live in what has been called a "settler state" that has imposed colonization on its traditional indigenous peoples.[60] The oppressive conditions of this colonization have created a federal dependency spawned from a racist paternalism and divisiveness about "Indian Identity." Government policies have made Native peoples subject to removal and relocation, and threatened cultural and political domains. Traditional Native peoples and their approach to life have stood in the way of development in mining and other profit-motive ventures, which have proven hazardous to the inhabitants' health, as well as the ecology of their natural environment.[61] An international perspective is needed for the Native peoples' situational affairs, as well as for local, regional, and national agendas, in order to connect the Indians' historical legacy with the present blight so that a more promising future for younger generations can be created.

With this historical legacy and the current state of affairs throughout Native America, it appears that for the Indians to survive in this country they must first perish, as is the lot of all mythological creatures. Yet, we can challenge this negation of us as relics of the past, and become the universal people we are meant to be. To accomplish this, we must resist the forces of our homogenization that are patriotic coercion for American nationalism. We need a call for our decolonization in alliance with other disenfranchised and dispossessed peoples. And we need to never lose sight of who we are in the circle we call humanity. This has nothing to do with race and racism, but is rooted historically in our cultural identity with the land and the environment.[62]

We also need to restore a strong sense of who we are as Native individuals and cultural groups in our own right. This is particularly urgent because there is a growing number of urban-based "ethnic" Indians, estimated at 60 percent of all Indians, and rising. Most Native American populations are found in the Western states; metropolitan Los Angeles is home to the largest Native population, at about 100,000, with Chicago next in line. The population of tribal-based Indians is dropping. The largest land-based groups are in the Southwest, with the exception of the Oklahoma Cherokees.[63] There is evidence that the neoconservative federally recognized tribal leadership in alliance with the Washington D.C. cultural brokers, are advocating the adoption of more restrictive qualifications for tribally recognized members among Native Americans. The federal government continues to determine rigid and inhumane racist categories that deny "mixed-blood" heritage in present times, even though such undesignated groups were traditionally considered members of the nations in pre-Columbian times. We question how some tribal leaders determine who gets on their tribal rolls and who gets taken off; at times these policies have appeared to be more influenced by tribal partisan politics than by the protection of membership rights. This is creating a problem in Indian and tribal identity politics, which is becoming the concern of human rights activists, as well as those who perceive a conflict in regard to democratic ideals and rights. Tribal leaders are now being pressured to include "civil rights codes" in their tribes' constitutions, which prohibit decisions about tribal membership that discriminate based on "race, creed, and/or national origin, as articulated in the U.S. Constitution and its Bill of Rights."[64] It is my assessment that gender should also be included among these rights because of noted court cases of tribal patriarchy, in which predominantly male-dominated tribal councils deny Native women and their offspring tribal status. These inequities are a result of U.S. colonization, and particularly due to the Indian Reorganization of tribal governance in 1934.

Haunani Kay Trask made this insightful assessment on the subject: "When you divide a people by race, you divide the people, themselves, from each other."[65] It is in this way we give up our ontology that is the ethos of our very existance, as *Indigenous to the Americas*. Granted that legal and entitlement considerations have come down to a recent "federal deficit" issue as part of the economic crisis in United States. Tribes and intertribal Indian organizations, until recently, were advocating more open policies to tribal enrollment and BIA certification. There has been abuse in this process, but it is probably a regional problem due to administrative mismanagement and even bureaucratic corruption. However, these problems do not require generic legislation via federal policy and congressional laws. Such McCarthyite tactics violate the human laws of Native individuals and groups who still trace their Indian identity through kinship and geneology, in stark contrast to any nationalist ideology based on racial constructs and racist formulations. As Vine Deloria once stated: "We should just drop the definitions, and concentrate on the development of programs for Indians wherever they are instead of keeping the myth alive that we follow very proper rules in determining who is eligible for federal service."[66] In this context, there is a need for resolutions of the ideological issues raised in terms of legal constructions of who is an American Indian and how that correlates with federal and state entitlements.

There is also a need to challenge the ahistoricism that exists in U.S. society, in order to acknowledge and comprehend the historiography of U.S. colonization put upon Tribal and Native groups of this continent. This understanding must also extend to how that U.S.–Indian construction is manifested in federal Indian policy in contrast to international human rights for indigenous peoples of the Americas. This is part of the decolonization process that is presently in motion, and what can be perceived as an indigenous liberation movement. Intertribal and regional organizations, such as the Confederated Chapters of the American Indian Movement, are the vanguard of this more global movement.[67] Their agendas focus on the decentralization of leadership within their own ranks as well as grassroots Native environmentalism to resist genocide, ethnocide, and ecocide while restoring ecological balance to their habitats and the planet—as Mother Earth. These liberation struggles also include the Native peoples in Third World countries as well as the United States and Canada.

On the basis of this research I make the following recommendations: (1) include community recognition, off as well as on reservation areas; (2) determine the definitions of a Tribal–Native community predicated on cultural traditions and indigenous rights that are predicated on cultural integrity; (3) reject the BIA Blood Quantum altogether, and replace it with a broader scope of kinship traditions that includes exogamy, naturalization, and adoption, as well as matrilineal or patrilineal ancestral lineage; (4) allow traditional Native peoples to determine tribal membership, which would acknowledge their landless and nonfederally recognized relations, and include a population among those who are referred to as "mixedblood." These recommendations need an international vision that would also address the need for the U.S. federal and state system to assist in the maintenance of traditional Native communities as cultural enclaves with indigenous rights. They would also assist in the restoration of groups who can claim grievances of acts of genocide and ethnocide on Native populations, which involve eugenics coding imposed upon them. This last recommendation also recognizes the impact of ecocide that has been wrought on Native lands as bioregional spheres in the natural environment, as a result of government and corporate intervention and exploitation of those homelands.[68] Indigenous groups should also be able to continue to solicit redress in international arenas, such as human rights forums, to hold the U.S. authorities accountable for past wrongdoing while the government makes amends by restitution and reparation to its colonized populations. Only then will Euroamerican imperialism and hegemony be confronted so the people, Native and non-Native among us, will be able to heal the wounds of our past and present for the sake of our future.

11

Exploring the Social Construction of Race: Sociology and the Study of Interracial Relationships

Abby L. Ferber

In this chapter, I discuss discourses of interracial heterosexual relationships and their underlying assumptions about racial categories. Then, proposing a postmodern rearticulation of race, I suggest some ways this changes our understanding of regulations regarding interracial heterosexual relationships. Consider this image.

A flyer distributed by Aryan Nations, a white supremacist group, reads across the top, in large letters, "The Death of the White Race." Beneath this heading is a photograph of a white woman with her arms wrapped around the neck of an African-American male. Beneath the photograph is the caption: "The Ultimate Abomination."[1]

Although this view may seem extremist, members of the far right are not the only ones to view miscegenation as problematic. Indeed, American society generally characterizes interracial relationships as a "problem." Each year, dozens of television talk shows focus on the problems of interracial dating, interracial marriage, mixed-race adoptions, and so forth. There have been numerous movies focusing on this problem, including *Imitation of Life*, *Guess Who's Coming To Dinner*, and more recently, *Jungle Fever*, *Mississippi Masala*, and *Made in America*.

Sociology of Interracial Sexuality

Historians, sociologists, and psychologists have devoted a great

155

deal of attention to the phenomena of race mixing. The majority of the literature on interracial relationships falls into two categories: historical; and sociological and social–psychological. The historical literature explores the history of laws regarding miscegenation, definitions of multiracial individuals, attitudes towards and patterns of intermarriage, achievements, experiences, and treatment of multiracial individuals; and comparisons of these factors in various countries.[2]

The majority of the sociological theories focus on discovering those elements of social structure and culture that shape rates and patterns of interracial and interethnic relationships. Paul Spickard has placed the major theories into four groups.[3]

One group explores those factors that contribute to rates of intermarriage, including unbalanced sex ratios,[4] the size of the minority group in a given location,[5] American society's increasing tolerance of racial diversity, and the generation since immigration.[6]

Another group studies which groups marry which groups, attempting to reveal certain patterns. One theorist in this group posits a triple melting-pot theory suggesting that the three major religious groupings each constitute a single melting pot.[7] Another suggests that boundaries between races are stronger than religious boundaries and that national origin boundaries are weakest.[8] More recent research has suggested that each ethnic group has its own unique hierarchy of preferences regarding intermarriage and suggests that cultural factors, such as the images and stereotypes a group has about itself and other groups, also play a role.[9]

A third group of theories predict the gender of those who outmarry; for example, the theory associated with Robert Merton suggests that outmarriage follows a pattern of hypogamy. This system assumes a hierarchy of ethnic groups based on status and suggests that women from higher status ethnic groups, who lack valued attributes such as wealth or beauty, marry down, that is, marry men of lower status ethnic groups, who possess valued attributes (e.g., beauty, talent, wealth, education). Conversely, some theorists suggest that informal sexual relations follow a pattern of hypergamy, with women of lower status ethnic groups involved in sexual relationships with males from higher status ethnic groups, but whom they are not likely to marry (because the males would have nothing to gain).[10]

A fourth group of theories explore the development of ethnic identity in mixed-race couples and their children: some theorists suggest that these families become part of the minority communities,[11] but others see intermarriage as a sign of assimilation by minorities into the majority.[12]

The literature on race mixing is largely empirical and presupposes the givenness of discrete races that are capable of engaging in race mixing. Little attention is given to what actually constitutes a racial group. Studies often rely on diverse indicators. Most research on Mexican–American intermarriage relies upon marriage records as a data source, and uses "Spanish-surname" to represent Mexican–American or Hispanic populations and "non-Spanish-surname" to represent Anglo-American populations. As authors often admit, "'Anglo' is often used somewhat loosely in this type of analysis and, not infrequently, becomes a residual category for all persons not explicitly identified as having a Spanish surname."[13] Similarly, research on Asian–American intermarriage often relies upon surname to establish ethnic identity. In the research conducted by Kitano, Yeung, Chai, and Hatanaka, they "selected every marriage license application having a Chinese, Japanese or Korean surname," and they explain that this "procedure missed the following Asians: (a) those who had anglicized their surnames, (b) those Asians born to non-Asian fathers, and (c) those whose surnames were not identified by our group."[14]

All of the attention focused on how to define or measure a racial community, including these examples that rely on last name, assumes that discrete races exist "out there," and that it is merely a methodological problem for social scientists to figure out how to best represent and measure those racial communities. This line of research assumes the givenness of discrete races which then engage in intermarriage, ignoring the fact of prior intermarriage, as well as the researcher's own role in defining racial communities. Little if any attention is given to discussing what constitutes a racial group—their givenness is assumed. There is no recognition of the complicity of social scientists in producing and defining specific racial categories. The sociological literature usually tries to draw implications from the research regarding the relative cohesiveness and solidarity or assimilation and breakdown of racial communities; however, this seems futile if little attention is devoted to considering what constitutes a racial community in the first place. When researchers fail to discuss what actually constitutes a racial group, they reproduce race as a naturally existing category.

Theoretical Foundations

The majority of the sociological research on intermarriage relies on an assimilationist framework. Michael Kearl and Edward Murguia explain that "one widely recognized indicator of minority assimilation into the majority society is the intermarriage between minority and majority groups."[15] Indeed, researchers frequently preface their data with such remarks, proffered as justification for undertaking research on intermarriage.

Michael Omi and Howard Winant explain that the assimilationist perspective arose within what they refer to as "ethnicity-based theory." "The ethnicity-based paradigm," they suggest, "arose in the 1920s and 1930s as an explicit challenge to the prevailing racial views of the period. . . . In contrast to biologically oriented approaches, the ethnicity-based paradigm was an insurgent theory which suggested that race was a *social* category."[16] From this perspective, race—usually defined as visible, physical differences—is simply one of many characteristics that identify ethnic groups.

Omi and Winant suggest that the major dispute within the ethnicity-based theory revolved around "the possibility of maintaining ethnic group identities over time."[17] The assimilationists and the cultural pluralists represented the two sides in this debate. The assimilationist perspective, introduced by Robert Park, presented a cycle of race relations eventually leading to the assimilation of minority groups into the majority culture. The notion of cultural pluralism, introduced by Horace Kallen, on the other hand, questioned the "inevitability or desirability of integration, assimilation, and amalgamation"[18] and "focused on the acceptance of different immigrant-based cultures."[19] Both of these perspectives, however, focus on white ethnics as their referent. That is, these theories were developed to explain the immigrant experiences of European, white, ethnic groups. Gunnar Myrdal's landmark, *An American Dilemma*, suggested that ethnicity-based theory be expanded to incorporate racial groups as well, arguing for the assimilation of blacks. Assimilation was presented as the cure-all for racism.

In the 1960s, Nathan Glazier and Daniel Moynihan's *Beyond the Melting Pot* drew on the assimilationist and pluralist perspectives, introducing the concept of political pluralism. They suggested that immigrant groups were transformed by the experience of assimilation, yet developed a distinct identity "which must sustain itself culturally and deliver tangible political gains . . . to the group. It was thus fundamental political interests, rather than factors such as primordial ties, cultural differences, or majoritarian resistance to incorporation which were ultimately decisive in the maintenance of ethnic identities."[20]

Omi and Winant discuss a number of problems with ethnicity-based theory: the failure of the immigrant analogy for addressing the experiences of racial minorities, its reduction of race to ethnicity, the attribution of differences in status to minority-group values and culture, and the erasure of ethnic differences among blacks and other racial minorities. They attribute these problems to "the application of a paradigm based in white ethnic history to a racially defined group."[21]

Because ethnicity theory is primarily preoccupied with the "*dynamics of incorporation* of minority groups into the dominant society . . . [and] therefore primarily concerned with questions of group identity,"[22] the phenomenon of intermarriage has been focused on as an important indicator of incorporation. Most sociological research on interracial relationships, therefore, has been approached from within this framework. Because this theory was developed to explain ethnic group identity, little discussion of the differences between race and ethnicity is found in the literature on intermarriage, and race is often reduced to a characteristic of ethnic groups. For this reason, researchers often make no distinction between "racial" and "ethnic" groups, and authors rarely explain their reasons for choosing one or the other term. In some studies Mexican Americans may be referred to as a racial group, in others, an ethnic group.

Although ethnicity-based theory attempts to move beyond race as a biological category and presents racial and ethnic identity as unfixed and open to change, researchers using this framework to study intermarriage still end up reproducing race as natural and given. Discrete racial and ethnic groups are assumed to exist and engage in intermarriage. So, for example, while sociologists may study Chicano–Anglo intermarriage and refute the biological fixity of race by conceptualizing intermarriage as a measure of assimilation, where minority groups may abandon or lose their previous racial or ethnic identity, these researchers never actually question their initial categorizations of Chicano and Anglo. These discrete groups are assumed to exist. There is no discussion of what constitutes a race or the role of social scientists in constructing the coherence of these racial categories—their complicity is erased.

More recent race theory moves beyond biological and assimilationist conceptualizations of race. Omi and Winant have advanced our understanding of race as a "preeminently sociohistorical concept." " Racial categories and the meaning of race," they explain, "are given concrete expression by the specific social relations and historical context in which they are embedded."[23] Today, many researchers acknowledge the social construction of race, and often a statement is offered, explaining that the authors do not believe in the existence of real biological races, and believe instead that they are socially constructed. However, it is often explained that because *others* (i.e., normal people "out there" in society) believe in the existence of races, race does exist as a subject of study. I do not believe this avoids the problems I have been noting. This form of research creates an artificial rift between sociologists, who merely represent society, and those people out there who are supposedly creating it.

Researchers studying intermarriage, whether working within the biological, ethnicity-based assimilationist or social constructionist frameworks, still take race as natural and given, and fail to explore the ways in which race is socially constructed. This research fails to recognize its own complicity in the production of race. If race is socially constructed and given concrete meaning and identity by the discourses in which it is embedded, then we, as researchers, contribute to that social construction. Attempts to ignore our own role in the social construction of race reproduce race as a natural and given category of identity. By failing to explore our own role in the construction of race and continuing to use it as a category of analysis, we produce race as a prediscursive category. We reproduce race as a given, obvious, natural category, existing outside of discourse. In other words, we counteract and delegitimize our very own claims that race is socially constructed. We must begin, then, to examine our own discourses as a site of the social construction of race.

Failing to interrogate the positions from which they write, social scientists have traditionally attempted to position themselves as objective observers. These efforts have served to mask the relations of power in which social scientists are situated. Informed by a postmodern approach to sociology, I would suggest that we need to explore the ways in which our own discourses are embedded in relations of power. As Steven Seidman explains:

> Social discourses . . . produced by demographers, criminologists, organizational sociologists, and so on, shape the social world by

creating normative frameworks of racial, gender, sexual, national, and other types of identity, social order, and institutional functioning that carry the intellectual and social authority of science. A discourse that bears the stamp of scientific knowledge gives its normative concepts of identity and order an authority.[24]

Social scientists take part in reproducing categories of identity as normative. Sociologists do not merely reflect and analyze existing relations, because in doing so they contribute to the consolidation of racial categories. In representing race as a given foundation, sociologists obscure the relationships of power that constitute race as a foundation. Social scientists are not outside of power struggles over identity formation, but situated necessarily within these struggles. As Judith Butler points out, "The juridical structures of language and politics constitute the contemporary field of power; hence, there is no position outside this field, but only a critical genealogy of its own legitimating practices."[25]

The Racialization of America, by Yehudi O. Webster, takes a number of steps in this direction, but encounters a number of problems. Webster criticizes social scientific research that ignores its own role in the racialization of the population, suggesting that:

> It is neither race nor racism that bedevils American society, but rather that racial classification enjoys a privileged status in social studies. . . . References to its realness are meant to consolidate and perpetuate its presence as something that cannot, or should not, be questioned.[26]

Sociological studies that examine race relations, in failing to examine their role in the construction of races, assume a biological or cultural basis for race. He suggests that

> Much of the controversy over the significance of racism can be avoided by conceiving racial classification *itself* as racism. . . . By implication, scholars should terminate the traditional moralistic focus on racism and address their own usage of racial classification and other elements of the racial theory.[27]

Racial classification, Webster contends, is the product of faulty reasoning. Because racial categories create groups on the basis of certain selected anatomical features, they are arbitrary, ambiguous, and illogical. In addition, the insurmountable differences, including class differences, that divide racial groups, lead Webster to conclude that "theories of race and ethnicity do not provide viable classifications of social relations. Any reference to a black situation can be controverted with the question: Which blacks?"[28] Webster attributes continued tolerance for such ambiguity to our educational system's failure to "cultivate respect for logical reasoning."[29]

Webster provides an important critique of the role of social science in the processes of racialization, and social scientists' failure to recognize and examine this role; a critique shaped by postmodern insights. As he asserts:

> Social scientists do not generally consider the logical implications of the claim that there is a real world that is separate and distinct from theories. This is especially pertinent to race relations studies whose most striking philosophical feature is their claim that race is a reality that is dealt with by various theories and models. However, over the last two decades, some philosophers have raised doubts about certain traditional philosophical propositions, such as: language as a representation, or mirror, of things beyond language; knowledge as a relationship between a theorizing subject and a real object; truth as a reflection of reality; and classifications as real, existing things. Their criticisms have deconstructive implications for the notion that race is a social reality that is investigated by social scientists.[30]

Webster's own arguments, however, end up falling back on these unquestioned propositions. Although he deconstructs attempts to posit racial identity as rooted in nature or biology, he then questions and bemoans the arbitrariness of race. However, precisely because there is no prediscursive, ontological grounding for race, it can only be arbitrary and ambiguous. And, I would add, that race and ethnicity are not the only socially constructed identities that shape our lives. Rather than asserting the social construction of *identities*, including race, ethnicity, nationality, sexualities, gender, and so forth, Webster contends that *race and ethnicity are false identities*, relying upon the notions of Truth and Reality he previously questioned. He claims that because race has no basis in reality and is arbitrary and ambiguous, it must be abandoned: "an effective approach to black socioeconomic rehabilitation would be an abandoning of racial classification. Black liberation demands the negation of blackness."[31] One is unsure, however, whether or not he would also recommend abandoning other constructed identities, such as gender, which is also ambiguous, classifies people based on certain specific anatomical differences, and erases class (and many other) differences among women.

Webster demands an abandonment of racial identities; he proposes instead that we adopt an identity based on common humanity. He explains that

> Protests against inhuman treatment and violations of human and civil rights suggest a hidden concern for persons as human beings. . . . These experiences suggest a terrible dehumanization. By implication, they are experiences of human beings; they are being racialized by the usage of the racial theory. Social scientists generally justify this usage with reference to a reality that is itself a product of the dissemination of the racial theory. Nevertheless, if racial consciousness is the source of discrimination and the scourge of human society, racial classification of persons should be abandoned, for it perpetuates the consciousness of difference that underlies dehumanization.[32]

Here we can see some of the contradictions in his arguments. Once again he criticizes social scientists' reliance upon a supposed reality from which they are detached observers, yet he argues for the abandonment of racial categories because they do not correspond with reality, and proposes a turn toward a common and essentialized human community whose reality remains unquestioned. Additionally, Webster assumes the existence of subjects as "human" outside of the processes of racialization.

A postmodern approach to understanding racial identity enables us to make the initial critique of social scientists' role in the construction of races, yet avoids reifying other categories of identity, including gender and humanity, and disrupts our truth–falsity dichotomies. A postmodern account of discourses of sexuality shifts our approach to understanding the "problem" of interracial relationships and exposes the discursive production of categories of identity, including race.

An Alternative Theoretical Perspective

In *The History of Sexuality, An Introduction*, Michel Foucault demonstrates that networks of power, extended through discourses of sexuality, actually produce and delimit bodies and subjects. "Fou-

cault points out that juridical systems of power produce the subjects they subsequently come to represent. Juridical notions of power
appear to regulate political life in purely negative terms. . . . But
the subjects regulated by such structures are, by virtue of being
subjected to them, formed, defined, and reproduced in accordance
with the requirements of those structures."[33]

While Foucault demonstrates the discursive production of subjects and identities, Judith Butler shows that this production occurs
through the construction of gendered identities. As Butler suggests

"persons" only become intelligible through becoming gendered in
conformity with recognizable standards of gender intelligibility.
. . . the very notion of "the person" is called into question by the
cultural emergence of those "incoherent" or "discontinuous" gendered
beings who appear to be persons but who fail to conform to the
gendered norms of cultural intelligibility by which persons are defined.[34]

Butler explores the construction of gendered subjects, but asks,
"What other foundational categories of identity . . . can be shown
as productions that create the effect of the natural, the original,
and the inevitable?"[35] Race, I suggest, is one of those categories of
identity. Paralleling Butler's discussion of "intelligible gender identities," Omi and Winant suggest that we also regulate intelligible
racial identities. They point out that

One of the first things we notice about people when we meet them
. . . is their race. We utilize race to provide clues about *who* a person is. This fact is made painfully obvious when we encounter someone
whom we cannot conveniently racially categorize—someone who is,
for example, racially "mixed" or of an ethnic/racial group with which
we are not familiar. Such an encounter becomes a source of discomfort and momentarily a crisis of racial meaning. Without a racial
identity, one is in danger of having no identity.[36]

Racialized identities govern our notions of culturally intelligible
humans. This, then, highlights a problem previously raised in the
discussion of Webster's argument: individuals are not culturally
intelligible humans prior to their racialization, as he maintains.

Regulatory practices governing sexuality produce culturally intelligible and coherent racialized identities. We can now briefly return
our discussion to an exploration of this production in white suprem-

acist discourses of interracial heterosexual relationships. Now that we have a different understanding of race, our understanding of these regulatory discourses also changes.

Regulations prohibiting interracial sexual relationships actually serve to produce and consolidate racial identities. Iris Marion Young explains that "any move to define an identity, a closed totality, always depends on excluding some elements, separating the pure from the impure. . . . the logic of identity seeks to keep those borders firmly drawn."[37] The construction of racial identities requires a policing of the borders; a maintenance of the boundaries between "one's own kind" and others. Butler points out a central insight of postmodernism: "'Inner' and 'outer' make sense only with reference to a mediating boundary that strives for stability. . . . Hence, 'inner' and 'outer' constitute a binary distinction that stabilizes and consolidates the coherent subject."[38]

This reading helps us to understand white supremacist discourse regarding interracial relationships. Recalling the image I began with, interracial heterosexual relationships are the "ultimate abomination." They are felt to actually threaten the community and identity of whiteness. The transgressive acts of an individual are felt to threaten the entire community, as well as the very possibility of a white identity.

The Turner Diaries by Andrew MacDonald is a novel widely read by members of various white supremacist groups. The futuristic novel describes a scenario of pervasive race mixing, which is seen as threatening to wipe out white existence, and traces a white supremacist organization's path to revolution and world domination.

As the organization attempts to establish a utopian society, the threat of miscegenation must be eliminated. Total racial separation must be established and all who have transgressed racial boundaries must be abolished. In the final stages of the revolution, we encounter

the Day of the Rope—a grim and bloody day, but an unavoidable one. . . . from tens of thousands of lampposts, power poles, and trees throughout this vast metropolitan area the grisly forms hang. . . . The first thing I saw in the moonlight was the placard with its legend in large, block letters: "I defiled my race." Above the placard leered the horribly bloated, purplish face of a young woman. . . . There are many thousands of hanging female corpses like that in this city tonight, all wearing identical placards around their necks.

They are the White women who were married to or living with Blacks,
with Jews, or with other non-White males.[39]

This excerpt serves as one example of white supremacist discourse that regulates sexual relations. Regulatory practices governing
heterosexual racial relations desire to produce the stable identity
of both the individual and community. Indeed, these regulations
produce these bodies themselves. In the preceding example, the
organization must draw and redraw the line defining who is and is
not white. The hung corpses are the bodies of those who appear
white, but whom the organization has declared polluted and no longer
allowed membership in the white race. The notion of sex pollution
"'expresses a desire to keep the body (physical and social) intact,'
suggesting that the naturalized notion of 'the' body is itself a consequence of taboos that render that body discrete by virtue of its
stable boundaries."[40] *The Turner Diaries* demonstrates the absolute
necessity of drawing boundaries to produce identities. The boundaries, however, are never "natural" boundaries, lying outside discrete subjects. Because race is not given, by nature, it must be
constructed and reconstructed, again and again, always a redraw-
ing of the boundaries. This reading, then, suggests that the actual
maintenance of the boundaries creates, reproduces, and consolidates
racialized identities. Discourses regulating heterosexual racial relations create the very same bodies they purport to protect.

Conclusions: New Beginnings

A postmodern reading of regulations regarding interracial heterosexual relationships exposes the discursive production of race.
While the traditional sociological literature has attempted to refute
biological notions of race, it has often ended up reproducing race
as a given and prediscursive category. Regulations regarding whom
members of a race could and could not marry have been viewed,
from this perspective, as serving "to maintain their cohesiveness
and identity,"[41] and rates and patterns of intermarriage have been
viewed as a "mechanism indicating maintenance and/or change of
. . . boundaries."[42] From this perspective, the racial identity of a
group is always represented as given and obvious from the beginning, and the question at hand is limited to one of the "maintenance" or "change" of identity.

I have tried to demonstrate that from a postmodern perspective, the construction and maintenance of boundaries to regulate interracial sexuality actually produce racial subjects themselves. While Foucault has suggested that discourses of sexuality produce subjects, here we see that the production of subjects occurs through the processes of racialization. Racial subjects are constructed in the process of establishing the boundaries between races. Regulations regarding interracial sexuality, then, are one site of the social construction of race.

Sociologists cannot merely assert the social construction of race and continue with business as usual. We must begin uncovering the multifarious processes that produce racialized identities as natural and given. Until sociologists begin to trace the production of racialized identities and their own role in this production, they will continue to be unwitting participants in the reification of race as a natural category, obscuring their own positions in relations of power. Sociologists are not detached observers, removed from the "reality" they study. A postmodern approach enables us to explore our own positions and to recognize the always, already-political nature of our work. The arguments presented here support Seidman's assertion that "Postmodernism underscores the practical and moral character of science. It sees the disciplines as implicated in heterogeneous struggles around gender, race, sexuality, the body, and the mind, to shape humanity."[43]

12

Therapeutic Perspectives on Biracial Identity Formation and Internalized Oppression

Helena Jia Hershel

Mental health professionals treating biracial individuals who are harmed by racial oppression need a special understanding of the biracial experience. This chapter discusses identity formation by examining phenomenological and psychological descriptions of oppression. Here, identity is explored within the context of biracial oppression, specifically as a consequence of racial projection and internalized alienating racial attitudes. The chapter concludes with some therapeutic recommendations on what is required for an individual of mixed race to maintain optimal psychological health.

Clinical anecdotes illustrate the effect of racial oppression on a population already in treatment.[1] Although much of the focus here is on the process of identity wounding and thus "worst case scenarios" to express the effect of racial oppression upon individuals from a clinical viewpoint, it is assumed that the reader understands that biracial people often have a very positive identity.

Belonging

The process of forming identity is a critical facet of selfhood. This process continues throughout one's life through personal and public relationships and is simultaneously influenced by broader social, cultural, and racial attitudes. Consequently, it is both an individual and a collective process. From birth onward, identity formation proceeds through internalizing one's relationship with others. The gaze of the mother and primary caretakers initiate the most early identifications of the child with another.[2] As one grows older, the identification with others grows in increasingly wider social circles and extends to membership in one's community and society.

The process of identity formation begins with "belonging." Belonging is fundamental to the organizational structure of humans and has survival value.[3] Belonging to a family implies physical similarities and shared characteristics such as race and appearance. In conflict with the familial belonging is the exceptional importance color and race perception have in the United States. When the biracial child does not racially look like either parent, that is, have the same hue, then outsiders may assume the child does not belong to this family because of the child's appearance.[4] This visibility and potential censorship are obviously inappropriate to a young child. Children are injured by others' lack of acceptance. They feel forced to choose monoracial identities, thus denying part of themselves. They may be unable to prevent the damage being caused to them.

Normally adolescence is the developmental phase in which awareness of being different and striving toward identity usually occurs. It is a developmental phase in which identity formation and a sense of belonging are integrated into the self. Belonging does not become an issue until exclusion (lack of acceptance) is communicated. The awareness of exclusion is imbued with painful feelings of "Where do I belong?" Consequently, being told "You don't belong" sets up a desire to belong. This desire is further frustrated by rejection, be it from friends, relatives, teachers, or members of monoracial groups.

Difficulties for biracial children may also be caused by cross-cultural or interracial marriages that are not accepted in the larger cultural arena or within the extended family. For example, extended families tend to fall into four typical patterns that can affect interracial marriages: protesting, sabotaging, disregarding, and integrating. Protesting families voice their demands outright if interracial/intercultural dating occurs. Threats are made to disinherit or exile the offending member from the family. Sabotaging families tend to blame any faults or failures on the outsider even when such behavior is initiated by their own family members. Disregarding families act as if the racial difference of the partner did not exist. The partner becomes invisible and problems ensue from that. Integrated families make concerted efforts to get acquainted with the other person's culture despite different styles of cultural expression or expectations.

Conflicts, resentment, or outright prejudice from either within the family or from society are often conveyed to the biracial child. Parents, grandparents, and extended family may have unresolved, collective, cultural and racial shame from the historical legacy of segregation. Parental secrets can add fuel to this dilemma by negatively affecting the integrity of the child's identity. For example, a biracial child may be kept secret from other family members; the child's missing parent may be of minority status; or the child may be adopted and not know her parentage. The following is rather a dramatic example of the effect of not knowing one's racial heritage.

> An eighteen-year old biracial girl was admitted to the hospital for visual hallucinations that were possibly related to the use of LSD. She refused to speak much English but responded in a quasi-Spanish that she admitted she learned in high school. She was adopted, but knew almost nothing about her biological parents except that she heard somewhere that her natural mother was "brown skinned" and a "prostitute." She did not identify with her white adopted parents. She was intent on identifying with this unknown mother even though she was still "a good girl." She stopped acting out and started to speak English when she came under the care of a biracial therapist who offered another role model, one more closely approximating her own identity.

Although this young woman had problems beyond the scope of this paper, she does illustrate discomfort at not knowing her parentage and the attempt to identify with her missing natural mother. The marginal status of children from mixed marriages in and of itself does not necessarily affect their self-concept or sense of achievement.[5] As part of the developmental process, a child may adopt the race of one parent, for example, the mother, and reject the race of the other, that is, the father, or go back and forth. Some studies suggest that trying on each parental racial identity in turn is part of the process of forming a new biracial synthesis.[6] The process of making one's own decisions about the self is an important way to avoid identifying with others' racial stereotypes.

Biracial Oppression

Oppression is the institutionalized enforcement of privileges based on racial, social, or physically inherited characteristics, that is, a person may have privileges based on color or class. The possession of privileges is determined by the established power structure. In some instances biracial persons may be identified with their majority status and in other instances with their minority status.[7] This is usually related to how the person's perceived race appears in the eyes of others.

Each racial identification confers a different set of advantages or disadvantages. For instance, the treatment received in an all-white community, all-black community, or all-Asian community is dependent to a degree on one's perceived ethnicity. In a racially divided community, survival may depend on perceived racial membership.

The biracial individual may become internally conflicted, not due to any psychological problems, but because of the need to protect one's self from social or racial discord, or both. Clinical experience shows that individuals in ongoing external conflict may begin to doubt themselves. When one's racial status is constantly and arbitrarily determined by others, self-doubts arise. One questions one's identity: "Do I have the same rights as others to belong?" "Am I the same person now as before?" "Who am I really?"

Identity and Alienation

Stability of the personality depends on the individual's ability to maintain a consistent sense of identity in various situations. Commonly, people attempt to identify the biracial person with rigid racial categories. The biracial person is seen now as a white person, now as a black person. Sometimes the biracial person is not recognized at all as belonging to any identifiable human group: this has a dehumanizing effect on the person.[8] The continual lack of social validation creates difficulty in maintaining a consistent sense of self and can produce intense anxiety and self-doubt. "How can I be me when others tell me I'm this race or that one?" One mother responded creatively to this dilemma when her child told her how he was being numerically divided into 50 percent Asian and 50 percent white by fellow students. She said he was, in fact, 100 percent Asian and 100 percent white. In this way she reframed what was perceived as a negative into a positive asset.

An individual's search for personal identity is the molding of a relationship between self-image and the world's perception of the self.[9] The mirroring of the self in a divisive manner, whether by significant others or by the general community in which one lives, confers upon the individual doubts of self-integrity, that is, a distrust in one's sense of self. Again this doubt can generate states of hypervigilance, feeling special or different, and heightened self-consciousness.

Self-doubt leads to self-alienation.[10] Living in an invalidating situation causes an internal split between one's ideal self-representation—who I am ideally—and one's socially constructed self—how I am perceived. This split is a psychological defense to protect from painful encounters and invalidation. However, such a defensive split also damages the self; it is an unconscious self-protectiveness, which adds a significant, though unnecessary, stressor to a person's life. Consequently, one begins to hide emotionally for protection. One ceases to show vulnerability in situations that threaten to be invalidating. The longer this protective process continues, the more difficult it is for the person to trust anyone else, and eventually oneself. Also, validating relationships with others are no longer expected, and the social sphere where validating relationships may be experienced shrinks to a private world of family and close friends.[11] Thus, one is ultimately immersed in the experience of what it is like to be (or feel) false, and within inauthentic communication with others. All one experiences is inauthenticity, so one's sense of self becomes inauthentic, that is, one is alienated.

> A young professional Latina of mixed heritage, passing as white, feels pressured to perform for others and to achieve success. She is chronically overworked, exhausted, and depressed. Her inner self tells her to slow down and spend more time in relationships, but her fears of exclusion result in overcompliance. "I can't say no to anyone." She feels inauthentic. She does not feel she belongs in corporate America. She does not make friends at work to avoid being found out. She thinks the people she works with do not know where she comes from, and she wants to keep it that way.

This woman faces the risk that she may be devalued or excluded if she is found out. To decline this risk of exclusion, she overcomplies. The consequences of accepting this self-alienation is that she feels inauthentic with a diminished sense of life.

The quality and degree of an internal split are lessened by the effect of positive internal objects and social support. The inability to resolve identity issues results in an alienated stance in the world, that is, one stands back and watches, not quite knowing how to participate or gain membership. The actions a person engages in may not affect the need for membership, a need that is profound and fundamental. A person can get caught between the strength of this need and the inability to fit in. Never knowing if someone will arbitrarily challenge who you are or where you come from will contribute to feelings of helplessness, hyperarousal, isolation, and identity crisis. To fit in, one has to find performance criteria that signify membership, as is suggested in the following case.

> A young Amerasian male expressed in treatment that he would try to behave like an Asian hoping that those around him would include him in their student groups. This was most problematic when encountering a new Asian group and trying to establish his identity. Part of behaving Asian was to not disclose much personal information and to present himself as reserved and polite. A psychological need was to have others know him and who he is, without having to tell them or constantly have to define himself. His need for acceptance from Asians was made all the more essential because he saw that white students discriminated against Asian students. He, too, had felt this same discrimination. At times, he suffered many insults as members of the group tried to discern his facial features, attempting to figure out who he was. Some Asians assumed he was white and therefore not really a part of the group. His membership was always precarious in these new groups and his isolation almost total.
>
> While growing up, family and friends had repeatedly referred to him as being "half," and this negative identity left him feeling unentitled and less than whole. A turning point in therapy came when he was able to tell people who he was racially and define himself rather than wait for others to define him. This happened only after his self esteem had been restored as he began to feel an internally integrated sense of self, a sense of wholeness.

The dilemma facing this young man is of being simultaneously discriminated against by the white students and being scrutinized by Asians. He is on a racially tense campus where racial identity is a political and social commodity that determines protection and status. Many students, cognizant of this racial climate, tend to stick with their own groups, maximizing their sense of belonging. The biraciality of the student seemed a disadvantage in the white campus community and seemed, at first, a disadvantage in the Asian campus community, as well. Besides his current reality at school, a history of growing up unsupported in his biraciality has hurt his self-esteem and has increased his vulnerability to non-acceptance by others.

Group Inclusion and Exclusion

Unfortunately, group membership, by its structural nature, is dependent on inclusion and exclusion group dynamics. This is a process of creating outsiders, in order to feel inner group cohesiveness. The in-group negatively sanctions those it regards as outsiders rendering them marginal. Being an outsider or marginal, in this instance, can occur on two levels: having a minority race status and being marginal to either race.

In mixed-race groups such as Mexican Americans, Native American Indians, and Native Hawaiians, ethnic awareness of behavior, language customs, beliefs, values, and attitudes may assume a similar or greater importance than physical characteristics. Exclusion in these cases follows the criteria of ethnic identity. Ethnic identity supplants race identity,[12] and positive identities of being mestizo (mixed) and happa (half) begin to form. Antagonism, however, may reappear when governmental and other agencies begin to assess the amount of race purity to determine institutional funding and ethnic entitlement programs.

Because of societal pressures and historical precedence, African Americans have had to absorb mixed-race persons as in the "one drop rule" and external definitions of who is black by state and federal statutes. Black in Mississippi equals 1/64 black; black in Louisiana equals 1/32 black. Social and political viability for blacks has often rested on not officially acknowledging a biracial or multiracial identity. Laws against black–white miscegenation and historical attempts to maintain white racial purity have contributed to the myth of two separate and distinct race groups. The black community has, for the most part, taken in people who are part black.[13]

Asian communities in the United States have a different history. They tend to be concerned with their racial purity to the extent that mixed persons of Asian heritage do not find it easy to assimilate into the Asian community. Amerasians, Eurasians, and Afro-Asians consequently may experience isolation within Asian communities to a degree greater than others of mixed heritage. They may find they gain more acceptance by the majority culture if they are part white or the black community if part black. Each biracial person consequently may have family and community issues that are quite distinct, given the variation and respective histories of their parentage. The greater the historical segregation of racial groups, the greater the person's exclusion, as in black–Asian ancestry.

Racial Projections and Internalized Oppression

The pathology of race oppression creates an additional burden that confronts the biracial person. Studies by Adorno, Allport, and Frenkle-Brunswick on the personality structures of racially and ethnically intolerant individuals have shown, among other traits, characterological rigidity linked with an inability to tolerate ambiguity.[14] People with rigid personalities have a predisposition to categorize and to stereotype. It is easier to objectify others especially when they belong to a class of individuals who are different and who impart a feeling of mutual strangeness. However, because biracial individuals often do not appear physically to belong to a specific racial category, they are "ambiguous" to some. A biracial person who does not fit into prescribed stereotypes can evoke an anxious ambiguous response in people whose main defensive psychological posture is to stereotype and categorize.[15]

Because of the ambiguity and anxiety created by their presence, multiracial persons or families may be used as a blank screen on which unresolved racial issues are projected, much like a projective test or inkblot. This accounts for the sometimes curious, sometimes voyeuristic interest people have in the multiracial person. All these factors contribute to a sense of vulnerability and harm one's sense of self with others. Racial pathology causes much harm, as illustrated by the example below.

> An elderly gentleman comes to therapy with the intent of working on cross-cultural issues. He feels that he has lived a fairly good life with one exception, that being the ridicule that he experienced throughout his life. He recalls growing up in a rural community. He describes how kids treated him like a freak. He suspects people were doing anthropology on him trying to discern if he had weird habits. As a boy he wished he were a movie star, popular and desired by the girls. Truth is he didn't have anyone to date. He didn't fit in anywhere. The girls rejected him because of his biracial heritage.

They would giggle, but refuse to go out with him. He didn't marry until late in life partially because he didn't think anyone would have him. He anticipates rejection and ridicule even within the therapy session.

Therapy provides this man with an opportunity to work out this social trauma that left painful emotional scars. The isolating circumstances of his youth convinced him that the negative image others held of him must be true. He progresses as he learns to trust, to become vulnerable again, and to test reality.

Projections take many forms. Sexual fantasies are often projected onto a person when that person is viewed as "Other."[16] A biracial female is particularly susceptible to having these sexual projections played out on her in several ways. First, she may be perceived as more sexually accessible than a monoracial girl, that is, less protected by sexual and racial taboos or defended by a kinship group that is seen as formidable. Second, this status of being perceived as different yet unknown contributes to the powerful projection of exotica. The boundaries and norms of appropriate behavior primarily govern only those that fall within its ranks, but those outside its ranks are often fair game.

Of course, sexual violation can happen to anyone regardless of race, gender, or age. When a traumatizing event occurs, it tends to seep into a preexisting generalized social wounding of the biracial person. The following is an example of how this occurs.

An older biracial woman in therapy recounts the vulnerability and shame she felt when she was raped as a girl. Her plight has been exacerbated by her inability to tell this story until now. The intense shame is augmented by her feelings of being seen as pathological, someone who is not perfect, not pure. It is hard for her to be proud of herself as a person when so much of her pain seems connected to how she felt perceived as marginal. She talks about how she blames herself. "I didn't fight back. It must have been my fault. It's because of me."

As with many victims of sexual violence, her feelings of guilt do not resolve themselves easily until it is clear just how groundless is her sense of responsibility. Her perceived social stigma of being a biracial woman needed to be distinguished from the stigma of being a victim of sexual assault. Specifically, her feelings of sexual impurity (on account of the rape) needed to be isolated from her preexisting feelings of racial impurity because of her biraciality.

Relationship Between
Oppressor and Oppressed

A closer look at the relationship between the oppressor and the oppressed provides insight on the difficulty of fending off the projections of the oppressor and of maintaining a consistent identity. The relationship between the oppressor and the oppressed is extremely ambivalent. Frequently, the oppressor projects his or her own sexual desires and aggressiveness onto the minority person. Projection is a method of repudiating feelings or desires that are felt to be repugnant or dangerous. The projector hates the person on whom he or she has projected, because that person now embodies that which the projector finds unacceptable in himself. At the same time the projector loves the other because that person now contains part of the projector himself. Thus the oppressor's projections form a love–hate paradox that entwines the oppressor with the oppressed. This process may be seen starkly in literary portrayals of minority groups as being savage, oversexed, dangerous, cunning, shrewd, dirty, and lazy.[17] These are typically the displaced images and projections of repressed cultural archetypes found within the individual and collective cultural psyche.

The oppressed person also has her or his own projections. The oppressed person projects ego needs such as self-esteem, entitlement, and power onto the oppressor. The aim is to create an idealization of personal wholeness, acceptance, and belonging by identifying with those who appear powerful and in the majority. The oppressed person's idealization and emulation of the oppressor not only empowers the oppressor but creates a libidinal bond with the oppressor. This bond is frustrated by envy of the oppressor. It is also frustrated by the desire to be an esteemed object, not a hated object.[18] The dialectic of oppression is contingent upon agreeing that there are at least two separate racial categories. This assumption is not valid in the case of biracial people. These considerations become clear when one considers the phenomenon of passing.

Passing or "passing for white" is being able, as a person of color, to go undetected as a member of a higher ranking racial group.

Historically, passing has been attendant with shame, fear of discovery, disclosure, and punishment. Passing is an interesting process because the person passing defies the accepted castelike boundaries of race. In the case of biracial persons, "passing" means pretending that one is only a single race. People who "pass" are criticized for identifying with the oppressor and for being in denial of their true race.[19]

It is important to distinguish between "passing" and the self-hatred that can be generated within an oppressive context when the person in question identifies not only with the privileges of the oppressor but also with the oppressor's projections of inferiority, sexuality, ugliness, unworthiness, and aggression. It is the identification with and internalization of these projections that constitutes internalized oppression.

Therapeutic Considerations

Much of this discussion has centered on the pathology of racial projections by society and internalized oppression within the individual. Although the consequences of racial pathology have been examined in detail above, equally important are the ways to obtain optimal psychological health. Obtaining and maintaining health begins with prevention. Prevention is paramount to minimize injury to a child's developing self-esteem and sense of self. The family with its integrity and identity as a multiracial unit is a good beginning. A strong family ethic that confronts intolerance by others and is caring and introspective enough to examine its own transmission of racial bias is helpful. This includes parents who are able to perceive the child's racial heritage as different from their own and can support this difference.[20] Often stories of how the parents met and how they managed opposition to the prevailing norms of their day offer a unifying ideology that gives the children a sense of pride and family identity. When a child has been given a sense of belonging and identity within the family, a very solid basis is established. This basis forms a template for continuing identity formation and is invaluable.

To maintain optimal health, it is useful to be prepared for questions of identity from without and from within. Some people have found it helpful to have ready-made responses to questions by others that are deemed friendly, neutral, or hostile. This preparedness helps offset the unexpected and random nature of questioning. Internal questions are of a different matter; they reflect an understanding, internal growth, and maturity.

Undertaking this endeavor involves understanding history, that is, how racial attitudes and aberrations came into being, and in doing so, beginning to undo the internalized oppression. For instance, many people assume that race is a biological reality rather than an intellectual idea with its own history and rationale. Most scholars have abandoned the concept of biological race because there tend to be more differences *within* a racial group than *between* racial groups.[21] Race also pervades one's thinking because it has been institutionalized within the society. Cognitive and emotional needs coupled with socioeconomic interests and rationales were among factors that upheld social conventions and legal barriers inhibiting the mixing of the races in the United States.[22]

For a biracial person to flourish, the social, political, and economic bifurcation along race lines must be ended. More than any other racial-group identity, the biracial person needs to be on guard against racism in all its forms, because racial strife confers no advantages, no belonging, but rather endangers one's very survival. People of mixed racial heritage are for the most part exquisitely aware of the pain associated with racial disharmony.

Psychotherapy has as one of its tasks the resolution of pain within the patient's psyche whenever possible or, at very least, helping the patient to cope with pain in a way that adds to the person's well-being. The individual presents her pain and feels it often in an isolated way as her personal trauma. When the process of identity-making has been injured by internalized oppressive beliefs and the pathology of racism, a person may not have the ability to acknowledge these faulty assumptions. There may be no experience or standard by which to judge these negative feelings. It is here the therapist is useful by introducing: perspective—cause and effect rather than self-blame; history—helping to understand the person within her own developmental process and particular "race" context; compassion—as an aid in helping a person toward more self-compassion; understanding—ending the isolation. The therapist reconnects the adult person with the renewed process of self-making and self-affirmation through the therapeutic relationship and the establishment of trust. Finally, the therapist can introduce the responsibility of living and being in the world in ways that promote health, understanding, and growth.

In-depth psychotherapy attempts to resolve internal conflicts and aid in the integration of the self. These internal conflicts, as I have pointed out, are not produced within a vacuum but as part of a social process that includes belonging, identity, and alienation within the family and within the community. The construction of the self is an intrapsychic and interpersonal process. Healing the wounds of an internal split may entail entering into a therapeutic relationship that provides a corrective emotional experience. Safety and trust are prerequisites in this process. Often, learning a defensive adaptation may be necessary to prevent the biracial person from reinjury within the ongoing racial pathology.

Conclusion

Our culture puts great emphasis on color and racial purity. Because racial division and tensions still prevail in our society, a person who does not physically appear to belong can be further marginalized. In a multiracial society where there is tolerance and pride in mixed heritage, color and racial purity are of lesser consequence, and positive identities arise as a natural course of events. It is essential to recognize that everyone has racial beliefs and prejudices, most often formed as young children.[23] Noticing how these messages are transmitted is an important step in furthering mutual understanding. Listening and educating ourselves about the different experiences of multiracial people is primary; we are not really talking so much about a group with shared characteristics as much as we are talking about how social and racial attitudes and historical oppression shape our tolerance for diversity.

Part IV
Public Policy

13

Grassroots Advocacy

Susan R. Graham

December 1993

June 30, 1993, was an important day for multiracial children in America. It was a step toward recognition of the success of a growing grassroots movement. On that day, a congressional subcommittee listened to our request for the federal government to accept a multiracial category. My written testimony follows this introduction.

Since its inception in 1991, Project RACE (Reclassify All Children Equally) members have been dedicated to the fight for the acceptance of the term "multiracial." We are advocates in school districts, counties, and states, and will continue on these local levels, if necessary, until the federal government accepts the combined heritage of our children.

It is not an easy road. It is a road with many manmade barriers. Fallacies about interracial unions and multiracial children exist in a history that has not been kind nor accepting. It is not easy to prove affronts to personal dignity. We are, therefore, continually frustrated by a bureaucracy that just "doesn't get it."

This fight will take a long time; but on days when I am ready to give up, I need only look at my own two children to be reminded of what this is all about.

Written Testimony for
Subcommittee on Census, Statistics and Postal Personnel
Committee on Post Office and Civil Service
United States House of Representatives
Washington, D.C.

by
Susan R. Graham
Executive Director
Project RACE, INC.
June 30, 1993

Mr. Chairman and Members of the Subcommittee:

I am Susan Graham, mother of two multiracial children and Executive Director of Project RACE, a national organization advocating for multiracial children.

When I received my 1990 Census form, I realized there was no "race category" for my children. I called the Census Bureau. After checking with supervisors, the bureau finally gave me their answer: the children should take the race of the mother. When I objected and asked why my children should be classified as their mother's race only and not their father's race at all, the U.S. Census Bureau representative said to me in a hushed voice, "Because in cases like these, we always know who the mother is and not the father."

I could not make a race choice from the five basic categories when I enrolled my son in kindergarten in Georgia. The only choice I had, like most other parents of multiracial children, was to leave "race" blank. I later found that my child's teacher was instructed to choose for him based on her "knowledge and observation" of my child. Ironically, my child has been white on the U.S. Census, black at school, and multiracial at home, all at the same time.

At about this same time, parents in Cincinnati, Ohio, began objecting to the lack of an appropriate category for their multiracial children on school forms. The Cincinnati schools agreed to put the category on all school forms. Chris Ashe, mother of a multiracial child in Cincinnati, approached State Majority Leader William Mallory to introduce statewide legislation. Mrs. Ashe joined Project RACE, and we worked with Representative Mallory to pass the first legislation for multiracial children in the country. The Ohio bill mandates the classification of multiracial on all school forms in the state, effective July 31, 1992. Representative Mallory was scheduled to be here today, but urgent state business prevented his testimony at this time. Therefore, an addendum to my testimony includes the racial breakdown from the Cincinnati Public Schools for three years, and an analysis of the data.[1]

After Representative Mallory's legislation passed in Ohio, I approached my child's school in Fulton County, Georgia. With the sanction of the superintendent and the approval of the School Board, Fulton County added the multiracial category to their school forms. Figures 1 and 2 in my testimony show the breakdown of students in Fulton County for the 1991–92 school year without the category and a representative month in 1993 with the multiracial data.[2]

Soon after, the Georgia State Department of Education agreed to accept and encourage the multiracial category from all districts in the state.

The members of Project RACE decided to pursue a legislative mandate for the classification. State Senator Ralph David Abernathy III (D-Atlanta) sponsored our bill. On March 4, 1993, it passed the Georgia Senate, *unanimously.*

This spring I enrolled my five-year-old daughter in kindergarten. Because of the progressive action in Georgia, there was, on the enrollment form a place for my daughter: a category called "Multiracial." She was not made to choose between her parents, and I hope she will never be forced to.

Children in Illinois will not have to choose soon. State Senator Howard Carroll (D-Chicago) introduced legislation for a multiracial category this year. It passed the House on May 13. We are awaiting the governor's signature.[3]

Children in Forsyth County, North Carolina, will not have to choose between their parents soon. Pressured by parents of multiracial children in Winston-Salem, their superintendent agreed just weeks ago to add multiracial to the list of accepted categories. Legislation is pending in Wisconsin, as well.

The worst part of my job is hearing heart-rending stories from all over our country. The multiracial teenager in North Carolina whose teacher asked in front of the class, "You're so light, are you sure your mother knows who your father is?" The child in Georgia whose teacher said, "You'd better go home and figure out what you are—you can't be both." The kindergartner in Maryland who was embarrassed when the school secretary came into her class and announced she was there to decide the child's race. And the multiracial engineer whose company, a government contractor, refused to let him classify himself as multiracial. The company solved its problem: they hired him as black and fired him as white.

The Civil Rights Act of 1964 was passed 29 years ago almost to the day. It prohibits discrimination based on race, color, religion, sex, or national origin. *Omission is a form of discrimination.* Congress was not thinking in 1964 about multiracial persons. But now we *are* thinking about them. And yet today they are still being omitted. Even in 1978 when OMB [Office of Management and Budget] Directive 15[4] was put into place, the multiracial numbers were small. The multiracial population is growing and its needs must be met.

I will address the two concerns we have about Directive 15. The first problem is that of how race is determined. The Directive states, "The category which most closely reflects the individual's recognition in his community should be used for purposes of reporting on persons who are of racially mixed and/or ethnic origins." We call this "eyeballing." It is a totally subjective and unfair method.

In a letter from Archie B. Meyer, the Regional Civil Rights Director for the U.S. Department of Education, Office for Civil Rights [OCR], Region IV, to the school attorney for the Forsyth County Schools, Mr. Meyer advised the schools, when dealing with multiracial students to ". . . reassign students to one of the five standard categories through observation." Based on Directive 15, Mr. Meyer further advised ". . . the classroom teacher may simply count the children according to the racial identification that best represents the child's race within the five categories available and report the total count broken down by race to the principal." The Regional Civil Rights Director concludes, "This method of collecting information may be preferable because it need not result in unwanted racial tags for any individual child."

What is a simple idea and preferable method to Mr. Meyer is a horrifying reality to parents of multiracial children, yet it happens all the time, sanctioned by the OMB and the OCR. *Self-identification is the only way to right this wrong.*

Our second concern is the necessity of a multiracial category. Parents, school districts, state legislatures, and organizations are showing us what they want. They want an accurate category for multiracial children, not mixed, not other, but multiracial. They don't want multiracial children to be forced to deny the race of one of their parents anymore.

Exhibits #1 and #2 outline our proposal for a revised Directive 15. It calls for a sixth category of "Multiracial."[5] It establishes a procedure for a variance *only* if more detailed information is necessary.[6] It gives our multiracial children, the stakeholders, the dignity they deserve.

A new procedure for collecting racial and ethnic statistics, which includes a multiracial category, has many positive applications. Data will be meaningless if you continue to pretend multiracial people don't exist. If accurate data are what we want, if equal minority representation is what we need, and if by affirmative action we truly mean protection of minority representation in the work place, we must change our skewed statistics. Can the current method, which results in the same child counted in the majority on the census and in the minority at his school, possibly be viewed as accurate? Can a system in which a company can hire a person as black and fire the same person as white possibly be viewed by anyone as fair?

I care about accurate data, too. But I'm not a scholar, statistician, attorney, or lawmaker. I'm just a mother. A mother who cares about children, and whether I like it or not, I realize that self-esteem is directly tied to accurate racial identity. More and more parents all over our country are instilling new pride in our multiracial children. Can we say we have succeeded if our children leave home only to be denied an equal place in our society?

I believe every one here today recognizes that we are addressing more than just statistics, we are concerned with human beings. I believe truly recognizing multiracial identity is part of our government's real objective for civil rights and equality for all.

The multiracial community has been very patient. While changes were discussed for the 1980 Census, my children had not even been born. While data analysis and consultation was conducted for the 1990 Census, my children were too young to know. My son will be sixteen when we receive the 2000 Census. We have been patient.

In 1963 Martin Luther King said, "Now is the time to make justice a reality for all God's children." I believe Dr. King was speaking thirty years ago for multiracial children, too. With your help, their time has finally come. Thank you.

14

Testimony of the Association of MultiEthnic Americans Before the Subcommittee on Census, Statistics, and Postal Personnel of the U.S. House of Representatives

Introduction
By Carlos A. Fernández
Coordinator for Law and Civil Rights,
President 1988-94,
The Association of MultiEthnic Americans (AMEA)

This written testimony was presented in June of 1993, together with our oral testimony, to the Subcommittee on Census, Statistics and Postal Personnel of the U.S. House of Representatives, chaired by Congressman Thomas Sawyer (D-Ohio).

This was the first time that the community of multiracial/multi-ethnic people in the United States was able to present its views in a formal setting at the federal level on the question of racial categories on government forms. Since then, we have also had the opportunity to present testimony to the Office of Management and Budget, the agency which defines racial categories at all levels of government throughout the United States, including the public schools, through its Statistical Directive 15, a copy of which appears at the end of this section.

Appended also is a copy of AMEA's proposal to revise OMB Directive 15 in such a way as to include the counting of people who are of more than one of the categories presently in use. It should be noted here that this proposal focuses not so much on the use of a stand-alone multiracial category, but rather, on the opportunity to signify what that means in terms of any of the other categories appearing on the form.

It was, and remains, AMEA's view that this approach best offers the detail and continuity required for various government interests such as civil rights enforcement, while at the same time providing for accurate responses by multiracial/ethnic individuals.

June 30, 1993
Presented by Carlos A. Fernández, Esq., President (San Francisco)
assisted by Edwin C. Darden, Vice President, Eastern Region (D.C.),
and Ramona E. Douglass, Vice President, Central Region (Chicago)

The Association of MultiEthnic Americans offers this testimony regarding the federal government's classification of people whose racial or ethnic identification encompasses more than one of the designated classifications currently in use.

(All appendixes and references to them which were attached to the original written testimony submitted to Congress have been omitted in the interest of space, the only exceptions being copies of OMB Directive 15 and AMEA's proposed revision to it which were Appendices 1 and 2 in the original.)

Introduction

The Association of MultiEthnic Americans (AMEA) is the only nationwide confederation of local multiethnic/interracial groups representing thousands of people from all walks of life and includes individuals and families of various racial and ethnic origins and mixtures. We represent one of the fastest-growing populations in the United States. (According to the Population Reference Bureau, children born to parents of different races went from 1 percent to 3.4 percent of total births from 1968 to 1989; from 1970 to 1991, the number of mixed-race couples excluding Hispanics increased from 310,000 to 994,000.)

AMEA was founded on November 12, 1988, by representatives of local interracial groups, many of which emerged around the country during the late 1970s and early 1980s. In many cases, these groups formed as parents, multiracial adults, and others began to challenge the official classification of multiracial, multiethnic people, particularly in connection with the public schools.

This issue of racial classification served to highlight the more general concerns of multiracial/multiethnic people in the United States and elsewhere. Of special concern to us then and now is that peculiar form of bigotry aimed at interracialism and interculturalism which is present in all ethnic communities. Many of us who fit into more than one of the official categories realize that our very identity is a challenge to this deeply ingrained prejudice of a divided world.

Consequently, AMEA's primary goal is to promote a positive awareness of interracial and multiethnic identity, for ourselves and for society as a whole.

We believe that every person, especially every child, who is multiethnic/interracial has the same right as any other person to assert an identity that embraces the fullness and integrity of their actual ancestry, and that every multiethnic/interracial family, whether biological or adoptive, has the same right to grow and develop as any other, and that our children have the right to love and respect each of their parents equally.

We also believe that a positive awareness of interracial and multicultural identity is an essential step toward resolving America's, and also the world's, profound difficulty with the issues of race and interethnic relations. We are convinced that our community is uniquely situated to confront these issues because of the special experiences and understanding we acquire in the intimacy of our families and our personalities.

AMEA seeks to accomplish its goals by winning recognition from government—local, state, and federal—as well as from the media, and engaging every opportunity to express our views and provide information on issues which concern our community. We have sought out and received the support of academics and professionals who recognize the social significance and magnitude of our concerns. We are establishing a national resource center and legal fund.

The Racial/Ethnic Classification Issue

The issue of racial/ethnic classifications on government-regulated forms is the most immediate tangible concern of most members of our community. Each and every time we confront one of these forms, we are faced yet again with the awkward, irrational, and for many of us, the offensive task of selecting a "race" or "ethnicity" which does not truthfully identify us and has the further result of failing to count our community.

This is why we are here today. To let you know our concerns about government racial classifications, and to offer our proposal for meeting these concerns in a workable manner.

Our Proposal—Acknowledging
Multiracial/Multiethnic People on Forms

In general, AMEA wants to see a government-wide reform to accommodate and acknowledge the particular identity of people whose racial or ethnic identification encompasses more than one of the designated classifications currently in use.

For instance, whenever a question calls for "racial" classification, the category "multiracial" should be included. Whenever a question calls for "ethnic" classification, the category "multiethnic" should be included. Whenever racial and ethnic information is sought in a combined format, the category "multiracial/multiethnic" should be included.

Additionally, the categories "multiracial," "multiethnic," and "multiracial/multiethnic" should each be followed by a listing of the racial and/or ethnic groups appearing on the main list. This secondary listing should be used to signify the racial/ethnic identifications or origins of the parents of the individual being tallied.

Current Government Race/Ethnic Classifications—
OMB Statistical Policy Directive 15

The most important and far-reaching rule affecting governmental classifications is set forth in Office of Management and Budget (OMB) Statistical Policy Directive 15 (Appendix 1). The stated purpose of this directive is to facilitate the exchange of racial and ethnic statistics among governmental agencies by standardizing the reporting of this information.

OMB Directive 15 affects all governmental agencies including the census, the public schools, Social Security, etc. Additionally, the Directive sets the example for the private sector. If reform is to be made affecting the counting of multiracial people anywhere in government, OMB Directive 15 must be changed.

OMB Directive 15 sets forth five racial/ethnic categories and requires reporting in one category only for each individual counted ("check-one-only"). "Other" is not one of the reporting categories.

OMB Directive 15 forces government agencies at all levels to design their racial/ethnic query forms in such a way that the information provided can be reported in terms of one of the Directive 15 categories only. Thus, people whose parentage encompasses more than one of the designated categories cannot be counted, except monoracially. This causes tremendous problems, not only for the individuals involved, but also for the government agencies who must develop forms and rules which offend both multiracial/ethnic people as well as any rational standard of accuracy.

AMEA proposes that OMB Statistical Directive 15 be changed in order to allow the accurate counting of multiracial/ethnic people. This change may be accomplished quite simply by (1) the addition of a "multiracial" and/or "multiethnic" category and (2) providing a subsection for those choosing to identify as multiracial/ethnic to signify their racial/ethnic parentage in terms of the other listed categories.

This proposal (1) counts people accurately according to their actual identity; (2) provides statistical continuity by accounting for the racial/ethnic component(s) which may be relevant for various government studies and programs; and (3) avoids unnecessary and unwarranted government influence and interference in the very sensitive and private matter of personal identity.

The Census

The 1990 Census, as in past censuses, maintains its own format for asking about racial/ethnic information. However, even the Census Bureau must ensure that its statistics are reportable in the terms dictated by OMB Directive 15. This meant that in 1990 monoracial/ethnic responses were required in the race and Hispanic questions (#4 & #7), although multiple answers were permitted in the ethnic ancestry question (#13) on the long form.

Census officials inform us that responses to "other race" were assigned to monoracial categories for OMB reporting purposes when the various racial components were stated. One version of the rule applied in these instances of which we are aware is that the first race stated was the one to which the response was assigned. Responses such as "multiracial" or "mixed" required either a visit by a census taker to obtain a monoracial response, or else they were not counted.

Additionally, responses such as "multiracial" when written in cannot be discovered from any publicly available reports of the Census Bureau although presumably, the individual responses are there.

Thus, one of the principal agencies of government charged with supplying important demographic information for government and business is hamstrung when it comes to counting the community we represent. This is primarily a consequence of the reporting requirements of OMB Statistical Directive 15.

The Public Schools

Perhaps nowhere is the impact of OMB Directive 15 more keenly felt by members of the multiracial/ethnic community than in the public education system. Indeed, the initial impetus in the formation of many local interracial groups across the country has been the classification of multiracial/ethnic children in public schools.

Beginning with the success of the AMEA-affiliated group "Interracial Intercultural Pride" (I-Pride) in California which succeeded in getting the Berkeley Public Schools to adopt an "Interracial" category in 1981 (limited to internal uses by OMB Dir 15) and continuing with the efforts of others, notably of Project RACE in Georgia, the Cincinnati Multiracial Alliance in Ohio, Michelle Erickson and her supporters in Illinois, Patricia Whitehead in San Diego, students at Harvard University, and of others including AMEA, the multiracial/ethnic community has been spurred on by the particularly offensive application of OMB Directive 15 in the realm of public education.

Why?

First, when government compels the multiracial, multiethnic family to signify a factually false identity for their child, it invades their fundamental right of privacy. Every multiracial/ethnic family is entitled to safeguard its integrity against unwarranted intrusions by the government. No child should be forced to favor one parent over the other by any governmental agency.

Second, it violates a fundamental right of privacy of the multiracial/ethnic individual to require that they deny their factual identity and heritage, including the right to their own distinctive identity as a multiracial/ethnic person. Such a requirement offends personal dignity and interferes in a negative way with the development of self-esteem of multiracial/ethnic students.

Third, it is especially offensive as well as a violation of privacy to require that school officials "visually inspect" for purposes of racially classifying a student who does not identify monoracially. This procedure has more in common with the sorting of animals than it does with the ordinary respect supposed to be accorded human beings. We cannot conceive of any reasonable basis for this procedure.

Fourth, it is appalling that an educational institution should require the giving of factually false information on school census forms. The teaching of facts and truth is the essence of education. A multiracial, multiethnic child or her parents cannot give a monoracial response and be truthful at the same time. It is wrong for government to make such a requirement of its citizens, parents and children alike.

There is also an argument to be made from the standpoint of religious belief. For example, the central tenet of the Baha'i Faith is the oneness of humanity. As a consequence, members are encouraged to marry across racial and cultural lines. For the offspring of such marriages, any requirement by school officials to identify by monoracial category places them in double jeopardy, challenging both their personal integrity and religious belief. (ref. Peter Adriance, National Spiritual Assembly of the Baha'is of the United States, Washington DC)

Public Health

The practice of not recognizing racial/ethnic mixture even reaches into the area of public health. Unbelievably, the National Center for Health Statistics denies the identity of multiracial, multiethnic people. In fact, this denial reached such absurd proportions that in 1989, the race of children of single mothers changed from race of the father to race of the mother! At no time was the race of the child recorded accurately as *multiracial* when this was actually the case. This sort of statistical method might serve someone's social views of race, but in public health where such statistics are required for life and death decisions such as allocation of research and health program funds or the rendering of medical assistance, there is no excuse.

Certainly, patterns of gene expression are different in racially and ethnically diverse individuals than they are in people whose genes are more closely similar. Thus, ignoring the fact of multiracial people in the gathering of these statistics can lead to false conclusions about the health needs of various population groups. Recent findings lend support to this conclusion. (See for instance the recent study in the *New England Journal of Medicine* showing significant differences in the metabolizing of drugs such as Inderal among different population groups; also, the ongoing efforts to improve the availability of compatible organ transplant donors.)

Moreover, we have anecdotal evidence of multiracial/ethnic people whose identity is confused by health care professionals, particularly in potentially life-threatening emergency situations.

Multiracial people can be characterized in various ways by different individuals, but rarely are we characterized as multiracial! This has as much to do with cultural training as with traditional, unscientific notions of race and race mixture inappropriately applied in the keeping and reporting of medical records and statistics.

Assessing the Needs of the
Multiracial/Ethnic Community

Disallowing the specific identity of multiracial/multiethnic people also deprives our community of basic data required to objectively assess or even discover those of its needs which might require legislative or even judicial action. Indeed, this is one of the rationales for keeping racial/ethnic statistics on the various other minority populations.

There is, for example, a form of discrimination arising from the special bigotry against racially mixed people which deserves attention and can only be gauged statistically if this population is counted specially and not just as "other" or as monoracial.

Certainly, there is no shortage of anecdotes and specific cases wherein bigotry against interracial people and families has occurred throughout U.S. history, continuing even today. One need look no further than the cases involving the anti-miscegenation laws for evidence of this fact. The record of the 1967 case of *Loving v. Virginia* which AMEA commemorated last year (see *New York Times,* June

12, 1992, Law page) was filled with the most nonsensical pseudo-scientific pap about the supposedly debilitated progeny of interracial unions, and hysterical fears that society might become "mongrelized" and thereby eventually collapse.

We are painfully aware that such prejudices persist in this country, even among members of minority groups. Whether these prejudices exist in patterns of discrimination can only be determined if accurate statistics are available. Because of current government classification rules, these patterns cannot at present be known with any reasonable certainty or accuracy.

Public Policy Considerations

In keeping with its origin in the Executive Branch of the Federal Government, OMB Statistical Directive 15 is supposed to aid the administration of government programs dealing with various racial and ethnic populations in the United States. In and of itself, Directive 15 in theory cannot dictate public policy, only facilitate its implementation.

Unfortunately, in its current form, Directive 15 unnecessarily incorporates a policy denying the fact of interracial/ethnic mixture, as well as failing to provide statistics that are accurate, a fundamental requirement if government is to function effectively, by mischaracterizing multiracial/ethnic people. It enshrines highly questionable and controversial notions of racial and ethnic group affiliation, in particular, the idea that individuals cannot transcend racial/ethnic lines even when they do!

It may be true that Directive 15 does not provide for the counting of multiracial/ethnic people only incidentally and inadvertently. This may be because the Legislative Branch, the Congress, has not acted to establish a public policy which explicitly acknowledges the existence of multiracial/ethnic people. Until it does so, OMB may not feel compelled to count us.

Now is the time for the Congress to make its concerns known to the Executive Branch in this area. Indeed, this hearing today is a positive development in that regard.

Congress has already enacted laws to encourage and improve the civil rights of all citizens, especially those who have historically suffered discrimination based on their race or ethnicity. One of the most important public policies upon which these enactments were made was, and remains, the desire to strengthen the unity of this country by eliminating barriers between individuals and communities based on race. Some of this was accomplished under the gun of Supreme Court decisions, some because it was believed to be sound public policy.

In keeping with this broad policy of national unity, it might be argued that racial and ethnic classifications should be done away with entirely. But such a view is utopian and also distorts the reality of continuing communal divisions based on race and ethnicity.

The better argument is that we must step up our efforts to improve the chances of all our citizens against the forces of prejudice, bigotry and separatism, thereby rendering racial and ethnic classifications increasingly irrelevant.

In the meantime, we should take advantage of the socially unifying force that is superbly represented by the multiracial, multiethnic community. As stated previously, our community is uniquely situated to confront racial and interethnic issues because of the special experiences and understanding we acquire in the intimacy of our families and our personalities. Ideally, our community has the potential to become the stable core around which the ethnic pluralism of the United States can be united.

In order to take advantage of the multiracial community's potential, this society must first recognize and acknowledge our existence. In concrete terms, this means accommodating our identity on official forms if not in common parlance. Once the concept of people whose identities transcend traditional racial and ethnic boundaries is accepted, the idea of social unity becomes easier to visualize. Without this concept, we enshrine racial and ethnic divisions.

Many sociologists agree that the degree of intermarriage and multiracial families in a society is a good gauge of the degree of racial/ethnic harmony of that society. (For citations, see Murguia, *Chicano Intermarriage*, Trinity University Press, 1982.) What that degree might be at any given moment and over time cannot be known accurately unless it is measured.

International Implications

Accommodating the multiracial/ethnic community in America by recognizing its specific identity also has important global implications. For instance, a recent study by the World Affairs Council of Northern California found that racism and ethnic division hurts the U.S. economically (*San Francisco Chronicle*, October 5, 1992). Conversely, it is reasonable to assume that racial and ethnic harmony, which is best represented by the multiracial community, can be an enormous advantage to this country. However, we cannot make full use of this advantage if we refuse to recognize the existence of the multiracial community, and we cannot recognize its existence if we deny its identity.

There is also the question of interracial, interethnic harmony across the world. This question bears on the health of the world economy as much as it does on the simple matter of peace.

Certainly, the experiences attendant to the breakup of the Soviet Union and Yugoslavia demonstrate the critical need for new thinking and new models for establishing and maintaining world peace and order. One important component of any new thinking must necessarily involve families and individuals whose very identities transcend racial and ethnic divisions and who therefore cannot abide the prejudices and bigotry that feed the fires of intercommunal wars. Of all the countries in the world, it should be the one whose motto is "E Pluribus Unum," the one nation that has the advantage of having drawn upon all the nations of the world for its people, the only nation that has the power, momentarily, to influence the other countries of the world in the ways of multiethnic living, that sets the example for others. Certainly this is at least an ideal to which we should aspire.

One important aspect of international relations of which we should be particularly concerned in this regard is the silence of the international community including the United States on the rights of multiethnic peoples caught in the conflicts between ethnic communities asserting their recognized rights of self-determination and sovereignty. This may seem a distant concern for consideration by this Subcommittee, but in fact, it is the same failure to recognize and acknowledge multiracial, multiethnic people there as here. We cannot hope to influence others to protect the rights of anyone if we cannot first demonstrate our own ability to do so within our own borders. We cannot do this if we cannot even recognize the existence of multiracial/ethnic people who are the links between our own diverse racial and ethnic communities.

Questions Submitted by the
Subcommittee and Responses

1. What are the primary purposes of the racial and ethnic categories?

A race question has appeared in every census beginning with the first one in 1790. The original utility of this question was to help ascertain the number of "free white persons" as distinguished mainly from black slaves and Native Americans. These two non-white groups were the only ones of any numerical consequence at the time.

Questions relating to ethnicity or "national origin" have appeared on most censuses, particularly in connection with the large-scale immigrations beginning in the late 19th century. Presumably the purpose here was to account for the newcomers in order to then legislate a restriction on their continued immigration.

The other most notable use of racial classifications occurred at the state level in the regulation of marriages and the tabulation of birth and death records, mainly for discriminatory purposes.

In recent years, racial and ethnic questions have been continued. However, their primary purpose has fundamentally changed. With the advent of the civil rights movement and the U.S. Supreme Court decisions that accompanied it, these questions have acquired a new importance. The information thus provided has become essential in the implementation of court decisions involving civil rights as well as in the allocation of government resources to meet the needs of various identifiable population groups who have suffered from discrimination. Recent court rulings have affirmed this purpose citing especially 13 USCS §141 (*Texas v. Mosbacher* 1992 SD Tex, 783 F. Supp 308).

The Office of Management and Budget (OMB) specifies its own purposes for the collection of racial and ethnic information. Statistical Policy Directive 15 which reaches to and affects all governmental entities including the census and the public schools, specifies that: "The minimum standard collection categories shall be utilized for reporting . . . Civil rights compliance reporting . . . General program administrative and grant reporting . . . (and) Statistical reporting" where required by statute or regulation.

2. How well are the current categories working (in terms of data accuracy and public acceptance)?

AMEA cannot answer this question except with respect to the interracial/multiethnic community we represent.

On behalf of this community, we state emphatically that the current categories on the census, school enrollment, and other governmental forms are wholly inadequate and grossly inaccurate in that there is no category or procedure by which multiracial/multiethnic people can identify themselves comfortably and accurately. The requirement on most forms to identify with only one specified category is a solicitation for inaccurate information when a factual response by a multiracial or multiethnic individual would require identification with more than one of the specified categories. This means (1) that multiracial people are not being accounted for and (2) other population groups are being mischaracterized.

Many people in the multiracial/multiethnic community are not accepting of the census categories currently employed and are often highly offended. They are particularly disturbed by the requirements of the OMB Directive 15 as it affects the forms used in the public schools and encountered by their children where even the option "other" is not available. And it must be said, the "other" category, when it is available, is also unacceptable to us, for both practical and philosophical reasons.

3. If the current categories are inadequate, how best can we increase their usefulness without compromising data comparability and public acceptance?

AMEA has outlined elsewhere in this written statement how questions calling for racial or ethnic information might be changed to accommodate the need for accuracy and acceptance by our community. We believe these proposals provide a method by which the need for statistical continuity can be met.

4. Would use of an ethnic identifier, or another set of categories, be more useful than a racial one?

Limited strictly to the question of "usefulness," racial and ethnic identifiers are probably equally effective. However, everything hinges on the meaning of the two terms "race" and "ethnicity." People typically use the terms interchangeably depending on what they are interested in (see *Saint Francis College v. Al-Khazraji*, 481 US 604 [1987]). There are individuals among the community we represent who choose to identify monoracially when what they really mean to indicate is the community to which they most closely interact (particularly if they grew up in a segregated environment) or for whose interests they wish to express support. In a real sense, they are identifying ethnically, although racially, strictly speaking, they would be considered multiracial. If the census and other governmental agencies wish to have any hope of getting a handle on all this, they must present the questions and categories in such a way that these phenomena can be properly discerned.

For instance, many if not most ethnically identified African Americans are "multiracial"; so, incidentally, are most "Hispanics." Thus, simply adding a multiracial category would introduce unnecessary confusion. A deracialized approach would serve better because it takes into account the actual divides between communities which are not based on the three-race theory, but rather on real cultural communities with historic origins in legal segregation and/or the presence of international borders; the multiracialism with which we are concerned is more properly a question of ethnicity, and therefore, the type of identity we are really concerned with is multiethnic in nature. And certainly, for most multiracial persons, the issues associated with this heritage have as much to do with the integration of different cultures as with the issue of skin color, even in the case of children of European-American and African-American parentage.

Of course, any deracializing of classifications on government forms must contend with the reality of popular perceptions. Thus it might make sense to employ a transitional scheme where "race" is used interchangeably with "ethnic." This is more easily understood by most people. "Ethnic" is a good term because properly, it incorporates both "race" and "culture," i.e., an ethnic group is primarily endogamous (racial) and shares a common culture based on social interactions occurring mainly within the community.

5. Should the federal government adopt a "bi-" or "multiracial" category, and what are the legal implications of such a category?

The census and all governmental entities should adopt a "multiracial" category when the question posed is "racial," "multiethnic" when the question is ethnicity, and both when racial and ethnic information is sought in a combined format. The prefix "multi-" is preferred to "bi-" since there are many instances of persons whose ancestry includes more than two racial or ethnic groups.

There is no particular legal implication that we can see arising from the adoption of a "multiracial/ethnic" category, though we do see legal problems arising from the current requirements of OMB Directive 15, some to which we have already alluded.

Of course, there is the question of how the adoption of such a category might impact various minority benefit programs since presumably, many persons now counted monoracially would then be counted as multiracial.

Furthermore, we understand the concern of government demographers and statisticians for continuity in their records.

Our proposal takes both of these questions into account by requiring that the races/ethnicities of parents be signified for each individual identifying as multiracial or multiethnic. In this way, it is possible to continue including multiracial people in various minority benefit programs if Congress deems such to be appropriate. Since many multiracial people have traditionally been discriminated against as if they were monoracial, their continued inclusion in at least some of these programs would seem justified. The need for continuity is preserved insofar as the sudden statistical "disappearance" of monoracial individuals from particular racial categories can be accounted for in the multiracial category in the manner proposed.

Conclusion

The Association of MultiEthnic Americans believes that now is the time for the Congress to take and recommend whatever actions are necessary to accommodate and acknowledge the particular identity of multiracial, multiethnic people. In particular, OMB Statistical Policy Directive 15 must be changed as we have proposed.

It is unacceptable to AMEA and the community it represents that what purports to be a mere administrative device should be the reason we are denied our identity. Directive 15 as it currently reads must be changed because (1) it fails its own test of accuracy and (2) it too conveniently corresponds to traditional notions of bigotry directed against so-called race mixing as well as the multiracial, multiethnic people thereby produced.

The multiracial, multiethnic community deserves, no less than any other community, the respect and dignity of recognition for who we really are. The changes we advocate are necessary as a matter of right as well as good public policy. They can be effected immediately with minimal or no adverse impact on anyone or any group, and with enormous benefit to all.

We thank the Subcommittee for hearing our views. We stand ready to be of further assistance as you may request.

Appendix 1
Race and Ethnic Standards for Federal Statistics and Administrative Reporting

This Directive provides standard classifications for recordkeeping, collection, and presentation of data on race and ethnicity in Federal program administrative reporting and statistical activities. These classifications should not be interpreted as being scientific or anthropological in nature, nor should they be viewed as determinants of eligibility for participation in any Federal program. They have been developed in response to needs expressed by both the executive branch and the Congress to provide for the collection and use of compatible, nonduplicated, exchangeable racial and ethnic data by Federal agencies.

Executive Office of Management and Budget
Statistical Directive No.15*

*Directive No. 15 supersedes section 7(h) and Exhibit F of OMB Circular No. A-46 dated May 3, 1974, and as revised May 12, 1977. Washington, D.C.

1. Definitions

The basic racial and ethnic categories for Federal statistics and program administrative reporting are defined as follows:
   a. *American Indian or Alaskan Native.* A person having origins in any of the original peoples of North America, and who maintains cultural identification through tribal affiliation or community recognition.
   b. *Asian or Pacific Islander.* A person having origins in any of the original peoples of the Far East, Southeast Asia, the Indian subcontinent, or the Pacific Islands. This area includes, for example, China, India, Japan, Korea, the Philippine Islands, and Samoa.
   c. *Black.* A person having origins in any of the black racial groups of Africa.

d. *Hispanic.* A person of Mexican, Puerto Rican, Cuban, Central or South American or other Spanish culture or origin, regardless of race.

e. *White.* A person having origins in any of the original peoples of Europe, North Africa, or the Middle East.

2. Utilization for Recordkeeping and Reporting

To provide flexibility, it is preferable to collect data on race and ethnicity separately. If separate race and ethnic categories are used, the minimum designations are:

a. *Race*:
— American Indian or Alaska Native
— Asian or Pacific Islander
— Black
— White
b. *Ethnicity*:
— Hispanic origin
— Not of Hispanic origin

When race and ethnicity are collected separately, the number of White and Black persons who are Hispanic must be identifiable, and capable of being reported in that category.

If a combined format is used to collect racial and ethnic data, the minimum acceptable categories are:

American Indian or Alaska Native
Asian or Pacific Islander
Black, not of Hispanic origin
Hispanic
White, not of Hispanic origin

The category which most closely reflects the individual's recognition in his community should be used for purposes of reporting on persons who are of mixed racial and/or ethnic origins. (emphasis added)

In no case should the provisions of this Directive be construed to limit the collection of data to the categories described above. However, any reporting required which uses more detail shall be organized in such a way that the additional categories can be aggregated into these basic racial/ethnic categories.

The minimum standard collection categories shall be utilized for reporting as follows:

a. *Civil rights compliance reporting.* The categories specified above will be used by all agencies in either the separate or combined format for civil rights compliance reporting and equal employment reporting for both the public and private sectors and for all levels of government. Any variation requiring less detailed data or data which cannot be aggregated into the basic categories will have to be specifically approved by the Office of Federal Statistical Policy and Standards for executive agencies. More detailed reporting which can be aggregated to the basic categories may be used at the agencies' discretion.

b. *General program administrative and grant reporting.* Whenever an agency subject to this Directive issues new or revised administrative reporting or recordkeeping requirements which include racial or ethnic data, the agency will use the race/ethnic categories described above. A variance can be specifically requested from the Office of Federal Statistical Policy and Standards, but such a variance will be granted only if the agency can demonstrate that it is not reasonable for the primary reporter to determine the racial or ethnic background in terms of the specified categories, and that such determination is not critical to the administration of the program in question, or if the specific program is directed to only one or a limited number of race/ethnic groups, e.g., Indian tribal activities.

c. *Statistical reporting.* The categories described in this Directive will be used at a minimum for federally sponsored statistical data collection where race and/or ethnicity is required, except when: the collection involves a sample of such size that the data on the smaller categories would be unreliable, or when the collection effort focuses on a specific racial or ethnic group. A repetitive survey shall be deemed to have an adequate sample size if the racial and ethnic data can be reliably aggregated on a biennial basis. Any other variation will have to be specifically authorized by OMB through the reports clearance process (see OMB Circular No.A-40). In those cases where the data collection is not subject to the reports clearance process, a direct request for a variance should be made to the OFSPS.

3. Effective Date

The provisions of this Directive are effective immediately for all *new* and *revised* recordkeeping or reporting requirements containing racial and/or ethnic information. All *existing* recordkeeping or reporting requirements shall be made consistent with this Directive at the time they are submitted for extension, or not later than January 1, 1980.

4. Presentation of Race/Ethnic Data

Displays of racial and ethnic compliance and statistical data will use the category designations listed above. The designation "non-white" is not acceptable for use in the presentation of Federal Government data. It is not to be used in any publication of compliance or statistical report.

In cases where the above designations are considered inappropriate for presentation of statistical data on particular regional areas, the sponsoring agency may use:

(1) The designations "Black and Other Races" or "All Other Races," as collective descriptions of minority races when the most summary distinction between the majority race and other races is appropriate; or

(2) The designations "White," "Black," and "All Other Races" when the distinction among the majority race, the principal minority race and other races is appropriate; or

(3) The designation of a particular minority race or races, and the inclusion of "Whites" with "All Other Races," if such a collective description is appropriate.

In displaying detailed information which represents a combination of race and ethnicity, the description of the data being displayed must clearly indicate that both bases of classification are being used.

When the primary focus of a statistical report is on two or more specific identifiable groups in the population, one or more of which is racial or ethnic, it is acceptable to display data for each of the particular groups separately and to describe data relating to the remainder of the population by an appropriate collective description.

Appendix 2
AMEA Proposed Revised Minimum Reporting Standards with Multiracial Multiethnic Categories

1. Race and Ethnicity Separated Format

   a. Race:
      1. American Indian/Alaskan Native
      2. Asian/Pacific Islander
      3. Black
      4. White
      5. Multiracial (persons of more than one of the listed groups only). For respondents in this category, specify races of parents.
           1. American Indian/Native American
           2. Asian/Pacific Islander
           3. Black
           4. White
   b. Ethnicity
      1. Hispanic origin
      2. Not of Hispanic origin
      3. Multiethnic (parent(s) of Hispanic and non-Hispanic origin)

2. Race and Ethnicity Combined Format

   1. American Indian/Alaskan Native
   2. Asian/Pacific Islander
   3. Black, not of Hispanic origin
   4. Hispanic
   5. White, not of Hispanic origin
   6. Multiracial/Multiethnic (persons of more than one of the listed groups only). For respondents in this category, specify races/ethnicities of parents.
        1. American Indian/Alaskan Native
        2. Asian/Pacific Islander
        3. Black, not of Hispanic origin
        4. Hispanic
        5. White, not of Hispanic origin

15

Multiracial Identity Assertion in the Sociopolitical Context of Primary Education

Jennifer Clancy

Historical perceptions of race have been reified by social institutions. For this reason, racial groups are socially understood as biological categories that are uniform and unmixed. This concept of race has survived generations. Although mixed-race people have succeeded in complicating social reality by their existence, they have not yet begun to enter into the next phase, that of shifting concepts of race in the larger culture. To shift racial paradigms, it is necessary for mixed-race scholars and activists to engage in the complex process of redefining social meanings of race and thereby making the assertion of multiracial identity tenable and legitimate. One possible site of struggle for mixed-race people is within the sociopolitical context of educational institutions, for it is there that the next generation can be taught not only how to challenge, but also how to actively transform social conceptions of race by uniting and struggling together.

Although it is true that "the presence of racially mixed persons defies the social order predicated upon race, blurs racial and ethnic group boundaries, and challenges generally accepted proscriptions and prescriptions regarding intergroup relations",[1] it is dangerous to portray the redefining of race and racial categories as acts that have already been accomplished. In doing so a false view of reality is created—the view that merely the passive presence of a community has the power to transform racial identity patterns within society.

In this chapter, I first analyze the limits of examining racial identity choice within the psychosocial framework that has been used by many scholars in this area.[2] I base my analysis on George Kich's developmental theory of biracial identity assertion and argue that examining racial identity choice through the lens of individualistic, psychosocial interpretations effaces the ways that the interrelationship between multiracial communities and monoracial culture influences the assertion of multiracial identification. I then explore the possibility of working within the sociopolitical framework of primary education as a strategy for shifting racial paradigms.

Racial Identity Choice: Psychosocial versus Sociopolitical Framework

George Kich[3] conducted empirical research to examine the possibility of asserting biracial identity as a developmental process. He studied fifteen biracial adults of Japanese and white heritage. Based on his research, Kich asserts, "Subsequent integration and continuing expression of a biracial identity involve a complex interplay among the dynamics of the family, the community, and oneself."[4] In other words, Kich believes that the ability to choose a multiracial identity develops through the resolution of psychosocial relationships, those that occur between individuals and their immediate social system. However, an examination of Kich's interpretation of his research reveals the limits of studying racial identity choice within a psychosocial framework.

Kich's theory of biracial identity choice posits three stages. During the initial stage, biracial individuals develop an awareness that they are different from their monoracial parents, friends, and peers. This experience of differentness leads to a devaluation of self and a feeling of not belonging. Although monoracial parents may be accepting of their biracial offspring, ultimately they cannot model for their children ways to resolve their racial identity conflict. Kich writes, "In the biracial person's quest for personal understanding and mastery, they begin to seek their own explanations for dissonance. . . ."[5]

It is this quest for personal understanding that moves the mixed-race person into the next stage. This second stage is a period of self-exploration. Biracial people begin this stage by seeking out the acceptance of others. The resolution of this stage, however, is marked by an acceptance of themselves as existing within a unique racial category that other people confront with misconceptions and rejection. "Biracial people," notes Kich, "at the end of the search-for-acceptance stage recognize the limitations of standard racial categories in general."[6]

Kich portrays the final developmental stage of biracial identity assertion as a potential that may never be fully reached. This is the period of self-acceptance, where mixed-race individuals attain the ability to define themselves. In addition to acquiring the ability to create self-definitions, the biracial person develops a tolerance for the limited views of race within the general society during this final developmental stage.

Kich's theory is limited in its scope of interaction. He portrays multiracial identification assertion as an act that is solely engendered and determined within the microsystems of the individual—the family and the immediate social community. This interpretation does not consider or recognize reciprocal interrelationship between the multiracial person's individual identification process and the larger culture's conceptions of race.

Kich's theory entails that the biracial person's individual need for self-mastery initiates the search for racial identification, and that the actions of their parents and extended family help to resolve identification conflict. Kich claims, "Parents are crucial facilitators of the biracial person's self-acceptance. . . . They can actively cultivate the family as an important medium through which a biracial sense of self develops."[7] But in addition to the effects of family are the less easily defined ways in which the larger monoracial culture shapes mixed-race persons' racial identity choices. For instance, educational institutions shape biracial persons' perceptions of race and racial categories within society. Since early in the century, scholars have recognized the role of schools in the socialization process of individuals. In 1916 John Dewey wrote, "Any education given by a group tends to socialize its members, but the quality and value of the socialization depends upon the habits and aims of the group."[8] Thus, the purpose of schools is not to provide equal education to the children of society, but instead to function as socialization tools of the dominant culture. Given the fact that all monoracial communities have specific investments in maintaining boundaries between different races, it would seem likely that educational institutions would resist legitimizing multiracial identity assertion because this would radically shift racial paradigms.

Because Kich focuses so closely on the liberating role of the family, his theory conceals the ways in which the socialization processes occurring within the schools and other macrolevel institutions thwart individuals' ability to identify as multiracial. He is, in fact, accomplishing the feat so lucidly described by Cynthia Nakashima[9] in her article "The Invisible Monster: The Creation and Denial of Mixed-Race People in America." Kich's theory portrays mixed-race people as having control over their identity choice, while it simultaneously veils the power of the larger culture to deny mixed-race identity assertion. An adequate theory of multiracial identification needs to be expanded beyond the context of individualistic, psychosocial relationships. Psychosocial theories do not fully reveal the contradictions inherent within multiracial experience.

Kich overlooks the extent to which the biracial identity choice is contingent upon the macroculture, and his theory therefore eclipses the potential power of mixed-race people to change conceptions of racial identification within the larger culture. For Kich society is a constant entity that will continuously misconceive of multiracial identification. He represents the final stage of biracial identity assertion as a period during which "they [biracial people] more clearly understand the confusion of the other person, essentially the confusion of the rest of society about race and ethnicity."[10] It seems that Kich is accepting the fact that the racial paradigms are immutable, and the most that mixed-race individuals can hope for is to reach a point where they can benevolently accept the larger society's limited perspectives on race and racial categories. By emphasizing only the psychosocial world of the biracial person, Kich obscures the potential of mixed-race people to influence racial categorization and social concepts of race within the larger sociopolitical environment. Frequently, mixed-race scholars and activists speak of acting as a bridge between the various racial communities. However, a bridge connotes the image of a connection between two solid, unchanging forms. The potential role of mixed-race people may not be only to act as the connecting link, but to radically change the forms themselves in such a way that their new shapes come together as a whole that has no need for external sources of connection.

An examination of multiracial identity development within a sociopolitical framework assumes that racial identification and categorizations function systematically through educational, legal, religious, economic, and other macrolevel social institutions, to benefit the dominant, white patriarchal society. In contrast to the psychosocial model, a sociopolitical perspective understands the assertion of a multiracial identity as a more complex process that involves not only microcontexts, but an interrelationship between the mixed-race individuals' immediate community and the social institutions that structure power balances and political reality within U.S. society.

Many scholars of multiraciality argue that the hierarchal structuring of racial categories is a social construct.[11] This entails that the distinctions between races have been created by groups of people to serve specific social, economic, and political purposes. Racial categories and boundaries have been established to maintain a hierarchal social structure. Race is related to biology because there are phenotypical differences among members of different racial groups, but the hierarchal values placed on these differences were created by society. Scholars in the field of multiraciality use social constructionist theory to prove that because reality is socially constructed, racial categories can be reconstructed.

Too often, however, multiracial theorists using constructionist theory seem to imply that because racial identity is produced by persons, any person can choose to change that identity at any time. The lack of realism of this reasoning is succinctly clarified by Amanda Udis-Kessler:

> While constructionism does imply fluidity across time and place, it does not necessarily imply willful choice or intentionality, either in an individual's life or in a given society. Cultures are not as malleable as we might like to think. . . .[12]

Often, constructionists imply the existence of choice by failing to recognize that social reality is not merely the product of an individual or groups of individuals acting upon a situation. Social reality is characterized instead by interaction among individuals and between groups of people, typically negotiated by the use of power and influence. In this way, social knowledge is produced through social collaboration. Although the individual or group may be capable of transforming their perspectives on reality in a myriad of ways, these perspectives are also limited by the historical and social context from which they are operating.

Kenneth Gergen asserts that a regularity in individual conceptions of reality develops because the concepts are established within specific historical contexts and shaped by the prevailing meaning systems of that period. "Intelligibility or 'sense making' is essentially a social product; if others do not agree that one's words are sensible, they are simply nonsense."[13] Thus, as Udis-Kessler explained, racial categories have the potential to change across time and place, but this fluidity is the result of interactions and reciprocal relationships, not the choice of isolated individuals or cultures.

In the process of legitimizing multiracial identification, mixed-race people are beginning to confront and deconstruct traditional racial paradigms. To radically transform current concepts of race, however, it needs to be understood that the developmental process of multiracial identity assertion takes place within a sociopolitical context, as well as psychosocially. If multiracial identity is to "make sense" to society at large, rather than be seen as legitimate only within the mixed-race community, scholars and activists must focus their attention on those institutions that shape the sociopolitical paradigm of race. Although currently many multiracial activists are attempting to effect change within the government institutions that control the racial categories included in the census, to be effective, scholars and activists need to expand their focus beyond governmental institutions. Therefore, I examine the possibility of working within elementary educational institutions to transform racial paradigms.

The Possibility for Multiracial Identity Assertion in Primary Education

Historically, it has been accepted that schools in the United States are apolitical. Any relationship between the educational system and unequal access to power and resources in the larger society has been routinely denied by the majority of U.S. educators.[14] However, critical education theorists believe this view is erroneous. Public elementary schools can be considered sociopolitical because they are institutions that function to produce and preserve ideology that benefits the dominant social class.[15] Educational institutions help maintain the status quo with practices that attempt to ensure dominant social positions in the larger society for white students and subordinate cultural positions for students of color. Schools emphasize "the basic values of uniformity, consensus, and ethnocentrism,"[16] in order for the European culture to maintain hegemony. There must be collective belief in the superiority of European students within the school ecology. Without this consensus among administrators, teachers, and students, the hierarchal social structure could not exist. Public schools, using institutionalized practices, teach students to uniformly believe that the unequal social order of the larger society is legitimate.

Because a collective opinion is necessary for the dominant culture, schools routinely validate uniform belief and value systems among students. For example, school curricula emphasize social conformity, social compromise, and political consensus.[17] Henry Giroux[18] believes that overvaluing political consensus functions to eclipse the social experiences and political realities of marginalized students; "This can be seen in the way that school curricula often ignore the histories of women, racial minorities, and the working class."[19] Educational practices efface the diversity that exists among people, and in the process, produce and validate myths of uniformity.

These myths of uniformity adversely affect the tenability of multiracial identity assertion by not only ignoring the experiences of students of color, but also functioning to silence discussions and dialogue within the classroom on race and racial categories. If the only social reality that is acknowledged within schools is that of the white race, then there is no forum within the classroom to discuss the variety of racial experiences that constitute social reality. This prohibits students from having the opportunity to reflect on, critique, and shift present concepts of race and racial identity. Schools socialize individuals to conceive of racial identity only in terms of single dimensions because monoracial categorization systems serve the dominant society. Conceiving of racial groups as consistent and unmixed creates strict boundary lines between the various racial communities. This accomplishes two types of division. It separates the white society from communities of color. Also, current racial boundary lines divide the various communities of color from one another. Thus, for the current social order to be maintained, it is necessary that racial categories continue to be considered exclusive. This is achieved through the systematic practices used within educational institutions. These practices deny students the opportunity to challenge the veracity of European social constructions of race. Consequentially, the shifting of racial paradigms has remained an arduous feat and society continues to deny multiracial identity assertion.

Because the development of monoracial paradigms within larger society is deeply embedded within the teaching practices and techniques used by schools, the primary goal of those working to legitimate multiracial identity assertion should be to restructure teaching practices within these institutions. One form of structural change necessary to accommodate multiracial identity assertion within schools is the development of multicultural education that is grounded in the educational philosophy of political activist Paulo Freire, critical pedagogy. It views education as political because it can be developed as a strategy for individual empowerment and social change. In this context, the term 'empowerment' is used to describe a process of self-determination, rather than a static state of being. Multicultural education based on the tenets of critical pedagogy has a variety of names: Christine Sleeter refers to it as "cultural democracy"; Louise Derman-Sparks calls this way of teaching "social transformation"; Antonia Darder uses the term "critical education"; while Margo Okazawa-Rey simply speaks of it as "revolution."[20] Here, I use the names interchangeably.

The social transformation approach to multicultural education, which grew out of the social activism and civil rights movements of the 1960s, directly confronts and challenges racism and the dominant-class myths of social equality. Sleeter notes that "cultural democracy attempts to redesign classrooms and schools to model an unoppressive, equal society that is also culturally diverse."[21] Critical education rebels against the notion that social reality is objective, a belief inherent in traditional education curricula. By contrast, the perspective of critical educators is that social meaning and knowledge are constructed through interactions between people; and knowledge has traditionally been created for the benefit of the dominant culture.[22] Instead of blaming the victim by viewing oppressed peoples' personal inadequacies as the cause of their unequal social status, educators who use cultural democracy place the responsibility for the problem on members of the dominant group. However, members of oppressed groups are capable of developing solutions to social problems. Cultural democracy changes the classroom into a forum for social problem solving by emphasizing dialogue among students and teachers, describing history from the perspectives of diverse racial groups, and promoting social participation.[23]

The essential aspects of this approach to multicultural education are empowerment and social change. Richard Ruiz[24] describes educators who are empowering as those who create the conditions where individuals can learn to believe in their own ability to act. In this definition, teachers are not benevolent helpers who empower their then indebted students. Instead, they are educators who develop curricula that create an environment where students learn how to think critically about social reality, build on the strengths they already possess, and to effect social change.[25] Because radical social change requires the efforts of groups of people, rather than individuals working alone, critical education emphasizes curricula that teach students how to work collectively to mobilize power and attain common interests.[26]

Critical education cannot provide a recipe for a classroom teaching practice that will legitimize multiracial identities. An important aspect of creating the environmental conditions for empowerment is to engage students in learning and teaching each other about their own historical and cultural contexts. A prefabricated curriculum does not allow for the particular cultural dynamics that are part of the individual personality of each classroom. Instead, Darder argues, cultural democracy "is meant to provide a set of critical educational principles that can guide and support teachers. . . ."[27] Social transformation education can create a classroom environment where multiracial and monoracial students are taught history that includes mixed-race people. Educators can promote and foster language that allows students to identify themselves as racially mixed, rather than expecting all students to identify monoracially. Teachers can teach students to question the basis of current racial paradigms that validate only monoracial identification. Also, a curriculum can be developed that illustrates the connections between racism and the denial of mixed-race people. When students learn about the history and specific social reasons for the denial of mixed-race people in the context of a culturally democratic classroom, they can use their social development skills to design an action plan to begin the process of legitimizing multiracial identity. The extent of the social change plan depends on the goals and design of the individuals involved in the project.

Teachers can be creative in designing their curriculum. They can dialogue with other cultural democracy educators and share ideas. Okazawa-Rey[28] believes that in a culturally democratic classroom a curriculum can be extensive and diverse; it can consist of art projects, writing projects, oral histories, and so forth. The book *Empowerment Through Multicultural Education*, edited by Christine E. Sleeter, provides some examples of curricula used by critical educators to teach multicultural education. However, in using critical education to legitimize multiracial identity, the focus should not be on the technique, but rather on the mission, which is to empower students to learn of their own ability to transform racial paradigms.

16

Yankee Imperialism and Imperialist Nostalgia: A View from the Inside

Mariella Squire-Hakey
Missisquoi Sokoki band, Western Abenaki of Vermont

My voice

In 1968 I was a young teenager in Vermont. It was the height of the urban counterculture, when affluent middle-class American young people found it fashionable to search for personal identity and to explore cultural ethnicity. The most fashionable culture was, and remains for them, American Indian. The most fashionable attire in the summer of 1968 was fringed leather vests, high boot moccasins, and beaded headbands. Vermont's largest city, Burlington, had a trendy downtown where shops and department stores sold Navajo rugs, Pueblo pottery, and Apache leather goods. Street peddlers, famous in the local scene, hawked cheap plastic dolls with brown skin and Anglo features dressed in beaded leather outfits with feathers. Bookstores did a brisk trade in books like Juan Carlos Castaneda's and sponsored courses on Native American shamanism which were taught by the local Unitarian minister.

I did not wear leather vests or beaded headbands. I never wore my moccasins where white people could see me, and my cheap, wonderful plastic Indian doll with her non-Indian face lived hidden in a bureau drawer. I loved her and I was ashamed of her. I would window shop through downtown Burlington and feel horribly, profoundly alien. I was an Indian, doggedly and silently Indian, and the expensive marketplace commercial world was not mine.

I would sometimes catch a glimpse of my reflection in the store windows and see it hang mistily above the Navajo rugs like a ghost.

I was a ghost in Vermont of 1968. The dominant culture, known as Vermont Yankee, was utterly convinced there were no Indians in Vermont. In the eyes of the Yankee hegemony neither my culture nor my ancestry was valid. The Yankee myth stated, unequivocally, that the last Indians of Vermont had left or died soon after 1800 and that no Indians had ever lived in the state on a permanent basis. The myth said we had been wanderers, that our homeland of Ndakinna was an uninhabited wilderness until settled by the Yankees. The fact that we Abenakis had been in Ndakinna for millennia was of no consequence. We simply did not exist.

The Yankee culture did admit that a few Indians from elsewhere might have drifted into modern Vermont. My mother, a Chippewa métis from Staten Island, had moved to Vermont in 1947. This was fine, she could be Indian—or Irish—or Roman Catholic—because her status was non-Yankee anyway. My mother, as a native of New York, could be Indian. My father, also a métis, had a more difficult identity. His grandfather had been one of the Yankee gentry, the landowning elite that descended from the first British colonists and that only married other Yankees. But my great-grandfather married an Abenaki. She was his mother's housekeeper; she passed as white. Had this mixed marriage been known in the late nineteenth-century Yankee gentry class, there would have been an unforgivable scandal. The Yankee hegemony believed such a mixed marriage could only result in inferior, degenerate, degraded offspring. There was such a class of people in Vermont, the so-called gypsies. Gypsies were the lowest of the social castes, below all whites like the immigrants, and even lower than blacks and Asians. They were abhorred by Yankees because they were presumed to be Vermont-born, and as nonwhite native Vermonters, they challenged the myth of racial purity.

The truth of great-grandmother's ethnicity has been kept a family secret for nearly a century. I was finally told it by an aunt, who prefaced the tale with "This won't matter so much to you, you're already an Indian. But don't tell your white cousins." These 'white' cousins descend from my (our) great-grandmother, but they are Yankee and therefore must be white.

As a child I thought my family were the only Indians in Vermont. Knowledge of other families and of our native ways was not known in the Yankee world and was closely kept secret in the Indian world. I thought of myself as Indian, but also knew this could never be spoken of publicly. As a child I remember seeing other Indians only once. My father and I were fishing along the Missisquoi River one summer and stopped at a small town for groceries. I saw a woman with two children in the parking lot. They had dark hair and gold skin, like my father and mother. They looked like my parents. I remember, even now, how delighted I was as I pointed them out to Dad. I remember, even now, how shocked I was when he said they were gypsies, and the way he said it left no room for discussion. The subject was closed and forever off-limits and we avoided that town afterwards.

It took me more than twenty years to find out that my father was a gypsy, a mixed-race Indian, just like my mother. No one in my family would ever speak about the gypsies of Vermont. But eventually I learned they were basketmakers who came to tourist areas each summer to sell their wares, and that they were migratory farmhands and domestics, an exploited and marginal pool of cheap labor within the agricultural economy of Vermont. I learned that the state of Vermont had authorized a campaign of forced sterilization against them in the 1920s and 1930s, when my father would have been a teenager. I learned about this program, called the Eugenics Survey, how it had been passed by the Vermont legislature and funded by the federal government through the Works Progress Administration (WPA) in the 1930s. Victims of eugenics were condemned on many grounds, such as pauperism, being migratory, being illiterate or alcoholic, or having diseases such as tuberculosis. The worst crime, however, was having Indian blood.[1] Abenaki oral tradition claims that county sheriffs legally abducted Indian children from parents deemed unfit by the eugenicists. Tradition holds that several hundred disappeared this way; the state's records are ambiguous. I have no direct evidence that any of my father's family were caught in the eugenics program, but I am convinced they knew of it. I think this is why my father was so adamant in denying the reality of my observation that we and that woman on the Missisquoi River were the same ethnic group.

Although I knew I was Indian, it never crossed my mind there was something wrong with this until my family moved to an exurb of Burlington in 1963 and I started fourth grade at an all-white school. I learned Vermont history from official textbooks where there was little room for non-Yankees and none at all for Indians. My fourth-grade textbook concluded its chapter of the French and Indian Wars with the official line, "Today, as part of an independent nation, descendents of the one-time French and English enemies live and work in Vermont. The unfortunate Indian has disappeared."[2] It was a lie. We had not disappeared. But I learned very quickly the harsh penalties of speaking out against the official story.

My schoolmates did not know I was Indian, but they did know I wasn't like them. The differences were subtle, but very real. Although I have blue eyes, light skin, brown hair, and can pass as white, I have "Indian features"—a broad face and wide cheekbones. I don't have a Yankee face. My schoolmates usually assumed I had African ancestry to account for the facial structure. I was called gorilla and nigger lips, racial insults that puzzled me more than they hurt, because I knew I wasn't African. But in a way I had to be 'nigger' because Indian did not exist in the cultural possibilities of my schoolmates' minds. This misconception continued throughout high school. On my last day, graduating from that all-white school, one girl slipped me a greeting card. In it was a poem entitled, "To black people from a white girl." The card said simply, "I'm sorry." Her gesture was unexpected and surprising, but I appreciated it. It was the only gesture concerning my race or ethnicity made toward me that had not been hostile, and even then it had to be clandestine.

Issues of ethnicity

The Yankee hegemony in New England generally has a hard time admitting that there are non-Yankee societies in the region. The various European ethnic groups that have entered New England since the seventeenth century have been thought to be absorbed into the Yankee system. If the descendants of the Welsh, Irish, Basque, French, Finns, Russians, Portuguese are not, in fact, from pre-1775 antecedents, they are at least white, Christian, and English speaking. They have been assimilated. It was policy to force assimilation, even on the Indians. But race is not assimilatable.[3]

For New England's Indians, assimilation has meant more than two centuries of unremitting cultural oppression. The purpose of the official history, of the eugenics program, of denial, was to transform Indians like my people from hunter–trapper–fisher people to clones of Yankee farmers, so that eventually we would come to reject our heritage and identify solely with our dominators.[4] We were written out of history, ignored, and rendered voiceless. For us to exist, even as the marginal gypsies, was to challenge the Yankee myth of cultural superiority.[5] We had to be silenced.

Silence is a tool of domination, which becomes oppressive "when it is characteristic of a dominated group and when the group is not allowed to break silence by its own choosing or by any means or medium controlled by the power group."[6] The group in power desires the silencing of the group it oppresses, for freedom to speak out challenges the status quo.[7] As John and Jean Comaroff have recently written, the most efficient hegemony is one in which there are no voices to speak against the system.[8] Silencing an oppressed group is extremely effective, because it ultimately prevents the survivors of oppression from considering the possibility that there might be others. As long as the scattered families of Abenakis in Vermont did not know of other families, nor that the culture was still carried in an underground oral tradition of which they were a part, the Yankee hegemony succeeded in its goal of ethnocide.

Another facet of ethnocide is the power that the dominant group exercises in defining the subordinate one. As Benjamin Ringer and Elinor Lawless put it, the dominant group

> sets the terms of adaptation and, furthermore, actively shapes the very character of the group itself, particularly if it is also a racially distinctive group. In some instances, the larger society recognizes the distinctiveness of an ethnic or racial group but defines and interprets this distinctiveness. In still other instances, it may refuse to recognize and/or legitimate the distinctiveness of a group which so views itself.[9]

The Yankee society of Vermont sets the terms of my existence as Indian even now. The Abenaki people were not and are not a recognized nation in Yankee eyes. In the laws of Vermont, we have no validity of culture or inherent land rights to our own ancestral territory, even though Ndakinna was never sold or exchanged in any treaty with any colonizing government. We never surrendered and we never made peace with the colonists. Our resistance is painted negatively in the hegemonic story. Our ancestors are vilified as bloodthirsty savages bent on annihilating the English, deserving of their genocide for standing in the way of the colonists and their God. Only rarely, and in individual biographies, are historic Indians portrayed as friendly. The way the texts read, it is obvious friendliness was a very unusual trait of Vermont's Indians. In either case, all knowledge of our present-day existence was omitted in the textbooks.

Looking back thirty years, I am not now surprised that the only Indians I knew of were my own family, and that we thought we were the last survivors of an ancient culture. Cultural and physical genocide has been so powerful a tool in Yankee imperialism that I am, at age 40, continually surprised to find there are so many Abenakis left. At last count, tribal enrollment was more than 3,000 adults.

The outright genocides of colonial imperialism have been replaced in the twentieth century by what Renato Rosaldo has termed "imperialist nostalgia." This is still imperialist. It is an essentializing, paradoxical agenda where a dominant culture "deliberately alters a way of life and then regrets things have not remained as they were. At one more remove, people destroy their environment and then they worship nature."[10] In imperialist nostalgia, the collective Indian becomes an icon of the lost paradise of preindustrialism. This strategy of white-generated romanticism redefines The Indian as a more natural and less cultural being possessing inherent essences that can only dimly be shared by the dominant society, the industrialists. The Indian is recast. No longer a savage to be destroyed, the Indian is now the savior–prophet of environmental awareness, a human extension of a romanticized wilderness, the voice of a voiceless natural world.

The use of Indians as icons of environmentalism and wisdom is as racist and pervasive a stereotype as the old-style imperialism, but unlike the savage of imperialism, the prophet is a seductive image. Old-style imperialism could be resisted[11] because one can fight back against conquest, but it is very hard to resist exaltation to a pedestal of semidivinity. We who are Indians may be spiritual people, and we may have a profound sense of our relationship with the universe and our homelands. If we try to live in harmony with all things, it is because of our beliefs that this is correct and moral behavior, not because we are mystical nonhuman beings. This new icon of environmental savior masks and distorts our individuality, our histories, and our ethnic diversity. It denies us our humanity. It is also profoundly ironic. We, who were and are victims of imperialism and ethnocide, are now expected to provide solutions for the flaws of a way of life that attempted our collective annihilation.

My voice again

I did not assert myself publicly as Indian until 1971, when I went to college and entered an even more alien, confusing, and paradoxical world. I was "discovered" by my anthropology professors, who then handed me over to folklorists like a piece of lost luggage. I lived with microphones, cassette recorders, and cameras. I felt like somebody's talking donkey. There was a paradox in that undergraduate anthropology department that has been expressed, in one way or another, by every department I have since been affiliated with. The paradox is that, while I may be Indian, white anthropologists don't think I look Indian enough. I could not be white growing up, because my face was against me. In the more urban but still stereotype-driven academic world, I cannot be Indian because of my coloring. I get comments such as "You can't be Indian, you have blue eyes." or "Looking at you, I wouldn't have guessed you are Indian." I can only imagine my various departments would prefer someone less phenotypically ambiguous to fill the sub rosa minority quota. I can only imagine they really would prefer me to have black hair, copper skin, and wear feathers. The stereotype of the copper-skinned Indian is unreal; it seems to assume the imperial forces that lightened the complexion of my African-American colleagues did not operate on my ancestors.

In 1973 the Abenaki nation of Vermont began asserting itself politically, with the long-term goal of regaining usurped land title. A tribal council was formed, a chief elected, and a constitution written, all in accordance with Bureau of Indian Affairs policies as established by the Indian Reorganization Act of 1934. Once again, the dominant society set limits on our existence. We now have to prove to the U.S. government that we really are Indians.

In the spring of 1993, Abenaki people came together for a festival of culture and education for the first time in several centuries. More than 5,000 people assembled at the Franklin County Airport near Swanton, where Missisquoi Abenaki Indians have lived for generations. The white governor and lieutenant governor made politically correct speeches praising our cultural heritage and hoping for a multicultural future.

Little was said about history or about the various lawsuits attempting to get a legal ruling on land rights in Vermont's courts. There was no mention of a Vermont Supreme Court decision of October 1992 that held our indigenous land rights may have once been valid but were now extinguished by the weight of history, as though 200 years of United States history could erase 10,000 years of native history.

At that festival I met many other Abenaki people who, like me, had grown up silenced and isolated. It was wonderful to hear them speak, to hear their stories, but after a while it became obvious their narratives were all the same story told differently. It was a story of invisible genocide, of an insidious and pernicious imperialism that made us nonpeople, ghosts, in our own homeland. It was also the story of survival against all odds of a people, a culture, and a history.

We are no longer silent, no longer scattered and separated from others like ourselves, although imperialism still dictates our lives and defines our identities. I am métis, a mixed-race Indian, neither white nor red, but living between both worlds the best I can. My nation, the Abenakis, live in many worlds as well—tribalism, the eco-savior, the minority ethnic group. I am Indian, we are Indian, with all of that complex identity and heritage. But we are no longer ghosts.

Part V
Identity Theory

17

The Multiracial Contribution to the Psychological Browning of America[1]

Maria P. P. Root

In the past two decades interracial marriage rates have increased almost fourfold.[2] The rate of multiracial births has increased at an even faster rate.[3] For example, multiracial black–white births have increased fivefold in this same twenty-year period compared with a growth rate of 27 percent for children born to two African-American parents. More children of Japanese-American heritage are born to interracial couples than same-race couples. Although Japanese Americans may have some of the highest rates of interracial unions, in general, there are now two-thirds as many multiracial births of persons with Asian or Pacific Island ancestry as births of children born of two parents of similar heritage. A conservative estimate of the whole picture estimates that in 1989, at least 117,000 children were born of mixed parentage. This figure only accounts for children born of two parents of ethnic–racial groups that have not adopted a multiracial identity such as the Latino population of this country.

While the anticipated change in demographics in the next few decades fuels discussions about the implications of the "browning" of America, this discussion largely ignores the contribution of multiracial Americans to this trend. The biracial baby boom has significant implications for reexamining current conceptual constructions and deconstructions of race—and for discussing the physical and psychological "browning of America."

Several factors shape the ethnic and racial identities an individual asserts, for example, family, history of race relations in different regions of the country, ratio of racial and ethnic groups in the community, birth country, social rejections based on perceived race, racism, family cutoffs. Root[4] and her colleagues[5,6,7] have opened the academic dialogue and critique of models of racial identity processes. Out of this discourse, multiracial persons are defining what the range of normative process is in identity development for racially mixed persons. In this discussion, observations of situational ethnicity, multiple identities, and transformed identities through the life cycle are discussed in the context of being a multiracial person in this country. These discussions make it clear that being a person of racially mixed heritage in the 1990s has different meaning and occurs in a different context than in the 1960s,[8,9] or earlier. These discussions also make it abundantly clear that the psychological processes of racial identity development described in the contemporary social science literature[10,11] reflect the pathology of our culture around notions of race that began in the seventeenth century.

The legacy of hypodescent, established to divest children of white male slave masters born to black slave women from privileges associated with paternity, assumed and legislated that the multiracial person of European heritage would be identified by the race of the mother and therefore identify as a person of color.[12] This legislation provided the origin for the decades in which the U.S. Census Bureau assigned a child's race based on the mother's race. Whereas centuries of efforts to preserve the purity of "white blood" have shaped the normative process of racial identity development for people monoracially identified, these same historical forces virtually negate the existence of the multiracial person contemporarily.

Racism in its various forms such as hypodescent, the assignment of an individual of racially mixed heritage to the social racial group of the parent with lower racial status, has been internalized. It is seldom questioned, and in fact, much conflict and misunderstanding pursue when a multiracial person insists on identifying as racially mixed. She or he may be required to pass tests of racial or ethnic legitimacy, or both, within their respective ethnic communities. The community is acting as though there is such a concept as ethnic purity and requiring stereotyped ways of being ethnic for the multiracial person to gain acceptance as bona fide African American or Asian American.

Hypodescent reflects a hierarchical notion of races. Thus, it exerts its influence even between communities of color; persons of African and Japanese-American heritages may be assigned to the social classification of black when they may identify as both.[13,14]

The combined effect of hypodescent, beliefs in racial purity, and the social distance between whites and blacks contributes to understanding why the discussion of multiraciality is largely viewed as a black–white issue. Although, the number of black–white marriages is a minority compared with other combinations of intermarriage,[15] white America is largely not concerned with the boundaries between groups of color. And now, much for psychological protection of identity, many persons in the African-American community insist on asserting a line between black and white. Subsequently, persons of racially mixed heritage of European descent may experience the "squeeze of oppression" between these two "warring" factions; persons born to two parents of color of different racial backgrounds are rendered invisible in the media discussions of multiracial identity.

Social science theories and definitions around racial and ethnic identity reflect the legacy of this racial caste system. Subsequently, the increasing trend for more multiracial persons to subvert and to challenge the rules of hypodescent by creating identity options is often misunderstood—particularly when these individuals, most often no longer born out of rape, assert access to membership and privileges of their multiple heritages. The normative experiences of fluid identities, situationally defined ethnicity and race, simultaneous identities, or defiance of rules of hypodescent have been interpreted as unhealthy, inviable choices. These declarations of identity that reveal the "truth" about the illogical racial system are instead viewed as misguided or symptoms of low self-esteem due to internalized racism. The illogical racial system has become so embedded in our social order that it is threatening to suggest that the "emperor is wearing no clothes." There has been a society-wide hypnotic induction into believing that race is a pure biological fact.

The question that has not been asked is, "What factors other than hypodescent lead a person to want to identify as a person of color when they are also of European heritage?" In other words, what if this is not a default identity? What if racially mixed persons of European heritage do not long to be accepted as white by the various white communities? There are at least four possible explanations of why a multiracial person of European heritage would choose to identify as African, Asian, or Native American regardless of how they are identified by others.

The first possibility derives from the security and groundedness of knowing one's ancestors and ethnic origins. Unfortunately, part of being American has required a willingness to shed cultural markers, such as language, religion, and holidays. As a result, the majority of Americans of European descent are without a continuous culture; they have forgotten their "ancestral stories" and struggles; they have lost connection to their roots.

Many young people of European heritage, other than recent immigrants, their children, and persons of Jewish heritage, know little about the lives of who has come before them. Subsequently, many parents of European heritage are at a loss as to how to help their elementary-age child respond to a teacher's assignment to bring something from home that represents part of their cultural heritage.

In contrast, many children of color are exposed to cultural traditions and icons of their ancestors. This exposure provides the foundation for knowing one's self in relationship to those who have come before; it provides rootedness and continuity. Thus, in a multiracial family where the parent of color can convey a history of who has come before with emotional memories and pride and the white parent has little information available, the multiracial person may came to identify primarily as a person of color, perhaps even monoethnically. The white ancestry is not rejected, but it is background to the ethnic heritage of the parent of color.

A second set of factors may originate in grandparents' reactions to their children's interracial partnerships. If there is going to be a cutoff, it is most likely to be by white parents. When white parents punish their children for interracially marrying by cutting them off physically and emotionally, the family that socializes the child is most likely to be the family associated with the parent of color. The love a child receives, and the faces that reflect who they are, are likely to be some shade of brown. The children will likely internalize an identification with those from whom they come.

Gallup polls over the past thirty years have shown a consistent trend of growing approval for interracial marriage for white respondents.[16] However, from a low of 17 percent in 1968 to a high of 44 percent in 1991, this rate is only approaching the approval rate of 48 percent by African Americans in 1968. Acceptance of intermarriage by whites is unlikely to reach the approval rate of 70 percent by blacks in 1991 for a long time.

The third factor, racism, creates shared life experiences that indelibly and insidiously exert a powerful orientation to life as a person of color. These experiences require the individual to develop the psychological skills and defenses to protect one's self as a person of color.[17,18] These experiences unwittingly bond many persons to their communities of color.

Fourth, though not in all cases, gender alignment between parents and children may exert influence on ethnic and racial socialization, particularly when they have good relationships and are mutually held in esteem. Thus, biracial sons may be more likely to identify with their fathers than their mothers and biracial daughters may be more likely to identify with their mothers than their fathers. Although C. C. I. Hall[19] did not find gender to be an independent variable affecting identity, recent studies on transracial adoption are suggesting that mediating variables may influence gender alignment including nationality of parents, personality matches, living arrangements,[20] birth order, and so forth. This last factor will be an important one to examine as differential rates of interracial marriage by race and gender exist.[21]

Lastly, the face of the racially mixed person shares features in common with many persons from many different places in the world. The brown face of different shades provides a linkage with the majority of the world's population.[22] In some individual cases this is a comfort to place one's location of belonging as a citizen of the world; this affords a cognitive way of coping with the daily insults of racism and the squeeze of oppression.

These five explanations for why a multiracial person of European heritage may assert an identity as a person of color and not long or desire to be accepted as white is neither exhaustive nor definitive. However, such a discussion requires us to consider factors other than strict hypodescent that lead to this identity formation. This discussion suggests that not only is America physically browning, but multiracial persons are contributing to a psychological browning of America and challenging the historical value of whiteness.

The psychological browning of America extends beyond skin color. This browning may help us connect with our humanity so that we may stop the oppression of racism, a form of psychological violence.

The choice, rather than the assumption and the imperative that multiracial people of color identify as people of color has significant implications for redefining assumptions about ethnicity and reexamining the factors that guide racial and ethnic identity.

We must reopen the dialogue on race. The existence of multiracial people provides a concrete vehicle through which we can explore how times have changed. Despite widespread racism, there is also hope that change is underway.

Those who were courageous to use love as a tool of revolution to defy centuries of legislation are appreciated. It is with their courage and the courage of those who follow in their footsteps, who dare to follow their hearts across the color lines, that we may tackle the "problem of the color line" in twentieth-century America.[23]

18

Made in the USA:
Racial Mixing 'n Matching

David Theo Goldberg

Man you ain't got to
Worry 'bout a thing
'Bout your daughter
Nah she ain't my type
(But supposin' she said she loved me)
Are you afraid of the mix of Black and White
We're livin' in a land where
The law say the mixing of race
Makes the blood impure
She's a woman I'm a man
But by the look on your face
See ya can't stand it[1]

Americans are trying to come to terms with the fact that racial purity is a thing of the past. There was a time, of course, and not so very long ago, when prevailing sentiment would have it as the wave of the future. Cast in this way, the racializing condition reveals the truth that common sense has so long denied, namely, that racial purity is nothing more than a thing of the imagination—scientific and social, political and cultural. The United States, perhaps, and more so than other countries, has begun to realize this, but continues to deny, to itself and anyone who cares to notice, the deep implications this realization has for the racializing project. For racial purity is an expressed commitment now only of the fringe right, and the racializing project is advanced more acceptably in terms of mixed race and multiculturalism.

We are, in the words announcing *Time Magazine*'s special issue

237

on "The New Face of America," the "World's First Multicultural Society."[2] This characterization reifies yesterday's common sense as it announces tomorrow's. For it silently denies the heterogeneity that so clearly marks human histories as it reinstates racialized characterization as the grounds of today's, or (perhaps) more hopefully tomorrow's, multicultural commitment.[3] Mixed race provides the metaphorical anchor. But the racial mix of this multicultural condition, not to put too fine a tautological point on it, is still the mixing of *races*. Race is equated now with culture, and it is simply reshaped, rather than dissolved, in once and, perhaps, still unconsciously illicit acts of miscegenation. And what may be socially illicit becomes electronically conceivable as test tube babies are produced by a Hollywood computer program where humans in the flesh fear to tread.

In its fall 1993 issue on multicultural America, *Time* invoked Hollywood's special effects program, Morph 2.0, used to create Michael Jackson's transformation in the *Black or White* video and the robot of *Terminator 2*, to 'predict' computer-graphically the ethnoracial outcome of progeny from mixed marriages between seven ethnoracially diverse men and women. That this special issue was about "America's Immigrant Challenge" perhaps explains the total absence throughout of reference to American Indians, including their omission from the representative mix of *Time*'s computer graphic experiment. Indigenous people are once more quite literally effaced in the silent extension of the doctrine of discovery. Empty lands for the taking. It should come as no surprise, then, that for its experiment *Time* chose the least diverse-looking representatives across ethnorace[4]—not to mention across class. Lest anyone object that these are naked headshots, hairstyles are something of a class giveaway. Progeny were projected by a "straight 50–50 combination of the physical characteristics of their progenitors." Although *Time*'s editors admit that "an entirely different *image*" (my emphasis) could have been produced by an input of different percentages, they fail to acknowledge that an even percentage split also involves choices, and so value assumptions, for human beings are hardly symmetrical within morphological traits. Halving the difference between straight blonde and curly black hair does not give you straight blonde hair—at least not non-presumptively. And genetically, there is no *literal* halving of the difference between (more-or-less) 'black' skin and 'white,' whatever these phenotypical hues signify.[5]

I am going to argue that this "new face of America" is being

colored with the revitalized cosmetics of the racialized condition.
The transformations in the body politic are being marked anew by
reconfigured racial categories. Thus the gauntlet thrown down in
the celebration of mixed-race identities is at best ambiguous, (re)fixing
the premises of the racializing project in place as it challenges that
project's very terms of articulation. I interrogate the possibilities
and limits of mixed-race formation through the examples of category construction in the U.S. census, focusing on the recent fashioning of "Hispanics," the creation of "Coloured" identity in South
Africa, and the moral panics prompted in relation to crossracial
adoption.

Fashioning Mixed Race

To comprehend the 'transforming continuities' characteristic of
the racializing condition in this apparent epistemological rupture
between yesterday's common sense and tomorrow's, and the implications it suggests for (re-)con-ceiving the body politic, we need
to understand the location of the concept of 'mixed race' in the
racial project. The best way of reaching such an understanding is
to establish the genealogy of the concept in the formal racial classification furnished by the history of census taking. The historical
imperatives to maintain a racially pure United States were reflected in the microtechnologies of administrative bureaucracy. From
its inception, the Republic required enumeration of racial groups,
formalized by constitutional mandate via census counts initiated in
1790. Formal racial *definition*, however, only came later, appearing first for the 1850 census. In the absence of explicit definitions
of the racial categories, the census relied in its first half century of
establishing the racial body count upon the 'common sense' judgments of its all-white enumerators. Persons were racially named,
the body politic measured, and resources distributed on the basis
of prevailing racial presumptions and mandated fractional assess-
ments. The society was literally marked, and marked only, in broad
strokes of black and white.

Distinctions began to appear in 1850 for those considered 'non-
white,' indicating, as it reflected, an emerging social commitment
to gradations in color consciousness. This perceptual color scale
no doubt was rooted in the implicit admission that the drive to
(maintain) purity is predicated upon the danger of its dissolute demise.
The growing complexity of these social distinctions seemed to demand

that enumerators be issued instruction schedules concerning the racial categories. Thus, in 1850, enumerators were asked to mark the color of "Free inhabitants," leaving the space under the heading "Color" blank for "whites," while "carefully" indicating others as "B" (for "black"), and for the first time marking off "black" from "mulatto" ("M"). Slaves were to be counted separately, and their color indicated also. The schedule of instructions cautioned enumerators to take special care in reporting "Mulatto (including quadroons, octoroons, and all persons having any perceptible trace of African blood," because *Important scientific results depend upon the correct determination of this class*" (my italics).

By 1880, the request for information about "Indians" had become more specific: The schedule for that decade's count specified Indian division between tribes, whether the person was a "full-blood" of the tribe or mixed with another; if mixed with "white," the person should be marked "W" (reflecting the presupposed closeness in the 'great chain of being' between 'Europeans' and 'Indians'); if mixed with "black" to be marked "B," and if mixed with "mulatto" to be marked "M," indicating the overriding presumption of 'black' otherness implicit in the principle of racial purity. Tribal adoptees were to be racially marked as "W.A." ("white adopted") or "B.A." ("black or mulatto adopted"). That enumerators were instructed not to accept answers they "know or have reason to believe are false" indicates the continued power of racial definition vested in the hands of all-white enumerators.

> Man calm your ass down, don't get mad
> I don't need your sistah
> (But supposin' she said she loved me)
> Would you still love her
> Or would you dismiss her
> What is pure? Who is pure?
> Is it European state of being, I'm not sure
> If the whole world was to come
> Thru peace and love
> Then what would we be made of?[6]

The schedule of instructions for the 1890 count reflected not only the rapid diversification of the U.S. population, but the intensifying administrative concern in the face of this expanding diversity with racial distinction, hierarchy, imposed division, and the symbolic and material challenges of miscegenational mix. Thus, while the categories for "white," "Chinese," and "Indian" remained unchanged, explicit and superficially specific distinctions were introduced between "black," "mulatto," "quadroon," and "octoroon." "Black" was to refer to any person with "three-fourths or more black blood"; "mulatto" referred to those having "from three-eighths to five-eighths black blood"; "quadroon" to those persons having "one-fourth black blood"; and "octoroon" to those "having one-eighth or any trace of black blood."

These fine distinctions of mixed-race formation scarcely hid the disgenic fear of sanguinary pollution: "Mixed-bloods" were considered as potentially polluting of the body politic as "full-blooded blacks." This fear manifested in 1900, when these finer distinctions began to collapse in the wake of the widespread social consideration that 'black' is any person "with but a drop of black blood." "Black" was indicated on the 1900 schedule as "a negro or of negro descent." Ten years later the category "other" was first introduced: Anyone not falling into the established census categories was to be so marked, and their race (assuming of course that it was identifiable) to be listed. Pertinently, the reintroduced definitions to distinguish "black" from "mulatto" shifted as they visibly struggled to balance the brand of blackness with the self-evident effects of miscegenation. Thus, the category "Black includes all persons who are *evidently* full-blooded negroes," whereas "Mulatto includes all persons having some proportion or *perceptible* trace of negro blood" (my emphases). In keeping with, but serving also to cement common comprehension at the time, race continued to be conceived eugenically in the confused mix of the literal and metaphorical as blood, a confusion that necessitated continuing to reduce the basis of distinction to nothing more than the enumerators'—or what was considered to be 'common'—perception.

By 1930 the prevailing institutional mandates of racialized segregation and immigration restriction in the United States had prompted the introduction of specific instructions for reporting race. Thus, enumerators were required to enter as "Negro" any person of "mixed white and Negro blood," irrespective of how small "the percentage of Negro blood." Moreover, a person "part Indian" and "part Negro" was to be listed as "Negro unless the Indian blood predominated and the person is generally accepted as Indian in the community." Similarly, someone of "mixed white and Indian blood" was to be counted as "Indian, except where the percentage of Indian blood" was deemed very small or the person was generally considered white in the community. In general, any "racially mixed person" with white parentage was to be designated according to the race of the parent not white; by contrast, "mixtures of colored races" were to be racially designated on the basis of the father's race, "except Negro–Indian." For the first time "Mexican" was introduced as a separate *racial* category and defined as "all persons born in Mexico, or having parents born in Mexico, and who are definitely not white, Negro, Indian, Chinese, or Japanese."

In the next count, however, partly in response to objections by the Mexican government and the U.S. State Department, "Mexicans" were to be listed as "white" unless they were "definitely Indian or some race other than white." Although the concern by 1940 with explicit racial purity may have been waning in the wake of 'Aryanism,' the growing 'ethno-coloring' of America seemed to demand a political technology for keeping US white.

These transformations in race designation were carried forward significantly into the 1980 census, in a way that altogether undermines any cross-census comparisons. The census introduced the underlying standard of racial *self*-identification that had begun in the early 1970s to be assumed in almost all the states of the union. For census purposes, however, the injunction to declare oneself what one chooses racially to be was circumscribed by *given* designations, a mix of traditionally racial, ethnic, and national categories from which respondents *were required* to choose. "Black" became a primary designation, though "Negro" was retained as an alternative reading. In becoming the overriding racial trope, this (self-) insistence on blackness was rendering explicit what had always been implicit in the racializing project. Similarly, those previously identified as of "Spanish" origin or descent could now also choose to identify themselves as "Hispanic" (but not Chicano or Latino). Where 'mixed-race' persons had difficulty placing themselves, enumerators were instructed to report the mother's race group, and where this was not acceptable, to list the first race cited by the respondent. For the Spanish-origin question, where someone reported mixed parentage with only the second category identifiable as "Spanish/ Hispanic" (e.g., Italian-Cuban), enumerators were instructed to deny "Spanish/Hispanic" designation.

Whatever happened to self-identification, including the *refusal* to identify oneself racially? The denial of such refusal, literally its abnegation, implies—if it does not presuppose—that race is a primary, indeed, a primal category of human classification, one so natural to the human condition that it can be ignored only on pain of self-denial. Underlying the imperative of racial self-identification is the presumption of naturalism: One is expected to identify oneself as what one 'naturally' is.[7] The democracy of self-naming is underpinned by the authoritarianism of imposed identity and identification. Those resisting literally become the 'new Others.'

> Excuse us for the news
> I question those accused
> Why does this fear of Black from White
> Influence who you choose?[8]

This apparent paradox of racial self-naming highlights the tensions faced by any body count committed to a racial numeration. Social identities belie simplicity, and the simplicity of bureaucratic–statistical requirements simply enforces the racializing imperative of the census and dominant social definition, and does so for political purposes. The general category of 'mixed race,' and the specific subcategories of racial identity it licenses, were admitted into the racial configuration as a way of cognizing this complexity, but cognizing it on (more precisely, *in*) racial terms. Thus, 'mixed race' may *seem* to capture in the most adequate fashion prevailing demographic heterogeneity, but it does so only by silently fixing in place the racializing project. It naturalizes racial assumption, marking mixed-ness as an aberrant condition, as transgressive, and at the extreme as purity polluting. It may seem to offer exciting proof positive that a deep social taboo has been transgressed, that racial discipline and order have been violated, that liberty's lure has once again undermined the condition of homogeneity by delimiting the constraints of the hegemonic. Yet it at once, and necessarily, reimposes the hegemony of racial duality—of blackness and whiteness—as the standard, the measure, of mixed-ness.

> Man c'mon now, I don't want your wife
> Stop screamin' it's not the end of your life
> (But supposin' she said she loved me)
> What's wrong with some color in your family tree
> I don't know[9]

There are serious implications, political as much as social, of remaining tied to the racializing project. Investing in the category of mixed race—giving it equal time in the media mix of America—serves to extend the insidious possibilities for these implications, to etherealize the deep historical divisions of wealth and power that continue to be effected and exercised under the sign of race, to license a politics of competitive division in the face of purportedly scarce social resources. Three examples will suffice to illustrate the material implications of this project.

Politics and the Power of Mixed Race

"Hispanic"

In the most recent census, the ethnoracial categories were once again altered. New categories were added, others disappeared, making intercensus comparisons all but useless. But the category that remains most problematic, the one whose fabrication carries the most straightforward political motivation and implication, is the hybrid "Hispanic." The 1990 census set the stakes for the end of one century, thereby to define the institution of a new one. To this end it introduced a separate question for those declaring "Spanish/Hispanic origin." This reflects the political history of nervous unsurety–if not outright insecurity—over the racial identity of those so self-identifying. Respondents under this category were asked to distinguish whether they are "Mexican, Mexican-American, or Chicano," "Puerto Rican," "Cuban," or "Other Spanish/Hispanic," which was taken to be exemplified by "Argentinean," "Colombian," "Dominican," "Nicaraguan," "Salvadoran," and "Spaniard." Although these categories were listed as "racial," they included a confused and confusing intersection of those deemed traditionally racial with national and ethnic configurations. The conceptual and political tensions in and between the categories were exacerbated by the appearance of a final question asking all respondents to list their "ancestry or ethnic origin." This was exemplified on the form by "German," "Afro-American," "Croatian," "Cape Verdean," "Dominican," "Cajun," "French Canadian," "Jamaican," "Korean," "Lebanese," "Mexican," "Nigerian," "Ukrainian," and so forth. Part of the projected 53 percent increase from 1980 to 1990 in "Hispanic origin population (of any race)," for example, was a function of the introduction of new explicit subcategories such as "Colombian" and "Dominican."

The qualifying afterthought "(of any race)" here signals deeper difficulties. The population of "Hispanic origin," the 1990 census reported, is greatest in the South and western United States (California, Arizona, New Mexico, Texas, and Florida). Nevertheless, those collected under "Hispanic origin" in the southwestern states differ, often dramatically, from those in the Southeast and in the large eastern cities like Washington, Philadelphia, and New York. Indeed, interests, culture, perhaps anything that could count as racial identification of "Hispanics" differ regionally. It is for this reason that contemporary census documents, in speaking of racial categories, commonly refer to "Race *and* Hispanic Origin." The category "Hispanic" is imposed: It *others* as it unites, marginalizes as it generalizes, stereotypes as it aggregates. It purports to extend specific identity to an entire subcontinent in the age of globalization and flexible accumulation, just as it seeks to create—to fabricate in the economic imaginary—a SuperSubject, a target market that abnegates the specificity of its constituents.[10] It is a category that has become fixed in the public mind—a given of common sense— through sociostatistical profiles and market research, the objective realism of numbers, the image underlying as it shores up the realism of tables, charts, and comparisons.

These racialized politics of numbers and numerical politics of racial naming and placing must be comprehended in the context of their primary legislative mandate. The point of the census in U.S. history, recall, has always been to manage effective resource distribution and voting access. These economic and political mandates in the United States have always been deeply racialized. The apparent contemporary democratizing of the census via self-identification and affirmative recognition of mixed-race identities serves at once to hide from view newly framed racialized tensions that remain as managed as they always were. It is in this context that the oft-cited 'fact' that "Hispanics" will catch "blacks" in percentage of the U.S. population by the end of the decade and pass them by the first decade of the next century becomes pregnant with meaning. "Hispanic" is a population category as manufactured—and as mixed in its extension—as 'black' was from its inception. Although "black" was created initially in the name of the project of racial purity, "Hispanic" was crafted to cut across racial designations, to reflect (ad-)mixture. In its generality, however, "Hispanic" has served and serves silently to reify a new racial category, to extend the project of purity, even as it is a product of mixture.

Racializing the body count in this way has, as it always had, significant implications for voting rights. The voting rights of blacks are now guaranteed in more or less complex ways by the 15th Amendment (1871), by the 1965 Voting Rights Act, and its 1982 Amendment. One of the subtly silent ways remaining available to dilute blacks' voting rights, perhaps one of the only permissible alternatives now, is to set them against 'other' statistically dominant 'minorities,' minorities whose racial configurations are precisely ambiguous. Blacks are marked hegemonically as politically and socially liberal (and in the 1980s liberal came to be cast as literally un-American); Hispanics (and perhaps also Asian Americans) are often cast as socially (and perhaps economically) conservative. There is some evidence for these claims. Given exactly what I have placed in question, namely the fixing of the racialized categories, 78 percent of black voters support the Democratic Party compared to 54 percent of "Hispanic" voters, and only 34 percent of whites.[11] In the managed tensions between liberals and conservatives that characterize U.S. politics, the drive to bring Hispanics under the 'right' wing is on (just as New Deal and especially Great Society Democrats sought to capture the black vote). A social statistics that purports to report the truth may be party to the next big lie, the new racialized dynamics. This new dynamic of racialized fabrication may be fueled paradoxically by the very instrument designed to democratize the social body count, namely, racial self-identification.

A key implication drawn by the State from the civil rights and independence struggles of the 1960s is the importance of self-naming. The imposition of group and individual designation was a central social technology of control under cultural colonialism and racialized domination. The formal introduction of self-identification as the standard of group definition in the 1970s reflected the apparent drive to democratize sociopolitical institutions in the United States. Nevertheless, the parameters of self-definition have never been open-ended, for the State has always furnished the range of available, of credible, and of reliable—that is, of licensed and so permissible—categories in terms of which self-definition may be effected. Simultaneously, as noted above, the overwhelmingly white-faced *image* throughout the history of the United States is giving in to its dramatic de facto shading. There is a sense, then, in which the nominal politics of Hispanicizing are serving to soften, if not to undermine, this racial transformation. In census terms, "Hispanic" is only ambiguously a racial category, placed alongside, as an additive to,

"Race." It is thus, at once, a mix of the racialized and deracialized: "Hispanics" may now be white or black. (As an indication of the politics of ambiguity at play here, recall George Bush's reference to one of his grandsons, whose mother is Mexican, as "the little brown one.") The former gatekeeping of blood counts that some were able, at considerable psychological cost, to evade through 'passing' has given over to a licensed and encouraged passing via redefinition, that is, a restructured white identity in racialized difference.[12] This restructured racial identity reflects material considerations: Witness the intersection of race and class interests around 'Mexicans' in the debate leading up to the congressional vote on NAFTA (the North American Free Trade Agreement), and the ongoing debate concerning extension of health care to 'illegal aliens.' The census promotion of "Hispanic" in the face of censoring categories such as 'Chicano' reorders the structure of whiteness as it strictures the boundaries of blackness. Mixed-race hybridity opens its (self-)referents to the shifting interests of those in control of the categories. Out of the barrios of blackness, Linda Chavez, and welcome to the whitened suburbs of your mediated dream.[13]

"Coloureds"

A second example reveals how the undertaking to undo the insidious implications of the racial project via mixed-race hybridity impales itself on its racializing assumptions. This concerns the constitution of "Coloured" in South Africa—that category of mixed-race formation in terms of which apartheid necessarily defined itself.

When the Dutch invaded the Cape to settle in 1652, they were greeted by indigenous San (still referred to in the local vernacular as "Bushmen" and "Hottentot"). The story goes that desire got the better of these European men who arrived without European women, and offspring of mixed race quickly followed. Shortly before the British took over colonial rule of the Cape at the end of the eighteenth century, the Dutch settlers had become so concerned with diminishing racial purity and the 'curse of bad blood' that they moved to circumscribe miscegenation. The challenge of desire to the imperative of purity was renewed with the Boer trek northward to escape British colonial rule in the 1830s, for the white trekkers quickly came into contact with other indigenous ethnic groups, variously defined under collective reference as "African," "Black," or "Bantu." Constrained by no law other than that perceived as God's, white men once more imposed themselves upon black women. The population considered of mixed race, which came to include Malaysian coolie laborers brought to the Cape in the late 1800s, was nominated "Coloured" before the close of the century.

People designated "Coloured" have always suffered ambiguous status in South Africa, with telling social, political, economic, and psychological effect. The very designation presupposes as the norm the stark disjunction between unshaded white and black.[14] The apartheid state formally instituted the category "Coloured" in the late 1940s and 1950s, outlawing mixed marriage and intercourse, while defining the (existing or future illegal) offspring of interracial relations and their progeny as "Coloured." Definition of the racial terms constitutive of apartheid's self-conception was offered first in the Population Registration Act of 1950 and was tightened in later amendments. So, "White person" came to be defined as:

> a. In appearance obviously is a white person and who is not generally accepted as a coloured person; and b. Is generally accepted as a white person and is not in appearance obviously not a white person. (*Population Registration Act*, 1950)

To prevent the likelihood of circular emptiness that this appeal to self-referential appearance obviates (a white person is one appearing white), the definition of "white" necessarily presupposes and explicitly invokes as its point of reference—as it conceptually must—the category of "coloured" (that euphemism in the South African vernacular for "mulatto" or "mixed race"). Likewise for the definition of "Black" or "African" (or "Negro," for that matter). The inevitable failure of the imperative of purity is that it is predisposed necessarily to predicate the definitions of the categories principal to the racializing project (black, white) upon the conceptual implications of 'mixed race.' Absent such predication, the categories of racial purity run the apparent danger of conceptual and referential emptiness.

The horrifying effects of apartheid's schema of racial classification were only outdone for those suffering reclassification (usually from "white" or "European" to "Coloured," or "Coloured" to "Non-European," or "Bantu," or "Native," or "African," and ever so occasionally and begrudgingly from "Coloured" to "white").[15] Mixed race thus came to mean mixed status: fewer rights and a more tenuous social position than whites, but significantly better conditions than those faced by the overwhelming majority of "Africans." With ambiguous status, however, came also the problematic ambiguity of political positionality and social identity. In the wars of position and maneuver that have marked South Africa at least since 1960, the prevailing consideration facing those defined as "Coloured"—a consideration they suffer much more heavily as a probing question than do those categorically shaded more lightly or darkly than they—has concerned where they stand. This political ambiguity and ambivalence (a taste of power, however marginal, has its lures) is tied directly to the configuration as mixed race. Indeed, the shifting fabrication of mixed-race status enables (in many ways, it is designed to promote) this marginalizing alienation at the center of racial definition.

The laws of South Africa restricting intermarriage and miscegenation were repealed in the 1980s and 1990s. And yet in the drive to configure an identity within racialized space—a space that overrides, if not exhausts, the range of available identity formation in South Africa—identification as and with the commitments of "Coloured" has taken hold. There is, in some nonreductive sense, a "Coloured" constituency and a "Coloured" vote, "Coloured" interests and "Coloured" concerns. There is, in an important identifiable sense, also a "Coloured" language and perhaps a "Coloured" culture.

But beyond this, and more problematically, forms of exclusion are promoted in the self-identifying mode, the name of 'Coloured.' The University of the Western Cape (UWC) was founded by the designers of apartheid as an institution for the separated higher education of 'Coloureds' in South Africa. In the late 1980s, it managed to redefine itself under astute leadership as the intellectual base of the African National Congress (ANC). Taking advantage of the liberalizing trajectory, UWC managed to institute in real terms the ANC's commitment to nonracialism, transforming an institution designed to circumscribe the possibilities of mixed race into one in which races would mix, if races would matter at all. However, the discursive arm of apartheid is considerably longer than this enlightened image would have it. A student survey conducted at the university in 1991 revealed that an overwhelming percentage of those students considering themselves 'Coloured' not only wished to maintain racially segregated dormitories (with 'Coloureds' especially kept apart from Black Africans), but insisted that

UWC remain a 'Coloured' institution, run by and for those deemed racially mixed in kind and culture. Gone in name, the separateness of apartheid lives on in legacy, disciplined by the normalized shadow boundaries of mixed-race definition.

I've been wonderin' why
Peoples livin' in fear
Of my shade
(Or my hi top fade)
I'm not the one that's runnin'
But they got me on the run
Treat me like I have a gun
All I got is genes and chromosomes
Consider me Black to the bone
All I want is peace and love
On this planet
(Ain't that how God planned it?)[16]

Mixed-Race Adoption

The politics of racialized mixed status are not nearly so formalized elsewhere as they have been in South Africa. Beyond the southern tip of Africa, therefore, the implications of mixed-race formation are played out mostly in the informalities of the broader social arena than they are directly in terms of law and political institutions. This is exemplified by considerations of cross-racial adoption in the United States. The debate around racialized adoption in America is in many ways complex, and I do not mean to belittle the complexity of the issues in by-passing them. Mixed-race considerations add considerably to this complexity, in ways that reify as they are meant to dissipate the racializing project in America. Mixed-race considerations in adoption are pulled between the liberalizing imperative to pay no heed to race in placing adoptive children and the racializing insistence by the likes of the National Association of Black Social Workers (NABSW), who insist that black children be placed only with black parents. The fact of the matter is that public and private adoption agencies in the United States make race one of the primary concerns in placement. This has special, and especially troubling, implications for children defined as racially mixed. While logically it may seem to imply that their pool of potential placement is enlarged, the history of racializing insists that mixed-race progeny are defined as *non*white (the 'one-drop rule'). If, for argument's sake, one accepts the NABSW insistence that black children placed with nonblack parents will necessarily lose the sustenance of black culture in facing off the heavy nihilistic weight of racism their blackness will necessarily burden them with,[17] mixed-race children with any black background will be so affected also. (If the argument holds for black children, perhaps it must be generalized for all defined racially as nonwhite; the same form of argument is forwarded by many American Indian groups.[18]) Thus the pool of placement in the case of mixed-race children is restricted to that for black (or in the more general case, for nonwhite) children. But, again logically, it is open to whites to object on the basis of the racialized premise that this restriction necessarily withholds from mixed children their white cultural heritage. The logical consequence of this line of deeply racialized analysis is that mixed-race children be adopted only by mixed-race parents, and perhaps most awkwardly only by parents of the precise racial mixture as themselves. The fact that nobody baldly claims (or hopefully believes) this is testament only to the poverty of the racializing premises.

If those committed to this line of analysis were prompted to give up the underlying biological insinuation in their conceptions of race, thus restricting race to cultural conception, mixed-race hybridity would become significantly more challenging, and in an interesting way. For mixed race then becomes conceivable explicitly as nothing more nor less than mixed culture, and cultural heterogeneity is the norm rather than the exception it is made out to be on the assumption of ethnoracial purity. Cultural heterogeneity has come to be almost all there is, in one degree or another. There was a time when, for some, group formation was considerably more localized and inward-looking than is now generally the case.[19] At some point, the insularity and isolation necessary to sustain homogeneity constrain cultural possibilities and are maintained only by the force of imposition. In modernity, the myth of homogeneity becomes nothing other than a narrative cultural members fashion for themselves in fabricating a binding identity.[20] Perhaps a future adoption standard conceived in the name of heterogeneity (and reflecting a changed commitment to advancing the interests of parentless children rather than the conflicted concerns of a racialized meat market)[21] will be represented in the willingness of adoption agencies to place a white child with willing black parents (just as we might talk about the desirability of whites choosing to move into—without taking over—black neighborhoods). But, in fact, that would require turning the racializing paradigm on its head.

> Excuse us for the news
> You might not be amused
> But did you know White comes from Black
> No need to be confused[22]

Cultural Hybrids, Mixed Race, and Hybrid Culture

Thus the normalcy, the seeming naturalness, of racial fabrication is at once fixed in place and challenged by the admission of mixed race-ness. The assumption of mixed race up-ends as it extends the racializing project. If in the social formation of (post-) modernity there is no escaping the confines of race, standing inside the mixed condition of hybridity confronts the proponents of purity with a telling query: How indeed do you really know you're *not* mixed?[23] That it should not matter reveals that the project of racial purity, even—one is tempted to say, especially—in its cultural instantiation, is nothing but political (self-)assertion. This politics of racialized self-assertion is exemplified by the insistence that Italian Americans be treated by City University of New York as a protected minority, subject thus to the benefits in terms of hiring, promotion, and institutional resources of preferential treatment.[24]

The cultural assumption of racial definition nevertheless presupposes yet another circuitous, if not straightforwardly circular, commitment. For it necessarily presumes cultural ownership by racial members. The claim of cultural property—'this is *my* (or *our*) culture'—artificially fences off cultural production as it polices the conditions of cultural consumption and exchange.[25] While one may pose the question of cultural ownership generally, it becomes especially fraught with respect to racially identified culture. The problematics of owning cultural artifacts via forceful or coerced or commodified appropriation is exemplified in the history of colonial museums. This reveals that static ownership of cultural artifacts is hardly synonymous with the experienced dynamism of cultural belonging. But beyond this, what makes some or other racialized culture mine or yours? Mere racial belonging? Attributed belonging, or a sense of belonging? As far as I can tell, my thinking is closer to Nelson Mandela's than it is to Norman Mailer's, to Toni Morrison's than to Helen Suzman's. I have been characterized, among other things, as white, European, Anglo, Jewish, and African American. What *racial* culture, exactly, is mine?

I do not mean to deny the existence of, say, 'black culture.' 'Black' here refers pragmatically to a history of experiences those identified or identifying themselves as 'black' have suffered and enjoyed, have been subjected to (in both senses of subjection) precisely *as* black. Ironically, because of this history of subjection and responses to it, there is a sense in which black culture, a culture deeply informed by its own history, now stands as vibrant, dynamic, and desirable, whereas what may be referred to as 'white culture,' if it exists at all, does so only tenuously. The history of racist culture has prompted self-defining cultures of resistance that at once challenge racialized parameters as they are partially defined by them. White culture, such as it is, defines itself for the most part not over and against that which it is not but as insular and homogeneous. In that sense, white culture has tended to become (if it was not always) a decadent culture, for the most part static, nostalgic, retrospective. Its romantic retrospection is tied to a historicism that displaces any historical memory of racialized terror in the name of Disneyesque dehistoricized theme parks. What energy white culture has, it acquires from, as it denies, the racialized cultures of otherness.[26]

Again, if the racialized conditions of cultural belonging could be established,[27] what, then, would a culture of mixed race amount to? Neither white nor black, but some hybrid mix of multiple components that, catalytically, generates something significantly and dynamically new. However, as the examples of "Coloured" in South Africa and "Hispanic" in the United States have revealed, this racialized product of cultural bricolage is not by that token beyond the constraints of cultural exclusivity and exclusion, of derogation and dismissal. It is the threatening ambiguity for the racializing project inherent in the relative lack of their racial definition that promotes alienation of mixed-race members. Racial characterization adds to group formation the fabrication of naturalism, the fixed and fast insinuation of community insider and outsider. In qualifying hybridity, it tends to delimit the (al-)chemical dynamics of cultural transformation by giving in to the racializing presumptions of ownership and selectivity, of purity and homogeneity, of the dangers of pollution.

At best, then, the condition of mixed-race formation constitutes an ambivalent challenge to the racial condition from within the fabric of the racializing project. It tugs dangerously at the limits of the racializing discourse it at once invokes, straddling ambiguously the sites of double consciousness—in and out of the racializing mode, rejecting as it defines itself in and through racial terms, dismissing as it reifies the racial project. Nevertheless, if we play up the mixing at the expense of racial matching, we begin to see that an insistent hybridity dissipates the political persistence of purity, if not the project of racial formation *tout court*. At the limit, the cultural imperative to renewed and improvisational hybrid mixing implies renunciation of the racial matching and definition reflected in the reification of the nominal case: whiteness, blackness, "mulatto," "Coloured."[28] The reiterative revisability of hybrid heterotopias in the final analysis confronts the command of homogeneity with the material and discursive conditions of its horizon, exploding the confines of fabricated racial identities again and again into something new.

In this sense, the multicultural babel that makes up the United States, a babel constituted emphatically out of already produced multiplicities, becomes an historically fashioned microcosm of an unfolding world and an experimental space for hybrid formation and transformation capable at least in principle of testing the limits of the political technologies of identities. Yet with a practical qualification: The history-effacing will to a presentist or future power expressed in the Madison Avenue injunction to 'Just Do It' must be made to carry along with it, and not so silently as we have become used to, the historically directed imperative in the case of racist exclusions, as a counter-T-shirt so eloquently puts, to "Just *Un*do It." The marvels of 'mutant power' to make new identities should not be allowed to efface the need to resist the exclusionary legacies of past or present ones. In this fashion, 'Made in the USA' may come to stand for racial dissolution through mixing rather than the racial fixing of matching. That is a social story we need to imagine, fashion, and narrate—again and again.

Besides the optimism of identity (re-)formation, however, the (*dis-*)rupture of Public Enemy's rap emphasizes that the play of textualized theory should not be allowed to drown out the call to resist and transform the marginalization in economic and sociopolitical power con-figured and en-gendered by racial formations. All I have argued is that such marginalization may be advanced as much in the name of mixed-race formation as the purportedly pure.[29]

19

Mestizo Identity

Linda Alcoff

We Latin Americans have never been able to take our racial or cultural identity for granted:

> Who are we? asks the Liberator [Venezuelan] Simon Bolivar: ". . . we are not Europeans, we are not Indians, but a species in between. . . . we find ourselves in the difficult position of challenging the natives for title of possession, and of upholding the country that saw us born against the opposition of the invaders. . . . It is impossible to identify correctly to what human family we belong."[1]

Part European, part indigenous, half colonialist aggressor, half colonized oppressed, we have never had an unproblematic relationship to the questions of culture, identity, race, ethnicity, or even liberation. Still, Latin American thought has been structured to a great extent by European ideas about race and culture—ideas which value racial purity and cultural authenticity—and the contradiction between those ideas and Latin American reality has produced a rich tradition of philosophical work on the concept of cultural identity and its relation to the self. In a situation where there is no hope of attaining purity, a different set of practices and concepts around identity has emerged, one not without its own racisms, but one that might evoke the beginnings of an alternative vision for mestizo peoples throughout the world.

This chapter is situated within Anglo-American discourses about identity and subjectivity. My aim is to contribute to new thinking about racial identity without purity for mixed-race peoples in the

United States. It may be thought that there already exists in the North American context an available alternative to racial purity, that is, assimilationism and the imagery of the melting pot. I discuss this in the second section and show why I believe it to be inadequate. I then draw from the work of Latin American and Latino philosophers and theorists to find transformative notions of identity, authenticity, and multiculturalism that can usefully inform debates here.

Raced Purely or Purely Erased

> Sometimes I feel like a socio-genetic experiment
> A petri-dish community's token of infection.
> —Disposable Heroes of Hiphoprisy

For a variety of reasons that I explore in the next section, Spanish colonizers generally did not operate through practices of genocide, but quickly began intermarrying with indigenous people. The result is that, although there are pockets in some countries where the people are almost wholly indigenous, nearly all the Hispanics of the region share indigenous or African heritage as well. Neocolonial relations between the United States and Latin America have created the conditions to continue this practice of intermarrying (the joke in Panama today is that the most lasting effect of the U.S. invasion is to be found neither in politics nor in the drug trade but in the several hundred marriages that resulted). My own family is a typical case. Neocolonial relations between Panama and the United States created the conditions in which my cholito (mixed Spanish, Indian, and African) Panamanian father married a white Anglo-Irish woman from the United States to produce my sister and me. And through his subsequent liaisons, I have a range of siblings from black to brown to tan to freckled, spanning five countries and three continents, at last count (Panama, Costa Rica, Spain, Venezuela, and the United States). Ours is truly the postcolonial, postmodernist family, an open-ended set of indeterminate national, cultural, racial, and even linguistic allegiances.

However, despite the normality of mestizo identity in Latin America, my own experience of my identity has been painful and at times confusing. In Panama, my sister and I were prized for our light skin. Because I was exceptionally light with auburn hair, my father named me "Linda," meaning pretty. There, the mix itself did not pose any difficulties; the issue of concern was the *nature* of the mix—lighter or darker—and we were of the appropriately valued lighter type. When my parents divorced, my sister and I moved with our mother to her parents' home in central Florida, and here the social meanings of our racial identity were wholly transformed. We were referred to as her "Latin daughters," and the fact that we were mixed made us objects of peculiarity. In the central Florida of the 1950s, a biracial system and the one-drop rule still reigned, and our mixed-race status meant that we could occupy white identity only precariously.[2] As much as was possible, we began to pass as simply white, which I was able to do more easily than my sister (she was older, darker, and spoke only Spanish at first). But for both of us, this coerced incorporation into the white Anglo community induced feelings of self-alienation, inferiority, and a strong desire to gain recognition and acceptance within the white community. It also, however, helped us to see through the Jim Crow system, for, through the experience of having racist whites unknowingly accept us, we could see all too clearly the speciousness of the biracial illusion as well as the hurtfulness and irrationality of racial hierarchies and systems of exclusion. I remember standing in the lunch line one day at school while a friend made racist remarks, feeling revolted by her attitude, and also thinking "you could be talking about me."

In cultures defined by racialized identities and divided by racial hierarchies, mixed white–nonwhite persons face an unresolvable status ambiguity. They are rejected by the dominant race as impure and therefore inferior, but also disliked by the oppressed race for their privileges of closer association with domination. Surprisingly consistent repudiations of mixing are found across differences of social status: oppressed and dominant communities disapprove of open mixing, both fail to acknowledge and accept mixed offspring, and both value a purity for racial identity. Thus, the mixed-race person has been denied that social recognition of self that Hegel understood as necessarily constitutive of self-consciousness and full self-development.[3] For those of us who could pass, our community acceptance was always at the price of misrecognition and the troubling knowledge that our social self was grounded on a lie.[4]

Interestingly, this problem has not been restricted to a single political ideology: left and right political discourses have placed a premium on racial purity. For the right, race mixing is a form of "pollution" that requires intermittent processes of ethnic cleansing, which can take the form of genocide, segregation, or simply rural terrorism (the kind practiced by the Ku Klux Klan, the Confederate Knights of America, and the White Aryan Resistance). The very concept of "rape as genocide"—the belief that a massive trans-community orchestrated series of rapes will result in the genocide of a culture—assumes purity as a necessary and prized cultural identity attribute. Right-wing nationalist movements have also been grounded, in some cases, on the claimed need for a separate political formation that is coextensive with a racial or ethnic identity; here the state becomes the representative of a race or ethnic group and the arbiter over questions of group inclusion.[5] The state must then make it its business to oversee the reproduction of this group, thus to engage in what Michel Foucault called bio-power, to ensure a continuation of its constituency.[6]

For the left, cultural autonomy and community integrity are held up as having an intrinsic value, resulting in mixed-race persons treated as symbols of colonial aggression or cultural dilution. The very demand for self-determination too often presupposes an authentic self, with clear, unambiguous commitments and allegiances. Thus, as Richard Rodriguez suggests sarcastically, the "Indian [has] become the mascot of an international ecology movement," but not just any Indian. "The industrial countries of the world romanticize the Indian who no longer exists [i.e., the authentic, culturally autonomous Indian without any connection to capitalist economic formations], ignoring the Indian who does—the Indian who is poised to chop down his rain forest, for example. Or the Indian who reads the *New York Times*.[7] The mythic authentic voice of the oppressed, valorized by the left, is culturally *un*changed, racially *un*mixed, and, as a matter of fact, extinct. The veneration of authenticity leads the left to disregard (when they do not scorn) the survivors of colonialism.

Thus, in many cultures today, mixed-race people are treated as the corporeal instantiation of a lack—the lack of an identity that can provide a public status. They (we) are turned away from as if from an unpleasant sight, the sight and mark of an unclean copulation, the product of a taboo, the sign of racial impurity, cultural dilution, colonial aggression, or even emasculation. Which particular attribution is chosen will reflect the particular community's cultural self-understanding and its position as dominant or subordinate. But the result is usually the same: Children with impure racial identities are treated as an unwanted reminder of something shameful or painful and are alienated (to a greater or lesser extent) from every community to which they have some claim of attachment.

Some theorists have suggested that when such a rigidity around racial identity manifests itself among oppressed people, it is the result of their internalization of oppression and acceptance of racist, self-denigrating cultural values.[8] But I am not sure that this is the cause in every case, or the whole story—the problem may be deeper, in that foundational concepts of self and identity are founded on purity, wholeness, and coherence. A self that is internally heterogeneous beyond repair or resolution becomes a candidate for pathology in a society where the integration of self is taken to be necessary for mental health. We need to reflect upon this premium put on internal coherence and racial purity and how this is manifested in Western concepts and practices of identity as a public persona as well as subjectivity as a foundational understanding of the self. We need to consider what role this preference for purity and racial separateness has had on dominant formulations of identity and subjectivity, and what the effects might be if this preference was no longer operative.

Behind my claim that an important relationship exists between purity and racial identity is of course the presupposition that an important relationship exists between race and identity, a relationship that may not always exist but one that appears quite resistant to imminent change. Today, it is easily apparent that acceptance and status within a community are tied to one's racial identification and *identifiability*. In the United States, census forms, as well as application forms of many types, confer various sorts of benefits or resources according to racial identity, thus affecting one's social status. Less formally, one's ability to be accepted in various kinds of social circles, religious groups, and neighborhoods is tied to one's (apparent) race. And I would also argue that not only social status is affected here, but one's lived interiority as well. Such things as government benefits and employment opportunities have an effect on one's subjectivity, one's sense of oneself as a unique, individuated person and as competent, acceptable, or inferior. Dominant discourses, whether they are publically regulated and institutionalized or more amorphous and decentralized, can affect the lived experience of subjectivity. Discourses and institutions implicitly invoke selves that have specific racial identities, which are correlated to those selves' specific legal status, discursive authority, epistemic credibility, and social standing.

During the building of the Panama Canal, workers were divided and identified by the United States owned and run Panama Canal Commission as "gold" (whites) and "silver" (West Indian blacks), denoting the form of currency in which they were paid. Gold and silver workers were given separate and differently constructed living quarters, different currency for wages, and different commissaries; they were assigned different tasks and also attributed different characteristics. In Canal Commission documents, gold workers were described as loyal, earnest, responsible, self-sacrificing, and enthusiastic. Silver workers were described as shiftless, inconstant, exasperating, irresponsible, carefree, "yet as reliable a workman as our own American cottonfield hand."[9] Here race explicitly determined economic and social status, but it also was understood by the dominant white authorities to be the determinate constitutive factor of subjectivity—involving personal character traits and internal constitution (blacks were thought to be more resistant to yellow fever).[10] Such publically instituted and circulated associations between race and subjectivity will always have an effect on the self-perceptions of those persons so described. The convincing portrait that has been drawn of subjectivity as constitutively relational by such theorists as Hegel, Fanon, and Irigaray, must persuade us that no self can withstand completely the substantive recognitions from external sources. Thus, racialized identities affect not only one's public status but one's experienced selfhood as well.

To the extent that this public and private self involves a racial construction, this self, outside of Latin America, has been constructed with a premium on purity and separation. The valorization of cultural integrity and autonomy found in diverse political orientations, from left to right, brings along with it the valorization of purity over dilution, of the authentic voice over the voice of collusion, and of autonomy over what might be called "bio-political intercourse."

Erasures of Race

What, then, is the American, this new man? . . . He is an American, who, leaving behind him all his ancient prejudices and manners, receives new ones from the new mode of the life he has embraced, the new government he obeys, and the new rank he holds.

—Hector St. Jean de Crevecoeur, 1782[11]

If it is generally true that selves are constituted in relationship to communities that have been racially constructed, what happens when there are multiple, conflicting communities through which a self is constituted? What would a concept of the self look like that did not valorize purity and coherence? If we reject the belief that retaining group integrity is an intrinsic good, how will this affect our political goals of resisting the oppression of racialized groups?

Within the United States, assimilationism has been the primary alternative to a racial purity and separateness, but it has notoriously been restricted to European ethnicities, and it has worked to assimilate them all to a Northern European WASP norm—thus Jewish and Roman Catholic Southern Europeans were more difficult to assimilate to this norm and never quite made it into the melting pot. And of course, the melting pot failed to diminish racial hierarchies because it was never really intended to include different races; no proponent of the melting pot ideology ever promoted miscegenation.[12]

Moreover, as Homi Bhabha remarks, "Fixity, as the sign of cultural/historical/racial difference in the discourse of colonialism, is a paradoxical mode of representation: it connotes rigidity and a unchanging order as well as disorder, degeneracy and daemonic repetition."[13] The fluidity of cultural identity promoted by the assimilationist discourse actually was used to bolster Northern European–Americans' claims to cultural superiority: Their (supposed) "fluidity" was contrasted with and presented as a higher cultural achievement than the (supposed) fixity and rigidity of colonized cultures. Here, fixity symbolized inferiority and flexibility symbolized superiority (although of course, in reality, the designation of "fixity" meant simply the inability or unwillingness to conform to the Northern European norm). This paradox of the meaning of fixity explains how it was possible that, simultaneous to the Panama Canal Commission's construction of rigid racial groups working on the Canal, the ideology at home (i.e., the United States) was dominated by the melting pot imagery. The WASPS could be fluid, tolerant, and evolving, but the natives could not. The very fluidity of identity that one might think would break down hierarchies was used to justify them. Given this, a prima facie danger exists in drawing on assimilationist rhetoric, as it was espoused in the United States, to reconfigure relations of domination.

Ironically, the fact of the matter is that throughout Latin America and the Caribbean, a true melting pot of peoples, cultures, and races was created unlike anything north of the border. The liberal, modernist-based vision of assimilation succeeded best in the pre-modernist, Roman Catholic, Iberian-influenced countries, while the proponents of secularism and modernism to the north were too busy to notice. Rodriguez points out that, still today,

> Mexico City is modern in ways that 'multiracial,' ethnically 'diverse' New York is not yet. Mexico City is centuries more modern than racially 'pure,' provincial Tokyo. . . . Mexico is the capital of modernity, for in the sixteenth century, . . . Mexico initiated the task of the twenty-first century—the renewal of the old, the known world, through miscegenation. Mexico carries the idea of a round world to its biological conclusion.[14]

Today, the liberalism that spawned assimilationism has metamorphosed into an ethic of appreciation for the diversity of cultures. In the name of preserving cultural diversity, and in the secret hope of appropriating native wisdom and the stimulation that only exotica can provide a consumption-weary middle class, indigenous cultures and peoples are commodified, fetishized and fossilized as standing outside of history and social evolution (if they are not totally different than "us," then they will not be exotic enough to have commodity value). Thus, an image of the American Indian straddling a snowmobile (as appeared in the *Times*) evokes affected protestations from educated Anglos about the tragic demise of a cultural identity, as if American Indian identity can only exist where it is pure, unsullied, fixed in time and place.[15] The project of "protecting" the cultural "integrity" of indigenous peoples in the guise of cultural appreciation secures a sense of superiority for those who see their own cultures as dynamic and evolving. Anglo culture can grow and improve through what it learns from "native" cultures, and thus the natives are prized for an exchange value that is dependent on their stagnation.

In North America, then, assimilationism and its heir apparent, cultural appreciation, have not led to a true mixing of races or cultures, or to an end to the relations of domination between cultures. However, interestingly, the concept and the practice of assimilation resonates very differently in South and Central America. As I discuss in the third section of this chapter, for Mexican philosophers such as Samuel Ramos and Leopoldo Zea, assimilation did not require conformity to a dominant norm; instead, assimilation was associated with an antixenophobic cosmopolitanism that sought to integrate diverse elements into a new formation.

What can account for the different practices and theories of assimilation in North and South cultures? And what were the elements involved in U.S. assimilationism that allowed it to coexist with racism rather than come into conflict with it? Finding the answer to such questions can be instructive for the project of developing a better alternative to identity constructions than those based on racial purity. Toward this, I have already suggested that assimilationism in the North was organized around an implicit normative identity (WASP) to which others were expected to conform; hence its exclusive application to Northern Europeans. And I have also suggested that the flexibility of identity claimed by assimilationists was used to bolster WASP claims to cultural superiority over the supposedly rigid peoples and cultures that could not be made to conform. I offer two further elements toward such an answer, one taken from cultural history and the other involving the Enlightenment concept of secular reason.

Latin American and North American countries have different cultural genealogies based on the different origins of their immigrants: respectively, Roman Catholic Iberia and Germano-Protestant England. In North America, race mixing generally was perceived with abhorrence. In the countries colonized by Spain, by contrast, "elaborate racial taxonomies gained official recognition from the outset . . . and these casta designations became distinct identities unto themselves, with legal rights as well as disabilities attaching to each."[16] After independence, the casta system was eliminated from official discourses, and racial discrimination was made illegal, because such practices of discrimination obviously could not work in countries where as few as 5 percent of the population were *not* mestizo of some varied racial combination.

According to Carlos Fernández and the historian A. Castro, this contrast in the practices around racial difference can be accounted for in the historical differences between "Nordic" and "Latin" cultures.

Due primarily to its imperial character, the Roman world of which Spain (Hispania) was an integral part developed over time a multiethnically tolerant culture, a culture virtually devoid of xenophobia. The Romans typically absorbed the cultures as well as the territories of the peoples they conquered. Outstanding among their cultural acquisitions were the Greek tradition and, later, the Judaic tradition. It was the Roman co-optation of Judaic Christianity that the Spanish inherited as Catholicism.[17]

Thus, in the missionary zeal of the Spanish Christians can be found the spirit of Roman imperialism, as well as its cosmopolitanism.

By contrast, the Germanic peoples of Northern Europe "emerged into history at the margins of the Roman empire, constantly at war with the legions, not fully conquered or assimilated into Roman life." Fernández hypothesizes that this "condition of perpetual resistance against an alien power and culture" produced the generally negative attitude of the Germans toward foreigners, especially because the Roman legions with which they fought included numerous ethnic groups. This attitude had profound historical results: "The persistence of the German peoples, born of their struggles against the Romans, can also be seen later in history as an important element in the Protestant schism with Rome accomplished by the German Martin Luther. It is no coincidence that Protestantism is primarily a phenomenon of Northwestern Europe while Catholicism is mainly associated with Southern Europe."[18]

Now this of course is not the whole story as to why genocide was so widespread in North America and not in the South: "The difference in the size and nature of the Native American populations in Anglo and Latin America also helps account for the emergence of different attitudes about race."[19] In the North, the indigenous peoples were generally nomadic and seminomadic, not very numerous, and there was a great technological distance between them and the European settlers; in the South, the indigenous peoples were numerous and "lived a settled, advanced (even by European standards) agricultural life with large cities and developed class systems."[20] So the resultant integrations between race and cultural formations that developed differently in the North and the South were the product not just of different European traditions but also their interaction with the different cultures in the New World.

And certainly Roman imperialism was not less oppressive than Germanic forms of domination: both perpetrated a strategy of domination. But it is instructive to note the different forms domination can take, and the different legacies each form has yielded in the present. In the North, the melting pot stopped at the border of German-Anglo ethnicities. To venture beyond that border endangered their incorporation into a Roman superpower, ethnically and racially diverse but centered always in Rome. Thus, for Nordic peoples, assimilation and cultural integrity were posed in conflict, and to maintain the distinctness of their borders, they were willing to commit sweeping annihilations. For Rome and Hispania, however, assimilation meant expansion, development, growth. Cultural supremacy did not require isolationism or separation but precisely the constant absorption and blending of difference into an ever larger, more complex, heterogeneous whole. Border control was thus not the highest priority or even considered an intrinsic good. This is why the concept of assimilationism has never had the same meaning in the South as it has in the North, either conceptually or in practice.

The second part of the story involves the Enlightenment concept of secular reason. The northern variant of assimilationism was strongly tied to the development of a Liberal antifeudal ideology that espoused humanism against the aristocracy and secularism against the fusion of church and civil society. The Enlightenment in Northern Europe put forward a vision of universal humanism with equality and civil freedoms for all citizens of a secular state. Diverse ethnicities and religious allegiances could coexist and unite under the auspices of a larger community founded on natural law, and that natural law could be discerned through the use of secular reason, which was conceived as the common denominator across cultural differences. Thus, reason became the means through which the Nordic immigrants to America could relax their borders enough to create a new ethnically mixed society.

But why was the banner of reason incapable of expanding beyond WASP communities? To understand this it helps to recall that the European Enlightenment was flourishing at exactly the same time that European countries were most successfully colonizing the globe—exploiting, enslaving, and in some cases eliminating indigenous populations.[21] But what can account for this juxtaposition between the invocations of liberty for all and the callous disregard of the liberty as well as well-being of non-Europeans? To answer this we need to look more critically at what grounded the claims to liberty.

Universalist humanism was based on a supposedly innate but unevenly developed capacity to reason, a reason conceptualized as entirely mental and thus capable of transcending the particularities of material contexts and specific individuals. Leopoldo Zea has written about the political uses that colonialism has made of the Western notion of reason.[22] Where the Frankfurt School analyzed the connection between Enlightenment reason and social domination, Zea provides a piece of the analysis noticeably missing from their account: the connection between reason and colonialism. "The marginalization of non-European peoples with respect to Europeans," Zea argues, "is related to a Eurocentric view of reason, which leads to the perception that non-Western people are inferior to Europeans in their capacity to reason, hence, in their status of human beings. Political questions of autonomy and the right of self-governance hang in the balance."[23] Universal standards and articulations of rationality are implicated in socially organized practices and institutions that implement colonial and neocolonial policies. When the paradigm of reason, construed as culturally neutral, is defined as the scientific practices of European-based countries, the result is a flattering contrast between Europe and its colonies. Reason is counterposed to ignorance, philosophies of mind to folk psychologies, religion to superstition, and history to myth, producing a cultural hierarchy that vindicates colonialist arrogance. And because this hierarchy is justified through a concept that is presented as culturally neutral, it cannot be assailed by political arguments nor can it be identified as an intellectual product of a particular culture. Thus its political effects become unassailable. Following this, Zea points out that the issue of identity must not be mistakenly thought to have relevance only within a conceptual or cultural realm. "It is a problem located in the public sector—in the public conception of reason and in the use of power."[24]

The capacity for reasoning and science on the Western model requires an ability to detach oneself, to be objective, to subdue one's own passionate attachments and emotions. Such a personality type was associated with Northern Europeans and contrasted with the passionate natures of Latin temperaments and the inferior intellects of darker peoples. Thus a humanism based on secular reason, far from conflicting with racism and cultural chauvinism, supported their continuation. In its most benign form, reason could only support Europe's role as beneficent teacher for the backward Other, but could never sustain a relationship of equality. It is for this reason that Zea concludes,

> The racial mestizahe that did not bother the Iberian conquerors and colonizers was to disturb greatly the creators of the new empires of America, Asia, and Africa. Christianity blessed the unity of men

and cultures regardless of race, more a function of their ability to be Christian. But modern civilization stressed racial purity, the having or lacking of particular habits and customs proper to a specific type of racial and cultural humanity.[25]

Thus, secularization actually promoted racial purity by replacing Christian values with culturally specific habits and customs. In challenging what is still a powerful orthodoxy—the claim that secularization has only progressive effects—Zea's critique of modernism strikes more deeply than even much of postmodernism. To today pretend that these existing concepts—of reason, of philosophy, and of religion—can be extracted from their cultural history and purged of their racial associations and racial content is a delusion. Reason, it turns out, is white, at least in its specific articulations in Western canonical discourses. Therefore, an account of the core of human nature that is based on a reasoning capacity is a racialized concept of the self *passing* for a universal one.

Given this history, then, it is no longer a surprise that the concept and practice of assimilationism that developed in this Northern European context sought to maintain its borders against the devouring capacities and polluting effects of other cultures, and to unite its diverse ethnic groups on the basis of a criterion that simultaneously excluded others (i.e., the capacity for reason and science in the mode of Northern Europe). Whether the concept of reason can be reconstructed is not my project here, though I certainly support such a project. Rather, my question here is, can the concept of assimilation be transformed and salvaged? This discussion will begin in the final section of this chapter.

But first, I want to look briefly at one other, more current, alternative to conceptions of identity based on purity—the very recently developed notion of nomad subjectivity in the work of Gilles Deleuze and Felix Guattari.[26] This concept is not analogous to assimilationism in being widely disseminated within dominant cultural discourses, but it is influential in many academic, theoretical circles and it gains support from some formulations of the new global world order. Nomad subjectivity announces that fluidity and indeterminateness will break up racial and cultural hierarchies that inflict oppression and subordination. Freed from state-imposed structures of identity by the indeterminate flows of capital, nomad subjectivity deterritorializes toward becoming like "a nomad, an immigrant, and a gypsy."[27] Within language, as within subjectivity,

> There is no longer any proper sense or figurative sense, but only a
> distribution of states that is part of the range of the word. The thing
> and other things are no longer anything but intensities overrun by
> deterritorialized sound or words that are following their lines of escape.
> . . . Instead, it is now a question of a becoming that includes the
> maximum of difference as a difference of intensity, the crossing of
> a barrier. . . .[28]

The flow of deterritorialization does not move between points but
"has abandoned points, coordinates, and measure, like a drunken
boat. . . ."[29] Deterritorializations thus have the effect of deconstructing
racial and morphological identity categories along with national,
cultural, and ethnic ones, and so the result is not a multiply situated subject but a nomadic subject without the concreteness implied
by situation.

This sort of view obviously connects more generally to a postmodernist notion of the indeterminate self, a self defined only by
its negation of or resistance to categories of identity.[30] And there is
a strand of this in academic feminism among theorists who repudiate identity-based politics in the name of antiessentialism. Liberation is associated with the refusal to be characterized, described,
or classified, and the only true strategy of resistance can be one of
negation, a kind of permanent revolution on the metaphysical front.
Unfortunately, nomadic subjectivity works no better than assimilationist doctrine to interpellate mixed identity: the nomad self is
bounded to no community and represents an absence of identity
rather than a multiply entangled and engaged identity. This is not
the situation of mixed-race peoples who have deep (even if problematic) ties to specific communities; to be a free-floating unbound
variable is not the same as being multiply categorized and ostracized by specific racial communities. It strikes me that the postmodern nomadic vision fits far better the multinational CEO with
fax machine and cellular phone in hand who is bound to, or by, no
national agenda, tax structure, cultural boundary, or geographical
border. And what this suggests is that a simplistic promotion of
fluidity will not suffice.

I am concerned with the way in which a refusal of identity might
be useful for the purposes of the current global market. The project
of global capitalism is to transform the whole world into postcolonial consumers and producers of goods in an acultural world commodity market, the Benetton-like vision where the only visible

differences are those that can be commodified and sold. Somewhere between that vision and the vision of a purist identity construction that requires intermittent ethnic cleansing we must develop a different alternative, an alternative which can offer a normative reconstruction of raced-identity applicable to mixed-race peoples.

Mestiza Race

Jose Vasconcelos, Mexican philosopher, envisaged una raza mestiza, una mezcla de razas afines, una raza de color—la primera raza sintesis del globo. He called it a cosmic race, la raza cosmica, a fifth race embracing the four major races of the world. Opposite to the theory of the pure Aryan. . . . his theory is one of inclusivity.

—Gloria Anzaldua[31]

We must begin to look South, where there already exists a long tradition of philosophical work on the intersection of identity, multiplicity, and politics. The specifically philosophical treatment of identity will certainly seem odd to Anglo philosophers, who on the whole leave such cultural specificities to sociologists or anthropologists, and instead prefer to concentrate on problems considered to have universal relevance and applicability. I am reminded here of a story that Michael Kimmel told recently at a talk he gave. As a graduate student in the History of Consciousness program at the University of California–Santa Cruz, he was taking a seminar in feminist theory when a debate occurred about the importance of race versus gender. In the midst of the discussion, bell hooks asked Bettina Aptheker what she saw when she looked in the mirror. Aptheker replied, "I see a woman." hooks responded that when she looked in the mirror, she saw a black woman. Kimmel reported feeling very uncomfortable at that moment, because he realized that when he looked in the mirror, what he saw was a human being. When your own particular and specific attributes are dominant *and* valorized, they can be taken for granted and ignored.

Because of their interest in contributing to the thinking about identity issues, many Latin American philosophers have developed a different understanding of the nature of philosophy itself. If philosophy is defined as raising only universal, general, and abstract problems, beyond the issues facing concrete individuals in the everyday world, there is no space within philosophy for discussions about cultural identity, and so such issues are left to the social sciences. Zea argues that such a view exemplifies the desire to be godlike on the part of philosophers, to transcend the "concrete capacity of vision of the one who asks."[32] Drawing on the views of Hans-Georg Gadamer and Karl-Otto Apel, Zea suggests that we need not abandon theoretical discourse to reject this delimitation of philosophical problems to abstract and universal issues:

> At stake here is not a choice [e.g., between theory and practice] but a reconstruction of problems that are inescapably linked among themselves because they have an origin in man. The philosopher does not have to give up being a philosopher to face the many problems of a reality different from theory. Without ceasing to be a philosopher he can philosophically, rationally, confront man's daily problems and seek possible solutions.[33]

So, without ceasing to be a philosopher, let me return to the problem of racial identity.

First, it seems clear that, within the context of racially based and organized systems of oppression, racial identity will continue to be a salient internal and external component of identity. Systems of oppression, segregated communities, and practices of discrimination create a collective experience and a shared history for a racialized grouping. It is that shared experience and history, more than any physiological or morphological features, that cements the community and creates connections with others along racial lines. And that history cannot be deconstructed by new scientific accounts that dispute the characterization of race as a natural kind.[34] Accounts of race as a social and historical identity, though this brings in elements that are temporally contingent and mutable, will probably prove to have more persistence than accounts of race that tie it to biology. Ironically, history will probably have more permanence than biology.

Moreover, I would argue that, given current social conditions, any materialist account of the self must take into account the element of race. This is not to deny that generic and universalist concepts of human being are both possible and necessary. Despite my concern expressed in the last section against formulating a universal humanism based on reason, connections do exist between persons that endure across differences of sexuality, race, culture, even class. My view is not that such connections do not exist, or that

they are trivial, or that in all cases a universalist humanism is politically pernicious. However, if we restrict a philosophical analysis of identity and subjectivity to only those elements that can be
universally applied, our resulting account will be too thin to do
much philosophical work. In the concrete everydayness of "actually existing" human life, the variabilities of racial designation me-
diate experience in ways we are just beginning to recognize.

Another reason to maintain the racial dimension of formulations
of identity is that universalist pretensions often produce alienation
in those whose identities are not dominant. When such false uni-
versalisms become influential in oppressed communities, the result
is that, for example, nonwhite peoples internalize the perspective
of white identity. In *The Bluest Eye*, Toni Morrison dramatically
captures this phenomenon for the young black child who wants blond
hair and blue eyes. Simone de Beauvoir and Sandra Bartky have
written about a form of female alienation in which women see themselves and their bodies through a generalized male gaze that rates
and ranks attributes, and disciplines behavior to a degree worthy
of Foucault's description of the Benthamite panopticon. And Samuel Ramos has argued that the veneration of Europe has led Mexicans to live "with a view of the world alien to their own cultural
reality," in effect, "to live outside their 'being'."[35]

Such patterns of alienation have profound effects on the capacity for self-knowledge, a capacity that philosophers as diverse as
Plato and Hegel have seen as critical for the possibility of any
knowledge whatsoever. If knowledge represents a concrete vision
correlated to a particular social location, then the alienation one
suffers from one's own perspectival vision will have ramifications
throughout one's life. And for mixed-race persons, this problem can
be particularly difficult to overcome. For them (us), it is not a question
of reorienting perspective from the alien to the familiar, because
no ready-made, available perspective captures their contradictory
experience. Without a social recognition of mixed identity, the mixed-
race person is told to choose one or another perspective. This creates not only alienation, but the sensation of having a mode of being
that is an incessant, unrecoverable lack and an unsurpassable inferiority. This blocks the possibility of self-knowledge. The epistemic authority and credibility that accrue to nearly everyone, at least
with respect to their "ownmost" perspective, is denied to the mixed-
race person. Vis-a-vis each community or social location to which

she or he might claim a connection, she or he can never claim authority to speak unproblematically for or from that position. Ramos warns that, without a connection to an ongoing history and community, "one lives only for the day . . . without regard to past or future."[36] Only communities have continuity beyond individual life; cast off from all communities, the individual has no historical identity, and thus is unlikely to value the community's future.

Identity is not, of course, monopolized by race, nor does race operate on identity as an autonomous determinant. Mixed-race persons probably notice more than others the extent to which "race" is a social construction, ontologically dependent on a host of contextual factors. The meanings of both race and such things as skin color are mediated by language, religion, nationality, and culture, to produce a racialized identity. As a result, a single individual's racial identity can change across communities, and a family's race can change across history. In the Dominican Republic, "black" is defined as Haitian, and dark-skinned Dominicans do not self-identify as black but as dark Indians or mestizos. Coming to the United States, Dominicans "become" black by the dominant standards. In the United States, I generally pass as a white angla; as soon as I land in Panama, I am recognized as Panamanian. In England, South Asians are identified as blacks. Every year in South Africa, numbers of people petition the government to change their official racial classification, resulting in odd official announcements from the Home Affairs Minister that, for example, "nine whites became coloured, 506 coloureds became white, two whites became Malay . . . 40 coloreds became black, 666 blacks became coloured, 87 coloreds became Indian. . . ."[37] The point here is not that racial identities are often misidentified, but that race does not stand alone; race identity is mediated by other factors, political as well as sociological ones. And appearance is also socially mediated; the dominant perspective in the United States on a person's racial identity or whether they "look" Latino or black is not natural. Appearances "appear" differently across cultural contexts.

Because nationality, culture, and language are so critical to identity, some propose that, for example, nationality should be taken as a more important distinguishing characteristic than race. Nationality could provide a strong connection across racialized communities, increasing their unity and sympathetic relationships. This phenomenon is emerging in the United States today as minority communities become antiimmigrant, even when the immigrants are of the same racial features or share a cultural background. Thus African-American school kids fight with West Indians in Brooklyn, and Cubans disdain the Central Americans flooding into Miami. Such conflict is sometimes based on class, but it is also based on a claim to the so-called "American" identity. In this way, U.S. minorities can ally with the (still) powerful white majority against new immigrants, and perhaps share in the feeling if not the reality of dominance. An identification that places nationality over race thus ensures, at least for the present, an increase in antiimmigrant violence.

The point of the preceding discussion is to suggest that race cannot and should not be eliminated as a salient identity in the near future. In my view, it should not be replaced by nationality, and its erasure only conceals the ongoing dominance of white Northern European values and perspectives. Some have argued that, given the socially constructed character of race, and the largely detrimental effects that racial classifications have had on all nonwhite peoples and mixed-race persons in particular, all forms of racial identity should be rejected. I would argue rather for developing a positive reconstruction of mixed-race identity. I will end by suggesting some ways this might be developed.

In her book *Borderlands/La Frontera*, Gloria Anzaldua has offered a powerful and lyrical vision of the difficulties mixed-race persons endure. She writes:

> The ambivalence from the clash of voices results in mental and emotional states of perplexity. Internal strife results in insecurity and indecisiveness. The mestiza's dual or multiple personality is plagued by psychic restlessness.[38]

Contrast that description with Deleuze and Guattari's romantic portrait of the nomad and the schizophrenic, as a paradigm of liberation.

Anzaldua worries that the shame and rootlessness of the mestizo can lead to excessive compensation, especially in the form of machismo. She writes:

> In the Gringo world, the Chicano suffers from excessive humility and self-effacement, shame of self and self-deprecation. Around Latinos he suffers from a sense of language inadequacy and its accompanying discomfort; with Native Americans he suffers from a racial amnesia which ignores our common blood, and from guilt because the Spanish part of him took their land and oppressed them. He has an excessive compensatory hubris when around Mexicans from the other

side. It overlays a deep sense of racial shame . . . which leads him
to put down women and even to brutalize them.[39]

For Anzaldua, an alternative positive articulation of mestiza consciousness and identity must be developed to provide some degree
of coherence and to avoid the incessant cultural collisions or violent compensations that result from the shame and frustration of
self-negation.

Toward this, Anzaldua sees the mixed-race person as engaged in
the valuable though often exhausting role of border crosser, negotiator, and mediator between races, and sometimes also between
cultures, nations, and linguistic communities. The mixed person is
a traveler often within her own home or neighborhood, translating
and negotiating the diversity of meanings, practices, and forms of
life. This vision provides a positive alternative to the mixed-race
person's usual representation as lack or as the tragically alienated
figure.

Such figures who can negotiate between cultures have of course
been notoriously useful for the dominant, who can use them to better
understand and thus control their colonized subjects. Thus, such
figures as Malinche and Pocahontas are often reviled for their cooperation with dominant communities and their love for specific
individuals from those communities. There is no question that such
border negotiation can exacerbate oppression. Today large numbers
of bilingual and biracial individuals are recruited by the U.S. military and the F.B.I. to infiltrate suspected gangs or communities
and countries designated as U.S. enemies. To my dismay, many
Latinos in the U.S. military were deployed in the invasion of Panama. Here again, an allegiance based on nationality is used to cir-
cumvent what might be a stronger racial or cultural tie.

I suspect that for mixed-race persons, especially those who have
suffered some degree of rejection from the communities to which
they have some attachment, such jobs hold a seductive attraction
as a way to overcome feelings of inferiority and to find advantage
for the first time in the situation of being mixed. Where I agree
with Anzaldua is the positive spin she puts on the mixed-race identity. (And I must say to Anglos who may have read her book, don't
underestimate the radical nature of what she has done: her use of
a mix of languages, including English, Spanish, Tex-Mex, and indigenous languages, is a practice that is reviled by most Spanish
speaking people in the United States and Latin America, even in-

cluding most Mexican Americans. Her insistence on linguistic mixes is very liberating.) But where I would place a note of caution concerns the uses to which such border crossings can be put: they are not all to the good.

Another element worth exploring is Samuel Ramos's concept of an assimilation that does not demand conformity to the dominant or consist in a kind of imitation. Rather, assimilation in Ramos's sense is an incorporation or absorption of different elements. This is similar to the Hegelian concept of sublation in the sense of a synthesis that does not simply unite differences but develops them into a higher and better formulation. In the context of Latin America, Ramos called for a new self-integration that would appropriate its European and Indian elements. "The practice of imitating European culture must be replaced by the assimilation of such a culture. 'Between the process of imitation and that of assimilation there lies the same difference,' he notes, 'as there is between what is mechanical and what is organic.'"[40] Ramos believes that this process of active assimilation cannot occur without reflective self-knowledge. An imitative stance toward the other, and a conformity to dominant norms, will occur unless the empty self-image of the Mexican is replaced by a more substantive perspective indexed to one's own cultural, political, and racial location.

I believe that the concept of mestizo consciousness and identity can contribute toward the development of such a perspective, by creating a linguistic, public, socially affirmed identity for mixed-race persons. Mestizo consciousness is a double vision, a conscious articulation of mixed identity, allegiances, and traditions. As I quote Anzaldua above, Jose Vasconcelos called this new identity the cosmic race, la raza cosmica, based on a rich inclusivity and mutability rather than purity. All forms of racial mixes could be included in this identity, thus avoiding the elaborate divisions that a proliferation of specific mixed identities could produce. Such a vision is not captured by the "United Colors of Benetton," but by the organic integration of a new human blend such as the world has never seen.

Only recently have I finally come to some acceptance of my ambiguous identity. I am not simply white nor simply Latina, and the gap that exists between my two identities—indeed, my two families—a gap that is cultural, racial, linguistic, and national, feels too wide and deep for me to span. I cannot bridge the gap, so I negotiate it, standing at one point here, and then there, moving between locations as events or other people's responses propel me. I never reach shore: I never wholly occupy either the Angla or the Latina identity. Paradoxically, in white society I feel my Latinness, in Latin society I feel my whiteness, as that which is left out, an invisible present, sometimes as intrusive as an elephant in the room and sometimes more as a pulled thread that alters the design of my fabricated self. Peace has come for me by living that gap, and no longer seeking some permanent home onshore. What I seek now is no longer a home, but perhaps a lighthouse, that might illuminate this place in which I live, for myself as much as for others.

20

Race and Racism: Marginalization within the Margins

Debra A. Barrath

As a South African woman of indeterminate class, "race," and culture, it is not surprising that I have been oppressed. What has complicated my existence, though, is the realisation that because I am euphemistically referred to as a middle-class "Coloured" woman, I cannot identify with either the privileged middle-class white women or even the less privileged middle-class black women. This is because the divisive political system of South Africa has controlled how we relate to each other on the basis of our racial origins. Such separation also prevents us from identifying any commonalities we may have in terms of our class or culture. It follows, therefore, that our only common ground is that we are South African women, and because of that we share at least one form of oppression, namely that based on gender. In this chapter I address my ambivalence as a "Coloured" woman who has been marginalized within the broader racial margins to which all South African "nonwhites" belong, but within which there is also a polarization toward black males of African descent. That is, I address the issue of black–white and male–female dualisms, which excludes many of us who are referred to as "others."

In South Africa, a "Coloured" may be defined as a person of mixed race, that is, any combination of white, African, or Asian. Because of this unique classification, whether I am of European, Asian, or African descent, I have no claim on the culture or traditions of my forbears. I have had to live with the feeling of having no roots. When everything around me speaks of cultural awareness, I am denied a voice—because I am "Coloured" and there is no distinct "Coloured" culture—although my peers would try to convince me that there is. This only deepens my sense of confusion, though, because the culture I see them aspiring to is that of Afro-Americans with which I have little in common, and therefore, cannot claim as mine, even when I enjoy certain aspects of it (e.g., the music or literature of Afro-Americans).

As a school child, I remember being rudely awakened to the reality of class distinctions while being bullied by my colleagues who thought that I felt that I was better than they were because I spoke and dressed differently and came to school with money. This was because my family was considered middle class, when many of my peers came from working-class families. Needless to say I was soon changed from that school to a "better" school with "better" people, that is, other middle-class "Coloured" children. It was much later when I started associating with white people at university and at my training hospital, that I realised that the experience of being a middle-class "Coloured" person was very different from that of being a middle-class white person. Our differences in color dictated that we should also belong to different social classes because my white counterpart had better access to the work that received higher pay than either my parents or I had. She was also likely to have had a better education than I did, and therefore, to have had a better chance of gaining access to tertiary educational institutions than I did. In fact I clearly remember a white, middle-class female professor telling the few "nonwhites" in my nursing class that we were privileged to be allowed to be in the university's nursing school at all, and therefore, that we should refrain from complaining when our white classmates were provided with free transportation to and from classes while most of us were not. Thus, by marking a distinction between the white students and ourselves, the dominant classist and racist structures were explained and perpetuated. My personal feelings of confusion at this time were intensified as the likelihood of ever finding a niche in an increasingly exclusive society diminished exponentially.

I was unable to establish common ground with most of the white students in my nursing class, even when they did deign to socialise with the remainder of us who were "nonwhite." It was around this time that I befriended an African classmate, and although this was my first association with a black person and I made many a racial faux pas, we developed a close professional and social alliance. She invited me to a meeting of the Black Students Society, to which I acquiesced with trepidation as the group was known to have links with the then-banned African National Congress, and my association with the group could have had very negative consequences (i.e., social censure, imprisonment). The experience was consciousness raising at its best; never before had I confronted the inconsistencies of our social system so frankly. At last I was beginning to understand what racial oppression really meant, and how much more it affected African women who were on the lowest rung of the ladder conferring socioeconomic status. Although this new insight gave me an advantage over some of my "Coloured" friends and family, social pressures soon precluded attendance at these "subversive" meetings, and once again I disappeared into that social cocoon that excuses our ignorance, complacency, and cowardice under the guise of preoccupation with other "more important" issues, such as my studies.

From then on, the issue of racial discrimination remained dormant until a few years later when I began attending a Canadian university as a graduate student. Shortly after arriving, I realised how guilty I felt about being a nonwhite South African in Canada. It was assumed that I was very knowledgeable on the subject of racism. In fact I was trying my hardest to ignore the subject because it made me realise that I could not identify with the majority of black South Africans or their struggle toward nationalism. Because of media and social restrictions in South Africa, I actually know very little about the experiences of racial oppression of black South Africans. I regret not having tried to learn more when I was in South Africa.

Although I have felt guilty for having been privileged socioeconomically, I am also aware that I am different, that many of my concerns differ from those of most Africans because of our racially based separation, and that however different we may be, our concerns are equally legitimate. I am also aware that merely reversing the existing political and racial power relations will have few benefits for oppressed, intermediate people like myself, as many will still be underrepresented socially and politically. This will continue for as long as we refuse to restructure the social relations that now separate us. We need to identify common goals in spite of the socially constructed racial, cultural, and class barriers that strive to deny the legitimacy of our concerns.

In South Africa whoever is not white is considered black. But within this broad racial category, there are other groups that have been identified collectively as African (also used interchangeably as black), "Coloured," and Indian. This classification becomes problematic when individuals are not easily identified or self-identified, as belonging to a specific racial group. It assumes a homogeneity that is not borne out by personal experience.

Because apartheid is based on physical appearances, people who are "more black" than others may be discriminated against by fairer skinned persons based on varying degrees of physical aberrations from the ideal of blond hair and blue eyes. Alternatively, the current move toward Afrocentricity means that, within the "Coloured" population, those who are fairer than the rest are also ostracised. Little girls and boys soon learn that being fairer or darker than your counterparts determines your degree of social acceptability. Sometimes these distinctions are made within their families. It is not uncommon for an adult to remark that one sibling is more attractive than another because they have straighter hair or fairer skin. More often, though, the distinctions are learned when children begin attending school or enter other social arenas. I still have occasional nightmares about my primary school days when I was bullied and labeled a "play-white" because my sisters and I were fairer and spoke differently than the other "Coloured" children. But the consequences of such discrimination extend far beyond the realm of dreams.

Being dismissed for not being black enough denies the fact that many of us *do* want to know more about our roots. It devalues our experiences, and hence, denies us our place in the world by too narrowly defining the meaning of being mixed race and of being racially oppressed. Being denied a place within the rest of the population, balances us precariously on the brink of invisibility. This is ironic because apartheid law (namely, the Population Registration Act of 1950), by classifying us according to our skin color, hair texture, and lip thickness, suggested that we were highly visible. Although this and similar apartheid laws have been dismantled, such thinking still determines social relations in South Africa. Racism continues to divide not only people of different colors, but also those of the same gender within the same racial group.

The phenomenon of multiple divisions extends to other forms of discrimination too, based on class, culture, ethnicity, age, religion, and heterosexism. This makes it difficult for members of any group or community to identify central concerns and common goals, and therefore, to organize. Thus, by obscuring common class and gender interests, apartheid has succeeded in its goal to "divide and conquer."

It is significant, therefore, that within this context, groups (such as women's collectives) have emerged that resist the status quo. Although political resistance groups are not new in South African history, the androcentricity inherent in their agenda alerted women to the need to redefine social change in terms of our existence as the largest oppressed group in the country. Women throughout South Africa representing a mosaic of racial, class, cultural, occupational, political, and religious groups have organized under the feminist banner to transform the oppressive social structures with which we live. Despite the aforementioned obstacles, central themes and common goals have been identified based on our only commonality, gender oppression as women.

Perhaps more so than in other countries we have had to expand definitions of feminism to include, not only gender-based oppression, but also racial oppression. Even broader definitions and categories of privilege, oppression, and exploitation emerge when we acknowledge the interaction of race and gender with class and other distinctions (such as age, ethnic, heterosexist, and religious differences). Hence, black women experience privilege and exploitation differently from black men and differently from white women, as victims of racism, sexism, and classism. On the individual and collective level, South African women have had to determine the relationship between racism and sexism, and how that impinges on our experiences and behavior. Where theories on class, race, and other power relations ignore the never-never land in which women of indeterminate class, race, or culture reside, feminism internationally, but particularly South African feminism, needs to explore and define these concerns as the only resistance group that represents an extensive cross-section of our society.

Very little literature is available on the experience of being "marginalized within the margins," that is, on the experience of not being acknowledged as a significant part of the "others," although one is categorised and oppressed within those broad margins. It disturbs me that with the strides being made toward "liberation" of blacks, it is only the needs of the African majority that are being addressed and not those of other "nonwhites" within its ranks. Without minimizing the significance of the oppression of Africans, I want to stress the importance of also addressing the needs of the less visible minorities before true liberation can be attained. For example, where discussions on black–white experiences include only the experiences of whites as oppressors and of blacks as oppressed, there is a need to include those who are not necessarily classified as black or white, but who are also oppressed by racist systems. For instance, in North America, an aboriginal, Hispanic, immigrant, or mixed-race woman should be able to discuss experiences of racist oppression without having to use the voice of African Americans with whom she may have little in common. More specifically this could include providing educational, political, and social opportunities for mixed-race persons to explore the meanings of their experiences, and to share knowledge of their racial and cultural heritage. As feminists, we are in the unique position to do this using nonhierarchical research methods for the exploration of experiences, the development of theory, and most importantly, social transformation by reconstructing the social relations that determine our places in society.

The generation of feminist theory within the South African context needs to go beyond those used in Europe and North America that have been criticised for their ethnocentrism. bell hooks and Mary Childers criticises the tendency of white, middle-class women to locate gender as more privileged than all other forms of difference.[1] Furthermore, while discussions of difference within white feminism are primarily concerned with differences between women and men, they fail to account for the fact that white feminists have addressed the concerns of non-existent universal women. As a result, issues such as racism, classism, and heterosexism, which may also transform women's oppression, are either subsumed or ignored. This view relegates the simultaneous discussions of black women's experiences of race, class, imperialism, and gender in black–white difference debates to the arena of "black deviance," that is, as exceptions to the white female norm. Consequently, white feminists have addressed the concerns of women as a whole, whereas black women alone have addressed the concerns of racially oppressed women. Instead of identifying white feminism as the adversary, as has been the trend, however, we need to confront the tendency to universalize *any* racial perspective as the norm.

I prefer a stance whereby we acknowledge our commonalities and differences, and the diffuse, constantly changing nature of discourse and practice. Women need to shape political discourse by developing more inclusive definitions while acknowledging the specific categories that describe our experiences. We need to explore all categories of "other" and what it means to be situated as such. We also need to explore the social construction of "other" in terms of "race," gender, class, sexual orientation, and culture. In identifying diversity and commonality among women, we need to identify the roles of men within such discourse because racially oppressed women often share interests and experiences with their male counterparts that are dissimilar to those of white women and men. Therefore, feminists need to break away from the fixed and oppositional identities that separate us from those who are similarly oppressed. We need to challenge the necessary use of labels and categories, to look at the political implications of naming our experiences, and to expose the social and ideological contexts within which names, labels, and categories of identity are produced. In Canada, for example, such a study could explore the meaning of being an aboriginal, immigrant or racially mixed woman, and how being referred to as "other" is related to experiences of race, sex, age, class, culture, and ethnicity.

21

Ethnic Transgressions: Confessions of an Assimilated Jew

Laurie Shrage

My aunt, who is now in her eighties, tells the following story. When her daughter was about six, she came home one day and told her parents that she didn't like the girl down the street because she was "jewith." My aunt says she was rather taken aback by her daughter's remark, to which she responded: "But Lisa, don't you know? You're Jewish too."

My mother-in-law used to tell the following story. When her daughter, Elizabeth, was around four, my mother-in-law discovered that Elizabeth had been telling their neighbors and friends that she was Catholic. According to my mother-in-law, her daughter formed her religious identity in the following way. Once when Elizabeth was visiting the larger extended family, she asked her cousin why she was not allowed to eat certain foods. Her cousin explained that it was because she was Jewish. Evidently Elizabeth reasoned that, because she was allowed to eat the forbidden foods, she must not be Jewish, and because she wasn't Jewish, she must be Catholic.

As the child of assimilated, nonobservant Jews, my discoveries of self were similarly comical and confusing. As I describe elsewhere,[1] my first-grade teacher is the first person I can remember who revealed to me that I was a Jew. This came about during an awkward show-and-tell presentation in which I attempted to repeat something my mother had told me. In one of her nostalgic moments, my mother sent me to school with a plate of hamentashen (a cookie made to celebrate Purim) and told me some story to go along with it. Evidently, in my mother's narration, I misheard *jewels* for *Jews*, and thus the story I told had to do with the former. My teacher caught my error, and in correcting my story she explained to the class what Jews were—and I was the primary means by which she did this.

I grew up in a very waspy part of northern California in the 60s. Once when one of my Brooklyn cousins was visiting us, she told me our household was too weird for her. She happened to be visiting us during some religious holiday (I can't remember which one). Now looking back on this, I think she found it strange that our daily routine was not in the least interrupted or changed during this holiday, and that we did not engage in any ritual or connect with other Jews in any way. At the time, I found her discomfort and proclaimed need to be with other Jews strange. I vaguely remember that my mother somehow arranged for her to go to a temple or be with a Jewish family during the holiday. What I learned from this and some other experiences was that, for some Jews, we were not Jews.

But strangely, to all non-Jews, we were Jews. I've been told by non-Jews (once I've indicated in some way that I am Jewish) that I look Jewish; and some non-Jewish men have told me how much they like Jewish girls, and how my Jewishness explains their perception that I talk too much, or that I can eat and talk at the same time, or some such thing. My college professors were often surprised to find out that I was a first-generation college student, that I was a financial-aid student, and that my parents thought my becoming a teacher was boring—they hoped I might aspire to something more glamourous, such as a stewardess. And my friends usually assume that my choice of a Jewish marital partner must have pleased my mother. Actually she always encouraged me to seek non-Jewish partners, having been limited by her own parents, but I rebelled.

A Polish-American I know tells the following story. Growing up in Poland, when he was asked what he was, he knew he was supposed to answer "Jewish." To be Jewish was to distinguish oneself from being "Polish," and vice versa. When he came to America, he was often asked what he was. The answer "Jewish" didn't seem to work. Eventually, he found out that the correct answer in this context was "Polish." Also, he learned that in giving this answer he did not erase his Jewishness—here he could be both.

After my own discovery, around the age of six, that the correct answer for me to the question "What are you?" was "Jewish," I started to wonder about what this attribute "Jewish" meant. Responding, in part, to my identity confusion, my mother decided that I ought to attend Jewish Sunday school so that I might learn something about my Jewish heritage. (I was about nine at this time.) To my surprise, the people at this religious school talked a lot about God. What did God have to do with being Jewish, I worried? Didn't they know God didn't exist, as my mother had so logically explained? After my first day of Sunday School, I told my mother that if being Jewish meant believing in God, then I wasn't Jewish. She told me it didn't mean that. Then what did it mean? Unfortunately, I never found out from attending Sunday school (I dropped out after the first month) or from my parents.

Being Jewish, at different historical moments and in different places, has been variously understood as being of a particular "race," "religion," or "ethnicity." In contemporary America it seems to be mostly a matter of "ethnicity." Ethnicities usually have something to do with the way we live, the values we hold, the customs we follow, the foods we eat, and the dialects we speak. I have several books that I call my "how to be Jewish" books. When I want to celebrate the Jewish holidays with my children, when I want to prepare Jewish foods, when I want to understand some Jewish expression, I now look them up in my books. Because I and my children are Jews to others—which is to say that we are Other to non-Jews—I want my children to associate this otherness with something other than pure otherness. This then is how I am dealing with the issue of difference. It indeed seems to be the favored solution of many—to claim one's otherness and then be the Other adequately or convincingly, that is, in a way that doesn't betray perhaps internalized anti-Semitism or racism, or inauthenticity. Had I married a non-Jew, it might have been different. I might have passed as something else or passed my children off as something else. But these assimilationist strategies seem less attractive than they must have to my parents' generation.

Although racial and ethnic assimilation, acculturation, and passing have problematic consequences and causes, the existing alternatives to assimilation are equally problematic. For persons like myself, the preferred alternative seems to be "finding my roots," learning about "my people," practicing "my traditions," or, in short, constructing a self that is more racially and ethnically pure. This is problematic to me for several reasons. One, many aspects of the traditions and roots I am supposed to seek appear patriarchal, misogynist, homophobic, and even racist or elitist toward non-Jews. Two, to seek to be more purely or thoroughly Jewish is to deny the part of me that grew up enjoying coloring Easter eggs or listening to gospel music. It also leads to seeing my upbringing as somehow deficient, shameful, or culturally and ethnically deprived. And three, to be more purely Jewish seems not at all to resist anti-Semitism, for the construction and reification of the Jew, as others have pointed out, may itself be a product of anti-Semitism.

Yet, to allow the Jewish part of my background to be crowded out by some intervening autobiographical and social circumstances communicates to others (especially to those to whom I look, act, "smell," or otherwise appear Jewish) the acceptance and internalization of the devaluation of things Jewish. Also, this "gentilization" of myself might appear opportunistic and selfish. It will look as if I am suppressing or deforming myself to profit individually in a system that oppresses my kind.

For people like myself, assimilation, acculturation, heterogeneity, and syncretism are not a choice, but something chosen for us by our parents (who then are often surprised by how ignorant their children are of their ethnic origins). For us the choice appears to be either to assimilate further into the dominant culture or to assimilate back to the communities our parents, and perhaps grandparents, rejected. Yet, while seeking to discover and express my Jewish "essence" in order to connect with a particular community is problematic in the ways indicated above, seeing myself as neither Jewish nor Gentile, that is, in ethnically blind terms, is also problematic. For as Patricia Williams argues in regard to blacks who do not identify as "black,"

> Neutrality is from this perspective a suppression, an institutionalization of psychic taboos as much as segregation was the institutionalization of physical boundaries. What the middle-class, propertied, upwardly mobile black striver must do, to accommodate a race-neutral world view, is to become an invisible black, a phantom black, by avoiding the label "black." . . . The words of race are like windows into the most private vulnerable parts of the self; the world looks in and the world will know, by the awesome, horrific revelation of a name.[2]

To echo Williams, what a person with Jewish ancestors must do to accommodate an ethnically neutral identity is to become an invisible Jew, a phantom Jew. In other words, because being Jewish carries a stigma, not to announce one's Jewishness is paramount to concealing it—to keeping it in the closet, so to speak. Yet, this socially construed act of concealing one's self is an act that serves to perpetuate an anti-Semitic social order—a system of power and privilege that serves to obliterate Jews and Jewishness. It is also pointless, as Williams's passage suggests, for the world will eventually find one's Jewish self because of the mere fact that there exist designations or names for it. In short, neither the choice to closet one's Jewishness and thereby assimilate further into the dominant social order, nor the choice to spring the Jewish self out of the closet for the world to observe and know, offers possibilities of resistance for partially assimilated, mixed-background people.

Naomi Zack has recently proposed that people who have both designated black and white ancestors should create mixed or hybrid identities that recognize their heterogeneous ethnic and racial origins.[3] For given that assimilation (identifying as white) and difference (identifying as black) are problematic choices for people of mixed racial backgrounds, Zack argues that it is unfair and damaging to such people to make them choose. Instead, people of mixed backgrounds should be allowed to identify (legally and informally) as persons of mixed race—as persons who are part black and white, or perhaps gray.

Although there is a need as Zack and others have shown to disrupt and denaturalize American racial and ethnic categories, deploying the metaphor of "mixing" categories may not be the most effective in this regard. Mixing suggests that there is some more pure stuff to be "mixed," and thus is consistent with racial ideologies that posit pure racial kinds. Though mixing recognizes the miscibility of different human kinds, the quality of the mixtures will still be determined by the quality of the stuff mixed. That is, the establishment of mixed identities may do little to challenge the valuations placed on different human kinds. Thus while claiming a mixed identity may marginally improve the treatment of mixed individuals, it will do little for unmixed people of the stigmatized races and ethnicities. Moreover, the recognition of mixed-race people may naturalize yet another racial group in a way that is divisive of economically and politically oppressed communities. Zack recognizes these aspects of positing mixed identities, but holds that racial identities and identifications serve important and meaningful functions in American society and will not be easily abolished. She thus proposes establishing mixed identities as an intermediate, temporary, or transitional remedy for the psychological harm and social injustice that our racial system imposes on persons of mixed backgrounds.

Perhaps there are other solutions. At least two other options present themselves. The first is the option Zack recognizes but dismisses for being perhaps unrealistic: the option of eschewing all racial and some ethnic identifications. The other option is that of claiming more than one racial or ethnic classification: of being *multi*racial or *multi*ethnic. This option is similar to the option of claiming a "mixed" identity, but it is different in the following way. The multiracial individual is not part black and white, but is both black and white. The multiethnic individual is not part-Jewish and part-Gentile, but is both a Jew and a Gentile. Moreover, multiracialism does not lead to an invention of new human kinds but calls our attention to areas of overlap between different categories. And finally, being multiracial and multiethnic may challenge pernicious customs of differentially valuing human kinds in the following way: if a black person can be white and a white person can be black, then black and white persons cannot have different degrees of moral worth by virtue of being black or white.

One might argue that under the current system of racial and ethnic classification in the United States, these multiple identities make little sense because American racial and ethnic categories are mutually exclusive, and thus multiple racial designations are contradictory designations. But the problem with mixed identities may be that they make too much sense given the existing systems of racial and ethnic classification, and thus they may fail to challenge the logic of these systems. Multiracial or multiethnic identities also may fail to challenge many pernicious aspects of the contemporary U.S. racial order. For multiple designations do not challenge the apparent necessity of the designations themselves or the apparent existence of racially differentiable human kinds.

Judith Butler has argued that identity categories are "sites of necessary trouble."[4] By communicating our membership in a particular category (lesbian, woman, black, Jew), we do not necessarily liberate or expose some intrinsic quality of ourselves, but rather we perpetuate the naturalization of categories that are themselves the byproducts of unliberatory discourses. Yet, Butler recognizes, like Williams, that we cannot simply refuse these identities, for such refusals perpetuate systems of power that oppress those subsumed under these categories. Nevertheless, our choices are not limited to either adopting or refusing these identities. For Butler, the challenge is, "How to use the sign and avow its temporal contingency at once?"[5] In other words, how can we assume these identities in ways that reflect or expose their nonnaturalness and historical specificity?

Writing about gender and sexual identity, Butler considers how particular identity categories become naturalized. She states that one way

> heterosexuality naturalizes itself [is] through setting up certain illusions of continuity between sex, gender, and desire. When Aretha Franklin sings, "you make me feel like a natural woman," she seems at first to suggest that some natural potential of her biological sex is actualized by her participation in the cultural position of "woman" as object of heterosexual recognition. Something in her "sex" is thus expressed by her "gender" which is then fully known and consecrated within the heterosexual scene. There is no breakage, no discontinuity between "sex" as biological facticity and essence, or between gender and sexuality. Although Aretha appears to be all too glad to have her naturalness confirmed, she also seems fully and paradoxically mindful that confirmation is never guaranteed, that the effect of naturalness is only achieved as a consequence of that moment of heterosexual recognition.[6]

Butler then goes on to consider how these illusions of continuity between sex, gender, and desire can be broken, so that we might glimpse how women are made by the operation of heterosexual norms, rather than born in some natural fashion with natural heterosexual desire. If the illusions of continuity are created in part by socially conventional expressions of biological sex and sexual desire, then these illusions might be disrupted by socially transgressive expressions of biological sex and sexual desire. Such transgressive performances are what are typically called "drag" and engaging in drag is indeed what Butler recommends both to claim particular identities and simultaneously subvert the very ideologies that produce them. For example, Butler asks us to imagine Aretha Franklin singing the same song to a female "impersonator," or to imagine Franklin singing this song to her, that is Butler herself.

Following Butler, we might try to see how particular systems of race and ethnicity in the United States naturalize themselves by setting up certain illusions of continuity between skin pigment, genealogy, race, ethnicity, character, behavior, ability, aspirations, dispositions, and so on. How might these illusions be interrupted so that we might glimpse how blacks and whites, Jews and Gentiles, are made by the operation of racial and ethnic norms, rather than born naturally possessing their notorious racial and ethnic traits? If these illusions of continuity are created, in part, by conforming to socially conventional interpretations of skin pigment and genealogy, then these illusions might be destroyed by attempts at transgressive interpretations of these facts. In this way, racial and ethnic drag might consist in blacks with one or more white ancestors taking up the mannerisms, personal styles, and vocations associated with whites, and "whites" with one or more black ancestors taking up the mannerisms, personal styles, and vocations associated with blacks.

When designated white persons[7] wear Afros or African clothing, and when designated black persons lighten and straighten their hair or wear formal European-style suits, we often see such people as confused, unauthentic, and, in the former kind of case, perhaps ridiculous. But why is this? Does the first kind of person represent the pathetic attempt of a "nonethnic" person to "go ethnic," and does the second kind of case represent the reverse? And why shouldn't whites "go ethnic" and those designated ethnic "go white"? One answer that comes to mind is that when whites "go ethnic" they engage in inappropriate cultural appropriation, and when ethnics whiten themselves they capitulate to hegemonic white values that threaten to obliterate nonwhite ethnicities.

When women of Asian descent have eyelid surgery and dark-pigmented persons use cosmetics to lighten their skin, these acts reflect the cultural hegemony of pernicious aesthetic and moral values that oppress many persons. And when New Age European Americans perform American Indian rituals, their acts reflect the illegitimate assumption of a particular type of cultural authority. But perhaps not all acts of "cross-dressing" and cross-behaving reflect and reproduce existing patterns of hegemony and marginalization. Moreover, our prudishness about ethnic-crossing places persons whose family backgrounds and personal lives are not ethnically pure in a bind. For example, Patricia Williams relates an incident where a particular white man and a particular black woman wondered if she, a law professor, saw herself as black. She states, "I heard the same-different words addressed to me, a perceived white-male-socialized black woman, as a challenge to mutually exclusive categorization. . . ."[8] Those who see her as predominantly a law professor see her blackness as irrelevant or suppressed, while those who see her as a black woman see her as an odd kind of law professor. In each case, her blackness or her professional status, respectively, are in constant jeopardy. De-essentializing racial and ethnic categories would alleviate the need to excuse or explain to ourselves some perceived crossings.

Commenting on the cross-gendered behavior of some lesbians and gay men, Butler states,

> It is important to recognize the ways in which heterosexual norms reappear within gay identities . . . but that they are *not* for that reason *determined* by them. They are running commentaries on those naturalized positions as well, parodic replays and resignifications. . . . But to be constituted or structured in part by the very heterosexual norms by which gay people are oppressed is not, I repeat, to be claimed or determined by those structures. And it is not necessary to think of such heterosexual constructs as the pernicious intrusion of "the straight mind," one that must be rooted out in its entirety. . . . The parodic replication and resignification of heterosexual constructs within non-heterosexual frames brings into relief the utterly constructed status of the so-called original. . . . The more the act is expropriated, the more the heterosexual claim to originality is exposed as illusory.[9]

Butler's comments might lead us to ask: are there ways for designated whites to "go ethnic" and for designated ethnics to "whiten" themselves that might call attention to the constructed status of whiteness and blackness? Can these transgressive ethnic crossings subvert pernicious racial norms and ideologies? Converging on a similar issue, Williams states:

> I think that the hard work of a nonracist sensibility is the boundary crossing, from safe circle into wilderness: the testing of boundary, the consecration of sacrilege. . . . The transgression is dizzyingly intense, a reminder of what it is to be alive. It is a sinful pleasure, this willing transgression of a line, which takes one into new awareness, a secret, lonely, and tabooed world—to survive transgression is terrifying and addictive. To know that everything has changed and yet that nothing has changed; and in leaping the chasm of this impossible division of self, a discovery of the self surviving, still well, still strong, and, as a curious consequence, renewed.[10]

By crossing the boundaries of ethnic and racial classification and incorporating the Other into ourselves, we do not necessarily betray, distort, or eradicate some more racially and ethnically pure self. When I light Hanukkah candles with my children one week and the next week decorate a Christmas tree with them, I am not claimed or determined (to borrow Butler's language) by the structures Jew and Gentile; I am deploying these constructs within a nonorthodox frame. And perhaps the sight of a Christmas tree, set under a Menorah and decorated with recycled dreidels, may draw attention to the temporal contingency of this sign. What this suggests is that we might usefully subject to critical reflection the discomfort we feel when a person's behavior and self-expression challenge the mutually exclusive categorization (to borrow Williams's words) of races, ethnicities, genders, and sexualities. In this regard, we need to distinguish when our discomfort results from crossings that indeed seem to perpetuate racism, heterosexism, and so on, and when our discomfort results from crossings that merely challenge our own essentialized notions of race, ethnicity, and gender. In short, it may be that some transgressions are destabilizing of gender, racial, sexual, and ethnic norms while others are not, and we need to be able to recognize the difference.

22

Life After Race

Naomi Zack

Microdiversity and the Life of the Mind

Sometimes, as with the Holocaust in Nazi Germany or Negro chattel slavery in the American South, the wrong thing is done on a great scale and subsequent generations are left with a terrible legacy of historical error. When the error is still not fully recognized by the majority or the dominant groups and individuals in society, those who must live under the error, with the knowledge that it is an error, are forced into hypothetical and theoretical modes of existence. If they are religious or mystical, they may retreat to a spiritual path. But if they are secular intellectuals, they can correct the error in the ordinary life of the mind. The present degree of intellectual freedom in American academic life is helpful to the secular project. Ideas formed in reaction to historical error can be written and discussed, without, as in other parts of the world, the necessity that intellectuals become political activists or revolutionaries. Writing like this can see the light of day without dire penalty and attempts can be made to correct the error within arts and letters. However, it is important not to forget that most American writing about and within microdiversity takes place in the life of the mind. Therefore, I want to introduce some philosophical reflections on what that means.

The term 'the life of the mind' has an irritating idealism associated with it in two senses: that such a life is better or more pure or noble than the lives that most human beings in fact live; that such a life takes place in an unreal realm. As to whether such a life is better than ordinary forms of life, the only reasonable answer is, "It depends." In the case of mixed-race existence, the life of the mind may be the only possible life at this time in American history, so in that sense it is better because life is better than nonlife (given all other things equal). As to the unreality of the place where the life of the mind is lived, it is real enough to philosophers and intellectuals generally.

In this "unreal" but real sense, the life of the mind is time spent by human beings writing, reading, thinking, and talking about a subject in a systematic way. These activities can take place privately (alone, except perhaps for talking), socially (among family and friends for no immediate gain), or publically (in some forum where the main relationships are formed in consequence of the activities in question). If these activities are important enough and one is prepared to make nonhedonistic commitments and develop bookish skills, then their public pursuit becomes professional. In the present (academic) context, this means either that one is officially connected to a college or university, or to publishers, or both.

Let's leave aside the fact that intellectuals are human beings in some same ways that nonintellectuals are, because that fact is presently well taken within the parameters of the contemporary scholarly triumvirate of Race, Class, and Gender. The contemporary (postmodern) scholar is expected to bring herself into her scholarly work, if not through direct autobiography, or in scholarship about a vulnerable group to which she belongs, then at least with an awareness that there are vulnerable groups in history and present society. Counter to that expectation, I want to argue, somewhat self-reflexively, that self-invention in contemporary intellectual emancipatory discussion, generally, and in the subject of mixed race, particularly, requires an identity that is not at all like anyone's ordinary life identity.

To write about one's mixed-race identity is as much to invent oneself or one's racial group, as to describe them. One invents oneself, on paper, as part of a theoretical inquiry, because outside of one's activities as an intellectual, that is, outside of the life of the mind, one has no secure racial existence. Mixed race is not recognized as an identity or form of culture by those individuals—the majority— who believe that they are racially pure. And, predictably, the self-invention of mixed-race identity is precarious.

First, mixed-race individuals, in America at least, are nonwhite and therefore members of minority groups that are not as privileged as the dominant white group in society. Insofar as the life of the mind lived by intellectuals requires a certain privilege or the relief from scrambling for food–clothing–shelter goods of survival, it is statistically more difficult for nonwhites to live it. Second, the self that is being invented in writing about mixed race is precarious because it cannot be decisively confirmed to exist outside of one's activities as an intellectual. Indeed, this lack of confirmation outside of the life of the mind is what may morally motivate the intellectual self-invention of mixed race: We have a right and certainly a need to be recognized for what we are racially—if anyone is anything racially.

Thus, the mixed-race self that invents itself on paper is a refugee to the life of the mind: Only on the printed page at this time can one begin to lay down the parameters of mixed-race identity and explore and criticize them. Outside one's professional life, mixed-race identity flashes on and off depending on whom one is interacting with. And administratively, within one's professional life, the record-keeping apparatus of the institution in question will most likely recategorize one in terms of the most disadvantaged or "under-represented" racial group that one has checked off on the relevant demographic form. Administrative compliance with Affirmative Action legal directives and the resultant financial rewards and humanitarian praise depend on such recategorization.

The foregoing uncertainties about identity mean that mixed-race identity can only be developed and preserved if one can develop and preserve one's intellectual identity, and that often requires success in the academic community. However, at each stage of academic progress the dearly coveted goal—be it a B.A., an M.A., a Ph.D., a first job, tenure, a first article published, a book, a fellowship, etc.—at each newly won achievement, one finds that the major problems of one's life have not been solved as one had hoped but that one has merely stepped into a new arena of struggle. And the dangers of one's purchase on the academic ledges are magnified, with less peer support, in one's existence as a writer who gets published in the hopes of being read, not just by anyone, but by the most intelligent and sensitive readers available, by one's imagined worst critics who will close the book or the journal with a sense of having been informed in an interesting way. So the mixed-race intellectual who is a refugee to the life of the mind could at any time lose her place, be found not to deserve it, or fail to advance to the next indicated position. That is, like anyone else in the intellectual community, she could lose her living as an intellectual (tenure not withstanding), but unlike anyone else, she would thereby also lose her racial identity.

There is very little security in this life of the mind. But, if one has a taste for what Thoreau called big conversation—and if one can make oneself heard, the stakes are high. The conversation is big because on one end it begins with the beginning of the whole human written record, and no one knows how long it will be to the other end. Of course, no one can think or read or write the whole of recorded history. One chooses as much as one can deal with within the systematicity of a discipline and one's own specialization within that. Even if one's discipline is not historical by consensus, it will nonetheless have a history that is situated within the larger history of the written record. This written record is conversational because it is open-ended, inconclusive, and constantly subject to revision. Voices come and go, the interpretation of past and present voices is never complete, and parts of the record get ignored or deleted. Still, the goal is to add one's own voice to that record, "for what it's worth." (Although whether, if one succeeds, it will have all been "worthwhile" can be no more than a personal decision.)

Philosophical Problems with 'Race'

The term 'mixed race' seems self-contradictory once it becomes clear that the term 'race' always connotes purity. Not only do racial populations need to have common traits to qualify as racial but when race is taken seriously, racial mixture is viewed as a problem. And that problem of mixed race which is a contradiction in terms and a contradiction in the facts of racial reality, leads to unavoidable trouble. In the final analysis all racial identities rest on ideologies that require energies of determination and control— of will—to maintain. One by-product of this kind of resolve around racial identity is an exaltation that seems "spiritual," in its own right, without recourse to non-natural agency. In the end, 'race' often comes down to something having to do with 'soul.' Those who think they can live honorably with that connection, because it is frequently associated with reactions against oppression, need to reflect on Alfred Rosenberg and his work, *The Myth of the Twen-*

tieth Century. Rosenberg is known for his claim that "soul is race viewed from within." However, Rosenberg was the main ideologist of the National Socialist Party under the Third Reich, and even Hitler found him an embarrassment.[1]

Because race means pure race, the opposite of race is not racelessness but racial impurity, or what I have here called microdiversity. The next step after microdiversity is racelessness. Racelessness is the next freeing stage after microdiversity and my continuing work in racial theory will address that subject.

I propose that we write ourselves out of race as a means of constructing racelessness or removing the constructions of race. And our language itself, or at least English, underscores such a move. The European word for race—in the sense of genealogical forebears—is a homonym of the word for a written mark, namely "line."[2] That is, given that race has no objective biological foundation, one must look to language for its origins and undoing. This homonymity of "line" is deeper than a pun if it is taken as a clue that language as a locus of race is, in an important dimension, written language. For example, when nineteenth-century pseudoscientists wanted to rationalize 'race' they produced learned texts; when the Harlem Renaissance writers glorified American Negro life, they wrote novels, poems, and plays; when contemporary racial theorists look for a foundation for African identity in a racial sense, they turn to writing.[3]

History has taught us too well that such lines can be genocidally erased in reality. But suppose one performs the erasure beforehand, in writing? Then, the targets of genocide, the objects of it, will have been removed. But, of course, only further written and spoken discussion on this topic can determine whether that would be a scorched earth policy or an (intellectual) opportunity for more fully human reality to rise from its own ashes.

Western philosophy is itself an historical culture that continually puts common sense on trial. When the ordinary American concept of race is held to this fire, the only kind of philosophical meaning retained by 'race' is a pragmatic one. I'd like to begin to show how we can write away 'race,' with an explanation of how 'race' evaporates in contact with philosophic meaning. Of course, philosophers hardly agree on the meaning of 'meaning' but there have been, since ancient Athens, several powerful philosophies of meaning, to which even their opponents concede plausibility. While there is no consensus, even among philosophers, favoring the disuse of terms that are philosophically bereft of meaning, the lack of such conceptual support is another reason to dispense with a term that is already a problem on other grounds.

Aristotle and his medieval followers connected meaning with doctrines of essence. According to this tradition, things are what they are because they contain the essences of the kinds to which they belong. Cats and trees, for example, have cat and tree essences. When the names of things are defined, their essential properties are described. By the time nineteenth-century scientists of race constructed taxonomies of human racial difference, the philosophical theory of essence, as a claim about the nature of reality, was long dead because no scientist had ever observed or measured an "essence"—of anything. However, this did not deter the nineteenth-century scientists of race from positing the existence of racial essences in a hierarchy with the white race at the top. Each race was (unempirically) held to have an "essence" or "genius" that was present in every one of its individual members in such a way that this essence was transmitted through human blood over subsequent generations. That alchemy of racial essence entailed that in any case of "mixture" between high and low, the "essence" of the "lower" race always predominated in the offspring.[4] That is, racial essentialism supported the one-drop rule.

The nonsense of racial essentialism, in the above context, is presently transparent, because of the absence of essences, and because racial differences are not literally differences in blood.[5] Still, terms for things other than races that were presumed to have essences, like cats and trees, have retained their meaning. The next relevant, and to this day plausible, philosophical account of meaning is nominalism.

John Locke shaped the modern form of nominalist theories of meaning. Locke held that what had been thought to be essences were human ideas, in the minds of human beings and constructed by them, with no unchanging and unavoidable correspondence to the way reality itself was divided. Locke even went so far as to claim that the different kinds of things in the world, such as plants and animals, were themselves arbitrarily imposed on the world by human thought. According to Locke, the meaning of a term describing a natural kind would be its definition.[6]

Although many philosophers accept some Lockean account of meaning, the arbitrary quality of Locke's extreme nominalism is usually modified to ensure a kind of empirical sensitivity of the language, particularly when a nominalist theory of meaning is applied to scientific terms. The traditional distinction between *intension* and *extension* does much of this work: The definition of a term is its intension; the class of objects, each one of which can be picked out by the definition, is the term's extension; and intension determines extension. Typically, the intension specifies what properties have to be present if an object is to belong to the extension of a term. Some terms may refer to groups of objects that do not all share the same properties but which have "family resemblances" to one another, for example, the words "chair" and "game"; in those cases, the intension lists the relevant properties of objects as alternatives (e.g., chairs have four legs, or they may not have any legs at all but people sit on them; games are forms of organized play done outdoors or indoors, or they are serious and done for their own sake, etc.). Furthermore, definitions by means of intension and extension cannot be vacuous or circular: it is not empirically sensitive to define a cat as an animal with only cats for parents, or wood as a stuff that is similar to other stuff called "wood."[7]

The problem with 'race' according to empirical nominalist meaning standards is that there is no non-vacuous and non-circular intensional meaning of the term. Take the American case of black and white race. Most Americans would be confident in their ability to distinguish between blacks and whites and would assume that there are real, factual differences between them. Suppose we grant, on the basis of the information given to the United States census, if nothing else, that the terms 'black' and 'white' do have extensions. Then, these terms should have intensions as well, which entails that there are some defining characteristics that all black Americans have in common, and likewise for whites. But there are no such defining or "necessary and sufficient" characteristics. The visual and cultural markers for membership in the black race differ too greatly for there to be any physical traits shared by all black individuals, and likewise for whites. There are, of course, genes that underlie physical characteristics that people associate with racial membership but the association of these characteristics with racial membership is determined by history and culture so it is no surprise that most members of the black group have genes that are racially significant for membership in the white group.

Biologists and anthropologists refer to races—and they are increasingly reluctant to do so within the empirical standards of their own sciences—as groups that have more of some inheritable physical traits than other groups. Scientifically, physical racial differences are statistical differences across groups of people and there are no known stable groups that could be called "racially pure."[8] And while there are genes associated with those traits that society has picked out as racial traits, there is nothing racial on a more general biological level, no chromosomal markers for race, as for instance there are for sex.

For sex, the presence of the chromosomal markers named by *XX* and *XY*, can be used to predict and explain the presence of less general sexual traits, such as the genes for ovaries or testicles. Even when XX or XY are imperfectly present or do not conform to the norm, these differences can be used to explain more specific differences from the norm (for example, the absence of external genitalia), in some cases. That is, not only do the overwhelming majority of human beings have either XX or XY in an unambiguous way, but it makes sense scientifically to refer to XX and XY as causes of other conditions.

In contrast to sexual markers, there is nothing on a general scientific level that can be used to explain the presence of the genes for those skin colors, hair textures, or other traits that may be considered "racial" within a culture. That is, the racial aspect of racial traits is a social characteristic and not a physical biological trait as sex is.[9] And yet, "society" is confident that the racial differences it has posited have a physical reality beyond the physical differences among human beings. Racial differences are believed to be more significant and more telling than differences in eye color, or height, for example. How do people manage to make racial distinctions if there really are no racial distinctions? In the case of black and white in America, the effective social mechanism for distinguishing between the two groups can be expressed by this "schema," or "program":

A person, P, is black if P has one black ancestor, any number of generations back. And a person, Q, is white if Q has no black ancestors, any number of generations back, and no other non-white ancestors of other races.

Obviously, this program is meaningful in one sense because Americans have used it effectively (whatever that means) for a very long time. But in the empirical nominalist sense of meaning that has been described earlier, there is a problem with the meaning of race, sociologically, because when people ascribe black or white race to themselves or others, they think they are doing something more than executing the foregoing "program." They think they are saying something physical about the individuals in question. And that belief that race refers to something physical (or biological) is simply false.

The American black and white schema means that race is determined by the race of a person's kin and the race of kin is determined by the race of their kin, and so on. A black person is someone with a black ancestor, who is someone with a black ancestor, and that is the only way in which all black people are racially similar. A white person does not have such a regress true of her. The regress built into the meaning of blackness and the exclusivity built into the meaning of whiteness underscore an unfairness in the very designations themselves. Blacks can never undo or dilute their race; whites have no positive definition of their race apart from its presumed purity. These strong value judgments and norms that are built into the very concepts of blackness and whiteness widen the distance between 'race' and other biological terms that do have nominalist empirical meaning. In effect, the social definitions of blackness and whiteness, and there are no other kinds of definitions of these terms, are more vacuous than defining a cat as an animal with two cat parents or wood as a stuff that resembles other wood.

There is another meaning of 'meaning' in contemporary Philosophy which at first looks as though it could rescue the ordinary concept of race because this kind of meaning, known as 'reference', locates meaning in the world or in what nominalists call extension. According to the "new theory of reference," as developed by Saul Kripke, Hilary Putnam, W. V. Quine, and others, a word for a natural kind of object, such as "cat" or "tree," is a *rigid designator*, something more like a proper name than a word that can be defined by necessary and sufficient conditions that objects must meet. People learn how to use these names of natural kinds over time, within cultures, and their meaning is not "in the head" but literally in the groups of objects to which they are applied.[10] Applying the new theory of reference to 'race', races would be what history has determined them to be and the meaning of the racial words "black" or "white" would be those people who are correctly designated by the words. What this would amount to is that an individual is a black person or a white person according to which group she has been assigned in her culture. However, this construction of meaning merely begs the questions raised by microdiversity. What if the cultural assignments do not fit an individual? What if the cultural assignments are based on past cultural errors?

Digging deeper into the new theory of reference, it becomes clear that this philosophical construction of meaning is an attempt to connect science with common sense. For example, an ordinary person may use the natural-kind words cat, tree, and lemon correctly based on superficial appearances, but she also assumes (in the back of her mind, so to speak) that within the relevant sciences there are more detailed technical descriptions of the traits that cats, trees, and lemons have in common among themselves.[11] But while her assumptions are correct for cats, trees, and lemons, they are not correct for blacks and whites, even though she uses the words for them correctly, within her culture.

Before leaving the new theory of reference, it is interesting to note that it does (unintentionally) yield another sense of meaning that is applicable to race—*attributive meaning*. Attributive meaning merely picks objects out for a present purpose.[12] For example, I refer to "the pen on the floor near the waste basket," or "the student near the window," not because being near the waste basket or the window is a definitive or important empirical characteristic of the pen or the student but because it distinguishes them for some reason. But when we refer to American blacks or whites, that may be the only kind of meaning the racial names for the groups have. When the offspring of slaves and whites were designated "negroes" or when scholars "of color" are thus focused on in contemporary academia, is not the racial designation used to pick them out for purposes that are unrelated to any "racial" characteristics they may have?

This last question leads into philosophical theories of *pragmatic meaning*. On a pragmatic account of its meaning, the meaning of 'race' would always refer to some purpose or value judgment.[13] It's easy to see that white racist designations of people as non-white have always been pragmatic in this sense. And, when Leonard Harris quotes Alain Locke on the pragmatic construction of the black race, as a necessary component of black culture, from a black point of view, so that "loyalty to the uplift of the race was, *mutatis mutandis*, loyalty to the uplift of the culture," the meaning of race is no less pragmatic.[14] The difference is that in the second case, the purpose is emancipation rather than oppression. But, the need for emancipation, in Alain Locke's day, as in our own, is a result of oppression, not the least of which is the oppressiveness of the false, presumed-objective descriptions of racial blackness as first constructed by American whites and subsequently assimilated by American blacks. Can a morally repugnant pragmatic meaning be successfully countered by a morally just pragmatic meaning? Surely, in meaning terms, the morally just pragmatic meaning is no better than the morally repugnant pragmatic meaning. What reason is there to think that 'race', with its false biological assumptions, can be successfully reconstructed for the purpose of more freedom, and that more freedom would result? Maybe a more direct, and less semantically compromised, route to freedom would be to simply let the whole idea of 'race' go.

The reader might respond with questions of how we are to function or imagine ourselves without race, and she could demand to know where we are to go from here. I suggest an historical path, a turn back in chronological time to the last period in Western history before the ordinary modern idea of race had been formulated. That would be the seventeenth century, the eve of modern European colonialism, when the ideas of race, gender, and even the self, that were first developed during the eighteenth-century Enlightenment, had no clear analogues.[15]

At first, this historical move would be possible only in "the life of the mind." But such a turn could intersect with twenty-first century revisions of ideas of human biology, whereby what used to be construed as the "physical facts" about people are no longer held to be essential or determining. This work of nonanachronistic reading and writing about the seventeenth century lies ahead and it may not be a very exciting solution for someone who wants to rush out and change the world directly. Neither is there a utopia at the end of the historical move because the African slave trade was already well underway during the seventeenth century.[16] But there may be clues to the motives behind constructions of race in that part of history. Such clues are important for present understanding because if microdiversity yields a lesson thus far, it is that the false reality of "race" requires as much attention as the evil of "racism."

Notes

Preface

1. Naomi Zack, *Race and Mixed Race* (Philadelphia: Temple University Press, 1993).

2. I made this reservation clear throughout my criticism of the lack of mixed-race identity for individuals with both black and white ancestry in the United States, but in chapter 14, "Nobility versus Good Faith," I argued against the project of constructing an identity of mixed race from scratch. See *Race and Mixed Race*, pp. 151–164.

3. F. James Davis, *Who is Black?* (University Park: Pennsylvania State University Press, 1991); Maria P. P. Root, *Racially Mixed People in America* (Newbury Park, Calif.: Sage, 1993).

Introduction

1. For changing views of race in the American social sciences, see R. Fred Wacker, *Ethnicity, Pluralism and Race* (Westwood, Conn.: Greenwood, 1983); for the contemporary, post–World War II consensus on the historical and not biological or racial origins of culture, see Claude Levi-Strauss, "Race and History," in *Race, Science and Society,* ed. Leo Kuper (New York: Columbia University Press, 1965).

2. This "common sense" view of race is so pervasive and widely accepted that instead of attempting to give scholarly references to it, it might be better to simply refer readers to their own experience or to the contemporary language of the popular media.

3. For contemporary statistics on mixed race among American blacks, which may be on the conservative side, and therefore are in no danger of overstating the case, see Joel Williamson, *New People* (New York: Free Press, 1980), pp. 110–113, 125–127.

4. For a more detailed analysis of the one-drop rule, see, for example, Zack, *Race and Mixed Race*, pp. 9–34.

5. Even where it would be useful to identify the race of an individual for clinical reasons because some diseases are statistically more prevalent in some "racial" groups than others, present medical reseachers have no reliable indicators. See, for example, the current inability to pick out likely suffer-

ers of sickle cell anemia based on race, in J. Jarrett Clinton, "From the Agency for Health Care Policy and Research," *Journal of the American Medical Association* 270, no. 18 (Nov. 10, 1993): 2158.

6. To speak of individuals as fractionally this race or that, for example, "one-quarter Chinese," or "one-eighth black," does not make sense given the genetic facts of human conception. We inherit one half of all our genes from our parents, and we have no way of knowing which genes each of them inherited from his or her parents, no way of knowing whether the genes society decides are definitive for racial membership have "dropped out" during any one instance of conception. For more detailed discussion and sources, see Zack, *Race and Mixed Race*, pp. 13–15.

7. Historians have traditionally assumed that Negroes were enslaved in the United States because they were Negroes, and not, as was the case, that anyone who was a slave, after about 1800, had to be a Negro. The clumsy historical assumption still carries over into liberal discussion. For example, John Immerwahr and Michael Burke write, "Only blacks were slaves and slaves were slaves because they were black," in "Race and the Modern Philosophy Course," *Teaching Philosophy* 16, no. 1 (March 1993): 27.

8. For details on the Harlem Renaissance constructions of blackness, and sources, see Zack, pp. 95–110.

9. On federally imposed restrictions about who can be an Indian, see Terry P. Wilson, "Blood Quantum: Native American Mixed Bloods," *Racially Mixed People in America,* ed. Maria P. P. Root (Newbury Park, Calif.: Sage, 1992), pp. 108–126.

Chapter 2

1. W. E. B. DuBois, *Black Reconstruction in America—1860–1880* (Cleveland, Ohio: World Publishing, 1968), p. 141.

2. W. E. B. DuBois, "The Function of the Negro Church," *The Black Church in America*, ed. H. Nelsen, R. Yokley, and A. Nelsen (New York: Basic Books, 1971), pp. 77–81.

3. DuBois, *Black Reconstruction,* p. 453.

4. J. Edward Kellough, "Affirmative Action in Government Employment," *The Annals* 523 (September 1992): 117-130.

Chapter 3

1. Maldwyn Allen Jones, *American Immigration* (Chicago: University of Chicago Press, 1960), p. 294.

2. Ibid.

3. Ibid.

4. But this does not stop Rastafarians, a religious group, from claiming ancestry from Ethiopia, which is on the east coast of Africa and not known to be slave-exporting. But if it serves to enable them to feel good about themselves, so be it.

5.   Frederick G. Cassidy, *Jamaica Talk: Three Hundred Years of the English Language in Jamaica*, 2nd ed. (London: Macmillan, 1971), p. 156.

6.   Thanks to my mother for this information.

7.   Cassidy, p. 163.

8.   J. Jarrett Clinton, "From the Agency for Health Care Policy and Research," *Journal of the American Medical Association* 270, no. 18 (Nov. 10, 1993): 2158.

9.   Ibid.

Chapter 4

1.   See bell hooks's *Feminist Theory: From Margin to Center* (Boston, Mass.: South End Press, 1984).

2.   See Sandra Harding, *Feminism and Methodology* (Bloomington: Indiana University Press, 1987).

3.   Trinidadian ethnic rhyme.

4.   Trevor Millette, *The Chinese in Trinidad* (Trinidad: Inprint Publication, 1993), pp. 30–49.

5.   Ibid., p. 50.

6.   The Convents are a chain of Catholic all-girls schools. The first was founded in the late nineteenth century in Port-of-Spain, Trinidad, and was built to educate the daughters of the French Creole and of the English expatriate families. The schools are still run by the Catholic Order of the Cluny Sisters. Because of its prestige as the leading girls' school in Trinidad, it is simply called "the Convent."

7.   "Vex Money" is money that young women carry with them in the event that there is a "vexation" between the woman and her date and she is forced to find her own way home.

8.   Baigan—a Hindi word for spinach. Because of the increasing numbers of Hindi speakers on the island, many Hindi words have been assimilated into the Trinidadian dialect.

9.   The French in the late nineteenth century were invited to the island to develop the plantations, which up to that time suffered from poor management. One of the many legacies left by the French is the "creole" names given to most of the fruits and vegetables. The word "gros Michel" means big Michael. It varies in length from ten to fourteen inches and is considered the most delicious of the bananas grown on the island. Like many French patois words, it has a double entendre referring to the size and length of a man's penis.

10.   "The Main" refers to the mainland of South America or more precisely to the northern regions of Venezuela.

11.   "Locura" means madness. Many Trinidadians still refer to the "pañols" as crazy probably because of their love of dancing, their fiery tempers, and their free-spiritedness. It may quite likely be a hang-over of the British arrogant racist description of people who lacked the stiff upper lip.

12.   "Parang" is a celebration of Spanish origin. "Paranderos," those who

take part in the celebrations, go from house to house singing songs of praise to the baby Jesus, to the Virgin Mary, and to St. Joseph. Annual parang competitions for the most outstanding choir have become very popular. The songs are composed by local lyricists and are in Spanish.

13. As in many other British colonies, elite schools were established to ensure that the sons of the expatriates had the same educational opportunities as their counterparts in England for qualifications to enter the universities of Oxford and Cambridge.

14. "Jammette" from the French "le diametre" meaning the margin.

15. See Eric Williams, *History of the People of Tinidad and Tobage* (London: Deutsch, 1964).

16. The steel pan, described as one of the few twentieth-century musical inventions, is made from discarded steel oil drums. This music continues to gain prestige and worldwide acceptance as a legitimate artform. It still has a dubious status in Trinidad, probably because it does not provide a steady income for musicians.

17. The season of Lent lasts for forty days. It begins on Ash Wednesday and ends on Glorious Saturday. It is a Christian period of fast and abstinence. Carnival celebrations occur in pre-Lenten season.

Chapter 5

1. As an illustration of this point, consider the following story. Recently, an African-American reporter was caught up short in Africa when he and others attempted to use a taxi outside a hotel. The reporter heard the doorman of the hotel say, "Let the white man have the taxi," and thought that he and the other black people were supposed to defer to some white man. Then he realized that he was the white man. In the eyes of white America (and thus in the eyes of everyone in America) the reporter was not white—he was black; in local African eyes, he was not black—he was white.

A conceptually sophisticated examination of the social and political nature of American racial classificatory systems—and their supposed roots in science—is given in Paul Spickard, "The Illogic of American Racial Categories," and in Maria P. P. Root, ed., *Racially Mixed People in America* (Newbury Park, Calif.: Sage Publications, 1992), pp. 12–23. Spickard concludes that "[r]ace . . . is primarily a social construct." In a footnote, he tells an interesting story of three brothers, who had the same mother and father and were born in Louisiana in the middle part of this century. The three brothers were classified as belonging to three different races (Negro, American Indian, and white) (Spickard, p. 23. fn. 8).

2. The U.S. Supreme Court noted that Plessy himself was 7/8ths white (*Plessy v. Ferguson*, 1986). But it allowed that the state of Louisiana was justified in requiring railway officials to accommodate him in the colored section of the railroad train. Then, if (at least for such purposes) Plessy counted as colored, and must be accommodated as a colored person, a hypothetical Plessy great-grandchild (all seven of whose other great-grandparents were, like Plessy's own, white) would also be colored. At this rate, no

descendant of Plessy, no matter how far into the future, will ever be white. Such a result makes puzzling the idea that there is some point at which the amount of a person's colored blood becomes too small to make a difference. On the one hand, Louisiana law specified that anyone who was 1/16th (or more) colored was colored—Louisiana appears to be measuring something. But on the other hand, the color factor does not seem to be capable of decreasing. It is not the case that Plessy's hypothetical descendants would gain more and more acceptance to the white car. (Was there thought to be some point at which some of these descendants would have to ride in the colored car while their own children would ride in the white car?)

Actual practice, in Louisiana and many other states, followed the so-called "one-drop rule," according to which a person who had "one drop" of colored blood was counted as colored. Even one drop of colored blood was far more socially consequential than very many drops of non-colored blood.

Note that whether one applies the legal standard of 1/16th part blood, or the one-drop rule, the power of the colored blood is regarded as very strong indeed. Even a small amount has serious consequences. The talk about blood makes it seem that the power in question here is biological, but it is clearly social. Even today, some African Americans report great power, for instance, in emptying swimming pools of all white people.

3. Bill Hosokawa, *Nisei: The Quiet Americans* (New York: William Morrow, 1969), p. 473.

4. Hosokawa, pp. 334ff.

5. In *Plessy*, racial classifications were made by railway officials.

6. For another view of this terminology, see Naomi Zack, *Race and Mixed Race* (Philadelphia: Temple University Press, 1993), esp. chapter 15.

7. I am uncertain about the terminology that would be best here. It is a commonplace that many so-called blacks are fairer than many so-called whites, and that in any case very few people are literally black or white in color, but the naming of the racial group that is the global majority—usually known as the Asian or oriental group—has difficulties of its own. "Asian," which will do in some contexts, and which I often use here, is not quite right, because native Indians, Pakistanis, and others are natives of Asian countries, but racially are generally Caucasians rather than Asians. "Oriental" has many of the same problems. In addition, "oriental" has been objected to as a designation of a racial group because it singles this group out by reference to where their homelands are from Europe. That is, east of Europe lies "the Orient," the homelands of such people. But if one had started from California, one would go west to find such homelands. So, it is concluded that the designation oriental (i.e., "eastern") is Eurocentric. But consider that what is generally known as Western Civilization has classical roots in (what are now) Italy and Greece, but is now widespread throughout Europe. Here, a phrase like "Western Civilization" serves mainly to distinguish that civilization from other traditional forms of civilization, especially Eastern (or Oriental) Civilization. Eastern and Western Civilization—and the Occident and the Orient, occidentals and orientals—are placed on a par with each other. Neither is presented as being inherently superior.

These considerations count decisively against the use of the term "Mongolian" here, although there is some reason in favor of that term. Caucasian children who suffered from what we now call Down's Syndrome were called "Mongolian idiots," who suffered from "Mongolism," because it was thought that Down's Syndrome represented the reappearance in a more advanced life form of features from a lower developmental stage, in this case, Asian or oriental features. For further details, see Stephen Jay Gould, *The Mismeasure of Man* (New York: W. W. Norton, 1981), pp. 134–135.

Chapter 6

1.   William Shatner and Chris Kreski, *Star Trek Memories* (New York: Harper Collins, 1993), p. 68.

2.   Melodrama is a dramatic genre that mixes elements of tragedy and comedy. The formula that is still used for this genre is rooted in the popular theater of the late eighteenth and early nineteenth centuries. Included in the formula is the concept of poetic justice, the idea that right will prevail indirectly, if not directly. Good and evil are clearly defined and personified by the hero and villain. Good is placed in jeopardy, a number of reversals or plot twists provide suspense, and there is usually some sort of violence involved. Emotions are extravagantly romantic. One feature of nineteenth-century stage melodrama is the "sensation scene," a visual spectacle, usually of some sort of cataclysmic event. Stock characters, readily identified as types, are a staple.

3.   The term "mulatto," originally coined to describe a person born of one black and one white parent, has become a descriptive term for any person of mixed race. The extrapolation of the word from mule, the crossbreeding of a horse and donkey, connotes the view of the dominant culture that such a union is bestial. A quadroon has one black grandparent. An octoroon is the offspring of a quadroon and a white. "Miscegenation," a term used to denote marriage or interbreeding between members of different races, is touched on in this essay, but the focus is on the children of interracial unions; thus, several stage and screen works have been either omitted or all but omitted. This terminology is used within the context of a historical study.

4.   Robert C. Toll, *Blacking Up: The Minstrel Show in Nineteenth-Century America* (New York: Oxford University Press, 1974), p. 76.

5.   Harriet Beecher Stowe, author of the novel, never wrote a dramatic adaptation. George Aiken was the first, and his version is often identified as the best, and most faithful to the original. *Uncle Tom's Cabin* became a phenomenally successful melodrama, with literally dozens of adaptations. References in this essay are made to the Aiken version from John Gassner, ed., *Best Plays of the Early American Theatre* (New York: Crown, 1967), pp. 136–184.

6.   Abolitionist societies often used drama as a teaching and propaganda tool. The character of mixed race was a figure of particular empathy. In J. T. Trowbridge's *Neighbor Jackwood* (1857), for example, the octoroon heroine

not only gains freedom, but escapes to Vermont and marries her Yankee benefactor.

7. In his essay, "Black is White/White is Black; Passing as a Strategy of Racial Compatability in Contemporary Hollywood Comedy," in *Unspeakable Images: Ethnicity and the American Cinema,* ed. Lester D. Friedman (Urbana: University of Illinois Press, 1991), Mark Winokur describes catharsis: "to act out the roles one fears becoming is to exorcise them from one's personality" (p. 196). Such a definition readily applies to the case of the mulatto character, but Winokur explains how this definition is applied to black comedians in contemporary films to please white audiences.

8. See Lerone Bennett Jr., *Before the Mayflower: A History of the Negro in America, 1619–1964* (New York: Penguin, 1980), chapter 10, "Miscegenation in America."

9. Brown is also the first African-American novelist to be published in the United States. *Clotel, or the President's Daughter, A Narrative of Slave Life in the United States,* which is primarily concerned with issues of miscegenation and mixed heritage within the context of slavery, appeared in 1854. His first play, *Experience, or How to Give a Northern Man a Backbone,* an antislavery satire in which a proslavery minister is sold as a slave, has been lost.

10. Kathy A. Perkins, *Black Female Playwrights: An Anthology of Plays Before 1950* (Bloomington: Indiana University Press, 1989), p. 11.

11. Leo Hamalian and James V. Hatch, eds., *The Roots of African-American Drama, An Anthology of Early Plays, 1858–1938* (Detroit: Wayne State University Press, 1991), pp. 207–230.

12. The producers of *Mulatto* had also produced *White Cargo* and wanted to exploit the sexual element of *Mulatto* as far as possible. The protagonist's sister, originally seen briefly in an earlier scene in the play, was brought back into the action near the end as the object of the lust of the white plantation overseer. The play went into production while Hughes was out of the country, and he was unable to excise the additions; published editions of the play omit the changes.

13. Paul Green, "In Abraham's Bosom," in *The Best Plays of 1926–1927,* ed. Burns Mantle (New York: Dodd, Mead and Co., 1927), p. 327.

14. Langston Hughes, *Five Plays by Langston Hughes* (Bloomington: University of Indiana Press, 1963), p. 2.

15. Hughes, p. 30.

16. Jeanne-Marie A. Miller, "Dramas by Black American Playwrights Produced on the New York Professional Stage from *The Chip Woman's Fortune* to *Five on the Black Hand Side*" (Ph.D. dissertation, Howard University, Washington, D.C., 1976), p. 406.

17. Mary Elizabeth Cronin, "Memoir Traces Mixed Roots," *Times Union,* Albany, N.Y., February 22, 1994, C 1, 4.

18. Charles Gordone, *No Place to Be Somebody* (Indianapolis: Bobbs-Merrill, 1969), p. 115.

19. This discussion of the tragic mulatto character is far from exhaus-

tive. More could be said about drama and film in the United States, as well as international views of the character, from *The Black Doctor* by Ira Aldridge to *The Bloodknot* by Athol Fugard.

20. It should be noted that the Code of the Motion Picture Producers and Distributers of America expressly forbade interracial sexual relationships on screen. Relationships between black and white characters were all but confined to servant and master to avoid even the implication that any deeper relationship could be possible. The Motion Picture Producers and Distributors of America Production Code was drafted in 1930 and amended or revised frequently thereafter until it was totally rewritten in 1966. The ban on miscegenation or the implication thereof was rescinded in 1956. See Richard S. Randall, *Censorship of the Movies: The Social and Political Control of a Mass Medium* (Madison: University of Wisconsin Press, 1968), pp. 102–103, 201. See also Edward De Grazia and Roger Kane Newman, *Banned Films, Movies, Censorship and the First Amendment* (New York: R.R. Bowker, 1982), pp. 34, 93.

21. Toni Morrison, *Playing in the Dark: Whiteness and the Literary Imagination* (Cambridge, Mass.: Harvard University Press, 1992), pp. 67–69.

22. Marcia Gillespie, "Lena Horne Finds Her Music," *MS*, August 1981, 45.

Chapter 7

I dedicate this work to UCSB's multiracial student organization, VARIATIONS, and to my brother and best friend *por vida,* Tracy Jay. I will only be able to acknowledge a small fraction of those who have nurtured my ideas that became the basis for this piece, "Theater of Identity." Thanks always to my family, Mom, Dad, Jay, Pinky, Brandy, and Pebbles, for they are the reason for everything I do. Special thanks to Sucheng Chan, Harsuku Suzuki, Hartie Suzuki, Hiromasa Suzuki, Yoneko Morino, Chieko Shimura, Tamiko Quint, Walter Allen, David Lopez, Don Nakanishi, Melvin Oliver, Naomi Zack, Maria Root, Christine Hall, Cynthia Nakashima, George Kich, Kip Fulbeck, Velina Houston, Setsuko Perry, Russell Leong, Shawn Griffin, Kenyon Chan, Nancy Brown, Kathy Shamey, Hauani-Kay Trask, David Stannard, Margo Okazawa-Rey, Michael Thornton, Stephen Murphy, Paul Spickard, Ari Rosner, Mari Sunaida, Dave Lemmel, Ruby Furrow, Kevin Yoshida, Jay Chan, Curtiss Rooks, my dearest friends at L.A.'s *Circus and Arena* (you know who you are), and forever Luis Alfredo Xicay-Santos. Shoutouts go to the brave students across all racial, ethnic, gender, sexual orientation, and class boundaries who continue to fight for ethnic and multiethnic studies on college campuses. Finally, I must thank all my students from Santa Monica College, Cal-State Northridge, UCLA, and UCSB.

1. Race is a social invention. It is a socially constructed and politically maintained category originally defined on the basis of so-called shared genetic characteristics. These so-called shared genetic characteristics were used as markers of differentiation and were formulated into a ranking system by

Europeans in the sixteenth century to support scientific racism and push forward European domination around the globe. Biological and phenotypical aspects of race are only significant because of their social use in further perpetuating a system of racial stratification based on physical and cultural likeness to the dominant group. According to Reynolds Farley and Walter Allen in *The Color Line and the Quality of Life in America* (Newbury Park, Calif.: Sage, 1987), p. 6: ". . . race in a heterogenous society like the United States is often no more than a socially constructed and defined characteristic. It is not at all uncommon in the United States, for example, to find considerable overlap between blacks and whites in terms of their values, personal histories, and blood lines." That is to say, "race" has been socially and culturally constructed and institutionally applied to systematically rank peoples according to these categories. Nevertheless, "race" continues to be a "sociological reality" and "exerts profound influence over the lives of people in this society," Farley and Allen concluded (p. 6). Therefore, my usage of the term is a combination of the social, political, and pseudo-biological definition of race and what race has meant in the United States. Social scientists have now come to distinguish between "biological race," "social race," "political race," and "race as identity." In actuality, when "race" is mentioned in popular culture and the social sciences, most people are really talking about the notion of "ethnicity." Along with racial characteristics, ethnicity includes cultural distinctiveness, religious background, identification by national origin, historical continuity, and a sense of peoplehood.

When one debates who is Asian, African American, Chicano, mixed, biracial, or monoracial, one is not talking about biological or even social "race" (see Maria P. P. Root, ed., *Racially Mixed People in America* [Newbury Park, Calif.: Sage, 1992]) one is putting forth his or her "identity." One's identity encompasses and crisscrosses multiple social boundaries that make up all of who he or she is—race, color, culture, language, nationality, gender, class, sexual orientation, personal temperament, etc. Along with phenotypical and genotypical characteristics—but not conclusively—our racial identity is shaped by our lived experiences, a historical consciousness, generational continuity, and a sense of peoplehood with others like us. Phenotypically, we may appear like an out-group member, yet our ancestry, socialization, and lived experiences may ground us in a particular racial identity or overlapping racial and ethnic identities. Without a sociopolitical and historical context, how can we explain the social phenomenon of African Americans "passing" as European American? (How does one "pass" for who he or she is truly not?) How do we make sense of a light-skinned black reality or a dark-skinned one? As Allen and Farley have put forth, the concept of "race" is "an attributed quality rather than a real one. . . . The idea of race is a much purer concept than the reality of race in American society" (p. 6).

2.   bell hooks's *Black Looks: Race and Representation* (Boston, Mass.: South End Press, 1992)—especially the chapter "Revolutionary Renegades" on the shared ancestries, histories, and experiences of African Americans

and Native Americans—and the poignant questions hooks asked at the sixth annual Black lesbian and gay leadership forum conference on Feb. 15, 1993, "If I can not share the truth of my existence, then how can you know or love me? And most importantly, how can you work for freedom on my behalf?", have inspired me to examine the racial representations of Eurasians and Afroasians because they have so powerfully influenced and shaped some of the earliest memories of my personal and public identity as a biracial person.

3. I apply the terms, "biracial," "multiracial," and "multiethnic," to Eurasian-Americans (Americans of European and Asian ancestries), Afroasian-Americans (Americans of African and Asian ancestries), and other mixed-race populations to convey the dual and multiple racial ancestries and cultural artifacts, affiliations, and loyalties these groups may have. Race is seen as a "racist" invention and socially constructed tool used to categorize and differentiate on the basis of perceived shared genetics and to support a racially ordered social structure. Ethnicity is conceptualized as a socially constructed way of creating and sustaining group boundaries in which processes of inclusion and exclusion simultaneously coexist on the basis of ancestry, lineage, perceived shared genetics, religion, language, culture, sense of peoplehood, and historical continuity (consciousness of kind). Both race and ethnicity are at once static and dynamic; rigid and fluid; and socially dictated and individually defined. That is to say, the lines of demarcation and the social forces of self/group imposition (based on race and ethnicity) continue to persist, while their definitions continually undergo shifts, changes, and transformations.

4. I have chosen to refer to people whose identity includes the awareness, acknowledgment, and affirmation of multiple racial and cultural (i.e., ethnic) ancestries. Some people who are products of interracial marriages may identify with only one parent group; although he or she is biracial (and likely, but not necessarily multicultural), he or she may center his or her experience in one group, thereby having a single-race/single-ethnic identity.

My choice for a *social name* would be "biracial" or "multiethnic" to include racial, cultural, and historical backgrounds and origins; however, I personally use "mixed" and "half" (*haafu*, in Japanese) to refer to myself because they are terms I have claimed since I was a young child. Throughout this chapter, I also use biracial, multiracial, mixed-race, racially mixed, and multiethnic to refer to these people. The terms "mixed-race" and "racially mixed" connote the purity of so-called unmixed peoples (usually whites), thereby furthering the notion of inherent biological separation and inequality between the races in which whites have been at the top. By replacing notions of impurity with multiplicity, variety, and fluidity, one can signify a powerful defiance to and subversion of the social boundaries that have been constructed for the maintenance of a racist, classist, sexist, heterosexist hierarchical system.

5. I distinguish between *articulated* identity and *intuitive* or *experiential* identity. One's articulated identity is what one calls oneself publically.

It is often a political statement. It may or may not be in concert with one's intuitive or experiential identity. For example, I call myself a "person of color," because of American racial history and therefore, my social locality in the United States. However, because of my cultural upbringing, my primary relationships with my European-American father, relatives, and ancestors, and my ambiguous phenotype that sometimes allows me to pass for white, I also understand intuitively and experientially that my European-American ancestry is an integral part of my personal and social identities. Identity is necessarily both personal and political. That is to say, identity is articulated, intuitive, and experiential. All of the socially constructed categories (race, ethnicity, gender, sex, sexual orientation, etc.) are problematic because they were never meant to capture the totality of our experiences and the complexity of our expressions. The terms I use are labels—labels that powerfully conceptualize images and attempt to put forth layers of meaning. Labels, terms, and definitions change with experience, politics, and time.

6. Monoracial and monoethnic, like multiracial and multiethnic, refer to the description of one's identity. For example, Native Americans, Latino Americans, African Americans, and Filipino Americans are groups that possess racial and cultural multiplicity and variety through centuries of blending, yet their national, racial, and ethnic identification has come to be based on a single identity. The distinction I make between "multi-" and "mono-" in this is not to further a racist discourse on notions of racial purity and reinforce racial apartheid, but to distinguish how people have made sense of who they are. For example, Lisa Bonet, Rae Dawn Chong, Jasmine Guy, Halley Berry, Vanessa Williams, Eartha Kitt, Vanity (Denise Matthews), Lena Horne, Paula Abdul, and Mariah Carey according to American racial definitions are considered black or belonging to the black community. They each have publically put forth their self-identifications. Some of them center their identification within the black experience and thus identify as black. Others of them have put forth many different terms of identification to try and capture their social realities. It's important to note that each individual experiences his or her own version of a racial–ethnic reality, while sharing an overarching one. To understand why one may "choose" an identification or come to see themselves as belonging to, partially belonging to, or not belonging to a particular group (especially when the individual possesses overlapping racial–ethnic ancestry and historical experiences with that group or groups), we must put the individual's life into historical and social context. Thus, I am not re-coding (nor I am suggesting one should re-code) all African Americans, Native Americans, Latino Americans, or European Americans as multiracial or multiethnic, unless members of those groups view their multiple ancestries as being an important part of their identity, history, and heritage.

7. For more, see F. James Davis, *Who Is Black? One Nation's Definition* (University Park: The Pennsylvania State University Press, 1991); Kathy Russell, Midge Wilson, and Ronald Hall, *The Color Complex: The Politics of Skin Color Among African Americans* (New York: Harcourt Brace Jovanovich,

1992); David Lemmel, *Outside the Color Lines: An Analysis of the External Influences Contributing to the Development of a Biracial Identity* (Unpublished senior thesis, Division of Social Studies, Bard College, November, 1992); Teresa Kay Williams, "The Mulatto Metaphor: The Embodiment of North America's Racial Contradiction" (Unpublished paper presented at the Pacific Sociological Association Conference, April, 1993).

8.   To confirm the separation, rigidity, purity of "racial" categories (i.e., white superior and people of color inferior), miscegenation as a concept came about, referring to the mixing and blending of two different races. Historically, it was used to refer to "race-mixing" between people of European descent and people of color (e.g., anti-miscegenation laws). Thus, like race it is an artificial concept. However, because we believe it to be real, as sociologist W. I. Thomas has put forth, the social consequences are real. For further discussion of "miscegenation," see W. E. B. DuBois's essay, "Miscegenation" (January 1935) Herbert Apetheker, ed., in *Against Racism: Unpublished Essays, Papers, Addresses, 1887–1961 W. E. B. DuBois* (Cambridge: University of Massachusetts, 1985).

9.   William Burkhardt, "Institutional Barriers, Marginality, and Adaptation Among the American-Japanese Mixed-Bloods in Japan," *Journal of Asian Studies* 42, no. 3 (May 1983): 519–544; H. Wagatsuma, "The Social Perception of Skin Color in Japan," *Daedalus* 96 (1967): 407–443; H. Wagatsuma, "Some Problems of Interracial Marriage for the Japanese," . Stuart and L. Abt, eds., *Interracial Marriage: Expectations and Realities* (New York: Grossman, 1973), pp. 247–264; H. Wagatsuma, *Culture and Identity* (Tokyo: Chiyoda Printing, 1986); Kazuyo Kaneko, *Emi yo* (Tokyo, 1954); Sumi Kosakai, *Kore wa Anata no Haha: Sawada Miki to Konketsujitachi* (Tokyo: Shuueisha, 1982); Hideo Honda, *Sonzai Shinai Kodomotachi* (*Children Who Haven't An Existence*) (Tokyo, 1982).

10.   Teresa Kay Williams, "Marriage Between Japanese Women and U.S. Servicemen since World War II," *Amerasia Journal* 17, no. 1 (1991).

11.   The television show, *Betwitched*, which I saw dubbed in Japanese on television in Japan (before bilingual adaptors and cable television), held special symbolic meaning for me and my family. Of all of the Japanese-dubbed American shows, it was always undoubtedly our favorite. Although I was not consciously aware of this until my brother pointed it out to me several years ago, the Stevenses are actually a "biracial" and "bicultural" family. Samantha is a witch. Darren is a mortal. Tabatha and Adam are part-witch (part-warlord) and part-mortal. Darren is against using witchcraft or having his children learning it. This is often a source of conflict for them. As long as Samantha appears like and behaves like a mortal, Darren is satisfied. He'll approve of witchcraft only to undo the mistakes and disasters it had created prior to and without his approval or knowledge. This show sends an explicit antibicultural, proassimilation message. Darren constantly pressures his wife and children to behave as a "normal," mainstream, middle-class, mortal, nuclear, European-American family would. In this case, difference

was powerfully other worldly and something that always had to be hidden, suppressed.

12. Erving Goffman, *The Presentation of Self in Everyday Life* (New York: Doubleday Anchor, 1959).

13. Michael Omi and Howard Winant, *Racial Formation in the U.S. 1960–1980* (New York: Routledge & Kegan Paul, 1986).

14. Warren Furutani, "Encore?," *Tozai Times*, September 1990.

15. George F. Will, "A Degradation of American Liberalism," *Los Angeles Times*, August 13, 1990.

16. Velina Hasu Houston, "It's Time to Overcome the Legacy of Racism in Theater," *Los Angeles Times*, August 13, 1990.

17. Paul Spickard, *Mixed Blood: Intermarriage and Ethnic Identity in Twentieth Century America* (Madison: University of Wisconsin Press, 1989), p. 346.

18. Ibid, p. 347.

19. Carla Bradshaw, "Beauty and the Beast: On Racial Ambiguity," in Root, pp. 77–90.

20. Maureen Orth, "Ciao, Tina," *Vanity Fair*, April 1993.

21. Ibid.

22. Candy Mills, "Unforgettable Woman of the Year," *Interrace*, March/April, 1990.

23. Naomi Hirahara, "Rising Sun Is Its Own Worst Enemy," *Rafu Shimpo*, July 21, 1993.

24. Cynthia Nakashima, "An Invisible Monster: The Creation and Denial of Mixed-Race People in America," in Root, pp. 162-180.

25. Karen Kablin, "LAPD's Multiculti Thing," *LA Weekly*, November 1992.

26. W. E. B. Dubois, *The Souls of Black Folk* (New York: Penguin Books, 1903/1989).

27. Ruthanne Lum McCunn, "Adrienne Telemaque versus Suzie Wong," in *Chinese American Portraits: Personal Histories 1828–1988* (San Francisco: Chronicle Books), pp. 132–134.

28. The term *hapa* (half) or *hapa haole* (half white) was originally used to refer to the offspring of Native Hawaiian women and European and European American men. With the large Asian population having peopled the Hawaiian Islands and gained social and political prominence, the term hapa has not only been extended to biracial–multiracial people of Asian descent, but now almost exclusively signifies the Eurasian.

29. W. E. B. Du Bois, *The Souls of Black Folk*.

30. Michael Thornton, *The Social History of a Multiethnic Identity: The Case of the Black Japanese* (Ph.D. Dissertation, University of Michigan, 1983), pp. 207–8.

31. Renato Rosaldo, *Culture and Truth: The Remaking of Social Analysis* (Boston: Beacon Press, 1989), p. 216; Luis Alfredo Xicay-Santos, "Reconcilable Differences: Soy Guatemalteco! Soy Mestizo!" *Interrace*, April 1994, pp. 28–30.

32.   Gloria Anzaldua, "La Conciencia de la Mestiza: Towards a New Consciousness," in *Making Face, Making Soul: Haciendo Caras* (San Francisco: Spinsters/Aunt Lute, 1990), p. 379.

Chapter 8

1.   Washington Irving, *A Tour on the Prairies* (New York: Vintage Books, 1969).
2.   William Faulkner, *Light in August* (New York: Modern Library, 1968).
3.   Diana Chang, *The Frontiers of Love* (New York: Random House, 1956).
4.   Louise Erdrich, *Tracks* (New York: Henry Holt, 1988).
5.   Judith R. Berzon, *Neither White Nor Black: The Mulatto Character in American Fiction* (New York: New York University Press, 1978).
6.   William J. Scheik, *The Half-Blood: A Cultural Symbol in 19th-Century American Fiction* (Lexington: University Press of Kentucky, 1979).
7.   See "Pioneers and Paradigms: The Eaton Sisters," in Amy Ling, *Between Worlds: Women Writers of Chinese Ancestry* (New York: Pergamon Press, 1990), pp. 21–55.
8.   Throughout this discussion I use the term "mixed blood" without the scare quotes. I mean it to be synonymous with mixed race in literature because most literary depictions use the (false) concept of blood. The term allows me to speak of the individual figure rather than to continually repeat the phrase "individuals of mixed race."
9.   See, for example, the editor's introduction in Henry Louis Gates, Jr., *"Race," Writing, and Difference* (Chicago: University of Chicago Press, 1986), pp. 1–20.
10.   See Adrienne Rich, "Readings of History," in *Snapshots of a Daughter-in-Law* (New York: Norton, 1967), pp. 36–40.
11.   Theodore Dreiser, *Jennie Gerhardt* (New York: Viking Penguin, 1989).
12.   Nella Larsen, *Quicksand and Passing* (New Brunswick: Rutgers University Press, 1989).
13.   Han Suyin, *The Crippled Tree* (New York: Putnam's Sons, 1965).
14.   Leslie Marmon Silko, *Ceremony* (New York: Penguin, 1986).
15.   See Larsen's *Quicksand and Passing*.
16.   Naomi Zack, *Race and Mixed Race* (Philadelphia: Temple University Press, 1993), p. 52.
17.   Julia Kristeva, *The Powers of Horror: An Essay on Abjection* (New York: Columbia University Press, 1982), p. 4.
18.   Winnifred Babcock Eaton (Otono Watanna), *Tama* (New York: Harper and Brothers, 1910), p. 31.
19.   Lanford Wilson, *The Redwood Curtain* (New York: Hill and Wang, 1993).
20.   Charles W. Chesnutt, *The House Behind the Cedars* (Ridgewood, N.J.: Gregg Press, 1968).
21.   See Walt Whitman's "The Half-Breed, a Tale of the Western Frontier," in *Short Stories by Walt Whitman*, ed. Thomas Olive Mabbot (New York: Colombia University Press, 1927), p. 24.
22.   Thomas Dixon, *The Clansman* (New York: Doubleday Page, 1905).

23. Kristeva, *Powers of Horror*, p. 5.

24. Donald M. Kartiganer, "The Meaning of Form in Light in August," in *William Faulkner's Light in August*, ed. Harold Bloom (New York: Chelsea House, 1988), p. 10.

25. Faulkner, *Light in August*, p. 363.

26. Kristeva, *Powers of Horror*, p. 8.

27. Ibid., p. 15.

28. Faulkner, *Light in August*, p. 440.

29. J. M. Coetzee, *White Writing* (New Haven: Yale University Press, 1988), p. 141.

30. William Gilmore Simms, *The Partisan: A Romance of the Revolution* (Chicago: Donahue and Henneberry, 1859).

31. Mark Twain, *The Tragedy of Pudd'nhead Wilson and Those Extraordinary Twins* (New York: Norton, 1980).

32. Toni Morrison, *The Bluest Eye* (New York: Washington Square, 1970).

33. See Andre Siniavski on Leila Sebbar, "Paroles d'Exil" in *Dossier 36*, no. 2 (July 1989): 38–39.

34. See Lauren Berlant, "National Brands, National Body," in *Comparative American Identities: Race, Sex, and Nationality in the Modern Text*, ed. Hortense J. Spillers (New York: Routledge, 1991), pp. 110–140.

35. Winnifred Babcock Eaton (Onoto Watanna), *The Heart of Hyacinth* (New York: Harper and Brothers, 1903).

36. Joel Williamson, *New People: Miscegenation and Mulattoes in the United States* (New York: The Free Press, 1980).

37. See Homi K. Bhabha, "Third Space," in *Identity*, ed. Johnathon Rutherford (London: Lawrence and Wishart, 1990), pp. 209–11. Bhabha's concept of the Third Space does not directly address the concept of mixed race, but much of his work on cultural hybridity—especially in the sense that the site of mixing is within—is applicable to the study of mixed race in literature.

38. Mourning Dove (Humishuma), *Cogewea, the Half Blood*, ed. Lucullus Virgin McWhorter (Lincoln: University of Nebraska Press, 1981).

39. Ibid., p. 41.

40. Ibid., p. 95.

41. Ibid., p. 232.

42. Ibid., p. 283.

43. Ibid., p. 285.

44. The example of Pauline points out the porosity of these categories. Even though I have employed the current categorization in order to show a thematic progression, they are not necessarily intended as discrete or discontinuous.

45. Silko's portrayals of these three mixed bloods are very different. Tayo is the protagonist and experiences the most conflict as a mixed blood.

46. Patricia Riley, "The Mixed Blood Writers as Interpreter and Mythmaker," in *Understanding Others: Cultural and Cross-Cultural Studies and the Teaching of Literature*, eds. Joseph Trimmer and Tilly Warnock (Urbana, Illinois: National Council of Teachers of English, 1992).

47.   Ana Castillo, *Sapogonia* (Tempe, Arizona: Bilingual Press/Editorial Bilingue, 1990).

48.   Leila Sebbar, *Le chinois vert d'afrique* (Paris: Stock, 1984).

49.   For a fuller discussion of "permanent disequilibrium" see Leila Sebbar's *Lettres parisiennes* (Paris: Stock, 1989).

50.   Zack, *Race and Mixed Race,* p. 164.

51.   Edith Eaton (Sui Sin Far), *Mrs. Spring Fragrance* (Chicago: A. C. McClurg, 1912).

52.   Edith Eaton (Sui Sin Far), "Leaves from the Mental Portfolio of an Eurasian" in *Heath Anthology of American Literature,* Vol. 2, ed. Paul Lauter (Lexington, Mass.: D.C. Heath, 1990).

53.   Ibid., p. 880.

54.   Ibid., p. 888.

55.   Ibid., p. 894.

56.   William Dean Howells, *An Imperative Duty* (New York: Harper and Brothers, 1892).

57.   W. E. B. DuBois, *The Souls of Black Folk* (New York: Penguin Books, 1969).

58.   Edith Eaton (Sui Sin Far), "Leaves," p. 890.

59.   Ibid., p. 895.

60.   Ibid., p. 890.

61.   Ibid., p. 895.

62.   Jessie Redmon Fauset, *There is Confusion* (New York: Boni and Liveright, 1924).

63.   Ibid., p. 288.

64.   See Jose Vasconcelos, *La Raza Cosmica: Mision de la Raza Ibero-Americana* (Mexico City: Aguilar S.A. de Ediciones, 1962).

65.   Richard Rodriguez, "Mixed Blood: A World Made Mestizo," in *Harpers* 203, no. 1698 (November 1991): 47–56.

66.   Gloria Anzaldua, *Borderlands/La Frontera: The New Mestiza* (San Francisco: Spinsters/Aunt Lute, 1987), p. 77. Anzaldua borrows the term from Mexican philosopher Jose Vasconcelos.

67.   Ibid., p. 78.

68.   Ibid., p. 3.

69.   Cherrie Moraga, *Loving in the War Years* (Boston: South End Press, 1983).

70.   Anzaldua, *Borderlands,* p. 81.

71.   Scheik, *The Half Blood,* Preface, p. ix.

Chapter 9

1.   Naomi Zack, "An Autobiographical View of Mixed Race and Deracination," *American Philosophical Association Newsletter on Philosophy and the Black Experience* 91, no. 1 (Spring 1992): 7.

2.   Brewton Berry and Henry L. Tischler, *Race and Ethnic Relations,* 4th ed. (Boston: Houghton Mifflin Co., 1978), pp. 97–98; F. James Davis, *Who Is Black? The American Definition* (University Park: The Pennsylvania

State University Press, 1991), pp. 5–6; Gunnar Myrdal, assisted by Richard Sterner and Arnold M. Rose, *An American Dilemma* (New York: Harper & Bros., 1944), pp. 60–67, 113–18; Paul R. Spickard, "The Illogic of American Racial Categories," Maria P. P. Root, ed., *Racially Mixed People in America* (Newbury Park, Calif.: Sage Publications, 1992), pp. 15–16; Joel Williamson, *New People: Miscegenation and Mulattoes in the United States* (New York: The Free Press, 1980), pp. 1–2.

3. Calvin Trillin, "American Chronicles: Black or White," *New Yorker,* April 4, 1986, 62–63, 71–74.

4. *State of Louisiana v. Jane Doe,* 485 So. 2d 60; 107 Sup. Ct. Reporter, interim ed. 638, 1986.

5. Amy Iwasaki Mass, "Interracial Japanese Americans: The Best of Both Worlds or the End of the Japanese American Community?" in Root, pp. 275–9.

6. Robin L. Miller, "The Human Ecology of Multiracial Identity," in Root, p. 29.

7. Eleanor C. Nordyke, "Blacks in Hawai'i: A Demographic and Historical Perspective," *The Hawaiian Journal of History* 22 (1988): 245–47.

8. Root, p. 9.

9. Ronald C. Johnson, "Offspring of Cross-Race and Cross-Ethnic Marriages in Hawaii," in Root, pp. 242–3.

10. Davis, *Who Is Black?,* pp. 81–122.

11. Kieu-Linh Caroline Valverde, "From Dust to Gold: The Vietnamese American Experience," in Root, pp. 144–61.

12. Brewton Berry, *Race and Ethnic Relations,* 3rd ed. (Boston: Houghton Mifflin Co., 1965), p. 192.

13. Terry P. Wilson, "Blood Quantum: Native American Mixed Bloods," in Root, pp. 118–25.

14. David Nicholls, "No Hawks or Pedlars: Levantines in the Caribbean," *Ethnic and Race Studies* 4 (October 1981): 427.

15. Teresa Kay Williams, "Prism Lives: Identity of Binational Amerasians," in Root, pp. 229–303.

16. Hubert M. Blalock, Jr., *Toward a Theory of Minority Group Relations* (New York: Capricorn Books, 1967), pp. 79–84.

17. Carlos A. Fernández, "La Raza and the Melting Pot: A Comparative Look at Multiethnicity," in Root, p. 13; Charles Wagley, ed., *Race and Class in Rural Brazil,* 2nd ed. (Paris: UNESCO, 1963), pp. 143–48.

18. Melvin Harris, *Patterns of Race in the Americas* (New York: W. W. Norton, 1964), pp. 57–61.

19. Mauricio Solaún and Sidney Kronus, *Discrimination Without Violence* (New York: John Wiley & Sons, 1973), pp. 3–9, 33–35, 56.

20. H. Hoetink, *Caribbean Race Relations: A Study of Two Variants* (London: Oxford University Press, 1967), pp. 39–41; Donald L. Horowitz, "Color Differentiation in the American Systems of Slavery," *Journal of Interdisciplinary History* 3 (Winter 1973): 510–13.

21. Virginia R. Dominguez, *White by Definition: Social Classification in*

Creole Louisiana (New Brunswick, N.J.: Rutgers University Press, 1986), pp. 273–7; Angela Jorge, "The Black Puerto Rican Woman in Contemporary American Society," in Edna Acosta-Belén, ed., *The Puerto Rican Woman* (New York: Praeger, 1979), pp. 134–35; Melvin M. Tumin, ed., *Comparative Perspectives on Race Relations* (Boston: Little, Brown & Co, 1969), pp. 204–14 and chapter 11.

22. Jorge, "The Black Puerto Rican Woman," pp. 135–41.

23. Williamson, *New People*, pp. 6–14.

24. Ira Berlin, *Slaves Without Masters: The Free Negro in the Antebellum South* (New York: Pantheon Books, 1975), pp. 49, 97–9.

25. Helen T. Caterall, *Judicial Cases Concerning American Slavery and the Negro* (Washington, D.C: Carnegie Institute of Washington, 5 vols., 1926–37), volume 2, p. 269.

26. John W. Blassingame, *Black New Orleans, 1860–1880* (Chicago: University of Chicago Press, 1973), pp. 17–21.

27. Dominguez, *White by Definition*, pp. 12–16, 23–26, 32, 94–151.

28. John W. Blassingame, *The Slave Community: Plantation Life in the Antebellum South* (New York: Oxford University Press, 1972), pp. 81–89; Waldo E. Martin, Jr., *The Mind of Frederick Douglass* (Chapel Hill: University of North Carolina Press, 1984), pp. 3–4.

29. Martin, *The Mind of Frederick Douglass*, pp. 3–4.

30. Berlin, *Slaves Without Masters*, pp. 365–6.

31. Dominguez, *White by Definition*, pp. 134–41.

32. Charles Staples Mangum, Jr., *The Legal Status of the Negro in the United States* (Chapel Hill: University of North Carolina Press, 1940), pp. 238–48.

33. Williamson, *New People*, pp. 88–91.

34. 109 U.S. 3., 1883.

35. *Plessy v. Ferguson*, 163 U.S. 537., 1896.

36. Cynthia L. Nakashima, "An Invisible Monster: The Creation and Denial of Mixed-Race People in America," in Root, p. 174.

37. Williamson, *New People*, p. 199.

38. James W. Vander Zanden, *American Minority Relations,* 3rd ed. (New York: Ronald Press Co., 1972), pp. 162–63.

39. Williamson, *New People*, p. 199.

40. Myrdal, *An American Dilemma*, pp. 60–61.

41. Arnold M. Rose and Caroline Rose, *America Divided* (New York: Alfred A. Knopf, 1948), pp. 154–65.

42. Dominguez, *White by Definition*, pp. 172–76; Williamson, *New People*, p. 190.

43. James E. Blackwell, *The Black Community: Diversity and Unity* (New York: Dodd, Mead & Co., 1975), pp. 73–94; Laurence Glasco, "The Mulatto: A Neglected Dimension of Afro-American Social Structure," paper given at the Convention of the Organization of American Historians, April 17–20, 1974, p. 33; J. Richard Udry et al., "Skin Color, Status, and Mate Selection," *American Journal of Sociology* 76 (January 1971): 722–23.

44. Williamson, *New People*, pp. 190–92.

45. Poppy Cannon, *A Gentle Knight: My Husband, Walter White* (New York: Rinehart, 1956), pp. 12–13; John Langston Gwaltney, *Drylongso: A Self-Portrait of Black America* (New York: Vintage Books, 1980), p.74; Lena Horne and Richard Schickel, *Lena* (Garden City, N.Y.: Doubleday, 1965), pp. 45–46.

46. Dawn Day, *The Adoption of Black Children: Counteracting Institutional Discrimination* (Lexington, Mass.: Lexington Books, D. C. Heath & Co., 1979), pp. 99–100.

47. Thomas F. Pettigrew, "Race, Mental Illness, and Intelligence: A Social Psychological View," in *The Biological and Social Meaning of Race*, ed. Richard H. Osborne (San Francisco: W. H. Freeman, 1971), p. xiii.

48. Wilson, "Blood Quantum," p. 111.

49. T. Edward Reed, "Caucasian Genes in American Negroes," *Science* 165 (August 22, 1969): 765.

50. Gwaltney, *Drylongso*, pp. 146–49.

51. Williamson, *New People*, p. 3.

52. G. Reginald Daniel, "Passers and Pluralists: Subverting the Racial Divide," in Root, pp. 91–107; Davis, *Who Is Black?*, pp. 132–7.

53. Brewton Berry, *Almost White* (New York: Macmillan, 1963), pp. 193–95.

54. Edmund Davis Cronon, *Black Moses* (Madison: University of Wisconsin Press, 1955), pp. 172–93.

55. Davis, *Who Is Black?*, pp. 142–56.

56. Gwaltney, *Drylongso*, pp. 71–74, 80–86.

57. Williamson, *New People*, pp. 98–108.

58. Davis, *Who Is Black?*, pp. 156–69.

59. Alan Howard, "Hawaiians," in *Harvard Encyclopedia of American Ethnic Groups*, ed. Stephan Thernstrom (Cambridge, Mass.: Harvard University Press, 1980), p. 449.

60. Johnson, "Offspring," p. 241.

61. Romanzo Adams, "The Unorthodox Race Doctrine of Hawaii," in Tumin, pp. 80–90; Berry, *Race and Ethnic Relations*, pp. 141–42.

62. A. Grove Day, *Hawaii and Its People* (New York: Duell, Sloan, & Pearce, 1960), p. 233; Howard, "Hawaiians," p. 450.

63. Berry, *Race and Ethnic Relations*, pp. 139–40.

64. Adams, "The Unorthodox Race Doctrine of Hawaii," p. 82.

65. Adams, "The Unorthodox Race Doctrine of Hawaii," p. 82; Berry, *Race and Ethnic Relations*, pp. 138–9.

66. Eleanor C. Nordyke, *Peopling of Hawai'i* (Honolulu: University of Hawaii Press, 1989), p. 132.

67. Johnson, "Offspring," pp. 243–5.

68. Howard, "Hawaiians," pp. 449–51.

69. Nordyke, "Blacks in Hawai'i," pp. 247–53.

70. Nakashima, "An Invisible Monster," pp. 177–8.

71. G. Reginald Daniel, "Beyond Black and White: The New Multiracial Consciousness," in Root, p. 334.

72. Ibid., p. 335.
73. Ibid., pp. 335–41.
74. Karen Grigsby Bates, "Color Complexity," *Emerge* (June 1993): 38–39.
75. Root, p. 344.
76. Daniel, "Beyond Black and White," pp. 339–41.

Chapter 10

1. On Tecumseh and a "Pan-Indian Federation," see Glenn Tucker, *Tecumseh: Vision of Glory* (Indianapolis: Bobbs-Merrill, 1959); also, a soon-to-be published paper by Rachel Buff, "Tecumseh, Tenskwatawa, and the National Popular: Myth, Historiography, and Popular Memory," *Historical Reflections, Cross-Cultural Contact*, special issue.

2. Alexandra Harmon, "When an Indian is not an Indian?, 'Friends of the Indian' and the Problem of Indian Identity," *Journal of Ethnic Studies* 18, no. 2 (1991): 95–123. Harmon bases her primary research on the *Proceedings of the 7th Annual Meeting of the Lake Mohonk Conference of Friends of the Indian (1886, 1889)*, in Lake Mohonk, N.Y.

3. See Stephen Jay Gould, *The Mismeasure of Man* (New York: Norton, 1981), pp. 50–60, on "Morton's Skulls," as a case of pseudoscientific racism that was later debunked for skewed research in the study of "craniometrics."

4. Ibid, pp. 98–103. The 1900s was the height of "scientific" racism that was predicated on American eugenics as well as the racial–racist doctrines of German social scientists of the time.

5. See Baird J. Callicott, *In Defense of the Land Ethic* (Binghamton: State University of New York Press, 1989), pp. 177–219, on American Indian Environmental Ethics and the Ojibways as illustration of attitudes towards nature, and an American Indian land wisdom.

6. Paula Gunn Allen, *The Sacred Hoop: Recovering the Feminine in American Indian Traditions* (Boston: Beacon Press, 1986). The author refers to native cultures as "matriarchies" and characterized as "gynocentric" in her pandering generalizations to feminism.

7. Established in 1820, within the U.S. (Continental) Office of War, the bureau is now under the auspices of the Department of the Interior. It has been criticized by Indians as a vehicle for colonist oppression; however, many Indians see it as a necessary evil because it symbolizes the federal obligations, which are based on treaties and other agreements. See M. A. Jaimes, "American Indian Indentification/Eligibility Policy in Federal Indian Service Programs," chapter 3, on BIA Origins, pp. 40–50 (Ph.D. dissertation, Arizona State University, 1990).

8. M. A. Jaimes with Theresa Halsey, "American Indian Women: At the Center of Indigenous Resistance in North America," *The State of Native America*, ed. M. A. Jaimes (Boston: South End Press, 1992), pp. 311–44.

9. M. A. Jaimes, "Federal Indian Identification Policy: A Usurpation of Indigenous Sovereignty in North America," in Jaimes, pp. 123–38. *The General Allotment Act of 1887*, also known as the *Dawes Act*, is described by

W. Churchill and G. Morris, "Table: Indian Laws and Cases," in Jaimes, p. 14.

10. Jaimes in Jaimes, *State of Native America*, p. 136.

11. Jack Weatherford, *Native Roots* (New York: Crown, 1991), pp. 19–36. For a fictional account, see Linda Hogan's excellent novel, *Mean Spirit* (New York: Atheneum, 1990), a story about a "white" man who married an Indian woman for her allotment, which led to her murder.

12. Ward Churchill, *Struggle for the Land* (Monroe, Maine: Common Courage Press, 1992–1993)—the theft of Indian lands is a main premise of this book.

13. *Cherokee Nation Application Form Letter* (p. 1, not dated), signed by R. Lee Fleming, Tribal Registrar, states:

> This letter is in reference to your inquiry concerning Cherokee Registration. To be eligible for Tribal membership with the Cherokee Nation, you must apply and be able to present necessary evidence. This evidence is a Certificate of Degree of Indian Blood (CBIB), issued by the Bureau of Indian Affairs.

14. "Cherokees Experience Population Boom," *The Circle*, Tulsa, Okla., February 18, 1994, 16.

15. Lynda Dixon Shaver, "Oklahoma Indians and the Cultural Deprivation of an Oklahoma Cherokee Family," presented at the Speech and Communication Association meeting, November 1993, Miami, Fla.

16. Shelly Davis, "Osage Adopt Constitution: U.S. Declared First Constitution Obsolete in 1881," in *News from Indian Country* (from Pawhuska, Okla.), February 1994, 15.

17. Edward Valandra, a graduate student working on his master's thesis in political science at the University of Colorado at Boulder, and former tribal council member for the Roseland Oglala Tribal Nation, has provided keen insights into the continuing practices of traditional kinship among his peoples in South Dakota. See also M. A. Jaimes's dissertation, "An American Indian International Perspective," pp. 159–69.

18. Peter Nabokov, ed., *Native American Testimony: A Chronicle of Indian–White Relations from Prophecy to the Present* (New York: Penguin Books, 1991), pp. 411–12; taken from 1969 Congressional hearings in Indian Education.

19. Russell Thornton, *American Indian Holocaust Survival: A Population History since 1492* (Norman: University of Oklahoma Press, 1987), p. 224. Quote is summary by James L. Simmons, 1977.

20. Jaimes in Jaimes, *State of Native America*, pp. 127–29.

21. Quote from Rayna Green on "ethnic cleansing" in Jerry Reynolds, "Indian Writers, Part II: The Good, the Bad, and the Ugly," *Indian Country Today*, Rapid City, S. Dakota, Sept. 15, 1993.

22. Elizabeth Cook-Lynn, ed., "Meeting of Indian Professors Takes Up Issues of 'Ethnic' Fraud," *Wicazo Sa Review* 1, no. 11 (Spring 1993): 57–59. Assessment of "ethnic fraud" position taken by the American Indian

Professoriate organization 1993 meeting at Arizona State University, Tempe, Ariz.; the position was spearheaded by Lakota ethnocentric Bea Medicine. The problem is that such inclusive claims to "documented abuse" on which this organization predicates its exclusionary position can be contradicted with violations that target those who have legitimate claims to being American Indian. It is therefore my assessment that the latter as exclusive abuse is more abusive, which leads me to conclude that the inconsistency of this policy is more about "Indian Identity" baiting motivated by professional self-interest in federal times of economic recession than not.

23. "The One-Drop Rule Defined" statement quotes Calvin Trillin, "American Chronicles: Black or White," *New Yorker* April 4, 1986, 76–78, about the Phipps case (*Jane Doe v. State of Louisiana*, 1983).

24. The "Twenty Points," 1973 statement in "On the Trail of Broken Treaties," is from "BIA, I'm Not Your Indian Anymore," *Akwesasne Notes*, Mohawk Nation, Roosevelt, N.Y. See also R. Burnett and J. Kostner, *The Road to Wounded Knee* (New York: Bantam Books, 1974); and "TREATY: The Campaign of Russell Means for the Presidency of the Oglala Sioux Tribe," *Porcupine*, S. Dakota, 1982.

25. See Emoke Szathmary, about research on "genetic markers" in his "Genetics of Aboriginal North Americans," *Evolutionary Anthropology* 1, no. 6 (1993): 202–20.

26. Native Hawaiian Peoples' International Tribunal, *Kanaka, Maoli Nation, Plaintiff, v. United States of America, Defendant*, held on the Hawaiian Islands, August 12–21, 1993, Interim Report on "Summary of Recognitions, Findings, and Recommendations" (to be followed by a complete final text from tribunal judges and rapporteur).

27. Haunani Kay Trask, taped presentation of "Native Hawaiian Sovereignty Rights and Indigenous Structures," from Feb. 22, 1994, University of Colorado at Boulder. See also H. K. Trask, *From a Native Daughter* (Monroe, Maine: Common Courage Press, 1993). This indigenous manifesto for Native Hawaiian liberation was presented as a documented testimony to the Native Hawaiian Peoples' International Tribunal, cited in note 26.

28. Stefan Kuhl, *The Nazi Connection: Eugenics, American Racism, and German National Socialism* (New York: Oxford University Press, 1994).

29. Hermann Raushning, *The Voice of Destruction* (New York: Putnam & Sons, 1940), esp. chapter 16, "Magic, Black and White" pp. 230–42.

30. Ward Churchill, "Genocide: Towards a Functional Definition," *Alternative Press* 2, no. 3 (July 1986): 403–30. See also Churchill, "In the Matter of Julius Streicher" on "Applying Nuremburg Precedents in the U.S.," in *Indians Are Us?*, ed. W. Churchill (Monroe, Maine: Common Courage Press, 1994), pp. 73–87; and M. A. Jaimes's citation of Churchill's work in *The State of Native America*, pp. 1–12.

31. M. Omi and H. Winant, *Racial Formation in the United States: From the 1960s to the 1980s* (New York: Routledge and Kegan Paul, 1986), pp. 105–43.

32. There is evidence that these racist practices are still in evidence, albeit in more covert manifestation as "instutional racism," which is still rooted in the southern United States with some such laws still on the books, but it is not exclusive to that region. Even more overt racism is evident in parts of the Northwest in Washington and Oregon, as well as along the economically eroded midwestern "Farmer's Belt," with particular emphasis in Idaho where paramilitary strongholds among the "white supremacy" racist groups are taking hold.

33. Tom Holm, "Patriots and Pawns: State Use of American Indians in the Military and the Process of Nativization in the U.S.," in Jaimes, pp. 345–70.

34. "And God blessed them, and God said onto them, 'Be fruitful, and multiply, and replenish the earth, and subdue it: and have dominion over the fish of the sea, and over the fowl of the air, and over every living thing that moveth upon the earth.'" Genesis 1:28, King James Translation of the Bible. This biblical reference is linked with the Spanish Sovereign Crown's "Doctrine of Discovery" that rationalized Spanish imperialism, later to be used as an international code by other imperialist seapowers beginning in the fifteenth century in the "New World." See J. H. Elliot, *Imperial Spain, 1469–1716* (New York: Penguin Books, 1990), p. 107.

35. Rudolf Acuna, *Occupied America*, 3rd ed. (New York: Harper Collins, 1988), p. 21, the Protestant Crusade, and pp. 202–76, Mexican American deportations. In addition, other respective seminal texts are Reginal Horsman, *Race and Manifest Destiny* (Cambridge, Mass.: Harvard University Press, 1981) on U.S. racial nationalism; Richard Drinnon, *Facing West* (New York: Schocken Books, 1980/1990) on the metaphysics of Indian-hating and Empire-building.

36. President Richard M. Nixon, before the Watergate scandal, was known for asserting to his cabinet that certain parts of the United States (at the time sitting on Indian reservation lands in Arizona and New Mexico) were to be unofficially declared "national sacrifice areas (NSAs)." These targeted areas included "expendable" Native peoples and their cultural communities on those lands, for the sake of prodevelopment interests around uranium and other mining operational enterprises (i.e., Peabody Coal Co.). For reference see W. Churchill and W. LaDuke, "Native North America: The Political Economy of Radioactive Colonialism," in Jaimes, pp. 241–66.

37. Marianna Guerrero, "American Indian Water Rights: The Blood of Life in Native North America," in Jaimes, pp. 189–216. This "water theft" premise is the thesis of her essay.

38. Eugene Linden, "Lost Tribes, Lost Knowledge," *Time*, September 23, 1991, 46–56; this cover story is about the "nomadic" Penans, Sarawak, and Malaysians in Borneo, Papua, New Guinea; the Aleuts, Unalaska, Alaska in the Aleutian Islands; Bayanga Pygmies in Central Africa; and Lacandan in Chiapas, Mexico, among indigenous peoples worldwide.

39. K. H. Redford, "The Ecological Nobel Savage" on the "Tasaday Hoax," *Cultural Survival Quarterly* 15, no. 1 (1991): 46–48.

40.   Bunty Anquoe, "Mescalero Apache Sign Agreement to Establish Facility for Nuclear Waste," *Indian Country Today* (Rapid City, S. Dakota) 13, no. 33 (Feb. 10, 1994):A1–A2. This case is really about money and what is being called "economy bribery." Therefore, Valerie Taliman ("Nuclear Guinea Pigs," *The Circle* [February 1994], p. 7) is more appropriate to assessing these kinds of economic enterprises that are hazardous to the health and environment of those living close to a "hosted" toxic dump site.

41.   Ward Churchill, "Since Predator Came: A Survey of Native America Since 1492," *The Current Wisdom* 1, no. 1 (1992):24–28.

42.   On the "Human Genome Diversity Project," see "Summary of Planning Workshop 3(B)" on "Ethical and Human Rights Implications," regarding the methods of research sampling, Stanford University, Stanford, Calif., cover letter dated May 17, 1994, and signed by Jean Dobie, Assistant Director, Morrison Institute for Populations and Resources Studies (involved in "selected dissemination of report"). This summation comprises more than 30 pages with an unattached tentative list of more than 600 indigenous groups targeted for DNA sampling worldwide (about 65 in North America, the United States, and Canada), with the data bank reputed to be in Los Alamos, New Mexico. It also lists thirteen participants of this session who are among the leading "genetic experts," several of whom are affiliated with the National Institutes of Health. This project is also indicated to be sponsored by private corporations, and it is different from the government-sponsored Human Genome Project that is collecting DNA samples for a larger data bank from the human population at large.

43.   Vandana Shiva, *The Violence of the Green Movement: Third World Agriculture, Ecology and Politics* (Zed Books and Third World Network, 1991). This "genetic engineering" in the plant world is a main premise in her work, which emphasizes the case of India. Of particular note is the chapter on "Miracle Seeds and the Destruction of Genetic Diversity," pp. 61–102. Another article which is pretty lame in comparison to Shiva's work on the issue of indigenous agrarian knowledge is by S. H. Davis, "Hard Choices: Indigenous Economic Development and Intellectual Property Rights," *Akwe:kon (All of Us)* 10, no. 4 (Winter 1993): 19–25 (from Cornell University, Ithaca, N.Y.).

44.   Sharon Venne, an international human rights activist for indigenous peoples and a Cree delegate to the United Nations since 1981, has shared this assessment with me. She was referring to the Human Rights proceedings at the "Working Group for Indigenous Populations (Peoples)," Geneva, Switzerland, 1993, at which she was a participant. She credits another delegate with the term "the Vampire Project" for referring to the "Human Genome Project" because it prefers blood samples to hair follicles and cheek scrapings for DNA genetic data.

45.   1993 Working Group; Venne and others from the international human rights arena asked such questions as, "Why (by what criteria) are the Native people and their respective cultures targeted on this list as "threatened" peoples in the first place? If this is in fact the case, what is being

humanely done to assist them in this genocide, ethnocide, and ecocide?" Such queries have prompted the indigenous non-governmental organizations of the United Nations to submit a declaration to cease and desist in the genetic research that is already underway. As Venne points out, the problem with this scenario is that while one area of the United Nations puts forth a declaration in protest, in another area of the monolithic, duplicitous bureaucracy, other agencies are funding the global project.

46. William Stanton, *The Leopard Spots: Scientific Attitudes Toward Race in America, 1819–59* (Chicago: University of Chicago, 1960). Of particular note is Stanton's "The Problem of the Free Hybrid," pp. 189–91.

47. Ibid.

48. Jack D. Forbes, *Black Africans and Native Americans: Color, Race, and Caste in the Evolution of Red–Black Peoples* (New York: Basil Blackwell, 1988). See also bell hooks, *Black Looks: Race and Representation* (Boston: South End Press, 1992); especially noted is her chapter "Revolutionary Renegades" (pp. 179–94) about "Red–Black Indian."

49. Thornton on Spanish obsession with interracial categories among *mestizo* offsprings of Spanish and Indian intermarriage and intermixing (*American Indian Holocaust Survival*, pp. 186–9). In addition, there is E. B. Reuter's dated but informative *Race Mixture: Studies in Intermarriage and Miscegenation* (New York: McGraw-Hill, 1931), which looks at "interracial" population groups.

50. Elliot on the Spanish notions of "Christian purity and race," which led to the ecclesiastical policy known as "limpiezas de sangre" (*Imperial Spain*, p. 107).

51. Thornton, *American Indian Holocaust Survival*, p. 55.

52. Harmon, "When an Indian is not an Indian?" pp. 108–11.

53. Vine Deloria, Jr., *A Better Day for Indians* (New York: Field Foundation, 1977), p. 20.

54. Vine Deloria, Jr., has commented on this phenomenon that he has run across in his examination of the older versions of some treaties between nations, which included sections about the "rights" of "mixed bloods" among tribal membership. This also seems to imply that the tribal leaders, as treaty delegates and negotiators, were using the language of the Europeans and American colonizers who were much more preoccupied with distinctions between "full bloods" and "half-breeds" among native groups.

55. Margaret Hacker, *Cynthia Ann Parker, the Life and Legend* (Austin: Texas Western Press, 1990).

56. Sandy Gonzales, "Intermarriage and Assimilation: The Beginning or the End?" *Wicazo Sa Review* 8, no. 2 (Fall 1992):48–52. Her research includes a table that provides more specific differences in intermarriage and exogamy between the Indian population genders. Gonzales provides good data, but I find her work too narrow in scope, particularly the implications of a rather pessimistic outlook. Thornton (*American Indian Holocaust Survival*, p. 236): In 1980, over 50% of *all* American Indians were married to non-Indians, while only about one (%) of whites and two (%) blacks were married to someone of another race.

57. Jack D. Forbes, "Undercounting Native Americans: the 1980 Census and the Manipulation of Racial Identity in the U.S.," *Wicazo Sa Review* 6, no. 1 (Spring 1990): 2–26. Forbes also refers to how President Richard Nixon, before Watergate, designated the use of the term "Hispanic" to diffuse and deter the sociopolical issues of Spanish-speaking populations in the United States, who in census-taking, opted to identify with the Native roots among indigenous peoples.

58. A reform movement is challenging the race "classifiers" in the United States; among them is *Mestizaje*, representing Chicano and Native activists in the western states, who are redefining cultural identity for themselves. There are also other "interracial groups" among blacks, Indians, and Asians, who are countering with grievances of "ethnic sorting," as in the case of "affirmative action" profiling. For example, American Indians are usually classified by a race coding and "federally recognized" tribal affiliation, in contrast to the Eurocentric label "Hispanics" imposed on all Spanish-speaking groups. The term Hispanic is supposed to be linked to Spanish culture, which denies many in this category their native heritage to the Americas. However, blacks and Asians are designated based on more distinct physical characteristics. These categories are inconsistent at best, and do not recognize the biological and cultural diversity among many, if not most, "mixed-blood identities" because of biological descendency and cultural heritage.

59. "Action Speaks Louder Than Words: Native Council of Canada Record on Native Women's Rights," *Native Women Journal* (Aug./Sept. 1992): 6–7. This record includes statements on "gender inequality in tribal governance and national recognition, among Métis Women's organizations with headquarters in Alberta.

60. Robert Stock, "The Settler State and the American Left," *New Studies on the Left* 14, no. 3 (Winter 1990–91): 72–78.

61. See W. Churchill and W. LaDuke on "radioactive colonization," in Jaimes, pp. 241–66.

62. M. A. Jaimes, "Native American Identity and Survival: Indigenism and Environmental Ethics" (forthcoming).

63. See Russell Thornton on Indian populations and demographics (*American Indian Holocaust Survival*); and 1980 census data and reports, Office of the U.S. Census, Washington, D.C.

64. John R. Wunder, *"Retained by the Peoples": A History of American Indians and the Bill of Rights* (New York: Oxford University Press, 1994).

65. H. K. Trask's presentation on "Native Hawaiian Sovereignty Rights."

66. Vine Deloria, Jr., "The Next Three Years: A Time for Change," *Indian Historian* 7, no. 2 (Spring 1974): 26.

67. Press release, March 28, 1994, from the International Confederation of Autonomous Chapters of the American Indian Movement, regarding summation of A.I.M. Tribunal held in San Francisco, March 26–26, 1994.

68. Al Gedicks, *The New Resource Wars: Native and Environmental Struggles Against Multinational Corporations* (Boston: South End Press, 1993).

Chapter 11

1. James Ridgeway, *Blood in the Face* (New York: Thundermouth Press, 1990).

2. See: F. James Davis, *Who Is Black? One Nation's Definition* (University Park: Pennsylvania State University Press, 1991); Carl N. Degler, *Neither Black Nor White: Slavery and Race Relations in Brazil and the United States* (New York: Macmillan Company, 1971); John G. Mencke, *Mulattoes and Race Mixture: American Attitudes and Images, 1865–1918* (Ann Arbor: University Microfilms Inc. Research Press, 1979); Edward Byron Reuter, *The Mulatto in the United States, Including a Study of the Role of Mixed-Blood Races Throughout the World* (Boston: Richard G. Badger, 1918); Joel Williamson, *New People: Miscegenation and Mulattoes in the U.S.* (New York: The Free Press, 1980).

3. Paul R. Spickard, *Mixed Blood: Intermarriage and Ethnic Identity in Twentieth-Century America* (Madison: University of Wisconsin Press, 1989).

4. Margaret A. Parkman and Jack Sawyer, "Dimensions of Ethnic Intermarriage in Hawaii," *American Sociological Review* 32 (1967): 593–608.

5. Romanzo Adams, *Interracial Marriage in Hawaii* (New York: MacMillan, 1937); Peter M. Blau, Terry C. Blum, and Joseph E. Schwartz, "Heterogeneity and Intermarriage," *American Sociological Review* 47 (February 1982): 45–62; Milton L. Barron, "Intergroup Aspects of Choosing a Mate," *The Blending American*, ed. Milton L. Barron (Chicago: Quandrangle Press, 1972).

6. Milton M. Gordon, *Assimilation in American Life* (New York: Oxford University Press, 1964).

7. Ruby Jo Reeves Kennedy, "Single or Triple Melting Pot? Intermarriage Trends in New Haven, 1870–1950," *American Journal of Sociology* 58 (1952).

8. Barron, *Blending American*; Parkman and Sawyer, "Dimensions of Intermarriage."

9. Spickard, *Mixed Blood*.

10. Robert K. Merton, "Intermarriage and the Social Structure," *Psychiatry* 4 (1941): 361–74; Kingsley Davis, "Intermarriage in Caste Societies," *American Anthropologist* 43 (1941): 376–95.

11. Merton, "Intermarriage and the Social Structure."

12. Ralph B. Cezares, Edward Murguia, and W. Parker Frisbie, "Mexican American Intermarriage In A Nonmetropolitan Context," *Social Science Quarterly* 65 (1984): 626–34; Gordon, *Assimilation*; Avelardo Valdez, "Recent Increases in Intermarriage by Mexican American Males: Bexar County, Texas, from 1971 to 1980," *Social Science Quarterly* 64 (1983): 136–44.

13. Edward Murguia and W. Parker Frisbie, "Trends in Mexican American Intermarriage: Recent Findings In Perspective," *Social Science Quarterly* 58 (1977): 375; See also Cezares, Murguia, and Frisbie, "Mexican American Intermarriage"; Michael C. Kearl and Edward Murguia, "Age

Differences of Spouses in Mexican American Intermarriage: Exploring the Cost of Minority Assimilation," *Social Science Quarterly* 66 (1985): 453–60.

14. Harry H. L. Kitano, Wai-Tsang Yeung, Lynn Chai, and Herbert Hatanaka, "Asian-American Interracial Marriage," *Journal of Marriage and the Family* 46 (February, 1984): 180.

15. Kearl and Murguia,"Age Differences," p. 453.

16. Michael Omi and Howard Winant, *Racial Formation in the United States: From the 1960s to the 1980s* (New York: Routledge, 1986), pp. 14–15.

17. Ibid., p. 16.

18. Kitano et al., "Asian-American Interracial Marriage," p. 179.

19. Omi and Winant, "Racial Formation," p. 16.

20. Ibid., p. 19.

21. Ibid., p. 23.

22. Ibid., p. 52.

23. Ibid., p. 60.

24. Steven Seidman, "The End of Sociological Theory: The Postmodern Hope," *Sociological Theory* 9, no. 2 (1991): 135.

25. Judith Butler, *Gender Trouble: Feminism and the Subversion of Identity* (New York: Routledge, 1990), p. 5.

26. Yehudi O. Webster, *The Racialization of America* (New York: St. Martin's Press, 1992), p. 2.

27. Ibid., p. 11.

28. Ibid., p. 194.

29. Ibid., p. 7.

30. Ibid., pp. 6–7.

31. Ibid., p. 193.

32. Ibid., p. 264.

33. Butler, *Gender Trouble,* p. 2.

34. Ibid., p. 17.

35. Ibid., p. x.

36. Omi and Winant, *Racial Formation,* p. 62.

37. Iris Marion Young, "The Ideal of Community and the Politics of Difference," *Feminism/Postmodernism,* ed. Linda J. Nicholson (New York: Routledge, 1990), p. 303

38. Butler, *Gender Trouble,* p. 134.

39. Andrew MacDonald, *The Turner Diaries* (Hillsboro, Virginia: National Vanguard Books, 1978), pp. 160–61.

40. Butler, *Gender Trouble,* p. 133.

41. Ernest Porterfield, "Black-American Intermarriage in the United States," *Marriage and Family Review* 5, no. 1 (Spring 1982): 17.

42. Edward Murguia, and Ralph B. Cazares, "Intermarriage of Mexican Americans," *Marriage and Family Review* 5, no. 1 (Spring 1982): 91.

43. Seidman, "End of Sociological Theory," p. 136.

Chapter 12

1. There is some controversy in presenting clinical materials given the concern that the clinical picture will be generalized to all biracial people. This is not my intention nor is it a valid generalization. The inclusion of clinical data is only to aid in understanding the complexity of internalized oppression and to enlighten the reader in approaching this matter with greater sensitivity.

2. For our purposes, it is assumed that the relationship with the primary caretakers is healthy, and the child is well mirrored in the eyes of the mother.

3. Maslow's hierarchy of human needs states that the most basic human needs are food and shelter. Once these physical needs are satisfied the next most pressing need is to belong. It is only after these three primary needs are satisfied that one can aspire toward self-respect, self-esteem, and self-actualization. Abraham Maslow, *Towards A Psychology of Being* (New York: Van Nostrand Reinhold Press, 1968).

4. Parental pride at the birth of a new baby often follows checking that it is healthy and determining sex if not already known, and then endless remarks are made about whom the baby resembles. It is also not uncommon for parents of color to anticipate how dark or light the baby will be as an indicator of social and community acceptance. It is understood by African-American parents that color and hair may change as the baby gets older and at puberty.

5. Cf. Theresa S. Chang's article "The Self-Concept of Children of Ethnically Different Marriages," *California Journal of Education Research* 25, no. 5 (1974): 245–52.

6. W. S. Carlos Poston, "The Biracial Identity Development Model: A Needed Addition," *Journal of Counseling & Development* 69 (Nov./Dec. 1990): 152–55; and George Kitahara Kich, "The Developmental Process of Asserting a Biracial Bicultural Identity," *Racially Mixed People in America*, ed. Maria P. P. Root (Newbury Park, Calif.: Sage, 1990), pp. 304–20.

7. Deborah Sebring, "Considerations in Counseling Interracial Children," *Journal of Non-White Concerns in Personnel and Guidance* 13, no.1 (January 1985): 6; and Cornelia Porter, "Social Reasons for Skin Tone Preferences of Black School-Age Children," *American Journal of Orthopsychiatry* 61, no. 1 (January 1991): 149–54, give examples of acceptance of children among peers according to skin color.

8. I choose this term dehumanizing because subjectively not belonging to a race is tantamount to not belonging to the human race.

9. Cf. Erik Erikson, *Identity and the Life Cycle* (New York: W. W. Norton & Co., 1980), pp. 122–27.

10. This can occur with additional stressors and a history of poor object relations, i.e., not being valued by one's parents or a lack of gratifying intimate relationships with significant others, or both.

11. In extreme cases, when one has grown up in grossly dysfunctional

families, even this reduced world of family and friends is not available because one never developed the trust to open up with them.

12. For a discussion of ethnic identity see Bernal et al., "The Development of Ethnic Identity in Mexican-American Children," *Hispanic Journal of Behavioral Sciences* 12, no. 1 (February 1990): 3–24.

13. See section on miscegenation in Eugene Genovese, *Roll Jordan Roll: The World The Slaves Made* (New York: Vintage, 1976), pp. 413–31.

14. T. W. Adorno et al., *The Authoritarian Personality* (New York: Wiley & Sons, 1964); Gordon Allport, *The Nature of Prejudice* (Reading, Mass.: Addison Wesley Publishing, 1985); E. Frenkel-Brunswick, "Intolerance of Ambiguity as an Emotional and Perceptual Personality Variable," *Journal of Personality* 18 (1949): 108–43; and E. Frankel-Brunswick, "Tolerance Toward Ambiguity as a Personality Variable," *American Psychologist* 3 (1968): 268.

15. It is interesting that some authors suggest that prejudice and intolerance are attributes of those who seek to bolster a weak identity and avoid their own self doubt. Bruno Bettelheim and Morris Janowitz, "Prejudice and the Search for Identity" in *Social Change and Prejudice* (New York: Free Press, 1975), pp. 56–60.

16. Sexualized race fantasies are far too complex to deal with within the scope of this paper. Two popularized books on this topic are Charles Herbert Stember, *Sexual Racism: The Emotional Barrier to an Integrated Society* (New York: Harper & Row, 1976), and Calvin Hernton, *Sex and Racism in America* (New York: Grove Press, 1965). Also Joel Kovel's *White Racism: A Psychohistory* (London: Free Association, 1988) is an excellent account of how the repressive denied sexuality of a dominant group is projected onto a minority population. See also the seminal work on the psychology of prejudice, Allport, *The Nature of Prejudice*, chapter 24 on "Projection."

17. This theme appears in many fine histories of race. Cf. Gilbert Osofsky, *The Burden of Race: A documentary History of Negro–White Relations in America* (New York: Harper & Row, 1967); and Ronald Takaki, *Iron Cages: Race and Culture in 19th Century America* (Seattle: University of Washington, 1982). Concerning anti-Semitism see Theodore Isaac Rubin, *Anti-Semitism: A Disease of the Mind* (New York: Continuum, 1990), chapter 2, where he discusses symbol sickness.

18. For a discussion of these dynamics that are prevalent in a colonial context see Albert Memmi, *The Colonizer and the Colonized* (Boston: Beacon, 1967), and by same author, *Dependence* (Boston: Beacon, 1984). See also O. Mannoni, *Prospero and Caliban: The Psychology of Colonization* (New York: Praeger, 1956).

19. For a fuller discussion of this issue, see G. Reginald Daniel, "Passers and Pluralists: Subverting the Racial Divide," in Root, pp. 91–107.

20. A discussion of assessing racial identity problems can be found in Ruth McRoy and Edith Freeman, "Racial-Identity Issues among Mixed-Race Children," *Social Work in Education* 8, no. 3 (January 1986): 164–74.

21. Cf. Ashley Montagu, *Man's Most Dangerous Myth: The Fallacy of*

Race (Cleveland, Ohio: World, 1964); Ashley Montagu, ed., *The Concept of Race* (London: Collier Books, 1969); Frank Livingstone, "On the Nonexistence of Human Races" in Montagu, p. 48.

22. As recently as 1967, antimiscegenation laws were still on the books in some states. In 1967 the Supreme Court in *Loving v. Virginia* overturned Virginia's law against interracial marriages. Sixteen other states held the same law, all of which were overturned by 1982.

23. It has been suggested that this process begins around three years of age. Doyle et al. "Developmental Patterns in the Flexibility of Children's Ethnic Attitudes," *Journal of Cross-Cultural Psychology* 19, no. 1 (March 1988): 3–6.

Chapter 13

1. Addendum analysis of Figures 1, 2, and 3. [Mentioned in text, but not included here—Ed.] The Cincinnati Public Schools present the most accurate data to date on the usage of the Multiracial category. The 1990–91 school year did not have "Other" or "Multiracial" on school forms. The 1991–92 school year used "Other," which was chosen by *489* students. A Multiracial category was not available that year. The following year, "Other" was removed and "Multiracial" was added. *527* students identified themselves as Multiracial in the Cincinnati Public Schools. Clearly, those students who identified as multiracial came mainly from the category of "Other." The multiracial students did *not* come from other racial categories. It is important to note that three minority categories, Asian, American Indian, and Hispanic, were chosen by fewer students than the multiracial group. In other words, if we can justify a classification for 18 American Indians in Cincinnati, we can surely justify a category for 527 multiracial children.

2. Analysis of Fulton County, Georgia, data shows 110 students (0.23%) utilizing the multiracial category in February of 1993 (the first year of use). In the previous year (1991–92), 17 students identified themselves in the "Other" category. A low percentage of black and white population was lost, apparently the result of the overall population shift to other areas. The Asian population showed a gain of 60 students, and the Native Indian/Alaskan and Hispanic populations reflected a gain of one student each. Of most interest, is that although the "Other" category was retained on the 1992–93 forms, *not one child chose to use the category of "Other,"* indicating that "Multiracial" was the preferable term.

3. Signed by Governor Jim Edgar, July 7, 1993. Effective date July 1, 1994.

4. Office of Management and Budget (OMB) Directive 15: "Race and Ethnic Standards for Federal Statistics and Administrative Reporting." The Directive provides standard classifications for record keeping, collection, and presentation of data on race and ethnicity in federal program administrative reporting and statistical activities. [See Appendix 1, Chapter 14—Ed.]

5. Defined as "f. Multiracial. A person whose parents have origins in two or more of the above racial and ethnic categories." The "above categories" as defined in Directive 15 are a. American Indian or Alaskan Native, b. Asian or Pacific Islander, c. Black, d. Hispanic, and e. White.

6. The acceptable variance in OMB Directive 15 would specify the combinations of origin. Data would then be assigned by fractions into the appropriate other five (a to e) racial and ethnic categories.

Chapter 14
List of Appendixes (3–11 not included here—Ed.)

1. Office of Management & Budget Statistical Policy Directive 15.

2. AMEA Proposed Revised OMB Minimum Reporting Standards With Multiracial, Multiethnic Categories.

3. 1990 Census Form, Race & Ethnic Origin Questions.

4. *Washington Post*, April 29, 1991, "Categorizing the Nation's Millions of Other Race."

5. Letter from U.S. Dept. of Education to AMEA dated Oct. 4, 1989, re: OMB Dir. 15.

6. Berkeley Public Schools Enrollment Form & Statistics, 1968–1992.

7. *Chicago Sun Times*, Feb. 8, 1993, "No Option in Schools"; *Chicago Sun Times*, Apr. 26, 1993, "Multiracial Category Sought on School Forms"; *Chicago Tribune*, May 3, 1993, "Multiracial People Want a Single Name That Fits."

8. Letter from American Civil Liberties Union to U.S. Department of Education dated Mar. 8, 1990, re: Baha'i student.

9. *Time Magazine*, Sept.4, 1989, "No Place For Mankind."

10. Personal Testimony of Ramona E. Douglass, AMEA Vice President, Central Region.

11. "Marital Status & Living Arrangements," U.S. Bureau of the Census, Current Population Reports Series P20-468.

Chapter 15

1. Maria P. P. Root, "Within, Between, and Beyond Race," in *Racially Mixed People in America,* ed. Maria P. P. Root (Newbury Park, Calif.: Sage, 1992), p. 3.

2. George Kich, "The Developmental Process of Asserting Biracial, Bicultural Identity," in Root, pp. 12–23; R. G. McRoy and E. Freeman, "Racial Identity Issues Among Mixed-race Children," *Social Work in Education* 8 (1986):164–174; Maria P. P. Root, "Within, Between, and Beyond Race," in Root, pp. 3–11; C. White-Stephan, "Mixed-Heritage Individuals: Ethnic Identity and Trait Characteristics," in Root, pp. 50–63.

3. Kich, "Developmental Process."

4. Ibid., p. 306.

5. Ibid., p. 309.

6. Ibid., p. 314.

7. Ibid., p. 317.

8. Cited in A. Darder, *Culture and Power in the Classroom: A Critical Foundation for Bicultural Education* (New York: Bergin & Garvey, 1991), p. 1.

9. Cynthia Nakashima, "An Invisible Monster: The Creation and Denial of Mixed Race People in America," in Root, pp. 162–178.

10. Kich, "Developmental Process," p. 315.

11. Nakashima, "Invisible Monster"; Root, "Within, Between, and Beyond Race"; P. R. Spickard, "The Illogic of American Racial Categories," in Root, pp. 12–23; M. Thornton, "Is Multiracial Status Unique? The Personal and Social Experience," in Root, pp. 321–5.

12. Amanda Udis-Kessler, "Bisexuality in an Essentialist World," *Bisexuality: A Reader and a Source Book*, ed. T. Geller (Ojai, Calif.: Times Change Press, 1990), p. 55.

13. Kenneth Gergen, *Toward Transformation in Social Knowledge* (New York: Springer-Verlag, 1984), p. 96.

14. Darder, *Culture and Power in the Classroom*; P. Freire and D. Macedo, *Literacy: Reading the Word and the World* (New York: Bergin & Garvey, 1987).

15. Darder, *Culture and Power in the Classroom*, p. 4.

16. Ibid.

17. Ibid., pp. 6–7.

18. Giroux, cited in Darder, *Culture and Power in the Classroom*, p. 7.

19. Aronowitz and Giroux, cited in Darder, *Culture and Power in the Classroom*, p. 20.

20. Darder, *Culture and Power in the Classroom*; L. Derman-Sparks, "Multicultural Education and Curriculum," 6th Annual Conference of the National Coalition of Education Activists, July 1993; C. E. Sleeter, "Introduction: Multicultural Education and Empowerment," in C. E. Sleeter, ed., *Empowerment Through Multicultural Education* (Albany, N.Y.: State University of New York Press, 1991), pp. 217–228.

21. Sleeter, "Introduction," p. 11.

22. J. A. Banks, "A Curriculum for Empowerment, Action, and Change," in Sleeter, pp. 125–142; Darder, *Culture and Power in the Classroom*.

23. Banks, "Curriculum."

24. R. Ruiz, "The Empowerment of Language-Minority Students," in Sleeter, pp. 217–228.

25. Sleeter, "Introduction," pp. 8–9.

26. Ibid., p. 12.

27. Darder, *Culture and Power in the Classroom*, 100.

28. Ibid.

Chapter 16

1. Kevin Dann, "From Degeneration to Regeneration: The Eugenics Survey of Vermont 1925–1936." *Vermont History* 1 (1991): 10–11.

2. Edmund Fuller, *Vermont: A History of the Green Mountain State* (Montpelier: State Board of Education, 1952), p. 47.

3. Virgil Vogel, *This Country Was Ours* (New York: Harper Torchbooks, 1972), p. 150.

4. Joan Rollins, ed., *Hidden Minorities: The Persistence of Ethnicity in American Life* (New York: University Press of America, 1981), p. 11.

5. Fuller, *Vermont*, p. 33.

6. Adam Jaworski, "How to Silence a Minority: The Case of Women," *International Journal of Sociology and Language* 94 (1992): 27.

7. Ibid., p. 28.

8. John Comaroff and Jean Comaroff, *Ethnography and the Historical Imagination* (Boulder: Westview, 1992), pp. 25–28.

9. Benjamin Ringer and Elinor Lawless, *Race, Ethnicity and Society* (New York: Routledge, Chapman and Hall, 1989), p. 18.

10. Renato Rosaldo, *Culture and Truth: The Remaking of Social Analysis* (Boston: Beacon Press, 1989), p. 70.

11. Rollins, *Hidden Minorities*, p. 13.

Chapter 17

1. Maria P. P. Root, "Reasons Racially Mixed Persons Identify as People of Color," *FOCUS* (Division 45 of the American Psychological Association, June 1994).

2. "Marital Status and Living Arrangements," March 1992, *Current Population Reports* (U.S. Department of Commerce, Bureau of the Census, Series P20-468, Washington, D.C., December 1992).

3. "Interracial Baby Boom Refocuses Racial Identity," *Minority Markets ALERT: Critical Trends Among Non-European Americans* (Brooklyn, N.Y.: EPM Communications, March 1992), p. 2.

4. M. P. P. Root, "Resolving 'Other' Status," in *Diversity and Complexity in Feminist Therapy*, eds. L. S. Brown and Maria P. P. Root (New York: Haworth Press, 1990), pp. 185–206.

5. Maria P. P. Root, ed., *Racially Mixed People in America* (Newbury Park, Calif.: Sage Publications, 1992).

6. Naomi Zack, *Race and Mixed Race* (Philadelphia: Temple University Press, 1993).

7. Maria P. P. Root, ed., *Racially Mixed People in a New Millenium* (Newbury Park, Calif.: Sage Publications, in preparation).

8. C. V. Willie, *Oreo: Race and Marginal Men and Women* (Wakefield, Mass.: Parameter Press, 1975).

9. F. Henriques, *Children of Conflict: A Study of Interracial Sex and Marriage* (New York: Dutton, 1974).

10. W. E. Cross, *Shades of Black: Diversity in African-American Identity* (Philadelphia: Temple University Press, 1991).

11. J. E. Helms, *Black and White Racial Identity: Theory, Research, and Practice* (New York: Greenwood Press, 1990).

12. L. R. Tenzer, *A Completely New Look at Interracial Sexuality: Pub-*

lic Opinion and Select Commentaries (Manahawkin, N.J.: Scholar's Publishing House, 1990).

13. C. C. I. Hall, *The Ethnic Identity of Racially Mixed People: A Study of Black-Japanese* (Los Angeles, University of California, Doctoral dissertation, 1980).

14. M. C. Thornton, *A Social History of a Multiethnic Identity: The Case of Black Japanese Americans* (Ann Arbor, University of Michigan, Doctoral Dissertation, 1983).

15. "Marital Status and Living Arrangements," Current Population Reports, Bureau of the Census, 1992.

16. "For the First Time, More Americans Approve of Interracial Marriage than Disapprove," *Gallup Poll Monthly* 311 (August 1991): 60–62.

17. R. Miller and B. Miller, "Mothering the Biracial Child: Bridging the Gaps Between African-American and White Parenting Styles," *Women and Therapy* 10 (1990): 169–80.

18. B. A. Greene, "What Has Gone Before: The Legacy of Racism and Sexism in the Lives of Black Mothers and Daughters," in L. S. Brown and Maria P. P. Root, pp. 207–30.

19. C. C. I. Hall, *Ethnic Identity*.

20. F. W. Twine, "Brown Skinned White Girls: Race, Class, and the Limits of White Identity Claims," in *Local Whiteness: Localizing White Identity*, ed. R. Frankenberg (Durham, N.C.: Duke University Press, in press).

21. P. R. Spickard, *Mixed Blood: Intermarriage and Ethnic Identity in Twentieth-Century America* (Madison: The University of Wisconsin Press, 1989).

22. J. Weisman provided helpful discussion in developing this linkage to the positive refuge in being a person of color.

23. W. E. B. Dubois, *The Souls of Black Folk* (New York: First Vintage Books/The Library of America Edition, 1990).

Chapter 18

1. Public Enemy, "Fear of a Black Planet," written by K. Shocklee, E. Sadler, and C. Ridenhour (Def Jam Records, 1990).

2. *Time*, 141, no. 2 "The New Face of America," Special Issue (Fall 1993).

3. Maria Root speaks of "The emergence of a racially mixed population . . . transforming the "face" of the United States. Root's "increasing presence of multiracial people" gives in to the premise of past purity. Maria P. P. Root, "Within, Between, and Beyond Race," in *Racially Mixed People*, ed. Maria P. P. Root (Newbury Park, Calif.: Sage, 1992), p. 3.

4. On "ethnorace," see David Theo Goldberg, *Racist Culture: Philosophy and the Politics of Meaning* (Oxford: Basil Blackwell, 1993), pp. 74–8.

5. *Time*, Fall 1993, 3, 66–7.

6. Public Enemy, "Fear of a Black Planet."

7. David Theo Goldberg, "The Semantics of Race," *Ethnic and Racial Studies* 15, no. 4 (October 1993), pp. 543–69.

8. Public Enemy, "Fear of a Black Planet."

9. Ibid.

10. Whereas the Census Bureau was initially under the Department of State, it is now notably part of the Department of Commerce. The census thus furnishes corporations free market research, effectively making a welfare payment to Wall Street.

11. Martin Kilson, "Anatomy of Black Conservatives," *Transition* 59 (1993): 4.

12. It was estimated on the basis of intercensal and birth-death rate comparisons that 25,000 blacks "passed into the general community" *each year* from 1900–1910. If these figures are even half accurate, they are remarkable. William Petersen, "Politics and the Measurement of Ethnicity," *The Politics of Numbers*, eds. William Alonso and Paul Starr (New York: Russell Sage Foundation, 1987), p. 212.

13. Cf. Linda Chavez, *Out of the Barrio: Toward a New Politics of Hispanic Assimilation* (New York: Basic Books), 1991.

14. The fabrication at work here is revealed in the ironic courtroom response of Steve Biko under prosecutorial interrogation during his trial. The exchange proceeded in something like the following terms. Prosecutor: Why does the Black Consciousness Movement characterize itself as 'black'? You're not black, but brown. To which Biko quickly retorted: Why 'white'? You're not white but pink.

15. See, for example, Roger Omond, *The Apartheid Handbook: A Guide to South Africa's Everyday Racial Policies* (Harmondsworth, U.K.: Penguin, 1985), pp. 21–5. As an example of multiple reclassifications, Omond cites the case of a Mr. Wilikinson, who found himself reclassified five times from "mixed" to "European (white)" to "Coloured" to "white" to "Coloured," the last time at his own request so as to be able to live legally with his wife, an Indian woman who at the same time applied successfully to be reclassified "Coloured."

16. Public Enemy, "Fear of a Black Planet."

17. On the "nihilistic threat" faced by blacks, cf. Cornel West, *Race Matters* (Boston: Beacon Press, 1993); and Richard Wright, *The Outsider* (New York: Harper and Row, 1965). On Wright's depiction of African-American nihilism, see Paul Gilroy, *The Black Atlantic: Modernity and Double Consciousness* (Cambridge, Mass.: Harvard University Press, 1993), p. 172; and on West's argument regarding black nihilism, see my "Whither West?", *Review of Education/Pedagogy/Cultural Studies* 1, no. 1 (1994): 1–13; and Adolph Reed, Jr., "Class Notes," *The Progressive* 57, no. 12 (December 1993):18–20.

18. See "A Cultural Gap May Swallow a Child," *New York Times*, Tuesday, October 8, 1993, A8. The Indian Welfare Act of 1978 grants American Indian tribes special preference in adopting children born to Indian parents. The case at hand in the report concerns a child fathered by an Oglala Sioux man and placed at birth by his white mother with white adoptive parents. The Oglala Sioux nation were suing the adoptive parents to re-place the now

four-year-old boy with Indian relatives on Pine Ridge Reservation. His biological father has since married a woman other than the boy's biological
mother, and according to the report has shown no interest in the child.

19.   Cf. Ernest Gellner, *Nations and Nationalism* (Oxford: Basil Blackwell,
1983), chapters 2 and 3. Eric Hobsbawm, "The New Threat to History," *New
York Review of Books* 40, no. 21 (December 1993): 62–65.

20.   Queen Victoria, that mythical figure of Englishness—of racialized
cultural homogeneity, precisely—illustrates the point. As Benedict Anderson notes, her own heritage is anything but completely English. Englishness, in any case, is itself a cultural hybrid. Cf. Benedict Anderson, *Imagined Communities* (London: Verso Books, 1983), pp. 84ff. Cf. Hugh A.
McDougall, *Racial Myth in English History: Trojans, Teutons, and Anglo-
Saxons* (Montreal: Harvest House, 1982). Alena Luter reminds me that what
Anderson cites as a monarchical commonplace generally characterizes the
aristocracy whose socioeconomic positionalities were maintained especially
in moments of crisis by negotiating transnationally the boundaries of their
local and homogeneous conditions and identities. Cf. David Theo Goldberg,
ed., *Multiculturalism: A Critical Reader* (Oxford: Basil Blackwell, 1994),
pp. 1–41.

21.   In its current arrangements, mixed-race adoption takes on more troubling implications yet, for it affords those adoptive parents who can afford
it the possibilities of a designer kid. The current yuppie flavor, reflecting
stereotypes of the model minority and ethnic intelligence, is Korean. For
approximately what it takes to buy a small Hyundai, and without import
duties or local bureaucracy, those with impeccably white credentials can
adopt a Korean kid (terms arrangeable no doubt for the right customer).
What, one might ask *Time Magazine*, happens to the child-as-property when
tastes change?

22.   Public Enemy, "Fear of a Black Planet."

23.   *Made in America* broaches the subject of mixed-race relations for
the 1990s, as *Guess Who's Coming to Dinner* did for the 1960s. While considerably more optimistic in conclusion than, say, *Jungle Fever, Made in
America* ends up implicitly reinserting the ban on mixed-race progeny (America
can breathe free again, Ted Danson is not the biological father of Whoopi
Goldberg's daughter) even as it calls for the exuberance of the intercultural
experience if not the commodified appropriation of the wonders of the Other's
cultural expression. I viewed the film in Mesa, Arizona, home to the second
largest Mormon population in America and outnumbered in this suburb of
Phoenix only by southwestern Catholics. The audience that chuckled ner-
vously at the thought of mixed-race offspring was virtually dancing in the
aisles during the celebratory finale.

24.   See "A Twist on Affirmative Action: Listing of Italian Americans as
Protected Group Triggers Debate at CUNY," *Chronicle of Higher Education*
(November 24, 1993): A13–14.

25.   Peter Caws points out that one's first culture, the one into which—
like one's first language—one is born, is not so much a culture that one

owns as that to which one belongs. Peter Caws, "Identity: Cultural, Transcultural, and Multicultural," in *Multiculturalism: A Critical Reader*, ed. David Theo Goldberg (Oxford: Basil Blackwell, 1994), pp. 371–387.

26.   Cf. Toni Morrison, *Playing in the Dark* (Cambridge, Mass.: Harvard University press, 1992); Paul Gilroy, *The Black Atlantic*, pp. 217–23.

27.   A theory of (deracinated) cultural membership is worked out by Asa Kasher in "Jewish Collective Identity," in *Jewish Identity*, eds. David Theo Goldberg and Michael Krausz (Philadelphia: Temple University Press, 1993), pp. 56–79.

28.   On the imperative to improvise, see Richard Wright, *Black Power: A Record of Reactions in a Land of Pathos* (New York: Harper and Brothers, 1954), pp. 346–47; and Paul Gilroy, *The Black Atlantic*, pp. 192–93.

29.   I am grateful to my good friend and colleague, Pat Lauderdale, whose insightful comments on an earlier draft reduced the probability of embarrassment. If there be further cause, nevertheless, the embarrassment will be mine alone.

Chapter 19

Epigraph to part 1: "Sociogenic Experiments," by Disposable Heroes of Hiphoprisy.

1.   Leopoldo Zea, "Identity: A Latin American Philosophical Problem," *The Philosophical Forum* 20 (Fall–Winter 1988–89):37.

2.   Latinos in the Florida of the 1950s were generally classified as "almost white" or as "black" depending on their color. But most lived in Miami and Tampa, which were even then cosmopolitan cities very different from the "deep south" cities in north Florida and other southern states. The biggest source of ostracism for Latinos then, as now, was language. Today, the many dark-skinned Latinos who have moved to south Florida are ostracized not only by white Anglos but by African Americans as well for their use of Spanish. Anglos of all colors ridicule the sound of the language, share jokes about uncomprehending sales clerks, and commiserate across their own racial and ethnic differences about the "difficulties" of living in a bilingual city. The experience of Latinos in the United States makes it very clear that so-called racial features never operate alone to determine identity but are always mediated by language, culture, nationality, and sometimes religion.

3.   "Self-consciousness exists in itself and for itself, in that, and by the fact that it exists for another self-consciousness; that is to say, it *is* only by being acknowledged or 'recognized'." G. W. F. Hegel, *The Phenomenology of Mind*, trs. J. B. Baillie (New York: Harper, 1967), p. 229.

4.   For a moving and insightful literary description of this situation, see Nella Larsen's brilliant novel, *Quicksand* (New Brunswick, N.J.: Rutgers University Press, 1993).

5.   For example, it seems likely that the problems Israeli feminists are having in gaining acceptance for a reproductive rights agenda has to do not

only with the close association between the Israeli state and Judaism, but also because the state's self-understood legitimation requires the literal reproduction of Jewish identity.

6. Michel Foucault, *The History of Sexuality, 1*, trs. Robert Hurley (New York: Random House, 1980).

7. Richard Rodriguez, *Days of Obligation* (New York: Penguin, 1992), p. 6.

8. See, e.g., Maria P. P. Root, "Within, Between, and Beyond Race," in *Racially Mixed People in America,* ed. Maria P. P. Root (Newbury Park, Calif.: Sage, 1992), pp. 3–11.

9. Frederic J. Haskin, *The Panama Canal* (Garden City, New York: Doubleday, 1913), p. 162.

10. See Stephen Frenkel's Ph.D. dissertation on the construction of the "other" in the building of the Panama Canal, Syracuse University, 1992.

11. Quoted in John Hope Franklin, *Race and History* (Baton Rouge: Louisiana State University Press, 1989), pp. 321–2.

12. See Franklin, *Race and History*.

13. Homi Bhabha, *The Location of Culture* (New York: Routledge, 1994), p. 66.

14. Rodriguez, pp. 24-25.

15. Rodriguez, p. 6.

16. Carlos A. Fernández, "La Raza and the Melting Pot: A Comparative Look at Multiethnicity," in Root, p. 135.

17. Fernández, p. 135.

18. Fernández, p. 136.

19. Fernández, p. 136.

20. Fernández, p. 137.

21. Just as feminist historians have countered the usual assessment of the Renaissance, arguing that in this period women's situation actually worsened and so there was no renaissance for women, so it has been argued that the Enlightenment offered nothing for those peoples of the world newly colonized. These epoch-dividing categories reflect the perspectives of the dominant.

22. Quoted in Ofelia Schutte, *Cultural Identity and Social Liberation in Latin American Thought* (Albany: State University Press of New York, 1993), p. 86.

23. Ibid.

24. Ibid.

25. Zea, "Identity: A Latin American Philosophical Problem," p. 37.

26. See Gilles Deleuze and Felix Guattari, *Kafka: Toward a Minor Literature*, trs. Dana Polan (Minneapolis: University of Minnesota Press, 1986); *Anti Oedipus*, trs. Robert Hurley et al. (Minneapolis: University of Minnesota Press, 1983); and *A Thousand Plateaus*, trs. Brian Massumi (Minneapolis: University of Minnesota Press, 1987). For a critique, see Caren Kaplan, "Deterritorializations: The Rewriting of Home and Exile in Western Feminist Discourse," *Cultural Critique* (Spring 1987):187–198.

27. *Kafka: Toward a Minor Literature*, p. 19.
28. Ibid., p. 22.
29. *A Thousand Plateaus*, p. 296.
30. See, e.g., Paul Smith, *Discerning the Subject* (Minneapolis: University of Minnesota Press, 1988). See also my review of this book in *American Literary History* (Summer 1993): 335–46.
31. Gloria Anzaldua, *Borderlands/La Frontera* (San Francisco: Spinsters/Aunt Lute, 1987), p. 77.
32. Zea, "Identity: A Latin American Philosophical Problem," pp. 33–34.
33. Ibid., p. 34.
34. See Naomi Zack, "Race and Philosophic Meaning," in *American Philosophical Association Newsletter on Philosophy and the Black Experience* 94, no. 1 (Fall 1994), pp. 14–20.
35. Schutte, *Cultural Identity*, p. 75.
36. Ibid., p. 77.
37. Quoted in Trinh T. Minh-Ha, *When the Moon Waxes Red* (New York: Routledge, 1991), p. 73. Notice that, as she points out, no whites applied to become black.
38. Anzaldua, *Borderlands/La Frontera*, p. 78.
39. Ibid., p. 83.
40. Schutte, *Cultural Identity*, p. 80.

Chapter 20

1. M. Childers and b. hooks, "A Conversation about Race and Class," in *Conflicts in Feminism*, eds. Marianne Hirsch and Evelyn Fox Keller (New York: Routledge, 1990).

Chapter 21

1. See my *Moral Dilemmas of Feminism: Prostitution, Adultery, and Abortion* (New York: Routledge, 1994), pp. 137–40.
2. Patricia Williams, *The Alchemy of Race and Rights* (Cambridge: Harvard University Press, 1991), p. 119.
3. Naomi Zack, *Race and Mixed Race* (Philadelphia: Temple University Press, 1993), pp. 143–7.
4. Judith Butler, "Imitation and Gender Insubordination," *The Lesbian and Gay Studies Reader*, eds. H. Abelove, M. Barale, and D. Halperin (New York: Routledge, 1993), p. 308. See also Judith Butler, *Gender Trouble: Feminism and the Subversion of Identity* (New York: Routledge, 1990).
5. Butler, "Imitation and Gender," p. 312.
6. Ibid., p. 317.
7. Here I follow Zack's practice of speaking of "designated whites and blacks" rather than just "whites" and "blacks" to underscore, as she does, that these are social constructs. See, for example, Zack, *Race and Mixed Race*, p. 27.

8. Williams, *Alchemy of Race and Rights,* p. 10.
9. Butler, "Imitation and Gender," p. 314. In her recent book, *Bodies That Matter* (New York: Routledge, 1993), Butler also considers drag performances that reproduce dominant cultural norms. Here she states

> Although many readers understood *Gender Trouble* to be arguing for the proliferation of drag performances as a way of subverting dominant gender norms, I want to underscore that there is no necessary relation between drag and subversion, and that drag may well be used in the service of both the denaturaliztion and idealization of hyperbolic heterosexual gender norms. (p. 125)

10. Williams, *Alchemy of Race and Rights*, pp. 129–30.

Chapter 22

1. Paul Edwards, ed., *The Encyclopedia of Philosophy* (New York: Macmillan, 1967), s.v. "German Philosophy and National Socialism," p. 315.
2. For further discussion of the concept of race as a line, see Naomi Zack, *Race and Mixed Race* (Philadelphia: Temple University Press, 1993), pp. 19–20.
3. For an attempt to construct African racial identity, at this time, through writing, based on a stated awareness of the conceptual problems with the term 'race,' and the "racial" diversity within Africa, see Anthony Appiah, *In My Father's House* (Oxford: Oxford University Press, 1992).
4. For more detailed discussion of nineteenth-century taxonomies of race, and further sources, see Zack, *Race and Mixed Race*, pp. 112–16; for historical analyses of how, given these hierarchies, measurements of the differences between races were biased and falsified by prominent American scientists, see Stephen Jay Gould, *The Mismeasure of Man* (New York: W. W. Norton, 1981), pp. 73–108.
5. The only empirical difference in blood types among groups of people, which is credited by scientists, is a somewhat geographical distribution of the four major blood types (so distinguished for transfusion purposes), over the surface of the planet. See, for example, N. P. Dubinin, "Race and Contemporary Genetics," in *Race, Science and Society*, ed. Leo Kuper (New York: Columbia University Press, 1975), pp. 71–74.
6. For Locke's explicit statements of his nominalism as summarized in this paper, see John Locke, *Essay Concerning Human Understanding*, ed. Peter H. Niddich (Oxford: Oxford University Press, 1990), as follows (page references are to this Niddich edition): that essences are things in the mind, and that they are made by the mind, *Essay,* III, III, 12, Niddich, pp. 414–15; that species (natural kinds) are imposed by the mind, *Essay*, III, VI, Section 27, Niddich, p. 454.
7. For typical empiricist restrictions to Lockean nominalism, see Irving M. Copi, *Introduction to Logic* (New York: Macmillan, 1961), pp. 107–12;

Merilee H. Salmon, *Introduction to Logic and Critical Thinking* (New York: Harcourt, Brace, Jovanovich, 1984), p. 330.

8. For this scientific consensus about race, see L. C. Dunn, "Race and Biology," in Kuper, *Race, Science and Society*, pp. 61–67; and, L. C. Dunn and Theodosius Dobzhansky, *Heredity, Race and society* (New York: Mentor, 1962), p. 114 et passim.

9. The identification and differentiation of XX and XY has been so successful scientifically that studies of genotypically sex-linked, nonsexual abnormalities, as well as the genetics of sexually indeterminate individuals, have been an important part of the epistemology of XX and XY as paradigm sexual markers. See, for example, Daniel J. Kevles, *In the Name of Eugenics* (Berkeley: University of California Press), pp. 238–50.

10. For an overview of the new theory of reference and its relationship to nominalism, see Stephen P. Schwartz, "Introduction," in *Meaning, Necessity and Natural Kinds*, ed. Stephen P. Schwartz (Ithaca: Cornell University Press, 1975).

11. See William K. Goosens, "Underlying Trait Terms," in Schwartz, *Meaning, Necessity and Natural Kinds*, pp. 133–54.

12. See Keith S. Donnellan, "Reference and Definite Descriptions," in Swartz, *Meaning, Necessity and Natural Kinds,* pp. 42–66.

13. This meaning of 'pragmatic' should be distinguished from a more general theory of pragmatic meaning in which all empirical terms, even terms that clear other sorts of meaning criteria, such as cats, trees, and lemons, would be viewed as having pragmatic meaning. For a more systematic, philosophical account of problems with the meaning of race, see Naomi Zack, "Race and Philosophic Meaning," in *American Philosophical Association Newsletter on Philosophy and the Black Experience* 94, no. 1 (Fall 1994): 14–20.

14. Leonard Harris, "Introduction," in Leonard Harris, ed., *The Philosophy of Alain Locke* (Philadelphia: Temple University Press, 1989), p. 20.

15. See Naomi Zack, *Bachelors of Science: Seventeenth Century Identity, Then and Now* (Philadelphia: Temple University Press, forthcomin..)

16. See ibid., chapter 12, "Slavery without Race."

Select
Bibliography

Preface and Introduction

Clinton, J. Jarrett. "From the Agency for Health Care Policy and Research." *Journal of the American Medical Association* 270, no. 18 (Nov. 10, 1993): 2158.

Davis, F. James. *Who is Black? One Nation's Definition.* University Park: Pennsylvania State University Press, 1991.

Kuper, Leo, ed. *Race, Science and Society.* New York: Columbia University Press, 1965.

Root, Maria P. P., ed. *Racially Mixed People in America.* Newbury Park, Calif.: Sage, 1993.

Wacker, R. Fred. *Ethnicity, Pluralism and Race.* Westwood, Conn.: Greenwood, 1983.

Williamson, Joel. *New People.* New York: Free Press, 1980.

Zack, Naomi. *Race and Mixed Race.* Philadelphia: Temple University Press, 1993.

Part I: Autobiography

Cassidy, Frederick G. *Jamaica Talk: Three Hundred Years of the English Language in Jamaica*, 2nd ed. London: Macmillan, 1971.

DuBois, W. E. B. *Black Reconstruction in America—1860–1880.* Cleveland, Ohio: World, 1968.

Gould, Stephen Jay. *The Mismeasure of Man.* New York: W. W. Norton, 1981.

Graham, Richard, ed. *The Idea of Race in Latin America, 1870–1940*. Austin, Texas: University of Texas Press, 1990.

Harding, Sandra. *Feminism and Methodology*. Bloomington, Ind: Indiana University Press, 1987.

hooks, bell. *Feminist Theory: From Margin to Center*. Boston, Mass.: South End Press, 1984.

Jones, Madlyn Allen. *American Immigration*. Chicago: University of Chicago Press, 1960.

Kellough, J. Edward. "Affirmative Action in Government Employment." *The Annals* 523 (September 1992): 117–30.

Millette, Trevor. *The Chinese in Trinidad*. Trinidad: Inprint Publication Inc., 1993.

Nelsen, H., R. Yokley and A. Nelsen, eds. *The Black Church in America*. New York: Basic Books, 1971.

Root, Maria P. P., ed. *Racially Mixed People in America*. Newbury Park, Calif.: Sage, 1993.

Williams, Eric. *History of the People of Trinidad and Tobage*. London: Deutsch, 1964.

Part II: Art

Anzaldua, Gloria. *Borderlands/La Frontera: The New Mestiza*. San Francisco: Spinsters/Aunt Lute, 1987.

Bennett, Lerone, Jr. *Before the Mayflower: A History of the Negro in America, 1619–1964*. New York: Penguin, 1980.

Berzon, Judith R. *Neither White Nor Black: The Mulatto Character in American Fiction*. New York: New York University Press, 1978.

Bone, Robert. *The Negro Novel in America*. New Haven: Yale University Press, 1958.

Breslin, R., ed. *Topics in Culture Learning*, vol. 2. Honolulu: East-West Center, 1974.

Chang, Diana. *The Frontiers of Love*. New York: Random House, 1956.

Chesnutt, Charles W. *The House Behind the Cedars*. Ridgewood, N.J.: Gregg Press, 1968.

Cohen, David W., and Jack P. Greene, eds. *Neither Slave nor Free: The Freedmen of African Descent in the Slave Societies of the New World*. Baltimore: Johns Hopkins University Press, 1972.

Davis, F. James. *Who Is Black? One Nation's Definition*. University Park: Pennsylvania State University Press, 1991.

Degler, Carl N. *Neither Black Nor White: Slavery and Race Relations in Brazil and the US*. New York: Macmillan, 1971.

Domínguez, Virginia. *White by Definition: Social Classification in Creole Louisiana.* New Brunswick, N.J.: Rutgers University Press, 1986.

DuBois, W. E. B. *The Souls of Black Folk.* New York: Penguin Books, 1903/1989.

Erdrich, Louise. *Tracks.* New York: Henry Holt, 1988.

Farley, Reynolds, and Walter Allen. *The Color Line and the Quality of Life in America.* Newbury Park, Calif.: Sage Publications, 1987.

Forbes, Jack D. *Black Africans and Native Americans: Color, Race and Caste in the Evolution of Red–Black Peoples.* London: Blackwell, 1988.

Freyre, Gilberto. *The Mansions and the Shanties,* tr. Harriet de Onís. New York: Alfred A. Knopf, 1963.

Friedman, Lester D., ed. *Unspeakable Images: Ethnicity and the American Cinema.* Urbana: University of Illinois Press, 1991.

Gates, Henry Louis, Jr. *"Race," Writing, and Difference.* Chicago: University of Chicago Press, 1986.

Gayle, Addison, Jr. *The Way of the New World: The Black Novel in America.* New York: Doubleday, 1976.

Goffman, Erving. *The Presentation of Self in Everyday Life.* New York: Doubleday Anchor, 1959.

Gordon, Charles. *No Place to Be Somebody.* Indianapolis: Bobbs-Merrill, 1969.

Hamalian, Leo, and James V. Hatch, eds. *The Roots of African-American Drama, An Anthology of Early Plays, 1858–1938.* Detroit: Wayne State University Press, 1991.

Hoetink, H. *Slavery and Race Relations in the Americas.* New York: Harper and Row, 1973.

Honda, Hideo. *Sonzai Shinai Kodomotachi (Children Who Haven't An Existence).* Tokyo: 1982.

hooks, bell. *Black Looks: Race and Representation.* Boston, Mass.: South End Press, 1992.

Jackson, Richard L. *Black Writers in Latin America.* Albuquerque: University of New Mexico Press, 1979.

Kaneko, Kazuyo. *Emi yo.* Tokyo: 1954.

Klein, Herbert. *African Slavery in Latin America and the Caribbean.* Oxford: Oxford University Press, 1986.

Kristeva, Julia. *The Powers of Horror: An Essay on Abjection.* New York: Colombia University Press, 1982.

Larsen, Nella. *Quicksand and Passing.* New Brunswick, N.J.: Rutgers University Press, 1989.

Ling, Amy. *Between Worlds: Women Writers of Chinese Ancestry.* New York: Pergamon Press, 1990.

Morrison, Toni. *Playing in the Dark: Whiteness and the Literary Imagination.* Cambridge, Mass.: Harvard University Press, 1992.

Morrison, Toni. *The Bluest Eye.* New York: Washington Square, 1970.

Omi, Michael, and Howard Winant. *Racial Formation in the U.S. 1960–1980.* New York: Routledge & Kegan Paul, 1986.

Perkins, Kathy A. *Black Female Playwrights: An Anthology of Plays Before 1950.* Bloomington: Indiana University Press, 1989.

Ramirez, Manuel, III. *Psychology of the Americas: Mestizo Perspectives on Personality and Mental Health.* New York: Pergamon Press, 1983.

Root, Maria P. P., ed. *Racially Mixed People in America.* Newbury Park, Calif.: Sage, 1992.

Rosaldo, Renato. *Culture and Truth: The Remaking of Social Analysis.* Boston: Beacon Press, 1989.

Russell, Kathy, Midge Wilson, and Ronald Hall. *The Color Complex: The Politics of Skin Color Among African Americans.* New York: Harcourt Brace Jovanovich, 1992.

Rutherford, Johnathan, ed. *Identity.* London: Lawrence and Wishart, 1990.

Scheik, William J. *The Half-Blood: A Cultural Symbol in 19th-Century American Fiction.* Lexington, Ky.: University Press of Kentucky, 1979.

Sebbar, Leila. *Lettres Parisiennes.* Paris: Stock, 1989.

Silko, Leslie Marmon. *Ceremony.* New York: Penguin, 1986.

Skidmore, Thomas E. *Black Into White: Race and National Identity in Brazilian Thought.* New York: Oxford University Press, 1974.

Spickard, Paul. *Mixed Blood: Intermarriage and Ethnic Identity in Twentieth Century America.* Madison, Wis.: University of Wisconsin Press, 1989.

Spillers, Hortense J., ed. *Comparative American Identities: Race, Sex, and Nationality in the Modern Text.* New York: Routledge, 1991.

Spitzer, Leo. *Lives in Between: Assimilation and Marginality in Austria, Brazil and West Africa, 1780–1945.* New York: Cambridge University Press, 1989.

Stuart, I., and L. Abt, eds. *Interracial Marriage: Expectations and Realities.* New York: Grossman Publishers, 1973.

Toll, Robert C. *Blacking Up: The Minstrel Show in Nineteenth Century America.* New York: Oxford University Press, 1974.

Trimmer, Joseph, and Tilly Warnock, eds. *Understanding Others:*

Cultural and Cross-Cultural Studies and the Teaching of Literature. Urbana, Ill.: NCTE, 1992.

Wagatsuma, H. *Culture and Identity*. Tokyo: Chiyoda Printing Co., 1986.

Williamson, Joel. *New People*. New York: Free Press, 1980.

Zack, Naomi. *Race and Mixed Race*. Philadelphia: Temple University Press, 1993.

Part III: Social Science

Acosta-Belén, Edna, ed. *The Puerto Rican Woman*. New York: Praeger, 1979.

Acuna, Rudolf. *Occupied America,* 3rd ed. New York: Harper Collins, 1988.

Adorno, T. W., et al. *The Authoritarian Personality*. New York: Wiley & Sons, 1964.

Allport, Gordon. *The Nature of Prejudice*. Reading, Mass.: Addison Wesley Publishing Co., 1985.

Barron, Milton, ed. *The Blending American*. Chicago: Quadrangle Books, 1972.

Berlin, Ira. *Slaves Without Masters: The Free Negro in the Antebellum South*. New York: Pantheon Books, 1975.

Berry, Brewton. *Almost White*. New York: Macmillan, 1963.

Berry, Brewton. *Race and Ethnic Relations*, 3rd. ed. Boston: Houghton Mifflin, 1965.

Berry, Brewton, and Henry L. Tischler. *Race and Ethnic Relations*, 3rd. ed. Boston: Houghton Mifflin, 1978.

Blackwell, James E. *The Black Community: Diversity and Unity*. New York: Dodd, Mead & Co., 1975.

Blalock, Hubert M., Jr. *Toward a Theory of Minority-Group Relations*. New York: Capricorn Books, 1967.

Blassingame, John W. *Black New Orleans, 1860–1880*. Chicago: University of Chicago Press, 1973.

Blassingame, John W. *The Slave Community: Plantation Life in the Antebellum South*. New York: Oxford University Press, 1972.

Blau, Peter M., Terry C. Blum, and Joseph E. Schwartz. "Heterogeneity and Intermarriage." *American Sociological Review* 47 (February 1982): 45–62.

Butler, Judith. *Gender Trouble: Feminism and the Subversion of Identity*. New York: Routledge, 1990.

Callicott, Baird J. *In Defense of the Land Ethic.* Albany: State University of New York Press, 1989.

Caterall, Helen T., ed. *Judicial Cases Concerning American Slavery and the Negro,* 5 vols. Washington, D.C: Carnegie Institute of Washington, 1926–37.

Cazares, Ralph B., Edward Murguia, and W. Parker Frisbie. "Mexican American Intermarriage In A Nonmetropolitan Context." *Social Science Quarterly* 65 (1984): 626–34.

Chang, Theresa S. "The Self-Concept of Children of Ethnically Different Marriages." *California Journal of Education Research* 25, no. 5 (November 1974): 245–252.

Churchill, Ward. *Struggle for the Land.* Monroe, Maine: Common Courage Press, 1992–93.

Cronon, Edmund Davis. *Black Moses.* Madison: University of Wisconsin Press, 1955.

Davis, F. James. *Who Is Black?* University Park: Pennsylvania State University Press, 1991.

Davis, Kingsley. "Intermarriage in Caste Societies." *American Anthropologist* 43 (1941): 376–95.

Day, A. Grove. *Hawaii and Its People,* rev. ed. New York: Duell, Sloan, & Pearce, 1960.

Day, Dawn. *The Adoption of Black Children: Counteracting Institutional Discrimination.* Lexington, Mass.: Lexington Books, D. C. Heath, 1979.

Degler, Carl N. *Neither Black Nor White: Slavery and Race Relations in Brazil and the United States.* New York: Macmillan, 1971.

Dominguez, Virginia R. *White by Definition: Social Classification in Creole Louisiana.* New Brunswick, N.J.: Rutgers University Press, 1986.

Doyle, Anna-Beth, et al. "Developmental Patterns in the Flexibility of Children's Ethnic Attitudes." *Journal of Cross-Cultural Psychology* 19, no. 1 (March 1988): 3–6.

Drinnon, Richard. *Facing West.* New York: Schocken Books, 1980–90.

Elliot, J. H. *Imperial Spain, 1469–1716.* New York: Penguin Books, 1990.

Erikson, Erik. *Identity and the Life Cycle.* New York: W. W. Norton, 1980.

Forbes, Jack D. *Black Africans and Native Americans: Color, Race and Caste in the Evolution of Red–Black Peoples.* London: Blackwell, 1988.

Forbes, Jack D. "Undercounting Native Americans: The 1980 Census and the Manipulation of Racial Identity in the U.S." *Wicazo Sa Review* 6, no .1 (Spring 1990): 2–26.

Frenkel-Brunswick, E. "Intolerance of Ambiguity as an Emotional and Perceptual Personality Variable." *Journal of Personality* 18 (1949): 108–43.

Frenkel-Brunswick, E. "Tolerance Toward Ambiguity as a Personality Variable." *American Psychologist* 3 (1968): 268.

Genovese, Eugene. *Roll Jordan Roll: The World The Slaves Made.* New York: Vintage, 1976.

Gordon, Milton M. *Assimilation in American Life.* New York: Oxford University Press, 1964.

Gould, Stephen Jay. *The Mismeasure of Man.* New York: W. W. Norton, 1981.

Gunn Allen, Paula. *The Sacred Hoop: Recovering the Feminine in American Indian Traditions.* Boston: Beacon Press, 1986.

Gwaltney, John Langston. *Drylongso: A Self-Portrait of Black America.* New York: Vintage Books, 1980.

Harmon, Alexandra. "When An Indian is Not an Indian? 'Friends of the Indian' and the Problem of Indian Identity." *Journal of Ethnic Studies* 18, no. 2 (1991): 95–123.

Harris, Melvin. *Patterns of Race in the Americas.* New York: W. W. Norton, 1964.

Hernton, Calvin. *Sex and Racism in America.* New York: Grove Press, 1965.

Hoetink, H. *Caribbean Race Relations: A Study of Two Variants.* London: Oxford University Press, 1964.

Hogan, Linda. *Mean Spirit.* New York: Atheneum, 1990.

Horowitz, Donald L. "Color Differentiation in the American Systems of Slavery." *Journal of Interdisciplinary History* 3 (Winter, 1973): 509–41.

Horsman, Reginald. *Race and Manifest Destiny.* Cambridge, Mass.: Harvard University Press, 1981.

Jaimes, M. A., ed. *The State of Native America.* Boston: South End Press, 1992.

Kearl, Michael C., and Edward Murguia. "Age Differences of Spouses in Mexican American Intermarriage: Exploring the Cost of Minority Assimilation." *Social Science Quarterly* 66 (1985): 453–60.

Kennedy, Ruby J. "Single or Triple Melting Pot? Intermarriage Trends in New Haven, 1870–1950." *American Journal of Sociology* 39 (1941): 331-39.

Kitano, Harry H. L., Wai-Tsang Yeung, Lynn Chai, and Herbert Hatanaka. "Asian-American Interracial Marriage." *Journal of Marriage and the Family* 46 (February 1984): 180.

Kovel, Joel. *White Racism: A Psychohistory.* London: Free Association, 1988.

Kuhl, Stefan. *The Nazi Connection: Eugenics, American Racism, and German National Socialism.* New York: Oxford University Press, 1994.

Macdonald, Andrew. *The Turner Diaries.* Hillsboro, Va.: National Vanguard Books, 1978.

Mangum, Charles Staples, Jr. *The Legal Status of the Negro in the United States.* Chapel Hill: University of North Carolina Press, 1940.

Mannoni, O. *Prospero and Caliban: The Psychology of Colonization.* New York: Praeger, 1956.

Martin, Waldo E., Jr. *The Mind of Frederick Douglass.* Chapel Hill: University of North Carolina Press, 1984.

Maslow, Abraham. *Towards A Psychology of Being.* New York: Van Nostrand Reinhold Press, 1968.

McKoy, Ruth, and Edith Freeman. "Racial-Identity Issues among Mixed-Race Children." *Social Workers in Education* (January 1986): 164–174.

Memmi, Albert. *The Colonizer and the Colonized.* Boston: Beacon, 1967.

Memmi, Albert. *Dependence.* Boston: Beacon, 1984.

Mencke, John G. *Mulattoes and Race Mixture: American Attitudes and Images, 1865–1918.* Ann Arbor: University Microfilms Inc. Research Press, 1979.

Merton, Robert K. "Intermarriage and the Social Structure." *Psychiatry* 4 (1941): 361–74.

Montagu, Ashley. *Man's Most Dangerous Myth: The Fallacy of Race.* Cleveland: World, 1964.

Montagu, Ashley. *The Concept of Race.* London: Collier Books, 1969.

Murguia, Edward, and Ralph B. Cazares. "Intermarriage of Mexican Americans." *Marriage and Family Review* 5, no. 1 (Spring, 1982): 91.

Murguia, Edward, and W. Parker Frisbie. "Trends in Mexican American Intermarriage: Recent Findings In Perspective." *Social Science Quarterly* 58 (1977):375.

Myrdal, Gunnar, assisted by Richard Sterner and Arnold M. Rose. *An American Dilemma.* New York: Harper & Bros., 1944.

Nabokov, Peter, ed. *Native American Testimony: A Cronicle of Indian–White Relations from Prophecy to the Present.* New York: Penguin Books, 1991.

Nicholls, David. "No Hawks or Pedlars: Levantines in the Caribbean." *Ethnic and Racial Studies* 4 (October 1981): 415–31.

Nicholson, Linda J., ed. *Feminism/Postmodernism.* New York: Routledge, 1990.

Nordyke, Eleanor C. "Blacks in Hawai'i: A Demographic and Historical Perspective." *The Hawaiian Journal of History* 22 (1988): 241–55.

Nordyke, Eleanor C. *Peopling of Hawai'i,* 2nd ed. Honolulu: University of Hawaii Press, 1989.

Omi, Michael, and Howard Winant. *Racial Formation in the United States: From the 1960s to the 1980s.* New York: Routledge and Kegan Paul, 1986.

Osofsky, Gilbert. *The Burden of Race: A Documentary History of Negro–White Relations in America.* New York: Harper & Row, 1967.

Parkman, Margaret A., and Jack Sawyer. "Dimensions of Ethnic Intermarriage in Hawaii." *American Sociological Review* 32 (1967): 513–608.

Porter, Cornelia. "Social Reasons for Skin Tone Preferences of Black School-Age Children." *American Journal of Orthopsychiatry* 61, no. 1 (January 1991): 149–154.

Porterfield, Ernest. "Black-American Intermarriage in the United States." *Marriage and Family Review* 5, no. 1 (Spring 1982): 17.

Poston, W. S. Carlos. "The Biracial Identity Development Model: A Needed Addition." *Journal of Counseling & Development* 69 (Nov./Dec. 1990): 152-55.

Raushning, Hermann. *The Voice of Destruction.* New York: Putnam & Sons, 1940.

Reuter, E. B. *Race Mixture: Studies in Intermarriage and Miscegenation.* New York: McGraw-Hill, 1931.

Reed, T. Edward. "Caucasian Genes in American Negroes." *Science* 165 (August 22, 1969): 762–68.

Reuter, Edward Byron. *The Mulatto in the United States, Including a Study of the Role of Mixed-Blood Races Throughout the World.* Boston: Richard G. Badger, 1918.

Ridgeway, James. *Blood in the Face.* New York: Thundermouth Press, 1990.

Root, Maria P. P., ed. *Racially Mixed People in America.* Newbury Park, Calif: Sage, 1992.

Rose, Arnold M., and Caroline Rose. *America Divided.* New York: Alfred A. Knopf, 1948.

Rubin, Theodore Isaac. *Anti-Semitism: A Disease of the Mind.* New York: Continuum, 1990.

Sebring, Deborah. "Considerations in Counseling Interracial Children." *Journal of Non-White Concerns in Personnel and Guidance* 13, no. 1 (January 1985): 6.

Seidman, Steven. "The End of Sociological Theory: The Postmodern Hope." *Sociological Theory* 9, no. 2 (1991): 134–36.

Solaún, Mauricio, and Sidney Kronus. *Discrimination Without Violence.* New York: John Wiley & Sons, 1973.

Spickard, Paul R. *Mixed Blood: Intermarriage and Ethnic Identity in Twentieth-Century America.* Madison: The University of Wisconsin Press, 1989.

Stanton, William. *The Leopard Spots: Scientific Attitudes Toward Race in America, 1819–59.* Chicago: University of Chicago Press, 1960.

Stember, Charles Herbert. *Sexual Racism: The Emotional Barrier to an Integrated Society.* New York: Harper & Row, 1976.

Stock, Robert. "The Settler State and the American Left." *New Studies on the Left* 14, no. 3 (Winter, 1990–91): 72–8.

Szathmary, Emoke. "Genetics of Aboriginal North Americans." *Evolutionary Anthropology* 1, no. 6 (1993): 202–20.

Takaki, Ronald. *Iron Cages: Race and Culture in 19th Century America.* Seattle: University of Washington, 1982.

Thornton, Russell. *American Indian Holocaust Survival: A Population History Since 1492.* Norman, Okla.: University of Oklahoma Press, 1987.

Trask, Haunani Kay. *From A Native Daughter.* Monroe, Maine: Common Courage Press, 1993.

Tumin, Melvin M., ed. *Comparative Perspectives on Race Relations.* Boston: Little, Brown & Co., 1969.

Udry, J. Richard, et al. "Skin Color, Status, and Mate Selection." *American Journal of Sociology* 76 (January 1971): 722–23.

Valdez, Avelardo. "Recent Increases in Intermarriage by Mexican American Males: Bexar County, Texas, from 1971 to 1980." *Social Science Quarterly* 64 (1983): 136–44.

Vander Zanden, James W. *American Minority Relations,* 3rd ed. New York: Ronald Press Co., 1972.

Wagley, Charles, ed. *Race and Class in Rural Brazil,* 2nd ed. Paris: UNESCO, 1963.

Weatherford, Jack. *Native Roots*. New York: Crown Publishers, 1991.

Webster, Yehudi O. *The Racialization of America*. New York: St. Martin's Press, 1992.

Wunder, John R. *"Retained by the Peoples": A History of American Indians and the Bill of Rights*. New York: Oxford University Press, 1994.

Zack, Naomi. "An Autobiographical View of Mixed Race and Deracination." *American Philosophical Association Newsletter on Philosophy and the Black Experience* 91, no. 1 (Spring 1991): 6–10.

Part IV: Public Policy

Adams, Romanzo C. *Interracial Marriage in Hawaii*. New York: AMS Press, republished 1969 (orig. publ. 1937).

Allen, James Paul, and Eugene James Turner, *We The People: An Atlas of America's Ethnic Diversity*. New York: Macmillan, 1988.

Barron, Milton. *The Blending American: Patterns of Intermarriage*. Chicago: Quadrangle Books, 1972.

Barzun, Jacques. *Race, A Study in Superstition*. New York: Harper and Row, 1965.

Berzon, J.R. *Neither Black nor White: The Mulatto Character in American Fiction*. New York: New York University Press, 1978.

Dann, Kevin. "From Degeneration to Regeneration: The Eugenics Survey of Vermont 1925–1936." *Vermont History* 1 (1991): 10–11.

Darder, A. *Culture and Power in the Classroom: A Critical Foundation for Bicultural Education*. New York: Bergin & Garvey, 1991.

Day, Beth. *Sexual Life Between Blacks and Whites: The Roots of Racism*. New York: World Publishing, Times Mirror, 1972.

Degler, Carl N. *Neither Black Nor White: Slavery and Race Relations in Brazil and the United States*. New York: Macmillan, 1971.

Early, Gerald, ed. *Lure and Loathing: Essays on Race, Identity, and the Ambivalence of Assimilation*. New York: Penguin, 1993.

Ferguson, R., M. Gever, T. T. Minh-ha, and C. West, eds. *Out There: Marginalization and Contemporary Cultures*. New York: The New Museum of Contemporary Art, 1990.

Freire, P. and D. Macedo. *Literacy: Reading the Word and the World*. New York: Bergin & Garvey, 1987.

Gay, Kathlyn. *The Rainbow Effect.* New York: Franklin Watts, 1987.

Gibbs, Jewelle, and L. N. Huang. *Children of Color.* San Francisco: Jossey-Bass, 1989.

Gossett, Thomas F. *Race: The History of an Idea in America.* New York: Schocken Press, 1965.

Hearst, Margo R., ed. *Interracial Identity: Celebration, Conflict, or Choice?* Chicago: Biracial Family Network, 1993.

Jaworski, Adam. "How to Silence a Minority: The Case of Women." *International Journal of Sociology and Language* 94 (1992): 27.

Japanese American Citizens League (JACL). Special issue on "Interracial Families." *Pacific Citizen* 101, no. 25 (December 20–27, 1985).

Johnston, James Hugo. *Miscegenation in the Ante-Bellum South.* New York: AMS Press, republished 1972 (orig. publ. 1939).

King, James C. *The Biology of Race.* Berkeley: University of California Press, 1981.

MacLachlan, Colin M., and Jaime E. Rodríguez. *The Forging of the Cosmic Race: A Reinterpretation of Colonial Mexico.* Berkeley: University of California Press, 1980.

Mathabane, Mark and Gail. *Love in Black and White.* New York: Harper Collins, 1992.

McCord, David, and William Cleveland. *Black and Red: The Historical Meeting of Africans and Native Americans.* Atlanta: Dreamkeeper Press, Inc., 1990.

McFee, Malcolm. "The 150% Man: A Product of Blackfoot Acculturation." *American Anthropologist* 70 (1968): 1096–1107.

McRoy, R. G., and E. Freeman. "Racial Identity Issues Among Mixed-race Children." *Social Work In Education* 8 (1986): 164–174.

Montagu, Ashley. *Man's Most Dangerous Myth: The Fallacy of Race,* 5th ed. London: Oxford University Press, 1974.

Morner, Magnus. *Race Mixture in the History of Latin America.* Boston: Little Brown, 1967.

Murguia, Edward. *Chicano Intermarriage.* Texas: Trinity University Press, 1982.

Owen, Lyla and Murphy. *The Creoles of New Orleans: People of Color.* New Orleans: First Quarter Publishing Company, 1987.

Poliakov, Leon. *The Aryan Myth: A History of Racist and Nationalist Ideas in Europe.* New York: New American Library, 1974.

Porterfield, Ernest. *Black and White Mixed Marriages.* Chicago: Nelson Hall Publishers, 1978.

Ringer, Benjamin, and Elinor Lawless. *Race, Ethnicity and Society.* New York: Routledge, Chapman and Hall, Inc., 1989.

Rollins, Joan, ed. *Hidden Minorities: The Persistence of Ethnicity in American Life.* New York: University Press of America, 1981.

Root, Maria P. P., ed. *Racially Mixed People in America.* Newbury Park, Calif.: Sage, 1992.

Rosaldo, Renato. *Culture and Truth: The Remaking of Social Analysis.* Boston: Beacon Press, 1989.

Russell, Kathy, Midge Wilson, and Ronald Hall. *The Color Complex: The Politics of Skin Color Among African Americans.* New York: Harcourt Brace Jovanovich, 1992.

Simon, Rita. *Adoption, Race & Identity: From Infancy Through Adolescence.* Westport, Conn.: Praeger Publishers (The Greenwood Group), 1992.

Sleeter, C.E., ed. *Empowerment through Multicultural Education.* Albany, N.Y.: State University of New York Press, 1991.

Spickard, Paul. *Mixed Blood: Intermarriage and Ethnic Identity in Twentieth Century America.* Madison, Wis.: University of Wisconsin Press, 1989.

Stepan, Nancy. *The Idea of Race in Science.* Hamden, Conn.: Archon Books, 1982.

Sung, Betty Lee. *Chinese American Intermarriage.* New York: Center for Migration Studies, 1990.

Thernstrom, Stephen, ed. *Harvard Encyclopedia of American Ethnic Groups.* Cambridge, Mass.: Belknap Press of Harvard University Press, 1980.

UNESCO. *The Race Concept.* Westport, Conn.: Greenwood Press, reprinted 1970.

Vasconcelos, José. *La Raza Cósmica,* tr. Didier T. Jaén. Los Angeles: Centro de Publicaciones, California State University, 1979 (first published in Mexico, 1925).

Vogel, Virgil. *This Country Was Ours.* New York: Harper Torchbooks, 1972.

White, Steve and Ruth. *Free Indeed: the Autobiography of an Interracial Couple.* Gardena, Calif.: A Place For Us Ministry, 1989.

Williamson, J. *New People.* New York: Free Press, 1980.

Part V: Identity Theory

Abelove, H., M. Barale, and D. Halperin, eds. *The Lesbian and Gay Studies Reader.* New York: Routledge, 1993.

Alonso, William, and Paul Starr, eds. *The Politics of Numbers.* New York: Russell Sage Foundation, 1987.

Anderson, Benedict. *Imagined Communities.* London: Verso Books, 1983.

Appiah, Anthony. *In My Father's House.* Oxford: Oxford University Press, 1992.

Augenbraum, Harold, and Ilan Stavans, eds. *Growing Up Latino.* Boston: Houghton Mifflin Company, 1993.

Bhabha, Homi. *The Location of Culture.* New York: Routledge, 1994.

Brown, L. S., and M. P. P. Root, eds. *Diversity and Complexity in Feminist Therapy.* New York: Haworth Press, 1990.

Chavez, Linda. *Out of the Barrio: Toward a New Politics of Hispanic Assimilation.* New York: Basic Books, 1991.

Cross, W. E. *Shades of Black: Diversity in African-American Identity.* Philadelphia: Temple University Press, 1991.

Davis, Marilyn P. *Mexican Voices/American Dreams.* New York: Henry Holt and Company, 1990.

DuBois, W. E. B. *The Souls of Black Folk.* New York: Penguin Books, 1903/1989.

Dunn, L.C., and Theodosius Dobzhansky. *Heredity, Race and Society.* New York: Mentor, 1962.

Foucault, Michel. *The History of Sexuality: 1,* tr. Robert Hurley. New York: Random House, 1980.

Franklin, John Hope. *Race and History.* Baton Rouge: Louisiana State University Press, 1989.

Gellner, Ernest. *Nations and Nationalism.* Oxford: Basil Blackwell, 1983.

Gilroy, Paul. *The Black Atlantic: Modernity and Double Consciousness.* Cambridge, Mass.: Harvard University Press, 1993.

Goldberg, David Theo, ed. *Multiculturalism: A Critical Reader.* Oxford: Basil Blackwell, 1994.

Goldberg, David Theo. *Racist Culture: Philosophy and the Politics of Meaning.* Oxford: Basil Blackwell, 1993.

Goldberg, David Theo. "The Semantics of Race." *Ethnic and Racial Studies* 15, no. 4 (October 1993): 543–69.

Goldberg, David Theo. "Whither West?" *Review of Education/Pedagogy/Cultural Studies* 1, no. 1 (1994): 1–13.

Goldberg, David Theo, and Michael Krausz, eds. *Jewish Identity.* Philadelphia: Temple University Press, 1993.

Hacker, Andrew. *Two Nations: Black and White, Separate, Hostile, Unequal.* New York: Ballantine Books, 1992.

Harris, Leonard, ed. *The Philosophy of Alain Locke.* Philadelphia: Temple University Press, 1989.

Haskin, Frederic J. *The Panama Canal.* Garden City, New York: Doubleday, 1913.

Hegel, G. W. F. *The Phenomenology of Mind,* tr. J. B. Baillie. New York: Harper, 1967.

Helms, J. E. *Black and White Racial Identity: Theory, Research, and Practice.* New York: Greenwood Press, 1990.

Henriques, F. *Children of Conflict: A Study of Interracial Sex and Marriage.* New York: Dutton, 1974.

Hirsch, Marianne and Evelyn Fox Keller, eds. *Conflicts in Feminism.* New York: Routledge, 1990.

Kevles, Daniel J. *In the Name of Eugenics.* Berkeley: University of California Press, 1985.

Kuper, Leo, ed. *Race, Science and Society.* New York: Columbia University Press, 1965.

Lechte, John, *Julia Kristeva.* New York: Routledge, 1990.

Locke, John. *Essay Concerning Human Understanding,* ed. Peter H. Niddich. Oxford: Oxford University Press, 1990.

McDougall, Hugh A. *Racial Myth in English History: Trojans, Teutons, and Anglo-Saxons.* Montreal: Harvest House, 1982.

Miller, R., and B. Miller. "Mothering the Biracial Child: Bridging the Gaps Between African-American and White Parenting Styles." *Women and Therapy* 10 (1990): 169–180.

Minh-Ha, Trinh T. *When the Moon Waxes Red.* New York: Routledge, 1991.

Morrison, Toni. *Playing in the Dark.* Cambridge, Mass.: Harvard University Press, 1992.

Myrdal, Gunnar. *An American Dilemma: The Negro Problem and Modern Democracy.* New York: Harper & Brothers Publishers, 1944.

Ormond, Roger. *The Apartheid Handbook: A Guide to South Africa's Everyday Racial Policies.* Harmondsworth, U.K.: Penguin, 1985.

Rodriguez, Richard. *Days of Obligation.* New York: Penguin, 1992.

Root, M. P. P. "Reasons Racially Mixed Persons Identify as People of Color." *FOCUS* (Division 45 of the American Psychological Association), June 1994: 14–16.

Root, Maria P. P., ed. *Racially Mixed People in America.* Newbury Park, Calif.: Sage, 1992.

Root, Maria P. P., ed. *Racially Mixed People in a New Millennium.* Newbury Park, Calif.: Sage Publications (in preparation).

Schutte, Ofelia. *Cultural Identity and Social Liberation in Latin*

American Thought. Albany: State University of New York Press, 1993.

Schwartz, Stephen P., ed. *Meaning, Necessity and Natural Kinds.* Ithaca: Cornell University Press, 1975.

Shrage, Laurie. *Moral Dilemmas of Feminism: Prostitution, Adultery, and Abortion.* New York: Routledge, 1994.

Spickard, P. R. *Mixed Blood: Intermarriage and Ethnic Identity in Twentieth-Century America.* Madison, Wis.: University of Wisconsin Press, 1989.

Tenzer, L. R. *A Completely New Look at Interracial Sexuality: Public Opinion and Select Commentaries.* Manahawkin, N.J.: Scholar's Publishing House, 1990.

Vega, Marta Morena, and Cheryll Y. Greene, eds. *Voices from the Battlefront: Achieving Cultural Equity.* Trenton: Africa World Press, Inc., 1993.

West, Cornel. *Race Matters.* Boston: Beacon Press, 1993.

Williams, Patricia. *The Alchemy of Race and Rights.* Cambridge: Harvard University Press, 1991.

Willie, C. V. *Oreo: Race and Marginal Men and Women.* Wakefield, Mass.: Parameter Press, 1975.

Wright, Richard. *Black Power: A Record of Reactions in a Land of Pathos.* New York: Harper and Brothers, 1954.

Wright, Richard. *The Outsider.* New York: Harper and Row, 1965.

Zack, Naomi. *Bachelors of Science: Seventeenth Century Identity Then and Now.* Philadelphia: Temple University Press (in preparation).

Zack, Naomi. *Race and Mixed Race.* Philadelphia: Temple University Press, 1993.

Zack, Naomi. "Race and Philosophic Meaning." *American Philosophical Association Newsletter on Philosophy and the Black Experience* 94, no. 1 (Fall 1994): 14–20.

Zea, Leopoldo. "Identity: A Latin American Philosophical Problem." *The Philosophical Forum* 20 (Fall-Winter 1988–89): 37.

Index

Abenaki. *See* Western Abenaki of Vermont
abjection, 100–103
adoption, 250–52; National Association of Black Social Workers and, 124, 129
Afroasians, depictions of in media, 92–94
Afrocentricity, and prejudice against light nonwhites, 282
Aiken, George, 65–66
alienation, 172–75
Allison, Hughes, 70
AMEA (Association of MultiEthnic Americans): congressional testimony of, 192–205; history and goals of, 192–93; proposal for amending Directive 15, 210
American colonies, 120–21
American Indian: feminism in Southwest tribes, 135; identity among youth, 138; intermarriage, 149; mixed race and movie portrayals of, 10; teenage suicide, 5; tribal definitions of race, 133–34; urban, 151; white nostalgia for, 150–51, 226, 260. *See also* Indian

American Indian Movement, and international connections, 152–53
American mixed race. *See* mixed race
Anderson, Garland, 69
antimiscegenation laws. *See* miscegenation
Anzaldua, Gloria, 95, 271, 275–76
apartheid: and fourfold segregation, 118–19; and racial classification, 249–49
Apteker, Bettina, 271
Aryan Nations, 155
Asians, appearance and racial classification, 59–60
assimilation, 120
assimilationist framework, applied to mixed race, 158
attributive meaning and race, 306; *See also* philosophic meaning and race

Baraka, Amiri (LeRoi Jones), 71–72
belonging, 172–76
Bhabha, Homi K., 105, 263, 323n37

About the
Contributors

Linda Alcoff, Ph.D., is Associate Professor of Philosophy and Women's Studies at Syracuse University. She is coeditor, with Elizabeth Potter, of *Feminist Epistemologies* (Routledge, 1993) and author of numerous articles, including "The Problem of Speaking for Others" (*Cultural Critique,* Winter 1991–2).

Debra Barrath is presently completing an M.A. in psychiatric/mental health nursing at Dalhousie University, Nova Scotia.

Jennifer Clancy recently earned an M.A. in social work from San Francisco State University, after extensive work experience in culturally diverse human service organizations. She is currently teaching and counseling at the middle school and high school of the Albuquerque Academy.

Susan Clements's poems, stories, and essays have been published in numerous literary journals and anthologies, most recently in *North Dakota Quarterly, Akwe:kon, a Journal of Indigenous Issues,* and *Unsettling America: An Anthology of Contemporary Multicultural Poetry* (Viking Penguin). She has two books of poetry, *The Broken Moon* and *In the Moon When the Deer Lose Their Horns*, and she was the recipient of a New York State Foundation for the Arts Poetry Fellowship in 1993.

F. James Davis, Ph.D., is Professor of Sociology, Emeritus, at Illinois State University. He also taught at the College of Wooster, Hamline University, and California State University–Fullerton. He has published numerous articles and books on the sociology of law, minority–dominant relations, social problems, and Turkey. The latest of his seven books is *Who Is Black?* (Pennsylvania State University Press, 1991).

Abby L. Ferber is Assistant Professor of Sociology at the University of Colorado at Colorado Springs. She recently received her Ph.D. from the University of Oregon and her dissertation explores the production of racialized, gendered subjects in contemporary white supremacist discourse. She has also published articles about race and gender in education.

Carlos A. Fernández, J.D., is currently the Coordinator for Law and Civil Rights of the Association of MultiEthnic Americans (AMEA). He helped found the AMEA and served as its first president from 1988–1994. He is an author and attorney in private practice in California. (AMEA can be contacted by phone at (510) 523–AMEA; by mail at P.O. Box 191726, San Francisco, CA 94119–1726; or by E-Mail at Internet amea@sgi.com.)

Susan R. Graham is the founder and Executive Director of Project RACE (Reclassify All Children Equally). She is a professional journalist who now writes a popular editorial column for an Atlanta newspaper. Graham has been interviewed about multiracial identification on the CBS news show "48 Hours," National Public Radio, and in national newspapers and magazines. She is married and has two multiracial children. (Project RACE can be contacted by phone at (404) 433–6076; by mail at 1425 Market Blvd. Ste. 1320–E6, Roswell, Georgia, 30076; and by E-Mail at ProjRace@aol.com.)

Freda Scott Giles, Ph.D., has been an actor, director, and teacher of theater for more than twenty years. She is currently Assistant Professor in the Theatre Department at the University at Albany, State University of New York. Her articles have been published in *Theatre Journal*, *Overture*, and *Harlem Renaissance Revaluations* (Amritjit Singh et al., eds., Garland, 1989).

David Theo Goldberg, Ph.D., is Professor of Justice Studies and Professor of the Ph.D. Committee on Law and Social Science at Arizona State University. He is cofounding editor of *Social Identities: A Journal for the Study of Race, Nation and Culture.* His publications include *Racist Culture: Philosophy and the Politics of Meaning* (Basil Blackwell, 1993) and *Ethical Theory and Social Issues* (Harcourt Brace 1994), as well as the edited anthologies *Multiculturalism: A Critical Reader* (Basil Blackwell, 1994), *Anatomy of Racism* (University of Minnesota Press, 1990), and *Jewish Identity* (Temple University Press, 1993). He is now working on a book on the racial state in governmentality.

Helena Jia Hershel, Ph.D., is a psychotherapist in private practice in Oakland, California. Her clinical speciality includes working with biracial individuals and with couples in multicultural relationships. She has taught at Dartmouth College and is Professor of Clinical Psychology at the Center for Psychological Studies. She has also published numerous articles and is a frequent lecturer on cross-cultural topics.

M. Annette Jaimes, Ed.D., (a.k.a. M. A. Jaimes*Guerrero) has developed and taught Indian studies at the Center for Studies of Ethnicity and Race in America, University of Colorado at Boulder. She edited *The State of Native America* (South End Press, 1992) and worked on *American Indians, American Racism* while on a grant at the Rockefeller Bellagio Center in Italy. She has been the recipient of United Nations postdoctoral fellowships for research in Mexico and Guatemala. She is presently Visiting Assistant Professor at the School of Justice Studies at Arizona State University where she teaches courses in qualitative research and American Indian justice.

Cecile Ann Lawrence, M.A., J.D., has held positions in teaching and higher education administration in the United States and in government administration in Jamaica.

Zena Moore, Ph.D., is Assistant Professor in the College of Education at the University of Texas at Austin. She has written five textbooks for teaching Spanish in secondary schools. Her most recent publication is "Portfolio and Culture Learning" (*Northeastern Conference Reports*, April 1994).

Maria P. P. Root, Ph.D., is a clinical psychologist in private practice in Seattle and Associate Professor at the University of Washington. She is the editor of *Racially Mixed People in America* (Sage, 1992); and the editor of the forthcoming *Racially Mixed people in a New Millennium* (Sage).

Stephen Satris, Ph.D., is Associate Professor of Philosophy at Clemson University. He is the author of *Ethical Emotivism* (Nijhoff, 1987) and the editor of *Taking Sides*, 3rd ed. (Dushkin, 1994).

Carol Roh Spaulding is a graduate student in the English Department of the University of Iowa, where she is writing her dissertation, *Blue-Eyed Asian Maidens: The Mixed-Race Heroines of Sui Sin Far, Onoto Watanna, Diana Chang and Han Suyin*.

Laurie Shrage, Ph.D., is Associate Professor of Philosophy at California State Polytechnic University, Pomona, where she teaches moral and political philosophy and gender, feminist, and sexuality studies. She is the author of *Moral Dilemmas of Feminism: Prostitution, Adultery and Abortion* (Routledge, 1994). She has also published articles on comparable worth and feminist film aesthetics.

Mariella Squire-Hakey has taught anthropology since 1982 and is currently completing her doctorate at the University at Albany, State University of New York. Her dissertation is *The Contemporary Western Abenaki: Maintaining, Reclaiming and Reconfiguring an American Indian Ethnic Identity*. She has the official post and vocation of Story Teller among the Western Abenaki of Vermont.

Teresa Kay Williams has M.A.s in Asian American studies and sociology, from the University of California—Los Angeles, where she is currently completing her doctorate. She teaches sociology and ethnic studies at UCLA and the University of California—Santa Barbara, including classes on multicultural identity.

Brunetta Reid Wolfman, Ph.D., has won many awards for educational and civic service over a distinguished career during which she has been Assistant Dean of Faculty and Assistant Professor of Urban Studies at Dartmouth College, Academic Dean and Professor of Education at Wheelock College, President of Roxbury Community College, and Associate Vice President for Academic Affairs at George Washington University, where she is also currently Professor of Education. She has presented and published numerous papers on black and ethnic studies, women in higher education, and curriculum development pertaining to women and minorities.

Naomi Zack, Ph.D., is Assistant Professor of Philosophy at the University at Albany, State University of New York. She is the author of *Race and Mixed Race* (Temple University Press, 1993) and is presently writing *Bachelors of Science* (Temple University Press, 1996).